Campfire Tales
And other stuff

By
Bernie McMellon

Campfire Tales
Copyright ©2021 Bernie McMellon

ISBN 978-1506-912-77-6 PBK
ISBN 978-1506-910-42-0 EBK

LCCN 2021905301

April 2021

Published and Distributed by
First Edition Design Publishing, Inc.
P.O. Box 17646, Sarasota, FL 34276-3217
www.firsteditiondesignpublishing.com

I wish to thank these two ladies for their special help and encouragement. Without them, this book would never have made it to press, My thanks and my love to you.

Ms. Joyce Spencer
Ms. Robin Maconochie

Contents

Across the Mountain

Chapter 1

Virginia land, 1758

Thomas and Virginia McMellon were young and very happy. Married only three months after four years of knowing that someday. Their love started when Virginia became aware of the big dark and curly haired boy that helped his father in the blacksmith's shop down the road. It took Thomas another four years to realize his devotion to her.

She was only twelve in this year of our Lord 1746, but already she had the mind of an adult in things that mattered in the keeping of a home. Her mother and father were very good to her, the only child, but they expected her to work at all of the things that would help a child grow into a responsible adult. Virginia's father was the only Baptist minister for miles around, so Virginia saw visitors from many places who came for the Sunday service. Many of them had little more than a team and a wagon to carry them to Saxson's Branch, the name of the little creek where twenty families had gathered to build their homes.

Often, Virginia and her mother were expected to feed a hungry passel of little tots before they started on the long journey home after the Sunday sermon. Fortunately, there was an abundance of food, for many of the parishioners paid their tithes in produce, or perhaps, chickens. This worked well as there was always enough to feed his family and any visitors that might come along.

During the warmer months of the year, many of the families were well on the way to the Sunday service soon after daybreak, having fed the cattle and done the milking well before dawn. Mother had fed the little ones and packed enough clean clothes to give them a change just before the service was to start. It was impossible for them to remain clean and tidy on the long wagon trip to Saxson's Branch church and Mother wanted them to be as presentable as possible. It was not unusual for the little boys to be in the creek, muddy, wet and much in need of dry clothes and a good calming down by Paw before the service was to start. Actually, service started almost as soon as they arrived, for these simple folk were a devout group of Christians. God was present for them as soon as they arrived on the church grounds.

Prayers of most could be heard before they left their wagon's, prayers of thanks for a safe trip, for the minister and the sermon he would soon deliver to them. Mothers had to take care of the food they had brought along for the noon meal. Some crocks were to be placed in the cold water of Saxson's Branch where the boys would not disturb and the many dogs were not able to get to them. After all, the boys had followers that would run along behind the wagon, usually in the shade of the wagon if the day was warm enough. Ole Ring was not going to stay at home on Sunday for he knew there would be lots of fun and much food after the service was over. Not only that, there would be others of his kind to run and frolic with, a good time for dogs and boys. After the service was over, mothers were busy placing food on the long bench that had been constructed for that purpose. There were hungry children under foot, boys trying to snatch a small morsel and even some of the men too hungry to stay clear until called. This was a time for great fellowship among the men who had much work on their minds, a time to question others who had successfully completed a special chore, or, perhaps, the best method of constructing a stone fireplace to replace the "stick and mud" chimney built with great haste when they first arrived last year. Dinner time was very soon after the service and a time for the women to share both food and recipes.

As a young boy newly arrived in Saxson's Branch, Thomas had the desire to roam as far as the eye could see. His dog, Ole Ring was always with him, no matter how far the day's trip would be. Thomas examined every rock, tree and bush with a desire to learn what it was, what caused it and what good it was. Although he was very good to help Peyton in the blacksmith shop, Peyton wanted him to be a boy and have fun while he was young. He never encouraged Thomas either way, figuring his boy would do the right thing. Peyton had brought him up to love the Lord and to do right by all men and in all circumstances. He also trusted Thomas to be very careful in watching for his directions so he would never be lost. He had taught Thomas the location of the stars and how to tell time by the location of the sun and the moon and Thomas was confident of his position at all times. Even though both Ole Ring and Thomas were always on the alert for danger, they were not so well trained that a sharp-eyed Indian had not been seen constantly watching them for weeks.

Konaya's wandering search took him through all of that summer and the following winter. He was still searching the day he saw young Thomas and his dog far from a settlement. Konaya's first impulse was either to hide or to kill the hated white. By now, he had come to hate all white settlers. Still, he could not help seeing how Thomas loved the woodland and how he was careful to examine everything he could touch.

Konaya had found a cavern at the head of a small stream. Upon entering the small opening, he found many signs of long ago use by his ancestors. There was a stone fire ring located far enough back so that light would not disclose the entrance by night. He also found the draft of air entering the opening that continued into the depths of the cavern so that his fire could not be seen either by light at night or by smoke in the day. With such a place to use as home, Konaya continued his search for White Deer through ever expanding territory. During this time, Konaya kept watch on Thomas and had followed him to Saxson's Branch where he learned more of white man's way. Not all white men were like the three who had taken his White Deer. He saw that most were helpful to their women and peaceful to each other. He also saw them gather from time to time at one log place and heard them singing in unfamiliar voices and tunes. He noted their seeming affection for each other by hand clasping and embracing, much like his own people he had not seen for several winters. What he was seeing was Christian love for all people, not just family by blood relationship.

The day came when the Indian chose to meet Thomas for he had observed the care Thomas used in his study of things around him. He made himself visible to Thomas at a time when he had neither knife nor bow. He was perfectly still when Ole Ring came on him at the crest of a small hill. Ole Ring barked but something in dogs lets them know the difference in friend and foe. The Indian helped matters very much by having a large offering of venison on a long stick, still smoking from the roasting fire. That vision and odor did it for both boy and dog.

By sign language of hands and facial expressions, The Indian made it clear he wanted Thomas to follow him to the roasting fire where meat was in abundance. As all three of them ate, words for different things were exchanged and in just a short time, both the Indian and Thomas understood words in the other's language.

Ole Ring was satisfied with a full stomach and the friendly chatter between man and boy so he decided a good long nap was in order.

From this time forward, Thomas spent as much time in the woods as he felt he could without shorting Peyton. He never failed to enter the woods and not find the Indian there to greet him. They exchanged words untill both understood the language of the other. By this time, they knew the other's name and only Ole Ring was left out. The Indian could not clearly speak the word Ring so it was "Ole wing" to him. Thomas now called the Indian Konaya as the best he could pronounce the word. This was good for all.

Chapter 2

The Saxson's Branch church building had been constructed of logs, lovingly cut and hewn to fit into a small but neat room, eighteen by thirty feet in size. Pride in the building was evident with the chinking of a mixture of clay and straw which made it almost air tight. Six small windows had been brought down from Portsmouth and were placed so that light came in from either side to allow light for reading of the Bible. This was never enough so there was always a need for candles which gave off a warm and welcome glow. Very few even had Bibles which was one of the reasons so many were in attendance. There was a hunger for God's word and the minister was the Shepherd of this little flock, the source of Bible understanding. Pews were arranged to seat sixty people with hopes that there would soon be enough to fill the room. In front and slightly off center stood a round, pot bellied stove that had a large square of tin on the floor under it. This was hopefully to keep coals from the fire away from the split log floor. The church was warm enough in winter but could become heated during the summer months and often during some of preacher Shelton's better sermons, even in the winter.

As in most communities, the ladies were most prominent at Sunday services, some to hear the word and some to show off the latest in finery and fashions. Since most of them, by necessity, had the ability to sew, it was not unusual to see the same garments week after week, the ladies having altered them with ribbons or other attachments in strategic places. Saxson's Branch had very little in the way of entertainment so it was up to the ladies to organize what was known as an "all day singing and dinner on the grounds." Of course, dinner was not served on the ground just as singing did not last all day. Dinner was supplied by covered dish from each of the ladies and served on a hewed log table placed outside. Singing was limited to a very few and for a very short time. Virginia had the seat of honor as it was she who supplied the music from the church pump organ.

For these special days, men would carry the church pump organ outside where it could be heard by all. For some of the town, that was as close to church as they were ever to come. Virginia loved music and had a natural talent for it. Her music was pleasant to the ear and caused most of the community to spend a pleasant part of the day, just to hear it. Without fail, every small boy in the community was present at the log table, both to eat his fill and to slip as much as possible into his pockets for his best friend, his dog. It was also a good time for the girls to eye the boys as they had only a small number to choose from. Boys also took stock of the girls but until they were about fourteen, their interest was very limited. Marbles, sling shot and huntin' dogs were more important. Since Saxson's Branch was small, every one was well acquainted with the neighbors, but there was something different about those lazy summer Sundays, something that would stick in fond memory for the remainder of their lives.

Men would gather to talk of the crops, those that would be planted or those that were ready for harvest. Horseshoe pitchin' and whittlin' seemed to occupy most of the men. It was almost certain that the younger men would see to the horse shoes for the older men found this a time of rest. Children were turned loose to roam for there was no fear of danger except when Saxson's Branch creek was unruly from recent rains. The older men delighted in the use of a sharp pocket knife and in the spring when sap was on the rise in the pawpaw bushes, they were kept busy making slide whistles for the smaller children. The men took pride in selecting the right size branch for the perfect whistle. It had to be about six inches long and about one half inch in diameter, perfect in shape from end to end. First the bark had to be loosened by tapping gently all around; then the whistle slot was cut and the mouth piece shaved to a pleasant slope. Next the bark was broken loose from the branch and slipped off. The plug for the whistle end had to be cut off just even with the whistle hole and a minor area shaved off so air could be passed over the whistle slot. By carefully reinserting the slick part of the inside branch and blowing into the whistle while moving the slide in or out, a reasonable tune could be generated. For a time after they got a few whistles made, the church yard was filled with every note and pitch in the musical scale. Some of the children were able to play a good rendition of hymns they were familiar with. By mid-afternoon, pawpaw whistles were drying so as to make the bark difficult to slide. Accordingly, the noise would fade and the younger ones would be placed on a quilt for a refreshing nap. The courting couples were seen at all times and would be sitting on quilts just outside hearing of others. This was a time of peace, a time that memories were made of.

Conversations were not much different from those of the last few days when neighbors were going about the chores of the week. Nothing much happened there and news was limited to the occasional visitor or the return of one of the residents who had made the long trip to Portsmouth for supplies. When a neighbor decided to make the trip, he would make it known at the Sunday meeting and would wait a week or so for everyone to give him a list of needed items. These special Sundays were so important to the community that they were held about every third Sunday. The first warm days of March would be the beginning and they would last until cold weather made it uncomfortable to remain outside. This would often be as late as November before they would decide to wait out another winter. Their goal was to have Thanksgiving services as a community gathering at the church and to have people from outlying homesteads gather with them. Perhaps this would be the last time of the year when they would see each other and it was certainly a time to sing praises to the Lord for their well being. The Reverend Shelton would perhaps deliver his best sermon of the year at this time for it was expected to be the last some would hear until spring.

The Reverend spent many hours in study and prayer for this sermon and he was usually rewarded with a message that contained lots of "love for our fellow man" followed by "fire and brimstone." Some of the less devout would choose to quietly leave before the real "fire and brimstone" part was to be delivered. He had a way of making them uncomfortable. Just as at all gatherings of this type, from the beginning of time, I suppose, at least one would bring a little brown jug. These less devout would usually find the fire part in the jug and the brimstone part could wait. Reverend Shelton, being aware of the less devout departure would simply raise his voice in an effort to keep them informed. The effect sometimes awakened the little children but just as often had the same effect on some of the men. Of course they had the excuse that hard work the day before had deprived them of much needed rest. Evidently, they did not need the rest so much that they could sleep through the Thanksgiving meal piled high on the outdoor log table. As stated before, this was a time when memories were made.

Saxson's Branch community was little different from dozens of other towns across the southern part of Virginia land. From somewhere, some place, Henry Saxson obtained the right or claimed the right to sell from a large tract of land in this part of Virginia land. Land was cheap but money was hard to come by, so by the standards of that day, few could afford to buy more than enough to have a large garden plot and a small pasture. Even to own more than two cows made that family well off. As the town of Saxson's Branch began to form, houses were placed far enough apart for the gardens to be beside the house for it was necessary to watch it carefully. Split rail fences would keep out the cows that roamed freely but some wild animals seemed to be drawn to produce that man had slaved over. Most families had a dog to help but that could not be relied on. The end result was that the town of Saxson's Branch was spread along the creek for nearly a mile. The wagon road running the length of town separated the stretch of homes from the sometimes unruly creek. From the front porch of every home, it was possible to see both ends of town and to look down into the creek bottoms. High water sometimes covered the land below the road, but the town itself was secure on higher ground.

The McMellon blacksmith shop was located at the end of town and near giant trees that had been there since the before Columbus thought he had discovered a new land. Obviously, Indians had discovered it long before he was born but they got little credit.

A wagon road of that time was usually along a creek bottom where the creek had played a good part in construction of cleared ground. Many times, the road was also the creek, until it became too deep or treacherous for the wagon. Men had no time for the clearing of trees and other obstacles when it was easier to drive around. Clearing woodland was usually done for the purpose of building a house from the timber or in the clearing of a garden spot. Burning was the only way to dispose of such massive trees and consequently, days when the wind was quiet, smoke columns could be seen for miles.

Saxson's Branch had been well chosen for a town as nature had been kind. Several hundred acres of land was almost free of giant timber, either from fires in the distant past or from the will of God that wanted to present man with a gift of open space. Some would say that life was hard in those times and perhaps they would be right. Those that lived there were there by choice and must have found hard work a small price to pay for freedom, some from the oppression of English rule in places such as Portsmouth, Philadelphia, or London, and some from the oppression of dictators in lands they had recently vacated.

Buildings in Saxson's Branch had a lot in common. All were made of logs with much labor. All were assembled with labor supplied by every man within a day's ride for it was a time when neighbors were absolutely necessary. Every man was used to working with an axe and the adze, for the adze was the tool of choice for dressing wood. With it, floors could be made smooth enough to walk on. With it, doors and frames could be made to fit well enough to keep out the cold. Then there was the crosscut Saw. With it, trees could be felled and ends squared. With it, lumber could be sawed and from that, furniture could be made. Every building was first constructedas a one room log structure with provisions for add-on's. This would get the family into a shelter and let the owner take care of later additions. Obviously, every building had a roof made of split shingles and for this, the froe was the tool of choice. That was the only way to split off shingles with any degree of accuracy and every carpenter made the froe an absolute necessity.

The blacksmith was also necessary to any community and Peyton McMellon had settled here when the community was young. He quickly found work from a wide area and others chose to settle here due to his presence. As a capable blacksmith, Peyton could make an axe or a froe, build a wagon or make a part for an English musket. If no urgent work was to be done, he would be making nails from a coil of wire. Every house in the community needed nails and Peyton found them good trade items for all sorts of things such as food and labor. During his slack time which was very little, Peyton considered the harnessing of Saxton's Branch with a dam so that in the future he might be able to operate a grist mill. Every community needed corn meal and cattle feed and at the present, meal had to come from a mill several miles down stream. Cattle had to do the best they could with shelled corn and much of the nutrition of corn was lost unless it was first ground into finer particles. Although Saxson's branch was a small stream of water in the dry season, it could become a raging torrent from rains upstream in the spring time. A dam would have to be constructed that would withstand the pressure of those floods and it would have to be completed in the very driest of times. Peyton would not be able to complete such a massive project alone, even if the creek was low for all of the summer. No doubt he would have the help of the local men, but even they would not be enough to move the massive amounts of rock and dirt necessary to complete a structure that would withstand a raging flood.

Every man for miles around would benefit from the building of such a dam and because they would, every man would be available once construction was started. It was also true that Peyton could use the power of water to do many chores for him. With a water wheel to turn the stones, he could also move a saw blade and from that, make reasonably smooth boards. Since the time to start the dam would have to wait for a dry summer, he could start the process of shaping mill stones with a hammer and a chisel, many hours of tedious work.

Life in Saxson's Branch was pleasant as the McMellon men continued to prosper and Thomas became more of a force in the blacksmith shop and in town. His knowledge of iron and wood increased with every minor mistake he was to make. Each time he failed at a task, he was encouraged by Peyton to start over and not make the same error a second time. Soon he became known as perhaps a better craftsman than his father, to the pride of Peyton. Saxson's Branch had more than one young lady with an eye for Thomas. He would be more than a good husband and father for he was known as a gentle man, slow to anger and quick to avoid trouble.

With these traits, it was only natural that the eye of every eligible young woman in the surrounding area was fixed on him as a possible husband. At eighteen, Thomas was perhaps at the peak of desirability but he had not yet found time for courtship nor had he considered married life to be for him. His mind was fixed on distant lands to the exclusion of all other thoughts of the future and of course he was planning for saw mills, grist mills and whatever else might present a challenge. Gentle though he might be, the day came when that would change for a brief period of time.

Chapter 3

That came about with the arrival of three men from parts unknown to Thomas. They came to the shop for repairs to a rifle which had been dropped, resulting in a broken hammer and trigger guard. They had been in the shop for less time than it took to tell Thomas what they wanted before Thomas knew them as bullies. Their vulgar language and demanding nature placed Thomas on edge and it was all he could do to keep from asking them to leave. Still, it was his duty, as the operator of the only blacksmith shop for many miles, to do the repairs as quickly and efficiently as possible. The sooner he accomplished this task, the sooner he would see them ride away, or so he thought.

After he finished and was reluctantly paid, dusk was creeping across the meadow so the men had decided to camp at the edge of town and to take advantage of a clear and fast flowing Saxson's Branch. This placed them within hearing of the shop so Thomas was still bothered by their rowdy presence, aggravated by the contents of a large brown jug they had tied behind a saddle. Thomas was in the process of banking the forge fire for the night when Virginia made her usual trip past his shop, hoping for the time when Thomas would give her more than a friendly few moment. Virginia by this time had grown to a lovely young woman, nearly sixteen. She was determined to have Thomas notice how she had filled out in all of the right places.

Perhaps Thomas had not noticed but the three men down by the creek did not fail to notice. The larger of the three, with his finger crooked through the eye of the jug, followed Virginia as she made her way toward the shop. Trailing behind him, the two others followed with drunken grins, knowing their leader was up to catching Virginia as darkness was near.

Unaware of the men, Virginia had timed her arrival at the shop at the edge of dark, knowing that Thomas had to close when he could no longer see to work. Virginia had no warning as a large, dirty hand closed over her mouth while another pinned her to the unseen form behind her. As the other hand closed over her small left breast, Virginia slumped forward in a frightened faint. She was not to know of the rage that overcame Thomas as he chose that moment to leave his shop and see Virginia wrapped in the arms of a man he had already come to despise. Thomas had no weapons except very large hands, bull strength, and rage at a man who would attack his Virginia.

Until that moment, it had never entered his mind that she was his Virginia. Now he was to claim her for life in a struggle that was beyond all that he thought himself capable of. With a rush of a charging bull, Thomas grabbed the man by the throat, causing him to drop the unconscious form and try to tear those large hands from his neck. He would not have lived more than a few moments had it not been for the attack made on Thomas from the other two men.

Now Thomas had three men to fight, all willing to kill him as soon as possible and no holds barred. Thomas realized that he would have to draw the fight away from Virginia to keep her from being hurt as she lay there unconscious. He also realized that he could lose the fight and Virginia would still be in great danger so it was desperation that drove him, even more so now that he had seen one of the men draw a large knife. He understood that to be momentarily pinned in the arms of one of them would allow the knife to do its final work. He understood that he could not defend himself and Virginia without a weapon and none was available.

He could not pick up Virginia and leave the fight as it was evident that nothing would satisfy the three men except to see his blood. As he struggled to land blows on the nearest man and at the same time, dodge the knife, he had drawn them away from Virginia and out into more open space, but he was becoming more winded and slower of movement. As Thomas backed away from the knife, he lost his footing for a moment, allowing the largest of the three to encircle and pin his arms. Now he was faced with the knife and too little time to break the hold he was under. Just before he might feel the knife slide through his rib cage, he saw a look of astonishment come across he face of his opponent and heard the familiar swish of Konaya's arrow as it penetrated a human heart.

As the knife fell to the ground, the man that had his arms pinned released his hold and turned in the direction from which the arrow came, just in time to receive the second arrow in the center of his own chest. Konaya had been watching these men ever since they arrived at Saxson's Branch for he had immediately recognized two of them as the men who had taken his bride, White Deer, over a year ago. He had planned to take them in their night camp as they had crept onto his camp that terrible night when he lost White Deer. He had hoped to find from them some trace of his bride, even though he had long since given her up for dead. These men probably would have killed her before going on into a white community, but he would never give up hope of either finding her or learning of her fate.

The following Sunday found Thomas at the Shelton table at the insistence of Virginia's mother. Nothing less would be acceptable since Thomas had saved Virginia from such a horrible trio of men. Mrs.Shelton sent Thomas and Virginia off for a walk after a delicious meal. Their stroll to the edge of town took them just north and up Saxson's Branch a short distance. The land gently sloped up to a wooded area that had never been cleared of great spreading trees. The forest floor here was so well shaded that there was very little undergrowth and the land nearer the branch was well covered in tall grass. Both young people had decided this was the place for them to build their home, even though neither had spoken to the other about it. Thomas mentioned the beauty of the place and Virginia quickly agreed. There on a beautiful Sunday afternoon, Thomas took both of her hands in his and with misty eyes asked, "Virginia, will you be my bride?" Her answer was to do what she had wanted to do for so very long, place her body as close to his as possible and tilt her face to him for the first kiss. Thus their pledge was sealed and the location for their home was chosen.

Thomas now considered speaking to preacher Shelton of their marriage date and should all agree, Thomas would make the necessary plans for the raising of their new home. There would be no shortage of both men and women to gather for the occasion. All of Saxson's Branch would gather for the cutting of timber and building of the home. As both Thomas and Virginia were well known and much loved, people would come with their tools and plenty of food. Covered wagons would be placed near the branch for the two or three days required for the building. It would be a grand time for all.

Virginia had been for some time working on her Hope Chest. It was half filled with items such as sheets and quilts, but with the plans for a house, she began in earnest on such necessities as curtains and cookware for a kitchen. Virginia's mother pitched in to help with suggestions and help with the more complicated items while her father tried to remain calm. If he had to lose his daughter, he was glad it was to be to someone like Thomas.

Thomas had built the house first in his mind then by scratching out the details on a piece of birch bark. The main structure was to be 30 feet long by 22 feet wide. Thirty feet was about the maximum length a log could be cut and remain near the same diameter from end to end. This structure would be the main living area with the kitchen on one end and bedrooms on the other. The main bedroom would be 10' x 12' with a child's bedroom across the narrow hall. The building would have a loft room with walls only four feet high on the sides but quickly sloping upward toward the center so that there would be eight feet of head room there. This would act as a future bedroom or perhaps more than one. Exposed rafters of cedar would make the room smell delightful for many years to come. Doors would be made of chestnut as well as the interior walls. Thomas had a love for beautiful wood grain patterns and chestnut would certainly supply both color and pattern. Later, Thomas would add a dog trot to allow a new kitchen away from the main living quarters. Heat from the kitchen during the hot part of the year was not welcome.

In the spring, March 1728, winds were blowing away the last of the snow clouds and Thomas, with a few of his close friends, had been cutting timber for a week. Peyton had worked from dawn to dusk to care for the shop so that Thomas would be free to build his future. His home with Virginia was his future, for he could think of little else. They were to be married in May and the Saxson's Branch ladies talked of little else. The house raising was to be a big affair when neighbors would come, even from distant farms, to help one of their own and to celebrate the marriage of the two most loved young people in town. At this time, it was too early to start spring plowing but would soon be necessary for every man to tend to his own fields. It was the best time for the men to gather for helping with the labor, even though it would be a little cool for the women to do their work of cooking and serving outdoors.

Mid March found the men gathered for the last of the timber preparation. Logs were cut and sized for the walls, leaving only the notching of the corner logs to be done last. Sizing of the logs required much labor if the house were to be square and presentable. Both the inside and the outside of the house would have log walls that had been shaved smooth with the foot adze. Care had to be taken to keep the logs the same thickness from end to end so each man using the foot adze had a joy stick. It was so called because it was a joy to complete the labor of shaving the log to the size indicated. Thomas had made several of these so- called sticks from iron, bent into a "u" shape so these where twelve inches inside. The log was shaved to a straight edge on one side, then the joy stick was used to shave the other side to a straight and equal thickness of twelve inches. Once this was completed, it was time for the logs to be sawed to exact length and notching of the ends. For the notching, a two foot saw blade between two sturdy pieces of split oak, called the verticals, which were then spread across a slightly longer oak beam. Opposite the saw blade, a heavy leather strap was wrapped completely around both verticals and secured as tight as possible. Then a small stick of the split oak was placed between the leather straps and twisted until the saw blade was stretched to the limit. This tool was called a buck saw and was used by one man to cut the small notches, one on each end of the log. twelve inches from the squared end, a saw cut was made, top and bottom, then the notch was finished with the foot adze. After locating the large flat stones for the foundation and placing them at the four corners and midway on the four sides, it was time for the foundation logs. On these, the floor joists were to be fitted. Floor joists were sawed straight and ready to fit.

Sawing had been done by four men, two above and two in the pit. The long saw was pulled up by two men on the top side with a little cut into the wood while two men in the pit pulled the saw down with a deep cut into the log. Even though the weather was cool, sawing was hot work and the men in the pit had an even more difficult job as sawdust continually fell on them with every pull of the saw. It soon became very uncomfortable with sawdust falling down inside collars. Thomas took more than his turn in the pit, glad to have the help of his neighbors.

While he was in the pit his mind was working on a plan to do the same job by water power. Details of how it could be done excited him and caused him to think of someday having a water mill for this hard work. What a wonderful thing it would be for water power to cut lumber, grind grain and perhaps do other chores while he had time to work at the things he loved, which was forming iron into useful items. Fitting of the floor joists was done as they were placed across the foundation logs. Each one was notched into the foundation log to an equal depth so the finished floor would be level and smooth. The final floor would be done after the roof was completed.

Now came the dangerous part, walking the logs up on top and into position. For this job, horses would do some of the hard labor and only the most gentle and obedient animals would do for the job. Two very long logs were placed as skid logs,one end on the ground and the other placed on the top log of the cabin.

Two ropes were used on the log to be raised and horse power would drag it up the skid logs. Once on top, man power was required to roll it into place. If care was taken, the notch would fit and the log would be in its final resting place for the next hundred years.

The last week in March found everything ready and word had been spread that Monday would be the day for all to gather. Sunday service at the church would find many people in attendance that came from distant points. They were in Saxson's Branch both for the time in church and for the following day when folks would gather, visiting and catching up on gossip, news and good stories. One story told was about two small boys who were regulars at preacher Shelton's every service, including burial services. They were seen digging a small hole out back of the church and a curious lady quietly listened to what was taking place. She saw one of them, with a dead bird in hand, gently place the bird in the grave with these words;"In the name of the Father, the Son, and in the holehegoes."

May 1728 arrived unseasonably warm which all of the folks of Saxson's Branch took as a good omen for the wedding to take place the first Sunday. Thomas had finished the house with the help of many friends, and

Virginia had hung curtains, placed throw rugs, and arranged the furniture Thomas had made. Most of the furniture Thomas had made was not up to his standards but would do until he had more time next winter. It made little difference to Virginia as anything he made was beautiful in her eyes. Her mother gave many items that she could do without or could share until Thomas found time to take Virginia to a city where manufactured goods could be purchased. Thomas was working every hour from dawn to well into the night, trying to make the house perfect for Virginia and also trying not to let his part of the shop work fall on his father. Four months back, Thomas and his father had started building a very well made and heavy wagon for Thomas, knowing that he would be using it to haul supplies to his new home. Now that it was almost finished, Thomas had decided to continue construction so it could be used as a comfortable home for Virginia on the several day's trip to Portsmouth. He considered the trip to Portsmouth to be a honeymoon and a shopping trip for Virginia. After a few weeks in their new home, the shopping list would grow to make the trip all the more exciting and profitable.

The wedding Sunday morning arrived, beautiful weather with many buggies and wagons arriving for preacher Shelton's usual fire and brimstone service. Today, no one was on the hot seat, no fire and no brimstone, just Proverbs 31:10:"Who can find a virtuous woman? For her price is far above rubies, the heart of her husband doth safely trust in her, so that he shall have no need of spoil. She will do him good and not evil all the days of her life." Again, Thomas felt that Preacher Shelton was speaking only to him, which he was. This time, he did not squirm with embarrassment, but he glowed with pride. Since it was the day of the wedding, which was to follow right after morning service, Virginia and many of the women were not in attendance. They were at the parsonage next door or preparing tables outside with food for the wedding feast following the ceremony. It was much appreciated that Preacher Shelton made the service short in order to continue with the wedding.

Mrs. Beckett was at the organ and at the request of the Minister, started softly playing the old hymn which Isaac Watts penned from the 118th Psalm in the early seventeen hundreds: "This is the day that the Lord hath made, we will rejoice and be glad in it." As the bridesmaids entered and took their places, Thomas stood facing the door, hardly believing the time had come when he would have title to his Virginia for life. As the bride stepped through the door, he was almost unable to breathe for he had never before seen such a lovely sight. Her snow-white gown in contrast to a radiant, youthful face caused more than one in the congregation to catch their breaths. Virginia was wearing her mother's wedding gown, possibly the most beautiful gown ever, having been made for her 20 years ago in

Philadelphia where they lived until after their marriage. Preacher Shelton was to perform the ceremony, provided he was able to speak past emotions constricting his throat. To see his lovely daughter dressed in the gown worn by his wife of the past twenty years was almost enough to deny him speech.

Warm winds of May had done a spectacular job of producing flowers in Saxon's Branch, both wild and cultivated. It seemed the ladies of the community had brought every flower from miles around, so many that even the floors were strewn with colorful blossoms. Two beautiful little girls were dressed in white, with pink sashes around their waists and pink ribbons in their hair. They were carrying arm loads of flowers to dress the pathway of Virginia to Thomas and her father. The bridesmaids were dressed in pale pink with white sashes around their waists and carrying bouquets of white wild roses. White apple blossom sprigs adorned their hair and made the entire scene almost unreal in beautiful colors.

Preacher Shelton had the double duty of giving his daughter's hand in marriage and also performing the ceremony. Neither duty was anything but pleasant but made his choice of words somewhat difficult:"I, Ezra Shelton give the hand of my daughter, Virginia Alice Shelton, to Thomas Jefferson McMellon in holy matrimony." The Reverend Ezra Shelton now asked"Virginia Alice, do you take this man as your lawful husband, to love and to serve until death do you part?" Virginia could hardly breathe much less say the word but she managed a whispered, "yes.""Thomas Jefferson McMellon, do you take Virginia Alice to be your lawfully wedded wife, to have, to love and to protect for so long as you shall live?" Thomas could hardly restrain himself from a whoop of joy that could be heard by all in the community. Instead, he managed to quietly say yes and add words of thanks to Reverend Shelton for the ceremony and for his most precious gift, the hand of his daughter.

After the ceremony, Thomas was allowed to accompany her to the parsonage for a change of clothing more suitable for the wedding feast. Later, they joined many people at tables laden with all manner of good foods. It seemed that every woman for miles around had brought the best she had and lots of it. There was so much that Thomas and Virginia could not possibly please everyone, but by taking small portions from each, they tried. They were so happy that no food at all would have been enough, so they sampled as much as possible. The afternoon passed so very slowly for them as they wanted to be in their own home, alone at last. Darkness was well surrounding the camp before they could slip away. Campfires were burning brightly all over the area as each wagon seemed to have a gathering, reluctant to call it a day.

At last, Thomas could lift his lovely Virginia in his arms and carry her across the threshold, into the home they had both worked on for so many weeks. Entry this time was so different.

Tonight they were one. To start a married life in their own home was almost more than either could believe, but both had worked hard for this wonderful start.

Thomas that had to be first and he did so by picking Virginia up in a loving embrace and taking her to the bedroom. Although Thomas was exceedingly strong, he was so gentle with Virginia that their first hours were filled with such delight as to never be repeated.

Chapter 4

The next three months were filled with hard work for Thomas, but delightful days for them as a newly married couple. Even with hard work and tired bodies, they found their time together to be filled with delight in each other. The wagon was ready for the trip to Portsmouth and both had a long shopping list for the home and the shop. Virginia was excited as she would have time to purchase gifts for her family, including Peyton. Her relationship with Peyton had developed to a love, equal to that of her own father. Peyton in turn had found a love for her that was equal to a daughter that he never had and for the first time since the loss of Mary, he became aware of his loneliness. With Thomas out of his house he faced long sleepless nights and sad memories of his life with Mary.

As much as he dared, he spent time with his children. He was fearful of making himself unwelcome, but Virginia never considered him other than family. Peyton, as well as Virginia's parents, also had a shopping list for the Portsmouth trip and Thomas figured it would take two or three days there to fill it all. As leaving time approached, Thomas and Peyton took great care to equip the wagon with all the comforts they could devise for Virginia. It would be her first trip away from home and her first trip where wagon travel would require cooking outside.

Camping would be a better name for it. In general, August would be a dry month with very warm nights so Thomas had little preparation for outside living except a canvas extending out from the side of the wagon. In case of a shower, this would be large enough to protect them while cooking or sleeping. Should bad weather develop, the covered wagon was more than sufficient for protection. It would be too warm to sleep inside at night unless rain did come so outside living was preferred.

Their first day on the road was one of the most exciting times in the young life of Virginia. They met many people along the road and at the pace the team was traveling, there was time to call out greetings. On occasion, they would rest the team for a spell while inquiring as to trace conditions ahead. Brief conversations with strangers changed them from strangers to friends for it was easy for Virginia to make friends.

Camping that first night was beside a clear stream where the horses could find plenty of grass and easy rest. They had not been used to long hours in harness as their riders were not used to travel in a bumpy wagon. Besides, Thomas wanted to give Virginia time to get well organized before dark on this their first night out. After all, this was supposed to be their honeymoon and Thomas had found the perfect place for them to sleep out under the moon and the stars. He need not have worried about Virginia's ability to adapt to this way of travel. She loved it and performed as if it was the only way of life she knew. Before Thomas had time to get a good cooking fire underway, she had skillets out with ham ready to fry, and biscuits were mixed and ready for buttermilk to be added. Potatoes were peeled and almost ready for the larger of the two skillets and the coffee pot had been filled from the clear stream just beside the wagon. Thomas had little to do except tend to the horses. They needed to be curried and hobbled for the night, but for the time they were up, he had them tied to a small area where grass was plentiful. Before bedding down for the night, he would hobble them and allow them to roam free.

After a supper fit for kings, Virginia placed bedding between the coals of the cooking fire and the wagon where the canvas would protect them from night dew which would settle as night air cooled.

Darkness fell with a complete blackness except from the stars in a clear sky. As they lay in a comfortable place where they could watch for the moon to appear in the eastern sky, they talked of heaven and how close they were to it tonight. Peace was so full around them that each felt no other couple had ever had the feeling before them. Each silently thanked God for such a wonderful companion and a peaceful time.

Both Thomas and Virginia were having such a good time that they deliberately made each day's trip end early. As a result, they were five days in reaching Portsmouth, and they thought it a bit too soon. Still, they had much to do and neither had seen such a lively place as Portsmouth turned out to be. They had to find a place to stable their team and a hotel for the two or three days expected. Nothing would do except for Thomas to be with Virginia while she did her shopping, most of it in ladies' stores. In those places, Thomas usually found a quiet corner and made himself invisible. Virginia in turn went with Thomas through many hardware stores for his purchase of tools and iron to be worked in the shop. They found most restaurants to their liking, but a few not so. Both preferred their camp food but it was nice to finish eating and leave without cleaning pans and dishes. Their last day in Portsmouth was hard work for them, gathering their purchases and loading the wagon. As it always turns out, there were a few items to buy at the last minute and a few they never located.

Nevertheless, the morning came to start the return trip, dawning clear but with the promise of a very hot and troubled sky. Thomas had a little trouble with the team as they seemed reluctant to leave the stable. He considered it to be what is known as "barn sour," or a lazy team due to the comforts of good hay in a cool barn. Soon they were on their way into open country going home. The wagon was laden with so many heavy goods that the team sensed they had work to do and they soon settled down. Even as they did, the sky became unruly with clouds racing across the horizon, and Thomas wondered about an August storm. His team worked hard but became increasingly nervous and hard to handle. It appeared they wanted to run and Thomas had to watch them carefully for fear they would take the wagon off the road he chose and perhaps break a wheel in a rut or on a rock. As the sky became even more unruly near noon time, Thomas decided to call it a day and find a camping place on higher ground. A storm, if it came, could cause the streams to rise quickly and he would rather not be camped near one.

Thunder rolled across the darkened sky as lightning flashed in almost a continuous bolt. Thomas had a very difficult time in holding the team from a mad dash for the other side of anyplace.

The team was so frightened they could only think of one thing...to run. Thomas gave the reins to Virginia with hopes she could hold them in check until he could reach the front of the team where his presence would calm the frightened animals.

When he did take the bridle of the lead animal and spoke in a calming voice, the horses seemed to believe he would take care of them. By this action, he was able to lead them to high ground at the edge of the woods. Here the wind was held in check by the trees and it seemed to calm all of them. Virginia was fearful that the wind would tear away the canvas covering leaving them exposed to wind and rain, as well as destroy their purchases. Thomas asked her to stay inside while he removed the harness from the horses and tethered them in under the trees. He understood the danger of lightning while under the trees but he also understood the need to keep the horses calm and this was the only way.

By this time the rain was coming not down but horizontal, driven by winds strong enough to cause him concern. He could do nothing but join Virginia inside the covering and wait it out. When he entered, he found Virginia on her knees in prayer. His heart melted with love for a companion who he knew would be with him until death. Virginia could not hear him enter over the noise of the storm so Thomas stood silently, watching her and then praying with her for their safety. Through the night, there was no thought of sleep as the wind and rain continued to pound the covering. Thomas was pleased with the way the wagon held against the storm. His work was something to be proud of. And he was grateful for the protection it gave his Virginia.

Toward dawn, the wind abated and with it, rain slacked. There had been no rest for either of them and none would be had this day until Thomas could care for the horses and Virginia could prepare food. After Thomas moved and staked the horses in a grassy area, he had to find wood suitable for a cooking fire. Everything was soaked, including him, but with a workout cutting wood, he would soon dry. By cutting a small dead tree, he was able to find dry wood and have a fire going in a short time. Even though it was August, the storm had made it seem like November with cold air on wet clothing, so when Thomas got the fire started, Virginia was glad for the warmth as she started cooking. They could not fail to see the stream where they would normally have camped, flooded with torrents of muddy water. Had they not found high ground, everything would have been lost, perhaps even their lives.

As it was, there was no possibility of continuing the trip home while water covered so much of the road ahead. By noon, they were well fed. The sun was quickly drying everything but there was still no possibility of continuing until the stream fell enough to clear the road. For the remainder of the day, Thomas and Virginia rested and prepared for the continuing trip of the next day. Virginia took advantage of the hot coals from the fire which had been burning for hours. It was the best kind of heat for baking and she had time to do so. Normally, bread would take several hours to rise, but she had placed dough in the bread box the day before and it was almost ready.

Thomas had checked the wagon for any problems the storm had caused but he had built it well and there was nothing for him to do except care for the horses and keep up the fire. He was never one to idle away his time and this would have made him restless except that he had wood and a knife. He had earlier chosen a small cherry tree for firewood, as it would burn well and with a sweet odor. Cherry was also excellent for carving and he wanted to carve a ladle for Virginia. It gave both of them great pleasure to be busy while waiting for the water to subside.

As dusk began to fall on their camp site, they had a wonderful meal of hot bread, ham and pinto beans. Virginia had put them over the fire in a large iron kettle early that morning and all day Thomas had been asking..."When??" Virginia had gathered dandelion greens for a salad to compliment what Thomas considered a perfect meal. She had treated the greens with a generous covering of buttermilk and spices purchased in Portsmouth. She had also made tea from a mixture of dried sassafras root and fresh bark from the spice bush which was a common bush and growing near their camp. Thomas gave the blessing as follows...

"Bless this food before us spread.
Our thanks oh Lord for this thy bread.
Be with those less fortunate than we.
Forgive us our sins, particularly me.
Lead us oh Lord in all that we do.
Prepare us oh God for eternity with you."

The earth was drying fast so it was certain that they would be leaving at dawn tomorrow. All day the sun had been drying their belongings and the water level had fallen. Thomas placed a canvas on the earth between the fire and their wagon for their bedding. Once again they had the very great pleasure of sleeping under the stars.

All too soon, dawn found them well rested and ready for the day's journey. Even the horses seemed ready for the day as Thomas placed the harness on them and hitched them to the wagon. At first light, they were on their way, anxious to return home now that they had lost a day of travel. It was to be another good day for them, bright sunshine and not too hot. The road was little more than a trail at best but after the flood many of what used to be ruts was now washed-out gullies across the trail. Thomas had to be constantly on the alert for these gullies and also for the rocks that had been exposed by flood waters. Either obstacle could break a wagon wheel in half and leave them stranded for perhaps days. Although Thomas could make a new wheel, it would be impossible without his tools and the iron for the tire. Making a tire was the most demanding of the blacksmith's trade for it had to be cut from a large roll of iron, curved, and fitted to the new wheel. Then it had to be welded into the correct size by heating the ends in the forge and hammering the metal into a continuous flowing circle. Next it had to be heated all around so the metal would expand and while very hot, it would be forced over the new wheel and quickly dropped into water. This would stop the metal from burning the wooden wheel and also shrink the metal tire so the wheel would be tightened into the spokes and held together firmly. Construction of the wooden parts of the wheel had to be made of dry and seasoned wood so that it would not shrink after the wheel was put to use. In very dry times, the wagon would be deliberately driven through water in order to keep the wheel tire tight. Today, that was not a worry to Thomas for he had to drive through muddy tracks and carefully cross the stream several times.

At noon time, they stopped only long enough for the team to rest and to eat the oats Thomas had brought for them. Virginia as usual had food prepared for them from breakfast time and from bread baked the day before. Neither of them had any idea of why they felt troubled and they did not speak of it to each other. Thomas had a feeling of dread or fear that he could not explain as everything seemed to be going so well. The small river they were following was almost quiet again and the road was almost dry. Certainly the home pasture was only a day or so ahead and Thomas was allowing them to travel at a brisk pace. Virginia had the same peculiar dread or fear in the pit of her stomach but she, like Thomas, said nothing. Without speaking of it, both were willing the horses to hurry.

On the evening of the third day, Saxson's Branch came into view and the feeling of dread was like a live knot in the pits of their stomachs. Both of them were glad to see their home still standing as both had a fear of fire. They also looked for signs of fire or trouble over the entire village as it came into view. Everything seemed to be well but the feeling was stronger than ever, especially since they had passed several people at the edge of town who waved but did not call out the usual greeting. Thomas directed the team to the blacksmith shop instead of to their home as he felt the need to see his father first. As he halted the team at the door, Peyton came out to meet them and it was obvious that he had not been working. His clothes and his hands were clean and this gave Thomas a greater feeling of dread than he had ever known. Peyton did not give the usual shout of welcome, instead he went to the far side and offered Virginia his hand to help her down. When she was down and facing him, he could not speak. He folded her in his arms with love and compassion as he told her of her parents.

Preacher Shelton and his wife had been over in the adjoining valley to minister to a sick family when the storm broke across the valley. From what had been learned, they had started for home just before the rain came in torrents. One of their team had returned to the stable with harness half off and several cuts and bruises. Yesterday, most of the men of the town had gone down river to search for them but so far, all that had been located was the remains of their wagon. It could only be speculated that they were both carried down stream in the flash flood and that their bodies would never be recovered. Peyton told them that a church service had been in place for several hours and that many of the people had returned home in exhaustion.

Nothing more could be done. In two days, there would be a memorial service for them and without the love of Thomas, Virginia would have found it unbearable. The entire community expressed Christian love for Virginia in every way possible but there was little they could do. Only God and time could heal the wound of losing both parents and never having their bodies where flowers could be placed by them. Virginia hated to leave the house and could not possibly go to the church where her father had been so often seen and heard. For her, every morning at waking was torture for she must go through the day seeing the things her mother had so lovingly helped her put together. After two weeks of this, she spoke to Thomas about moving to another county, far enough away to help her forget the tragedy she had to face every day. Thomas was torn between the love for his father and for Virginia but he remembered the words of Virginia's father, so often spoke from the pulpit. "That a man must cleave to his wife" was the words that echoed in his mind and Thomas needed no biblical encouragement to do just that. Thomas would leave his father.

Chapter 5

October

Now that both Thomas and Virginia had a desire to move to a new land, preparations were started. The land beyond the mountains came to life again. Beautiful streams and rolling hills. New land to explore and to tame his desires. In his mind's eye, he could see the stream with a small dam and water doing his bidding. A grist mill, saw mill and a beautiful home for Virginia, but the picture was always blurred by the thought of Peyton being left behind.

Already the chill night air spoke of the promise of a coming winter, with snows and winds that would bite through the best of woolen clothing. He had to start thinking of March of next year, a time to leave, of work to do, or mountain trails cut out by migrating buffalo over generations past. It would require much preparation, much thought and much hard work. He must build another wagon, one that would protect his one and only love, Virginia. It must be strong enough to carry his iron tools and supplies and little else, for with them and his hands, he would build a home for Virginia.

Although Thomas and Virginia lived in a time and a place where twenty or thirty families could be considered a town, it was still necessary to keep cattle and horses nearby. Farm work was hard and both were well versed in the animal care. Thomas worked every day except Sunday, repairing or building wagons and farm implements, shoeing horses and forming iron parts for many things. He had worked in his father's shop since a small child, running errands, bringing in wood for the heater and quenching the fire at just the right time to make charcoal for the forge. Thomas had developed strength and stature early and now at nineteen, he was a giant in comparison to his peers. He was strong but very gentle with people and with the animals under his care. Many hours of using a hammer and tongs at the forge had given Thomas hands large enough to almost encircle the tiny waist of his petite Virginia. Petite though she might be, at sixteen Virginia was more than capable of holding her own in any kitchen or on any farm. She shared with Thomas the love of animals and often held the bridle of a nervous horse as Thomas applied shoes. Virginia's calm and soothing voice could do wonders with the wildest of animals.

Thomas could not delay talking to his father any longer. He could not consider such an undertaking without his father's blessing. After many sleepless and prayerful nights, he would speak to Peyton as father and equal. He was filled with sadness at the prospect of leaving Peyton behind, thinking him too old for such a journey. He also considered his father's place in the community to be so firmly entrenched as to be irreplaceable. After the death of preacher Shelton, his father had become the church leader, trying to serve as pastor until another minister could be found. What Thomas did not consider was that God would have a hand in the undertaking.

Before he could bring himself to speak to his father, a remarkable thing happened. Saxson's Branch community became Saxsonville. Land developers had arrived and with them came merchants with an interest in a large general store. Many things Peyton had been expected to make for his neighbors would now be sold in the new general store, manufactured in the north and freighted to Saxsonville. Even so, the need for a blacksmith shop was still much in demand. More people arriving would bring more horses, wagons and other farm implements to repair. Along with the new arrivals came the will of God in the form of a blacksmith with money and a desire to buy a growing business. It was then that Thomas told his father of the plan to move across the mountains and it was then that Peyton made the decision to sell and go with his children. Peyton lost no time in striking a deal where the new owner would allow Thomas and Peyton the use of the shop to prepare for the journey.

The new owner had anticipated having a blacksmith shop somewhere south of Portsmouth but he did not know at the time how he would come to that end. In order to have the labor he would need, he had brought Henry and Mary Spears with him. Henry was not yet trained as a blacksmith but he was young and strong, also a very willing worker. Mary was much like Henry, not yet trained to wilderness life but a very eager to learn young woman. The community pitched in to make a place for them to live while the new owner prepared a place for himself in the shop.

November arrived with cold nights and balmy days. October colors had faded to brown and clear skies at night gave Thomas and Virginia a restful time they would cherish for the remainder of their lives. Crops were all laid by, and fruits and berries had all been canned, dried or preserved for the winter to come.

The last of the fall work that both dreaded was butchering of hogs, still to come. The work was not what they dreaded so much but the killing of animals. Somehow, killing a wild turkey or a henhouse chicken did not affect either of them as it did to butcher a pig that had been given a name. "Old Snort" or "Miss Squeelie" may not be much of a name but it still carried the familiarity of part of the family. By the time the hogs were in the smoke house, salted down and wrapped in a thick film of hickory smoke, the name Old Snort and Miss Whatchamacallit were almost forgotten. Now was the time to gather the last of the bounty provided by

the endless hills and woods. Hickory nuts, chestnuts, walnuts and butternuts were there by the bushels. Townspeople who kept many hogs let them run free in the woods to feast on the fallen nuts for two or three months. So long as there was food close by, the hogs would not wander far.

Thomas loved to spend time with his Virginia when the evening stars began to show. He loved to walk the fields, to the edge of the woods, where there was a place to sit and rest. Most of all, he loved to cradle her petite form under his arm and to feel her hair against his cheek while they watched the stars begin to appear. Although Thomas could look at the stars and know that Heaven was out there, to him Heaven was to hold Virginia next to him. God's Heaven was distant in both time and space. He could not use the word Heaven to describe his feeling for Virginia, but he knew she was a gift from his God.

There in the bliss of evening rest, Thomas did much of the planning of how he would build a home for Virginia and perhaps a son to carry on his name. He often thought of a daughter who would be an exact copy of Virginia so he could watch her grow from childhood to become like the beautiful woman he now held underhis arm. There, at those times, was when Thomas became a true child of God. Then and there he held all that was dear to him and in his heart he spoke to God of his love of life and of blessings, too many to name.

Winter was fast approaching and the new owner was doing more than his share of the work in the blacksmith shop. This left Thomas and Peyton more time and it was much needed for now they had decided to leave Saxsonville and move across the Appalachian Mountains. For this, they needed much larger and more sturdy wagons.

It was decided that they would take a large supply of iron and tools with them as they would find it much easier to set up a new shop if they did not have to make new tools. Since they had little knowledge of their final destination, they could not know what they would need, but they did know a good supply of these items would make life easier.

Obviously, it would require more of their wagons and it would also require four oxen to each wagon as well as horses. This meant more animal food to carry and it seemed never ending to put together the list of items to go with them. They understood that many items of food could be bought from people along the way but they could not depend on this. As for animal food, they felt that they could do with the grass found most of the way, but grass was scarce if not nonexistent in the deep woods that they expected to travel through. Virginia was to be considered above all else. Of concern was her kitchen for the trail as well as the items she would need to set up a new home. Thomas would allow her to decide on the things she would need and if necessary, he would leave some of his things off the list.

Thomas and Peyton had a good stock of seasoned oak and sassafras they had sawed in years past. It was select wood as it had been racked and dried with care. From this stock, they chose the best for their wagons. Oak for the frame work was used for the strength and sassafras for sides that did not require so much strength. Sassafras had a natural oil that made it better for turning water and it was lighter in weight. It was also easier to cut and shape and gave off a nice odor while it was being worked.

Neither Thomas nor Peyton would think of themselves as wheel-wrights or specialists in the construction of wheels, but they did know the trade and they did know the necessity of a strong wheel. This was to be the first and most difficult part of building their wagons and they would need eight wheels, plus four spares. Each of the four front and the four back wheels had to be interchangeable so the replacement of a wheel would fit the axel. Next would be the framework which would be built on four level corner posts set in the ground so that the structure would be down at a more convenient working level and also aid them in keeping the wagon straight and level.

Construction plans were to build a wagon bed nineteen feet in length and six feet wide. The sides were to be four feet high with at least two feet of height at the rear. Above this two foot end, there would be another two feet of drop tailgate and the hopes were to make the wagons as near boat-like as possible. Keeping the wagons narrow would help in passing through trees when the time came that it could not be avoided. The wagons had to be capable of carrying about two or three tons each since there would be no way to return for additional supplies for perhaps many years.

Peyton made the list to be purchased from a Ships Chandler in Portsmouth and to buy bolts and rivets which he would not have time to make at the forge. He also needed to take along enough sail cloth to cover the wagons and for tents as temporary housing in the new land. Although it seemed to him that he might be over doing it, he decided on a thousand feet of one inch rope and enough caulking to make both wagons as near water proof as possible. Caulking would be a very precious commodity in the construction and for repairs on the trail. This material was made of a mixture of cotton and hemp fiber saturated with melted tar. He also decided to take along a good supply of this tar for the purpose of renewing the waterproofing of the wagons.

There would be many streams to cross and he would not know the extent of these hazards until he faced them on the trail. Peyton would be at least three and perhaps four weeks on the trip to Portsmouth and would need two regular wagons and teams of horses for the load he would have. Thomas agreed to stay and help the new owner so Henry could go with Peyton and leave Thomas to care for the shop and start the frame construction of the two new wagons.

Peyton and Henry made good time to Portsmouth and caught a favorable time to do the shopping and loading of his wagons. Peyton thought the prices were much too high but with no choice, he made the purchases as necessary. This would be the last place to buy anything, perhaps for many years. In fact, he thought there would be little use for money at their new location, not for many years to come. It was during this trip that Henry decided his and Mary's future lay with the McMellon's.

The return trip was without incident and they arrived a full week before expected. Of course, Thomas was delighted to see the mountain of goods for it was his future in the wilderness.

Before Thomas could do much in the way of looking through the wagons, he caught the sound of an animal in one of the wagons. Fearful of being bitten or otherwise maimed, he cautiously lifted each box and covering until he found Peyton's gift to him. He lifted it up and held it close under his chin in order to quiet its uneasy whining, delighted to see that it had the very same marking as Ole Ring. Virginia had the pleasure of holding it and giving it a name. Being a female companion for Ole Ring made it an easy choice, Lil Ringo. Perhaps Peyton thought the pup was for Thomas but he was wrong. Ringo was taken to heart by all of them and became a constant companion of Ole Ring as well.

December. Thomas worked on the new wagons as long as there was light to see. Virginia and Mary made certain he did not want for food and water. Christmas this year was just between the family with very little done in the church. It seemed too sad for Thomas and Virginia and, of course, Peyton saw it in the entire community. Building the frame work of their wagons was the critical part as it required a gentle curve with the center, to be lower by 1 ½ feet. This would help stabilize the load as the wagons were going up or down steep trails. With the exception of Christmas day, Thomas never stopped working. The wagons were too important to leave for more than a day.

After it was built, the entire wagon bed would be jacked up and wheels put on the axels. Last would be the fitting of canvas stays or bows and then the canvas would be made to fit.

By February, the wagons were completed and it was well as the weather turned cold, almost too cold to work outside. Thomas had little to do outside except care for his animals and search for more animals to purchase for their trip. During this part of the year, horses did little work and some of them looked in poor shape, partly from lack of good grazing and partly from lack of grooming. Thomas had good knowledge of horse flesh and was in a good position of timing to buy. By the first of March, he had four well fed and cared for horses as well as the eight oxen. Virginia had lost much of her interest in her home since the loss of her parents, but she found new direction when Thomas asked her to help care for the horses. He needed no help but he recognized Virginia's need to have something to care for. With her love for the animals, she soon had them loving her and showing it by coming to her whenever she went to the barn. Sometimes it looked to be dangerous for her to see all of them trying to get close to her. There was even a little jealousy among them and sometimes they would bite each other causing a commotion which looked as if she could be trampled.

During this time of very cold weather, Thomas worried about his friend Konaya. He had not spent much time with him since his marriage to Virginia. He had taken Virginia with him to the woods last summer and the three of them had walked to some of Konaya's favorite places. The Indian had never allowed either Thomas or Virginia to know where he stayed and it seemed that he always knew when Thomas was in the woods. Thomas had assumed he lived in a nearby and secure place, but with such cold weather, he had to worry. The Indian had never been one to visit the home of Thomas and Virginia, but with the addition of horses and the frequent trips she made to the barn, Konaya began to visit the barn. He and Virginia became very close friends and Virginia began to talk to him of her God. Konaya had a very strong belief in a great spirit but he had no understanding of words written about the God of Virginia. He told her of watching many people go to the Sunday service and told her of how his family used to gather at certain times to call on the great spirit. He never explained more about his family and although Virginia had a burning curiosity, she never asked.

Konaya had so little knowledge of Jesus the Christ that Thomas and Virginia were eager to teach him by reading to him. However, old English was too difficult for Konaya to grasp, so they made every effort to get him in their church group discussions, even if some would object. His limited understanding of the English language also made this difficult. His desire to learn was evident to Virginia and it seemed necessary to have him in her home more frequently so that she and Thomas could teach with more patience than was exhibited by the church group.

Virginia and Thomas took great pleasure in teaching Konaya English and the Bible, and he was eager to learn both. By the time they learned a small part of Konaya's story, a firm bond had been secured and Konaya became part of their family. Konaya seemed to have a natural affinity for horses and spent many hours in grooming them. While he was caring for the horses, Virginia would often use this time to read to him from the Bible.

Konaya loved to hear Virginia tell and read of "Eternal life"as promised by her God. Most of all he wanted her to tell of how she would see her father and mother again and be with them forever. Virginia deduced from this that Konaya had lost all of his family and was lonesome. This was reason enough for her to spend more time in the stables and more time telling the Indian about her God. The day came when he asked her how he could be certain of this wonderful gift of life and it gave her great pleasure to tell him of Jesus and the cross. She was privileged to have a Bible and understand the words of Paul when he said in Romans 10: 9-13: "That if thou shall confess with thy mouth the LORD JESUS, and shalt believe in thine heart that GOD hath raised him from the dead, thou shalt be saved.—For with the heart man believeth unto righteousness and with the mouth confession is made unto salvation.—For the scripture saith, whosoever believeth on him shall not be ashamed.- –For there is no difference between the Jew and the Greek: For the same LORD over all is rich unto all that call unto him.—For whosoever shall call upon the name of the LORD shall be saved." Although Konaya could think of no sins he had committed, he gladly asked for forgiveness for all past and future sins and accepted the saving grace of Jesus the Christ. Now he was a brother to Thomas, Virginia and Peyton.

Chapter 6

In 1663-64-Gabriel Arthur was the first recorded Englishman to see the mouth of the Kanawha River, then known as the "Conoy" from a Shawnee tribe. They controlled the lower river and produced salt for sale and trade.

The Conoy Indians had a permanent camp about sixty miles up the Conoy River and another six miles up past the Elk River mouth.

In 1669 the French out of Montreal started exploring the Ohio Valley but left no records of having crossed the Ohio River.

1671, Governor William Berkley sent an expedition to explore the Kanawha Valley. Thomas Batts and Robert Fallam set out September 1,1671, crossing through the Roanoke River gap and up the Shenandoah Valley. They neared the head waters of the Kanawha before turning back. They retreated in fear of the Conoy salt works Indians when they met a lone white man who claimed to have nearly lost his life to them.

Little is known of the next 25 years except that the French claimed all the land drained by the Ohio River. Their claim was based on a claim of Sieur De La Salle that he had discovered the Ohio River in 1669.

It was not until 1755 that the first English hunters came in numbers and this was the beginning of the French and Indian wars. These next eight years were bloody on all sides.

1726, Irish, Scottish and German immigrants began to pour into the Shenandoah Valley, seeking cheap land. William Penn's heirs began selling 100 acre plots for 10 pounds. The old wagon road up the valley became crowded with settlers building log cabins. Many continued on south into North Carolina where the Tuscarora Indian nation was being driven out. Already, some had crossed the Blue Ridge mountains, sending word back of a fabulous land. A few hardy men had continued across the Appalachian Mountain chain and returned with almost unbelievable stories of mountains, streams of clear water and unlimited game for hunting.

By 1740, Thomas had heard stories enough to fill him with a desire to see these wonderful sites. The English had moved south from Canada in an effort to claim the Ohio-Indiana territory. They had also extended the long arm of taxation to Saxsonville. It was not a reasonable tax but oppressive and demanding. In 1725 there were only 5 newspapers in the 13 Continental Colonies.

When copies of one of these weekly papers did arrive in Saxsonville, it was usually worn thin but contained enough for Thomas and Virginia to learn of England's unfair control of all except the English rulers. As this news continued to arrive, telling of even more English control, Thomas, Peyton and Henry set their westward goal even further west across the Appalachians. Of course, Virginia was delighted that Mary was to be a member of their party westward.As they became closer and more understanding of the lonely existence of Konaya, they found him to be from the Cherokee tribe, far to the west. His story was one of great loss and tragedy.

Konaya had been given a beautiful young maiden as wife several winters past. They had enjoyed a short season together west of the Appalachian Mountains. They had been hunting and fishing in the headwaters of that river he called the beautiful Conoy, which translated to mean unhealthy. All was at peace with them so they had no fear of night camp troubles as long as a fire blazed to keep animals at bay. The blazing fire brought their downfall as it was seen by three white men in an area where none was ever known before. Konaya was awakened by a cry from his woman, White Deer. Her cry gave him only enough time to see by the firelight that she was held by one man and the club descending on him by another white.

Daybreak found Konaya struggling to regain his senses by a cold fire and no sign of White Deer. With all of the strength he could muster, Konaya picked up the trail of three men and signs of bare feet, his woman, being half dragged up stream. He had no idea of when he had been clubbed and left for dead, but by the signs left behind, he knew they had hours of head start. They had left him nothing in his night camp. No weapon, no robe, no food and little more than his life. Even that they had intended to take. They were keeping to the stream course deeper into the mountains to the southeast.

To Konaya, that indicated no fear of pursuit as they thought him dead. His first concern was to find weapons and to recover from the terrible blows to his upper body and head. He could not follow for two days but felt that traveling alone would allow him to catch up and rescue White Deer. When he was able to follow,

he found the trail and, as suspected, it followed the stream. Even so, he was not able to overtake them before the stream ended at a pass through the mountains. Konaya, heartsick, continued into unknown land in a futile search. By now, rains and weather had erased their signs of a trail. All he could do was continue the path of least resistance, thinking his enemies would also take the easy path. Konaya wandered through many miles of Virginia land with little to guide him. When he did encounter a settler's log cabin, he did not approach it. He would stay out of sight and watch for any sign of his White Deer or her captors.

Chapter 7

Thomas began to tell Konaya more of his plan to cross the mountains to the west and to find a new home. Thomas noted a gleam in the eye of Konaya, but it was some time later that Konaya expressed a desire to accompany them. Nothing could have given Thomas more pleasure than to have Konaya act as guide, friend and brother in Christ for the difficult journey. As they planned the trip, Konaya outlined the path he had been over as being mountainous and difficult, but not impossible. It would be best to cross the southernmost tip of the Blue Ridge mountain chain and then follow the valley north to the old buffalo migration trail that headed west.

It would be possible to go to the warm springs held sacred by all Indian tribes and much used by buffalo, for it was known as "white stinking water springs" and as a cure for old and infirm bones that ached with changes in weather.

As plans were made, Thomas realized he must take animals with him that were common in Saxsonville but not available in the new land such as chickens, hogs and cows. It would not be possible to keep hogs in the wagons and not possible to drive them as he could do with cows. He could only expect Peyton and himself to drive an oxen team; therefore, he was limited to two wagons, or was he?

After discussion with Peyton, they decided to build a small, single axel trailer to hitch behind either large wagon. This trailing wagon would be only large enough to carry 6 newborn pigs and twelve chickens. It would also carry the spare wagon wheels and food for the animals. It would use the same large wheels as used by the two wagons which would be like spares if the need arose. Riding horses and cows would be tied behind the other wagon. Their animals would consist of eight oxen, four horses with saddles for three as Konaya preferred to ride bare back, one milk cow just freshened and her calf, to be placed in the wagon with pigs and chickens until it became strong enough to walk. This would cause the cow to stay close. Also, there would be one yearling bull and two yearling heifers. With the pigs and chickens added to this list, Thomas felt prepared to start his home away from any nearby settlement.

Up to this time, Thomas and Peyton had made a good supply of axes, knives and tools to be used on the journey. In view of Konaya's great contribution, they had located and purchased a fine rifle and all the necessary accruements for him. Thomas spent time to teach him how to quickly load and fire with accuracy. Konaya was reluctant to give up his bow, but soon found the rifle to be far superior. He would not give up his buffalo robe in favor of a blanket for he found blankets inferior. Certainly, white man's clothes were inferior to deerskin leggings and jacket.

At the suggestion of Konaya, trade goods were also added to the list. These consisted mostly of mirrors and factory-made knives that were inferior to those he could make. It was necessary to buy them as he now had little time, and the new store owner in Saxsonville had just arrived with a good supply. Other items he would take as trade stock had to be small and lightweight. He chose glass beads, needles, and thread to complete the list.

March arrived with cold wind and snow flurries, but it was time to load. It would take every day available to reach a new land before winter snows, and excitement ran high with the six of them. It was difficult to do the loading and final preparation as it seemed all of the townspeople wanted to be helpful and to say goodbye. Thomas had sold their home and now the new owners were there in hopes of keeping all that Virginia was forced to leave behind. She had several friends there, some of which she had promised items she could not take along. It seemed as a flock of geese at feeding time to Konaya, and more than once, he considered running for the woods.

Eventually, all was in order. Thomas was in the first wagon with Virginia beside him. Peyton was driving the second wagon with Mary beside him and Henry riding beside the oxen and horses tied behind. Only Konaya was free to ride ahead and enjoy separation from grunting pigs and creaking wagons. Mid-morning found them well away from Saxsonville where Thomas called a halt. There he gathered them into a circle and thanked God for a timely start as well as His guidance and protection for the journey. With none of their friends there to disturb Thomas, he concluded his prayer and made a quick inspection of chains, ropes and other fasteners. This done, the journey was underway again without so much as a backward glance.

Through the lowlands of Virginia, travel was easy and they were able to cover about 15 miles before halting for the first night. Thomas did not wish to push the oxen for he knew it would require all of their strength and stamina when reaching the mountains. He also wanted Virginia to have time to establish some routine for the preparation of the one big meal of the day. She was to cook only once each day and breakfast would be hot coffee and leftovers. That is, so long as the coffee lasted. Thomas and Peyton divided chores of caring for the animals and gathering wood for the supper and night fire.

Konaya provided game for the evening cook fire and, when necessary, carried the night watch. Being a light sleeper and able to doze while riding daytime,he had the ability always to be on the alert at night. Thomas and

Peyton found this to be of great comfort, for it allowed them a full night of rest from their labor. Later, Virginia became much more aware of night sounds and acted as additional night watch. She was able to catch some sleep in the wagon when the road was not too rough.

Nights were cold in March, so Thomas and Virginia used a bed they had prepared inside their wagon. Peyton's wagon also had a bed for Henry and Mary. Konaya would not consider sleeping in camp, much less in a wagon bed, so Peyton made his bed under a heavy canvas near where they would have a night fire.Konaya did accept an oiled canvas which he used as a ground cover, except when raining, for then it was a head covering.

For this first night of trail rest, Konaya had brought a young deer to be roasted over an evening fire. Since nights were cold, a large bed of coals was welcome. He and Thomas built two fires so the venison could be roasted in smaller pieces and so it would be more comfortable for Virginia to work between the two rather than over one large one. Virginia was grateful for this consideration and she set out to make bread for two or three days. She had brought her box of bread risings which, when a small portion was added to bread dough, it soon began to ferment and bring her bread loaves to a light and fluffy state. Keeping the dough warm between the two fires helped the yeast to work faster. By dark that evening, she had a supper of roast venison and light sourdough bread. The three men had hobbled the horses in a meadow where winter grass was in abundance. The oxen and cows would not leave this meadow, so it was only necessary for them to put bells around the neck of each animal. Ole Ring seemed to be the happiest dog in all of Virginia land.

He was everywhere with Thomas and would run downwind of the fire every few minutes. He was just checking the mouth-watering odor of supper on the spit. Ole Ring had the intelligence endowed to very few dogs. It seemed to Thomas and Virginia that he could read their minds and certainly did understand English. At times, Virginia would say, "Thomas, did you hear Ole Ring speak?" It would usually be something that could pose danger to one of them if Ole Ring were to try to form words. When Thomas and Virginia slept outside near the fire, Ole Ring would be outside the fire light, but as close to them as was practical. When they were sleeping inside the wagon, Ole Ring was directly below. It was a great comfort to have him constantly watching over her, and Virginia never failed to speak his name when he came near.

Although Konaya tried to become close to Ole Ring, he could never call the dog out of sight of either Thomas or Virginia. On occasion, Thomas would allow Virginia to drive while he took a short ride ahead on his saddle horse. Konaya would ride his horse beside Virginia's wagon, in part to keep her company, and also to make certain she had no trouble with the oxen. At these times, Ole Ring would stay with Thomas, for he remembered his times as a pup being Thomas' best friend.

They had become inseparable companions from the time Thomas had lifted him out of the saddle bag of a traveler. Thomas was able to trade his work of new shoes on the horse for a pup that was considered excess baggage. From that time on, Thomas set him on the floor of the shop. Pup, as he was called, was never underfoot. He found a way to climb onto the lower shelf of a work bench so that he could see all that was taking place. Pup never left this sheltered place until Thomas called or picked him up for a run outside. With the beautiful white ring that formed around his neck as he grew, and the intelligence of a much older dog, Pup soon became known as Ole Ring.

After supper that first night, the six of them sat around the one fire that had been fed with green wood so it would last through the night. The sky was so clear that a billion stars competed with each other to give more light to a grateful camp. Ole Ring sat between Thomas and Virginia, first leaning on one and then on the other. He had equal love for both of them and tried to show equal attention. Konaya was only familiar with Indian dogs that had served as beasts of burden and were used to carrying saddle packs or being ignored. He found that he was coming to love Ole Ring.

As they finished the day, Peyton remarked on the beauty of the night sky and spoke of the depth of endless stars. He related his belief that eternity was much like that, endless and with more beauty than man could understand. Virginia spoke words her father had often used from the pulpit, "As a believer in Christ, I will someday travel among those stars. My faith in Jesus will be my ticket to visit any of them I wish." Konaya silently thanked God for sending him to this loving family.

Well before dawn, the men were up and adding fuel of dry wood to the coals. The water kettle was filled before they left the fireside to gather the animals and to allow Virginia and Mary privacy of dressing for the day. First the oxen were brought in and placed under yoke. The calf was placed in the small trailing wagon so that the cow would follow close behind. The young bull and two young heifers would trail close behind the cow. Since the horses had been hobbled, they were close and easy to catch. By the time this was done, Virginia had hot coffee and reheated choice cuts of venison. Bread she had baked the night before tasted extra good when slathered with Virginia's blackberry jam from last season's crop. By first light, all was in order and Peyton in the lead wagon gave the commanding crack of the whip to move out. March grass was just beginning to green up the meadows so it was easy for Peyton to see rocks and rough places ahead. He could choose the wagon path to take advantage of the better direction. It was up to Konaya to ride ahead and search out the best course for all of the day ahead.

By noon time, Thomas called a halt for the rest and grazing of the oxen. An hour spent at noon would give the animals time to recover, just as people needed a resting time. Both Thomas and Peyton were kind to the animals and it would certainly be to their advantage in the rough mountain travel they would soon be faced with. As for food at noon, Thomas was the only one in need and his hunger was satisfied with a cold piece of venison and a drink from the brook they had been following. During the afternoon, the land was rising toward distant mountains and easy travel through meadows along the stream bed was being reduced. Giant trees on either side sent out limbs and roots toward the creek, seeking both water and sunlight. The effect was to limit grasslands and produce a tunnel through which they found both strange and beautiful.

Konaya had left early morning for the foothills in order to seek the best route. So long as the stream course was best, he left no sign of his passage. When it would become necessary to leave this easy route, Konaya would leave sign of a hatchet mark on a tree for Peyton to follow. Long before evening, Konaya had traveled miles ahead and returned to the wagons. He had been back with the wagons only a short time before Ole Ring started giving low growls and doing strange things. He would run ahead a short distance and with hair standing up on his back, he would growl and stand in front of Peyton's oxen. Peyton and Konaya became alarmed and called a halt on the pretext of a trouble wagon wheel. Konaya rode back the trail they had came in on, far enough to be out of sight. He turned off into a wide circle around the wagons and back on to their proposed path about a mile in front. Then he dismounted and tied his horse so he could walk back to the wagons. Ole Ring continued looking ahead and with low growls kept leaning against Thomas' leg as if to push him aside.

Peyton and Thomas checked the priming of their rifles and continued to act as if a wagon wheel was in trouble. Virginia was instructed to stay in the wagon and out of sight. For the better part of an hour, tension continued to mount and Ole Ring never let up his growl and peering into the gloom ahead. Suddenly, a shot rang out through the forest followed by a few moments of silence. Then a second shot. Thomas and Peyton stood ready to use their rifles, but all was silent for several minutes. Ole Ring gave a happy, tail-wagging bark just before Konaya came into sight, leading a strange horse. Thomas recognized the horse as one stolen back in Saxsonville over a month ago. From Konaya, they heard the rest of the story.

Konaya had walked almost a mile from where he had tethered his horse, keeping an eye out for trouble ahead. Ole Ring had somehow known that 300 yards ahead, two men were hidden in ambush positions, one on each side of the trail they would be forced to travel. Ole Ring had warned them in time to prevent their being murdered for their wagons and plunder. Konaya had spotted both of them and had recognized one of them as the man who had attacked Virginia back in Saxsonville. Konaya had a visceral hatred for this man and had seen him more than once near Saxsonville during these past few years, but considered him no threat until after he attacked Virginia. Today, seeing him in waiting to kill his friends, it was too much and Konaya took the only safe way. He shot this man first and reloaded as fast as possible. The other man lost no time in leaping astride his horse for a rapid departure. Konaya threw a shot at his retreating behind, but did not know if he connected. He then took the dead man's horse, leading it to the wagons so he could watch for the possibility of another attempted ambush from the second man.

Konaya's horse was tethered in an open glen about a mile ahead, so it was there that they camped for the second night. It was excellent camp ground, well supplied with all they needed. Although it was too early to stop for the night, the men thought it wise for Konaya to follow the trail of the second man to be certain he posed no threat to them during the coming night.

While Thomas and Peyton set up camp, Konaya backtracked to the ambush area. There, he picked up the trail of a running horse and followed it at a rapid pace for two or three miles. When he was certain the man was making fast tracks toward Saxsonville, he started the return trip with more care, in hopes of spotting game. Evening shadows made it difficult to see much, but his trained eye caught sight of a turkey flying almost straight up to a night roost. By leaving his horse, he was able to get within one hundred yards and spot the turkey settling down for the night. A carefully placed shot brought the turkey down, and tonight, they would feast on roast turkey.

The stolen horse was somewhat of a problem to Thomas and Peyton. It was much too far back for them to return it, so to turn it loose seemed the only answer. Horses usually return to their home when released from not too far distant points. Perhaps this one would remember its place in Saxsonville, but then, it may consider home as the place where it had been kept by the thief. Thomas had little choice. He removed all metal rings, snaps and fasteners from both the old saddle and the bridle and discarded the leather. When he released the horse, he fully expected it to run toward Saxsonville. It did nothing but start to graze nearby. It seemed to prefer their company and refused to leave. Over the next few days, Thomas would not hobble the horse at night as he did his own. He almost thought of that as stealing it all over again. During the day, the horse followed them, keeping one or two hundred yards behind.

The next several days found them covering only five to ten miles each day. Giant trees crowded even closer to the ever-smaller stream and it was sometimes difficult to find passage without wending their way through on a course to either side of the stream. Crossing the stream was no problem since it was usually only inches deep. Besides, it was good for the wagon wheels to be wetted so that joints would expand and tighten. Konaya rode many extra miles each day in order to select the best route. His contribution was above price and, as added bonus, he always brought game to the evening cook fire.

The approach of April brought rain showers that gave some discomfort but no real danger. Swollen creeks were usually fast to recede and gave no problems. Flat lands were behind them and mountains were ahead. Thomas looked at the rising timbered shores ahead and wondered if they did not present an impenetrable barrier. Only when Konaya returned each night with assurance that there was a way did Thomas rest easy. Never having seen mountains of this size, it took much reassurance. April was a time when trees did not yet leaf out, so sunlight found its way to the forest floor. New grass was in fair supply and would remain so until leaves cut off the supply of sunlight. Accordingly, they spent extra time in camp to allow their animals to take advantage of this. Soon the supply would become very scarce.

For the past two days, Konaya had been talking of the sacred place called "White Stinking Springs." About noon they arrived at this place of wonder. Much land was clear of trees in this valley, seemingly kept clear by movement of herds of buffalo, elk, deer and bear. It seemed to be a place where animals would gather without fear of each other and where soil was good to grass but not to trees. Although there were a few lone trees, little underbrush cluttered the area. It had several small bubbling springs of very warm and stinking water which Peyton was quick to determine was sulfur. Other springs close by delivered wonderful cold and clear water. No wonder Indians thought of this place as sacred. Evidence all around proved that many visited, but none for long.

Thomas chose to make this a camp for at least two days. April showers had done a superb job of producing grass and besides, they wanted time to soak their tired bodies in such wonderful luxury. Konaya would not kill animals or birds in this sacred spot, even for food.

He would ride out for some distance before gathering from the bountiful supply. His first foray was for their favorite wild food, and Konaya was successful in bringing in six large grouse. Virginia dressed three of them for frying and three for roasting. Before placing them on the spit, she filled the body cavity with chestnuts, wild sage and Spicewood bark. Later, Thomas remarked that the inside was almost as good as the outside.

May arrived with little change except warm nights and a little less rain. Travel was more difficult now that the oxen had to work harder on even steeper ground. Thomas insisted on resting them frequently as he was told by Konaya, "Ahead is much more bad." Konaya had scouted the route well enough to find open bench land where in recent years fire had cleaned the land, and where there was not only level camp space, but a good supply of grass. On one of these areas, Konaya had found a small herd of ten buffalo. He had taken one of the small ones for meat and after dressing it out to cool, he pulled over small saplings and tied meat to them so they would straighten and lift meat out of the reach of wolves. On returning to this clearing with the wagons, they lost no time in setting up camp and with the camp fire now burned down to hot coals, buffalo back strap was now being turned on a hickory spit.

As usual, their horses and cattle remained close by if grass was plentiful. Still behind them, the stolen horse was at the far end of the meadow, perhaps two hundred yards away. Work was done and they were at rest, waiting on Virginia's word that supper was ready. Konaya, as usual, had placed himself so he had a good view of their surroundings. He was first to see and call attention to the lone wolf approaching the stolen horse. They all recognized at once that the wolf was rabid, and that it would probably catch the stolen horse unaware. Konaya was first to fire his rifle. He did so quickly, knowing he would probably miss but hoping to alarm the horse into running away. It did alarm the horse, but not as he had expected. The horse made an effort to turn quickly and found himself face to face with the wolf. Rabies causes blindness and rage, which caused the wolf to charge. The horse turned around again to kick but was too late to avoid a slashing set of teeth into a front leg.

From then on, Virginia and the men could do nothing but watch as the two animals fought, each in their own way. Blindness in the wolf did not allow it to see both steel shod hooves coming at its head. It was over in an instant, but neither of the men wanted to approach the wolf or the horse. Nothing could be done for either except a well-placed bullet to end the life of the stolen horse.

At the close of each day, both Thomas and Peyton had cut a small notch in the tongue of their wagons. The Sunday notch was always cut a little longer so they could keep track of Sunday service days. Although this was not Sunday, Peyton called for a prayer service to thank God for deliverance from the rabid wolf. It could have been one of them instead of the stolen horse. After prayer, Virginia sang a hymn of praise and thanksgiving followed by a prayer of thanks for food and continued travel mercy.

For the first time in his young life, Ole Ring was tied inside the wagon that night. All except Konaya slept inside for fear of other rabid animals. Konaya sat by the fire all night, keeping it well fed with dry wood. None slept well, and long before dawn, they were hitched and moving out.

Late the next day, Konaya led them through a low saddle in the mountain where it was obvious that buffalo had cleared a run over generations past. From the crest of this pass, they could look to the west and see many miles ahead ofdense forest with lots of clearing that looked like tended pasture land. Buffalo and elk had found this to be favorable grazing land, and Thomas was eager to get to the lower lands ahead. He felt that he had had enough of mountain runs.

Late May was a time of refreshing of the land with new grass and newly clothed trees. Flowers were growing alongside every brook and in every spot where they could find sunlight. The air was fresh as only a new spring breeze could supply. Virginia's spirits were lifted and for the first time she could go an entire day without wondering what happened to her parents. There was little in this new land to remind her of that fateful day. She now had something else to think about,something that would enrich her life and something that would worry Thomas for a time.

She was now certain that she would add a third member to their family near Christmas time, and Thomas would be even more concerned for her comfort and safety. She determined not to tell him until it would be impossible to keep it a secret.

With all of her caution and care, Thomas could see the happy look on her face and how she was careful not to jump from the wagon as she had often done. Neither of them spoke of it as if it were a secret from Thomas, but soon Virginia knew he had guessed the truth. Now it became a subject that occupied most of their quiet time. Thomas wanted to call a halt to their westward move while Virginia wanted to continue. They all felt they were still much too close to English rule for a permanent home, for they knew England was relentless in seeking westward settlements for the purpose of taxation. Thomas and Peyton wanted far enough west to avoid this for years to come and Konaya wanted to go home to his people, still far to the west. Thomas understood that it might be years before his sawmill and gristmill would be in demand, but he also knew it might take years to build. There was also the comfort of being among Konaya's family, for now they considered Konaya as their own family. Surely his family would be theirs, also.

By the ending of May, they were traveling over rolling hills with much grassland and some forest land so dense as to defy passage of two oxen side by side. Konaya was able to find easy routes around these impenetrable areas of forest land and for the most part, going was slow but easy. They had just forded a beautiful river without trouble so now all looked exciting and every day brought more fair weather and wonderful sights.

Toward noon, Konaya returned to the wagons with news of caverns ahead. They were places he had not seen before but he had heard of from his people. These caverns were used by his people as well as other tribes for shelter when they were in the area and Konaya expected to find some of his tribe there now. He hoped they would be either Cherokee or a friendly tribe that they might visit in peace. As they approached the area, Thomas and Peyton had to stop for a time while Konaya scouted ahead. He was cautious in his approach, and it was well that he was, for there was at least twenty people near the major cavern entrance. After watching for a while, he determined women and children outnumbered adult men. This was an indication of a peaceful group, so Konaya walked toward them with his rifle across his shoulder and his hands out with palms upturned. At first they watched him with bows at ready, for none had rifles. To them, he posed a danger because of his mixed dress and white man's weapon. Konaya had left his horse tethered out of sight where he could return and mount quickly in case of real danger.

After a few minutes, he was accepted as a friend, even though they were of the Mingo nation. A word from their leader brought more women and children out of the cavern entrance, and Konaya began to wonder where their men were. About this time young women came from the cavern with food-filled clay bowls,some steaming hot. Konaya felt he could relax as it looked to be more than a temporary camp.

Their cooking fires were inside the cavern and no doubt they were using the caverns for night shelter also. After sharing their food, Konaya answered many questions about himself and in return found that their men were here for taking young buffalo. The skins of young buffalo were softer and of better weight to be used for women and children clothing. The men may be away for several days as this area was exceptionally good for spring calving. Konaya then told them of his party, two or three miles back, and his desire to bring them in. Blue Heron, their leader, called two of his men to accompany Konaya and gave them presents of heavy buffalo hide moccasins to present to Peyton and Thomas.

Konaya led them to his tethered horse but since they were on foot, he chose to run with them, leading his horse. On their return to the hunters campground, Konaya directed Thomas to keep back knives and hatchets but offer gifts of mirrors, needles and thread. These gifts were well received and in return, these people offered gifts of fine leather items. There was much talk between Konaya and the men and only very late that night did calmness come over the camp. Konaya and Ole Ring sat close to Virginia's wagon to keep watch through the night. Konaya was also aware of a night watch just inside the cavern.

The following morning, camp came alive early and Virginia had prepared coffee as usual. With warmed over buffalo roast and coffee, they were soon to move out. Blue Heron came to their campfire to bid them good travel and Virginia offered him a tin cup of coffee. He took the cup and after blowing on it several times, he took a sip. Immediately he spit it out and looked as if he had been given some sort of witches brew. Konaya, fearing he would think it poisonous, took the cup from him and drank the hot liquid. He then made a face as if he thought it bad, but then broke into laughter. With this all had a good laugh and they were able to depart in peace.

Two more easy traveling days brought them to Sunday, a day when no work was to be done except to care for the animals.

Of course, a woman's work is never done so Virginia and Mary had much to do. Saturday night was a very busy time as they had to locate a suitable campsite in order for the women to prepare. They had a weeks clothing to wash in mostly cold water and lye soap. There wasample food to cook for Saturday night and Sunday. Although it was not always possible, they liked to hang out bedding to air and in some cases, wash blankets. Thomas tried to help but Virginia found him mostly in her way. By Sunday morning, she was glad to recognize it as a day of rest, after of course feeding her men and washing up dishes, pots and pans.

Later in the day, she would have to gather clothes and blankets from bushes all over the clearing, check them for dryness, fold and store them, and rest in between. Still, she looked forward to Peyton's service. She did not consider him her husband's father at this time. He was her pastor, her minister. His service was as if he spoke to thirty, not just three.

This Sunday morning, Peyton was careful to thank God first for their safe trip and for the beautiful weather. Peyton chose an unusual text. Isaiah 55:12 was to him alive with promise for all around them was the works of his hand. God said, "For ye shall go out with joy, and be led forth with peace; the mountains and the hills shall break forth before you in singing, and all the trees of the field shall clap their hands." Peyton explained that this speaks of far future and everlasting salvation, but it is wonderful to know that as Christians, we will see that time. As for today, Peyton explained that for him, the wind in the tree branches was a song of praise. Only God could make a tree. Only God could carry them safely to their destination.

This beautiful June morning found them with wagons loaded and ready to move out. Konaya and two of his friends had scouted the trail ahead for many miles. They thought it would be free of trouble for the oxen to pull without having to double up for the steep slope upward, although it did appear, they would have to cut trees to secure behind for the descent of some of the steeper mountain trails. The wagons did have brakes but they were almost useless for the run down steep places. Without the tree to drag behind, the wagon would overrun the oxen and perhaps overturn , even injure or kill the oxen. Their first day on the south trail was without incident, and Virginia spent most of her day by riding her horse or walking and leading him. The Indians were to come and go, seemingly without reason or pattern. It was a source of comfort to Thomas that they seemed to be aware of all that was around them, for it was possible to encounter danger from many sources.

During the times when they were in camp for the nights, Thomas, Henry and Peyton learned many things from the Indians, As they learned the Cherokee language, they also learned more about the Shawnee tribe called the "Salt Indians." who made it dangerous to travel down the Conoy river. It was understood that the salt works just off the river belonged to them, and it was also the reason for the buffalo trail through the mountains. For generations the Shawnee tribe had gathered salt and buffalo hides at the same location.Elk and deer also loved to go there for the salt. Thomas did not know this when he bought four crock churns of salt for this trip but it would have made little difference since he would not have know how to trade for it.

They also learned of how coal was available to be picked up along the lower river. It was to be found in great slabs along the mountain sides where it would break off from time to time. Land slides or erosion would expose layers of it and since it was lighter than stone, it would wash down the mountains and into the river. The Shawnee had learned to burn it in the process of extracting salt from the brine that bubbled up from the ground.

It seemed that God had provided the salt and the method of drying it, all within easy reach of the river. They also told of another wonder where the salt Indians had a permanent camp. Two of them had seen it when they were part of a trading party going there to obtain salt. They told of how it was a large burning on the earth that had no source of fuel. No wood and none of the black rock the Shawnee called coal. It was a place the Indians thought to be home of evil spirits and none dared to approach it, even though it would have been a source of warmth during cold winter days and nights. Thomas and Peyton had knowledge of gas and surmised this to be gas escaping from the earth.

For the next several weeks, travel would be more difficult than they had imagined. Not only were there mountain but also rapid flowing streams and narrow valleys, sometimes too narrow for them to get through. These valleys would have to be avoided at all cost and alternate routes chosen over the tops of mountains. Some roads would have to be made with the axe and sweat, with much prayer mixed in,some so dangerous that Virginia would have to walk, staying clear of a possible wrecked wagon. Their one encouraging point was that buffalo had used this route for untold generations and they had chosen the most direct east to west trail.

But where a buffalo could walk did not mean a wagon could go. They could only guess the reason for the buffalo migration from east to west, but they were told by Konaya of how his people took advantage of this migration each fall in order to gather the winter's supply of dried meat and hides. It was also apparent that many Indians used this trail and they could only hope and pray any they met would be friendly. Few white men had penetrated this far west and those that did usually brought trade goods. Fair trading so far had kept the whites and Indians in a peaceable relationship. Their major concern was that Konaya would be considered an enemy should they meet a party of Shawnee from north of the Ohio River. No one remembered just why they were enemies.

June came with both days and nights warm and with a full head of leaves on all giant trees. Most of the woodland they traveled through was lighted with soft green light, filtered through dense tree tops. Some trees were so large that it took three of them holding hands to reach around. For thousands of years, these trees had competed for sunlight, and to obtain a full share meant they had to grow tall and straight. Some would reach a height of sixty feet before their first limb. Peyton and Thomas looked in wonder at such an awesome sight, for never had they been faced with a mountain to cross that had such massive timber.

Konaya had scouted for miles to locate the best path through this wilderness. The river route was out of the question even though buffalo had used this narrow stream bed as their passage. Mountains on both sides were very steep and started their rise at rivers edge. The river was swift but that was not the problem. Huge rocks were everywhere, seemingly placed just for the purpose of preventing wagon travel. Mountains on either side of the stream were also steep, but on the north side, this mountain seemed to be mostly clear of rock and undergrowth.

Thomas and Peyton walked to the summit, marking well the trail they must use. This also required their attention to the down side for it would be impossible to change direction going down. Should they come upon a rock cliff, all would be lost. Konaya had marked a trail, but they were afraid he may have missed or overlooked a dangerous part of the down slope.

Thomas continued inspection of the trail down, marking it well while Peyton returned to the wagons below. By the time Thomas returned, Peyton had hitched all eight oxen to the lead wagon. It would be impossible for a team of four to pull a wagon up the steeper slopes.

As most mountains are, this one had steep parts followed by a bench where it was possible to stop and rest the oxen. Since the trees were so large, they were spread apart enough to allow easy wagon passage. Fearful of such a heavy load, Thomas, Henry and Peyton removed several hundred pounds of iron before starting up. It was well that they did, for the oxen struggled to reach the first of three benches. Virginia climbed to this bench well clear of the wagon. Leading their horses and with cattle following close behind, Thomas and Peyton walked, one to each side of the lead oxen, partly to encourage them and also to guide them. Should they decide on their own to turn for an angled climb up the mountain, the sideways pressure on wagon wheels would snap spokes and cause the wagon to roll over.

Three hours of combined labor, rest and prayer found the first wagon on the summit. Thomas and Peyton wasted no time returning for the second wagon, for they did not want darkness to catch them in the process of moving. After removing some weight from the second wagon and leaving the chicken trailing wagon behind, they again made the difficult climb to the summit.

Evening was now too close for the final run but first, one of the wagons had to be unloaded before it could return for the last of their gear. Virginia took care of the evening meal while Thomas and Peyton selected three small trees from further out the ridge. These would be needed for the descent and while there was still light, they cut and dragged one back to camp. Along this ridge, there was no grass and the oxen had done a very hard day's work. This was a time when their precious supply of animal food became necessary.

Chapter 8

This night was lighted only by a quarter moon and that filtered through the heavy covering of tree tops. Being very tired, all bedded down at dusk, leaving a good green wood fire and Ole Ring to stand night watch. Konaya lay on his buffalo robe, sleeping as only he could do. His eyes were closed but his mind was alert. Soon after dark a wolf howl could be heard from the valley below and another answering call from a distant ridge. Ole Ring was instantly standing with his neck hair erect. Konaya became fully awake and spoke quietly to Ole Ring, for he knew there was no immediate danger. Over the next hour, several more answering howls were heard and they seem to be congregating directly below. Konaya stood up and walked to the ridge break where they had come up. Then he was certain that wolves were trying to get to the trailing wagon animals. Now he could hear the desperate squeal of pigs under attack by many wolves. He could hear them well enough to know there was at least a dozen and that the wagon was still secure. Considering they would not break into the wagon, Konaya became fearful they may follow scent to their camp and attack the horses, cows or oxen. He called Thomas,Peyton and Henry awake to help bring their animals into close protection of their fires and rifles.

As quickly as possible, all of their animals were brought close in and tied securely. Fires were started outside the ring of animals and none too soon, for they could now hear the excited bark of more than a dozen wolves. Colder air on the ridge had carried their animals' scent down to the valley and now the wolves had given up trying for the pigs. For the second time in his life, Ole Ring was tied inside a wagon. Should a wolf break into the ring of protection, Ole Ring would be the first animal attacked and he would stand no chance. He would also likely run outside the protection of their camp in a futile effort to protect his family.

Although wolves would be afraid of fire and would stay back from it, their fires were too far apart to hold them at bay. Soon the glow of reflected fire marked the eyes of several wolves. In preparation for this, Konaya had told them he would fire first and except to stop a bushel of several wolves, they were not to fire. It would be best to always keep two rifles at the ready while he reloaded and picked one off at each shot. After killing the second wolf, they understood the noise of a rifle meant danger to them.

Horses and cattle were keeping a clamorous confusion of fear to the point of making it difficult for the men to converse, other than in a shout. This only served to excite their animals all the more. Throughout the night, fires consumed all of the wood they could safely reach. In desperation they had to begin firing at every glimpse of an eye reflecting light from a dying fire.

Toward morning, they were desperate for firewood and with trees all around that seemed ludicrous. All were too large to fell and too tall for the taking of lower limbs. Virginia had the answer which was to strip the dry parts of bark from all trees within reach. This carried them through until first light of dawn and no more was seen or heard of the wolf pack except six dead ones scattered out from their camp.

Although none had rested or slept, it was necessary to go for the supplies and the trailing wagon left behind. Soon after hot coffee and warmed-over roasted elk haunch, Thomas and Peyton hitched to the empty wagon for the return trip. All eight oxen were hitched and a small tree was fastened to the rear axel, but first, the trip down had to have drag on the wagon in order to keep it from running up on the oxen. At the base, they found pigs and chickens safe but in need of food and water. The top and sides of the trailing wagon had suffered a ferocious attack from sharp teeth of several wolves. Thomas had used green split hickory for the top and sides and this had dried and hardened to almost the strength of iron.

Pigs and chickens were cared for and the wagon was loaded with the last of their iron supplies. The oxen weregiven the command to move out and again Thomas and Peyton took position on either side of the lead oxen. Since the wagon was not loaded nearly as heavy as yesterday, they had no trouble reaching the summit camp site. Several hours were used in order to rearrange and load both wagons. Two good sized trees were cut and hitched to the rear axel of both wagons. This had to be done with care on the trailing wagon since the pig wagon was not strong enough to drag a tree. A long pole was used to attach to the wagon axel and extended to the rear of the trailing pig wagon. Then the butt of the dragging tree was chained to this long pole.

At last, late afternoon saw them on the way down with Peyton's wagon in the lead and Virginia leading horses and cows bringing up the rear. They made camp at the base of the mountain where again the fast flowing stream, now a young river, had opened up several acres of flood lands. At normal river flow the flat land was alive with grass and flowers. This was a wonderful camp site and place where both animals and people could recover from the harrowing night just past.

Konaya had now scouted miles ahead to be certain the old buffalo trail still led them westward and presented no major obstacle. For many miles ahead, there was no sign of river or creek, just rolling hills and an occasional brook. It looked to be easy going and good game land so they would always have fresh meat.

June was hot by day and pleasant at night. By this time, they had all had become efficient travelers. Little pigs were now hogs and too large to remain in the trailing wagon, so it was necessary to round them up each morning after allowing them to run free for an hour before dawn. They could find enough food in that time to do them without using their dwindling grain supply. They became more of a burden than they were worth for now it was up to Virginia to walk behind and drive them to keep up. The animals' natural tendency was to follow food and herd together but hogs were not so inclined. Virginia sometimes rode her mare, but Thomas did not want her to do so. He had a great fear that the horse would be startled and perhaps throw Virginia.

Even though game was plentiful, Thomas made the decision to shoot one of the hogs for food. His temper was kindled mightily when their leader continued to turn to the side and would run when Virginia tried to direct them to follow the wagons. Toward evening, Virginia was having a difficult time with "Old Stubborn" as she had named him. Thomas saw her trying to run him back onto the trail and he kept leading the others away. It was too much for Thomas, so with rising anger, he called a halt to the wagons. He called Virginia in and promptly dispatched Old Stubborn.

June was not the time to butcher hogs, but some good could be made of it. That evening found them all very busy. While Virginia roasted one back strap on a spit, she fried another after cutting it into one inch thick slabs. No game animal could match the flavor of fried back strap, and it was feast time for them. Thomas was busy with butchering Old Stubborn and since meat could not be kept long, it was necessary to use only select parts to salt preserve.

Thomas had brought four crock churns of salt from Saxsonville knowing its value and scarcity, so he was reluctant to use very much. Virginia took the time to render as much lard as she thought would keep. Soon, another hog had taken his place as the leader, but Peyton was ready for this one. He had Thomas and Konaya help catch the new leader and hold him while Peyton fitted a newly made harness. From then on, he was tied to the trailing wagon and had to follow. The other hogs then stayed close behind.

Now that they were nearing the land where Konaya had been when his woman, White Deer, was taken from him, he spent much time alone. Thomas understood his sadness, for to lose Virginia would be worse than anything he could imagine. He tried to draw Konaya into a conversation about that day but it only served to upset him more. Had it not been for the love he had for Thomas and Virginia, Konaya would have gone ahead to find his people. For what reason he could not understand, for that would not have assuaged his memory. White Deer meant too much to him for another to take her place.

As boys became men in the Indian way, a new name was attached
and the old name was forgotten, forever. The new name was usually
tied to some brave deed having been done by the young man, but not
always. The new name could be attached by some accident or stupid act
the young man did that gave the tribe reason to repeat the story and have
another good laugh. Obviously this caused most young men to strive for
an act of bravery in hopes of receiving a name to be proud of. One special
name came to Bear Claw by his act of killing a large bear with only his
knife, thereby saving a child from certain death. Bear Claw had the honor
of the new name and also the special honor of wearing a necklace of bear
claws for the rest of his life. Since Thomas had named Konaya so long ago,
Konaya liked the name and promptly forgot his boyhood name.

Along the buffalo trail, more signs of Indians appeared each
day. Caution was necessary now, and more than ever. They had made
contact with small groups and twice with lone Indians. They were always
friendly. Even though whites had penetrated this far before, there had
been no sign of any along their trail. Apparently, no trouble had developed
between white and red men which made the McMellon men very happy.

This Sunday morning the wagons were parked in a grassy meadow
beside a fast-flowing stream. Water falling over a rocky outcrop was
almost more than a rapid, but not quite a falls. The noise of rushing water
and the noise of dozens of ducks made this a perfect place for Peyton to
hold the usual morning prayer. After breakfast would come the Sunday
services and rest for the day. Not often had they found such a pleasant
place and never before on a Saturday night. Only Konaya was unhappy,not
because of the scenery or the meadow, but because the noise would not
allow him to hear well should danger approach.

All morning was pleasant to the point of being perfect. Peyton
conducted the morning service just as if he had a congregation of
dozens. He still did have the ducks which paid about as much attention as
children usually do, occasionally raising their voices either in protest or
agreement. Peyton took their occasional outbreak as shouts of "amen"
and singing praises to the Lord. He could even glory in the knowledge that
most of his flock were baptizing themselves by total immersion. After the
service, Konaya and Thomas located fish hooks and line from one of the
wagons. So far on this journey they had found neither the time or place to
use them, but Konaya had noticed that below the falls or rapids, fish were
almost fighting for a place to call their own. Bass and pike had both been
feeding on flying insects that got too close to water's surface, and it was
too much for the men to resist.

Virginia and Mary was not to work on Sunday, but this was not
considered work. Peyton said that God must be providing manna from

heaven and it was up to them to gather and eat. Whoever heard of fishing as work? Of course, Virginia could not let God's manna go to waste, so that was not work in the true description of labor.

Catching fish until they had all they could use was not enough. Fishing for the fun of catch and release became all consuming and with whoops and shouts of joy, caution was abandoned. Only Ole Ring was aware of the approach of several Indians and he could not make the men understand. The three of them thought Ole Ring was just enjoying the fun, so his warning barks were unheeded until too late.

Virginia was first to look away from the direction of the men. She saw Ole Ring looking at her and then running toward her with neck hair standing erect. With alarm, she turned to face several Indians who had walked close enough almost to touch her but did nothing to harm her. Ole Ring was at her side, ready to defend her if necessary. In a quiet voice, one Indian spoke to the dog and extended his hand. We will never know how dogs determine who is friend and who is to be avoided, but Ole Ring quickly determined the Indian to be friend.

It was only after a short time that Konaya, Henry and the McMellon men turned to see Virginia feeding her visitors with their lunch. Fortunately, Virginia had fried a large amount of bass filleted in a light dusting of salt and corn meal. Lard from Old Stubborn made up the perfect combination to attract her visitors from a mile away. Konaya was first to approach their visitors, for he at once recognized the dress of his own tribe. Even though Konaya had adopted some of white man's clothing and trappings, his tribe members recognized him as one of their tribe and much Cherokee speech took place with greetings and explanations.

Thomas had learned some of the Cherokee language and strained to follow, but he had no need to for Konaya was proud to be the central figure. He spoke as rapidly as possible to make known the thoughts and speech of each to the other. Konaya's tribal friends were going no place but where the desire took them. The frying fish had brought them to Virginia. Now she was expected to provide more. This was all the excuse Thomas and Peyton needed to fish on. Konaya and friends could clean and filet, Virginia could fry and all could eat. Poor Virginia did not have to work on Sunday, for this was fun and fun could not be labor.

The fishing party lasted well into the night as some wanted to dry filets by fire light that night and the following day. Konaya was catching up on news from his tribe and also trying to act as interpreter. With all of the excitement, Virginia felt left out, and as soon as possible, secluded herself in her wagon. Poles were cut and racks were built that could be placed near enough to fires to almost cook sixteen inch filets. These thin slices dried very quickly and as soon as fires were down to hot coals, the racks were moved over and green hickory bark and branches were placed on the coals. All that night and the following day, Konaya and his friends kept hickory smoke curling around the drying fish. Thomas, Henry and Peyton fell into the activity, delighted to have so many friendly people in their camp.

Konaya, in his desire to translate, began a serious teaching effort which both sides joined in, much like children. By day's end Thomas and Virginia were settled in their wagon bed, discussing what they had learned. They were amazed at the results of one day's lessons and happy to have Konaya's friends as theirs.

After much discussion with his friends, Konaya and they decided on the best route to continue with the wagons. By this time all had decided it would be a great honor to bring Konaya and the whites to their tribe and present them to their chief. It would also provide great fun to be with wagons and oxen. None had seen wagons and oxen like this before and besides, the wagons held great treasures.

The heat in July was repressive except in the deep woods where sunlight never got to the floor and where grass never grew. Konaya's friends were aware of the river trail ahead, withrocky gorges, rapids and buffalo trails that no wagon could negotiate. They were also much afraid of the salt works. Shawnees controlled the lower branches of this river. For them, the only way was the ridge line trail used by Indians for hundreds of years. Many ridges were clear of timber and would make wagon traffic easier. Where mountains were steep, it would be great fun for them to help oxen along. This trail ran far south of the river route but would take them to their home village. Konaya had not known either of them in his youth but he knew the tribe and its location as home. He was pleased to tell Thomas and Peyton of their decision to accompany them over the south mountain trail.

Two days and nights of drying and smoking fish gave them all they wanted. Virginia had fried fish until it was making her wonder where these men were putting it. She was glad to hear that tomorrow they could go. That evening was a busy time again, sorting and loading. It made them wonder where all of their goods came from, and where to put it all.

Peyton and Thomas had discussed the friendly relationship and after discussing it with Konaya, presented a knife to each of them. Nothing could have cemented a friendship as solidly as this gift and each member tried to express that friendship as best he could.

Although women of their tribe were not considered and respected as Virginia was, they took quickly to treating Virginia as Konaya, Thomas and Peyton did. With her long blonde hair, she was thought to be something of a goddess or a princess, and they treated her so. Virginia was grateful for the respect and worked even harder to show her appreciation. Cooking for eight Indians plus her three men would have been too much except that Konaya and one other now made up the scouting party. Three or four others were usually off either hunting or just roaming the woods. Most of the time, they would eat only once each day and that was fresh game roasted on a spit by the night fire.

Konaya found less time to be near the wagons and more time to be with his friends. For many days, he was very protective of Virginia and he now made certain to sleep near Virginia's wagon. Thomas wondered if it was concern for fear of an encounter with hostile Indians, but he never asked. He was grateful for Konaya and the love he held for Virginia. He was also learning more Cherokee words and often heard Konaya speaking to his friends, using the words God and Jesus. How he wished he could tell them in English about his savior, Jesus, the Christ.

Konaya usually slept far enough away from the wagons to be outside fire light. If danger should approach, he wanted to be in darkness. Ole Ring wanted to be close to Thomas and Virginia, so he was next to their bed if weather permitted them to be on the ground. If they were inside the wagon, Ole Ring was directly below. In the dark hours after midnight, fire light had burned out and Ole Ring heard a noise. Thomas and Virginia in the wagon could not hear it and Konaya was too far away. Ole Ring could see the approach and he gave a low warning growl. He was ignored so he growled a little louder. Still no results. By now he was standing and facing the intruder, teeth bared, hair erect, ready for battle. With stiff legs, tail straight behind, Ole Ring made it known that the intruder must about face. He did, and fired a shot which blinded and took Ole Ring's breath. With tail held high, Mr. Skunk pranced off into the night.

Thomas heard the yelp of pain and was immediately engulfed in a cloud of odor much like blue smoke. Virginia was fearful of choking and tried burrowing under covers, to no avail. Konaya, now standing behind a large tree, gun in hand and ready for trouble, got his first wave of blue cloud skunk. He had to struggle mightily to hold laughter in check for Thomas was in a fit of turmoil. He was prancing around the hot coals trying to get a fire light going. Poor Ole Ring was now crying and trying to get close to Thomas for comfort. Lucky Lil Ringo was safely in the wagon when the intruder fired that one winning shot. Thomas had been keeping her inside due to her small size and tendency to wander off into darkness where she could become wolf food.

For all of the following day, Virginia did not have to cook for anyone and no Indian came into camp. Thomas, Peyton and Henry reckoned this to be the best possible defense against hostile Indians. It certainly worked well enough with friendly ones.

They had one more day of easy travel across fields of grass and small patches of woodland. It looked as if fire had been deliberately set here for many years past. Thomas asked Konaya if he understood the bare spaces and was not too surprised when Konaya told him it was deliberate. Indians from all tribes made it a habit to set fall fires where there was grass fields. By doing so, they maintained good grazing fields for buffalo and deer. These grass fields were prime hunting grounds and were to be protected by all who roamed here. Fires were usually set in the late fall when grass was beginning to turn but not too late so as to destroy all grazing just before snow falls. This left a month or so for the grass to renew and allow game animals to have plenty of feed before true winter made it scarce.

On the second day of moving westward, the Indians were leading them on a more northerly course and toward what looked like a cut through the Appalachian Mountain chain. This particular range of mountains was known to Konaya as the Blue Ridge mountains and just on the other side was home to his tribe. Just over the ridge they seemed close to arriving at their destination, but Konaya did not tell Thomas that the distance was still many days and across several ridges. Their total trip was just over half way to where Konaya wanted to see his living sisters.

At the base of the second mountain, they could look back and see where they came from and wondered if they would ever make it to the top of this one. Thomas, Peyton and Henry decided the climb would be very hard on their horses and oxen. One day was needed, being a Sunday by his reckoning, for them to catch up on feed in the new grass before taking on the rugged climb to what Thomas figured was a very long day, if they could make it in one day. This day was also a day of rest for Virginia and Thomas saw to it that she did very little in hard work. He was careful to keep her from lifting anything of any weight except in cooking. She did not like the restraint but understood and loved Thomas all the more for his concern.

Their worship service attracted the Indians and caused them to lie around much like the men back home did. Sunday afternoon naps were common with the men and also the children back in Saxsonville who tired from their play and had to be made to be quiet for a spell. Most paid no attention to the service but a few were touched at the tears that were shed during prayers. They did not understand the love for their God that would make them cry. The Indian God was kind and fearful at the same time. He left no reason to cry because the Indian did not cry from fear. It took them some time to realize the white people cried from love, not from fear. This made an impression on them that they did not understand, loving a God so much they cried for Him.

The answer could only come from Konaya since he also cried and would be able to understand the question in their language. Konaya did not know it at the time, but he just became the first missionary west of the first mountain range.

Late Sunday evening, the McMellon family held the evening service as they were used to doing. This service was to be just a little different in that they had visitors who were very curious to know more about their God. By asking Konaya for more details and his bringing it to Peyton, the decision was made for Peyton to make this evening service more of a teaching time than a worship service. He spoke slowly so Konaya had time to translate and pass on questions about their God. Peyton was blessed to be the source of information to the Indian tribe and he made it clear he talked to God as a father, not a remote something that could not answer.

Over the next two days, the wagons were taken to the top of this mountain by repeatedly moving small amounts of the load on each successive trip. Virginia had been carried up with the first load by being seated on one of their most gentle horses being led by Thomas. He would take no chance on her falling or being on a rough wagon that might overturn. Her life was his life and too valuable for him to risk.

The friends of Konaya roamed far and wide in the search of game or just for the fun of it. They had no responsibility other than to gather prime animal skins and this was not the season for prime furs. Camp meat was secondary because deer and bear were plentiful and there was no need to carry meat very far when it could be found near the camp each evening. Because they cared for Virginia, it was their prime purpose to locate the best wagon route through cuts in the mountain range and to avoid steep places, if possible. In many cases, it would seem to Peyton, Thomas and Henry the route they chose was in the wrong direction but Konaya assured them it was their best route. Going was fairly easy when they traveled along the ridge line of the many mountains that had to be crossed. The route chosen would lead them to a gap in the mountain range where it was much easier to descend and cross the valley ahead. Every valley they crossed had grass for the animals and resting time for the people. Every valley crossed made the rest of the trip a little easier for Konaya's friends understood the need for Virginia to have an easy time of traveling.

Although this was wilderness, there were still many people scattered throughout the mountains. All of them so far had been friends of Konaya's tribe, and the ones spotted that might be enemies were carefully avoided. In other times, they might have had battle with them as was their nature but again, they were avoiding trouble for the love of Virginia and her family.

All of them loved the times in their camp where Virginia was both cook and friend. She had come to love them as little children and delighted in teaching them her ways and her language.Obviously, she was in a very good position to learn from them and was soon proficient in their language. By this time, Virginia was so busy and happy that she had lost the deep longing for her mother and father. Thomas had become more protective of her and his love for her was growing stronger every day, if that were possible.

This hot summer day in July, they saw the first women of Konaya's tribe. Their party of roaming friends had found the small, herb gathering group of women and brought them to meet Virginia. As women were everywhere, the chatter was such that men could make no sense of it. Much of it was pertaining to Virginia's swollen belly and the food she was in the process of preparing for the evening meal. The women had been gathering herbs and along with them had brought several wild greens to feed their men with. Virginia had some knowledge of wild greens but the Indian women had much to share with her. They had brought a large deer hide bag of green leaves from the Sochan plant which was to be boiled and served much like spinach Virginia had not heard of this plant and was excited to know about a plant that was everywhere and would feed her family the much needed greens throughout the summer months. This plant grows about ten feet tall and has a very distinctive three inch flower head. The Indians referred to it as the "Corn Flower". It was at its best in early spring as was the onion-like plant known as the ramp.

This plant was also boiled and eaten with anything like meat or potatoes. It was a wonderful food but with a rich and somewhat unpleasant smell. Later in the fall, the onion bulb was also used to flavor stews and even some fresh greens if used sparingly. Of course Virginia was familiar with the Polk bush but the Indian women set much store by it as a food all summer long, just by taking the top sprouts from several stalks. These were everywhere and would keep well into the fall days. This plant was also good when the stalk was sliced boiled then fried like okra which Virginia was familiar with. Lamb's Quarters was another plant the Indian women brought with them. It was also prepared much like spinach but was just a bit more tangy. They told her about Branch Lettuce, Creecy greens and wild mustard. Virginia was delighted to learn so much from them here and looked forward to the time when she would live among them and learn more of their wild life.

By this time, their evening meal was all from the woods and fields near by, except for the corn meal Thomas had insisted they bring by the barrel. Cornbread was a staple that would fill out any dish prepared of a game animal. It would even be a welcome meal with nothing else but water. Even so, Thomas had also seen fit to bring a large barrel of dry beans. He had treated them before hand by smoking and heating them, just enough to kill any existing larva or stray bug that might exist on a diet of his beans. Besides, smoked beans made them all the better, if that were possible. Beans bubbling in an iron pot was the odor next to heaven, especially if cornpone and onions were available. Filled with this wonder food, they needed nothing for dessert except a long drink of water from a cold, clear creek.

The most precious part of their food cargo was seed that Thomas did not expect to find in the wilderness. Some of this was already known to the Indians but at the beginning he had no way of knowing just what they would find when they settled in the new location. The seeds he had brought were protected from moisture and bugs by carefully drying and wrapping in cloth and as a final protection, he had dipped the cloth bag in a heavy coat of hot bees' wax. The seeds he thought would be most precious were wheat and rye. He had some corn even though Konaya had told him there was corn at his home place. There were also beans of several varieties, along with apple, peach, cherry and pear seeds.

August brought the heat of late summer was making travel a little more difficult, their Indian guides were choosing travel by streams as much as possible. Finding cold, clear water at every hand made travel almost a pleasure. Even so, there was yet another mountain to cross, lesser in size than those past but still difficult. Certain supplies were running low, coffee being one of them. The Indian women came to the rescue by introducing Virginia to baked and ground acorns,not the best but certainly a good substitute when added to other dried roots the Indians produced from their carry bags. Virginia and the men were pleased with the substitute, even if it was not coffee but had the same effect as the caffeine in coffee.

This day dawned with a clear and hot sky which made the mountain ahead seem like almost too much for the oxen to drag the wagons over. Konaya returned with a party of six of his brothers to tell them how the land on the other side leveled out. It was not exactly level but there would no longer be a need to unload the wagons to traverse the higher ridge of this one. From this point on, they would be following an ever widening valley stream flowing to the west. In just a few more days, they would be arriving at the home they were looking for.

Berries were ripe all along the trail and the Paw Paw trees were about to give off their fruit. This was known as the American banana bush, a very mellow fruit that could be eaten in many ways. This fruit had a dark green skin and was delicious when fully ripe but somewhat like a persimmon in it's bitterness when still a little less than ripe. Soon there would be chestnut trees dropping nuts by the bushels. These trees reached far into the skies and were the perfect tree for lumber. They were tall and straight, sometimes reaching twenty feet to the lowest limb. The best nut of all though was the Butternut, from a tree that might reach sixty feet in height and be fifty feet across the top. This tree was not so plentiful but was prized for the sweet kernel, somewhat like a black walnut but in a soft shell. The Indians had these trees well located and watched for the ripe nuts to fall since wild animals made short work of the nuts.

Thomas was pushing hard to make their destination before the trees had shed all of their leaves. He felt the need to construct a solid home for Virginia, one that could be kept warm through the coldest winter months and one that would protect their first born from the dangers of the frontier. At this time of the year, the trees were no longer pulling moisture from the earth and the results was a dryer timber that would last much longer. It would also be lighter to handle and easier to cut.

In spite of all he could do, the Indians found this a time of plenty and they were like children, running through the fields and woods, gathering berries and other edible items. Virginia was overburdened with the food items they brought for her to cook. She delighted in doing for their new friends and was surprised every day or so, to see a new face. It seemed they were getting close to their home and now and then, a new wanderer would join the crowd for a visit to see the wonder woman, Virginia. Her delight was to always have food ready to feed all of them, even if it was cold. She found from the beginning the Indians were not picky eaters. Anything they were fed, they would eat without a grumble.

Late this afternoon, Konaya rode in to meet the wagon train. He had good news, that which all were eager to hear. If they pushed hard, it would be possible to reach the Indian town before moon rise. Thomas, Peyton and Henry voted to pull up and camp for the night at the first place where water was available. Tomorrow would be a very busy day and they needed to face it well-rested for it was certainly going to be a busy day. Well before dusk, everything had been done for a peaceful night, the last one before their new home. Even the animals sensed the end was near by feeding early and lying down at dusk. The cow had done her best to keep up a supply of milk but with the rigors of travel and less feeding time, it was a lost cause. Virginia had saved her milk as long as possible so as to have a small amount of butter. Virginia and Mary had time to prepare a very large meal of corn cakes with a generous supply of salt cured ham. The last of their trail dinners was to be remembered well, if Virginia had anything to do with it. Tomorrow might not fare so well with so many Indians to meet and possibly feed from her dwindling supply.

Dawn found the entire wagon train wide awake and doing little things to keep busy while breakfast was under way. Virginia had been keeping her limited number of eggs back for several days. Hens did not like to lay eggs in a moving trailer. With the three she had, she used the last of her flour to make pancakes cooked in butter and sweetened with the very last of her small stock of maple syrup. That with some of the left over ham from last night made a very tasty breakfast. For once she was glad Konaya and his friends had chosen to stay with their people last night. There was far too little to go around as it was.

Packing for today's travel took almost no time since most had been done the night before. It was the work of cleaning up the breakfast things by Virginia and Mary that held them back for just a short time. They were more than ready for travel when Konaya and a large group of men, women and children rode into their camp. It was to be a very great day for the Indians as well as the McMellon tribe. Konaya was obviously the leader of the pack and in his glory. To be bringing such riches into the Indian camp was a great honor to him and he made the most of it. Being able to converse freely in the white man's tongue was enough to make him a celebrity and place him before the tribal chief with the honor of introductions. First he had to make known the new name of Konaya he carried and to explain it to his chief. He did so with pride and was paid high tribute by the chief.

Chapter 9

Perhaps a half mile outside the Indian town, the wagons were met by what seemed like a multitude of Indian children. Virginia looked on all of them as children, even if some bore the wrinkles of many years of living with the elements, just a buffalo skin away. Their homes were no doubt comfortable to them, but Virginia could not understand why they did not have warmer log structures for the bitter cold months. With so much building material at hand, she thought it would be easy to construct a warm place of logs and earth. It did not occur to her that they had no reasonable way to cut trees and make a log shelter of them. When she spoke to Thomas of this matter, he assured her it would be different once he had set up a sawmill and passed out tools to the Indians. The ownership of an axe was unknown to them at this time and they would have to be carefully trained so as to prevent serious injury to the user. The best tool they had was known as the Tomahawk, so named by the white settlers who first saw this weapon of war. Some were of cheap iron blade which came to them as trade goods from the French or English in Canada, hardly worth calling a hatchet or an axe.

It was at the time of celebration for the fall crops that runners arrived in the town of Chief Night Bird to tell of the white people and wagons approaching the town of Bear Claw. White Deer asked for permission to take a few warriors with her to meet the wagons approaching the town. It was her hope that the men who had abducted her would be with these wagons, and her warriors would be there to punish them. With permission, their party left the same morning and arrived the day before Thomas and his party. White Deer and her warriors chose to stay well in the background so as to see before being seen, if the men she sought were really with the wagons.

The wagons pulled into the center of their compound just before noon and were immediately surrounded by people of all ages and stature. Many were from the tribe that had their home across several hills from here and among them was a young woman who caught Virginia's eye. This young woman seemed to be aged far beyond her years and had a look of being either an outcast or one that was suffering from a major hurt. Virginia called this woman to the attention of Thomas and he felt great compassion for her, even though he did not know what her troubles were. As they sat and contemplated approaching her, to perhaps offer her words or help, whichever was needed, they saw her face light up in a radiant smile. She was at the back of the crowd when they saw her smile and then start a frantic effort to part the people and get to their wagon. They did not understand until they saw Konaya also break into a smile and leap off the wagon to engulf the young woman in his arms. He now knew that White Deer did not die at the hands of those three men. Konaya could not speak for several minutes, but when he could, he told Thomas and Virginia what they had already guessed. With such a momentous occasion, Virginia and Thomas both openly shed tears of joy. It was more than an hour later when Konaya was able to continuewith the introductions to his chief, Bear Claw. Yes, this Indian wore a necklace of many bear claws for he had proven his bravery many times and had multiple scars to prove it.

The honor of meeting this man was stirring to Thomas, Peyton and Henry, making them wonder what kind of gift to offer. They had no good rifles to spare and to give him one lesser than one Konaya had was to insult him. In much haste, they discussed it with Virginia and it was she that came up with the answer. It hurt her very much to part with it but it was for a very good cause. The quilt of many colors her mother made for their wedding night was precious to her and would set Bear Claw apart like no other gift. When Virginia removed it from the chest and shook it out for all to see, the women and the men were awed by the rainbow of colors. Nothing would have pleased Chief Bear Claw so much as this gift did.

Later, they assembled in the round house where the elders and leaders met for the purpose of smoking the peace pipe and exchanging blood from cuts in their hands. This was the Indian way of mixing blood in the palm of their hands to seal forever the act of becoming blood brothers. After this ceremony, Thomas passed out hunting knives to every man. Their welcome was such that it lasted for days. It also gained them willing workers to help with the construction of storage buildings so the wagons could be unloaded. This was necessary since the wagons would have to do for their living quarters until log homes could be constructed.

Virginia and Mary were eager to hear the story of what happened to White Deer that time so long ago when Konaya thought her lost forever. Obviously they could not yet converse with her but they took her in as a sister which pleased Konaya very much.

Chapter 10

In the little time they had before turning in that night, White Deer explained she was captive for three days and two nights. The three men made a slave of her and treated her as common goods for their pleasure. They forced her to cook for them and beat her when it was not satisfactory. She was allowed some freedom as long as she was busy at their food preparation. At night she was tied to one of them so her every move was reason for her to be struck again. They confirmed her thoughts that her husband was dead since she saw him clubbed to unconsciousness and left on the ground for dead. She had no way of returning to the location where she last saw Konaya for in their travels they went to the east, and she had been blindfolded much of the way. She was determined to escape and return to her people, no matter the cost. She did her best to please the men into thinking she liked being with them.

On the third evening, they relaxed their guard while she prepared the evening meal. They had allowed her the use of one of their knives while cooking. When she had to go to the creek for water, she had waited until dusk. This evening she had been able to conceal the knife for this break. When out of sight for just a few moments, she made a run for freedom. They were unable to see her and therefore she made an all night run in what she hoped was to the west. As best as she could see on such a dark night when clouds covered the sky most of the night, she used the north star to continue west. At dawn, she found a small cave and there rested for that first day. The need for food drove her out well before full darkness and she used the dusk time to locate an opossum. As unsavory as this animal is, it was food for a starving woman who had been deprived of a good meal for the past four days.

The small fire she was able to keep in the confines of the cave she had slept in most of the day was enough to allow her to roast the animal. As cook and slave to those men, she had the use of the knife taken from one of her captors. which she now used to prepare the opossums. Starting a fire had been the only real problem she had encountered. That she had solved with the rawhide string the man gave her for her belt when he took her beautiful, beaded belt for his headband. With that string, she was able to make a bow and use it to spin a stick of dry wood into another dry piece of wood. With the friction from this spinning stick, she developed enough heat for starting her much needed fire.

While she had a fire going, she managed to find a hickory sprout, just right for a combination walking stick and long enough to act as a spear, if needed. She earlier had found a rock with enough silica to make a good sharpening stone. Her knife needed much work but she had the time to get it as sharp as a trade knife could be. With the smaller end of the stick shaved to a long point, she fire-hardened it enough to make a serious weapon.

She knew enough about the three men to know they would give up following her after an hour or so. The next day they would try to follow her trail but this would become too tiring for lazy men well before noon. White Deer felt safer traveling in full light than after dark, in part because the panther hunted at night and also the rattle snake hunted at night. These mountains were plagued with an abundance of these dangerous snakes and a bite from one of them would be the end of her.

During the time when she was first captured and taken east, White Deer had enough knowledge to keep their direction firmly fixed in her mind. She had watched the shadow of trees to plot their course almost due east. Now all she had to do was reverse this course and she would soon encounter people of her own tribe.

The next morning, she was well rested from a night and a day in her little cave home. Starting in the cool of dawn, she set out for a hard day of traveling and on only a small portion of the left-over opossum. As unsavory as it was, she managed, but with the full intention of finding better food in her travels today.

Around mid afternoon of the second day she found a small lake with an abundance of catfish in shallow water. It appeared the water level had been dropping for some reason which was a blessing to her. With her walking stick spear, she made short work of one that was as long as her arm, from elbow to finger tip. Just the right size to split down the middle and bake over a slow fire. She cleaned it and removed every part that was not edible. Gathering the long leaves from the Cattail/latifolia growing just inside the edge of the pond, she used these to wrap the fish for cooking at day's end. As for food just now, there was nothing better than the tender stems and roots of the cattail which tasted much like asparagus or, some believe, like celery. In either case, White Deer made a meal of these tender shoots and continued on west without a fire. Toward dusk, she located an overhanging rock shelf that was to be her home for the night. Gathering dry wood that would not give off much smoke, she started another cook fire. While this was burning down to hot coals, she gathered pine branches for her bed which was to be between the fire and the back of the overhang. This would discourage any animal or snake that looked for a warm body, either to eat or to rest next to during the colder morning hours. It was well understood that the rattlesnake roams throughout the warm night but when temperatures fall, it looks for a warm place like under a rock. The sun-warmed rock holds heat for hours where the snake rests until sun-up, then it comes out and usually lies on top of the rock until well warmed. It has been known to find a sleeping body to get next to for the warmth, not very comforting to the awakening person.

After the fire had burned down to a bed of coals, White Deer placed a layer of cattail leaves on the coals, then the fish and more leaves on top of that. A half hour later, she had food fit for her Gods and enough to make her sleep well for the night.

White Deer traveled ever westward this fourth day of her freedom, always on the lookout for other humans. It was possible that she would be taken captive again unless she encountered members of her own tribe. Caution slowed her travel until she could do no more than a few miles each day. Time did not worry her though; just the thoughts of her husband lying back there where the three men had killed him was enough to make her super cautious.

Finding food was not too much of a problem but cooking was. She always had to make the fire where smoke would not give her presence away and this meant under a rock ledge or a cave of some sort. She was always on the search for rabbits since they were very good to eat and usually easier to catch than other game. Because of an abundance of panthers, the rabbit population was rather thin so she did not have much luck. It was from the creeks and ponds where food was easy. Other than fish, there were turtles and mussels in plentiful supply. It took several mussels to make a good meal but when she found them, it was just a matter of picking them up.

On the evening of the ninth day, she spotted several men on the opposite mountain. They were not doing much to hide their party so she figured they were in their home territory. By carefully moving across the valley between, she carefully approached the men until she was certain they were from her own tribe. She was dressed in the rags left to her by her captors and not easily identified as a woman except when she got rather close to them. When she stepped out from behind a large tree, it was in such a way as to not excite them into shooting an arrow her way.

After identifying her as one of their tribe, they could not do enough for her. Sharing their food was the first act of kindness she had seen since the loss of her husband and she could not have been more overjoyed at their actions. She knew some of the men and was known as the woman who would never return. As soon as she had eaten just a few bites, she started telling these men where she came from and how she had been captured by white men. Of course, this led them to believe all white men were to be treated as enemy and killed on sight. It was only the better part of one day back to their town and they left at once, arriving just before dark. There she was embraced by her sister and her father as they had thought her dead. Her honeymoon should have been finished weeks ago and neither she or her husband had returned. According to tradition, they were given a ceremony to help them find their way home, at least all of the family and most of the tribe prayed for their safe return.

Chapter 11

As the welcome home ceremony was a good excuse for all to eat and dance all night, this was not one to be passed off lightly since White Deer was so well thought of by all of her tribe. Her marriage to another clan would have meant seeing her only frequently in future years and she would have been sorely missed. Her return today was like setting the clock of time backward and this made her many friends and all of her family very happy and ready for the all night celebration.

Within any group of people, there is always a trouble maker willing to use any excuse to create violence. This tribe was no different except perhaps there had to be two of the same mind. To them, it was not enough that White Deer was safely home; they wanted to go immediately to the nearest white settlement and take revenge. All they needed was three or four more whipped up to the same level of vengeance to form a war party. This night of celebration was not the right time for stirring up the trouble.They wanted it to end only after a few days.

The following day the issue was brought before chief Night Bird and the elders as a need to punish the white men for their treatment of the Indians, White Deer being the example they used. Of course, the elders were sympathetic with the daughter that had been violated and at least one thought action was needed. However, the chief and other elders made a positive statement that only the exact culprit was to be punished and that by death. This was not the answer wanted by Horned Owl, the leader of the forming war party. In spite of the elders' ruling, Horned Owl made his war party aware and set the time for visiting the incoming whites just a few days after their arrival. He was in hopes the trouble he planned would have started well before he got there and the killing of the whites could be blamed on the other clan, that of chief Bear Claw.

After two days and nights of celebration, Thomas was able to get the work started on the first shelter. He got the help of several men who wanted in on the fun of doing things the white man's way and gaining possession of the wonderful axe they were passing out. First came the work of cutting trees of the proper size and trimming them to cabin length. To fell the trees, a crosscut saw was used, pulled through the cut by a man on each end. The Indians had never seen a saw and the work was fascinating to them to see. How a piece of flat metal could slice through a tree that would never have given way to the cheap axes they owned and used. And then to see the sharp axe that would cut limbs off and never seem to grow dull. What fun it was to use white man's tools. That first day of cutting produced enough logs to build the 20 X 30 shelter Virginia and

Thomas would call home for many months to come. The second day was also a new experience to the Indians and one they delighted in doing,raising and fitting the logs as fast as Thomas and Peyton could notch the ends. Henry was very busy in selecting the proper log for the next round and before it seemed possible, the structure was up and a roof had been placed with smaller logs. While this was being done, another group of Indians was in the process of cutting a large chestnut tree into short pieces, just long enough to make shingles when split into layers about an inch thick. These were spread out in sunlight to dry as much as possible before they needed to be placed on the roof. Shrinkage was best before being nailed down and would keep them from splitting later.

Work continued for several days toward building a cabin for Henry and Mary and another for Peyton which would also serve to house the more valuable of the wagon cargo. As work progressed, Thomas and Peyton were continually passing out small gifts and Virginia, with Mary's help, was feeding the men the best they possibly could. There was never a shortage of buffalo and this was the basis for their cooking. Virginia was having a wonderful time as the Indian women were right with her in cooking and teaching her the use of their spices. It was truly a time of celebration with so much food and such a good relationship between all of them, almost like play time.

Peyton took advantage of this by holding worship services around the evening fire when all were resting with a full stomach. He and his party were having a wonderful time teaching them to sing hymns and at the same time telling them what the songs meant. He was wise enough to know all would be sleeping in fifteen minutes with a plain sermon so the mixture was doing the job well. Of course, Konaya was doing his share of teaching about Jesus for he understood and could translate with accuracy. White Deer was the first to accept the teachings of Peyton and Konaya. She wanted baptism as soon as possible for she understood the importance of following her husband who had followed the Bible teaching of Peyton. Truly, God had instigated this meeting,thought Peyton. How else could he have reached so many in such a short time? How could he have gained these followers of Jesus without the help of Konaya? He preached love to them with tears flowing down his cheeks which at first made the Indians wonder if he was a mite touched. But as time passed and they began to understand, they also shed tears.

White Deer and her warriors had arrived days ago and having seen the love of the whites, decided to stay on for a time and enjoy the fun. They also came under the spell of Peyton's God, even though they did not understand the emotion they felt in their hearts. We are told in, Titus 2:11: "For the grace of God that bringeth salvation hath appeared to all men." And in John 1:9,"That was the true light which lighteth every man that cometh into the world."

In John 12:32, Jesus said, "And I, if I be lifted up from the earth, will draw all men unto me."

How could we deny that God has placed in the heart of every man who ever lived, the conscience of God's existence? All Peyton was doing was awakening the spirit in the hearts of men who already had inert knowledge of our God? They were born with it and it was through Peyton it came to life.

Chapter 12

It was the start of a busy day in mid-September when both cabins were finished shells. The work of cutting doors and windows was Peyton's work while Thomas and Henry went to the woods with several Indians. Konaya was still running slow in the morning hours for he was intent on staying with White Deer until she had prepared breakfast for the two of them. In part, it was the fear of losing White Deer again that made him almost desert his friends. He did not like for her to get out of his sight and he did not like to be caught without his rifle close by. It was this thought that made Konaya take his rifle with him as he started for the woods where Thomas was cutting trees.

Horned Owl and three of his followers entered the town just as Konaya was leaving. Horned Owl saw Peyton across the compound as he was just starting to work and since he came here to kill whites, what better place to start? As he started a screaming run toward Peyton with his Tomahawk lifted for the killing blow, Konaya saw in time to place a bullet in Horned Owl's back. Most of the men had gone to the work site, and only the women saw the next move by the followers of Horned Owl. These two must have thought another white man had fired the shot, for Konaya was wearing mostly white man's clothes. They both started toward Konaya who was now unarmed since he had no time to reload. Their trouble started when the women took up the fight by rushing the men with knives, fire tongs and bare hands. The fight lasted only seconds before all three were dead. White Deer recognized them as from her town and told the people that her Chief Night Bird had ordered them to not form a war party. Because of White Deer seeing all of the fight, it was decided she and Konaya were to go to the families of the three and tell the story so there would be no thought of reprisals from their town. Konaya and White Deer were invited to stay for a few days so his story could be heard by all. Even though he would rather be working with Thomas, he was obligated to tell his story to White Deer's relatives. That night and all of the next day was another celebration for with so little to amuse themselves, celebrations were looked forward to and lasted as long as possible.

Now that Konaya was a Christian and had a believing wife, he took great pleasure in telling the part of the story where he first saw white people in prayer and how it touched him. He told of looking from his hiding place and seeing them kneeling in prayer, singing and holding their hands to heaven in supplication to their God. He told how he was received in love when he first met the boy, Thomas and how the family took him in. His best part of the story was how their God also took him in and changed his life, forever.

Time to return to his friends and the work that they were doing left a little sadness as always when parting from people we really love. To his surprise, four men and their wives made it clear they would return with Konaya. They said they would not be happy until they heard more about this God that had so much love. They must hear it from Peyton, their chief.

On returning from White Deer's town with converts, Konaya introduced them to Peyton. As usual, Peyton lifted his hands to Heaven and thanked God for the addition to his flock.

Now all work on their homes had to stop. Peyton felt it was necessary to have a permanent place to call their church building. In fact, he thought it a good idea to make the building large enough and strong enough to withstand a major storm. Tornados were not known in this part of the world but very strong winds and thunder storms were common. The buffalo hide structures the Indians lived in were sometimes destroyed from these winds and all would appreciate a strong building when these winds struck.

It was with much enthusiasm that the entire tribe joined in the fun of having a community building. Even the women wanted to be a part of the construction and so Peyton found work for them in the form of making mud pies, mud chinking made from the red clay found near the creek edge. Water mixed with this clay and again mixed with grass gathered from the same place made a thick and durable cement. With this placed between the logs as they were erected, a wall as solid as could be found on the frontier became the church and the community center. In addition to the walls, Peyton had them construct a fireplace large enough to stand in. He thought this would give them a place to take refuge from about any form of danger that might come and at the same time give them warmth and a place to cook. As for the roof, it took a lot of extra time since it was a larger building than usual, twenty-eight by forty-eight feet, and he wanted it to last.

First he had chestnut logs cut to extra long lengths, about to length of a man, then split into shingles at least well over a foot wide. Placing smaller split logs on the roof first, with the flat side up. Shingles made an almost air tight roof and one that would last for many years. For windows, He sacrificed the glass he had brought for his home which gave the building four small windows, not enough to read by in day time but enough for the gatherings to light candles when needed.

The building became the most secure west of Philadelphia which made all of them very proud. Because of the time lost on Peyton's home, Thomas and Virginia insisted he move his things in until a time when they could catch up. Since the building was so large that most of it was not yet needed,

Peyton did move into one corner near the fire place.

Now that November chill was in the air, the home Virginia moved into was only one large room but she made short work of using her quilts and canvas to divide the area. This made it more comfortable near the fireplace and added privacy for their sleeping area. It was very hard work for her, and Mary would not allow her to step up on anything that she might fall from. Thomas had brought enough canvas to separate the room in half, from floor to ceiling, and this was well used since very cold weather was on the way. Their living quarters near the fire place would stay warm even in the coldest part of winter to come. For the hanging of this canvas, Thomas would use Henry for help and securely fasten it to the ceiling beams so that no heat was lost. For the door, it was only a slit in the canvas but Virginia had taken a piece of left over canvas and sewed a covering for the slit. The was nearly an air-tight enclosure and one that Virginia would need very soon. Her baby was due in perhaps another thirty days and the baby would need to be kept warm. Weather could often reach below zero and stay there for days, while snow would build to well over a foot in depth. It was well that enough firewood had been cut in the process of building the cabins that no more would be needed this coming winter.

Henry and Mary's cabin was also finished but Mary did nothing toward furnishing hers until Virginia was well taken care of. Mary's place did have a good fireplace and she did move in with most of her belongings but they were mighty scarce,just enough to cooking and sleeping. Henry had made their bed and table, both temporary but satisfactory for the time. During the long winter months of December through March, Henry would make permanent tables, chairs and a bed which could be done inside their cabin. Thomas and Peyton would also be making their furnishings inside.

All three men would work outside when a break in the weather permitted, for the blacksmith shop needed to have a roof and three sides. The back of this shop building would have a small enclosed space for valuable items such as those the Indians might be tempted to take. Items such as guns, powder and shot were moved into Henry's cabin. All food supplies were stored inside both of the cabins where the women would have easy access and supplies could be protected from weather and varmints. In addition to the building, Peyton supervised the construction of a forge. This was mostly made of clay bricks made by the women of Konaya's following. They had been busy making bricks back in July and were happy to be playing in the clay and forming bricks was just another way to do something for Peyton. They pitched into the chore while laughing and having a good time as they sometimes threw clay balls at each other. As the clay slowly dried into bricks, they were ready for the forge when Peyton placed them in a platform shape with a recessed bowl in the center. Here the air would be sent under the coals from a bellows made of leather and slabs of chestnut wood. Peyton had brought a section of metal pipe which was placed so as to send air under the coals when the bellows was pumped. As soon as it was ready for fire, Peyton built a small fire in it to help dry and bake the bricks into a permanent forge. This fire would also help keep the place warm enough during the coming cold spells when it was necessary to do wood work on the wheels and cogs for both saw and grist mills.

December, 1760 found a deep snow in which very few Indians were ever seen outside. Virginia was not able to do much work and Mary was a God-send helper. She did almost all cooking for their party of five and left Virginia alone only during the night when Thomas was staying in. Konaya and White Deer had a place of their own and were often visitors to Virginia's home. White Deer had an old medicine woman visit Virginia on occasion, just to become friends and know she would help with the birth of the new one. Peyton was trying to hold services as much as possible during this coldest part of the year. These services were not as well attended as he had hoped but some were brave and curious enough to gather for his service. He had learned much of their language and was able to present a vivid picture of the birth of Christ but could not make them understand the virgin part. In an effort to be the good Shepherd and pastor to the Indians, he made an effort to visit with them in their Tepees and found them to be very comfortable and wonderful hosts. He was constantly being fed something and had to curtail his visits to keep from being overfed. Before the winter was over, he had made a visit to every tepee in this town and was liked every where he went. The place he liked to visit most was at the tepee of Konaya and White Deer. There, he could converse in English for by now, Konaya had taught his wife to speak English fluently. Konaya had been faithful in telling his people about his God and it was well known that Konaya was blessed with much knowledge. He and Peyton made some progress in Christianizing several of them and was delighted to have them want baptizing as soon as the river was free of ice.

December thirteenth, 1730 arrived, cold and clear. This day was also marked with the arrival of the new one, named Boyce James, much like Thomas, already well filled out with muscles in the right places. The medicine woman had arrived about dawn, knowing in some un-fathomable way that a new boy was due today. Her help was with knowledge from delivery of a hundred babies before. Virginia did have some struggle, but it was a good birth and the pain would soon be forgotten. Boyce was worth it all and turned out to be a very quiet baby, contented to sleep most of the day and all of the nights. Thomas was such a proud father he was reluctant to place Boyce in his mother's arms when feeding time arrived. Thomas was content to sit by the fire and cuddle Boyce for as long as he could hold out against sleep.

December 22nd and Virginia, with Mary's help, had made the community center as beautiful as possible by hanging pine, cedar and holly branches all over the building. With the newness of the cut logs and the trimmings being placed everywhere, there was a wonderful, clean smell about the place. Logs split in half and with short legs added, it became more like a church ready for the Christmas ceremony. Days before, Peyton had been preaching about the birth of Christ and the coming celebration. By this time, the community was excited about the Christmas meeting and had plans for bringing food to the church for an all day meeting. Many of the Indians did not understand why all the fuss over a baby being born but they went along with it for the fun of something different, if nothing else. Although Thanksgiving time is considered turkey time, the Indians recognized the difficulty in obtaining the elusive turkey, so it was prized enough untill several hunted for them days in advance. Arriving on Christmas morning, many families came with offerings of buffalo hump, venison and the few turkeys found. Many dishes of Indian delicacy arrived, mostly of unknown contents to the whites and not all considered gourmet food by Thomas. Still it was necessary to partake of at least a trial run or the possibility of offending their friends. The day progressed with several sermons given by Peyton, mostly about love but with an effort to tell about the God-given conception of Jesus, the Christ. Few understood but the seed of Christianity was planted this day.

Virginia had decorated their home as best she could and had made a gift of gloves or mittens for Thomas and another pair for Peyton. She had used her time while too close to delivery for the purpose of sewing them from the supply of deer skins Konaya had supplied. These were made of two flat pieces of the leather, cut to cover the hand and long enough to tie around the wrist. On the thumb side, the mitten was left open so the thumb and forefinger or the entire hand could be removed quickly. This was similar to the ones Konaya was wearing and seemed to be the most practical for a working man. There was so little she could do to express her love for the men in her life, including the little man, Boyce.

Chapter 13

Soon began week's of bitter cold weather with never a sight of bare ground and no running water to be seen in the river. Everything was frozen and food for the animals was running very short. It was a struggle for Thomas to break the river ice every day so the animals could drink. They were turned loose to forage whatever they could find to supplement the meager food Thomas could give them. Fortunately, they had been very saving with the grain brought from Saxsonville, and Thomas, with the help of Henry had gathered what grass they could find to cut and store while it was still standing back in September.

There was no need to keep the animals confined except at night and then it was their habit to return on their own, just for the few bites of grain Thomas could give them. His fear was the loss of their animals to wolves which howled all night long now that they too were hungry. There was the danger of a daytime attack from the wolves so all of the men kept their rifles at ready, just in case. Water for their use was also a problem which caused the men to carry water from the river when the cattle were watered. Under the ice, the river ran clear which was a blessing, but Thomas made a promise to dig a well as soon as the ground thawed enough to allow digging. Peyton wondered about where the Indians got their water and asked Konaya for an explanation. He was told they did not need much and kept a large pot on their fire which snow and ice was added to from time to time.

The closing of their first winter of March 1731 winds coming and with them a warming trend to reduce the snow that had piled up to about two feet in places. There was no shortage of fire wood logs but some shortage in cut wood since the Indians had been taking advantage of that which was cut during the last summer and fall. It was good for all and Thomas had no trouble forming a work party for the purpose of cutting firewood for the winter to come, even though it was still ten months in the future. For the Indians, they never had a winter before that they did not have to struggle for fire wood throughout the cold months. Spring was soon to turn the trees into-sap filled logs, unsuitable for building material. Even though it was still very cold, Thomas had the work party felling suitable trees and leaving them un-trimmed. In effect, he was killing the tree before it had time to bring water up from the roots and make the log too heavy to be used for buildings. Of course, logs filled with water or sap as it really was, would rot much faster and was not suitable for using in a cabin or building.

He also had the dream of a dam across this small river that would be used for his grist mill, saw mill and blacksmith shop. Working while he could in cold weather made it far more comfortable than waiting until heat made work times less productive. While all of this work was underway, he was looking for rocks and a place where he could quarry slabs of stone. He would need a lot of it for the dam.

By early April, he had enough logs cut and trimmed to finish all of the buildings planned for. He also had several that would help in the construction of the dam, even though that would not start until the dry season coming in July and August. The last planned building was for the home of Peyton and was to be finished well before summer.

Chapter 14

May,1731 was also time for the preparation of a garden large enough to feed all of his family.

Two of his oxen were well trained to the plow but the work was extremely difficult. Even though he had selected a place where no trees had been cut, the ground was a tangled mass of roots. Thankfully there was very little in the way of stones to contend with. It appeared this had been a river bottom in ages past and the soil was deep in rich dirt.

By the end of April, he had completed his garden with some seeds planted. He had started his fruit tree seeds in pots inside a month earlier by taking them out every day the weather was warm enough. Some things like tomato and pepper plants had a head start the same way. Potato buds were showing on their seed potatoes and it was time to plant them. All hands turned out in late April to help with the garden, even Virginia with Boyce in a large basket at garden's edge. All was well except for the varmints that loved gardens. Thomas paid the Indian boys a bounty on animals caught in the garden,raccoons being the worst and rabbits second, but at night time it was the deer that gave them the most trouble. Now Lil Ringo came into her own. Between her and Ole Ring, deer had a hard time of getting much out of their garden. Both dogs were seemingly knowledgeable as to the value of this garden plot and guarded it day and night. Thomas and Peyton built a high split rail fence that was secure enough to keep out only his oxen, cattle and horses. The rest was up to them and to the dogs.

May of this first spring and the garden was complete. Now it needed constant care to protect it from a dozen different things that wanted to eat it before harvest time. Lil Ringo and their cow, all had young ones in the oven. Lil Ringo should give her young before July first and their cow, before mid June. Mary on the other hand was to hold on until next December, Christmas she hoped. Except work from well before dawn untill the darkness of night, this family had nothing to do, that is to say, no loafing time. Peyton insisted on Sunday's being free from work for them and for their animals. It was not long before the Indians fell into the same pattern of church in the morning and again in the evening. Peyton considered the restless nature of the children and cut his sermons very short. He was delighted that almost every one of the town would show up at the meeting house for both sermons. Of late, Virginia had been referring to their settlement as a town.Soon, Mary picked up the reference to it as a town. Peyton continued, in every way possible to teach love as being the first commandment. He was very careful to keep the other commandments back until he understood the traditions of his followers. Time would take care of that. Now that he was so familiar with the names of all of them, he made it a point in greeting each of them in their tongue and expressing love for them. After all, they were his children. Thomas welcomed this day as a time when he could spend a little time with Boyce and a lot more time in the shade of a large tree outside their back yard. Sleep was foremost on his mind on those lazy Sunday afternoons. It goes without saying that Virginia and Mary had no real free day except that sometimes Mary would take over and cook while caring for Boyce and give Virginia a free Sunday afternoon with Thomas.

On these days, Thomas would walk the river's edge with Virginia and tell her of his plans for their future. Virginia mentioned to Thomas several times that she would like to try for a little girl. Although he would like to have the baby girl, he hesitated to agree because of the fear of losing Virginia. He remembered his childhood when he had no mother and he understood the risk. However, nature has a way of doing the natural thing and before the summer's end, Virginia broke the news of another in their future.

July found the weather very hot and beginning to get dry from lack of rain.The river had been dropping all spring and now summer found it low enough for Thomas to start the dam. He had already gathered many hugh rocks with the oxen and had them where they could be quickly placed across the bottom of the river. He had already dug a channel that would be used to divert the river until the dam could be completed and later used as the spillway for his water wheel. Digging the spillway was a heavy job and could only be done with two oxen and a slip scraper. This item was a large shovel-like pan with handles much like a wheelbarrow with no wheels. The oxen would pull it while Thomas would regulate the depth of the cut by raising or lowering the handles. When the scraper was full,he would drop the handles until the oxen pulled the load to a dumping spot. There Thomas would raise the handles so the scraper would up-end and dump the load. It sounds like quite a detailed job but was actually very simple and quickly done. Now that the river was diverted, Thomas could move the largest rocks into place and build the dam with ever smaller rocks. All the time he was building, the dam was wide enough at the base for the oxen to pull slip scraper loads of rock and clay across, building the dam with enough width and height to fill the river channel. Thomas, Peyton and Henry worked as if madness had set in just so they could finish well before fall rains started. All of this time, the women had to tend the garden and were really surprised that Konaya and two other men came to help. They had brought their wives who did most of the garden work while Konaya and the men helped on the dam. It was then that the shale rock slabs came into use. The walls of the bypass channel had to be lined so as to keep the river from making a new main channel. This one was to be used to direct the force of the river to turn a water wheel. In the main dam, they had made a sluice gate which would allow the river to overflow the dam when turning the water wheel was not needed. Now it was time to build the grist mill building and set up the parts Thomas had brought from Portsmouth, Old Virginia.

Considering food to be more important than lumber, Thomas and Peyton set to work on the grist mill first. The most difficult job of all in the making of a grist mill was the forming of the grinding stones. From the time they left Saxsonville, Thomas had been looking for and trying to remember where he saw suitable stone for the ones he needed. About two days back along the trail they came in on, he had located just the right place for these stones. Getting them was a task for as many Indian friends as he felt he could depend on and with a great deal of labor. Thomas had located a place where the mountain had fallen away, probably in a prolonged rain, and shelf rock stuck out of the mountain. The slab rock looked to be about a foot or slightly thicker and very smooth on the top side. It appeared to be such that he could remove some top soil and cut away slabs about three feet in diameter.

The day he left with Konaya and three of his friends, they took as many tools and as much ropes as Thomas thought they might need. Food for the trip would mostly be from the land so they only took a small amount of cooking utensils and no solid food except for the first evening on the trail. The second day they arrived and with a closer inspection, Thomas was delighted in how easy it would be to cut out the stone he needed. It would take time and much labor to get out two pieces. As he was to rough cut the stone with hammer and chisel, he cut wide and with care so as not to break the stone in an unusable way. After cutting one of them, he had the oxen team move the wagon in position to allow the stone to be drug on board. First, he had to cut small logs to make a ramp from the hillside, down to the tailgate of the wagon. Securing the wagon so it would not move, he hitched the oxen to the stone and dragged it to the front. After this, cutting out the second stone and repeating the process , he had both on the wagon for a very heavy load. Both Thomas and Peyton worked to set up a shaping process whereby the stones could be made near perfectly round,one with a round hole in the center and the best one with a five inch square hole in the center. This stone would have the burs or grinding notches cut in the surface at an angle so grain being ground would be gradually moved to the outside and off the edge. The top stone would remain stable as a mate to the grinding process. Making the water wheel and the gear wheels was everyday work for Peyton as he had been doing this kind of work for years. In a matter of three weeks, the water was turned through the water sluice and the grinding wheel turned for the first time.

In mid September, this years corn crop was very good and some of it was almost dry enough to grind. It had to be placed in the sun as much as possible for the next few days in order for it to make good meal and not clog the grinding groves. All thought it well worth the waiting time.

October saw their first crop to be very good with an abundance of green beans, now dry on the vine. Bushels of them had been placed on strings and hung from every place in the buildings that could be spared. Peppers, both hot and mild, were hanging everywhere, even out in the shop. Corn had been picked and placed in wire cages where mice could not get to it. Thomas had thoughtfully brought enough wire to build a small enclosure for this purpose.

Unfortunately, there would be no fruit for another two years but there was a plentiful supply of wild plums. The Indians had been good to bring Virginia much of the bounty of the wilds, including honey and many berries. Blackberries and blueberries were everywhere and Virginia filled every jar she had been able to bring to their new home. Jam made from the wilds needed very little sugar and what she did need, honey was more than satisfactory. A good crop of turnips had been planned for and would last them far into the winter. Some things such as potatoes would keep well in the garden pit where it was buried until needed.Poor Thomas was run from dawn to well after dusk caring for the winter supply of food and wanting desperately to start n the saw mill.

November, the grist mill was ready for use and the first run of corn meal had been a whopping success. Peyton took on the job of grinding enough for their use and much more for the Indian women. He could not afford the time to do more than a months supply and would have to make another run when time permitted, perhaps in December. Thomas was more than ready to start on the saw mill part. This was just a matter of building another wheel with the crosscut saw attached to one side so as the wheel turned, the saw would back away from the log on the upstroke and bite into the log on the down stroke. All of this was attached to the water wheel so a ratchet fed the log into the saw blade. Even so, it took all winter to complete the sawmill and have it working by early spring. During the cold winter months, he could work only part time on the wheels and cogs necessary for his mill, but he did fill in the coldest times with cutting logs suitable for the mill.

The forge was in constant use that winter as Thomas and Peyton spent much of their time close to heat while they formed wheels and pegs for the saw mill operation. This was a little more complicated than the grist mill since the only function of the grinding stone was to turn in the same direction all of the time. The saw mill had to turn the cutting wheel the same direction but the feeder part had to have some complicated cogs to feed the log into the saw only on the down stroke of the saw. The ratchet wheel that did this part was much like a large watch ratchet in that every revolution of the wheel triggered a forward movement of the log bed. To make the pins all the same, it was necessary for Peyton to use the lathe run by foot power. It operated much like the early sewing machines that used a foot treadle for power. Dozens of these pegs were needed and for replacements, many more were turned while Peyton was set up for the best method to duplicate shape and size.

As cold as it was, Virginia made it a duty to spend time in the blacksmith shop with her man while he worked. She would bundle up baby Boyce in a thick bear skin robe and sit close to the forge fire. By pulling on the bellows rope from time to time, a good fire was always burning brightly. It made her feel as if she was contributing to their welfare to bring a good meal out to the place where the three men were doing their best to finish a saw mill part. To carry Boyce and the large pot of stew, she had to be very careful not to slip and fall on snow and ice. Thomas was always looking for her to step outside for fire wood or any other reason. When she did show up with a cast iron pot, he was quick to drop every thing and go to meet her.

Sometime last summer, Peyton had cut a large tree butt into a suitable length to set the anvil on. It had to be cut square on both ends so as to set solid for the hammer blows to come. Henry used this anvil and forge to make nails when he was not needed for the heavy work of turning a wheel. Peyton had brought a large roll of wire about one eighth inch in diameter so that Henry had to cut it to lengthonly and form a head on one end and sharpen the other end. They had a plentiful supply on hand but the day would come that more would be needed. Thomas had a dream of some day having neighbors and this becoming a frontier settlement like no other.

He also wanted to duplicate the house they had to leave behind in Saxsonville. Virginia had loved that house and not just because it was made of lumber instead of logs. It was their design and built with the future in mind where children would have their own bedroom or rooms. As soon as the sawmill was up and running, he planned to cut lumber to start the new house. Why he thought there would soon be new settlers coming, there was no way of knowing. Perhaps it was just wishful thinking but he did plan for it to happen some day. The house he and Virginia now lived in would be a welcome home to any new arrivals.

Visitors from White Deer's people came often but would never consider living in a log house, not even for a short visit. In the mean time, it would do well as a storage building and as they were soon to find out, there was never enough storage space.

December 23, Mary had been looking forward to this date for the past nine months and in spite of her best efforts, she could not hold it off for another day. Her desire was to have it on the celebrated birthday of Jesus. But then she realized, it was better on the 23rd so as to give her a day of recuperation before the big day the entire town of "Miltown", would celebrate in the new church building. Virginia had been given the privilege of choosing the name and a future church service would be held to dedicate their town to service for the Lord.

The same Indian woman that delivered for Virginia came to help Mary, and as was expected, she did very well. Her daughter was petite but very strong, both in will and noise output. Henry was delighted with the baby girl and right away chose the name of Eva Lola Spears. He said he thought this little girl will make a fine bride for Boyce some day and Mary quickly agreed.

December chill hit like a hammer blow. Fall season had been very mild and much work had been done outside. Peyton had added sides and a front to the blacksmith's shop so he could work there through the coldest winter months. Stables had been built for the horses and separate stalls for the cows and the bull. As sometimes happens, their bull became mean and dangerous. It reached the point where Thomas and Peyton had to do something both hated to do. Put a ring in his nose to keep him under control. They understood it would hurt the bull to be maimed in this way, but better that than have him hurt one of them. This was to be a very dangerous undertaking. First, the bull had to be tied in such a way that he could not kick, swing his head or move much in any direction. He had to be immobilized on the floor of his stall and done with extreme care. Since they could not enter the stall with him, they had to make slip knots in rope that could be pushed under the lower stall logs. The loop had to be opened and spread out till the time the bull had both front feet in the loop. Then it had to be jerked tight so as to tie front feet together. This process was to be repeated until the rear feet were caught, then both ropes pulled tight enough to cause the bull to fall on his side. Ropes then had to be securely tied to the barn posts so there was no way for him to kick. Next, his head had to be caught in the same type of loop and when drawn tight, he could no longer move his head. This was almost enough to cut off his air by choking him into submission. Then it was safe to enter the stall and apply more rope to further secure his legs and head. Even so, it was still dangerous and scary to be that close to an animal that would like nothing more than to kill any person available.

Prior to this, Peyton had made a large ring that would pierce the septum which is the dividing wall between the nostrils . This ring was made to close and never be opened again. On this ring, Peyton had secured their largest chain which was long enough to reach a post set deep in the ground just outside the stall. While the bull was still tied down, the back wall of the stall was removed so the bull could go outside or stay inside. He would be fed and watered there for the rest of his existence. This action is something that has to be done to keep breeding stock under control and no one understands just why a gentle animal like this will turn mean and become a killer.

December 25, Christmas day and the church was full to the front door. Indians of both Konaya's and White Deer's relatives and friends had gathered to hear Peyton tell how the birth of Christ could be without a father. Last Christmas, he made it clear to very few who had tried to pass along the truth but only succeeded in creating more questions. It was also in expectations of plenty of good food and perhaps some presents. As for the presents, their numbers overwhelmed Peyton's supply of needles, beads and trade items. As for food, everyone brought something, not all to Virginia's liking but she could not dodge the offerings made to her by some of the women. Their food was not always made from items Virginia was used to eating but she closed her mind and tried everything. Due to the arrival of Eva Lola, Mary had not been able to help with the decorations, so the building was not near so festive as last year. Due to the many people inside, the fireplace was not so much in demand. Peyton's sermon was a little hot also for it was time to turn on some "Fire and Brimstone" preaching. Not everyone would respond to the "Love" sermon so it was necessary to tell them about Hell. They certainly understood this because they already had this well factored into their religion. It was the birth and death of Jesus that eliminated the fear of Hell and took the attention of every one there. Peyton did manage to get several Indians to accept the birth of Jesus as fact because they did accept the fact that the powers of Heaven created the earth and all that is on it. Christmas day was truly a great success for there was no anger over anything and all left well fed, both with food and the spirit of God.

January 1732 was extremely cold and kept Thomas, Peyton and Henry in the shop most of the time. During the last days of fall, October and November, Thomas and Henry had spent some time in the woods for the purpose of finding the winter supply of meat, mostly buffalo and some elk. Hunting bear was not necessary for the bear would hunt them when they had a good kill to clean and process. It was necessary to keep their rifles loaded and a sharp eye out for them and when they did come into their range, Thomas and Henry would take the bear for its hide. A bearskin coat was the prime reason but it was also nice to have a bearskin rug beside the bed when the need came to hit the floor in the morning.

Processing elk, buffalo and venison for all winter storage was mostly a matter of salting the surface and hanging over a cold fire where the object was to smoke the meat. A small enclosed room was made for the smoking process, in part to hold the smoke close and in part to keep hungry animals from destroying their winter supply. Green hickory wood would be placed on hot coals and as much as possible, air to the fire would be restricted. This process would last for two months or even all winter. There was no loss to the nutrition but only a better smoked flavor and the smoke discouraged all forms of animal life from trying to take the meat.

Chapter 15

February fifteenth, just when everything seemed to be in perfect shape for the coming of a new spring and summer, when all were looking forward to warmer weather, Peyton became very sick from some unknown cause. He had gone to bed the night before and in the dawn of a new day when he should have been up, Virginia sent Thomas to see about him. When Thomas got no answer to his knock, he opened the door to a cold room. The fire had been out for most of the night and Peyton was still deep under covering of every quilt he could have piled on. Thomas heard a dry cough from under the covers and knew Peyton was awake so he spoke to Peyton with the question, what can I do to help you?

Peyton spoke as if he was out of breath and followed that with another dry cough. Thomas felt his brow and found indication of low grade temperature. Not certain as to what to do, he first built up the fire and then went to see if Virginia or Mary would know.Virginia asked Mary to go to the Indian village for help from the medicine woman since neither of them were quite sure what to do.

Medicine woman came at once, bringing her grandson, Swift Fox along as her helper and protégé. This young man seemed to be about fourteen and very solemn for a youth of that age. She asked that she and her grandson be alone with Peyton for a time. Her questions to Peyton made her decide that Thomas should move Peyton to his home where Virginia could be in constant care over the next few days. Thomas did not hesitate to pick Peyton and his bed up and carry him home. He was surprised at how light Peyton had become since leaving Saxsonville and it made him wonder if Peyton was losing weight or was it that Thomas ws gaining strength. With the very hard work of building things, surely it had to be his gaining of strength.

By the time Thomas had Peyton well placed near the fireplace, medicine woman had returned with her deer skin bag of herbs. Her decision was to treat him for congested lungs since he did not have elevated temperature and only a dry cough. Her treatment was as much water as could be forced down Peyton, day and night for as long as he was sick.

Along with this, she had a mixture of horseradish, mullein, ginseng, garlic and wild indigo which was to be added to the water in just enough to see floating on top of the water he was to drink. He was to be kept warm but not hot and fed only small portions of meat soup. By the time Peyton had been treated all of the first day, he was feeling better, but there was a long way to go.

Swift Fox became an every day visitor and sometimes stayed all day. He seemed to be concerned with Peyton and Virginia's ability to care for him so the young man made it a practice to do for Peyton as long as he could stay each day. Virginia found him to be very pleasant company and very eager to learn as much about the white people as possible. He was one continuous question, even as he worked to make Peyton comfortable. From him, Virginia learned much of his ways and became more respectful of all Indian customs. Virginia learned the young man wanted to become the tribal medicine man and it was from him that she learned the use of herbs that was being given to Peyton. It was from her that Swift Fox learned the true meaning of Christianity and finally understood the virgin birth of Jesus. Virginia considered this almost a miracle, the trading of Peyton's continued life for the new life of Swift Fox. This young man became one of their best converts and students, just as Konaya had. He became one of the family over the next two months, even after Peyton was well enough to care for himself. Swift Fox used every excuse to delay the return of Peyton to his own home for this meant the end of his education under Virginia.

Peyton wanted to return to his shop for light work and saw the excuse to take Swift Fox under his care, to teach him as much as possible. His first thought was to rename Swift Fox to something more suitable for a student and helper. What better name could he choose than DOC? It had meaning and promise for the future. How about "Doc White"?

April 1732 From the beginning, Peyton thought it was necessary to teach the first of his students to read and write. He did have the thought of a school some time in the future when he was too old to do a good day's work. He considered it necessary to please God by working until his death. Teaching school would fill this belief and in the process, give the Indians some hope of a future with the coming white invasion. He had no doubt that the day would come when whites would come streaming over the mountains in droves.

April showers were to bring May flowers and so they did, in profusion. Mary now had Eva to care for and it was little extra for her to also keep Boyce. Thomas and Virginia had a busy time of trying to prepare a new garden while Peyton did not feel well enough to be of much help. He spent most of his time in the blacksmith shop, even though he often failed to light a fire in the forge. Much of this time was spent with Doc as student while Peyton acted as master.

Chapter 16

Peyton had never told Thomas much about his early life and very little about the mother Thomas never knew. It grieved him too much to talk about the love of his life leaving him so soon. He had never told Thomas that he had been educated in Edinburgh, Scotland, at St. Andrews University where only the wealthy were admitted. His major was engineering and science, paid for by a wealthy family who expected him to marry into more money and continue the family business. Peyton never told Thomas that his mother was just a lowly serving maid who had stolen his fathers heart and caused his family to deny him his birthright. Peyton was without a recognized family when they gave him a small amount of money and a passage to the new world for him and his new wife.

Arriving in Portsmouth after many weeks at sea, Peyton had a wife who was sick and not able to care for herself. Peyton tried for a position at engineering firms but found nothing readily available. The shipping industry had many jobs but most of them required more time away from his wife than he could afford. When he had just about given up, he stopped in a blacksmith shop with hopes of finding a need for an engineer. What he did find was a need for an iron monger which he gladly accepted. His education allowed him to speak with ships owners, and through these contacts he was able to sell his employer's products. In a short time Peyton was working at the forge, making items too complicated for the owner's experience. His engineering background served him well in this trade and soon he was thinking of a shop of his own.

Thomas was born when his mother was in a weakened condition, so she was not able to survive the delivery. Peyton now had a baby to care for and the only way was to hire a woman to feed and care for him until he was old enough for Peyton to leave Portsmouth.This had become a hated place as he never got free of grief from the loss of his wife. Moving south seemed to be the only way.

Peyton had accumulated some money with which he could buy the needed items for a new shop and a wagon with team for the move to a new place. With no destination in mind, Peyton traveled south until he found the peaceful little settlement of Saxon's Branch and no blacksmith shop for many miles. He and Thomas had found home.

Chapter 17

June found Thomas very busy at the mill and Peyton mostly at the shop, hardly ever lighting a fire in the forge. He was doing what he loved to do while regaining his strength and renewing his desire to accomplish the task of building a new town. He was remembering his lost wife and feeling somewhat useless, as if the years had piled up on him much too fast. Salvation would come in the form of a small Indian lad who wanted to learn all there was to learn about the world he lived in.

Doc was a very good student, just as Thomas had been. The difference was that Doc had to be taught the alphabet and numbers, along with the English language. Peyton might have given up on such a demanding task had it not been for the fact that he was now tired most of the time. He found teaching to be restful as well as satisfying. Doc would arrive at the shop just after dawn and stay until Peyton asked him to leave. When Peyton was trying to work, Doc was watching every move and trying to anticipate the need for particular tool. He was soon Peyton's right hand and able to converse in English most of the time. Peyton tried to make teaching numbers a game by asking for number two or six tool. He had numbered everything so as to teach and it worked very well. At the same time, he was making Doc learn the tools by spelling the name or the number. It seemed that Doc

learned faster than Peyton could devise new teaching methods, and becoming fast friends made it easier for Thomas to go about other, outside tasks and not worry so much about his father.

Virginia had the undivided loyalty of White Deer for her everyday companion and Thomas had both Henry and Konaya.

Work progressed down at the sawmill better than Thomas ever hoped for and by July the saw mill was finished and ready for the first log. Thomas was so excited about having it this far along that he ran this first one with no preparation yet made for either a new log skid or a finished lumber skid. It would be necessary to make the incoming log skid first. Otherwise, it would take enormous strength of two men to roll the log into place where it could be easily rolled to the saw blade. This was done by placing two very large logs on a slight downfall toward the blade. Logs could be hauled into place at the top of the skid by the oxen and from there, gently rolled down to the blade. As for the lumber output, the same method was used but now a downward skid, away from the blade. It took Thomas, Konaya and Henry three days to prepare the required slope and then set the four skid logs. This was the last labor to prepare the mill for lumber output.

August heat slowed the action around their work site but it continued even if a bit slower. Virginia and Mary were already putting up food for the coming winter. Berries were ripe and this took much time to pick them and then the canning process. They had some luck in making a form of honey/jam with blackberries which could be placed in containers and covered with melted bee's wax. This would keep better than the raw honey or the berries alone. Some garden produce started to come in about mid-month and then the work really became heavy. Thanks to the help of White Deer in caring for the children and her advice on the Indian way, much food was stored. Virginia had a very limited number of jars from Saxonville and no lids to spare. White Deer told them of the Indian ways of a layer of bees wax and that covered with a thin layer of clay. That was to keep bugs and air from the wax. White Deer told them the Indian way was to use clay pots in much the same way and through her help, Virginia managed to obtain four nice large pots. With these, she was able to make kraut from their abundance of cabbage and to pickle corn in the same way.

September continued hot and dry with some of the crops still producing, mostly potatoes and carrots. These were to be placed in the straw lined pit along with cabbage and covered for the winter. Next year, there would be apples but not this year. The trees were just starting and they would be lucky to get fruit by next year.

Thomas and Konaya were sawing lumber as fast as the saw would work with limited water supply. Real work from the saw would have to wait until rains upstream supplied mre power. Still, there was the need for logs and they were kept busy in sawing and hauling logs to the mill. There was no immediate need for lumber but it would take some drying time for good lumber to season, so it was necessary for it to be cut weeks in advance of the need.

During this fall season, Thomas would be on the lookout for special grain configuration in butternut logs. These boards would be kept back to air for at least a year before being used to make furniture. He and Virginia believed the grain of this wood was the most beautiful of all God had supplied and she wanted all of her furniture made of it in the future.

October 1741. Corn was ready for cutting and building into shocks in the field. Pumpkins were not far behind as many of the vines were already dying or dead. All green beans had been picked and dried, ready for shelling in the cold winter months ahead. Some beans had been picked while still green and placed on the roof of their buildings to dry in the shell. These would be cooked in the shell and known as "Leather Britches," cooked a long time with a good chunk of pork from the smoke house. This and a pan of cornbread would be a wonderful evening meal when the snow was a foot deep outside.

Chapter 18

November brought the first of a cold wind and spitting snow to the valley. It also brought a visitor from back across the mountains. Ebenezer Spurlock was one of the early mountain men who was just curious as to what was on the other side of the mountain. He had no destination in mind and no particular hurry to find one. To his amazement, the Indians welcomed him instead of shooting him full of arrows. He was fortunate to be found by Konaya and friends before he wandered too far north and encountered the Salt Indians. He was also amazed to see Konaya carrying the same French manufactured rifle that he carried. He had considered it the latest and no other like it west of the mountains. Although this was a French design, some makers of guns in the New England area had started to copy and make some minor improvements which was apparent on both the rifle he carried as well as the one held by Konaya. Of course he was more amazed to hear Konaya speak in English and ask if he was a Christian. Konaya liked to take any new information directly to his chief Bear Claw and this was very important news. Konaya delivered Ebenezer to his chief where Eb got another surprise. Many of the Indians spoke to him in good English and asked many times if he was friend to Thomas and Peyton. Of course, he had no idea who they were asking about and could only ask in return, who are they?

He told his story of wandering across the mountains and seeing no one for many days. He told little about the place he startled from, but the Indians were not curious; he was just a friend. He was given a place to bed down that night in a smaller Tepee since it was raining. He was well fed as an honored guest and in the morning, he was well fed again. As soon as polite, he was asking about Peyton and Thomas which Konaya was pleased to tell of his friends. He offered to take Eb across the low hills to where Peyton and Thomas had their home.

Crossing the ridge line gave Eb a first look at the settlement Thomas and Peyton had put together. This sight was enhanced by the many Indian tee-pee homes of at least thirty families. Already this morning, there was at least that many children playing in the creek below the dam. The mill was running and Eb almost gave way to shock to see a town in the making so far from what he thought was civilization. Konaya was in his glory, being able to present Eb to Thomas, Virginia and Peyton. Peyton was not the first of these people to ask if he was Christian but he was first to offer his hand in Christian love. His invitation for Eb to stay for a time was in earnest. It is doubtful that Eb decided that moment, but he did decide to stay, permanently. Ebenezer Spurlock was a very stout young man of twenty years, having lived mostly in the open country and working at whatever jobs came handy. He had arrived in Portsmouth from Scotland as a boy who lost his parents on the voyage to America. He had worked on the docks for a time and later for a carpenter. His strength and experience was sorely needed in this town and Peyton welcomed him with as much fatherly love as he thought Eb would accept. Becoming tired of working for very small wages and having the curiosity of land beyond the mountains, Eb saved his money for a travel pack and a rifle. As soon as he could, he struck out west with no destination and no one left behind to miss him.

Thanksgiving time was a joyous occasion for Peyton for he had many new converts and church services were being held now for those truly interested in God, and no longer just because of the novelty of it. The tables at the church were loaded with a multitude of offerings, mostly from the garden recently harvested but also from the abundance of game. The table had offerings of venison, turkey, grouse, elk and buffalo hump,as well as many offerings of small game such as rabbit and squirrel. The supply of food was almost too much to be consumed but everyone did their best to help.

Thomas had plenty of work for the newest addition to their town and he lost no time in setting forth the chores needed to be attended to. Eb took this in stride and seemed happy to be a part of the community. Virginia and Mary discussed the situation and decided he needed a wife if he was to stay in their community. Eb did not yet know it but he was being set up for the responsibility of a wife and a permanent place. Both women realized that Peyton was beginning to show his years and that Thomas needed another strong hand if they were to survive here on the frontier.

The women also decided it was time to declare a permanent name for their community if it was to be recognized as a true town. Two weeks later after church services, they gathered at the home of Virginia and Thomas for a noontime meal and the naming. As a party it was not much more than all of them crowded into a small space and eating a very little before the naming started. Thomas and Virginia did not tell them of the decision last fall. He was in hopes that someone would suggest the name Miltown. The name of Thomasville and also Peyton's place were offered but both men spoke a quick, no. Thomas proposed they name it in such a way as to be recognized from a distant point for what it was, a mill town. The final name had been selected long ago as Miltown. All agreed this would serve them well.

December 1732

Christmas was a time of plenty and mild weather. An early storm had dropped several inches of snow, but warming weather had brought one of those rare days when it was pleasant to be outside with a temperature just at the freezing point. Sunshine made the world look clean and Thomas took advantage of it to treat his family to a sleigh ride. He quickly mounted two benches across the work sled where eight people could sit facing forward. When he hitched their best horse to it, he drove to the cabins of Henry and Mary, to pick up Peyton and Eb. With Virginia beside him and Boyce well wrapped on her lap, they headed across the hill to visit with Konaya and White Deer. When they arrived, White Deer was so glad to see them she asked if it would do for her to bring her little sister and Konaya to ride with them. Of course the sled had the room, if no extra seats. Eb quickly gave his seat to the little sister of White Deer and Peyton made room for White Deer and little Eva. An hour of sleigh ride along the frozen creek was enough time for Eb to fall in love with little sister, Blue Bird.

Now that Eb was in love, he could think of little else, but that never got in the way of his work. What he did think of was soon to be mentioned to Thomas in the form of a request for a home of his own. He could not hold his secret much longer and who better to confide in than Thomas? As soon as he asked for a home to be built for him, Thomas guessed and was delighted to settle on the sleigh ride and the attention paid to Blue Bird. It was such a delightful thought that Thomas could not keep it from Virginia and she followed with a whispered message to Mary, from there to Henry and from there to Konaya. The rest was just a matter of time, all of several minutes until Blue Bird heard the word. Being a beautiful sixteen-year-old, she had several suitors who would not be happy with the loss of Blue Bird. It could have been a source of trouble but Peyton had done a good job of creating peace and Christianity in both camps.

January 1733 was still in a mild temperature phase so Thomas lost no time in starting the new home for Eb. It was to be the first building in Millerton made of powered sawmill lumber, mostly sawed and dried weeks before. The men were all happy to be in the building trade again and the women pitched in with some of the best food prepared in Millerton to date.

During this time, White Deer and Konaya made the trip to the new building site, both for the company and so Konaya could do his part in construction. White Deer made certain to take Blue Bird with her because she wanted the exposure to Eb to be such that he would have the chance to propose marriage.

Everyone knew the reason and all made the excuse whenever possible for Blue Bird to be near Eb and to also serve him when food was placed on tables set up in the church meeting room. They took a noon time rest in the church due to working outside in cold weather. Peyton, as usual, took advantage of the confinement to do a little preaching. His congregation had all accepted the saving grace of Jesus the Christ; however, they all needed to know more about the way God expected them to live.

In latter February, the last shingle had been placed and the last door was hung, all gathered in the new house to dedicate it to their God. It was now time for Eb to speak of his desire and Blue Bird was filled with expectation. She tried to stay at the back of the room, out of sight as much as this small gathering would allow, but her fingers tingled and her heart raced for she had fallen in love with Eb, even though neither of them had spoken of it.

Eb had a prepared speech that did not come out as planned. Instead, he took the hand of Blue Bird, led her to the front and asked her if she would like to make this her home with him there to protect her. Not the usual proposal but very effective in that Blue Bird fell into his arms where she had wanted to be for the past several weeks.

Since the fire place chimney had been built well before the roof was on, they had kept a small fire going on order to dry the mud used in building it. Now that it ws dry and roofed over, it was safe to build a larger fire which made the house a warm place to stay. Eb moved in that very night and started the process of building furniture. Thomas and Henry were more than happy to contribute all of their tools and expertise toward the goal of a marriage ceremony in April, just five weeks away.

Chapter 19

1745

Peace and tranquility reigned supreme for the next twelve years.

The family of Thomas and Virginia had grown to include four boys and three girls. Henry and Mary had fared well with four boys and two girls. Eb and Blue Bird had two boys and one girl. Konaya and White Deer were blessed with five warriors and one lovely daughter.

The Indian medicine woman had passed on to the happy place and now Doc White had the chore of doctoring all of both his community as well as Miltown.His reputation for treating the sick, and the lame had traveled far, and many came to seek his magical cures. Peyton had taught him all of the white man's ways in doctoring, leaving out the questionable cure of bleeding the patient. With the Indian way and that learned from Peyton, he did have a very high success rate. Because of the need to know more and for some medicine not available elsewhere, Peyton asked Konaya to accompany him back across the mountains for much needed supplies. Peyton was getting very frail in his latter years but he was sure he was up to the trip if there was no hurry.

It was decided to leave in June 1745 with one pack horse and two riding horses.

Peyton felt the Indian items of beaded moccasins, purses and belts would trade well and give the Indians some special items as well. They were in need of items such as needles and factory made thread. Other items not so important but useful would be left up to Peyton and Konaya to decide on.

On their entry into eastern Virginia, Peyton was shocked at the progress and the numbers of people, right up to the edge of the first mountain. Riding on in to larger towns gave them a better selection of goods they needed and also better prices. As soon as they could fill their shopping list and add such items as they thought would be welcomed back home, they purchased two extra pack horses and left eastern Virginia. At the base of the first mountain, there was a small camp of two men, their wives and two children, all fitted with pack animals, riding horses and mules. They had become acquainted with Peyton on the way east, heard about his town out west and decided to join them on the way back. Nothing Peyton could say would discourage the men or their wives leaving nothing but to welcome them to the remainder of their trip west. The return trip took five days in which Peyton felt the strain of traveling on horseback. Of course this was not the real reason he felt bad; it was his age and not sufficient rest at night. Konaya began to worry about his condition and did all of the work in camps along the way. This seemed to help but it became evident to Konaya that would not be enough.

Their arrival back home was none too soon for Peyton since he had to go immediately to his bed. Virginia did everything possible for him and Doc White was in constant attendance. All was in vain for time caught up with Peyton on the sad day of September 23rd, 1745.

Thomas felt alone now, or so he thought. Losing the last parent is something every person faces and it is like the end of a secure life. Having that last parent still alive, even though helpless, gives the child a feeling of a place to turn when everything is falling apart. For some time after the loss of that last parent, there is something like fear of facing the future without the perceived protection of a parent. Thomas, like millions before him, took up the reins of life and worked toward his own time of departure.

With the addition of two new families, Thomas felt the strain double on him. To prepare a home for these families was not enough. He had the additional job of assigning the men work to do. He was enormously pleased to learn that Lonnie France was an experienced sawmill operator. That took care of his most urgent need, for the extra time he spent there was keeping all other work from being addressed. It was well that the other family had been their friends for some time which meant they could work together. The sawmill did need at least two men to make it work and the third would be welcome. This meant that Eb could be more useful to the town. Now Thomas was in position to oversee the building of two more houses which Lonnie would saw the lumber for.

In a few weeks the town was running smooth again, even though Peyton was much missed. His grandchildren were coming of age and already they were beginning to look for lifetime partners, some of the boys looking at Indian maidens. No doubt they were beautiful people and better trained to live on the frontier than the daughters of whites. With a contented town so far out in the wilderness, it seemed there was no need to be concerned with the rest of the world but, not so.

More people from the Virginia colonies were coming across the mountains and from all of the horrid stories they had heard, Indians were their enemies and needed to be killed on sight. Accordingly, one of the wagons working westward in a train of four encountered the salt Indians at the head of the Conoy river. In the mistaken notion that they were in immediate danger, one man opened fire which changed the entire frontier. Within weeks, there was a division between the white settlers and the Indians, including the peaceful tribe of Konoya's people.

From that day forth, Thomas was destined to travel with the peaceful

Indians of his towns in an effort to make peace with all incoming settlers. Many did gather with him and settle in the valleys near his sawmill, and many were saved by his actions. Thomas and Virginia lived long lives, never seeing a time when there was complete peace, but their legacy lived on with many Indians and whites finding peace with God as sufficient for this life.

The Adkins

My home is in the foot hills of West Virginia, not far removed from the coal-fields, and where my grandparents have spent their lives. These tales are not to say that I am educated, nor am I ignorant. But I do know about a lot of things that came to me in the years that I made it to hunting camps for over forty years. Around those camp fires when the day is ended and tired men brought out the soothing elixir of whatever they refused to name, but nursed as if it were liquid gold, then the education started. Now, I recognize that not every tale was truthful and I will attempt to stay away from the tall ones, especially the ones when told causes the eyes of the teller to bulge and grow wide.

I learned long ago to watch the eyes of those who tend to lie, about anything. Now, I will not LYE to you. Being absolutely truthful is the only way to get through this world alive. Even dead it's better to be truthful. Campfires and good mountain water from the hills of West Virginia and Kentucky will expose secrets that the FBI and National Intelligence people should pay attention to and, use when needed to exact the truth from saboteurs. Lying is to be expected from some but not from me or those setting around a good camp fire with a Mason jar of clear mountain water at hand.

This story came to me across a very large campfire when the night temperature was close to zero. The resultant flames were such that I could well see the eyes of the teller, and I will state emphatically that his eyes did not grow large. The watering of those eyes could have been from smoke of the fire, or possibly even the strength of the water in his fruit jar.

In either case, his story was one that made the hair on the back of my neck stand out, and made me want to place one foot before the other, and at a rapidly accelerating pace. Only the fear of those dark woods around us held me glued to the log I was setting on.

Now I need to tell you that I was about sixteen, and the old man telling this story was at least seventy. He had told us that he was born in 1880 so with that much age and experience, I had no doubt that he was worth listening to. He was telling us how it was back when he was a young man and that death then was not like it is now. I wondered how death could change over the years for after all, when you're dead, you're dead. Of course, some of you will take issue with that statement for it is a known fact that the dead roam this earth when the moon is dark, and spirits are restless. That is another story that must be told later in this book of truths.

I also know for a fact that animals, such as dogs, also roam the nether land. I am told by some of the old timers that, to be bitten by one of these will doom you forever. I have been cautioned to never try feeding one by hand. It is much too dangerous to be feeding dogs that you can't see.

The old man continued with the description of how the dead were treated back then. and how the caskets were laid out in the living room for viewing by the morbid, as well as the bereaved. Now as I write this, I am old enough to remember setting up with my mother at a neighbor's house where the father had died a day or so past. I do remember that it was cold in that house because all the windows were open and no fire in the grate. Mom took me on her lap and wrapped me in a small blanket for the night. I don't remember any ghosts or much of anything because come daylight, I found myself in a bed along with three other small boys.

I suppose the title, "living room" should have been temporarily changed to "the dead room".

Back then, there was no such thing as embalming so burial had to be done PDQ or even before that, unless it was very cold weather such as we had that night.

The story teller, having been a young man, now older, could speak of an old man as being "wore out" in the coal fields. Even though the old man he spoke of was only about forty five, or fifty. So his story was about Paw and Maw Adkins, both in their fifties. Their only child had moved to Detroit to work for Henry Ford when the lure of a horseless carriage was just a dream in the coal fields. Now Paw Adkins had worked in the mines since he became old enough to work, eleven that is.

Being small, he was sent to the coal seam that was only four foot thick and the boy had to learn to dig coal in a bent over position. Several years of this and you can imagine what happened to his spine. Well, anyway, he got the urge to have a wife when he reached adulthood at sixteen, so he crossed over to the next holler, valley to you. In that holler, he found the love of his life, Lilly June, his first cousin. They were married at once, and because he worked for the mines, he was assigned a company house near the company store.

As you probably know, the mine owners printed their own money, known as script. They also minted small coins for change but about all it was needed for was to play poker with on Sunday. Payday did not come in the form of a check, what they got was a credit voucher, good only at the company store. No other store was allowed in the area the mines controlled. Everything needed by the miners was ready to be placed against his credit tab. This made it a credit issue with predictable results. Even ordering from Sears and Roebuck was frowned on since the mines also controlled the US Post Office. Buying a money order for Sears and

Roebuck had to be paid to the postmaster in mine issued script, so the postmaster had to clear it with the mine foreman. What this meant was that ten dollars to Sears and roebuck cost fourteen in script. Two dollars each to the postmaster, and two to the mine foreman.

Paw Adkins was a valued employee at the age of sixteen, after four years of digging coal in the same four-foot seam. Accordingly, he had full credit at the company store and there he and Lilly June went for their furniture. They picked up a bed, table, two chairs and a stock of groceries, all on credit. What he didn't know was that he would still owe for that when he retired, or died. I'm kinda getting' off the story.

Paw Adkins must have been about twenty when there was a slate fall in his mine, and Paw was injured such that he was confined to bed for about a year. Credit at the company store continued on a much reduced level, and interest increased on a much elevated level. When Paw could go back to the four-foot seam, he was better qualified than ever.

During that year in bed, he found he could not rest except in the fetal position, similar to the position he had to work while in the mine. Accordingly, his spine took a permanent set and from that day forth, he had to walk in a bent over position, looking straight at the ground.

Of course the mine owners were delighted to have a form fitted employee working that shaft and they complimented him on his production, but not with a raise in pay. Maw found his condition great burden on her as well as an almost impossible condition for him except when working. His ability to dress himself became more than he could handle alone.

Maw had to help him with almost every chore he faced, and dressing himself was the worst of the trials he worried with. It also became necessary for her to modify the bib overalls he got at the company store. Larger sizes were bought and the fronts altered to shorten them. Maw became a very good hand with a needle since the company store would not sell her a sewing machine until paw worked off some of the debt accumulated while in bed. The debt was such that interest on it took about everything paw could shovel out of the mine. Most friends thought it hopeless but what to do?

Well, Paw Adkins was wore out at fifty, and had to give up the ghost. Maw Adkins was not far behind since she had spent her life washing coal dust out of his clothes and off the floors, table and herself. Being bent over the wash tub all those "black Dust" years had taken their toll. Not only did Paw Adkins have trouble breathing through coal laden lungs, so did Maw. Well Paw Adkins was dead and the neighbors had to step in and do their thing. Prep the body and procure the casket from the company owned lumber yard.

Now then, they had two kinds of caskets, one that had the removable lid, and had to be nailed down at the grave site. This one cost twenty five dollars, and one with a brass hinged cover and with a fancy brass latch, painted with left over house paint, cost fifty dollars.

Since Paw still had some mine script and wages credit at the company store, they were aware of the amount. Accordingly, they sold them a hinged casket. Not to worry about Maw, she could go live with a relative across to the next holler.

Well now, it was cold during the fall when Paw died, and there was every reason to keep him on display for as long as possible. He had relations that would not be able to make it until late the next day. As everyone there was aware of, to preserve anything you either had to smoke it, salt it or place it in alcohol. Smoking Paw was out of the question since it took too long. Salting him down was not practical since the company store charged too much and it weren't sightly. That left Alcohol and there was plenty of that from all of the local stills. It was decided to fill Paw with at least a gallon of the uncut, straight stuff, and in order to keep it inside him, he had to have a tight cord around his neck. This would not uncomfort him in the least since he weren't breathing anyway, and besides, there was the problem of him wanting to set upright. Well, the cord around his neck could serve another purpose such as holding him stretched out in the sublime position, which he had not been in for over thirty years. Two nails in the bottom of the coffin box, one on each side of the neck and fastened to the cord would hold him down. Another tight rope around his feet, also nailed to the bottom of the coffin and paw was ready for the wake.

Properly pickled and nailed down, Paw Adkins was the picture of a man at rest. As was the custom in those times, neighbors brought food, and many of them sat with the casket through the long ordeal. That night was a cold one so all windows and the front door was left open.This helped to preserve Paw for the few extra hours needed. Two men and several ladies were there, all bundled against the cold. The ladies were mostly wrapped in handmade quilts, and sitting in upright chairs. Talk was of the weather, the church services next Sunday.General gossip and for the most part, the men were quiet. Around midnight, one of the men mentioned that he was hearing noise from the casket box that was strange, and he wondered what it could be. The other man said he wondered if Paw was choking from the cord too tight around his neck. They both listened and asked the ladies to be quiet for a spell. Maw was a-sittin' at the foot of the casket which was placed on two short saw horses. She was able to see over the foot of the box, and see Paw a-restin' in peace.

Then as it got real quiet, they all heard a sound similar to pulling a nail out of new wood.

That was what the men thought it was. It was----the nails gave way. and Paw sat up with a whooshing sound. He faced Maw and for the first time, she saw the cord tied tightly around Paw's neck.

For a short time, there was total silence, until it was apparent that Maw had lost control of her bowels, lost her breath, suffered a heart attack and died on the spot. What a tragedy. When several of the ladies were recovered from their fainting spell, order was restored by the men that understood what had happened.

Now, what to do about Maw Adkins? There is no more money or credit from the company store and now that she was in need, it was up to the neighbors to come up with a plan.

First, the company owners would not allow two to be buried in the same casket as it would cheat them out of the price of one more. Next, it was against company policy to bury them on company property without a casket, supplied by the company sawmill and the woods for miles around belonged to the coal companies. Now it was up to the neighbors to come up with funds or find a way to cheat the company. Most still worked for the same company so they were somewhat afraid to cheat as it could cost them their job if found out and of course loss of the company house. Now the company had millions of acres of trees, lumber was free for the company sawmill but employees were not allowed to cut trees for their own use so they couldn't build their own casket.

After a closed door meeting between the men of the community, it was decided to fill Maw Adkins with the same output from the same stills, thereby buying time for the next move. As it was, Maw Adkins was a lot smaller than Paw Adkins so it took only three quarts to fill her and it did take a tighter cord around her neck to retain that shot. Word was sent out for the benefit of the company man that Maw had become too sick to attend the funeral and she had been taken to her relatives over in the next holler. Now both Maw and Paw had been underfed for years and both were very skinny.

Take note that the company sawmill had been constructing the same casket design for years. All sizes were the same, "extrie large" to fit whatever needed to be buried. The perfect solution was to place both Paw and Maw in the same "extrie large" casket, face to face. This would accomplish the problem of holding Paw in the straight position and sendin' them off to glorie land in the same position they had so much enjoyed in the early years of their marriage. All went well until some brownnoser slipped word to the company foreman what they planned to do. He, being a devout company man placed himself in the edge of the woods by the cemetery to wait until they showed up with the casket. He planned to take one last look and place the extra casket charge on them, even if they didn't need it.

As coal camps go, gossip soon warned the neighbors about the company man and another plan was put into action. They waited until dark, knowing that the bodies would hold safe for another day since both were filled with the best spirits available on their side of the mountain.

The following day at dawn, six men got around the double filled casket and headed up the mountain, away from the cemetery. About noon, they reached a place where company men and revenuers' never trod. There they dug the grave and had a send-off service fittin' for the much revered Adkins couple. Preacher Ronald Black had the usual box of rattlers and on the way up, he had picked up another serpent meant to show faith that the company man would never find the grave site. After the "sermon on the mount" (they were on the mountain) preacher Black passed the previously handled serpents around and kept the newer one to himself. It was a little agitated and he feared they might have to carry one of his parishioners down the mountain if a lesser experienced handler did not have enough faith.

All went well and so far as we know, the coal company men are still looking for the grave site casket. They now know they were cheated and are determined to get even by removing the brass hinges and latch.

Some of you might get the idea that I have no love for the coal companies that have destroyed this beautiful state. This is not exactly true--The real truth is that I leave it to God. He will send them all to the place where coal is not needed. God uses Brimstone.

Barboursville Boyhood

College Street in Barboursville, WV had a new addition to the human race on the morning of December 13th, 1926. My immediate rejection of the cold of this world led me to let out a squall that exceeded those of my sister, Jewel. She had been the apple of mom's eye and now that was over. Not to say that I was an apple of her eye, but to say that I demanded more attention than did Jewel. I believe she still resents that intrusion into her secure little world.

Of course I do not remember much about that day, except that it was cold, very cold.

About that time, dad realized he needed more room, I think he had just discovered what brought on babies and he had no intention of stopping the process of reproducing. Therefore, he had to make arrangements for additional bed rooms and some hired help.

Grand dad McMellon had purchased a larger home on McClung Avenue and somehow dad managed to secure title to the place. Perhaps it was pity for mom since she guessed what was coming. More of the same, five more.

Well it was necessary for dad to get help with the move and along came Kenneth, dad's younger brother who was sixteen. Not only did he help, he decided to stay on for an extended time, just in case dad needed more moving help. In fact he did need more moving help the winter of 1936 when the move was made to the Fudge Creek farm. That is another story since I am writing only about Barboursville. This part of the story ended December 28, 1936 which made me just over ten years old.

In the new house on McClung, Kenneth had little to do so mom made him a baby sitter while she tended to her Kroger shopping over on main street. Now the time is still winter of 1926 and I am still cold. Kenneth had the duty of diapers as well as trying to comfort me. He rightfully concluded that I was cold since he was and that house was solid but not too well insulated. Kenneth had the solution of warming the kitchen by lighting the gas oven and I do believe he also had a little nip of his favorite Kentucky Bourbon to warm his insides. Mom had pure hatred for booze and Kenneth had to slip it in and keep it out of sight. I suppose he always had the penchant for a gut warmer. Well, on this cold morning he decided I needed warming a little more than usual so he partially wrapped me in a blanket, placed me in a large oval dish pan and set me on top of the gas cook stove. Now the squalling really started and no telling where it would have ended if mom had not returned just then. She dropped her grocery sack and grabbed me out of the fire, literally. Kenneth in his gut warming state did not realize that my back was against the bare edge on the roasting pan. I have a twelve inch burn scar to prove that I was not cold for the rest of that day. Neither was Kenneth for mom seared his hide with words I don't think she ever used before of afterward.

With that behind us, mom still needed help and Kenneth could not be trusted. The solution was to ask cousin Mamie Spurlock (Cute) to live with us as she attended high school. There was so many of dad's cousins who dropped in for a visit and stayed for months that I can't remember all of them. Of course mom had some family from up in the coal fields of Logan County that needed a rest and recovery (at mom's expense).

In my early years, I can only remember a never-ending stream of visitors who mostly came to eat, sleep and rest. Mom got little of the latter.

A few things stick out in my memory such as the time Thurmond and I stood at the front fence which was much higher than our heads and called a black man what we had heard blacks referred to as----. It turned out to be a very nice old man that lived a block behind us where the colored grade school was located. He said nothing to us but he did to mom as soon as he could get to the back door. Mom made us apologize and then to reinforce the lesson, we both got a peach tree limb switching. I suppose there was much talk in our house about the black race since we had so many visitors and since there was a steady stream of black kids going past our house to the school. Segregation was much in vogue back then.

Later, I was allowed to watch the old black man slaughter a steer for dad and mom. It took place in his outbuilding and I was so troubled by that scene that it is still vivid in my memory today. He did not kill that animal in the usual manner and that is too much for me to write about today.

Next door to us and between ours and where the Forth's lived stood dad's garage. This was where I took part in a play where the three Forth girls and another girl I can't remember or name set up the housekeeping play. As it turned out, I was the youngest, perhaps three or four years old. My part was to be the baby and cry once in a while.

I well remember all went well until the oldest girl dropped the top of her dress and wanted to breast feed me. Right then and there, I broke up the play house. What a difference fifteen or twenty years make.

Down back of our house, we had a hog pen with at least two hogs all year long. Dad never seemed to mind butchering a hog but he did not like to do it to cattle. It seemed all winter long mom was canning beef and pork. I know it was not a pleasure to her except that it allowed her to give her children the very best. In that respect, I was lucky to be the oldest boy because I always got the new "Overalls" and Thurmond got the hand-me-downs.

I remember the morning mom and I went to the barn for the morning feed and milking and found her favorite cow dead. Mom always managed to have a cow named Susie and this morning I best remember her cry of "Oh Susie, Oh Susie". It broke her heart that we had left Susie with her head fastened in the stanchion where she was to be milked. She had tried to get up after falling and had choked to death.

Funny how memory is so clear that I can still see things in my mind's eye, just as I did so many years ago. Across the street from us came Alene. She was about my age and I remember her as a tomboy, always wanting to do the same things I did. She was good at climbing trees of which we only had one besides the apple trees. Mom said we were not allowed to pester the apple trees since they were too busy trying to feed us. Well anyway, I got to be five years old in the late summer of 1931 and by now I had developed a burning curiosity as to why Alene's mother would keep telling Alene not to climb trees anymore. I asked her why her momma spoiled our fun and she said it was not nice for little girls to show her hiney to boys. Now I am really curious. What is under those drawers made out of feed sacks that boys are not supposed to see? I pondered this for many days and finally reached the point where I had to find out. This hot, sunny afternoon when my older sister jewel, Alene and I were in the shade of our front porch, I told Alene I would give her my two cents if she would pull her drawers down so I could see what was so taboo down there. I never noticed that my sister went in the house because I was doing what men have done since Adam first became curious about what Eve was hiding. Well, Alene needed the money and a deal was struck. She took my two cents and in one quick motion, lifted her skirt and dropped her drawers. Just then, my mother and my tattletale sister stood just inside the screen door and mom said "Shame on you son and Alene, you go home." I was filled with shame and disgust for what had just happened. Not for what mom thought but because I had spent my last two cents and felt cheated. There was nothing there. I at least had something to show, she didn't so I was cheated.

My memory has been a puzzle to me. I have excellent memory of my youth, all the way back to when I was about four years old. As an example, I well remember when my sister, two years older than me went to school for her first day. I cried because I couldn't start when she did. This was 1930 and the depression was in full bloom. We lived in a small town where dad had a decent job with the railroad.

His paycheck was small but steady and mom made the best of it by keeping a large garden, two cows and making use of every small apple that grew on our two trees. It seemed to me that we almost lived on cow butter and apple butter, supplemented with beans and cornbread. Mom really did much better than that though. Her garden supplied vegetables all year around; a cellar filled with canned goods was far more than our neighbors had. Since dad worked for the railroad, we lived close to the point where a branch line connected with the main rail line. Trains almost came to a walking speed when they approached the junction and this allowed rail bums to get on and off without much danger. I call them rail bums but they were not really bums, they were men

out of work and hungry. They rode the rails in search of work and perhaps a better chance for their families back there somewhere. My mother had great compassion for those men and made certain to put a very large pot of beans on to cook every morning for several years. Those hungry men seemed to know where there was food to be had and several showed up every day. I remember most all of them wanted to work at something to pay for the food.

Sometimes mom allowed them to work in her garden and she never complained when she saw one of them pocket a raw potato or turnip. Her attitude was that God supplied our needs and he also made a little extra for the hungry man sent her back door.

We had a small plot at the edge of town but not enough land to keep cows on grass land. We did have a small barn to keep them in overnight but every morning and evening, it was my job to move the cows from rented pasture about ½ mile away. I first remember doing this before I started school so I must have been about five. Of course the cows knew they were supposed to make the journey to the barn for milking or to the pasture for the day. My job was just to see to the gate but it made me feel like a real cowboy. I carried a whip which was nothing more than a piece of string and the cowboy hat I wore was one that had long ago become too ragged for any discerning man to wear. The only problem I had was the house I had to pass just before the pasture gate. Jimmy the bully lived there. He was a few years older than me and took great delight in chasing the cows off the designated course. He would throw rocks at the cows and laugh when I would chase and cry. As time went on, he expanded his bullying to throwing rocks at me and later still, hitting me until I finally had to ask dad for help. I am not certain what took place but after dad visited his home, jimmy the bully was very careful to avoid me.

Life in a small town in the 1930's was so much different. Children went all over town without fear and parents did not hesitate to send a child to the store with a note and money for whatever was needed. During warm summer evenings we would be at the ball field well after dark and no one was concerned. Life was simple and safe. We had a radio which was the only one on the block and often we would have a visitor to listen to Lum & Abner. This program was a favorite of all of us and it was on every week in a continued series. I remember when Lum & Abner was gathered around the pot belly stove at the store with several other men of the town. In comes an insurance salesman and over several weeks, he sells the men a group health policy. Soon thereafter, Abner gets sick and has to spend time in the local hospital. On recovery, he returns to the store and when all of the men are around the stove, in comes the insurance salesman. Abner is happy to see him as the hospital bill has just arrived. Next week we gather around the radio to hear how much the hospital bill is. Toward the end of the broadcast, the insurance man speaks, "Were you the only one to get sick?" "Of course he was said Lum." "Well I'm sorry we can't pay the bill because it's a group policy and ya'll gotta get sick at the same time." I believe this to be near the truth today, if the insurance company can find any excuse, they will use it.

I think it was 1935 when dad brought home a small goat which he said was given to him. He thought it might become useful to start a goat herd, perhaps for milk, or something. My little brother Don who would have been about three then took up with the goat. They were about the same size and I remember he cried a lot since mom refused to allow him to keep it in the house. It was summer time and the lone maple tree we had was perfect for climbing and lying along one of the big limbs not too high above the ground. Thurman, my brother and I had climbed the tree but Don could not leave his goat. The grass below the tree was scarce and recently cut so Thurman and I watched Don fall asleep with the goat in his arms. Goat did not care for being held so tight so he or she, whichever it was removed itself from the clutches of Don and took a new position beside the sleeping Don. Thurman and I watched the goat start chewing on Don's long blond hair. That goat had teeth like scissors and soon had cut all of Don's hair it could reach easily. When it started trying for hair on the bottom side, Don woke up. Thurman and I were rolling in laughter, seeing Don almost bald on one side only. Of course Don ran to mom, crying "see what they did to me?" Guess what, I was the guilty one and I was the one that took the licking. To this day, we refer to a bad haircut as "goat cut".

My sister, Jewel was about ten or eleven when Brother Don was still using a high chair when eating at the table. I remember one cold morning when we were in a rush for school and Jewel was particularly bossy. She was across the table from Don and giving him h--- for something she didn't like. Don was half way through a bowl of oatmeal which I remember to be rather thick. Why I would remember it as thick makes no difference to the end result except I can still see a gob of it stuck where it hit. I remember Don had a spoon full on the way to his mouth when she said something which acted as a trigger. Without changing course, the spoon continued to a throwing position where Don let it fly. Point of impact was across the table and almost center of the forehead. Don was using a very large spoon and it left a cut and a gob of oatmeal on Jewel. Today the oatmeal is gone but the scar is still there. Why mom did not blame me is still a mystery but in either case, she did not punish Don.

Mom hated booze with unmitigated passion and I could only surmise that she had seen Uncle Kenneth become addicted while still in his teens and she remembered the episode of dad and Kenneth making a batch of home brew when I was about eight. At that time, probation was just about over and most drinking men had learned to make home brew in vast quantities. I have to believe this was their first experience since it turned out to be a disaster of major proportions and was never repeated. To explain the magnitude of dad's shame, I have to explain the layout of our home and the placement of our cellar. Down over the hill behind the house, our cellar was set into the ground so it was cool and perfect for canned goods as well as a place for apples and big crocks of sour kraut. It had a heavy wood door to help the contents stay cool and keep out those that did not take the time to do their own canning. Although we never locked the house, we did have a neighbor that was considered a little lazy and untrustworthy. Around the interior, shelves were placed such that dozens of quart jars could be placed. Mom was very particular in arranging them so she could know what was where and how long it had been there. This fits into the disaster soon to be revealed.

As dad and Kenneth proceeded with their project, Kenneth brought home numerous beer bottles and Dad procured the bottle capper and caps. In this cellar, mom had allowed a ten gallon crock to be filled with their concoction which they watched and tasted every day. Considering it ready to bottle when it made them a little tipsy and the foam began to settle down, they set about filling and capping the many beer bottles. Kenneth was capping and placing the bottles on every vacant space between moms preserves, peaches and green beans. I remember it was great fun for them since the more bottles they filled and the more they sampled, the more they laughed. Mostly I sat on the ground outside and just watched, wondering what was so funny.

A few days later I was near the cellar when I heard a gunshot, coming from the cellar I thought. I ran to the house and told Dad someone was in the cellar and had shot at me. He grabbed his .38 revolver and with Kenneth close behind set out to shoot the SOB that would shoot at his little boy. Of course I was behind them even if I was told to stay in the house. When dad got to the cellar, he saw the door still locked and was wondering where the shooter could have been. Just then, a second shot was heard from inside the cellar, followed quickly with a third and a fourth. Now mom was with us and I can still remember her telling dad to call John Dodd, our local law man who lived just down the road. We had no such thing as a phone but a loud call would have reached him since he hardly ever left the swing on his front porch. Kenneth being more experienced than the rest of us, made the statement that it had to be a homebrew explosion and much too dangerous to enter the cellar. By now we were hearing them like two or three shots in quick succession and seeing foam running out from under the door. It didn't take long for mom to notice fragments and color of her canned black berries, oozing out from under the door. According to Kenneth and dad, it was too dangerous to try saving the canned goods so poor mom just stood there and cried. The following day, all was quiet and dad had to shovel out the remains and mom was so sick she had to stay in bed. No wonder she was somewhat opposed to the Devil's brew.

Just a block from our house, the sidewalk started to climb to the next level of our town. This made a perfect place for the boys of our community to coast down a full block without gaining too much speed. We enjoyed making carts of every description and also using the little RED FLYER wagons that some of us boys got. All seemed to be well except the crotchity old man living on that street thought it would wear out his side walk. I believe his name was Burke but in either case we named him Mr. Puke. It did not help his disposition when some one called him that name and from then on, it was war. From then on it was not unusual to see chalk or crayon markings on his private walk.

I suppose it is well to tell you about the Holiness church mom and I attended where preacher Musgrave held services. I was all of five when I decided it was time for me to accept Jesus.

I remember the service and surely I must have embarrased mom. I got happy just as they did and somehow, I overdid it. Mom took me home and gave me a serious talking to. This day is cloudy in my memory and so I really don't know if Jesus laughed at me or with me.

Other memorable happenings was the time John Dodd, our local police department shot and killed a mad dog with a pistol, almost a block away. He was the talk of the town for some time afterward and a hero to we boys in the neighborhood. I made out best because Detective Dodd lived almost across the street from us. Obviously I was in demand to tell the story to boys on the other side of town. Not too long after that a similar happening occurred with dad, in our back yard. We had a small dog, not much more than a pup and he was tied to the back steps overnight.

I don't know why since the entire place was behind a very secure fence. He should have been free to run the lot. In either case, at the breakfast table one morning, we heard an awful dog fight under the kitchen. Dad looked out the back door and saw a large rabid dog looking at the screen door where he was standing. Dad quickly closed the door and ran for his .38 pistol. When he returned, he opened the door just enough to see the dog still staring at the noise of the door.

Dad took careful aim and killed the dog with one clean shot. We were not allowed out of the house that day until after lime had been spread all over the back yard. Unfortunately, our little dog was taken away.

Just outside the back door and very near where the dog was shot, our well supplied the only source of water. It was well sealed from ground water but the health department had lime also put down the well. I don't remember that it changed the taste of the water but mom was very concerned and boiled our drinking water for some time after that.

Mrs. Holsteen lived across the street and up toward the railroad crossing about two houses.

She hired me many Saturdays through the summers and I was expected to stay busy, pulling weeds, cutting grass and a multitude of chores her bad back would not let her on her knees to do.

I was paid a nickel for a days work which I thought was at least ten hours but I now believe it was more like two hours. Doctor Bourne paid me much more for my services which entailed hauling a wagon load of medicine bottles over to the river bank and dumping them. I remember it was ten cents a load and I was very glad to get two loads a week. Other than that, I used my wagon for orher jobs that paid little or nothing.

One year when I was eight, Kenneth went to either Georgia or South Carolina for a truck load of peaches. This is where I became aware of my future in sales. Since I have made my life's work in sales, the peach incident has stuck in my mind as clearly as if it took place yesterday.

Dad loaded the little red wagon. with peaches which I had strict instruction to sell, door to door for 25 cents a basket. At eight years old, this was quite an undertaking so he sent my 6-year-old brother to supervise. We left McClung avenue one Saturday morning with a full load and believe me, it was a reluctant journey. As we headed toward downtown Barboursville where the better homes were located, I knocked on door after door and got the same answer at all except one lady near the Holiness church decided she could use two baskets. Overjoyed with 50 cents in my pocket we continued on with several "NO SALES" and Thurman was beginning to grumble.

We passed under the railroad on the way to town and as soon as we cleared the underpass, the school was on our side of the street so we crossed the road to where the senior center is now located. There was a very large brick house at the end of that street and I was beginning to feel like a failure. When I knocked on the door, a very nice lady answered and I gave her my sales pitch which went something like this. "My daddy told me to sell these peaches before I could come home" About this time, Thurmond said "Orvice, let's go home, I'm tired."

That lady asked the price and said, "OH you dear boys, wait right here" and with that she closed the screen door and disappeared. Curious as I was, I had to press my face against the screen to look inside and wonder where she went. When she returned, she said "You have seven baskets and here is two dollars. Now little boys you can go home".

When I got home, mom told me to go look in the mirror at my face. I did and what I saw convinced me I was destined to become a peeping tom. My face was a crosshatch of dirty screen wire and from the looks of it, I must have pressed hard enough to leave an imprint of my face in her screen door. Many times, during my 50 sales years, I have wished I had Thurmond along to help me close a deal.

It was about this time that I saw my first movie, black & white and silent except for the piano in the background. Kenneth took me to the Saturday afternoon show and I well remember the story line. It really had no story, just a line of things dogs do. I suppose Kenneth enjoyed it as much as I did since I laughed much of the time because he was laughing. I still don't know what was so funny about a dog dragging clothes off the line the overworked woman had just hung out to dry.

Personally I would have kicked the s--- out of my dog for pulling that trick. I had watched mom too many times scrubbing over a washboard. Twerent funny. What was funny were the times we had in the back seat of a Hugh, convertible Hupmobile on the way to West Hamlin where granddad had the grist mil and the blacksmith shop.. There was enough room in the back seat to hold five kids and allow us to fight or sleep as desired. That big monster had very hard tires and virtually no springs. The road to West Hamlin was paved with brick and every brick was at a different level which kept your teeth in a continuous chatter. We loved to go to West Hamlin and I truly believe it was because grandpa was the epitome of gentle fun and love. At least he was to his grandchildren.

He died January 19, 1934 and I so well remember sitting under his casket the next day, crying all day and refusing to go downstairs with the rest of the family, I still miss him today.

I spent a lot of summer time with him and he always had something for me to do in the blacksmith shop or at the grist mill. I was either pumping the forge or changing sacks as the ground corn fell from the mill. I was even allowed to measure out the amount of grain he charged for grinding, be it cornmeal or animal feed. I was made to feel important and was usually paid in candy or small change. Both acceptable.

It was in these early years that dad and Kenneth got the motorcycle fever. They had a big Harley and complete with cap and goggles, they were the stuff. Of course I was fascinated with the machine and decided to ride it one day when I was alone with it in the garage. To explain what happened, I need to describe the garage floor. Where cars were parked, the floor was dirt and gravel. In the back there was a work area with a high step up onto a wood floor. This day I decided to ride it, I put on the cap and goggles and from the raised work floor, leaped into the saddle. My leap fell short and the motorcycle fell toward me, pinned me to the floor. I was saved from being swashed by the raised floor since it supported most of the weight of that monster. Still I was helpless and for some time, I could do nothing except cry for help. Thankfully Kenneth came out of the house and heard my pitiful sobs. I never did get to ride that bike.

Seems as if I was always in trouble for something, either what I did or what I allowed Don to do.

This time, Don had nothing to do with my accident. Dad and Kenneth decided to dig a basement under the house. When they were in the mood, they would dig and wheelbarrow dirt down over the back hill. During their lazy time when no digging was taking place, I was moved to do my part. Dad had a big railroad pick which had a very sharp point. I felt capable of swinging that pick and proceeded to finish the basement while they were resting up in the house. It must have been about the third of fourth swing that the pick hit the floor joist above me. That diverted my swing from dirt to foot. That pick point entered my fight foot, through the shoe and on into the ground. My screech must have awakened the entire city block but it got me help and a trip to Doctor Bourne.

I recall another accident which happened about 2AM on a Sunday morning. What conceivable accident could occur at that time in the morning? To explain this accident, it is first necessary to explain my relationship with Kenneth. He was more than a big brother to me. He was the one that taught me to do for myself. He and I took a stake body truck apart and made it into a dump truck. Only he had the patients, like grandpa, to let me learn and do things that made me feel useful. I really loved him and this explains why I hid his whisky from mom. Every Sunday morning, he would come staggering in to our bedroom, smelling like a hog pen and looking as if he just got out of the trough with the other pigs, which he had. He would pull off his clothes and hand me a bottle that he called "The hair of the dog that bit me". I was to hide it from mom because he needed a drink when he finally made it out of bed and started the Sunday sobering process. This particular Sunday morning, I had gotten up and hid the "HAIR" and was back in bed with covers up under my chin. I had moved to the complete back side since it was not pleasant to be close to him when he was this soused. Kenneth was so polluted he failed to turn off the light and he literally fell on the bed, passed out. Now this bed was made of heavy iron bars and reached almost to the ceiling. The bed could only stand so much weight and Kenneth passes the legal limit. the bed collapsed and that heavy head board came down across me in such a way that I was between two rails with my arms pinned beside me. I could not move and I could not get Kenneth awake. I was afraid to scream loud enough to get mom for she would have shot Kenneth. With the light on and helpless the remainder of that night, I wondered what would happen if there was a fire. I didn't burn but I must admit I was burning with anger.

In this same bedroom which was originally intended as the front living room, we had a large ornate front door with an oval glass filling most of the door. There was no other window in the room and it was filled with two large chests and I believe some boxes of cardboard filled with stuff----mom's storage room. There was a time when I was five that I was afraid in the dark.

This scary night when we had company, I suppose I was acting up and the result was that dad locked me in this room and took the lamp with him. It was dark, spooky and I lost control.

All I could find to throw was a wash pan and throw it , I did. It hit that glass door and I remember that I was screaming with fear when I threw it. After that, I was screaming with pain from the belt dad wrapped around my hiney. I remember that bed room as if it was last week and not a pleasant memory.

I well remember my first day at school. I was still five and would not make it to six for another three months. Mom assigned the chore of taking me there to Jewel who had already become quite bossy. I remember walking through the several streets on the way to the underpass and that there was a whole passel of kids heading the same way. None was as excited as I and all seemed to be having a good time. I suppose I loved school for I never remember crying as so many of the newcomers did. Later I found the fastest way from school was out the back and over the railroad. I don't think mom ever approved of that route but we did it anyway. She often said we were to watch out for the HOBO's but so far as I was concerned, they were just nice men, mostly ragged and hungry. I think what I loved most about school was so simple that I hesitate to tell it.

Nothing pleased me more than to get a new pencil and tablet. I hated to make the first mark in it.

At this writing, it is 5:30 Christmas Eve and I have a flood of memories of when an orange and a banana was big time Christmas. Other than chocolate candy with white sugar centers and peppermint sticks by the hand full, English walnuts and nigr toes, peanuts and hot drops, there was little else from the store in the way of sweets. Mom was very efficient in making Christmas a lot of fun . Mom had plenty of home baked cookies and wonderful food. We were usually so candy and nut stuffed, we never really noticed the wonderful table she set. Presents were not expensive junk but clothes and practical things and we were more fortunate than our friends since some of them got nothing. The little red wagon came from Brady hardware and was for all three boys. It was also practical since mom had visions of it's use in the garden, and it did serve that purpose. I think this was the one time in the year that Thurmond got new clothes because he got my "hand-me-downs" . I never remember him complaining..

Mom was partial to Don from the day of his birth. I remember her dedicating him to the Lord as a minister before he could even spell BIBLE. Thurmond and I resented his treatment at times

But we never made it known. We would usually send him to try the dangerous things first since we understood that God would protect him. At least mom would. Of course we three got into lots of things that should not have been, such as corn cob battles with the Hutchinson boys in later years. As for Barboursville, we delighted in sending him down the sidewalk where we knew old man Puke would come out and rave at him. Don was too young to pay any attention to that crotchety old man but he was old enough to steer the wagon and enjoy the trip.

I must tell you about the time Don did get in trouble with dad, even though mom objected.

Her reasoning was that I was to blame since I saw him throw the rock. We three boys were out on the side walk in front of our house when a man drove a new CORD automobile convertible down our street. He was so proud of it he drove slow so all could see what a fine car he had. I remember his jaunty big car as he looked at us. Don, quick as a flash, picked up a good sized

rock and let it fly toward that man. It would have been a perfect throw except the windshield was in the way. This was before safety glass and that rock made a thousand pieces of that windshield.

The man had no speed so he just turned into our garage entrance, got out and to the back door.

Mom was near fainting when she heard what happened. Of course dad had to pay a hefty repair bill, I got a switching and Don got a good talking to. I remember Thurmond crying and telling dad I didn't do it.

Mom was a fair woman except when it came to Don and I believe she was blinded by his blond hair and what appeared to be an angelic bearing.

Even so, he did mostly act like a boy when mom was not around. I was not the only one that took a spanking on his behalf.

There was the time when Don was still too young to talk but not too young to know what he wanted. Mom had gone up the street about two houses toward the railroad to visit with the lady there. I don't remember her name but I do remember mom left Jewel in total charge of Don, Thurmond and me. I suspect an hour passed with Don crying most of the time. Jewel was doing everything she could to stop his crying. She said to me,"Don must be sick and I don't know what to do. Would you go get mom?" I suppose I refused because I next remember following Jewel up to the house where mom was. Thurmond and I were close behind and Don was squalling fit to be heard long before we got to the front door. Mom met us at the door and before Jewel said a word, mom took Don and he immediately stopped crying. I don't remember the words that were spoken but I do remember mom breaking off a switch with which she whipped Jewel all the way home.

Thurmond and I were both crying and telling mom not whip Jewel. I certainly hope brother Don does not deny a relationship to me because I write of such things.

Life in the 30's when depression was at the deepest point was not easy, even though Dad had a good job. I often wonder how he did it with so many children and visitors that stayed on for years. He certainly got no help from his mother or sisters. I remember he bought a new car from Vernon Sharp. The Graham Paige was a classy automobile and we were very proud of it. Bea came down from Chicago, I think that was the place. After a week with us, she somehow talked dad into selling her the car ,,,,on time....

A time and times and times passed and I know dad never got the first payment for that car. Mom shed many tears over that and I suppose dad also shed them, but not in public as mom did.

Christmas 1936 passed and we were so packed up to move, excitement was not for Christmas but for our new country home.

I Wont tarry here but move on to FUDGE CREEK

Between Christmas and New Year of 1936, we moved to a large farm where we no longer had water, gas and electric. To some this would be devastating. To me, it was the best part of my life. I had just turned ten years old and to go to the country was wonderful. We had a fireplace and a wood cook stove. We had cold bedrooms and heavy quilts. We had almost 400 acres to explore, plus all of the neighbor's fields and streams. I got to ride a school bus for the first time. We inherited a farm dog and two horses and very soon I was given a bicycle. We also got some extra cows and I no longer had to drive cows to pasture. They came in without being driven but now it was my job to feed them hay and grain and learn to milk one or two each morning and evening. Life was sweet. By this time my brother, Thurmond who was eight and brother Don who was six. The farm next to ours had boys the same age, Alonzo, Richard and Melvin. We became fast friends well before summer. They had very little to do since theirs was not really a farm but a small home in the country. With time on their hands, they became very frequent visitors, sometimes pitching in to help me with our work. Since I was the oldest of the three of us, it was up to me to see that work was done. In other words, I was the boss boy. My sister who was two years older than me was the big boss woman and she took her job seriously, sometimes to extreme. My little brother, Don was mom's pet, so we thought. At any rate, I took several whippings for allowing him to get into trouble.

Along the ridge back of our barn, there stood a line of old oak trees, Hugh and solid where the cows had shaded for many years. Grass under those majestic trees had long since ceased to grow. If the cows had not come in by milking time, I would go after them and almost always found them there if the temperature was high. We also had an apple orchard of about 40 trees on the back side of the pasture. Frequently the two older boys, Alonzo and Richard would join Thurman and me on a run to the apple orchard. Sometimes we went to eat apples or just because it was something to do. Never can I remember a time that we did not throw apples at each other. Sometimes like playing ball or if we could find a good ripe one, let it fly when you caught someone with their back to you. Frequently this horseplay would continue to the ridge where the cows liked to rest. We probably were not the first boys to discover dry cow manure makes great Frisbee's. When we ran out of dry discs to sail at each other, we found it was just as much fun to throw wet ones. Fortunately we lived next to a stream that would wash away most all traces of a battle won or lost, as the case may be. Just after one of these washings, we spotted fish swimming close to shore and decided it was time to catch some. I believe it was Melvin that ran home and returned with string and hooks. We cut willow poles and dug worms close to the stream bank where soil was soft. Perhaps I should have said minnows instead of fish .What we caught averaged about four inches long and I had caught one and tied it to my big toe. Having bare feet and setting where my feet was under water, this was a natural place to keep a string attached, I had not been fishing long until I felt the little fellow tied to my toe begin to pull harder than normal. All I had to do was lift my foot about 18 inches to discover that a snake had swallowed my catch. I do not recall what happened during the next few minutes but I do remember I was half way home and with a sore toe when I discovered the snake was no longer with me.

Around this time I had a desire for a RED RIDER BB gun. There was a company that made and sold a wonder salve, guaranteed to cure anything. I believe the name was CLOVERENE, sold only door to door. Considering myself to be a good salesman and considering one of the rewards for selling 24 containers of this wonder product, a RED RIDER BB gun, I contacted them and arranged to become their star salesman for my territory. That territory was as far as I could ride on my bicycle, perhaps fifty country houses. I rode most of the summer and finally peddled all 24 cans, sending the money to Cloverene as I sold the stuff. The day arrived when my new Red Rider came by way of the rural postman. It even had a small container of BB's and a manly looking strap for shoulder carry. Talkin' about proud- I truly was. In the front yard of our house stood an old apple tree with little nubbin apples on it, too small to be of much use except as targets for my Red Rider. Perhaps 30 shots later, I had found where to hold aim which was not in line with the sights. No fault though, I thought that was normal. Sister Jewel came out to see the new rifle and asked to shoot it. No problem except I didn't tell her to hold left of where she wanted to hit. About five shots and five misses later, she said "this thing isn't loaded "and with that, she took it by the barrel and with one mighty swing, wrapped it around the apple tree. I was more broken than the Red Rider and not too old to cry.

That evening when dad came home from work at the railroad, I gave him the sad story expecting him to give her a thrashing with a willow stick. He said nothing and did nothing so I was more broken hearted than ever. Next evening when he came home from work, he gave me my first real gun, a much used .22 rifle. Now I was glad my sister did me the favor. I might add that I became very good with that rifle and wish I had it today. It was in the house we lived in when the house burned. That rifle helped me get qualified as an expert rifleman in WWII.

About a year later, dad gave me a single shot pistol in .410 gauge which being a shotgun with a 10 inch barrel would be considered illegal in today's gun world. He gave it to me as a method of ridding the place of rats around the barn. For each rat I turned in, he gave me another shell and it didn't take long for me to increase my ammo supply by the simple way of being patient. Wait until I caught two or more close together. That shotgun would spread shot enough to cover a wide angle and my record was seven with one shot. Dad never caught on and I had ammo to rabbit hunt with. My favorite place to wait for rats to congregate was on the corn crib roof which was attached to the barn. One day I told mom I was going rat hunting and my sister, Betty, age 3 wanted to go with me. She promised to be very still so I took her to the shed roof with me. That day the roofing tin was under a direct sun and very hot. Betty did not have what we called "overalls" so I suppose the hot tin roof got to her nearly bare rear end. She squirmed and scooted on that roof until every rat in the county hid to laugh at us. Our hunting trip that hot afternoon did not last long. "Overalls" then was the accepted wear for boys. I had three pairs which I rotated two of them for day wear and used the newer pair for Sunday. For Christmas and my birthday, combined, I usually got two new pairs to accommodate for my rapid growth. I don't know how mom did it but she managed to have four of us so near Christmas that we never got a separate birthday gift. Again, the house fire did this wonderful, little pistol in.

When I joined the US Army in WW11, I found my experience with guns to be a great help and I am reminded of the statement made by a Japanese general when he said they could not afford to invade the shores of the USA since too many men and boys were armed.

The little stream next to our house was a source of many happy times. We children had the only place that was suitable for a swimmin' hole right in front of the house. Neighbors came from nearby farms to swim and the local Baptist church used the same place for Baptismal services. Many sins were washed away there, that is if water only did the trick. Sometimes it worked and sometimes it lasted for only a few days.

Then there was Old Tiger, a Hugh striped bull dog who considered his life's work to care for children, any child. All of the children of the neighborhood loved Old Tiger and loved to tease him at the water hole. Tiger loved the water but when we were in it, he roamed the bank and watched us like a concerned mother. To tease him, one of us would yell "Help" and go under. Then is when Old Tiger did his stuff. Sometimes his teeth would dig in a little deep when he pulled you out to the bank but, pull you out he did. T o this day, I believe we hurt his feelings when we then all had a good laugh at his expense. He would actually turn his rear end to us until we stopped laughing. Where ever we roamed in the woods and fields, Tiger was with us. He seemed to always know when there was danger and many times we have seen him run before us to grab and kill a snake. Tiger was killed while still in his prime and all of his charges cried, this included our mother who would not let animals stay in her house.

Tiger was with us the day Thurman, Alonzo, Richard and I came across a small skunk in the apple orchard. Tiger wanted to give it a wide berth but as boys sometimes think, we were primed for trouble. I don't remember which of us started it but it came as a dare to grab the skunk by the tail. The dog stayed clear until last but he finally took his turn. That was either fortunate or a wise decision on his part since by the time he grabbed the skunk it was about out of ammunition so he did not get any in his eyes. Now that we all gave off the same stench we had to worry about going home and facing mom. She was in the garden when we came down off the hill. Tiger couldn't wait to tell on us so he ran to mom ahead of us. One whiff and she knew what to do. "You boys go to the barn and stay there until." She brought some of her extra strong lye soap and a stiff bristle brush with orders to wash each other and our clothes in cold water until we were fit to come out. Several hours later, near dark, she brought clean overalls for all four of us and told us that we would have to sleep in the hayloft that night. Sometime later, she brought four plates of cornbread and four chunks of ham along with some leftovers for Tiger. Sleeping in the hay loft was not really punishment. That was to come the next day.

The next day-----just after daylight, mom brought us a big breakfast, ham eggs, gravy and hot biscuits. She also brought the milk buckets for me to milk 6 cows and told us the milk we would drink this morning would be delivered by me and the cows. Normally I would have to milk three of them and she would milk the other three. Part of my punishment was under way as it was my fault so I had to stand the worst punishment. Being the oldest boy was not always something to be proud of. When we took the milk to the house, mom laid out the master plan for the day which was all day in the corn field. Then we had to hoe corn by cutting out the weeds, thinning each hill by removing the smaller corn shoot to leave only the two larger ones. That was real punishment since we had five acres of corn and the day was blistering hot. Alonzo and Richard had parents that cared not at all if they never came home so missing over night meant little to them. We loved that family and I often wondered if they didn't care or if there was so many that maw and paw lost count. I think maw would miss Richard only when she yelled for him to "come bring me a bucket of water" and Richard didn't respond. Well, those boys stayed with us for most of the day because we made it a fun game to work a row to the end and jump in the creek. The field ran beside the creek for a half mile and so we spent more time in the creek than in the corn. Bib overalls had several advantages that belted jeans do not have today. We only needed to unfasten one shoulder strap, let everything fall to the ground and hit the creek naked. I well remember that our dog "Tiger" was well ahead of us when we got near the creek. I blamed him for our failure to finish the corn work that day. How could boys resist going into the creek to save our dog? I might add that when we saw mom coming to the field with lunch, we were making the weeds fly and wet overalls never gave us away. Sweat on our brow and wet hair was supposed to attest to our diligence in working the corn.

Marvin

Today I wonder how we got by without something being broken every few days. Legs, arms, ribs and heads all suffered minor bruises but otherwise, God was showed much mercy to mom since she had enough to do without caring for injured children. Doing acrobatics in the hay loft was very minor and fun that all seven of us enjoyed from time to time. We would climb to the top of the loft and do all sorts of dangerous things before we hit the hay below. Of course we needed to include Marvin in our fun but first I need to describe Marvin. He was a first cousin, raised and protected by our grandmother to the point that he was useless. No doubt he had lost some of his brain power due to a high temperature as a child. Grandma did the rest by protecting him as a baby for as long as she lived. He caused so much trouble in school that he never got past the first grade. My parents brought grandma down out of the mountains to live close to us where mom could take care of her mother. Marvin did not have to go to school, even though he was perhaps twelve when they moved next to us. He was already very tall and skinny, had a good nature and fell right into our need for someone to play jokes on.

Our house sat on a knoll with a driveway running down to the county road and was about a quarter mile long. On each side of the driven there was a row of cherry and pear trees, perfect for our next joke on Marvin. Uncle Kenneth lived with us from the time I was born until he got married when I was about thirteen. It was some time before he got married that he took Thurman, Don, Marvin and me to a movie. As well as I can remember it was our first and a very exciting movie. Marvin got so excited we thought he was losing it, just because the bicycle race had several people in it and the winner went through the ribbon with his hands held high. Marvin disturbed the audience by holding his hands up and mumbling something we did not understand. Well, this was Saturday evening and we got home in time to do the chores, milking and feeding the cattle, pigs and old Tiger. Sunday, Mom made us go to church but Marvin did not have to go. Sunday afternoon, Marvin was still talking about the man on the bicycle and still waving his hands in the air so we decided to help Marvin with his fantasy as a winner.

The best we could find was a plow line, 3/8 inch rope needed to control the horse team. With this, Thurman, Alonzo and I tied it across the drive way at the foot of the hill. From the Cherry tree to a fence post across the driveway, banjo string tight and at the chest height necessary for Marvin to get the full impact of the winner's breathless joy.

Well, the drive way was down hill enough to allow Marvin to gain the necessary speed for the winner to cut the ribbon but not the plow line. We stood at the top of the hill and watched Marvin hit the rope with hands held high, mouth wide open with a winners yell . It sounded more like a fire truck siren and it ended with breathless silence. What we saw was a cherry tree shaking off ripe cherries, the bicycle continuing on down to the main road and Marvin hanging bent over the rope. All of a sudden, it ceased to be funny. By the time we got to him, Marvin had regained his breath and was able to stand up, only slightly bent over. I figured I would be in for a willow switching over that one but soon Marvin was laughing about it. Boys are hard to injure. Mom's prayers were loud and plentiful. I wondered at times if she thought God was hard of hearing. Never the less, they worked for we had many close to death experiences and God had sent a particularly busy Angel to care for us.

I suppose I need to tell you how I learned to chew tobacco since dad used the stuff and I wanted to be a man like him. We had an old man living on the farm who had to put up with the antics of boys from the adjoining farm up the road from us and from Alonzo, Melvin and Richard. Nine of us could find more to get into than any man should have to tolerate. Don being the youngest of all seemed to be the cause of more than his share of it. There's more about Don later. Right now I need to tell you how old man Morrison taught me to chew tobacco. He told me it would make me sick unless I followed his directions to the letter. Take a large chew from dad's Mail Pouch and a large chunk of cornbread up to the orchard where I could enjoy it alone. Find a good shade tree and take that chew, as much as I could get in my mouth. Chew and spit like a man for as long as I could stand it, then eat the corn bread and all would be well. I suppose you could think I was gullible but at age twelve, what boy isn't? At any rate, all went well for about ten minutes and then I staggered up to get my cornbread off the fence post where I had placed it for safe keeping from old tiger. Perhaps tiger was hungry or perhaps he knew I needed a lesson because just as I got near the fence post, tiger jumped up and got the cornbread. From that point on, my memory is kinda faded except remembering the long time it took me to crawl down to the barn.

It must have another of those near death experiences we hear so much about.

Old man Morrison never asked me if I had learned to chew but I am certain he either heard or saw me in the barn, too sick to open my eyes. I know he laughed at me but I set out to get even. At that time he owned an old Ford truck, probably a 1930 model with half doors on the sides and canvas to cover where windows were later used. It had a choke knob on the passenger side that extended down through the floor and between the passengers feet. Every Saturday mom would make me go to the city market with him, to either buy or sell produce. Since I had a score to settle with him anyway, I used my feet to gently grasp the choke rod and slowly lift it. As I did, that old truck would cough and sputter, slow down to the point he would be pulling off the road side. Then I would let the choke loose and we would take off with him cussin' a blue streak. In the ten miles to the market, I had him so mad he was threatening to beat the h*** out of that old sumvbich when he got it home. I figured I got even on the way down so I refrained from my wicked ways on the way home. Needless to say, old man Morrison changed the oil in that old truck and pronounced that to be the cure. I'm almost afraid to meet him in Heaven some day as I know he will be waiting for me.

The Well

Back before television it was usual for mom to let us run all over the farm until we got tired and came in to bed. I can't ever remember when she said anything like "bed time boys". Dad usually said something like, "you boys go to bed and be quiet, or else". The "or else" usually meant the belt and I can still remember how that belt felt on bare skin. Our favorite play then was "hide and seek" which Don took to mean, don't let them find me. I can't remember how old he was but I do remember mom aged about five years as we searched for him. Out back of our house there was a very deep well encased with a waist high stone wall around the well. On top there was a full cover which had a small, round sliding cover to allow only the bucket to enter the well. It must have been almost an hour that all of us were calling and searching for him, panic in our calls. Brother Don was secure in his hiding place inside the well cover. I remember his call, "I'm in the well, help me out". I remember this so well but yet I can't remember if dad whipped him or not. I know mom protected him so much that I don't think dad dared to overrule her.   Mom often told us she had dedicated Don to the Lord and some day he would be a preacher. Perhaps this explains why he did not fall into the well and drown. What a shame that would have been, for him to contaminate the water we had to drink. God does work in mysterious ways.

As for me, I was a very, very good boy. Never got into trouble, never lyed (notice the spelling) and was always on time. Still, it was my job to watch over Thurman and Don. I suppose I did a fair job, just enough to rate myself one notch above F minus. My failing was curiosity and for this reason, mom could not keep an alarm clock. I needed the gears for whatever project I was working on at the time.

One time my curious nature almost got me. I had some items like sulphur, black powder and a few other restricted items which needed to be mixed. I had enough knowledge to know it was likely to set the house or barn on fire so I took it to the middle of the front yard for the final mix. Good thing I did since it flared up into a roaring fire, shooting a mixture of burning oil all over me. If not for mom thinking fast and rolling me in a blanket, I would have become roasted and toasted. This explains why I never became a chemical engineer. Today I am cautious about mixing flammable items such as iced tea and sugar. Laugh if you will but if you read the bible much, you know God made the water burn, just to prove that he was the only God.

Wine and Home Brew

My first experience with wine came when I was about twelve. I decided wine was in my future because old man Morrison was putting thoughts in my head. He made wine sound like the nectar of the gods and was known to quoting the bible enough that he often came across the place where Jesus turned water into wine. How come I reasoned, if it was OK by Jesus, why did Mom hate "that old stuff"? After all, she prayed to Jesus every morning and again at night so I supposed she had failed to read that part. I could only surmise that she had seen Uncle Kenneth become addicted while still in his teens and she remembered the episode of dad and Kenneth making a batch of home brew when I was about eight. At that time, probation was just about over and most drinking men had learned to make home brew in vast quantities. I have to believe this was their first experience since it turned out to be a disaster of major proportions and never to be repeated.

Well, to continue with my own experience in wine making.

As I said before, I was about twelve and old man Morrison was the influence a twelve year old needed to really get into trouble. He gave me the particulars on mixing and setting blackberry wine.

I was to use blackberries mom had canned earlier in the season. We had an old building called the milk house that had been converted to storage of unused furniture and some extra chicken feed. There is where my sin took root with a stolen quart of blackberries and a cup of sugar. I started it in a gallon jug and placed it under an old desk that had not been moved for at least fifty years or since the south lost the war. All went well for about four or five days, until it started to foam and put out fumes of what old man Morrison claimed was "Nectar of the Gods odors". Maybe that was what it was but whatever, mom homed in on it like a blood hound on dirty bloomers. I think she had not been in that building since last Christmas or so but walking past it from a hundred yards out, she caught the scent. The hogs got a treat of freshly fermented blackberry wine and I got dragged into the house by the ear. I told her it was old man Morrison's and he denied knowing about. Guess who won? About six hogs got that quart so none got the full impact, but I did, with a willow switch.

126

The Biscuit Pan Arrest

Now you will find this story almost too much to swallow but if you care to do so, check the Lincoln County Tennessee Court records of 1975 and you will find names of the participants. In this story, I will not use the true names of the assisting officers or the persons I was forced to prosecute, but I will use the true names of places where this theft occurred.

About 1975, I lived in Huntsville, Alabama where I ran my business. Twenty five miles north is the small berg of Taft, Tennessee where farm land was available and where my family could spend the weekends and keep horses which we had been boarding at the edge of Huntsville. My wife and daughter found a farm near Taft that had a log house and a log barn which was still usable and where we spent many a happy weekend. This farm was located a good ways back from the public dirt road which made it very private. After we had spent many very hot weekends there, I decided to have the power company install a new line and this allowed the installation of a central air conditioner. Of course, the locals thought this was the height of ignorance, to put this much money in an old log house. Through the remainder of that summer, we enjoyed the old log house and I continued to do repairs on both the house and the barn. It became our weekend home away from home, and we loved every hour of it.

By early fall I had quite a lot of tools there and four expensive saddles. The log house had a wonderful old fireplace and we were beginning to have a fire in it on cooler evenings and cold nights. It was the only source of heat except in the kitchen where we had a wood burning cook stove. My lovely wife spent many hours at that old stove, just like her grandmother did at hers. Believe me, I loved her biscuits covered in gravy, with a thick pork chop, or a large sausage patty on the side.

About November, my daughter who was eighteen at the time, had what she called a pajamas party for her girlfriends. They spent Friday and Saturday night there and I understand they had a wonderful time. For this party, my wife had bought lots of food and some unnecessary items such as a very large plastic bag of tiny marshmallows for the fireplace, and hot chocolate. This bag was very large, probably three gallons, and I still wonder why she bought such a large volume. The girls cut the top open and must have used all of a pint of those little things and left the bag open, standing next to the fireplace. I should add that they were about the size of a pencil eraser and of every color imaginable.

Because we were not there except on Friday and Saturday nights, it was necessary to feed the four horses by an automatic method. Being somewhat handy with tools, I made an automatic - feeding system that dropped corn down plastic pipes to the four stalls and it did so at five PM, every day. Now the horses were lured to the barn where we could catch them on Friday evening without a fuss. It was delightful to be standing in the barn at about ten minutes to five and hear those horses come tearing in from the back pasture, right on time. They had the run of a hundred acres and before the automatic feeder, it was sometimes difficult to catch them.

When I decided to have central air installed, the nearest dealer was in Huntsville where there were at least six or eight places I could have used to do the job. The one I chose agreed to make the installation on a Saturday while we could be there. As it turned out, the foreman of that crew was a horse lover and spent some time at our place.

Not too many weeks passed before we arrived at the farm on Friday evening and found that we no longer had saddles or tools. I called the local Sheriff but his department took no interest in a common theft.

It was too far out of his town of Fayetteville, Tennessee and besides, it was Friday night. Saturday morning, I went to the neighbors along that country road to ask if they had seen anything or noticed an out of place vehicle.

Sure enough, one neighbor said they had seen a pickup truck with air conditioning repairs written on the door. On the way back to the farm, I noticed colored spots beside the road. I stopped for a closer look and discovered they were marshmallows. At the farm I found the bag belonging to my daughter was missing so I went back to the road and followed a trail that made the two turns onto the highway toward Huntsville. Sunday morning, I was back in Huntsville looking for the truck that fit my neighbor's description. When I found one parked at a closed business location, I worked my way through the fence for a closer look. Viola!

It had colored marshmallows on the floor and it had my hatchet lying there with my initials cut in the handle.

Now all I had to do was call the local law for an arrest.

Sorry, we can't do anything about it since the crime was committed in Tennessee and this is Alabama. OK, so now I call the sheriff in Tennessee. Sorry, I can't do anything about it since they are located in Alabama and this is Tennessee.

Now it is up to me to locate the driver this truck is assigned to. By Monday morning, I had the address and the night before I had been a peeping tom and looked in his window. There sat the foreman who had installed my heat air conditioning unit.

In plain sight, in the middle of the floor, there lay my saddles, topped off with my biscuit pan. Now what?

I called a city patrolman that has become a close friend, for life. He agreed to park his patrol car down the street while I made a citizen's arrest. All I had to do was fire a shot and he then comes up with lights flashing and calling for backup.

Now, I am nervous, so I again peeped in under a drawn blind and saw three men at the kitchen table.

One of the men had my jacket on and in the middle of the table stood a gallon size can of pork & beans. The lid had been cut almost totally loose and folded up to where I could read the writing on the lid. Just a few days before, my daughter had given me this gallon of beans for my Thanksgiving deer hunt. She did it as a joke and had used a black, felt pen to write "TO DADDY, EAT WELL. I am not certain if they were eating beans for breakfast or if it had happened the night before but in either case it made me very angry.

Now, five years later, I write the story. From this point on, I wanted to be certain I had not lost the facts, so I called the retired detective of the Huntsville police department to refresh my memory. Roger agrees with me on every detail so I can assure you the story is true to the last period.

I kicked the door in and with my .38 held in shaking hands; spoke in a squeaky voice,

"Hands up, you are under arrest". I fired one shot into the ceiling to emphasize the fact that I was in command. When Roger heard the shot, things happened so fast that I can't really remember the next few minutes. I do remember that before long, the place on Drake Mountain had its share of detectives, officers and the local TV news Cameraman. I do remember the name of that cameraman, Van valkenberg because he got a great story.

After the arrest, it was evident there was stolen articles from several companies and from the military in that house. Of the three men, one was wanted for parole violation on the charge of burglary. One was a teenager who was taken directly to juvenile detention. The last was one, I was forced to prosecute since I had made the arrest. During the search of that house, Roger, the city patrolman, located a stash of marijuana.

Just at that time, my wife arrived with my truck which one of the lawmen had called her to bring the truck in order to haul away my property. As she drove up to the crime scene, Roger walked over with the plastic container to show her what we had uncovered.

The major TV station in Huntsville had sent their best cameraman, Van valkenberg, who was filming this, along with me and my wife. Later that evening, it made national news as "The REAL McMellon and Wife."

The following day, Before the news cast was finished, I had to answer the phone. It was my mother who was watching the news 500 miles away in West Virginia. ARE you in real trouble son? I told her no but then I did not know the end of the story.

At the time of this arrest, The Lincoln County district attorney had trouble bring the case to trial. It went on for several months, each time I had to take a truck load of saddles and tools to the center of the courtroom floor as evidence. There was delay after delay. The accused had a good attorney who managed to get delays, due to sickness, a broken arm and other unfortunate accidents. Meantime, my life was threatened more than once. Tennessee did not have a concealed weapon permit at that time but the Sheriff told me to carry anyway and he would protect me if it became necessary.

Finally, the state prosecuting attorney from Nashville arrived in Fayetteville to take over the case. This day started same as several others in the past with me lugging saddles and tools to the center of the court room. I also brought my beloved biscuit pan and placed it on top of the pile, just as it was in the house the day of the arrest. I really don't know why I brought the empty bean can but I did and placed it beside the biscuit pan.

I met with that attorney before the trial and gave him the same story as I have just written it.

By this time the story was all over Lincoln County and the court room was filled. Huntsville police department had sent Roger to the trial in case his testimony was needed.

As it went, neither he nor I had to testify. The attorney took off like any good preacher about to deliver a telling sermon, which he did. I can't remember much of the defense attorney because he hardly had time to speak. I do well remember the closing speech from the prosecutor though. It went much like this---

"Ladies and gentlemen of the jury, you have heard of the innocence of the accused from his able attorney, but we must ignore all of it. There was a trail of marshmallows leading to the accused. There is nothing to be said other than the accused shows his guilt by wearing the jacket of Mr. McMellon. He had the evidence on him, he ate the beans, he had the evidence in him and besides that, he stole the beloved biscuit pan." With that he sat down. The jury was out and back in such a short time, they never had time to set down. Guilty! The accused got seven years and I got off the hook with the determination to never make another arrest.

Well, the story did not end here. as it should have. The jailed local man had a son who was just as far from the law as his father had been. I *will call him Junior because I do not remember his name.* He was guilty of sending me threats on the life and safety of my daughter. During the year following the arrest, my wife and daughter had to always be together for safety. In fact, I met a man in the parking lot of Lowe's who drew a switch blade knife, triggered the blade out before me with these words. "You had better watch your back, and keep your daughter home". With that, he closed the knife and walked away.

A year passed before Junior showed up at my door. I answered the door with my .38 in hand, expecting real trouble. The shock I got was totally unnerving as Junior backed away from the door. He was on crutches, and almost helpless which made my first thought to step out and give him a hand. Still I stood just inside with my pistol hand just out of sight. Junior started his speech as follows; "Mr. McMellon, I am truly sorry for all the misery my father and I have placed on you and your family. I was under the influence of drugs and angry at you and my father. I have found Jesus and changed my life. Please forgive me and my family?"

I carefully slipped the pistol in my back pocket and walked the three steps out to him. I placed my arm over his shoulder and said, "Of course you and your father are forgiven". With that, he turned and limped to his car which someone else was driving.

I never saw him again, but a year later, his father was released.

Someone told me Junior died of drug overdose and was the real reason his father got parole.

Boyd's Song

Boyd did not see anything but a blur when he opened his eyes. The light hurt something fierce so he quickly closed them again. Now he began to hear sounds that made no sense to his throbbing head.

He heard sounds much like ten thousand bees and, through this buzz, he could hear what sounded like children and he was certain he heard a dog bark. The dog sound was all he could recognize from the jumble of roaring and thumping in his head. No wonder he did not want to open his eyes again. As he lay there wondering why he hurt all over, he tried to place his hand on his forehead but found it too hard to move. He was helpless. Now he began to know the feeling of fear, on top of waves of nausea, when he realized he was unable to sit up, no matter how hard he tried. Was it real or was it a dream? He did manage to pinch his thigh and it hurt so it must be real. He groaned with pain as he tried to lift his arm again. It was too much and Boyd fell asleep again.

Football is a tough sport when every high school boy on the team is competing for honors. He shows how tough he is because he knows the choice of girls is his reward. Boyd was one of the toughest and Maryann was the reward. He was so deeply in love that he carried her picture in his pocket and in his mind. She was just as much in love with Boyd, and it was well known that they were matched for life. Maryann was the sweet sixteen that seems to be the turning point in a girl's life where she often thinks she is in love but does not yet understand what love really is. Her parents had no objection to Boyd as they knew him to be one of the most desirable and trustworthy young men in the small town where they lived. They had complete faith in both Boyd and Maryann.

As Boyd lay in a state of half consciousness, his mind was working around holding Maryann close on the day he had to leave for military service. The warm and slender young body next to him was so real that he was back at the train station telling her he would be back soon. Maryann is telling him that she would wait forever and she was dreading the lonely months ahead. Boyd still felt that last lingering kiss and fought to hold on to the taste of her as he heard the boarding call.

Much later he was awakened by the sound of children's voices in what he took to be the tune to the Christian song of "Amazing Grace", but he didn't understand the words. Perhaps his head was so out of gear from the hurting that he no longer understood speech. As he lay there listening, he could also hear that dog bark and other strange voices amid the buzzing of a monumental head-ache. Boyd must have fallen asleep again with the tune "Amazing Grace" firmly planted in his troubled brain. Throughout his youth, Boyd had attended the small country church where Baptist's used that song every service, so Boyd had no trouble remembering the words. When he awakened again, he realized he could remember those words and many other things, such as why he was hurting so.

Boyd started to remember the "before" time. Before the flight, he was assigned to leave the island base. Leaving in the early morning, the Douglas DC3 was the workhorse of the army, and it was overloaded with supplies for the forward army troops. The time was February 1943 and Boyd was the radio operator, gunner, and coffee-getter-for the pilot and the co-pilot. In fact, he was the gofer and nothing else. He was helpless when the plane started to lose altitude, and the pilots could do nothing except look for an island in the Pacific where they might find a place to do a controlled crash. The storm they were caught in was not unusual, just the unexpected change in South Pacific weather patterns. Being in the area of the Mariana Islands gave them no comfort since all of these islands were occupied by Japanese forces. Boyd could only hang on and wonder how high they were and if they would make land.

The pilot was not much better informed since he could see nothing except the blurred outline of mountains and the instrument panel. When the crash came, it was expected but still a surprise to Boyd. The surprise was that he was able to feel the tearing of trees and metal as they slammed into jungle growth. Then the world went dark.

His groan of pain brought a very dark woman to his side who looked down at him and made some foreign sounds Boyd realized they were in a language he had never heard before. As he did not know the meaning, all he could do was stare back and try to say his name and United States Air Force. When this failed, the woman left but soon returned with a cup of some hot soup that smelled like beef broth. Whatever it was made no difference to Boyd for he was famished. The woman held the cup for him until it was finished. Then she left saying another string of that words that Boyd could not understand. Again, sleep took over Boyd's body for the rest he needed.

Much later, he was awake again and heard the sound of children as well as adult voices. He did not understand the words but he did understand that he was in the care of natives that spoke their own language. After the prolonged sleep he had been under, his body was healing enough for him to raise his arm and feel his head. It seemed to be intact even if it did feel like it was about three sizes too large. He could now look around with some understanding. He was in a grass hut and was lying on a grass matt on the ground. Around him were natives dressed in grass skirts and very little of that. Men had almost nothing to hide their private parts, and, in fact, those parts were not very private at all. When one of them saw Boyd looking at them, he spoke in words Boyd thought to be English but there were not really clear to him. This man-made gestures to indicate his name was something like Adam. With many signs and broken English, this man made it clear to Boyd he was safe from soldiers. Boyd did not need to ask for he knew he was in Japanese territory and the natives had him under their protection.

Days later, Boyd had been well fed and cared for. He had been able to hobble out on a crutch the native he called Adam had made for him. Once outside the grass hut, it was clear to Boyd that this was a temporary structure and he guessed it had been made just to shelter him for a short period of time. The jungle was barely open enough for the hut and, again Boyd gathered this was in order to keep it hidden from the air as well as from ground observation.

Almost a month passed before Boyd was able to walk without his crutch. He still hurt in places but not so much that he had to stay confined to the hut area. He had also learned some of the words used by the natives and understood there were a lot of English, as well as French, in their conversation.

He learned the names of animals they brought in for food and this gave him the basic meaning of other words. Many people, including children, came and went while he was there, and he thought this was just a clearing, not far removed from their main village, probably to hide him from the soldiers. He did hear and see aircraft from time to time but they were always too high for him to identify. It made no difference anyway; he had no way to contact them if they were American and he dared not chance letting the Japanese know of his presence.

As Boyd grew stronger, the natives took him with them on short trips into the surrounding jungle. Hunting consisted mostly of searching the trees for monkeys as they provided most of the meat the natives had. There were some other small animals Boyd had never seen before and had no idea what they were, but that they made a good stew. The natives began to teach him their words for surrounding objects and it was astonishing to him that he could learn so fast. Part of his education was on their trips deeper into the jungle where he learned their ways and names of the people. He also learned to use the blow gun they used for almost all of their hunting. The bow and arrows they used were not as certain to kill as were the poisoned darts, so it was rarely used. Boyd liked the silent way these men traveled through the dense vegetation, and it took a great deal of training on his part to travel with them.

Time passed quickly and soon he was rewarded with a trip to their village where he was warmly welcomed. Their children were a delight to Boyd. They were always bringing him something they thought might interest him. Boyd was from the hill country of West Virginia and certainly was no stranger to living off the land so he was quick to jump in and help the women with camp chores. It was not certain to him if the men approved or if he was breaking their rules, but the women really loved him for his efforts. As part of his education, the younger men tried to help him learn to use the bow and arrow. He tried teaching them some of his West Virginia skills which such as the use of the sling. This was a new weapon to them and Boyd delighted in constructing slings and teaching them the use of it. As a boy, he had been taught to make one from two leather straps about one half inch wide and eighteen inches long. With these fastened to a small pouch in the middle, a good sized creek rock could be thrown the length of a football field. At thirty yards, the rock could be a deadly projectile and Boyd had enough practice to be deadly with it. Proof of the force and accuracy was written in the Bible where David, the shepherd boy, killed the giant with one.

Occasionally, Japanese soldiers made a scouting party trip through the mountainous area where this village was located. The natives always knew when and where they were and took Boyd deep into the jungle when they were due a visit from the enemy. There was no doubt the Japs were their enemy. When they visited their village, anything of value had to be hidden and the young women had to be well hidden. The soldiers were brutal when they managed to catch one of their young women, and the natives dared not interfere. They had heard of other villages being totally wiped out because of interference. Boyd had some difficulty converting his manner of dress to that of the natives, but the time came when he had little choice. His clothing was tattered from the crash and what was left soon became little better than rags. Modesty was something he had to leave by the wayside for it soon became necessary for him to cover himself with the same skimpy pieces of animal skin as that used by the men.

Living with the natives for a year was enough for him to be accepted into the tribe as one of them. Now that he had learned the language and hunted with them as quietly and efficiently as they, he managed to bring in his part of the game animals. He used his sling as well as their blow guns but he never became proficient with the bow. He was not certain when the tribe decided it was time for him to take a mate, but the decision was made for him. Before he was fully aware of their plans, it was too late. He found himself a part of a ritual marriage dance and his bride was presented to him. Boyd was certain the women of that tribe who cared for him when he was helpless after the crash knew he had totally lost his manhood. Certainly the men he had fished and bathed with for the past year could not help but know he was injured and deformed; he was no longer a man.

This seemed to be of no concern to Makoco, his bride, for she went about moving into his shelter and taking over as if she had always been there. For Boyd, there was still enough of the West Virginia boy in him to be embarrassed for a time, but it soon faded when he realized Makoco had no problem with it. His greatest concern was Maryann who never left his mind and his heart. He wondered if Maryann would wait on him since he would now be listed as "missing in action" and there was no way of knowing how long he would stay that way.

He also wondered if she would still want him in his deformed state when she found it would never be possible to consummate a marriage. Boyd had not forgotten the power of prayer and he also honored his savior every day and long into restless nights. Certainly Boyd understood the saying that "absence makes the heart grow fonder" for his love for Maryann was stronger than ever before. Ten thousand miles across restless oceans had no dampening effect on his memory or his love for Maryann. He suffered, though, thinking that his report of "missing in action" would cause her to give him up.

Now that he had a woman in his hut to prepare his food and look after him, he became a man of leisure. He spent more time out with the men on hunting parties and often took chances of visiting the Japanese camp for the purpose of stealing anything they could get their hands on. Some items they stole meant nothing to them, but to Boyd, they were valuable items of destruction and needed to be carefully hidden. There would come a day when he intended to do everything he could to rid this island of Japanese. For one thing, he saw them as an enemy of the United States but it went much further than that now. They were a danger to his people; his, being the ones he lived with and had learned to love.

As near as Boyd could tell from the records he had kept, it was about April 1944 when he began to see and hear aircraft almost constantly. Through the binoculars his friends had stolen from the Japs, he saw they were all from Japan. It gave him a sinking feeling that he saw no American or friendly aircraft. It made him wonder if the USA was losing the war. Several days of this action and the morning came when he heard the sound of many aircraft and gunfire well off in the distant sky. He was so excited to think guns were being fired at the Japanese. It had to be friendly forces to the USA; perhaps the same air force of which he was a member.

He and his native family headed for the mountain top where they hoped to see the action, and he prayed it was the Americans he would see. What he did see was to be called the "Marianas Turkey Shoot" in which the Japanese lost three hundred -sixty five planes over the next few days. He saw the battle come to him whereby he could lie on his back, and look up, and see plane after plane burst into flame, all of them Japanese. What a glorious feeling and what a desire to join in the destruction of Japan and the troops that had been so cruel to his people here on this island.

Boyd and his friend whom he called Adam, gathered three other strong men and opened their hiding place of stolen Japanese shells and explosives. While the Japanese were in such turmoil, it was time to strike a blow for freedom from them. Running through his head was "Amazing Grace," the children's song, apparently the only song they knew. He learned there had been missionaries on the island just before war broke out who left when the Japanese had killed one of them and threatened the others. "Amazing Grace" was what he had running through his head, night and day. He thought it fit well now that he had a chance to do something for his people and his country. Amazing grace, how sweet the thought— blow them Japs to number nought.

A week later they were ready to eliminate as many solders and as much of their supplies as possible with stolen explosives. Well after midnight when the moon was down, Boyd and his friends slipped into the compound with a large load of powder removed from artillery shells. They had also managed to get fifty pounds of plastic explosives and a long reel of Primacord detonation explosive. Boyd was no explosive genius but his basic training had been enough to let him know how to rig a grand explosion. None of them could read Japanese but Boyd had been trained in the use of explosives well enough to know they had stolen a box of delayed action fuses. He remembered the instructor showing them how acid in a glass vial would eat through the fuse link and set off the explosion at a pre-determined time. Just how long this time was had to be printed in Japanese but he had no way to tell.

Of course, the answer was to break one and count periods of sixty, then make a mark indicating one minute. From this, Boyd learned he had delayed action fuses set for close to fifteen minutes. By removing powder from shells to add to their stolen plastic explosive, they had enough to make a grand firework display.

From previous night explorations, he had learned that their supply of ammunition was placed a short distance away from their living quarters, and they had only one guard at each end of the storage area. The night came when the moon would set in the early morning hours and total darkness could be expected. Boyd placed one of his friends at each end of the storage area where he could get a clean hit on the guard with his blow gun. That was the one great thing about that weapon; it was silent and deadly. With a triple dose of curare on the dart and placed in the neck, it was instant death and the coast was clear. Boyd managed to locate the cases of plastic explosive by feel since he had spotted them and marked the location in his mind when there was enough moonlight to see. By moving at a crawl and sliding cases of this, Boyd and one other were able to get two cases across the compound and placed under the barracks where most of the troops were sleeping. Primacord tied the two together so that one fuse set both off at the same time.

Boyd was fearful of a failure with the fuses so he tied two together in case one failed. When that job was finished, he returned to the ammunition stockpile and carefully placed small plastic charges all along the length of the stacks. He tied all of these together with Primacord and again set two delayed action fuses. He placed Adam where that fuse was and sent all of the other men back into the jungle to a safe distance. Crawling back to the barracks fuse, he broke the glass vials and quickly returned to Adam's location where Adam was to break his fuse vials as soon as Boyd got close enough to whisper the OK. Knowing this was to be a violent explosion, the two men crawled only as long as necessary to be out of sight in case they were seen or heard. Boyd had been counting the minutes as best as he could, and well before he reached the expected time, the explosions came almost simultaneously. Being careful to be as far removed from the destruction as possible, they did not stop until they were back in their village. There was the possibility that many men would have escaped and would be filled with vengeance against any native found.

Leaving only the elderly men and women in the village, Boyd and the rest took everything necessary for survival and headed deeper into the jungle. It gave him great pleasure to see more air battles over the next few days and always the defeat of the Japanese. It meant that someday soon he hoped he would be in contact with Americans and even the possibility he would be on his way back to West Virginia. Now he spent every waking moment thinking of Maryann and wondering if she would still love him. It was agony but he could not erase the fear from his mind. Perhaps she had found, or would find, another.

Boyd guessed that they were near the center of the mountain range since he could climb a tree and not see any other higher mountain. During the next month, several tribes were in contact with Boyd's tribe as the entire population was under threat from the remaining Japs. They were vicious in their retaliation and when young men were found, they were shot on sight. Every visit with another tribe brought better news. The

Japanese were leaving the island and American planes had dropped bombs on the port where the main camp of the Japanese was located.

Two weeks later, word came by way of a native runner that the Americans had landed and a fierce battle was under way. At the end of this battle, all Japanese had been killed or captured except a very few who had escaped to the hills. No doubt the natives and their trusty blow guns would account for them in time. Boyd was ecstatic. It was time for him to see American soldiers and be on his way home. On July 21, 1944, Guam was liberated. Boyd had been a guest of a wonderful native village for eighteen months and he would always consider the natives his family.

Contact with the Americans was the most wonderful feeling Boyd could ever remember and, yet, it was a very sad day. He would never forget the woman he was married to and in fact had learned to love. Certainly he had never consummated that marriage in the usual sense, but the bonds of love go far beyond a sexual relationship. This point made it one of the saddest he could remember. It also made him think that Maryann might be able to accept him the way he was. He knew in his heart that no man ever loved a woman more than he loved Maryann and, without her, death would be desirable.

Because Boyd had been missing for so long, the military treated him as a released prisoner of war and made arrangements for his flight to Walter Reed Army Medical Center where he would be thoroughly checked and then discharged. As soon as he was under the army's care, his family was notified but he could not contact them until he was back stateside. At the first phone he could locate, he got help from the operator and placed a collect call home. His family could get little from him until they answered his question, "Is Maryann waiting for me?"

Travel restrictions would not allow Maryann to go to Boyd, and Boyd had to wait the thirty days before he was free to leave for home. During this thirty-day period, Boyd agonized over telling Maryann anything except his love for her. Minutes seemed like hours and hours like days but eventually he was released. On his arrival at the home train station, he could see his family and Maryann on the platform well before the train stopped. This was probably the happiest and most fearful time in the life of any returning soldier. Seeing his family and his beloved Maryann watching for him and wondering if Maryann would turn her back on a deformed soldier was almost more than he could bear.

After a wonderful dinner that had been prepared by his mother and Maryann, the family settled down in the living room to hear about where he had been. Boyd was aching to be alone with Maryann but at the same time he was glad he did not have to face telling her the truth. He quickly glossed over the plane crash, being rescued and given a home with the natives. Bryan was careful to avoid his relationship with Makoco and his marriage to her. He had to tell Maryann but never his parents. It would not be fair to Maryann to allow her to believe all was well. As much as he loved her, he could not bear the thought of losing her, but it must be done, tonight.

Just before darkness set the day's end, Boyd's father handed him the keys to the 1941 Plymouth with the words, "Take care of it and Maryann."Boyd knew the only place to take Maryann was the same place down by the river park where they had spent their last hours before he left, over two years ago.

With an aching heart, Boyd would not allow even a kiss before he had to tell her of his real experience and his injury. As he spoke, he could hear sobs being held in and he wanted with all of his heart to take her in his arms. But, no, he had to get the truth out to Maryann and allow her to make the decision for it was her life that would suffer because of his condition.

Before Boyd could finish his story, Maryann threw her arms around him with the words, "I will love you forever and we will overcome any problems we will ever have to face. "It was then that Boyd heard the words "Amazing Grace, how sweet the sound."

This is a true story. Boyd was my high school friend. He entered the armed forces just ahead of my enlistment and we lost touch shortly after he completed his basic training.Maryann never gave up hope and stayed with Boyd until his death thirty years later. The interesting part of this story must be said after it seems we have reached the end. Boyd and Maryann were able to return to Guam in 1947 where they met Boyd's second family. Maryann never knew that Makoco was Boyd's wife , but she did see the love for Boyd that Makoco had for him. Because he was considered a part of their tribe, when he asked about adopting two babies. mothers gladly offered their children to him. Boyd and Maryann raised two great members of their family .in their Florida home. The end of the end.

Clean Earth

Forty years of mixing with hunters all over the USA has made me aware of a real truth.

Almost every man I ever hunted or, camped with is much concerned about the trash scattered all over the highways and throughout our river system. In Elk hunting season in the Rockies and deer season in West Virginia, I have seen hunters return to camp at the day's end, open their pockets or day pack, and remove trash they did not drop in the woods. I remember the time Fred and I spent a half day hiking to a spot in the Monongahela National Forest that the forest warden had recommended as the most beautiful place in the mountains. He was right in the nomination and we were truly rewarded. This place was almost level, situated on top of a smaller mountain. It was totally covered with pine and cedar needles and had a thick covering of moss almost everywhere. No other trees were in this spot, just very large cedar and pine. It looked as if it had survived the lumberjack for a hundred years.

When Fred and I got there, all we cared to do was look. We found a moss covered log to sit on and ate our Vienna sausage and cracker lunch. I suppose we sat there for well over an hour and talked about how wonderful it was to be where man had not trod for years. When lunch was finished and time to move on, Fred leaned backward over the log in order to bury a chewing gum wrapper. He had already put the empty can and cracker wrapper in his pack but a chewing wrapper was small enough to be buried. Fred said, "O my Gosh, what's this?" He held a new Buck hunting knife up for me to see, with not a speck of rust on it. Some person had been here not more than a day ahead of us. In a way, this was a letdown but it did serve to prove that people who love the woods tend to carry their trash out. This person did not leave an intentional sign of having been there. Later that same afternoon and not too far from that spot, I found my lucky horse shoe.

Now I do not really believe in lucky objects, but this seemed to be special and one deserving of the special place it holds today. I had that shoe silver plated and it hangs by my back door where I can see the inscription of "W.Va. 1969" engraved in the metal. This horse shoe is 6 ½ inches wide and 7 ½ inches long, very large, and very well worn. It has been hand forged from layered steel which in itself is unusual. I believe it is from the mid 1800's when Clydesdale draft horses were used to drag virgin timber out of those mountains. Those massive horses were of Scottish origin and known for their gentle nature. So far as I know, few of them exist now in the USA except for the Budweiser teams that we see on TV in beer advertising.

My love for the state of West Virginia may seem too much for some but it makes me sick to see trash scattered by the roadside and along the river banks, I don't understand the need to throw trash around when it is just as easy to place it in a garbage bag. I do know that littering is against the law but it is almost impossible to catch offenders. Just two years ago, I photographed an automobile with people throwing trash out about every few hundred feet. I took the film to the WV State Police and was told nothing could be done about it.

About 1999, we had garbage pickup by a private individual in Tennessee where I lived at that time. This man used a pickup truck with high side boards. We paid something like fifteen dollars each month for the service. The trouble was he did not use a cover over the garbage and windblown garbage was common near the end of his run to the dump. As he left our area, he had a two mile stretch where he usually drove at a high speed. This stretch was garbage strewn to almost a continuous layer. I had made several complaints but nothing was done, so I followed him and did a video showing even a full bag of garbage falling off. I took this to the county health department with another complaint. The end result was that the garbage man knocked on my door and asked to be paid in full. I gave him a check as usual, then he told me he would no longer take my garbage. Nothing else changed.

It would be so effective and at so little cost for the states to place garbage disposal bins along state highways for public use. I have traveled in some western states where this is the practice and it was noticeable that road sides were cleaner. Certain counties in Tennessee had containers for public use but it was sometimes necessary for you to show a drivers license before using the garbage bins. This was, in my opinion, totally unnecessary since they were placed there in order to prevent garbage from being dumped at the roadside. Perhaps it's too late. Should we just try learning to live with it?

CLEAN EARTH

There is a stream flowing, almost still,
where I seek retreat when I am weary and ill.
It is here that I find peace in this wooded glen,
where my troubled thoughts can turn within.
One day I sought peace and drifted into sleep.
The quiet sounds of nature were mine to keep.
But, I still heard the birds in their wild song,
blending with a voice that was calling me along.
Then while I lay dreaming, free of all strife,
my body was changing and possibly my life.
I took on soft wings of gossamer strands,
that carried me aloft with movement of hands.
the breeze gently lifted and carried me up high
So now I could view earth from a cloudless sky.
But because I was dreaming, I saw not man's earth,
but those things that were given by God at its birth.
Flowers that were colored in beautiful arrays,
illuminated by sunlight in magnificent ways.
By motion of hands I gained control of my flight,
so I climbed even higher for a wonderful sight.
Suddenly, I realized I was here before man.
The Garden of Eden was under my hand.
The dilemma of death had not yet come about,
I could live forever if man would stay out.
Higher and higher I wanted to soar,
to see mountains and rivers, and much, much more.
Clean fields and streams far beyond my sight.
But, it was time to return, to end my flight.
So I circled and drifted till I settled to ground.
I was back where trash was scattered around.
Oh ! But to see a clean earth just once more.
So, what can I do that will help earth restore?

Eb Spurlock

His true name, Ebenezer Spurlock came from Scotland, Loch Arkaig in Lochabar. Some of his people were moved under force in order to populate Crown Lands by Loch Tay. Ebenezer and some of his people moved on south to Galloway where they formed an extensive colony in the Glenkens district of Stewarty. Ebenezer was soon to be fourteen, by his reckoning, and without parents, he was his own man, and not content to abide by the crown rules. British rules made him crown property and he was treated as such. As soon as he found a way to remove himself from the crown overseer, he made his way to Portpatrick. There he searched for a seaman's berth on any ship heading to America. Finding a berth was no trouble for every captain was on the lookout for boys that could be had for nothing more than food, and a place to sleep. In fact, he did not have to ask for a place for it was just turning dark when he was snatched from an alley way, tied, gagged, and carried aboard a sailing vessel. The captain never spoke to him but the master gave him a good understanding of what the whip could do, if he failed to carry out orders from any able seaman.

Life aboard a sailing ship was no better so far as freedom was concerned. His position was cabin boy which meant he was under orders from any person aboard. Much of his time was cleaning behind men who cared less about conditions and used any chamber pot available. Kitchen duties and deck cleaning was only part of his duties since he was also expected to keep the living quarters clean. What he expected was to jump ship in America but the captain was wise to this and kept all new hands in closed quarters during their time in port. Eb never saw land except from a distance much too far to swim and he never knew which port they visited.

From Portpatrick, they sailed to South America and eventually returned to a British port. Again it was confinement to quarters to keep him on board for another trip across the Atlantic. Eb decided to play a part of loving the sea and great admiration for his captain. The result was more freedom and when he undertook to learn celestial navigation, then his efforts were rewarded. The captain took him under his care and taught him as if he were the only pupil in a college class room. Ebenezer's early education was poor, and he never learned much about how the world worked. But this gave the captain something to do with many days of boredom on a calm sea. Navigation was the subject that held the most interest for both teacher and pupil so it was that Eb learned how the world was sectioned off in grid patterns. For starters, he had to learn the location of the stars and the direction their ship was headed. Actually, this was to serve him well in later life but for now, it got him the freedom to roam the boat at will, and also relieved him of many onerous duties. Part of his education was to learn that the world was divided into latitude and longitude.

Earth is divided into 360-degree division lines, both north to south and east to west. On the east to west lines, they start at zero at a point near Greenwich, near London and every 15 degrees there is an imaginary line from the north to the south pole called Longitude. As for the line divisions running around the earth, starting at the center or zero line which is the Equator. Every 15 degree north of that is considered a Northern Latitude line.

One of the most important things Eb learned was that this would be helpful in the wilderness. the ability to know where he was and where he was headed. A compass would serve the purpose of keeping him in the right direction, but suppose he lost both compass and his prized watch at a river crossing. Telling time and direction with the timepiece was very easy but with the loss of his watch, he would have to rely on a make do watch and compass. Not so difficult when a little sun is shining through and a noon time could be spared. Making a sundial was easy for knowing the exact time at noon but not so easy any other part of the day. Simply place a thin stick vertical in a bare spot and watch the shadow. When it is directly in line with the stick. It is noon. At night he would have to rely on the north star which is very easy to spot. The big dipper in the north sky is usually standing out very plainly. The open end of the dipper has two bright stars and following the line from there as if water is poured out of the dipper. Then the bright star directly in line is the star Polaris or the north star. To be certain, you can make out the little dipper if you consider the north star is the last one in the handle of the little dipper. To assure you are seeing the right place, the dippers have handles pointing in opposite directions and the open part of both dippers almost face each other. Knowing the direction north made it possible to set a course any direction on the compass. Eb was grateful for the education far more than the captain could even guess. Eb planned to travel alone through all of the west and he wanted to know where he was and where he needed to go.

The second year at sea and Eb never got the privilege of setting foot on dry land, nor on a planked harbor either. He ached to find a way to free himself from slavery, even worse than when he was back in Loch Arkaig. One thing he was good at was keeping an ear open for scuttlebutt among the crew. His efforts paid off on more than one occasion for he was able to make two of the crew show him some respect when he overheard them talking of mutiny.

March, 1727 when their ship docked in Hampton harbor, America, Eb had made himself the captains boy. He was hated by most of the crew but he cared nothing for that since he would be long gone if allowed to set foot on dry land. Their ship was unloaded of heavy machinery which was a difficult task and took the better part of a long day. The following day they were in the process of loading goods from the colony such as tobacco, molasses, and wheat when the captain called for Ebenezer to take the bill of lading to the harbormaster. Even though the harbormaster's office was in close proximity to the ship, Eb knew this would be his last chance and he determined to make it good. As he had learned he must do, his savings from his years at sea was in the form of gold coins belted round his waist. With one eye on the captain and the other looking for the best route to run, Ebenezer dropped the bill of lading in front of the office and continued to the corner where he could turn and be out of sight in just moments. An hour later, he was in farming country where he felt safe in asking for work and since he was very mannerly and very stout in appearance, the first farmer was delighted to hire him. Pay was almost nothing but food and shelter was his goal. He needed to have a reason for traveling alone so he told the farm family the story of leaving Scotland with his parents and how they died on the way over.

Being a sympathetic couple, this man and his wife made him a part of their family, giving him a room in their home. Eb was very much aware of the daughter Becky, but he had no interest in her as more than a sister. He was very careful to never be alone with her for fear of a lasting commitment. It did bother him that he was living a lie with these wonderful and simple people.

Spending the long summer months on the farm helped Eb become even stronger and taught him much about how to live off the land. Miss Becky was the only child of this farmer and his wife.

In a very short time it was decided by all that Becky was to be Eb's wife, that is to say, all except Eb. He said little or nothing that did not have to be said except about farming and what could be gathered from the wilds as food. He wanted only to know all he could gather from them about living off the land.

October 1727. With a summer well spent on the farm, Eb decided it was time to return to the docks where he could seek a paying berth. There he found the ship "Milverton", a square rigged, four mast schooner of 250 tons. It was in need of a master before it could leave for the Orkney Islands of Scotland. It was a break for Eb since this was a shipping center near his home place and he was familiar with the docks there. The captain did little to confirm his qualifications since he claimed to be able to navigate and did know the destination port.

Captain Robert Thelen gave Eb very few instructions because he was supposed to know how to get under way. Eb did have a lot of knowledge but he had never had full command over the departure of a ship and this left him very nervous. Carefully, he thought of the times he had watched the captain of other ships go through this maneuver and he acted as if he was in full command and knowledge, successfully departing dockside. As this was being taken care of, he did not have time to see that Captain Thelen was watching every motion of Eb's hands. By the time they cleared the harbor, Captain Thelen knew he had found a prize in his new master.

Ebenezer Spurlock had signed on for a year or two voyages to foreign ports, which ever came first. As it turned out, he liked the ship and made the captain a very able hand. After the first passage to the Orkney's and two trips to the south Atlantic islands, he was free of his commitment but chose to stay on. His pay was very good and now the captain gave him a percentage of the profits to act as master. Almost two more years of hard work and living completely on the ship, he managed to save every coin he was paid, and ended his sailing days a very wealthy young man.

Entering the port of Portsmouth, Virginia was the time of decision for Eb. His long-term plan was to see America and make a new life for himself. Parting from his captain was done with much fondness for he had come to love the old man. His life at sea had educated Eb in many things for the captain had loved teaching him and treated almost as a son. At this port city, there was no shortage of positions Eb could have filled and made himself a permanent citizen. Still, this was not for Eb as he was looking westward for the freedom, he knew was his for the taking.

August 1729 now 18

Ebenezer Spurlock was a very careful young man, knowing he would be killed for the money he carried in gold. He did not want stand out as man of wealth so he took a job as helper in a blacksmith shop. When he could, he also worked as a carpenter along the docks. His training was necessary for the time when he would be all alone on the frontier. He had to learn how to put shoes on a horse, as well as ride and care for one. He dressed as a poor man but bought the very best items he knew he would need when he finally made the break from eastern society.

He chose well in buying his horse for he planned to keep him for life. This animal would be his only companion for many years, or so he thought. In part, Eb would not stay in a hotel or boarding house for fear of being robbed so he made it a necessity to have the best in a rifle and two pistols. He would camp well out of town each night and only stay in Portsmouth long enough to gather his travel gear. It was also because of his desire to be his own man, to be free of any other that might give him trouble. Even so, he failed in the department of covering his tracks and being safe from intruders. John Dexter Had spotted Eb in town and had watched what was being purchased. From what he saw, he guessed Eb was headed into the wilderness and he determined to become a partner. His destination was much the same since he had no idea where he wanted to go, except westward.

Neither man had the training to set up a camp that would ensure privacy and neither had woodland training in tracking. The result was a camp site that John had no trouble finding and no trouble in approaching. He did so with the fear of being shot as an intruder. As darkness fell, John was nearby, only waiting to see by firelight how well Eb was set to protect himself. When he deemed it safe enough, he gave a friendly call and asked for permission to visit for a time. Eb had thought he was well away from any trail or place that was likely to be visited during the night so he was very cautious. John approached with great care for he understood Eb had chosen to be alone and might feel some degree of danger.

It was not very long before they were comfortable with each other and had made clear the reason for camping well out of town. When it was known that both men had no family and both were expecting to travel across the mountains for a new start., a partnership was made. John proved to be about as well prepared with guns and supplies as Eb was so it was evident to Eb that John had been planning to go it alone. It was fortunate they were both so well prepared as this left no reason for another day in town. Both men had fine riding horses and both had chosen mules for their pack animals. Both had everything they owned either on their horse or placed on a pack saddle for the mules. Ebenezer had a much larger pack for his mule than John and he guessed it to be that he had purchased a good supply of trade items such as needles, thread and some knives. Perhaps they would later move some of Eb's load over to John's mule for a better balance and better traveling time. Eb also had a good supply of gold on his belt but no idea what John had. It would not make much difference as soon as they cleared civilization at the base of the first mountain range. There would be nothing to buy except the possibility of meeting another man in the vast wilderness before them.

October 1729 found them well into the depths of the Appalachian chain of mountains and in no hurry for they had found the mountain streams to be filled with trout and the woods loaded with game. At one point where the valley they were in was wider than usual, they discussed the possibility of staying there for a long winter to come. Both understood the rigors of a cold winter without shelter could be disastrous, so it was decided to make this their winter shelter. There was an ample supply of grass land and even enough that they might be able to gather enough for winter feed for their animals. Without proper tools, this would be a difficult undertaking but with so much available, it would be quite easy to gather by arm loads. It was thought by Eb that the animals did not need help with hay because he was a seaman but John knew it might be too difficult for the animals when snow covered everything. Both men had an axe and knowledge of how to construct a tight cabin for themselves and how to make the lean-to beside this for shelter for their animals. They chose a site well for the nearness of small timber and for the shelter of a rock cliff behind. This rock facing would make it easy for the back side, both for their cabin and for the lean-to. By using this, they only had to construct a roof and one side. For the back side of the cabin, they figured to use natural cracks in the rocks for securing the cabin walls to the rock face. This would also be the place where they would have a fire since the rocks would hold heat long after the fire died down at night. To construct a chimney required some heavy mud hauling from the creek bed which was done by remaking one of the pack saddles as a mud carrier. They worked well into late October before they were satisfied, they could have a comfortable winter dwelling place.

As winter approached, John did most of the hunting and Eb did most of the gathering of chestnuts and the preparation of food for their everyday use. His time as kitchen helper on ship board came as good experience so they were well fed. He also did almost all of the animal care, seeing that they did not wander off too far and seeing to it that they returned to the shelter every night. To allow them free roam would mean the possibility of one of them becoming bear food. It was necessary at first to hobble them during the day so they could be caught for confinement at night. Processing the hides of elk and smaller game animals that John brought in was almost a full time job for Eb but he loved doing it. It was a certainty they would need the Elk hides for lining the interior of their cabin as well as make warm beds possible.

Christmas time came with their first heavy snow fall and then they were rewarded for their decision to spent the winter here. The mountains around them was almost breathtaking for the beauty of massive trees with almost no undergrowth to limit their vision and with the quiet stillness of freedom. Eb was almost to the point of tears to think this was a sight before him that he had dreamed of for so many years. Although Eb had seen enough of Christianity in his native Scotland where the people were almost in slavery to it, he was now feeling the call of a true God. How else could what he was seeing be there before him other than that there was a loving God. Scotland had long before his time managed to destroy everything close to the beauty of these wooded mountains. Nowhere in all of Scotland did they have one tree of this size to feast the eyes on. Thinking of this, Eb was quick to dress against the cold and just wander through these woods and thank God for what he saw and the freedom he had to enjoy it. Perhaps this was the first time Eb had ever talked to God in a loving way. Perhaps this was the hour he became a Christian. He deemed it necessary to speak of this experience with John when they were settled down for the night.

These giant trees around them gave some degree of shelter from heavy wind but when the temperature fell to freezing, it was comfortable for both men and animals. Even though snow covered everything, their horses and mules still found more than enough to satisfy their needs. Tall grass heads stuck out of the snow all over the valley and just below these markers, heavy grass could be had by pawing the snow away. The men did have some grass stored in bundles and tied to high tree limbs where it could be lowered when needed. Even though they did have a good supply of rope, they choose not to use it for hay storage. Instead, they made rope from cutting circles in elk hides such that starting in the center of a hide and cutting ever larger circles, a rope of some forty to fifty feet could be made. Nothing was wasted for every scrap of animal hides was made into garments and leather for future use. John did some trapping for small game since they had a limited number of traps. They caught some animals for their prime fur and some such as rabbits for food. There was never a shortage of some needed chore to do and never a time when they did not enjoy every day of it.

JANUARY 1730. With all of the trees free of leaves, it was possible to see long distances and this was what Eb and John needed to do. The cold gave a brief spell of relief in late January and snow melted to show lots of bare earth. This made it a perfect time for them to climb the highest mountain within their range and from the top, see how the mountains looked and see if there was a pass of some kind to the west. Mostly they did not need a pass since they could climb most of the mountains on foot but it might be profitable to know where passes were, if any.

Not knowing how long they would be away and what they might encounter, they decided to take all four of their animals with pack saddles on the mules. It certainly would be safer for the animals to stay under their protection instead of leaving them behind. There was no shortage of wolves and mountain lions that would kill their animals if left alone. Too often in the months just passed, they had to protect them by killing a wolf or two and in one case killing a very large mountain lion. The first day they traveled westward and up the mountain behind their cabin, travel was relatively easy. There was just enough snow to cover the ground in patches and that was melting during the day when sunlight could penetrate the trees. Night would be much colder so they decided to stop as soon as they reached a good vantage point, even though there would be no streams for water. With so much snow melt, they figured to find a small pond or puddle to supply their horses and mules. For their use, they had carried a small amount of water in leather bags. They also brought along a large enough piece of canvas to make their night lean-to stay dry in case of rain or snow fall. Well before darkness set in, they had constructed a lean-to large enough for comfort and gathered enough fire wood to have a good fire in front through the long night. Hobbling their animals in a grassy clearing gave them some food and they were allowed to stay there until it was too dark for their safety. Then they were brought in close and tethered to trees very near their fire.

Dawn found them finishing a breakfast of dried venison and sassafras tea. The animals had been released but hobbled and allowed an hour or so in what grass there was left. Sunlight had just begun touching the tops of the highest trees when they were packed and ready to move in a north westerly direction, This was the way the ridge ran and seemed to be leading them to the highest peak for many miles where they could get a view of mountain tops for as far as the eye could see.

This turned out to be much more than one day of travel as there were many places where they had to find a way around rock clefts and impassable steep places. As they traveled, Eb was continually making mental notes of features which would help him travel this way again, in either direction. John seemed to pay no attention but in reality, he was taking it all in while noting every bush and tree they passed. It was this observation that allow him to see the impassable places such as rhododendron thickets far ahead of Eb. These bushes were almost impenetrable to everything except small animals and sometimes deer would find a path through them. Beautiful they may be, but a real terror to fight a way through. After a full day of travel, they were too tired to do much more than heat water for sassafras tea to go with dry pemmican, John had learned how to make this from animal parts mixed with herbs, nuts and berries. Then dried to perfection. For the remaining time they were together, they were never without a good supply. Only once during the long winter night did they have to replenish the fire, and that was because their animals were upset over the pack of wolves nearby. It seemed there were either wolves or mountain lions getting too close to their horses and mules. When they got up to rekindled the fire, their animals settled down. Eb remained awake and watchful for some time but John was slept well.

At dawn, they were loaded and, on their way, back to their cabin. It was a beautiful day with no regard for any possible danger. And so it goes, when you least expect it, lightning strikes. John slipped on a flat rock that was covered in light snow. Before he could regain balance, he fell sideways and heard the bone in his leg snap. He became helpless even to move to a setting position. Eb was now the only way for survival for the coming winter. As master of a sailing ship, Eb had seen his share of accidents and, had become quite proficient at dressing wounds. This was not the first broken limb Ed had found needing his care. First, he had to find suitable small branches for holding the leg straight. Even before tending to John's leg, Ed had something to do. He told John he felt so very small in this wilderness, and facing a task as important as this, prayer was in order. John said nothing as Ed knelt in prayer. Dear heavenly father, we have traveled many a safe mile without once stopping to thank you for our safety and guidance. Now that we are in trouble, like many Christians have done from the beginning, we have stopped to ask for mercy. We have little chance to read your word but I remember scripture where you told me to ask in faith and it will be done. It has been years since I really thought I needed your guidance, but I must have it now. Without your help, John could lose his leg, or even his life, so I plead with you to make this easy on John and guide my hands that I set the bone in perfect alignment. Thank you, Father God, for the answer to this prayer and for your son and our savior, Jesus Christ. Through and by him alone, Amen

Next came the very painful problem of pulling the leg far enough out to allow it to reset in the proper alignment. All John could do was hold on so the leg could be stretched. Eb found it necessary to call on God to help him as this was the first he had to do alone. By cutting one of the elk hides into strips, Eb had the necessary binding to hold John's leg in position to heal properly. Fortunately, there was no indication of bone splintering, and John was satisfied of a clean healing.

From there back to the cabin was a very slow trip, with John holding his animal back for an easy ride. Darkness found them back at the cabin, and Eb having to build a fire to prepare a meal. John was in such pain as to be almost helpless. They were very glad they had cut an ample supply of fire wood and salted down a very large elk. Now, all they had to do was hunker down until Johns leg healed. Mostly for something to do, Eb set about making a table and chairs. He was amazed at how much his time on a sailing vessel was helping him now, in the heart of the eastern mountains.

Winter passed ever so slowly for the first two months. Eb was reluctant to leave John alone even though he felt the need to set a trap line. That would have to wait for the next winter when they would be west of the mountain range. At this time there was no set plan as to what they would do, or where they would stop for the next winter. So far, they had seen no Indians, just lots of signs of their temporary camps. Neither had heard of Indians being unfriendly, so they did little about night watch. Also, they thought they might be the first white men to penetrate this far into the western wilderness. Their object was to locate at least a mile of cleared land along a river where they could establish a permanent home. Knowing that many rivers had changed course and left much cleared land above flood plain, the hope was to find just that. It was not their intention to wander forever, but just long enough to be the first to settle on prime land. Spring would soon change the landscape and make it easier to travel. John's leg had healed very well and he was soon walking, on the lookout for elk and deer. They needed several hides for their next winter quarters, possibly for their permanent home. John would take his mule for a pack animal and could even ride him if he became lame. Eb stayed closer to camp and tended the hides John brought back. It was a very good arrangement, and both were content

MARCH 1730 found them well on their way westward. Some of the valleys still held snow too deep to travel, but they were content to stay along the ridges where it was mostly clear. JD still favored the broken leg, but insisted it gave him no trouble. That accident had made both of them super cautious, and Eb was still asking, "John are you sure you are fit to walk so much?" Their pack animals had now been given the extra load of hides gathered during the past winter. Because of this, both John and wasEd chose to place some of the extra burden on the saddle horses and walk.

For several days, they continued with ever improving weather. Indian signs were becoming more frequent, but as yet, they had not seen one. From Indian tales back in Portsmouth, they had heard the name of the Indians was Cherokee, and mostly friendly. Eb, having heard this decided to buy things such as needles, knives and other small, useful items. It was a wise choice since mostly the weight was low and the value was the highest.

The first week in April, they came upon a hunting party of about a dozen men. It was difficult to count them as they were cautious enough to never be in a small group. Eb was also cautious in letting them know what he had to trade with. First, he presented them with a needle each. These were heavy construction, with a very large eye to facilitate animal sinew. Of course, thread was unknown and the sinew of all animals had been in use since man had killed his first animal. After this gift, the Indians became much more friendly. They had been in a semi camp site a mile or so away for several days. Now they invited the Eb and John to their camp for a good visit and a place to spend the night. Conversation consisted of many grunts and hand signs, but it did not take long for them to begin to understand each other. At camp, Ed started to set up their canvas shelter and to place the hides inside where they would stay dry and make a good bed. John seemed to have a better grasp of their language and hand signs. It appeared that his years on a sailing ship helped him understand better than John. Perhaps this was because he was used to living with men from many places who spoke many foreign languages. The next day, all of them were content to stay in camp for it was so unusual to have strangers to converse with. They were all trying hard to learn the language of the other, and it was showing progress. John showed a great interest in the bow and arrows carried by their new friends, just as the Indians wanted to know all about their rifles. John wanted to know from a practical standpoint. He knew that someday he would run out of powder and lead. Then it would be crucial to his survival to know how to construct and use a bow. In this camp, the Indians had been drying choice strips of meat while fleshing hides and curing them with ashes and bark of the oak tree. Tannin came from the oak bark and did a quick job of curing the hides into leather. Although Ed knew this process, he had a lot to learn from the Indian way of doing it.

The weather was warming up very rapidly which made it difficult to cure meat and hides. Before Ed and JD understood just what the Indians were up to, they had almost broken camp and ready to move out. Neither of them understood the invitation given to them to pack up and move with them. The younger of the group was called by a name that sounded like owayee, and he was the one that started to pick up their belongings and carried them to their pack animals. By this and the motions of several of them, it was decided they wanted Ed and JD to follow them. Since there was no indication of anything other than friendship, they began the task of loading the animals. Looming ahead of them was the most formable mountain so far. It was hoped the Indians were headed that way and would reveal a passage over.

Two days later, they were at the top of the highest mountain in this chain. From there it was possible to see what looked like a hundred miles of nothing except an ocean of gigantic trees. There seemed to be no trails except the one cut deep into the woodland soil by animal tracks, looking mostly like cattle. As they traveled this trail down and westward Ed told JD it looked like a midland trail through almost impenetrable forest land. What streams they saw were fast flowing and getting larger as they traveled down them. Two more days of travel and they began to meet other Indians who were excited about their presence. All wanting to stop them to talk. In every case, the leader of their party called something that sounded like "swift eagle" indicated a need to quickly move on. By the time they reached land that was not considered mountainous, they had picked up a large following of both men and women. It appeared most of them had been gathering green plants and buds from certain trees No doubt it was food that neither Ed nor JD was familiar with. This was good to know and so both watched as these items were picked and stored in leather containers. They would have to wait in order to discover how they were processed, and if in fact were for food.

What was first considered a camp was in fact a town. Permanent as Indian towns seem to be, and consisting of well over two hundred dwellings. All were made of animal hides, mostly very large animals. Inside the dwellings were floorings of a very thick fur of the same animal which they soon learned were buffalo. Both men had heard all about the massive numbers of the buffalo, but neither knew they roamed all the way to the Atlantic Ocean. Already, the settlers on the east coast had thinned the herds until they were rarely seen. Also, the floors of some of the Tipi homes were covered in bear skins. There seemed to be only a few of these, even though bears were plentiful. Ed surmised it was because the brown bear was quite a lot harder to kill. After a long time of being scrutinized, Ed and John were astonished to see the men start gathering their hides and building a tipi next to the leader, Swift Eagle. It appeared he was a great leader and so an honor to have a tipi next to him. It was also time to meet his wife and two children. All three of them were perfectly mannered, and Ed was taken with the beauty of his wife.

Over the next few months, both men learned enough of their language to converse almost freely. They had also learned to use the bow and arrow as well as make, and use the spear. They learned the art of making a spear point as sharp as iron by the use of fire hardening the point. Good grade of flint was not so easily come by, but there was enough of it for their friends to teach them the art of making good arrow heads. Both men had considered themselves well enough educated to living in the wilds, but soon found out just how ignorant they really were. Making friends was no problem for them since both had outgoing personalities. Both were well built and very strong. This appealed to the young women which made it almost impossible to find time alone. The unmarried girls all seemed to have a hook and line baited for them. Both men were in the prime of life and could not help but be excited over being courted. Of course, this had to lead to a choice, and before they were quite ready, they found themselves, hooked for life. They had been there for only about eight months when chief Swift Eagle made the announcement of their coming marriage to two of the choice young women of the tribe. Even though they had told each other it would never happen, it did and they loved it. Winter was coming on fast and both would welcome a bed mate for the cold nights to come. Of a certainty, it was well to get the marriage on as soon as possible. They needed to set up their winter home and this was mostly the job of the women. The ceremony was by our standards, a very short action by chief Swift Eagle who made a very small cut in the hands of all four of them. They were then told to mingle their blood for a pact that would last forever. Such a short ceremony meant much to the women of this tribe, and it was touching to Eb more so than to John. Eb considered it to be ordained by God while John still had some doubts about God. Even so, John did fall deeply in love with his bride. That made it last for as long as he lived.

With the arrival of winter, it was time to gather their supply of food. The entire tribe set about gathering nuts, mostly walnuts and butternuts, Hickory nuts were everywhere but considered too difficult to pick the kernels from. The chestnut that fell was almost thick enough to walk on under the multitude of trees. Butternut was not so plentiful but had a far superior taste, and was very easy to retrieve from the shell. Ed joined a hunting party to travel northward up a smaller river. It was believed to have more elk as well as some late migrating buffalo. This was to be the first hunt Ed would be on with bow and arrow only. They took several pack animals since they were expecting to gather meat and hides for the entire settlement. During this hunt which would last until snow fall made it difficult for the pack animals, they expected to bring back at least twenty large elk. Perhaps they would be lucky enough to gather two or three buffalo. Most of the hides would have been fleshed out and trimmed of all fat during the evening times by a community fire. Also, much meat would have been trimmed of fat and dried by the fire. One or two would always be on guard, and would tend the fire. Guard duty was necessary if for no other reason than that wolves and bears would be drawn by the smell of fresh meat.

John, by virtue of his sailing and fishing experience would be with a party of another twenty or so. They would be traveling down stream to the big river the Indians knew as Beautiful River. That name when spoken of in their native language sounded like ohoho to John, so he promptly shortened it to Ohio. In ten canoes, they set off for a trip that had no schedule. Just go fishing and catch all they can and dry almost all they catch. One long day of travel brought them to the confluence of two great rivers. At the point of land extending well out into both rivers, there was only two trees with much bare ground. This made it a perfect place to set up their temporary camp. There was also a good supply of drift wood trees, perfect for fire wood. Needed both for cooking and drying fish. The river was still low at this time of the year which made it great for the harvest of fish. Both rivers contained trout, bass, walleye, sturgeon and muskellunge. In order to catch a large supply, it was necessary to build traps. These were made of willow branches that were plentiful near the river. Willow needed much water in order to thrive, so it was possible for several traps to be under construction at once. By the second day, traps were placed upstream of both rivers and the first catch was ready for the evening fire. Fishing was well done by the by the first of December, and snow was in the air. With the first traces of snow on the ground, and two canoes loaded with fish, it was decided to return to their families. Eb was by this time, anxious to return to his new wife. He knew she would have their winter home ready for his return. He also realized just how much he loved his companion. For the next two days of travel upstream, Eb talked to God, with continuous thanksgiving. He realized just how blessed he was to have found a home where he was loved, nothing like back in Scotland.

Now, I must confess, this is not my story alone. Much of it comes from my father's niece, Mable Spurlock of Lincoln county West Virginia. In her diary was the names and dates of the Spurlock clan, all the way back to Ebenezer Spurlock in Scotland.

I confess that I may have some of the spelling and dates wrong, but her writing was not so perfect either. I did the best I could since I am 94 years old and have lost much of my eyesight. As a young man, I spent some time with Mable at her home in Griffithsville, Lincoln County, West Virginia.

I have reason to believe that JD, or John Deagan was her teen-age flame. I see no connection other than she wrote love notes to him in her diary. I doubt anything ever came from that silent courtship. She never wrote his last name or ever spoke of where he lived. So he could be a name she gave the boy next to her in school, perhaps in order to conceal his true identify. I find myself in these last years, wishing I had asked many more questions, about many things. I suppose that is the dilemma of many old folks. I console myself with the thought that soon, I will meet God, and he will tell me all I need to know in order to spend eternity with him.

Please, my reader friend! Make your preparations to meet God, for I wish to spend eternity with you.

Eddie's Visit

On one of our hunting trips into the mountains of West Virginia, we were blessed with the presence of a very old local man. We first met him as we drove up toward Middle Mountain where we intended to set up camp for about ten days. After leaving the main hard surface road, we had about fifteen miles of dirt road to navigate to our favorite camping spot. I suppose we had covered about ten of those when we came to a ragged old pickup truck parked off the road shoulder. Sticking out from under that old truck was a pair of ragged jeans and old work boots. It was near dark on Friday evening and, we hoped to set up our tents before full dark but it was not absolutely necessary.

Of course we had no choice but to try to help a stranded motorist in that wild and lonely place. It could be the next day before another vehicle passed by this place and there was no hunting trip that would cause me to pass a human in trouble here.

When I stopped and got out, the man crawled out from under the truck and quickly told me he had it fixed. I asked what the trouble had been, and he hesitated before asking about my Alabama license plates. Instead of answering my question, he asked why I had traveled so far for deer season. Of course my answer was that my party was more interested in camping and enjoying the wild and wonderful state than in bagging deer.

I believe he decided to trust us and tell the true reason why he was under the truck since we were not from the law. With that, he dropped to the ground and reached under the truck for his weapon. It turned out to be a .410 single shot with an arrow in the barrel. I looked at what I considered to be a dangerous combination even though he had removed the shot from the shell casing, and decided not to ask about it. There was no need to ask for he had decided to tell us of the need for deer meat.

His story was that he was too poor to buy what he, his wife, and crippled son needed, and this was his way of feeding them. He explained this was the last day of bow season and any deer checked in this Friday and Saturday had to be taken with bow and arrow. His truck was parked near a deer crossing, and he hoped to shoot one from under his truck as he had done in the past. He also told us that he knew others that had taken deer the same way.

He explained that his reason for telling us this story was in hopes that if we got deer and did not wish to haul them back to Alabama, he would love to have them. We told him where we usually set up our camp and wished him luck before we continued on our way.

My camp was a very large, two tent campsite and we usually had a great fire going every evening just outside the cook tent. Monday morning was the start of gun season and a very exciting time in deer camps all over West Virginia. We were usually out well before daybreak, and would return to camp just after dark. I said we but I meant they, since it was up to me to get in early and prepare the evening meal. This was something I loved to do and my party loved to have a first class camp cook. About all they had to do was eat prepared meals, then sit by the fire and tell tall tales. Once in a while, the mountain water from an unknown still appeared which served to loosen their tongues.

If I remember correctly, there were no deer taken that Monday but there was one or two the following day. In either case, Tuesday evening while I was still the only one in camp and in the process of frying potatoes, the old man in his battered pickup pulled in. He told me he had seen deer but were too far away for the reach of his shotgun.

He was wondering if we might have had better luck. So far as I knew then, the answer was no but my party was not due in till dark. I asked him to stay for supper with us, and I could tell he was overjoyed.

Right away he asked if he could help in any way so I set him to gathering fire wood and building a much bigger fire because the temperature was going to be near zero in another hour or so. Just a few minutes before dark, Fred came into camp dragging a small buck that he had field dressed back in the woods. There must have been about an inch of snow then because Fred was able to drag that deer without much trouble. Snow that night was expected in inches, along with a zero night. Tent sleeping would have been intolerable if not for the small gas heater I had rigged for the sleeping part of our camp tent. Even so, inside could and did get as low as about thirty-five which made us get up and get dressed in just seconds, not minutes.

The old man told us his name was Eddie and he was from Elkins where he had not worked for some time. He said he was originally from down in the coal fields where he had worked twenty years in a deep mine. My guess was that he would be about sixty-five or seventy because he had a lot of trouble getting around, particularly difficult for him to get up from a seting position. Also, he told stories about the mines when he lived and/or worked there since the early nineteen twenties.

By the time all of my party was in and half starved, so they said, I had plenty ready. As usual, there was in addition to potatoes, pinto beans, cornbread and onion,and a generous supply of celery as a salad. I found many years ago that celery was about all I could keep in an ice chest for the full week we were there. The extreme cold required an ice chest to keep from freezing such things as eggs, milk, and salads.

I did have an accident one morning in years past that could have been fatal if not for pure chance that I had to get bacon and eggs from the chest. That morning the temperature was well below zero and I was ready to work on the bacon and eggs. I had set the coffee on the wood burning stove inside and it was perking merrily along. My ice chest and my gasoline cook stove were outside under a tent awning and on a makeshift work counter. I turned the gasoline stove on high, set the fourteen-inch iron skillet on the flame, and bent over to get the bacon from the ice chest which was on the ground. At that moment, there was an explosion, and iron pieces of the skillet flew in every direction. It was similar to a hand grenade with pieces of that skillet flying over me and out of sight. Fortunately, all others in my party were still in their sleeping bags when pieces of the iron skillet passed over them. I later figured the super cold skillet was so large that when placed on a gas burner, heat in the middle caused expansion to occur so rapidly that it had to explode.

We invited Eddie to eat with us and there was no hesitation. He was starved and we quickly disposed of enough food for eight men rather than the five we were. Eddie seemed to be in no hurry to leave for his camp as our bed time approached. At last, someone said it was time for him to turn in and Eddie said he was ready for some sleep also. We wondered what he planned to do since he just sat and stared into the fire.

I finally asked where he was camped and was stunned when he told me he slept in the cab of his truck. That was a good way to freeze to death, and, if he survived that, he would get very little rest. As I said before, my cook tent had no canvas floor but it did have a small heat and cook stove.

It could get quite warm with a good hot fire blazing, and, at least, the ground was dry inside. I offered Eddie a place to sleep on the ground inside the cook tent, and, again, he was quick to accept. He brought in the two blankets he had and I removed the tarp from my small trailer which he placed on the ground. I know it must have been miserable but it was the best we had to offer. All during the night, I could hear Eddie stoking the wood stove for a little more heat but I could offer nothing better.

OLD BLUE

Eddie stayed with us for the remainder of that week and we were rewarded with some stories from the mining camp where he spent his youth. Believable or not, they were entertaining and for the most part, I thought hewas telling the truth. Now I have had some experiences in coal camps that caused me to believe, but the rest of my party might not.

Anyway, Eddie told this story without the slightest indication of anything but the truth. In his words--------.

When I was digging coal for Acme mines, we used black powder and squibs for blasting coal seams loose so we could load it on flat cars. Because powder and squibs were free for taking home if we needed to blast something, most of us had a few extra shots for the fourth of July. There was little to celebrate then, but, we did the best we could to break the monotony of six days down in the pit.

This explains why Jim Shelley had blasting stuff at home when he decided he had to dig a pit for the new privy. Instead of using the shovel he turned to explosives, and, the knowledge he had gained down in the mine. Jim figured correctly that a small charge, just eighteen inches deep would blow enough dirt out that he could go deeper with a second charge. This worked as planned and, now, he was down to about the two-foot level. He reasoned that one more, heavy charge would finish the job. It is a rule when triggering a charge, and it fails to explode, stay well clear of it for at least thirty minutes. Sometimes a failed charge is due to a faulty fuse, and will explode minutes later. On this last heavy charge, Jim forgot or ignored the safety rule, and waited only about ten minutes after the charge should have blown. He had lit a timed fuse of only five minutes, so after ten or fifteen minutes he walked up to the hole with Old Blue at his side. Fortunately, Old Blue did not jump down into the hole as Jim did. His arthritis made him move very slow and, jumping was out of the question. He was just peering over the edge when the explosion came. Just as Jim's feet hit the bottom, his course was reversed, from down, to up. Before Jim made it back to earth, Old Blue had become un-restrained and made it to the far side of the house and under the porch.

We would never have heard of this sad story if Jim had been able to work next day. As it was, coal camps need all the excitement they can get and before the day was over, the entire camp could express sorrow for Old Blue.

SNAKE BITE

As for my personal experience with coal camps, my grandfather worked the mines near Man, West Virginia, during those same years. The miners were a tough breed of men and their wives had to be even tougher to survive the coal dust and difficult living conditions. I marvel at the toughness of granddad who, while picking blueberries on the mountain was bitten by a rattle snake on the left index finger. Knowing the distance to the house and the even greater distance to help, he had little choice. He used his pocket knife and cut off his finger before poison could enter the main blood stream. As he told the story, he was afraid of being bitten again so he placed his foot on the head of that snake until he had the time to cut off its head. That takes more nerve than I have ever had.

COMPANY PROPERTY

My grandparents lived in a company house that was made of plain sawed lumber with no insulation and with cracks that were open to the weather. The cure for the cracks was newspapers and cardboard glued to the walls. They never burned paper for it was needed as insulation. I remember being taken to see them when I was a child of about six or seven, about 1932. My mother's parents were tied to the coal mines, and, even though my parents were willing to help, they did not want to leave the mountains. Life was very hard during the late thirties and on into the late sixties. I was a young man at the time of my last visit to their home. Soon after that visit, both died and my relationship with miners ceased. Grandpa had a small place in the hill back of his house where coal was sticking out of the ground. He was very fortunate since the coal companies never gave a break to the men that worked for them.

They were even restricted from removing trees for firewood since the coal companies wanted everything the men earned to come back to them for necessities purchased at the company owned store.

The company theater was located across the dirt road from the company store, and, when I was a child, the price of admission was a dime in script, company money. If that was not available, the theatre would take anything that could be resold in the company store such as garden produce. My grandpa had a garden on the side of the mountain that, to this day, I don't know how he managed. He had no horse or mule, and, if he did, he would not have been able to use a plow up there. He did raise corn there, though, and I remember in 1937 that we children went to the Saturday show for the admission price of one ear of corn each. I realize today that he made a real sacrifice to give us the corn. It belonged on grandmother's table.

Another thing happened to my cousins because of the plentiful supply of explosives. Two of them brought explosives into the house one very warm fall evening. Grandpa always had the fireplace grate filled with kindling and coal for starting a fire with no more trouble than striking a match to the lowest part where fine shavings were placed. The two boys were sleeping in the bedroom where the fireplace was located, and when Grandpa got up, it was a very cold morning. He went to that room and lit the kindling. Shortly after he walked out of the room, there was an explosion that killed the cousin sleeping on the side next to the fireplace.

It turned out the boys had hidden the stolen powder in the fireplace.

THE OLDSMOBILE GHOST

This hunting trip took place in 1969, and I had moved to Huntsville, Alabama, where NASA was firing up for the race to the moon. Prior to this, I had been sent to Columbus, Ohio, where I met my hunting buddy of so many years. Fred Engle and I shared many hunting and fishing trips to the mountains of West Virginia. Although I had been born in that state, as had Fred, we loved to camp in the mountains and returned every chance we found. Work conditions moved us to other states and never allowed Fred to live in West Virginia again. As for me, I have returned to the place of my birth after seventy years.

We finally learned Eddie's last name to be Haynor. He was not much inclined to talk until he had a snort or two from the Mason jar he carried in his truck. We did learn by the end of the week that he made it himself, but only in small quantities. None of my party would consider sharing his brew and I think it was mostly because none of us really liked alcohol. At any rate, Eddie could be inclined to spin another tale when he had about three snorts of mountain spring water. No tale around a night time camp fire would be complete without spooks coming in to enjoy the warmth of a big blaze on a cold night. Eddie had this to say about strange happenings in the valley where he was a youth.

"When I was eight years old, my Mom n' Daddy lived up the holler in the last house. Then the holler was so narrow that our front porch needed about twenty steps from the ground up. Daddy could spit tobacco juice into the creek without leaning over the porch railin'. Momma planted climbing beans in front of the house and by fall, she could stand on the porch and pick beans off the vine tops. Now I mean to tell you that holler was so narrow the horse and buggy had to come up the middle of the creek for a road. We didn't have no buggy; in fact, we didn't have no horse. If we did, there was no grass for it up there. All we did have was trees and big rocks. All that held them big rocks from rollin down on us was them big trees.

I remember when the sawmill people came to take them big trees away, how sick I was to see our creek change. I remember when I could step in water so clear it looked like it was ankle deep but I would find that I was in till my bottom was wet.

"Now what I wanted to tell you was about the time when we was a settin' on the porch just before dark and we heard this thing a commin' up the creek road that sounded like a pop, pop, pop and a rattlin' like a wheelbarrow full of tin cans. It came up the creek, right to our front porch, then turned around and went a rattlin down the way it came.

We sat there for a long time a wonderin' what it could have been when Uncle Henry said he had heard down in the mine town that the super had bought an old contraption called a buggy with an engine in it. He thought it was called an Oldsmobile but, at any way, the super had started home with it from town. There bein' no roads except creeks and wagon trails on the side of the mountain where creeks wuz too narrow, he never made it home. A week later, word come that he had rolled that contraption down the mountain, tore it up, and killed his self. We learned later that the super had been driving all over the coal company property, just a seein, to the company holdings."

WEST VIRGINIA TIMBER

We could not quite believe Eddie's story but it did cause me to look into when big trees were cut in West Virginia. I was surprised to learn that one tree cut in Tucker County in 1913 was a white oak that measured thirteen feet in diameter and at sixteen feet above the ground. Ten men could stand side by side on the stump. Also, in Tucker county, yellow poplar trees stood higher than 120 feet, about the same as a 12-story building. One tree they cut was eighty feet to the first limb, and sawing provided 12,400 feet of lumber. At today's prices, that tree would have been worth about 31,000 dollars. I can't help but wonder what it took for mere man to move such massive logs to the mill. No circular saw of that time could have made lumber out of such a giant of a tree, but since the band saw was introduced to West Virginia in 1881, the forest was doomed.

When the first settlers arrived in this state around 1750 to 1800, it must have been a sight never to be seen again.

Trees were so large and so thick that it would be impossible to see more than a few hundred feet. Certainly, it would be impossible to see across the mountains and valleys in order to hold to a direction. Traveling had to be done by following streams and game trails. It is said that US Route 60 across the state is the original buffalo migration trail, kept open by the tens of thousands of animals moving west to east and back again. The area just east of Charleston and where US 60 passes through has very large salt deposits. This alone would be enough to lure the animals through this valley. History tells us that the rivers in this country were the roads to penetration of the wilderness. Oh, how I wish I could have seen the forest before man destroyed all of the virgin timber.

THE PANTHER

Eddie had another story for us the last night in camp. By this time he had the field-dressed and frozen carcasses of three deer. He was leaving right after breakfast Saturday morning, and, by this time, we had become fond of him and his mountain ways and sayings. We had even invited him to join our party the next year. He was about to run out of the Mason jar water and needed to go home for a refill, if nothing else. Eddie's last story.

"When I was about twelve years old, papa took me with him to a town across the mountain where things could be bought or traded in a store that was not owned by the coal company. Poppa had a gift for finding ginsang and yeller root. Both would bring a good price away from the company store. I remember the morning we left before daylight with Poppa, carrying a burlap sack over his shoulder, and me, a-carin-a' coal-oil lantern. Momma had fixed us a sack full of vittles so we could have plenty to eat that day. We would not get there till well after dark. I carried a goodly-sized load cause I had to carry a blanket for us to sleep under the next night. I wore it like a coat till it got warmer up in the day, then Poppa rolled it up to a small bundle and tied it across my shoulders. His burlap sack had to be heavy and a hard to carry 'cause it had two gallon jugs of something and lots of dried roots. The jugs were wrapped in skins Poppa had cured from coons and one from bobcat.

Poppa never went to the woods without his rifle ceptin' this trip. We wuz so burdened a goin' and a commin' that we couldn't carry it. That night I wuz so tired we curled up in a barn full of some man's hay and I think I died. Poppa brought me back to life before daylight the next day and before the store opened, we wuz a settin' on their porch. The last biscuits we had with us didn't do much to fill my empty spaces, and I wuz a hopen' Poppa had it in mind to buy some bacon or just anything we could eat in a hurry. I do remember he did a lot of tradin' before we could leave, and it must have been nearly noon and I was nearly starved to death before we got outta there. Poppa had got some cheese and dried apples, and I never forgot the sweet taste of them apples and the smooth cheese a runnin' down my tongue.

It was just after noon; I could tell by the sun a goin' west that it was. We started back up the mountains we had to cross on our way home. Poppa said if we hurry, we could be home afore midnight unless we got turned around. With the stars well out and not too many clouds, we could make it. All afternoon, we trudged up that mountain and the load on my back got to a growin' heaverier'n heaverier. Poppa said I wuz lookin at it from reverse. I wuz to think lighter'n lighter, and I did and it still got heaverier'n heaverier.

Long about dark, me n'Poppa stopped for a rest and some of that bacon he brung. We built a small fire and set two forked sticks in the ground on each side. Then we speared that thick bacon through with a bigger stick and laid it 'cross the fire where it could drip and smell up a hundred acres. I like to a died a waitin' on that bacon, but when it wuz about done, Poppa handed me a chunk of cheese and plopped a chunk of bacon on it and low and behold, I came back to livin again.

'Bout this time, it came full dark and we could see the stars. That big old north star shined like it wuz just for us and we headed across the ridges leading toward home. I had to carry the lantern and follow Poppa 'cause he didn't trust me to watch out for coppers and rattlin' snakes that came out at night. I wuz kinda glad I didn't have to watch out where my feet stumbled fer I wuz too tired to much care.

Well, anyway, long 'bout half-way home, I heard a noise behind me and when I looked back, there wuz them two, big, green eyes that looked to be about a foot apart. I almost dropped the lantern when I grabbed Poppa by the legs and caused him to drop his heavy sack of sugar, salt, and good eatin' stuff. When he looked back, he said that has to be the biggest panther in the whole country. Then I really got scared. Poppa picked up a tree limb and threw it at that panther and all it did was scream at us. We stood there for a time and poppa said he thought it was just curious and we better be a movin' on. Curious or not, I well remember the wet overalls I had to wear the rest of that night. I think it wuz the only time in my life when I lost control of my water. Poppa did let me walk in front for a time by telling' me every minute or so to watch out for the snakes. I didn't see any, but I did worry some which would be worse, snake bite or panther bite? That thing followed us till we almost got home and Poppa hoped it would follow us to the front door where he could get his shootin' gun. A panther hide that big would cover my bedroom floor, and I truly wanted that hide. I wanted to walk on that thing from now to eternity for scarin' me so bad."

Eddie left us the next morning with a promise to join us again next year. We looked for him the following year but he failed to show. By the time we broke camp and loaded everything for the return trip home, snow was starting to fall again, and, I must admit it was a comfort to pack everything before the snow really came down.

Ghost Dogs

Chapter 1

It was probably 1952 or '53 when I was sent to Richwood, West Virginia, to install x-ray equipment in their new hospital. I lived there for the month it took to finish the installation and then another week to teach its use. During this week, I learned to love the people and their way of life. Richwood then was a town built around the timber industry. The smell of wood smoke in the early morning while fog was still heavy on the river got to me in a way that I will always cherish. For the past 40+ years, I have returned to that area for what I like to call deer season. I have always had the privilege of taking a customer or friend with me and introducing him to what Richwood was like. As an example, for several years I would arrange to meet my party in Charleston and then drive on to deer camp. It was the practice several years back for coffee and donuts to be passed out beside the road to incoming hunters. Hotel reservations were set a year in advance and the town was in a festive mood. To this day, some of my friends from the 50's still return to that area when possible, either on vacation or to hunt during turkey or deer season. The number of deer or turkey have very little to do with the choice of most of us

We choose to hunt there for the same reasons noted above and for the wild beauty of the forest surrounding Richwood. I now have hanging over my door a very large horse shoe that I found deep in the woods the first year I hunted there in 1953. It was a handmade shoe and was very badly rusted. It had to have been lost there around the turn of the century or probably in the eighteen hundreds and must to have been made for a Clydesdale horse.

I don't have to guess for I just measured it as six and one half inches wide by seven inches long. Those beautiful animals were used when virgin timber was taken from that area and pictures prove some of the trees were large enough for three men to stand in the first cut.It took the most powerful horses available to work those logs out, and I am a great admirer of the animals used as the Budweiser commercials show them. In remembrance of the first hunt there, I have had that shoe treated for removal of all rust and it is now silver plated.

About 1970, I had a party of four from Ohio, Texas, Alabama and I was there from Tennessee. We were ham radio operators and had brought a radio and generator to use in our tent on Bear Mountain. You have to understand that hams got the name HAM due to the love of talking and this was a perfect time. Our radio seldom got a rest because while there we communicated with friends all over the south and made some new ones in other parts of the world. Hunting consisted of probably an hour each morning and the rest of the day, eat, sleep and hunt for new radio contacts. As I said, we do not really hunt for deer, we hunt for seclusion and camping in the mountains around Richwood is the perfect place

It was on this trip that we got to know the Alabama dog lover, Ken. He was a story teller that never seemed to run out of words and the one that hogged the radio. One story he told sticks out above all others and I will try to give it to you as he told it.

"As you guys know, Alabama has its mountains and rural areas not much different than here. Just twenty miles out of Huntsville at a place called Gurley, the mountain range starts, and believe me, it has its share of moonshine stills and places where you can get lost, forever. I know of a place where you could fall off the edge and fall for so long that your buddy would not hear your body hit the bottom. Those mountains are riddled with limestone caves and holes in the earth. It is told that the ghost of murdered people roam those woods and that some animals have fallen in there and their ghost is part of the pack that roam with them. Now I don't want to stretch the truth for the straight truth is much better than fiction, so I will tell you exactly what happened the day I went to a friend's still for a gallon of reprocessed water.

I have heard the reprocessed water from the state of West Virginia is second to none and I will admit it is good for gout, arthritis and lumbago. It even helps the meek to speak up and say what is on the mind. Hey, Mac, pass me that jug. I need to refresh my memory.

As I was saying, I went to the mountain for another jug and at that time, I had my dog Phiado with me. Now my dog was not much for hunting but he was a mean SOB and one I wanted to be by my side when we visited this neck of the woods. He would tackle the Devil's beast if it looked like it wanted to hurt me. Well, I got deep in the woods when Phiado started to growl and when I looked at him, I could see his hair standing up and his lips retracted to show those deadly teeth. Looking in the same direction as Phiado did, I could see nothing so now my hair was beginning to stand out. It became much worse when I saw Phiado begin to circle around something that I did not see. Just then, it would have been possible to run, to climb a tree or to do something, but I didn't know which way to run.

Right then, Phiado tangled with something that seemed to be larger than he was; and then I saw he was taking a beating. Teeth marks were appearing on his neck and shoulders and blood was beginning to flow. I don't mind telling you, something else was flowing down my leg and I still didn't know which way to run. I had no idea what to do to help Phiado since I could see nothing except that he was almost done in. I just stood there and watched my sweet old dog pass away. In his dying quivers, I felt something pulling on the leg of my jeans. I looked down and could see the jeans leg being pulled as if a dog had a bite just below my knee and was pulling me away from my Phiado. RUN? Impossible! Fear had me by the throat and my bowels were locked up for the next thirty days.

Seems like I didn't have no choice but to go where that "thing" was a pullin' me.

I took off a walkin' and that thing would pull on one leg or t'other to guide me.

Purty soon I come into this place by the crek when a man stepped out with a greeting, "Howdy mister, looks like Buster brung me another customer." With that, he leaned over and, in a motion, I took to be a pettin' a dog's head, he said, Thanke Buster and then he produced a wiener and held it out---it disappeared without a sound.

Over the next few minutes, I got control of my bowels and my voice. That old man was

generous with samples of his product and when I was thoroughly doctored, he told me about Buster. "Gimme that jug again, I have a dry mouth.-----Thankye!"

He said that Buster was the son of Willie and Bettie.

Seems he was in Africa during the big war when he was on scouting duty with another soldier. He, being corporal Adam Crosley, and Private Lewis with him were miles from their base and were lost in their third day of wandering. They were about out of food and had little knowledge of how to live off the land. They had a compass but for some reason, neither had any idea which way to point it for their base camp. In their wanderings, they had to dodge Japs as well as swamp areas where they might get eaten by alligators or other jungle animals. By this time, their captain would have notified headquarters of MIA or missing in action. Certainly no one would be looking for them. They were moving as quietly as possible through the jungle when they heard Japs shouting as if they did not fear being overheard. Crawling through the tangled undergrowth toward the noise, they came up on a clearing in which twenty-one people were lined up before a firing squad of Jap soldiers. Seeing the need to move fast, the two of them ran screaming into the clearing with automatic weapons chattering. In the attack, his buddy was killed but all of the Japs were finished. Of course, he was adopted at once, fed and served in every way possible. Being lost and also being treated like a king, he decided to stay lost until the war was over. He didn't like the idea of going back to where he thought his company was since he didn't know even the direction to start. Right away he was led to a grass lean-to and several young woman started to undress him for the ritual of adoption into their tribe.

During his long stay there, he saw the unusual actions of something being fed, food disappearing without a sight or sound, just food gone. As difficult as it was, he soon learned the word for food, and after a year there, he had learned the language of these generous people so he got up the nerve to ask the village elder about that strange action.

It took some prodding but eventually he learned of the Ghost Dogs. Then he learned the tribe had been in possession of them for ages past, handed down through the ages, to be protected and never be allowed to trade or sell them. By this time, he had become aware of the presence of one, even though he could not see it. Just stick out his hand and he could feel the dog and pet its head. It seemed he had been adopted by more than the tribe. This dog had also adopted him. From then on, he lost his fear of being alone in the jungle which was all around him. He could always stick out his hand and the dog would be there. He had come to understand that his dog understood the spoken word so long as it was in the native tongue, but for some reason, he wanted the dog to understand English. He supposed it was because he was lonesome for someone to talk with in his own language.

Before many months had passed, he could speak to the dog in English and know he was understood. He became bolder in wandering through the jungle and since he had a good and serviceable automatic rifle, he could hunt without fear of any animal he might encounter. He named the dog BO, as he thought it was short for brother and this dog had become a brother and a companion to him.

He had also picked up an admirer in one of the first young women who had helped undress him. Possibly she had been ordered to accompany him but it made no difference to him. She was good company and with her, they wandered further and further from their home.

One day a messenger came to tell the tribe that the Japs were gone and the American soldiers were loading ships to leave forever. Then Adam knew it was time to leave his friends who had cared for him for the past three years. He had nothing to give them except his well-worn knife and bayonet, but giving with love and thanks, he did. In return, the elder gave him the greatest gift of all. He was given a male and a female pup. He was also told the dogs had a life span of at least twenty years, so he would never be without a companion. He just had to promise to care for them and be certain the breed did not become spread all over the world. The elder had him place his hands out to where he was touching the two pups and a bond was made that would last forever. Although he could feel their soft fur in his hands, he could not see them, but there was a warm and vibrating feeling in his heart. A life long bond was sealed and it was time to leave.

Catching the last ship to leave for America, he was well aware of the presence of his new companions but, apparently, no one else was. He had assigned names to the dogs, the male he called "Weinie" because this dog could dispatch a wiener in one gulp. The female he called "Bunns" because buns go with hot dogs. Weinie was like most other friendly dogs. He liked to place his front paws on Adam in greeting. Bunns was more likely to take his hand in her mouth and just hold it for comfort. Both were loving companions.

His major problem on the passage home was in the care and feeding of his charges. There was so much joy and confusion in going home after the war that none noticed his sometimes strange actions.

Back home in Alabama was wonderful after being gone for almost five years. Home to him was the mountains where coal used to be mined and was now abandoned. This mountain range was remote enough to remind him of his friends back in Africa and also great for his companion Ghost Dogs. But there was no way to make a living since all he ever did was soldier and loaf. The answer of course was in good moonshine. He had learned how to make a special kind of brew while he lived with the tribe in Africa and it was just a start to doing it well in Alabama.

Adam was now well trained in the art of living off the land. Deer and other game were plentiful in his chosen mountain home so he had it made. Huntsville, and later Birmingham, were both prime for the sale of his product and best of all, his ghost dogs were good at protecting him and bringing him customers. Adam had been living here for twenty years and had made a good home for himself and his dogs. His rare trips to town were to take a few gallons of reprocessed water to special buyers and to pick up a few supplies. While in Birmingham, he would stay with his widowed and overweight sister who lived in a very high crime area of the city. It was then he decided to introduce Sis to the breed and give her Little Bunns for her protection. Now Sis had never been a dog lover but after being introduced to this lovable dog, she became one.

It was not too long before she found just how useful "Little Bunns" could be.

The dog missed the mountain retreat Adam called home but with love from Sis, she soon became used to the city. One evening as she was nearing bed time, two young men broke in her back door, demanding money. Little

Bunns was quick to take action and the two left so quickly, the door was bypassed in favor of diving out the still closed window. One left the rear end of his jeans behind and both lost control of bowels. Sis was never troubled again for word got out quickly, that that woman was a witch. She delighted in taking Little Bunns downtown on the city bus since she could take her anywhere dogs were not permitted. Feeding her at the "ALL UCN EAT" cafeteria was a delight to both of them. Sis was endowed with a more than ample baggage on her behind and sometimes had trouble climbing the steps onto the bus. Local folks still wonder why she got half way on and looking behind herself and said, "Come on Little Bunns, time to go home."

Ken was obviously running out of steam and we wanted to know the rest of the story so Fred handed him the jug. Ken continued telling his story and we were wondering if he ever had the chance to own one of those ghost dogs.

Ken continued. "On the way back to his mountain home, Adam had a similar experience in Huntsville when he was standing in line to board the bus to Gurley. Just outside the local bus station a group of scantily clad girls passed and his dog, Weinie, was acting like he wanted to make friends with one of them. Other passengers were startled when Adam looked down and said, "Behave yourself Weinie."

Back on the mountain, Adam continued the exacting efforts to make better shine.The last time I visited him it was for my yearly supply. His first two dogs were gone to the happy hunting grounds and Adam was becoming feeble. He was surrounded by several happy ghost dogs which Adam loved and cared for as best he could. Even though I wanted to take some of them to friends in Huntsville and Birmingham, Adam would not let me have them. I told him he might not make it through another winter and asked what about the welfare of the dogs. His answer was that for the past few months, he realized he might not live much longer and that he had been teaching the dogs to hunt for themselves.

It was good that he did so since that last time I went to the mountain, Adam was gone. His ghost dogs were around and I could sense them but they did not come to me when I called. It appears they have gone wild and that ends the story of Adam's retreat and his dogs. I suppose they are still there but are not friendly to people any more.

No doubt they have taken up with all of the other ghosts that roam those mountains.

Chapter 2

Several years have passed and now I am completely alone in this world. I have lost my wife and, for the most part, I have been deserted by all that I thought cared for me. Perhaps it is that I no longer have money or the promise of wealth that makes me an undesirable. No one wants to take on the burden of an old man who is beginning to show signs of frailty and who might become a responsibility in the near future. With money and greed combined most older people can find someone who will say, "I love you" and will make at least a halfhearted effort to care for the elderly.

Having reached the point I just described, I started remembering the one love I had that was unconditional here on earth. That was the dogs, Bunns and Weinie, who never asked for more than to be beside me and never seemed to care when I was unable to give them much more than a cold biscuit. Now, I do not doubt the love of my wife, not even for a second of her busy life. We had many wonderful years together and now that I am seventy and alone, I realize just how much she cared for me. I was not very lovable for most of my life because I had very stressful work and I took it home with me. As I look back over the years, I wonder why she did not leave me at some point when I was at my worst. Certainly she was blessed with looks and personality that would have allowed her to choose a better husband than I have been.

Sometimes I remember with regret the sales meetings I had to attend in foreign countries where I could have taken her along and did not. She would want to go but I found reasons to leave her behind simply because there were places I wanted to see that she would not. I liked to tour, places that made military equipment such as guns and heavy equipment. These were men's tours and she would have refused to accompany me so I would have to forego these places in favor of perhaps a garment factory. I had a great fear of leaving her alone in another country, even for an hour or so. Her presence when I did factory tours of my principals was different in that I had to go and she was always willing to stand by my side even when it held no interest whatsoever to her.

It is well over five hundred miles back to the mountain where I last felt the presence of ghost dogs but not so far as to discourage me on my endeavor to be among them again. I determined to find another dog or dogs that I might become friends with, those being offspring of Weinie and Bunns.

At my age and condition, no one would miss me if I left and never returned so I made the arrangements to leave forever. I sold my little cottage and gave my old furniture to the Salvation Army. I traded my car for an older four wheel drive pick-up truck which would become my home for the foreseeable future. On this, I bought and had installed an older camper top that would do for an old man to finish his life in. To complete my gear, I added a rifle, axe, shovel and as many basic food items as I could think of. Mostly I bought survival food boxes with unsavory dry beans, carrots, potatoes and whatever else that could be dried and stored. The only items that were in cans was dog food and I bought a very large amount of that. To supplement it, I added several containers of sealed, dried dog food. Containers for cooking and holding a small supply of water completed my arrangements for an extended stay on Coal Mine Mountain in Alabama.

Two days on the road and I was there at the base of Coal Mine Mountain and then I discovered the road was not as good as I remembered it. In years past, the road had been used by timber companies and was originally built by the company that tried to open a successful mine. The coal was inferior so it failed. Timber lasted only so long then it was gone. Now the road was used only by hunters and sometimes by recreational vehicles which left it barely usable for my truck. I cared little if I never got out but I was determined to get in. It took two days of slowly dodging ruts and large rocks that magically appear when the road is left to return to nature. Late in the evening of the second day, I found the site of the old camp and whiskey still that Ken had described so well. It was well marked by some aluminum pans still hanging from tree branches, just as Ken had said.

There was no sign that any man had been here for years and this was very much to my liking. I managed to back my truck into a thicket where it was not too easily seen in case a hunter did wander into the area. Setting up camp was easy this first night since all I had to do was open the back door of my camper and go to bed. But first, I had to build a small fire to heat food I had bought in town just before I left the main road through this valley. It was to be the last food I had before I had to start cooking for myself. I quickly dispatched the reheated cold hamburgers and soggy French fries to their intended place, made a cup of hot tea and hit the bed

I found I was unable to sleep because of the excitement of being where I knew there was some very lovable dogs around my camp. Come morning, I planned to warm a can of the best dog food so it would release a good doggie odor, then place it some distance from my camp so as to lure the dogs in. I wanted to know if they were still there but I felt they would not approach the food so long as I was watching. All I could do was leave it there and check the flat rock tomorrow. I did not use any of the pans still left there for fear they might avoid even those. After I set out the food the next morning, I waited until dusk before checking and finding the food gone. This time I placed the food in a pan from one of the tree limbs and left it for the night. During that first day, I had spent my time being as quiet as possible while setting up camp. I had a bow saw which allowed me to cut small trees and use them for tables and benches. Being a good furniture maker, I knew how to make locking joints that required no nails, so my tables were a cinch to make. To get the most stability, I placed them between two trees. I suppose I needed only one work table but as I got into it, I found much enjoyment in my work and continued to build work space.

Now that I knew something was taking the food, I had to wonder if it could be another animal such as a raccoon. They are notable as thieves and dog food would certainly be appealing. I dared not set any form of trap, so it became necessary for me to move the feeding place close enough for me to watch it during the day and possibly hear a night time visitor. This went on for five days and nights and I never saw the food disappear nor did I see a raccoon. It could only mean that the ghost dogs were here and silently taking the food. I was overjoyed at the prospect of having them that close and I determined to move the food closer and closer to my camp every time I placed a new serving out. By the tenth day, I had moved the pan to the outer edge of what I called my compound. Reverting back to my army days, this meant the area where I was determined to defend at the cost of my life.

I began to wonder if the dogs were afraid of me because I never showed myself as being vulnerable. I think everyone has seen the actions of a dog that wishes to show its self at the mercy of another, larger dog. The subservient animal will lie on its back and expose its throat and belly to the dominate dog, thereby showing trust and obedience, if necessary. I had shown the opposite by closing my door at night for protection against whatever might harm me as I slept. This understanding led me to construct a shed at the outer edge of my compound, one that would protect me from rain if it should occur during the night. Under this, I made a bed of poles very close to the ground and covered it with grass I could gather from the open areas I found in the heavy woods. It took much searching and gathering but I did finally have a comfortable bed outside.

By this time, I had become accustomed to talking to the dogs as if they were my friends, which they were. I had to wonder if there could be one or more of them that would remember Adam, the man they loved and who passed on some time back. I had to also wonder what had become of his remains. Would I someday be in the same position of death and no one to see to my proper burial? Well, no matter. I cared little about my remains for I was a firm believer that God said he would gather the dead from the dust of the earth and we would live again as flesh in the Heaven he has prepared for those that love him. He said I would have a new body and that is enough for me.

In just a few short weeks, the dogs were eating food I left out for them within my compound. I was sleeping very well under the shed roof and the first rain I had proved that I had learned my military lessons well. It did not leak through the stripped bark I had made my roof. The poplar tree gives up its bark quite easily during the spring months as it was now. I was careful to pull the bark only from a tree I intended to use later, either for fire wood or to split for table wood. Poplar makes very poor fire wood but it is usually easy to split for making boards or benches. One fairly large tree cut into eight foot sections made the perfect roof shingles and also were the perfect length for a table. One tree also provided enough bark for me to have a solid roof since I could cut it into three lengths of eight foot each.

I had no way of knowing how many dogs there were except that now I was supplying dry dog food and they seemed to love it and consume a very large amount. What would I do when I ran out? I don't want to face that just yet because I did bring several hundred pounds of dry food. It was a certainty that I could kill deer and cook it for them and for myself. The woods was overrun with them and I suspect that was what the dogs had been living on since Adam had left. Even so, the change to prepared dog food must have been a welcome treat for them and it would be another to get cooked venison.

Now as I go to my bed at dusk, I may be imagining it but I think I hear the dogs breathing beside me. It is a comfort to think they are near me while I sleep and I do hope one day soon I will be able to reach out and touch one of them.

It is worth note that the ridge line I am on is the lower end of the Appalachian mountain chain. From my location, it is approximately thirty miles northeast as the crow flies before coming to a road that crosses this mountain chain. To the southwest, it is just a little shorter distance but very rugged. I doubt there will be any sign of visitors until next November when deer season is open again. Even then, it is not too likely because deer are located in much easier terrain to hunt. It could be years before this compound sees another human and the dogs are quite safe from accidental shooting or trapping.

The one and only thing I feared about this venture was sickness. I had brought a good supply of emergency bandages and salves, three different kinds of heating rub for sore muscles and bones, laxatives, iodine, bandages, prescription pain medication such as Hydrocodone and a few other items I thought I might need. I was very careful not to cut myself with the axe or the knife but being careful could not avoid some internal sickness that I could not even diagnose much less treat. Just as I feared, that kind of sickness came to me one morning as I was still half asleep on my outdoor cot. I had to hurry to empty my bowels and my stomach, both at the same time. I had a splitting headache that even a double dose of Hydrocodone would not temper. I tried drinking lots of water but it immediately came back up and left me with the fear of inhaling it into my lungs and from that develop pneumonia. I was far too sick to feed the dogs and even to work my way into the truck camper was out of the question. As I mentioned earlier, I am not afraid of dying for I know I am going to a better place, a place where I am loved and not for money or what I can do for someone. I lay there all day and well into the night before I could get up for more water. This time I took very small sips, just enough to get another pain pill down. I am not certain about the next few hours because I do believe I was unconscious rather than sleeping. My body was wet from top to the end of my toes and I was chilling to the point of a violent shiver. I had a very thin cover to pull over me because it had been a wonderful season with warm nights and no need for covers. Now I needed something but was unable to crawl to the camper much less to get up the steps and inside it. Sometime during the night I remember the feel of a rough cloth across my forehead and only a fleeting thought of, who is it? Much later I felt a warm blanket laid across my body and from then on, I believe I was sleeping instead of being unconscious.

Another day passed and I was still unable to get up and still was not aware of who my savior was that laid the warm blanket over me. I know I was delirious because I was talking to my wife, and getting no answer. I suppose I was angry at her but I have no remembrance of raising my voice at her for I loved her too much for that. It seemed she was telling me to get up and prepare food for her and, of course, it was never like that. She was always doing for me and never asking for anything in return.

Well into the second night, I began to feel a little better and discovered the blanket had been removed. My nurse must have taken my temperature and decided I no longer needed it. While I was lying there and wondering who had taken care of me and if they were in my camper bed or where they could be, I decided to stay where I was and remain as quiet as possible.

It was so dark that I could not see my hand before my face and I had no way of making a fire light and no other way of seeing, I felt at peace just lying there and resting.

It was at that time when I felt the rough cloth pass over the back of my hand, not once but three times. Then I realized it was the tongue of one of the ghost dogs. Had I not been so weak, I would have shouted for joy. To think that my nurse was the very thing I had come here for and it had found me too sick to respond. But with some inner strength, I raised my hand and lowered it to the top of that dog's head. Words failed me. Joy filled my very soul and I wanted so desperately to take that creature in my arms and tell it how much I loved it.

It was total darkness, and I could see nothing, but, never mind, the dog was invisible any way.I now believe it was better that way for I could use my hands to see with and the dog seemed to enjoy being felt all over. I had to know what it looked like and for the first time in my life, I understood the nature of a blind person seeing with his fingers. First I gave the dog's head a good examination and determined he would stand about knee height to me and that he had massive jaws, not like a bulldog but more like a German police dog. He had very tall and straight ears that stood straight up. These reminded me of the pictures I have seen of the wild dogs of Africa, and, I suppose, he could have had that kind of blood since that is where his ancestors came from. As I continued to pet him and feel all over his body I found that he was covered in a rather coarse hair that was not quite like what we find on dogs such as the Jack Russell but more like that found on a horse in winter time. His feet were enormous compared to the rest of his body and he had very strong leg muscles. His tail was not real long but neither would it be described as short. All in all, I would describe him as a very stocky-built dog such as a bulldog but nothing like the head and nose of that breed.

By the time I had petted him and examined him all over, he was sitting on the ground as close to my bed as he could get. When I had no more strength to sit up, I lay back and he immediately laid his head across my chest. Now I realize the blanket that was placed over me in my worst hour was the body of this or another dog. I would venture to say that two dogs lay with me, one on either side and I do believe they were my salvation. What a wonderful feeling to have found such a friend in the wilds of north Alabama.

By late that evening, I was up and feeling very well, also starved as I believe my friend was. Now I had a way to find out if there was more than one dog and I really wanted to know if there were more and if so, how many? I got busy with a fire and began cooking some of the dried food for myself. While doing this, I opened four of the canned food and placed them where they would get very warm but not hot--Just enough to smell delicious. Next, I placed each can in a different dish so I could put them down in different places. I knew this would have to be fast because the dominant dog would eat the first one like lightning and quickly move on to the second dish. I certainly did not want to scold him so the others could eat but I must work fast if I was to find a count from this.

I placed the dishes as far apart as I could without throwing them and watched the first dish disappear almost at once. The second dish was beginning to disappear when it was a certainty that the dominate dog was there to claim it. Now I saw in very rapid succession, all four dishes were emptied, and then I watched as all four were being licked clean at the same time. There was no doubt, I had four friends.

Over the next few days, I took care to have feed in both hands, one on each side of my body so two dogs could eat at the same time. Then I moved to pet the second dog and was successful to the point that I now knew she was a she. No matter how hard I tried, I never got to pet the last two dogs as I did the one I called Adam, in remembrance of the man who first brought this breed to our country. Of course, that meant the female had to be Eve. As I petted and felt all over her body. It became apparent to me that she was with pups which made me glad. Just why I was happy about that I can't say but I suppose I had become a great admirer of the two that I know saved my life and I hoped they would be happy with a new family.

Many days passed and we were in mid-summer when it should be hot weather but it was very pleasant. I had no thermometer but I guessed the temperature to be in the mid-seventies since I was almost on top of the highest mountain around north Alabama. I loved it here and I believe the dogs really enjoyed my company because they were always within my reach. Although I had a lot of time to move down to lower ground before winter, I never made any arrangements to do anything except to shore up my shed with two sides and a back. Winters here can get below zero and I have seen four inches of snow in down town Huntsville. I suppose it could get as much as twenty degrees colder up here on the mountain but I had plenty of fire wood and food to do me for at least a year. One thing I did without thinking of it as winter shelter was to build a circular stone place for my fire. The abandon coal mine had left lots of flat slate and rock at the old mine entrance and it was not very far from where I had set up my camp. I could get my exercise by carrying stone up to my camp. I did realize there was a great danger in allowing a fire to get out of control in the dry months of fall, so I made the stone walls just a little higher than my head and about eight feet across. I left a very narrow door and made a heavy pole gate to keep the wind from pulling firebrands out into the woods. It did work out well right away because I could bank a fire in there and it would burn for many hours. That saved me the trouble of starting a new one every morning.

Then there was a bonus from a bed of coals. I would place my only iron pot in the red ashes with a hand full of dry beans and the slow cooker made the best meal I could have on a rainy day. With nothing much to do except build something around camp, I decided to build another shed roof over the stone room. I had to make it high enough that fire would not reach up and start one that I didn't want. It also had to be high enough to let smoke rise freely so the room below would stay dry and comfortable without the choking smoke any fire will sometimes make. During the fall and early winter months, this place became my outside home when weather was less that good. In fact, I found the dogs would come in with me if the fire had burned down to red ashes. If it blazed up, I could hear their movement out of there quickly. I know the round pile of rock did not meet building code but it was strong enough to withstand anything short of an earthquake. I did consider the fact that my fire at night could be as much as I wanted for it could not be seen through bare trees during the fall.

As the colder days of fall came and trees began to shed their leaves, I delighted in the colors that were all mine. I was living in a dreamland of beauty and had the most lovable companions available to man. Eve had not placed her head in my lap for some time and I began to wonder if she was all right. I guessed she had left the compound for delivery of her family but she should have returned some time back. There was nothing I could do except wait and hope. There was something peculiar about these dogs in that they never made a sound except as a warning to an intruder. I had noticed the lack of other animals and assumed the dogs kept them at bay, but I never heard a sound until afternoon when I was relaxed in what I called my recliner, a pole bed made to slant upward about forty degrees. This was my favorite place to take twenty winks, a nap that is. The foot of it was on the ground and the head was almost waist high, just enough to make me relax. I was about to nod off into dreamland when Eve dropped a little ball of fur on my stomach. It was making a mewing sound much like a small cat and when I picked it up, it became totally silent. Momma had already trained it to keep silent. I held that little thing under my chin and talked to it as if it were a small child and was already fully trained. What a joy, to be trusted with the son of Eve. Well, not only the son for she returned almost at once and dropped another one on me, then two more to be exact. I felt like a grandfather holding my own, the first from my daughter and I loved every moment of it.

Then cold weather came like a roaring giant out of the north. I was so glad that I had spent the time to construct the round room for holding my fire within safe walls for it turned out to be my salvation. The storm was so unexpected that I had little time to bring in enough wood to keep the fire going over the next three days. I had plenty of wood cut but it was covered with snow and not very close to my shelter.

It was also necessary to bring in water and some food from my truck. Some that would freeze and ruin which I never gave a thought to until it was too late. I managed to feed the dogs but not near enough for them to weather the storm and certainly not enough for eve that was still feeding the pups. I did invite her in by taking an armload of them and bringing them into the shelter but Eve did not follow. I suppose she had wintered this area before and had prepared a den close by where they would all make it through without my help.I heard and felt no more of them for several days.

As the weather cleared and some warming took place, I tried to make some improvements to my place I now called home. There was little I could do as it was still too cold to work outside and like the greenhorn I was, I had brought no clothing suitable for this kind of weather. Alabama? I never gave a thought to a blizzard and zero weather this far south so now I was in a predicament that made it apparent I needed to get out and buy more clothes.

I had not started my truck since last spring and that was another drastic mistake. I did give it a try but found a dead battery and there was no way but to walk out. Perhaps it would be best to stay here until some really warm weather came, at least enough for the battery to regain some semblance of life and the engine would not be so stiff with cold.

It was far too cold to use the camper now so I moved some necessities into my round house, including my typewriter and writing material. I had to keep the fire going and as I would occasionally go to the wood pile, I would see some tracks in the snow telling me the dogs were here, at least two of them. No doubt, they would all den together and only the hunters would venture out in search of food. If only people were as caring for each other as those dogs were for their family, the world would be a better place.

I thought my troubles would be over with warmer weather but the heat wave I longed for never came. I had kept track of the weeks and days to the point that I knew it was the first week of February when I developed this deep chest congestion. It never had warmed up enough for the truck battery to do more than click the starter. It was dead and, therefore, my truck was just as dead. I had given up hope of going into town and was glad I had constructed a bed well above the ground in my house. With a very small fire and the limited blankets I had brought with me, I managed to stay very comfortable. My time was spent in writing and sleeping and I had almost stopped eating. Even drinking water was not to my liking which brought on constipation and more pain in my chest. I would gather enough strength to carry in a few loads of wood then, I would fall to my bed exhausted. Try as I might, I found it more difficult to write and chose to spend more time in my bed. The wood pile is so far away I would take in only one load -- and then---No one was close enough to hear the dogs howl a long and lonesome farewell.

Grandma Casey At the Race

Now as deer camp goes, stories are usually about previous hunts or fishing trips. Sometimes they are about sports, but, since some of us do not follow ball games, golf, football and baseball are rarely mentioned. During my years as an independent salesman, I learned to despise ballgame talk simply because it took so much of my valuable time. Neither did I like auto races, but fast cars come up in campfire tales quite often since they are much in demand for the transportation of liquid lightning. The same stuff seems to appear at every hunting camp I have ever attended. It is lovingly referred to as Poppas well water and carried in Mason fruit jars.

From all I have been able to learn, it is mostly available in the mountains of West Virginia and Kentucky, primarily in the coal fields. I suppose it has something to do with the water found in mountain streams.

Fast cars are used to transport a few gallons at a time from somewhere in the mountains down to Atlanta or over to Charlotte. I know very little about this since I never see it or hear about it except in deer camp.

What I do know about fast cars and Mason jar water is that organized crime really took hold in America when

Prohibition took effect with the VOLSTEAD ACT of October 28, 1919. President Wilson vetoed that bill but the House of Representatives and the Senate voted to override the veto. So the 18th Amendment took effect on January 17, 1920. The Volstead Act covered all intoxicating liquors making it illegal to manufacture liquor but not the use of it. Crime came into the picture when liquor was used but not taxed. Organized crime filled the desire of the American public for the next twelve years. During this time it became necessary for the runners of illegal liquor to move faster than the local sheriff and also to haul a paying load. Consequently, 1920/1932 Fords were overhauled with heavy springs and undercarriages and then with high horsepower engines. By keeping the cars normal looking they hoped to slip a load of liquor past the law, but if not, they hoped to outrun them. Then in 1933, the 21st Amendment ended the Volstead Act which was the only instance of an Amendment's repeal.

In August of 1932, Herbert Hoover spoke to the American public pertaining to the 18th Amendment. Excerpts from this speech-

Mr. Chairman and my fellow citizens,

We must recognize the difficulties which have developed in making the 18th Amendment effective and that grave abuses have grown up. In order to secure the enforcement of the Amendment under our dual form of government, the constitutional provision called for concurrent action on one hand by the state and local authorities, and on the other by the Federal Government. Its enforcement requires, therefore, independent but coincident action of both agencies. An increasing number of states and municipalities are proving themselves unwilling to engage in that enforcement. Due to these forces there is in large sections increasing illegal traffic in liquor. But worse than this there has been in those areas a spread of disrespect not only for this law but for all laws, grave dangers of practical nullification of the constitution, an increase in subsidized crime and violence. I cannot consent to a continuation of that regime.

Now deer camp is no place to argue on the legality of liquor but it is a place to discuss what happened to almost destroy our nation. The crash of our stock market in 1929 was somewhat blamed on the liquor trade but many world factors had to be considered. That is history that has no bearing on fast cars. But what I wanted to bring out was that those years were somewhat related to fast cars and baseball.

A Ballad of the Republic "CASEY AT THE BAT" was written in 1888. Ernest Thayer wrote it for the San Francisco Examiner and it was later popularized by DeWolfe Hopper in many vaudeville performances. Thayer wrote 13 verses about the fictional town and baseball team of MUDVILLE and their star player, Casey. He was known as The Mighty Casey for his ability to bat the winning game. In the poem of 13 verses, Casey was to bat the last and winning run. He was so certain of his ability, he let the first two balls pass without a care and intended to bat number three out of the ball park. Now I give you the last, number thirteen verse----

Oh, somewhere in this favored land the sun is shining bright;
The band is playing somewhere, and somewhere hearts are light,
And somewhere men are laughing, and somewhere children shout;
But there is no joy in Mudville---mighty Casey has struck out.

I doubt that there has been a parody of this poem done relating to prohibition and race cars before my effort to do so, but I have made the effort to eulogize Grandma Casey in my parody.

I believe you may now see why the race car industry came into being. With all of those fast cars around and no great need for them after the repeal, it was only natural for the owners to engage in racing for sport. Well, that's my version and the one I presented at my turn for a story around the campfire.

GRANDMA CASEY AT THE RACE

Bernie McMellon

Grandma had a dream so wild
Ever since she was a child
To drive a car in a mighty race,
On oval track or any place.

The roar of engines filled her ears,
The flag is out and start time nears.
Smoke and dust roll across the track
And every Ford is painted black.

The young girl stood, entranced by all,
From this first race, she felt the call.
While still young and a freckled youth,
Grandma discovered a profound truth.

Her goal in life would someday be,
a race car driver for all to see.

Now years have flown, Grandma can attest
as she sits in her rocker, just takin' a rest.
But her goal in life is still the same
Even though age has made her lame.
5
Maybe now I should tell you my well-known name.
I'm Buckwheat Jones of race car fame.
So when my crew gathers at the race,
My Grandma takes her front row place.

Now the story goes on to last Saturday's date
When Grandma arranged for me to be late.
So in padded suit and with helmet in place,
The driver's last call put her in my place.

Grandma's joy was near complete,
With the pedal to the metal, she did compete.
Around and around the five mile track
While car after car began to fall back.

For fifty years she had studied race car winners
And watched them eradicate most beginners.
Grandma was an expert on tricks of the trade,
If her engine would hold, she had it made.

With smoking tires and a one-car lead,
Grandma pushed for higher speed.
"Eat my dust she screamed with glee."
The fans were standing, the better to see.

Now Grandma knew the tricks of the race
And she wanted more than just first place.
But her hearing had suffered with old age
And fate was about to turn a page.

One half a lap was still to go
When Grandma's engine had to blow.
All she could do was steer straight and pray,
Perhaps she could coast and save the day.

Car number two caused the lead to diminish
And nose to nose they crossed the finish.
If she had won, there was some doubt,
but----Grandma Casey had struck out.

BUT WAIT, there was confusion on the track.
The judges called---run the camera back.
Car number two had come up fast
But the camera had proven---it came in last.

As you can see, Grandma Casey did win the race, unlike her cousin, The Mighty Casey who lost the game. I just could not see her losing that race after so many years planning for it. It's my soft heart.

Perhaps I should tell you that I have only attended one 500-mile race and at that time, I took a sworn oath never to do it again. It was a very hot day in Daytona, Florida and I did not have a shaded place to rest my buns. By the time 200 miles had been done, I was done---cooked as well as finished. I wanted to leave but my ride said no, there could possibly be a wreck and we would miss it. I gathered from that statement, all he wanted to see was a wreck and blood on the track. From the excitement of a minor fender bender, I believe this covered most of the fans.

Murder by Proxy

Grace had been on trial and fighting for her life for the past three days. Now the jury was out and all she could do was pray that her life would be spared. She recognized that she was guilty of the most heinous crime a woman had ever committed. While she was setting where the accused sat at the court table with her attorney, she could look over her shoulder and see her husband of twelve years, Lonnie Hutchins. She could not help but wonder if he was really on her side or was he there for show? It was also a fact that he had been investigated thoroughly by the detectives in hopes of finding another woman in his life, hopes that they could implicate him in the murder. Not so, he came up so clean he could have been a saint. Not even a parking ticket, no flirtations at the office, nothing. She was into this murder all on her own.

Gracie's parents were very wealthy due to having oil wells on their Texas property and because they hated to spend it. Grace was just as they were, stingy to the core, but now she had to spend it on attorneys. She was losing the battle and Lonnie still sat near the front of the court room but with very little emotion on his face. That expression, or the lack of one made Grace even more certain that something was rotten in Denmark, or here in the court.

Twelve years back Gracie was too deliriously happy to see anything except Lonnie. He was all she could hope for so she set out to get him while the getting was good. Too late, Lonnie found all that glitters is not gold and what you see in the dark won't look the same in the light of day. But to his credit, he made the best of it and became a model husband, never seeing any need to look over the fence or around the next curve, be it road or body.

Grace also did her part in being a model wife for she realized she had made a catch of her lifetime.

No second chance for her, she had it all except money and dad and mom would see to that in time.

Now Lonnie had other thoughts but was very good at long range planning. His present position would allow him all the freedom any man could want but then, some are not satisfied with more than enough, they want more, and more, and more. Stop ?

Grace had her garden club as well as the ladies weekly gin rummy card game. Mostly they met at her house due to the cost of hosting a nice game. That was one thing that Grace did not hesitate to spend for, a nice presentation of her home and her wealth.

These days were the ones Lonnie spent down at the shooting club where he could pop some ammo at paper that needed killing. Now Lonnie had a wonderful wife and he knew it. She was very attractive and more than Lonnie could have expected but as I said, some men never appreciate her until she is gone. Lonnie had yet to learn many lessons in life and it is a certainty that God will teach at just the right time.

Now Lonnie had been in the planning stage since dad had turned the oil field over to grace. He did not specify that Lonnie was to be on the deed but somehow it slipped by without his name where he would have liked it. No of course, Texas law said it made no difference at the time of death, Lonnie would automatically be the owner when she died, except he would have some taxes to pay. Never mind that, it just didn't set well with him to be left out. Now Lonnie never did play around even though he was much desired by those women he came into contact within the course of his duties. He had no desire and back then, he did believe his wife was the best the world had to offer. Well, he still thought so but then there was the fact that she had left him off the property deed. What else was she capable of? Would her dad leave him out of the will and Grace would have it all? Would that make him kept man? Would his reputation down at the shooting gallery go out the window with a bang? He didn't think he would be able to face his ridin' & shootin' buddies if that should happen.

Graces attorney had been frank with Lonnie, it looked as if she would go up the river for a very long spell, possibly life with no parole and this left Lonnie with many points to ponder. He thought of seeking legal advise from an attorney on the other side of Texas, but he did not know how close the attorneys stayed in touch and it might leak that he wanted the answer to some sticky questions.

Almost three years ago, Lonnie had the notion that he could be much happier with total ownership of all his wife and her parents owned. With that kind of money he could and would spend his winters in the south Atlantic islands where he would live the life of the leisurely rich. No reason why he could not have the services of a lovely young woman, one that could be changed for a new one as he desired.

Both Grace and Lonnie called her father 'Dad" which pleased the old man very much.

He really envied Lonnie and tried to see how much he could help the one he called "My Boy". Partly he felt sorry for Lonnie as "My Boy" never had a father to do for him.

Lonnie was educated by hard work on his part with no help from his mother or anyone else. Two jobs and college at the same time was almost too much for any young man. It was because of this that Grace's dad helped him with finding a good job but not working in his company. Dad wanted him to feel he was on his own so he called in a debt from a friend to place Lonnie where a good income was set for starters.

Lonnie pondered the thought of death and an inheritance. The more he thought about it, the more it seemed only natural that people who had lived till their late seventies had been in the world long enough.

Two years ago, Grace's parents decided it was time to give their only child the deed to their property so she could have the income and also because she would be the one to contend with attorneys and tax people.

Dad was just tired of them all and he had more than he could spend if he lived another hundred years. Dad liked and treated Lonnie as a son and also wanted him to have the income that would allow him to quit a job that he hated. Lonnie had in fact, taken an early retirement bonus and left with no regrets.

Now he could go shooting and riding his bike through the woods at leisure. Defining a bike means it has only two wheels, unless it was a three wheeler that lost a limb. He could buy the toys he desired without having regrets and as far as Grace was concerned, she was glad he was out of the house. It seemed as if both of them were feeling the need to go places alone and this is not the good feelings of a successful marriage.

Murder was out of the question. Lonnie could not stand the thought of hurting even the pesky animals that needed to be removed. He would almost wreck his automobile to dodge an animal in the road, be it dog or rat. Yes, murder was not in his system. Still, that seemed the only way to gain control of the entire fortune. Grace and her parents, Mr. and Mrs. Herbert and Julia Myers was blessed with just too much money for Lonnie to forget. Murder? Out of the question for Lonnie but perhaps there is another way.

Now Grace and Lonnie had experimented with party drugs, nothing to be ashamed of and nothing addictive, so they thought. As Lonnie pondered the question, drugs came to mind but he never even thought of getting Grace's parents to try them. They were very straight laced and attended religious services weekly. No sir, no drugs for them. But it dawned on him that Grace would be a pushover. All he had to do was give her so much attention that she would do anything for him, even take a short sniff of the hard stuff just before he made mad love to her. Obviously, he could get much pleasure from feeding her just the right amount of drugs and allow her to think he was taking the same amount.

First, Lonnie had to locate a good supply of the hard stuff and buy enough of it to assure he would not have to locate more at a critical time. Being very careful but taking somewhat of a chance, he chose to buy in a distant city and buy enough to make it appear he was dealing. This way, he would get a good price and leave no trail back to him.

On returning to his home, he had to find a place to hide it where even the drug sniffing dogs would not locate it. After some thought, he remembered that the smell of gasoline killed the olfactory nerves in the dogs nose and they would be unable to identify anything else for some time. Now he had it. Hide it in the tool shed where the lawnmower gasoline was kept. But, this would look peculiar Grace since they hired a lawn care service and left him no reason to go to that shed. As much as he hated work it looked as if he would have to dismiss the lawn service company and take up the chore of lawn boy. He would need to change a lot for dad to believe what he was seeing but then, he did need the exercise and dad would appreciate his effort to better himself.

In preparation for hiding the drugs in plain sight, he would need to buy new gasoline cans of the five gallon plastic size. With care, he could make a small opening in the bottom of one where drug packs could be inserted and then close the cleverly made door.

When setting on the floor, it would appear to be just another empty gas container.

Now all he had to do was keep the real one nearly full and keep spilling a little gas on the empty container from time to time. With a little on the floor and on the can, no dog would ever find his stash. It looked as if his plan was a good one except he now had to do the lawn care and this was almost more than he could stand. A year or two of this and he would really be in good physical shape as well as monetarily fixed.

Herb and Julia were frequent visitors since Grace was their only child and since she now controlled the bulk of their fortune. It was the nature of Herbert to watch carefully for a time, just be certain that Grace was up to the task . It would not do for her to become lax with so much responsibility and Herb wanted to be certain that she understood the nature of his business. This irritated Lonnie but he never said or acted the part of one that was being left out of the picture. After all, some day soon he would have it all. During their visits, he made himself scarce by working at some trivial project at his basement work bench. Dad soon realized the change but said nothing except to Grace that she should be more attentive toward Lonnie.

Grace did try to include Lonnie in more of her activities but he was not interested in the things women liked. What he did like was their cozy evenings when Grace did pay more attention and when he could introduce small amounts of the chosen drug. As days and weeks passed, he did increase the dosage in minute amounts which made Grace more pliable to his desires. Of course he was also taking small amounts but with the determination to never allow it to become a habit and never enough that he would need it for any reason.

Mom and Dad soon realized Grace was on drugs and took the chance of confronting her. Lonnie was not there but he could hear the outburst from his basement work bench and it pleased him very much. This very night he made the first comment which was to say that mom and dad had no business messing with her life. He had planted the seed of destruction which would only require a little watering from time to time.

Because of the interference from her mother and dad, Grace was delighted to accompany Lonnie on an extended vacation around the world. It would be very upsetting with her parents that she would leave the business to her accountant for the three months they would be gone. Dad was furious with Grace but helpless since he had signed almost everything over to her. There was no turning back now but he did resolve to leave the balance of his estate to Lonnie and not to her. In all of this, he was positive that Lonnie was not on drugs so Grace got the full blame. It seemed Lonnie's plan was working better that he had thought it would.

Grace and Lonnie arrived in Rome the first week of their vacation and Lonnie was well prepared to purchase whatever drugs he needed, regardless of price. He had done his homework and understood the market in the USA as well as in Italy, France and other countries they would be visiting. He was firm in the demand that Grace talk to her dad every day because he knew dad would never let up on criticism and Grace would only

become angrier with every passing day.

Good! This was part of the plan. Now he had to fan the fire by telling Grace how her parents were trying to take every thing back from her and they had come to hate her. That word "Hate" was a little harsh but necessary if his plan was to work.

Three months in Rome was about all he could take of grandiose monuments of ancient origin, no matter if the rest of the world thought it was to be revered. Paris was more to his liking where he would have no trouble finding the drugs and entertainment he enjoyed. Night clubs were his thing and Grace would also like them since he had her bombed half out of her mind anyway. Sleeping it off the next morning and prepping for another night on the town was just what Grace needed and It would help fan the flame of hate he wanted. He would see that Grace spoke to her father every day and that she would not be in complete control of her speech when she did. Dad would blast her again for not taking care of business at home and for the obvious drunken stupor he noticed in her voice.

Two months of this and dad dropped a bomb shell. Grace must come home at once if she wanted to see her mother again. Julia had been diagnosed with a rare form of cancer that would take her life in a very short time. Dad was broken hearted when he tried to tell Grace the bad news but he found Grace unable to understand the reality of sudden death from cancer. He tried but succeeded only in making Grace angry. Dad did not understand that Lonnie had been building a wall of hate between Grace and himself for the past several weeks and that drugs were almost in complete control. Herb gave up on Grace and asked Lonnie if he would please bring Grace home, at least for the short time Julia had left and with hopes that he could make it in time.

Lonnie went to the task with intention of causing Grace to believe dad had ordered her home instead of asking, just another fortunate occurrence to help him build the wall of hate toward dad. Lonnie made the arrangements for departure the next day. He told Grace it was for her mother and definitely not her father and by increasing the drug dose, he was able to convince her that it was out of his hands. He also started the lie that dad was working on retaking all of his property back from a drunken daughter. Grace was not of sound mind at this time or she would have realized that move was impossible but, it made the wall of hate just a little higher.

At the hospital, Grace and Lonnie found Julia in a comatose condition, mostly from pain medication since they expected her to die any hour. Dad was with Julia when they arrived and saw at once that Grace was drunk with a combination of drugs and alcohol.

He was heartbroken that Julia might know the condition of her daughter during her last hours. He said little but could not hold back the tears for it was evident that Grace did not know what she was seeing. Her mother was unable to speak and Grace made no effort to communicate with either her or her father. Dad asked Lonnie what brought on this addiction and Lonnie had made the excuse that Grace had been hospitalized in Rome where she was given too much for too long and a prescription for even more. He said he did not let them know because it would only worry them since the doctors had promised that it was not serious. They diagnosed the problem as common Tachycardia brought on by stress and giving her a dangerous heart rate of 115 beats per minute. The doctors insisted that she must stay for two weeks in order to be well rested. To them, her problem was stress and her heart was perfectly normal. Recovery was from rest and total departure from her business. Lonnie said that during those two weeks, he had been asked to keep his visits very short and far between. He never saw a drug problem until she was out and needed to excuse herself for a fix. Herb could see and feel a great change in Grace. Her hatred was not well concealed, just as if she wanted it to show. Herb was more confused than ever but could do little about it since Grace did not talk to him at all.

Three days later, Julia passed away and this brought Grace to her senses for a time. She could not do with out her drugs but leaving off most of the alcohol, she was able to attend funeral services. During this time she remained aloof to Herb, avoiding any contact where she might have to suffer another reprimand from Herb. Lonnie was making every effort to keep Herb from the truth while trying to be the good son-in-law. At the same time fanning the flame of hate in the mind of Grace. Everything was going as he planned it and soon he would be rich.

In a fatherly effort to win Grace back to her other self, he asked Lonnie to please make some excuse to have them spend a few days with him. Tell her dad is really in need of our comfort with the loss of Julia or tell her the sky is blue, just tell her anything to get her to stay in her old room for a few days. Again the course of time has played into his plan for total control of the Myers fortune. Grace was so firmly hooked that she would do anything for another fix and Lonnie had control of her medicine, so he called it. With this control over her, it was no trouble to get her to spend a few days in the room she had used since childhood. Lonnie spent much of the daytime hours with her but left her alone at night. Dad thought she was improving as Lonnie had told him her med was being reduced so she could sleep it off. In fact, Lonnie was increasing the dose and at the same time telling her dad had her prisoner.

A week of this confinement was telling on Grace and she was near insanity, just where Lonnie wanted her. This day he made the suggestion that dad should die and the way was his gun collection he kept in his basement study. He was telling Grace he would like to do it but as she understood, he always fainted at the sight of blood.

He was too sure he would chicken out at the last moment and dad would have him in jail Grace would have to be the one to finish it since it was she that he hated. Lonnie continued to prep her on how and when but he had no need to tell her about guns. She had been target shooting with Lonnie many times and after all, dad was just another target.

Lonnie now needed to stay clear of her room at night after giving her a heavy dose of her med. It was the usual pattern for him to leave the house after dad was soundly sleeping and walking about a mile to the local bar. He seldom had more than one beer but spent a lot of time at the pool table with the deliberate loss of small bets. He really was a poor pool player so it was no problem to find a man to take his money. He was in fact, paying for an alibi. At two AM closing time, he tried to keep one or more men in a conversation for as long as possible before walking home again.

A week of this and it was wearing thin on him. He was losing sleep and needed to speed up the process some way. After giving it some thought, he brought one of dad's revolvers

to Grace, telling her it was for her protection as there had been a number of home invasions in the area. Grace was too bombed out to understand anything except the gun was in her bedside drawer and now Lonnie had to push a little harder on dad to give her a fatherly talking to. To the credit of a good father, Herb tried to reason with her but she showed such hatred, he was at a loss for words. Grace became so very angry, dad just stopped trying and told Lonnie he must place her in a secure drying out center. Nothing would do except that he had to try one more time to talk to Grace. His effort was to plead with her then threaten her with confinement if she made no effort to control her anger.

That night, Lonnie went to the bar as usual, played pool and lost small amounts until two in the morning. On leaving, one of his new found friends wanted to give Lonnie a ride to his home. When they arrived, every light in the house was on and a number of official cars were all over the lawn. Right away, he knew it was all over and somehow he needed to get rid of the gas can with cocaine in it. He had kept very little drugs in the house and these were in Grace's room. They had not been in their home but a very short time after returning from Europe and this was just long enough for Lonnie to do the lawn care work it needed. He had contracted a lawn service company to do this job while he was away and he made certain they furnished their own mowers and fuel. Even so, he had placed a good lock on the tool shed door just to make certain all was left intact.

Grace had been taken to a hospital under guard where she would be confined until she was drug free. He was questioned by the investigators but he had the friend from the bar to vouch for his last five hours, as well as every night for the past several evenings.

The arresting officer had done a good job of keeping all evidence intact and had dutifully read Grace her rights. She had been in positive control of her senses to the point that she readily admitted shooting her father, because she hated him. That admission might not stand in court but it was damaging enough. Very little investigation was done after the admission of Grace so Lonnie was free to continue his normal routine., being careful to not make a minor mistake though, like when he stopped visiting the bar and playing pool with his new friends. That could look like a time of mourning but Lonnie never resumed the visits to the bar and to the investigating officer it would appear he did not need the alibi now that the deed was done.

A few weeks ago one of the lawn care part timers had been dutifully cutting the grass near the door of Lonnie's tool shed. He could not help but notice the extra heavy hasp and lock on such a building as this. Why? That lock began to trouble him and it became a possibility that something of real value was locked inside. Since he had been here two times before, he was certain no one lived here and that made it all the more reason to check it out By carefully removing two boards on the back side where it could not be seen from the street, he was inside and with the flashlight he had brought, he began a careful search. At first it appeared just the normal tools for lawn care but there had to be a reason for such security. Carefully picking each item for close examination, he picked the first gas can and found it nearly full. The second can smelled like gas but was very light and did not sound like liquid when shaken. Carefully he turned it upside down and there was the false bottom.

With over a hundred small bags of white powder, he knew he had dope but not what kind? He also knew it was worth a lot of money and dangerous to be caught with so he took all of it out and placed it in a large plastic bag, then hid it buried in another bag of fertilizer.

No need to place the boards back for it would make no difference in the end. It was just necessary to get out of there and try to locate someone who knew what he had. Taking one small bag to the place where he had seen dope sold to passing automobiles, he asked the seller to look at what he had. Right away he was questioned and refused to give an answer but told the seller he had three bags to sell. Not knowing prices, he was happy to get twenty dollars for them and left.

Weeks passed and nothing else was done to investigate the murder of Herbert Myers. So far as the investigators were concerned, they had a sure-fire case so It was closed. The prosecuting attorney was satisfied he could get a quick conviction so nothing more was required for him. The trial was held almost as a formality and Grace was pronounced guilty on all counts with no real effort to get her off on temporary insanity. It looked as if she was finished for the next fifty years which was the sentence the judge gave her.

Lonnie was jubilant but dared not let it show. Not only did he get control of the Myers fortune, he also got the insurance on the old man's life. The plot had worked and Lonnie was so proud of his plan it was almost more than he could do to keep it to himself.

Across town where drugs could be bought and sold almost with immunity, the lawn boy tried for another small sale, this time with six bags thinking forty dollars. He did not see the original buyer so he approached a nattily dressed man leaning against the fence where the other buyer had been. A sale was quickly made and yard boy was ready to leave when he felt the handcuff's close on his wrist. The loiter turned out to be an under cover cop and he was arrested as a dealer.

Down at the station, he was soon telling all and it was apparent that he knew very little about drugs. Before he was questioned more than a half hour, he admitted to theft and gave them the address of his find.

Detective Tim Ford realized this was the same house where he had made an arrest over a year back and the trial was just over a month ago. Remembering that the woman was bombed out of her mind when he arrested her, he gave this some serious thought. Her husband was not on drugs at the time and it was very unlikely that a woman would hide her dope in a gasoline can. This was definitely a mans drug stash. Obviously, there would not be more drugs in the same location so it would not do for a search warrant. He had no probable cause and no way to find if the husband, Lonnie Hutchins was on drugs.

It was going to be a cat & mouse game for the next few weeks and detective Ford had all the time necessary to watch the mouse, or should he say, the rat.

Lonnie made short work of disposing of Grace's personal items. It was if he never knew her and that was another reason Tim Ford had for close observation. As he watched day after day, he never caught Lonnie near a drug dealer or even in the area where they were known to hang out. Facts were beginning to add up to murder and not by Grace as charged. To be certain he was on the right track, Tim had a fellow undercover officer offer Lonnie drugs at a party and as suspected, Lonnie refused with the words, "Never touch the stuff".

Weeks pass while detective Ford is trying to locate the source of the drugs found in Lonnie's tool shed. With no luck in this direction, it was time to take a new course, one that would require the help of his commander. Orlando, the yard boy had to be recruited for help, a sting set-up for Lonnie. To make it work, Orlando had to be sprung from a short sentence in the county jail and carefully coached on the plan. With several plain clothes officers watching, Orlando is to approach Lonnie for help.

He is to admit to the theft of Lonnie's drugs and tell him he needed more and demand help in buying it. If Lonnie acts as they think he will, he will tell Orlando to "Bug off", at which time Orlando is to threaten Lonnie of going to the police. Either way, Lonnie is in a tight place, knowing he might get caught buying again and knowing he might expose himself to Dad Myers death if he goes either way. The answer is to rid himself of Orlando once and for all. He promises Orlando he will try to set it up and tells Orlando to meet him here tomorrow night.

When they meet again, Lonnie has a plan of action that will end it now. He set it for a meeting and a buy at midnight the next night in front of the old abandoned factory building at town's edge. He told Orlando to bring a thousand dollars and come alone, walking instead of driving. Lonnie had a very good plan, to shoot Orlando and place the body in the trunk of his automobile where he had prepared a plastic lined place. . Orlando would leave no sign of his presence later. His body would be easy to drag to the grave he had dug earlier in the day. A place far out in the country where only hunters visited during hunting season.

He really did not care if the body was found later since there was nothing to connect him to Orlando. Even the gun he would use was stolen and purchased from a questionable source in another town, many miles away. It too would be wiped clean and buried with Orlando. Lonnie went over the plan many times, looking for the one mistake could cost him his freedom. Perhaps it would be netter to buy Orlando off since he had more money than he could ever spend and Orlando was obviously in need. Just in case, he would take the gun and a very large stack of bills, mostly in small denominations, so it would look good to the yard boy. He would offer the money first and if that failed, he would take the next step.

Orlando was fitted with a wire and coached on his every remark. He was to give the marked money to Lonnie and accept the promise of delivery at the same place one night later. He was not to argue or question Lonnie in any fashion, the money changing hands would be enough.

With enough plain clothed police placed in strategic places, Orlando was coached on where to stand, where to try getting Lonnie to face so the night vision camera could get the proper picture and to listen for a certain signal. Detective Ford had some fear for Orlando's life so he arranged for a car to be placed well out of sight but on station to signal Orlando. If it looked as if it might get out of hand, Tim Ford would radio the remote car to sound his horn. By being well away from the action, Tim hoped Lonnie would not catch the signal but Orlando would and remove himself from danger.

Orlando was to wait until Lonnie was parked and then he was to approach the car on foot.

It was necessary for Lonnie to get out of the car so Orlando was instructed to stand well clear, forcing Lonnie to approach him in dim lighting from a security light on the old factory building. All went as planned by detective Ford and Lonnie took a small travel bag from the trunk of his car. This served the purpose of leaving the trunk lid open and ready to receive the body, if necessary. Lonnie had a powerful flashlight which he used to take a quick look at the wall of the old building.

He did not see the well concealed officers on either side of his location so he opened the bag and showed Orlando a large pile of bills. He said to drop the need for dope since that was too risky and besides, this amount of money far surpassed the profit from any dope he could get and sell. Orlando and Tim Ford were both caught off guard and no plan for this had been put in place.

Acting on what he would do if this was for real, Orlando decided to take the money.

It looked to him as if the evidence Tim Ford needed was in the bag and along with the taped conversation.

Lonnie felt good. Dad's money had bought him freedom and now it was time to take a trip, back to Europe where he could really live it up. Detective Tim Ford was somewhat disappointed but not finished with the trap.

The next day, before Lonnie had time to become fully awake, Orlando was ringing his door bell with vigor. Lonnie saw who it was and decided to treat Orlando as a friend, the best way to catch him off guard. Invite him in for coffee and a conversation. Orlando understood he might lose radio contact with Tim if he went inside so he refused but insisted they talk. Lonnie chose to speak with him only because he could see no one and no automobiles close. Orlando told him that he had counted the money and was angry because it was not as much as he needed and angry because of small bills intended to fool him. He wanted more and he wanted it tonight at the same place same time. With that said, Orlando walked away, leaving Lonnie to ponder when it might end. Should he pay or should he end it with a bullet?

By early afternoon, he had made the decision to pay and then leave for Europe at once. Orlando would never find him there and the shakedown would end without bloodshed.

This time Tim Ford and his fellow detectives were better prepared for either eventually.

They had in fact decided that Lonnie would choose to kill Orlando and steps were taken for a sniper rifle to be on Lonnie at all times. Should he show a gun, he was to be taken out immediately. Orlando was to insist on counting the money before he would allow Lonnie to leave. He was to make a big fuss over being cheated the other time and he was not about to let that happen again. His instructions were to antagonize Lonnie every way he could. Tell him he had found the reason for the drugs and that he knew Grace was paying the price. Tell him he had been to the police to inquire of how Grace had been convicted. Spread the money on the ground and count slowly so Lonnie would have time to build enough anger to act. Stay close to the ground all the time he was counting money.

Lonnie was building anger while trying to stay in control of his actions. He came to the conclusion that Orlando had to die. He would wait until Orlando counted the money and returned it to the bag. He did not want to leave this as evidence and he could not afford the time to pick it up and bag it after shooting Orlando.

When Orlando heard the shot, he realized he had been instructed to stay low in order to protect him from a sniper's bullet. When he looked up.

Lonnie was in the process of falling, with a gun in his hand meant to be used on Orlando. He had been shot in the right shoulder where he was out of commission but definitely not dead. The police needed him very much alive if they had any hopes of convicting him and helping to free Grace. Orlando was rewarded for his good work by having his sentence cancelled. He was a free man and determined to never cross the police again. He had learned the futility of trying to outwit a dedicated detective like Tim Ford.

My West Virginia Hills

If only I could sing clear notes of praise,
I would direct my voice to the ANCIENT OF DAYS   *
If only I could sing as some others do,
Blessed with a voice that rings out true.

I would sing to the hills of the beauty I see,
Of life in the forest and in every tree.
Magnificent hills; God shaped by hand.
Mountains and valleys; a part of this land.

Clothed in a forest of Elm, Cedar and Oak,
Both summer and winter, a glorious cloak.
Trees with fall colors of red, green and yellow,
Those bearing apples, some tart and some mellow.

Hickory and Walnut, yes blackberries on vine,
These hills are covered with food that is fine.
But my voice can't do justice to each little tree,
So let the wind in their branches sing praises for me.

*Daniel 7:9

The Garden of Eden

The Garden of Eden had no trash,
but soon came taxes, then, excess cash.
Politicians got busy on how to spend;
too much cash was easy to mend.
So bottles and cans were created by loads
for people to drop on public roads.
More taxes came next to pay the road crew.
Politicians explain, what else could we do ?
The chief politician hired his nephew.
Taxes paid him to direct the road crew.
Paychecks increased at a prodigious rate,
and trash now covers most of the state
Trash pickup has made little change
since political hiring covers the range.

An old Obituary

Let us wander back through the years to the year1849 when Julia McMellon was in hard labor. She and her husband had made the crossing through Cumberland Gap from the area round what is now Roanoke, Virginia. Their destination was the area of Guyan valley where his grandfather had settled in territory known only to the Shawnee Indians. Only a very few trappers had penetrated that country , and most that entered never returned to tell of it's beauty.. Thomas McMellon had settled there with the help of friendly Indians, mostly because he and his family were very generous. Their settlement was not far off the valley of the Kanawha river which was known by the Indians as ths conoy river valley.

Gabriel Arthur was noted as the first man to see the mouth of the Conoy river in 1863/4 , although Thomas McMellon was really the first in 1798. It is not well known that Thomas had the experience of a great friendship with the Shawnee Indians who worked the salt works not far above what is now known as Charleston, West Virginia. It appears they were very protective of the supply of salt from a spring on the bank of the Kanawha. They worked this source of salt and traded with Indians all over their part of the country.

In 1753, the Virginia governor Robert Dinwiddie sent George Washington to southwestern Pennsylvania with a written order, demanding French forces vacate the Ohio valley territory. which they refused to do. A year later, Washington returned with a force of hundreds, ambushed a small scouting party, May 1754. This was the beginning of the French & Indian war. Twenty years of conflict between the British and the French ended with the ratification of the treaty of Paris February 10th; 1763.

The French & Indian war had little effect on the Ohio valley during this conflict. It was not until later when Britain found itself in deep debt from paying its forces to continue the war for so long. As a result, it enacted the Sugar act of 1764, the stamp act of 1765

the Townsend Act of 1767, as well as other ways to raise funds from its 13 American colonies. This brought on a rebellion against "Taxation without representation"

Britain had issued a Proclamation in 1763 which banned colonial settlement west of the Appalachian Mountains. This also contributed to discontent among the colonist which led to armed conflict rebellion in

1775. Thomas McMellon had crossed the Appalachian mountains in 1798, long before this ban.

The name Thomas originated in Scotland, too far back to be traced. The name McMellon also came from Scotland , but was incorrectly translated from McMillan.. This name of Thomas McMellon has been carried down through the years since the first arrival.

It is known that the McMillan or the McMellon brothers came to America with a trade of "Iron Mongers" which we know as "Blacksmiths". It is also known that the elder brother worked his way north, into New York and on to the Boston area. The younger, Thomas found a need for blacksmith work on the frontier, further south. There seems to be other men by the name Thomas McMellon, mostly lost in history.

We do know there was a slave owner in south Georgia that carried the name, Thomas McMellon. This story is about one, Thomas James McMellon. who was a Baptist minister in and around the counties of Lincoln, West Virginia. Thomas was a veteran of the Civil War, fighting for the north. He was severely wounded and could do little work on his farm near Griffithville, WV: Thomas traveled widely in the service of the Lord, preaching in the several counties within riding distance for him and his horse. He seemed to be very well known in the territory between Huntington ,Charleston and Logan. His obituary was written by a fellow preacher in Hurricane, WV, even though his body was laid to rest in the family cemetery at Yawkey. I believe this cemetery was part of the farm he owned and that it came to him by a grant for his war service. I have not taken time to look up the original deed, so I can't vouch for this.

AN OBITUARY

In memory of T.J. McMellon. Brother McMellon departed this life Nov.4th 1921 aged 72 years. He was the father of eight children, three boys, Thomas, Pomp and James. Five daughters, Mary, Julia, Poca, Gustava, and Maude, four of whom preceded him to the grave. Maud died about1808, thirteen years ago. Julia in the early spring, of last year. Mary in the early spring of this year. James in the spring of this year. The loss of so many of his children in so rapid succession was a greater strain on him than he was able to bear and, soon after the death of James, his health gave way and he was an invalid the rest of his life, but he was carefully nursed and cared for by aged wife, and children until the end.

He united with the Providence Church of Regular Baptist Faith and Order about thirty seven years ago, and soon after was ordained to the ministry which work he served faithfully for twenty five years. During the last twelve years he was not physically able to devote much time to the ministerial work, but remained faithful to the church, to his family, neighbors, and friends, exemplifying Christ in his life.

The writer preached his funeral at the old home-stead near Griffithville, on November of 1921. A large crowd attended his funeral and there was much weeping because a great father in Israel had fallen. At the conclusion of the services he was laid to rest in the family cemetery to await the resurrection of the just. We, in our closing remarks, wish to say to the widow and children that their loss is his eternal gain. Weep not as those that have no hope. Your father can not come back to you, but you can go to him where parting will be no more.

LEONARD OXLEY
Hurricane, W.Va.

The son, James was shot and killed while in the church yard where his father was preaching. The reason as best I have been able to discern was a jealous man over the love of a girl. I have often thought of the trauma of losing a child like that, while trying to carry on God's work. It is no wonder to me as to why Thomas lost the will to live.

Thomas Jefferson was my great grandfather. His son Thomas Peyton was my grandfather who lived and died a great Christian. For many years, until his death, he was the local blacksmith and grist mill operator located in West Hamlin, W.Va. From the time I was about six years old, my dad allowed me to spend a month each summer with him.

I delighted in being in his cavernous shop where the mill ran for most of the day and where the forge kept a glowing fire while granddad placed new shoes on a horse.

Grandfather was blessed with much land and gas wells on his property. Gas was the fuel for a monstrous engine used to turn the many machines in his shop. I often watched him start that giant in the morning. He did so by climbing up on to the center of that giant flywheel and stepping out to the end of one of the great spokes. When he did, the wheel would start to turn and granddad jumped off just before being thrown off. I do remember the flywheel was tall enough that the center hub was about even with the top of my head. In the same building and on the other end, there was located the forge. In those years, farmers would drive their wagons in one end of the building, drop off the grain that needed to be ground into flour or cattle feed. Then they would move their horses on down to the forge where they got new shoes or the old ones relocated. My grand father passed away in 1934 and his funeral was preached in the church where he was an ordained deacon. This church still stands on the property grand father donated to the church from the end of his property. It is my burning desire to see my wonderful granddad in the Heaven where

I know he is and I will be, very soon.

I need to take this story a bit further by telling you that my father was named Boyce James. I never heard him called James but he did go by BJ to a lot of folks. Dad was also a devout Christian, one that set too high a standard for me. In fact, I am a devout Christian but have not always led the life of one. I have many regrets for my actions in my early life, regrets that fill my head with sorrow at times. I know Jesus died on the cross to eliminate my sins, but he has not yet cleared my memory of them. I started my first public job in 1940, a full year before Pearl Harbor, and the beginning of WW11. When my time arrived, I served in the uniform of the United States armed forces. My mother was truly a prayer warrior and was in constant prayer for my safety. I truly believe God had his hand on me the better part of my life, all because Mom was constantly asking him to.

Part 2, my life,

I was born in Barboursville, west Virginia, December 13, 1926, just one year after my father left the coal mines of Logan County, WV: He became an employee of the C & O railroad where he worked for over forty years. My first nine years were spent in that small town where my mother tried to feed a very large and growing family through the depression of the late thirties. Mom had a large garden and spent every possible hour of the summer in it. She also had about four cows and provided her family with the best of garden and dairy food. As far back as I can remember, it was my duty to drive the cows from the barn to the pasture, and returnm. I learned very early to milk cows and to tend the rows of vegetables.

As for school. I did very well, even though I was very introverted and had little to do with the other children my age. I considered myself a country boy among city kids, just because we lived on the last street in town and had cows.

Uncle Kenneth was dad's younger brother who had chosen to live with us from the time I was born. He was about 15 when he came to live in Barboursville from his parents home in West Hamlin, WV: He became my big brother and lived with us until he married and started his family. He was responsible for much of my early training, simply because dad was always too busy.

In December, 1936 my parents bought a large farm with a very old house on it. We moved into that house just after Christmas where life really became the best part of my young life memories. A very old country school with no city kids gave me a bus ride every day. It also gave me new duties at home because mom was in her glory. A very large garden and now twenty or more cows to care for. two hundred acres of pasture, a peach and apple orchard. I had many duties and loved it.

Peanut Butter

During my years as a manufacturer's representative, I worked with many manufacturers all over the eight southeastern states, and with their engineers, and purchasing agents. To sell my product, it was necessary to become well acquainted with these men. What better way than to spend a week with them in a hunting camp. It was my practice to invite one of the key men to accompany me on the annual deer hunt, in either West Virginia, or in Colorado, for elk. While I truly enjoyed the week in the wilderness, it was a treat to do so at the expense of IRS, since I could write it off as legitimate sales expense. Interesting stories came from most of them, somewho had little experience and never camped in a tent, much less in a snow storm. Some of these men had more experience in camping out in the mountains than I, and all were truly enjoyable, even the novice which took most of my time in watching out for his safety.

My long time hunting buddy was Fred Engle, and for most of those years we lived hundreds of miles apart. That never prevented us from planning ahead for at least eleven months, where we would camp, and how. I had been the camp cook for thirty years or more, and loved doing it. Somehow we became fixed on a place called Middle Mountain where we saw the same group of men every year. It became a tradition that I would get the first deer killed in the camps and with it, prepare Thanksgiving dinner of venison stew. The men from the camps on either side of us were old timers and the same members came every year. I always took the necessary vegetables and other items for a good Thanksgiving spread.

Usually the hunters were in camp by mid-afternoon in anticipation of the dinner I was preparing. For this gathering, a very large campfire was built so that coals were glowing just before dusk. About twenty of us would enjoy enough stew to satisfy the most serious appetite and with full stomach lethargy, gather around the fire for the remainder of the day. It was then that many stories were told, mostly about past hunts and mostly true.

One of the best that Fred used to tell every year was "The Peanut Butter Story". Even though it was well known to all except perhaps, one new comer, Fred was able to embellish the story to the point of having all of us in stitches.

About 1970, we were camping in my large, two room tent that had a wood burning stove in the cooking area but no heat in the sleeping area.

That year I had invited the chief engineer from a company in South Georgia to be with us as my guest. I had not planned on his assistant but since he asked, I had no choice but to extend the invitation, Let me call the engineer Jerry and his assistant Kent. As it turned out, Kent had no idea what it was all about so we had to give him a list of needed clothing and camp items such as a good sleeping bag. Jerry took him out one weekend and taught him to shoot a borrowed rifle which was totally unnecessary since he never left camp when we did get there. Kent had heard one too many stories of men being lost in the deep woods of West Virginia so he spent his days burning our supply of firewood. We were afraid to allow him to use the axe since he seemed to be helpless in all other camp chores. He was so helpless that Jerry apologized for him when he ask someone to help rig his sleeping bag and air mattress.

In preparation for a long day of travel and setting up camp when we arrived, Dixie, my wife had baked a five pound beef roast, wrapped in several layers of aluminum foil over Friday night. We were to have it for the evening meal on Saturday, after camp was secured for the night. With this, I had added green beans, potatoes wrapped in aluminum foil and thrown directly into the coals of our camp fire., gravy and cornbread. Our salad was plain celery and dessert was one more cup of mint tea.

Now the story goes back to the selection of food for the week. I had planned every meal, using items that took little space and would give us better than average camp grub. We always had bacon, sausage, eggs, gravy and biscuits for breakfast. Since we were to be in the field all day, I had brought only enough sliced bread for 6 days of sandwich's which the four of us used to make our field lunch with. I took two large jars of jelly for breakfast and one large peanut butter containers for both breakfast and field lunch sandwiches . I had previously found this to be more than sufficient. Dinner time was usually cornbread and/or biscuits. Over the years, I had found a way to make biscuits over a camp fire that was near perfect. It was astonishing to see how much food placed before men who had been out in the cold mountains all day, disappeared in moments.

A few days before we were to leave, Jerry told me he thought I should take some hot dogs since Kent had told him about their eating habits at home. Jerry relayed the story to me and I thought it was funny but I thought Kent would enjoy some good food for a change.

I did not take hotdogs because I had never failed to prepare much better meals and I saw no reason to change, just because Kent liked hot dogs.

As the story was told to Jerry, both Kent and his wife worked and had little time for their home and children (two boys). They had a large microwave oven and a large freezer which did the trick. This was the time when microwave ovens were very expensive and not many people had them. Kent said that payday shopping was the time they bought a month's supply of food, took it home and spent the entire evening putting it together and placing it in the freezer. Now, all they had to do was open the freezer, get the proper number of hot dogs out for the microwave. The boys never had to ask for food, they just helped themselves. What a time saver. Jerry did not ask but he assumed the family did not use such things as vegetables and salads. Kent never mentioned the use of a cook stove even though he and Jerry worked side by side for years. Perhaps this explained why Kent was grossly over weight.

The trouble started when we were ready to set down to that large chunk of roast beef.

Kent said nothing until he watched me peel off the several layers of aluminum foil. To heat the beef, I had left it wrapped and placed it on a rack above the camp fire. Since it had been cooked for about eight hours and never unwrapped, it just needed to be warmed. Kent made no other comment except "We don't eat leftovers at our house" and with that, he got out the peanut butter, jelly and bread. Sunday morning, with bacon, eggs and biscuits available, he returned to the peanut butter and jelly. He made certain we would not get into his supply of jelly by licking his spoon several times and stirring the jelly.

We said nothing about his strange behavior while in camp but wondered about it when we were alone in the woods.

Wednesday morning came when I had to go into town for the purpose of calling my office and returning calls from my customers. In Hillsboro, West Virginia there was a small store with a telephone and a nice old lady running it. She lived in the back part of the store and never seemed to have customers. Usually Fred and I went there together so that he could call his wife. This morning as we were in the truck, ready to leave camp, Kent called out, "Be sure you bring some peanut butter, bread and jelly, be sure it's crunchy." We were well aware of the shortage because he had eaten nothing for three days except that and water. We drove to Hillsboro, laughing about how Kent was gaining weight while we were doing all the exercise and losing weight. Kent had consumed almost all of our weeks supply of sliced bread, a large container of jelly and another of peanut butter. At the store, we asked the old lady for crunchy peanut butter and were told, "Only smooth in stock". I asked her if she would loan me a small plate and spoon which she went in back for without a word. When she returned, I removed most of the peanut butter and added two large packages of whole and hot barbecue peanuts. Carefully mixed and returned to fill the jar, the old lady looked at me as if I am nuts and by now Fred had caught on to the coming attraction.

Back in camp, Jerry had just returned from his morning hunt and was setting by a large fire with snow falling heavy and already about two inches. Kent also hugged the fire but when we arrived, he came to life at once and went for the peanut butter.

We had no time to tell Jerry about the mixture so all Fred and I could do was keep our backs to Kent and watch Jerry's face as Kent made a sandwich. Jerry must have thought Fred and I were in pain from the look on our faces and I don't know what he thought when Kent started to smear peanut butter on soft bread. He later told us that Kent made a small pass over the bread and stood frozen for a long time while he stared at the mess on his bread. Jerry said he thought Kent might be sick and about to pass out since he went from white to red and back again. Fred and I were afraid to look at Kent for fear of losing it. Much later, Jerry went down the trail with Fred and me, supposedly to get firewood. When out of hearing from camp. We told Jerry what we had done and I thought he would collapse from laughter. He had watched Kent smear that awful mixture on bread and turn his back to us when he ate it. Jerry did not know until this time that the whole nuts were salt and barbecue, laced with red pepper and that made Jerry lose his breath with laughter. For a time I thought we would need a doctor for Jerry---perhaps even Kent.

To the credit of Kent, he ate that stuff for the remainder of the week without a word. Saturday morning, we broke camp and dropped them in town where Jerry had left his car.

On their way back to Georgia, Kent told Jerry what a dirty trick Bernie and Fred had played on him and asked him to please stop at the first hamburger joint they came to. Jerry had to deny any knowledge of the prank since he had to work with Kent but ever after, when I went to that plant, Jerry had to go outside with me for another good laugh.

The following year, Jerry was to go with us again. I doubted Kent would ask to accompany us this year but to be on the safe side, I took a case of restaurant size jelly packages to be certain we would have clean jelly. No way would Kent be able to lick all of those 500 little packets. Kent never asked to accompany us to the hunting camp again.

He never said anything to me again either, except what was necessary in the course of our business. I was truly glad that Jerry was his boss, otherwise I would have lost a very good customer.

Fred could not wait to tell that story again in future hunting and fishing camps, and I suspect he is still telling it in Heaven.

Perfect Earth

For well over forty years of going to the woods every chance I have had, I have learned to appreciate the earth such that few people can understand. My long-time hunting buddy, Fred Engle, shared my love for the untamed forest of West Virginia. Too many years to remember found us in the woods over the Thanksgiving week which we and a million others called "deer season." For Fred and me, it was never that we wanted to kill an animal but that we found indescribable pleasure in sharing the week in camp and in the woods. Exactly why we chose to camp in the most remote and coldest place in West Virginia might be a mystery to some but not to us. Middle Mountain, a long and high ridge that must have the highest winds combined with horizontal snow fall, fits that description. There we found what we were looking for--few hunters to clutter the woods.

Frequently, we determined to find the most uncluttered place on the map and make that the destination for our hike there, even if it meant staying out overnight. We would look at the forest service map for that kind of place, no roads or trails shown and, by measured distance, as far in as possible from people. Of course, we were young then, able to hike all of those mountain miles with a day pack and a rifle, taking enough food for two days and also a good poncho in case of snow. Many times, we needed all we had with us. We usually arrived at our choice of camps on the Friday evening before deer season opened at sunrise on the following Monday. Setting up a quick camp Friday night and refining it Saturday, we loafed and ate, open fire cooked food fit for the kings. We also cut firewood for the week, and, if there were other hunters within sight, we would visit and make ourselves known. That was a good idea because we never knew when someone would need help. For the last few years we hunted together, we got to know the hunters next camp from ours since they were much like us, there for the experience more than to kill a deer. I was cooking for our church in those years and so it was a natural for me to prepare the Thanksgiving dinner. I usually took the necessary vegetables and seasonings, and, the first deer killed in either camp supplied the turkey. At those gatherings my camp would host a four PM dinner with all welcome. My reputation for free food got a little out of hand when as many as a dozen strangers would show up. It reached the point that we had to stop having Thanksgiving dinner open to all.

I remember the time when we were caught in a terrible snow storm about two miles from camp and darkness was setting in. As long as it was snow, we could keep going but this time it turned to rain. Torrents of it came in waves and we had no choice but try to sit tight and wait it out. There was no rock cleft that we knew about so we could use our poncho and huddle in as small a ball as possible. Both for warmth and to make two ponchos cover as much of us as possible, we sat close together with our back to a fallen log. Alternately, rain and sleet fell until it was well after dark, and, as we sat there, close behind us we heard the squall of a wild cat or panther. It was very close and we talked in a normal voice, wondering why it was not afraid of the human presence. I must admit it made my hair stand out when it screamed just a few feet behind us. I think it must have been close to midnight before the rain and sleet let up enough for us to continue on to our camp. I love the woods but not in a sleet storm at midnight.

As wild as West Virginia is, it pays to be prepared when venturing into the wilderness and some people fail to take the necessary precautions. It is the custom in areas where lots of hunters gather, for local towns to turn on the fire sirens at night when a hunter is reported lost or missing. I have heard these sirens wailing for an hour or more which served to give the lost person a direction to head for, and also time for search parties to gather. The sirens usually started near midnight when it is certain a man is missing and when his buddies have gone into town and reported him lost. The search parties need every man they can get. There is nothing I dread to hear more when I am comfortably wrapped in a warm sleeping bag. Nothing else will do except to crawl out and head for town. I have been fortunate in that I have had military survival training. It has served me well in those years in the mountains. The word "panic" comes to mind when I hear the siren start, not my panic, but the poor soul who is lost. The universal signal for help is three shots. At night, to hear three shots from somewhere up on the mountain is a sure sign of need. It may be a lost soul or it may be an injury. In either case, it is a call to action. Nothing will do except to dress and prepare to head out with whatever search party is forming.

Not all stories of hunting are pleasant and some just show how unsafe it is, not always from nature but sometimes from man. Emory, who worked with me for several years had an experience that could have been very serious, even deadly and by the hand of man. Emory and his brother Dan always hunted together and were very close, in part because Emory had spent three years working in a Japanese coal mine as slave labor and was very frail. He was a small man to begin with and had never regained his weight and stamina after the army had rescued him. After three months in an army hospital, they released him, still almost too frail to get around, and not able to work. Emory was usually sick and was forced to rest frequently while working with me. I was a signal maintainer on the railroad and Emory was my assistant. Neither of us had much work to do except repair signals when they failed, and I could carry the load for both of us. Repairing trouble spots was usually an electrical problem in a junction box, but, on occasion, it was a broken line wire. Emory was unable to climb the poles so I did all of that kind of work. The railroad supervisor would have discharged Emory, if possible, but both of our jobs were protected by the US Government for returning vets.

Dan took care of Emory from childhood and when it came to hunting, Dan was never far from Emory. In 1954, those two were hunting in Webster County near the end of a dirt road. They had left their vehicle parked where two others were parked and had walked up the hill, perhaps a mile. Emory ran out of steam and decided to take a stand where it was possible to see deer crossing at a low place in the hills. Dan continued on about another 200 yards in order to give Emory some chance to see deer and also to stay close in case he was needed. Late in the afternoon, Emory spotted a very large, perhaps trophy buck and was fortunate in getting a perfect shot. Dan heard the shot and was certain it came from Emory, so he decided to take his time and still hunt on the way back where he knew he would be the one to drag a deer out to their truck. Shortly, he saw Emory coming up toward him, waving his arms frantically. When Dan heard the story, they both got in a great hurry. Emory told him that he had indeed taken what looked to be a real trophy, and while field dressing it, two men came and watched him dress out the buck.

According to West Virginia law, Emory had unloaded his rifle and leaned it against a tree while dressing the Buck. He had also removed his jacket and dropped it next to his rifle. When he finished the dirty work, one man held a rifle pointed at Emory and said "You took our deer." The other man made certain Emory's rifle was unloaded and then went through the jacket and took all of Emory's ammunition. Laughing at the big joke, they proceeded to carry his deer down the hill toward their parked vehicle.

Dan and Emory used the same ammunition which was 30.06 and quite powerful. Dan had a full box of twenty rounds, plus six in his rifle. As they hurried to catch up with the two men, they divided the ammo. When they were still fifty yards from the two men, they could see Emory's deer in the back of the new Chevy truck, and the men were just getting into it. Dan and Emory stopped and took the prone shooting position. Just as the engine started, both fired into the engine compartment as fast as they could reload and fire again. The last of those two men were seen they were heading into the timber on the other side of the road.

I asked Emory of they had thought a stray bullet might have killed one of those men.His answer was, "Good Riddance, who cares?" It never pays to under estimate the little man you plan to steal from, does it?

All of this is to say that my love for the wilderness is such that I will never get enough of it. My vacation time now is spent in searching for beautiful things to photograph, such as flowers, trees, rivers or mountains. I may offend some who like to speak of "Mother earth" but I never use that term. God gave us the earth and we have failed to protect it. Mother had nothing to do with it.

PERFECT EARTH
The earth was perfect when God gave it to man.
He formed it and blessed it by his great holy hand.
The fields and the streams were clean in his sight.
Then, he blessed his creation with a glorious light.
For thousands of years earth gave without reason.
Trees gave us shelter and nuts, each in their season.
Earth gave us fruit and grapes from their vine,
sweet apples and pears, red and white wine.
Food from the forest and the fields for the taking.
A mist from the earth to help in the making.
But man was not happy with a pristine land,
Destruction of goodness fell under his hand.
Fresh water was flowing from a high mountain glen.
Creeks, rivers and pools were clean for all men.
But man became lazy and used rivers for dumps,
Throwing trash in our rivers in massive clumps.
God watched the destruction with tears in his eyes
While man pollutes the waters and high in the skies.
Mountains are destroyed for the coal and the oil,
Pollution and destruction for the water and soil.
How long can man continue to destroy this great land?
How soon will our great rivers be polluted dry sand?
We must stop the desecration and clean up our ways
Or soon face the results and the end of our days.

Sheldon Church

Yemassee, South Carolina

This has been a sad day here at the plantation, sad because we laid my father to rest in the family plot. It is now up to me to care for the multitude of details of working a thousand acres of prime South Carolina land In the Prince William Parish. Father devoted his life to the land and to the church which was being rebuilt in 1826, the year I was born. December 13th to be exact. Part of the Newberry plantation land owned by William Bull was used to build the church. I had been very happy in those years and spent much time with father there on the grounds. He had taken on the duties of grounds keeper so I had the privilege of playing all around the grounds.

The church ruins had been a lonesome place since the British troops had burned it in 1779 but the original building had been founded in1740 and the first service held there in 1757. Construction was done with such sturdy love that almost all of the walls were untouched. Much of the original membership had moved on long ago, leaving the old Sheldon church to waste away with time. I thought father was an old man when I was born and I am not sure how he managed a young woman such as my mother. I do remember her as a very prominent member in the ladies meetings at the church and that she was very stern with me, making certain I was not led astray by Satan and wayward boys who had little supervision. Father had made it quite clear that he was to be laid to rest in the church grounds where he loved to spend most all of his time but mother had her way as usual and the family plot it was. Fathers death came in 1872 when he had reached the ripe old age of sixty seven. The south was beginning to stabilize after the war was over. Most of our blacks were still with us even though they were free to do as they pleased. Father was always very good to them and when Lincoln made them free, father made them free to go or stay as they chose but with the offer of reasonable wages, most stayed.

The same day I was born, Boo was born to the young girl who was helper to our cook.

Father had, from the very beginning chose to buy only light skinned blacks, believing them to be mixed with the white race and therefore of higher intelligence.

Of course that was not the belief of any of our neighbors but this resulted in father having many blacks with the chosen last name of Brown. This made the boy born on my birthday to be named Boo Brown and to explain the Boo part, one only had to look at him. From birth he was so large as to almost destroy his mother. In part, he was helped out of the birth canal with metal tongs that deformed his head. It is a wonder that he survived birth and except for his size, other boys would have made life miserable for him. Father gave him to me as companion and protector so he led a sheltered life on the plantation.

Boo was privileged to sleep on the floor beside my bed and to run with me where ever I chose to go. Kitchen privileges' were two fold in that Boo's mother was soon elevated to cook and that assured our choice of food. It was a certainty that we were to have a package of the best when we made it known we planned to be out all day. Mostly we stayed clear of the field hands since we were afraid we might have to work. It was not unusual for us to spend the entire day in the woods with the house still in sight.

When it came time for me to attend school, I took Boo with me but he was not allowed inside the class room. After class, I tried to teach Boo as much as I remembered which was very little for the first two or three years. School was close enough to our place that Boo usually went to be with his people during the middle of the day. He was learning the ways of his people and in turn teaching me much of it.

Well before I was born, father had become instrumental in the rebuilding of the Sheldon church building. Although the reconstruction was well over fifteen years in progress, work was still being done when I was a small child. I suppose work on the building never stopped until the Yankees burned it again in 1865. I was not present at the time it supposedly burned, so I can not vouch for the way it was destroyed. Many years later, a South Carolina historian wrote that it did not burn but that black and some whites removed the interior for the purpose of building their own homes. During the construction, there was always more carved panels to put into place that took years to finish. Such love for the building and the place where God chose to visit with them at least twice each week would never be finished. I can still remember the scaffolding that allowed men to do finish work on the ceiling and upper walls. Detail work was such that each man had a part in finishing the wood work and trim. Perhaps it would never be inspected by a critical eye but even the detail work on the ceiling was perfection. Only God would see and know how much love went into the carving and trim moldings.

Father had taken the best of his blacks to church with him in order to complete the reconstruction as soon as possible. Many of the plantation owners for miles around supplied money for the rebuilding and some of them supplied the massive timbers that had to be hewed and finished before elevating into place on the roof.

Mostly the blacks of these plantations did the work, supervised by the owners or their white supervisors. So far as I was ever able to determine, all of the plantation owners treated their blacks with care and not like cattle. Cotton, cane, peanuts, rice and other crops were needed to supply a hungry nation and a happy nigra did a much better job of caring for the owners Property than did an abused man or woman.

December 20, 1860, South Carolina secedes from the union. I was thirty four at the time and dreaded the thought of killing my fellow man.

In 1861, Jefferson Davis assumed the position of provisional confederate president and military commander from the state house in Charleston, South Carolina. In 1861 the provisional confederate congress passed additional military legislation to establish a permanent Confederate army. From this day on, it was the duty of every southern male to become a soldier or to help in the supply of military troops. For the most part, the confederate army was in a continuous state of loss and it all ended April 9, 1865 when General Robert E. Lee surrendered, unconditionally to Ulysses S. Grant.

In 1864 the war was running full steam all around us and it was time that I had to leave the plantation for service to my homeland here in the south. I had been able to avoid service on the necessity of supplying vital food and monetary aid to the cause.

Sherman had left Atlanta in flames and was moving south toward Savannah at a very rapid rate and destruction was positive and complete.

Boo was with me as a constant companion and when I had to join the ranks as a soldier, so did Boo. He had never looked on himself as a slave so it was not a problem for him to fight for the cause of slavery. He was simply Boo Brown, free man and my companion.

We chose two of our finest riding mounts and made our way to Charleston where we went directly to the headquarters of General Beauregard at the south west corner of Meeting and John street. There I was well received since my plantation had been instrumental in the supply of much needed food for the confederate army. Although Boo was left in the outer room of the generals office, he was certainly welcomed into service to act as my aid. General Beauregard commissioned me a Lieutenant and assigned me to the position of supply officer at his headquarters.

From there he sent me to see Col. A.J. Gonzales who was chief of artillery and was at that time in his office at 46 Rutledge st: in Charleston. Col Rutledge welcomed me with the news that it would be necessary for me to act immediately in order for the troops at fort Moultre to obtain supplies for the coming attack from an overpowering Federal army.

April 1863 the Federal ironclad ships were pounding Ft Moultre and for the next twenty months, the bombardment continued unabated. In February 1865, Ft Moultre was abandoned with the troops moving into Charleston. General P.G.T. Beauregard had his command post and living quarters in the Mills House hotel which was now coming under fire from Federal artillery. To this time, I had been unable to garner much in the way of supplies for our troops. The south was running dry and to make matters worse, the Confederate army's supply of powder was stored in the old Charleston train station.

Also in 1865, children playing in the train station set fire to something that quickly got out of control. The result was an explosion that killed over 150 and injured hundreds. The Roper hospital was overflowing with troops and now this. Even so, this hospital was never fired on by either army and stood intact throughout all of the many bombardments and fires Charleston withstood.

After the south failed to gain independence, many trials and tribulations fell on the south and my plantation was not excluded. Had it not been for BOO and the many loyal blacks, I would have lost all. Many Yankee carpetbaggers came and laid claim to my property. My salvation was that both me and my father before me had treated our blacks with respect and they now stood with me to drive off intruders. Legally, from the laws of the federal government , I could not hold on to my plantation but because I had given many plots of land to my blacks, I had their support and the federals did not take everything. I retained enough to live out my life in reasonable comfort but I was not assured a place in the Sheldon Church cemetery.

Terror of Teddy

This Thursday started off just as a hundred other days for Teddy since he had been named top salesman for Master Sales Company. He usually made the same customer calls every two weeks and in the same general time slot. Today was different only in that it was an exceptional spring morning when even the birds were feeling the mating call. Ted, at forty, was much in love with his wife of fifteen years but there was just something special about this day that made him think of young love, the excitement of the chase. As he drove west on Rt.29 for his last call of the day, he remembered the face and figure of the most luscious secretary of all on his route. His motto had been, "look but don't touch." However, Marla was different. His mind had been able to call her up, both face and figure, and dwell there for extended periods of time even though he did not like the idea so much.

Now as he had done so many times in the past, he forced himself to recall the past weekend with his wife and to their plan for the coming week with her in the country. Not that they ever did anything exciting, but there was comfort in being with Diane. She had become a little fixed in her ways which came of having a comfortable income and time on her hands. The garden club seemed to have become the most important thing in her life. Even Poochie, her little mutt, had been able to get her attention when Ted could not.

Poochie was tolerated but certainly not loved by Teddy. So far as he was concerned, Poochie belonged outside while he was at home but that never happened. That little dog always took Ted's favorite chair and made it stick while Diane was in the room. To Ted, she thought more of the dog than she did of him.

On the way to his last customer call where that luscious Marla held court, Ted drove at a moderate speed and took in the beauty of spring. New leaves on the trees, the smell of new grass in lush fields and children playing in the warm breeze of a near perfect day.

Ducks on farm ponds in pairs, swimming as if they were in love and had not a care in the world. Just being together was all that was necessary and this made Teddy think of Diane and wish they were that close again. Now his mind moved faster than the car and he was thinking of that lovely Marla just a few miles ahead, and it made him wonder if she was as pleasant at home as she was at the office. He wondered if she had a husband or if there was some other living condition? He wondered if----

well, he shouldn't wonder about these things. Ted had a wife and a little monster dog to feed and worry about.

Saturday, three weeks away, was to be special since they were hosting a birthday party for Al who lived next door. Jeannie, his wife, had set it up as a surprise for Al and being close friends, Diane had set up the party without consulting Ted. Of course it made little difference since they usually had a card game every Saturday night anyway, either at their house or Al and Jeannie's place. The only variation of this schedule was when they would cater a fancy feed, as Ted would say, for a surprise birthday party for either of them.

Ted entered the parking lot of his last call today. This was Thursday and he was one day ahead of schedule and he was thinking of how to close the order and be on his way. He hoped to visit a sporting goods store this evening and pick up some tips on upstate New York fishing and perhaps buy some fishing tackle. He had been planning since Christmas to get in a weekend of fishing when the weather got warm enough. His father had taken him to a small lake about three hours drive north of the location where Ted's last customer was located. Ted remembered the trip as one of great freedom and he longed for a repeat of that feeling. Although it happened over twenty five years ago, it was fresh in his memory. At that time, Ted remembered it as primeval forest with totally free and clear streams. He only had that one memory of his father when there was no stress and Ted longed for that feeling again. Ted's father had passed away over twenty years back and Ted's marriage and job had filled his leisure time. Perhaps it was time for Ted to live it up for a change. Ted hoped to locate the same lake as he remembered it, but thought it wise to ask the locals for directions and he might also pick up some tips on how to catch fish.

At his last customer call, Ted told himself it would not do for him to spend much time in the same room with that luscious lady, Marla. She would locate his buyers for him, direct him to the proper office, and, with luck he would be out of there in less than an hour. He would even avoid lobby time with Marla since it gave him uncomfortable thoughts. This weekend was his for the next three wonderful days. No boss, no phone, no card game, and best of all, no Poochie. The prospect of this trip was well worth the lie he had to tell Diane about how he would have to work with a customer over the weekend on a very difficult project.

Ted was not in luck this day. His buyer was delayed so that Ted was forced to take a comfortable chair facing Marla and wait out the next hour. He tried reading Purchasing News and Business Today but for all the effort he put into it, he could only read a line or two before he had to sneak a look over the top of the page at that luscious Marla. She in turn had tried to stay busy but he caught her staring at him a few times. And this let his mind go into an ecstasy of day dreams--those fantasies of things that are real in the mind but not so real as to give a man trouble later. Behind his eye lids, he could see Marla across the dinner table from him, candle light and silver, her evening dress cut low with little sparkles like diamonds on the dress and in her eyes.

He held her hand with the gentleness of perfect love and looked into her eyes as she told him how perfect he was. Ted, darling, you have the most perfect physique, the most dazzling teeth, and your perfectly groomed hair is my favorite color. How did your mother ever produce such a perfect and gorgeous man? Ted let his mind ramble where it would, accelerating through the evening till the time when he would take her in his arms and plant his sensuous lips on her luscious mouth. He was into it deep now so he let his mind continue to where he had drawn her close in his arms and was about to get the kiss he so richly deserved. Then he heard a gruff male voice call his name.

Ted, I'll be with you in about half an hour. My meeting time is running over . Perhaps Marla would take you back to the coffee room. Might help you stay awake, HA ! Ha !

Fat chance he would fall asleep with his heart pounding and blood racing through his temples until he was almost dizzy. Marla seemed to be waiting for an excuse to speak to Ted of things other than business, and the coffee room was that chance. Ted realized she really was attracted to him and, just maybe, he really was gorgeous . With this fresh new thought, his shoulders pulled up stomach in and chest out, he followed her down the hallway to the coffee room, thinking of how she moved. She was perfect, just as he thought he was. His walk improved as he considered that he was in perfect condition since he walked two miles every day, and Diane often told him what a great hunk of a man he was. He wished Diane had stayed out of this conversation. She had no business interrupting this appraisal he was having of himself.

Marla prepared coffee for him without asking his preference, and he never noticed that it had sugar and he never liked it that way. Ted was trying desperately to think of something witty to say but all he could think of was that he was going fishing next weekend in up-state New York. "Gee you must be some great outdoors man and I especially love a man that loves to fish." There it was again he thought. She was fishing. Ted caught himself day dreaming again but only for a moment. He was standing on the bank of a beautiful lake, fishing rod bent to the maximum while Marla stood behind him cheering him on to land the fourth large fish in only an hour.

Marla pulled him out of the trance by asking where he planned to go for this special trip and how long did he plan to stay? When he told her it was Whitewater lake, she gave a little cry of delight and told him it was close to her mother's home and she had played on that lake shore many times as a little girl. So now his fishing trip was delayed for a later weekend.

On this Friday afternoon, his thoughts were half way home and half way back to Mega where Marla would be just now cleaning off her desk for the last work day of the week. On arrival home, the package had just arrived from L.L. Bean, and Diane had placed it in his study room without looking at the contents or where it was from.

Ted was glad to be the one to open it since it would be hard to explain rubber waders that covered his feet and legs, all the way to his crotch. Ted just did not want to explain to Diane that he planned to slip off for a weekend alone. He just had to get away from Poochie and the hum-drum home life for a time. He knew Diane would laugh at him if he mentioned a fishing trip or anything that moved him to departure from the ordinary existence of a salesman. She had the idea he should be as ordinary as she was with her garden club meetings and same every day existence, but it was not to be. Perhaps some time with his wife would help him forget Marla, at least for another week because he was always glad to get home from a week on the road. He was thinking of home, a good dinner, and then his favorite chair if he could beat the mutt to it or if Diane was out of the room long enough for him to dispatch Poochie.

Ted had purchased some other fishing gear the night before and he planned to spend some time in the basement looking it over this evening, and he did not want Al to know about his planned weekend. Al might want to come along and this was to be his free week end, not another party. Al and Jeannie were close friends as well as next door neighbors, and, for many months, every Saturday night had been spent with them in a card game. It was with some degree of guilt that he realized it was Al and Jeannie that he wished to be away from, at least for one long weekend.

Perhaps this would be the Friday evening that Diane would greet him with a kiss and a good roast beef dinner. Later, a shower, some cuddle time on the couch and some love that he was much in need of and fully deserved.

During the last hour of the drive home, Ted allowed his mind to drift off into fantasy land which he was very good at. He arrived home just as Diane was putting finishing touches on a wonderful dinner and Poochie would be at the front drive with wagging tail to greet him with doggie kisses. He would enter the side door into the kitchen and be greeted with the odor of roast beef, smothered in onions, fresh blackberry pie just out of the oven, and best, of all, his favorite perfume on Diane's neck. Her gown was a little much for an evening at home but Ted understood. Nothing but the best for a hard-working husband who had been on the road for a week. She wore an expensive gown he never failed to appreciate and this evening she would cater to his every whim.

It was not to be. Poochie was under the weather so Diane said. Another dog had been hanging around the back door all day and Poochie wanted out, but Diane was worried and kept her inside. Poochie was agitated and when Ted failed to close the door fast enough, Poochie shot out the crack too fast for him to stop her. Diane still had morning curlers in her hair so Ted was less than pleased with the coming home response. Ted tried not to show his disappointment but it was hard to fall from heaven to the basement just by entering the kitchen door.

Well, this was the perfect time to lay out the fishing gear in the basement an look it over. At least he would have the entire evening all to himself. He could read the book on how to become the great fisherman and would be able to hold his own with any other fisherman he might encounter at the lake. The store clerk had filled his order list and had added many other essential items. Some things he recognized and some others he thought might have been invented since he had last wet a hook. He remembered seeing his father place hooks and lures in his hat but for the life of him, he failed to see just how this would work with the hard, plastic hat the salesman sold him. He also wondered why the hat needed batteries but would not ask the salesman for fear he would expose his ignorance. The batteries had something to do with the little container on top of the hat and he guessed the lures would be placed in the hat's side pockets as they were less likely to grab limbs or hands. The hard hat did have some features he liked, in part because he always did like lots of pockets.

First, he had to try on the rubber boots. They were a little large but he ordered them that way so there would be no chance of having to send them back. Next he put on the special fishing jacket the knowledgeable salesman had recommended. Much to his liking, it was loaded with pockets which the salesman had explained was a necessity for a full day at the lake. It came complete with emergency water wings, just in case a large fish should drag him into deep water. All he had to do was squeeze his arms tightly to his sides and the wings would expand with gusto. This was so that he would be able to keep both hands free to fight a fish that large, a real trophy. High on the back, just below the collar was an expandable pocket to be used for dry matches, fire starting chips and other fire starting paraphernalia. It was placed in this strategic location so as to remain high and dry when that fish pulled him into deep water and the salvation wings expanded. After all, it could have rained the night before and there would be a shortage of dry wood. It could be dangerous for a man to be fishing alone and fall into deep water.

High on both sleeves were zippered pockets for those items frequently needed. These pockets were large enough to hold cigarettes on one side and a beer can on the other.

The reserve beer can pocket was located low on the left side where it would be submerged most of the time, helping it to stay cool. It would also be out of the way of his right hand casting motion. Ted marveled at the engineering know how applied to the design of such a garment. There were still more pockets in reserve, including the king sized and expandable, zippered pockets on the upper left and right chest area. One of them was marked "INSULATED FOR SANDWICHES." The other chest pocket contained survival gear, complete with compass, mirror, needle with black thread, small flashlight, band aids, sunburn cream, chap stick, matches, candle, toilet paper and a shiny police whistle. The salesman had thrown in a map of New York state for free which Ted thought he might need if he should wander too far around the lake.

To make him a safer fisherman, the salesman sold him a shoulder mounted flashlight with a large battery pack that would fit in still another pocket high in the center of his back where the weight would not be so noticeable. The best pocket of all was the one located on the very tail end of his jacket and was placed there so the big fish he caught would be close to water so it could be submerged from time to time. This was absolutely necessary in order to keep the fish from becoming restless, so the salesman said.

Ted looked over the hat and decided it went well with the jacket As he read the instructions it became clear to him that great engineering talent went into the design of the hat. Each little door around the periphery of that marvel could be opened for the storage of another fishing lure. All he had to do was memorize the location of the lure he needed to catch a particular fish. Ted loved little pockets and storage places and this hat was an expensive marvel. As he read the instructions, he found the explanation for the cable attached to the back of the hat. It explained that the cable was to be attached to the ring on the right shoulder of his jacket, a necessity to keep it from being lost if a large fish were to pull him under. Now that he had read the instructions, he wondered why he had not thought of that himself.

He read that the little compartment on top with attached batteries was to carry worms. Some worms were not accustomed to cold night air or the early morning cold that he might be fishing in and they might grow stiff with the cold. No self respecting fish would go for a cold, stiff worm. Ted guessed that a stiff worm might be a problem to any fisherman isolated as he would be out on the lake shore. So much for that .

He placed himself before the mirror while holding his new fishing rod and admired the figure of the perfectly dressed fisherman. No doubt he could grace the cover of

FISHING WORLD as the most perfect figure available at the time.

Poochie had spent the day lost out where she could not or would not answer the call of Diane but when she returned at dark, she had a contented look on her hairy snout. Ted was still looking in the mirror when Poochie chose that moment to break into his dream with a trip to the basement. She was half way across the basement before she saw the strange apparition from another world standing before the mirror. To her it looked like two of the strangest demons she had ever seen and it was directly in her path. Too late to check her momentum in the forward direction, she chose to do what any scared dog would do, take a bite out of it on the way up the steps to where Diane would protect her. Her sharp little teeth made a good sized hole in the new waders. It happened too fast for Ted to react, slowed as he was by heavy boots and a much heavier jacket. Besides he did not want to create a scene that might bring Diane into the picture. It was enough that Poochie was upstairs, barking as if all the demons in the world had taken up residence in the basement. Ted could only look at the large tear in on the back of the left leg and dislike the dog even more. What else could this dog do to spoil his evening? Much, much more as it turned out. Diane took the little dog on her lap and spoke the loving things a dog of culture wants to hear.

After a restless night in the guest room because Poochie needed the care of Diane, Ted faced Saturday morning with a gloomy attitude. His work around the house was less than perfection and resulted in more work than he had to start with. That big male dog was continually in his way, following his every step and hoping Ted would make the mistake of entering the house and leaving a crack in the door--all he needed to slip out for another visit with his new-found lady friend. Poochie had to stay in but she was never far from the door, just in case Ted forgot. Ted never cared for dogs the way most people did but he liked them when they were in their place, outside and out of the way.

He finally gave up the effort to do the chores and decided to practice with his new casting rod. This required a lot of space outdoors, and, since he did not have the back lawn for it, he chose to take it along with his clubs down to the club house. There he got the feel of the rod and obtained some degree of accuracy, deciding he was as good as most fishermen. With this experience, he thought, "Look out big fishes, here comes Teddy." Ted had to be careful that his friends, Doc and Al, did not see him with the fishing gear. Doc in particular was a good golfing buddy but knew nothing about the finer arts of fishing, and Ted did not have the time nor desire to include Doc in his plans.

When Doc arrived, they played the usual eighteen holes with a beer at every hole. It mattered not that other players played through, leaving Ted and Doc to partake of shade and more beer. Both of them loved to cheat and got great pleasure out of telling the big lies that go with golfing. Ted loved to tell how he got three birdies and an eagle last week.

Unless he had to, he would never tell that his rules were a little different from the norm. In his rules, if he sliced to the left, it was a birdie and if he sliced to the right, it was an eagle. With these rules, he could not be beaten, not even by Doc who could slice all day after the first beer. Ted had his mind on next weekend and so lost ten dollars to Doc, mostly because he forgot to lie enough.

Diane had disappointed him last night. Poochie had snapped at him and almost ruined his new boots, and the only pleasant time he had this week end was the thoughts of Marla.

Ted was serious about the fishing trip that would start soon after he left Mega Manufacturing where Marla worked. He would feast his eyes on that luscious creature for a short time and then leave there and be on the lake before dark Thursday. He would set up his tent, grill a choice steak, and with a few beers, get a good nights sleep.

On the way home from the club, he remembered to stop at a gas station for a large container of tire and tube patching. It only came in red and his boots were olive, but he guessed the patch would be under water most of the time so other fishermen would not notice. It was a good thing that he purchased the large container because Poochie had been busy while he was at the club. Diane said the poor thing had been so nervous that she had to have something to chew on and all Diane could find that Poochie liked was the rubber stuff in the basement. Since they were rubber, Diane thought the dog could do no harm. Ted picked up the remains and calculated patches versus holes and decided to patch rather than forego his fishing trip. Besides, he had told Diane that he needed them in order to do an on site job for a client next weekend. It would not do for him to change his story now. By the time he finished, it was almost time for Al and Jeannie to arrive for the usual Saturday night card game. Diane had been on edge for most of the day and it was altogether due to the peculiar actions of the mutt. Ted was inclined to ignore the dog, but on these occasions when he could not get Diane's attention away from the mutt, he was irritated and was likely to make faces at the mutt and dare it to react. Ted wanted the excuse to put the dog outside as punishment for sins, real or imagined but since it was acting this way, it was impossible. Diane became even more hostile to Ted and the valley between them became wider as the evening wore on.

Interest in the game was less than thrilling. Ted had the next weekend in mind, Diane had the dog on hers while Al and Jeannie had their own thoughts far from the game. The conversation between Dianne and Jeannie went on as woman chatter. At one point in the chatter, Ted distinctly heard Jeannie say that she would kill Al if she ever caught him involved with another woman. He hears Diane second that motion and resolved to never get caught in that situation. Marla crossed his mind but he quickly cast it aside as just another customer with a great deal of "look but don't touch" pleasure.

Soon it became apparent the game was wearing thin. Al completed the last hand and announced that the next Saturday night game was off. He had been given a two week lay-off notice at the plant and he was taking Jeannie for a vacation. No place in particular but they considered driving down to Virginia to see Jeannie's mother. It had been such a long time and her mother was getting kind of old. Al never mentioned that he would also be on a long weekend vacation. If he had, he considered that Dianne would want to accompany him since Jeannie would be away. He had thought this over since January when he ordered the L.L. Bean boots and he had made the arrangements to leave off the Friday customers for that coming weekend. He also knew Diane would never hear to a fishing and camping trip since her idea of camping started at the Ritz and ended at the same place. He also knew he could not tolerate Poochie in a tent with him.

Sunday noon found Ted and Doc on the Golf course again. Doc had noticed the far away look in Ted's eyes and diagnosed it as too much work and responsibility on his job. He lied and cheated through another eighteen holes and took six beers plus ten bucks from Ted. Then he proceeded to give Ted some free medical advice. "Without question" said Doc, "you need to get close to Diane and stop the worry about your job. Nothing takes away the worry as well as an intimate night with your wife." "For this," Doc told him, " no charge and don't thank me, just pay the ten bucks you lost." Ted was thinking how right Doc was but he said nothing as it was out of Doc's hands. It was definitely between Diane, Poochie and him and the dog was planted square in the middle. He resolved to try again and be on his best behavior tonight. Let nature take its course as they say. Unfortunately, nature was taking its course with Poochie.

Ted arrived home from the club and was greeted by a worried Diane and a very restless dog. Diane said she wished the vet's office was open on Sunday as she thought sweet little Poochie needed something like tranquilizing pills. Ted thought he knew how to quiet the mutt but his life would be on the line if he spoke the thought. Inside, his anger mounted but he held it in check while he drifted off into dream world again. This time he saw himself let Poochie outside while six large male dogs waited in canine anticipation. He thought he saw Poochie take off across the field, running for her life with the six big ones on her tail and she losing the race. He could even hear the barking and the fighting among the six big ones as to which would have the pleasure of sinking teeth in her little rump.

Ted grinned with deep satisfaction due to the entire pack disappearing over the horizon and out of sight forever. Good riddance he spoke out loud, not hearing Diane say she was off to the druggist for some help for Poochie. She was just exiting the door when she heard the muttered words meant for Poochie and took them to be meant for her. Well, she was just glad to know how he felt about her, so she turned from the kitchen door to the bedroom door, locking herself in for the night. Ted was stuck with the dog and considered doing as he had day dreamed a short time ago, send that dog out to face the six big ones.

Problem was, he didn't have the nerve to face Diane the next morning if something drastic happened to that mutt. The best he could do was watch television and try to pass the evening dreaming of Marla.

About eleven that night, he and the dog heard Diane groan and both went to the door. Poochie was very restless and wanted to either go in with her or outside. Poochie was shivering and let out a doggie groan. Diane opened the door a crack to let the dog in but she made it clear Ted was not welcome and he groaned. Diane said it sounded like they both had come down with the same bug or worm. Ted agreed they had and told Poochie to come take a cold shower with him and they would then split a can of Kennel Ration. Ted spent a restless night on the couch and a murder mystery on TV It held little attraction for him except it was about a jilted wife planning to kill her husband for the insurance. As she formulated a plan, Ted tried to give her some pointers such as don't let blood get on you and become evidence. Do it in the shower so it could be washed down the drain with ease. As poison was considered, he had little advice to offer except it should be given with food. He was only thinking it should be a good dinner since it would be his last meal and it would make dieing a little more pleasant. Right now, he was thinking that death would be a little easier than at most times. He thought about people on death row and realized there was always the desire to live, even if a cantankerous wife and a miserable mutt did make life so unpleasant.

Toward morning, Ted got a little sleep and was in fair shape to face another week on the road. Perhaps this one would go fast since the trunk of his car was loaded with fishing and camping gear. Four days of work then three days of being alone, away from that mutt.

He decided to take breakfast downtown and not see Diane and that miserable mutt before leaving for the next two weeks. Diane would be angry but so was he.Monday mornings were usually spent at the office where Ted did last week's reports and the new week's planned activity schedule. This Monday was unusual since his automobile held a slightly different cargo, and, once he was away from the house, Ted had a different attitude. Mr. Bud Billings, his over weight and overbearing boss gave his usual Monday morning pep talk. Ted took it in stride since he knew the boss had to do something to make it appear he had something to do with success. Ted listened with respect but found these morning meetings to be only good for a last cup of coffee before facing the rigors of the road. He knew he was the only sensible driver out there and that he had to watch out for idiots.

He also had to be careful due to the necessity of making excuses about his Nikon camera. His boss wanted it at a greatly reduced price and Ted was not about to give it to him. Bud Billings had the way about him that inferred the salesmen should treat him with respect or suffer the consequences. Selling him his trusted camera at half price was expected, but Ted made one excuse after another. Ted thought he treated the old windbag right by just listening to the same stories every Monday and giving the proper strained laughter. Bud told the same hunting story week after week in which he and his hunting partner were on horseback through the mountains in bear country. The story goes that his partner, Jim, got off the horse and walked into the bushes to relieve himself where he met a bear that let out a roar. Jim screamed, "Run for your life," and promptly outran the horse with his trousers around his ankles. Ted thought this was funny but he had changed the story to see in his mind's eye-- Bud Billings doing the running. He was laughing at the image of old lard butt on the run with his butt exposed to the elements.

Before Ted could get out of the office that morning, a phone call came in from Marla. Ted was much surprised and pleased to hear from her, for any reason. He thought at first that her boss might have a large or rush order to place with him and it was unusual for this company to give him large orders. Instead, Marla told him all weekend she had been thinking about her mother. This morning she had asked her boss for Friday off, and, although she was needed in the morning, he had given her the afternoon off. Since Ted had told her he planned a trip up to Whitewater Lake and it was near her mother's, could she please ride up there with him Friday and back on Sunday?

Ted started to tell her he planned to go up Thursday night but he quickly decided to forego fishing until Friday late evening. Marla said she knew him to be such a gentleman that she felt comfortable in asking this favor of him. Ted would be making a call on her boss that Thursday so he would just wait around until Marla was free of work. Ted had a case of nervous jitters, not entirely unexpected, but it was certainly a mixture of fear and wild expectation.

The automobile trunk was filled with camping and fishing gear, and Ted was filled with excitement and anticipation. It was a fine spring morning and off we went. Ted drove to his only customer for Mondays and hardly realized he had made the trip. His mind was filled with fantasies and plans with no room left for Diane and Poochie. Marla was nice and she was beautiful. Ted thought how nice it would be to have a long conversation with a beautiful person for several hours, and he started thinking of witty things to say. No doubt the conversation would be about the place where she worked since it was about the only thing they had in common. Tuesday was filled with many orders and rapid customer contact. Very little time was available for Ted to think of anything except work. Wednesday went much the same way and by motel time that evening, he started thinking again of Marla. After the day's orders were written and the motel desk was cleared, Ted turned on the TV for late news and some relaxation before bed time. Ted never saw the news because his eyelids became a movie screen for his latest departure from reality. He had driven north to Marla's mother's place and Marla was introducing him to her mom. She was telling the old lady what a gentleman Ted was.

Ted had the uncomfortable feeling that mom was very little older than he but since this was fantasy, he parked that thought in the "Forget it" column. He felt Marla's hand take him by the arm as she told mom what a wonderful gentleman he was and how sweet he was on the drive up. Mom asked them to come in for the dinner she had prepared and Ted could smell the roast beef smothered in onions, and he got a whiff of blackberry pie fresh from the oven.

Ted got the feeling he had been there many times before, and, come to think of it, he had been there in his mind's eye. Dinner was excellent and conversation was witty with Ted doing most of the talking. The two women were starved for intelligent male conversation and Ted was at his best. Sometimes conversations didn't go just as Ted wanted them to, and, this was one time he was not in complete control. Mom started leading the conversation to marriage for her daughter and Ted had to scramble it back to reality before it got out of hand. He wished he had been able to stay for the blackberry pie.

Thursday morning was almost more than Teddy could bear. He had one call to make before driving to Mega Manufacturing where Marla worked. This call was almost useless since he said all the wrong things about his products and only obtained one small order, and that was for essential items. This call was lost money since he had his mind on the next call and the last one for the week. By this time, he had forgotten all about the fishing trip. It was all about the company of Marla. At last he arrived at Mega and there was Marla, just as efficient and beautiful as he remembered, if not more so. She had set his appointment with the buyers in such a way as to allow time to talk to him between buyers.

She told him how great it was to see him and how much she was looking forward to seeing her mom. She even said she would enjoy being with Ted for the few travel hours this week end. Ted almost choked on things he almost said and did his best to act the part of an efficient salesman and how he was used to giving customers a ride. After all, he did take customers to lunch many times during any given month and this was no different !

Marla had it well planned but she told Ted only the part he wanted to hear for the moment. Ted was to pick her up at her apartment at two o'clock this Friday afternoon.

He arrived promptly, and, just before turning off the engine, he took a furtive look up and down the street as if he expected to be caught with his hand in the cookie jar. Seeing no one he was acquainted with, he slipped out of the car and went to the door trying desperately to quench the feeling of fear or guilt, which ever. Then the remembrance of the day dream of Marla in her nightgown made him feel somewhat better, but he was not so certain that Diane could read his mind, even at this distance. Then Marla came to the door with suitcase in hand, acting like a little girl, and when Ted saw how lovely she was, he forgot all about Diane. He forgot about his job, that despicable mutt back home, and everything except "Carpe Diem," Latin for seize the moment. In this case, seize the weekend. Now he took on the air of a youthful Don Juan, gallant and witty.

They traveled north for the next two hours, driving as slow as possible in order to view the scenery,, so Ted said, but in reality he did not want this trip to pass too quickly. Marla was well aware of the effect she had on him, so it was unnecessary for her to do much more than smile at his attempts at witticisms. Ted was half here and half there, thinking what it would be like to have her for the full weekend. Just in case mom was away for the weekend, he would play the gentleman and offer to take her to a relative or even return her to her apartment. Ted had planned the drive up thoroughly. He had planned to say he was hungry just before a suitable restaurant came in sight. Marla was receptive to a prolonged dinner stop, and Ted never realized that she had no place to go and was in no hurry to get there. At dinner, Ted was all thumbs and so intent on impressing Marla with his cosmopolitan manners that he made one mistake after another.

He dropped his fork and continued eating with his spoon, as if Marla would not notice. He dropped his napkin so many times that he failed to notice he was using the corner of the table cloth. Marla knew she had him captivated so she continued acting the part of a sweet little girl, right to the end.

Ted, the experienced traveling man was at a loss as to what to say since he was trying to stay on safe ground. He failed to realize he was already in mud up to the arm pits. He must be careful to say nothing about home, Diane or the mutt as this would probably dampen the mood and destroy his weekend. He was having enough trouble with the conversation and his penchant for falling into a trance about things that pleased or worried him. Marla was trying to carry the conversation and be coy enough to to show herself as the perfect lady. She thought it would be safe to ask him about his preference in music, sports, and hobbies. "Ted, what do you do with your time on weekends?" The question was innocent for Marla but loaded for Ted. Before he could answer, he was off into the trance of "Never, Never Land" where Poochie was at his heels as he cut grass and Diane was sitting at the lawn table with iced tea and glasses. Ted stopped long enough to join her in a cold glass of her wonderful tea and a brief rest. They spoke of their beautiful home and Ted's love for an immaculate lawn and garden. He realized he loved golf and classical music and the Saturday night card game with Al and Jeannie, the four of them around the kitchen table. He loved potato chips and beer at the card game and he was lost in the trance of all the things he loved. Marla prompted him with the question again.

Only briefly did he come out of the trance long enough to say he enjoyed living and all the things that go with having a good income. At once his mind returned to the card game where he could talk to Al about anything. They were brothers. While he carried a conversation with Al, he distinctly remembered the conversation Diane and Jeanne were having in which Jeannie was telling about the lady down at the beauty parlor who just got a settlement from her divorce. She got everything. Al was speaking to him but he was hearing Jeannie say she would kill the SOB for the insurance as well. He also heard Diane say killing him for his unfaithfulness was definitely in order. The SOB should die a lingering death.

POP! His mind was back at the table where the lovely Marla sat across from him and he realized his brow was covered with beads of sweat. Ted wanted to say that he needed to get on with the fishing trip but, somehow, the words were not available. Ted quickly moved his thoughts from home to his job. Now he could tell Marla about how important his job is and how stressed out he is every weekend. This served to explain the perspiration which appeared for no apparent reason on his forehead, and now he could relate the need for a fishing trip. He told her about Doc and his golf games with the old crook and then he recited the poem he wrote last week.

And now I face a stressful day.
The pressure is on to work and pay.
With pounding heart and racing blood,
I swim in troubles as in a flood.
Irate customers are demanding,
Do or die my boss is commanding
The phone demands immediate attention,
My muddled brain has lost retention.
Then comes a minor break in pace,
I send a prayer to outer space.
Help me Lord, my God almighty.
Help me make it through till Friday.
My doctor tells me to worry not
For money pressures kill a lot.
He sends his bill for lots of cash
My budget does a Wall Street crash
And again, I face a stressful day.

TED DOESN'T KNOW WHAT STRESS IS JUST YET.

Marla laughs and tells him she thinks he is a very clever and flamboyant character. She has loads of sympathy for him and reaches across the table for his hand. The first intimate contact and Ted feels the blood pressure rise to a dangerous level. He thinks he is very clever to have pulled off a dinner with such a lovely female, and now the perspiration appears on his forehead again. For the first time, Ted becomes reckless and speaks a word which he would not have used in his right mind. "Marla, dear, do you think we should be on our way?" There it was, the word "Dear" and she failed to react, at least in so far as Ted could tell. Up to now, Marla was fishing and now, she was ready to set the hook.

Now , thought Marla, time to be on our way to mom's place and we do need to go. Ted thought the drive would be too short but, at the same time, he hoped it would end so he could be on his way to the lake. Short bursts of fear hit him, but desire overpowered all other thoughts.

They arrived at mom's house only to find it dark and apparently deserted. By calling on the neighbor next door, they learned that mom was visiting her sister and would be away for the next two weeks, and, no, they did not have a spare key. Ted's fantasy had come true. He had been through this in his dream world, so he expressed sympathy and offered to drive her to a relative or even back to her apartment in the city. Marla liked neither and said so. Ted jokingly offered her his tent but Marla had a better idea. "Ted, I know where there is an old hotel that was bypassed by the new interstate a few years back. It is a lovely vacation place and nobody goes there any more. It should not be expensive and I wonder if you would be a gentleman and take me there?" Ted was on the line, good and solid, just as Marla planned had when she heard that her mother was to be away for this weekend. Well, for Ted, this was culmination of his most erotic dream, and, if he had had complete control, he could not have planned it better. As it turned out, the old hotel was close enough for them to arrive about ten thirty. On the way there, Marla had again expressed her faith in his gentlemanly manners . "Ted, I know I can trust you completely, so why don't we take a two-bedroom suite so we can talk?" Ted fell for the gentleman's angle, or did he?

At the hotel, Ted carried their suitcases up to the old man at the counter and asked for a two-bedroom suite as Mr. and Mrs. Teddley. The old man told him the rooms were at the top of the stairs and the elevator was out of service. In truth, the elevator had been broken for almost three years and they would have to climb the stairs. Ted was so delighted at how he had maneuvered this deal that he was willing to climb twenty floors. Ted took the key and picked up a bag in each hand. As he did an about face toward the stairs, he looked across the lobby for the first time. Al was grinning at him and Jeannie was giving him the death glare, for real, no dream, no trance, no escape. Ted felt himself going faint and weak in the legs, his breath was very short and his heart was about to jump out of his chest. In that instant of indecision, there was a flashback to the card game and Jeannie saying, "I would kill Al." In this moment, he makes the decision to bluff it out and pretend to be someone else. He changed his voice and spoke loudly to the old man, "Call us at six, our children will be meeting us for breakfast." Marla thought he was joking with her and laughed as she thought she was supposed to.

The old man said "six it is and good night". Ted knew this was not going to be a good night as he climbed the ten thousand steps to doom. One step after another sounded like, sorry *SOB, sorry SOB, sorry SOB.*

The hotel room was beautiful old Victorian with almost everything done in white. Even the carpet was deep pile in white on white. Marla was elated as it appeared that they had been given the bridal suite. It fit well in her plans, and poor Ted had no idea of the color or lack of such in the entire room. Everything looked black to him and some things refused to settle down and stay in one place. Even when he sat in a white Queen Anne chair, with his eyes closed, everything looked black. The inside of his eyelids looked black with flashes of red, like war over the horizon. Marla could not help but see the change in him and she attributed it to his being a bashful gentleman. That was all the more reason why she would have to take the lead, and this required a shower and the proper night gown. Ted finally got the black screen before his eyes to return to near normal focus, but he did not like the picture and could do nothing to change it. He could see Al and Jeanie rushing to their room to pack for a middle of the night departure-- destination home as fast as they could drive it in the wee still hours of the morning, knocking on Diane's door for an early morning discussion of how to kill an unfaithful husband. Al, his friend would help dispose of the body, and, from Al's grin down in the lobby a short time ago, Ted was certain Al was already anticipating digging a shallow grave.

Ted was not hearing the things Marla was saying from the bathroom where she had left the door half way open. She told Ted they could talk while she showered but Ted failed to hear that part. In fact, he was not hearing anything she said for he was hearing Diane saying, "The SOB should die a lingering death." Marla thought her looks and words held Ted speechless and this was part of her little girl act. She came out of the bathroom dressed in the most seductive, off-white gown that money could buy--one that she could not afford except as bait for her fishing trip. She had purchased the gown over a year ago and had been waiting for just the right man to come along. She now looked the part of what she really was, a designing woman out for blood. She wanted a man that had been tried in marriage and seemed to be happy with it. He needed to be successful in business and reasonable in looks. His family meant nothing to her and she did not want his children, so a good divorce settlement would leave his children with a jilted wife. So be it.

Marla walked over to him and placed a gentle hand on his cheek. Again Ted was speechless, but the condition was brought on by the vision of a lovely woman who he had been thinking of for weeks. He even had to admit that he had dreamed of just such a situation as he was in with Marla like this. But now, he had to face facts, that he was already guilty in Al and Jeannie's eyes.   Ok, then. He decides to forget all else and enjoy the time and the beautiful offering before him. In the shower under a hot stream of water, Ted took stock and knew he could never explain this to anyone. Guilty, guilty, they would all say and they would be right so he might as well make the best of it.

Next week when he returned for his personal articles at what used to be his home, he would soon enough face the music. But, as he continued to shower and contemplate, he got the vision of Poochie meeting him at the driveway, shaking her head, and Marla wringing her hands and asking, "Why? why? Why?" He couldn't do it !

Ted returned to the bedroom dressed in his pajamas with every button up tight. He was slightly bent over and holding his stomach as if in great pain (which he mentally was). Marla saw the contorted look on his face of great pain and became much concerned.

Ted asked her to bring him a glass of water so he could take the special pill Doc had prescribed. While she was out of sight, Ted got the aspirin tablet from his PJ pocket so Marla could see him take the all-important pill. He swallowed it and took the fetal position on the couch, claming he would be all right in a few hours. Marla, not willing to give up this chance to set the hook on this fishing trip, sat on the edge of the couch and massaged his back and shoulders. She smothered him with what she thought was motherly concern. She had no experience in combating abject fear, so it was in vain. About two thirty Saturday morning, she gave up and went to bed, alone.

Ted lay on the couch for a long time before he dropped off into a very troubled sleep. He had no more than dozed off until he was in a dream series again, this time just arriving home to face Diane. When he got out of the car in his driveway, Poochie ran up to meet him, teeth bared and determined to chew his leg off up to the place where Diane would take over and continue chewing. She carried a king sized shotgun with which she held him at bay while she and Poochie chewed. Diane had said about all there was to say as she raised the shotgun to his chest level. Her final words were, "Die you miserable son of a b****". BANG went Ted's eyelids as they popped open to face the horrors of the rest of that night in the bridal suite.

At five in the morning, Ted could stand no more. He called Marla and told her he was no better (gross understatement) and needed see Doc. He now had a headache and a stomach that really did feel sick. Marla believed he had a bad case of ulcers which a lot of hard working men seem to have. Most salesmen have a boss that helps the ulcers along, and Bud Billings, who he had told her about, seemed to be the worst kind. At check out time, Ted was on edge. Sure enough, when Ted asked about Al and Jeannie, he was told that they had checked out some time ago. In either case, they would already be with Diane or soon to arrive. There was nothing he could do now. It was far too late, so he must prepare to die soon. By now, Ted was unable to carry on a conversation with Marla. She was doubly concerned when Ted did not want breakfast, not even coffee. He just wanted to be on the road home---to see Doc, so he said.

At mid morning when Ted dropped Marla at her apartment, he was in worse shape than at dawn and still had almost two hours to drive home. Marla tried to keep him there by offering to get a doctor to make a house call for him, but she had no way of knowing that a medical doctor would be useless. She believed that she might still have a chance if she could just keep him there over the rest of the weekend. Also, she thought her kind of bed rest would do wonders for him, not knowing that Ted's problem was just plain remorse and fear. Well, Ted was remorseful all right but only because he got caught. He remembered that famous line spoken by President Roosevelt at the beginning of World War II: "We have nothing to fear but fear itself." Ted remembered those lines, and, for the first time in his life, he knew and understood abject and unremitting terror. Ted drove out to the highway and stopped at the first public telephone he could locate He called Diane to tell her the job was cut short (it really was), and he said he would be home in about four hours. He very carefully asked if she had heard from Jeannie of if they had returned. Diane was somewhat concerned, as she could hear the fear in Ted's voice and did not recognize the meaning, but she understood that Ted wanted very much to be home. She said, "Please be careful on the road, Ted, dear. Take your time and I will have dinner ready when you arrive." Ted had not eaten since dinner yesterday and he did not plan to eat for the rest of his life. He figured there was no reason to since he was to die soon and it might be easier on an empty stomach. Surely, Al and Jeannie would be there soon and death would quickly follow.

Ted drove rather slow and remembered nothing about the towns and traffic he passed, except, an ambulance passed him and he wondered if it would follow him home in order to remove his dead body. He did see the face of the injured man on the stretcher and wondered if Diane would use a method that would let him last long enough to reach the hospital. He wondered if it would be a knife, the shotgun, or poison. With this, he drifted off into another of his day dreams.

He was in his driveway and about to get out of his car. Before him stood a very large man dressed as a sheriff with a badge the size of a gallon milk jug pinned to a massive chest. In his hand he held a large envelope marked with the heavy black words, DIVORCE PROCEEDINGS. The sign on the front door said in bold letters, DIANE'S RESIDENCE, and scattered on the front lawn, lay all of his clothes and personal things. Poochie stood beside the sheriff with teeth bared, ready to take off his leg. Poochie's boy friend was beside his golf clubs with a leg cocked up and spoiling his clubs.

By this time he had his eyes closed and was crying out, I didn't do it--I couldn't do it, I'm not guilty. While in this state off remorse, he drifted across the center line and was awakened by the blast of a semi truck horn. After a short lifetime, Ted arrived at the dreaded driveway. There was no car in Al's driveway, no lights in the house, and no sign they were at home or had been. Ted is at a loss for thought but he must still face Diane. At the front door, Poochie is barking and Ted thinks at any moment he will feel those sharp little teeth, but he must face it. He must try to take it like a man even though he felt like a mouse. He pushed the door open and there stood Poochie with wagging tail and a welcome jump to let him know all was well. Diane called a warm greeting from the kitchen and the house was filled with the smell of his favorite roast beef, smothered in onions. Blackberry pie and Diane was wearing his favorite perfume. Relief floods Ted's soul but he still has to ask if Al or Jeannie had called. Yes, she called about noon. There was no further statement from Diane and Ted had to wait for the axe to fall because he dared not ask another question. Instead he asked about Poochie's health and was told that the dog got out on Monday and did not return until Thursday morning. Diane said she came back well and happy. Poochie was listening to this conversation and had a silly and contented grin on her face. Ted had a grin on his face but it was far from contented. It was silly with the knowledge they would soon have pups. Diane seemed to be totally unaware of the reason Poochie left home for those three days. Diane noticed the peaked look on Ted's face and asked about his health. Ted told her he had caught a bad case of stomach something and would see Doc soon. Diane said she thought he might be overworked and perhaps he should go out and get some of whatever Poochie got that made her come home all bouncy and happy. If it was so easy for Poochie to locate, it surely should do Ted a world of good.

Dinner was excellent with all of the food that Ted would die for. Did he really think that? Anyway, this Saturday night was not the usual, so Ted ate very little. He was somewhat afraid that there was a taste of poison in every dish. He watched Diane closely and would only taste it after he saw Diane eat it or feed Poochie a little of it. When Diane placed a tasty morsel on his plate in order to tempt him, Ted would slip Poochie a sample first. As long as she continued to stand, he figured it was safe for him. Still, he knew very little about poisons so he was still apprehensive. Eventually, dinner was over and Ted was relieved that he felt no adverse effects of an unknown substance in his stomach and Poochie was still a happy dog. Could this mean that he would live through another night?

He remembered reading a detective story where the victim lived for weeks, slowly succumbing to the poison with increasing agony near the end. Still, he had seen Diane feed her little dog and he knew that dog was more important to her than he was. After dinner Diane suggested that they go to the living room for a little TV before bedtime. Poochie heard the suggestion and the word TV and raced to be there first to take control of Ted's favorite chair. When Ted arrived, it would have been normal for Diane to tell Ted to find another chair since Poochie was there first, but this evening Poochie took one sorrowful look at Ted and jumped to the floor at Ted's feet. Some say that dogs have a sixth sense about impending death of a human, and, this evening, Ted would have agreed with the author of that statement.

Diane got the TV set to where she thought Ted was engrossed in the screen, but, in fact, he was staring at the moving lights and seeing his own version of a drama. Diane slipped out to their bedroom where she took a shower and soon returned, prepared for an intimate evening with her husband. On returning to the living room, she told Ted how sorry she was for the rejection last weekend and, by the flickering TV lights, Ted saw she had on the identical articles of clothing as those worn by Marla last evening. Now he was certain, tonight he was to die. Diane knew and was out to torture him to the last second of his life. Even Poochie was in on the plot to destroy him. How? Time was short for him to find out, but when Diane asked him to shower and join her in bed, he thought he had the answer. She would open the shower door and stab him so he wouldn't bleed on the floor. Nothing else but to face it, so he undressed and said a prayer before entering the shower.

Now I lay me down to sleep,
I pray, O Lord, my soul to keep.
And when she stabs me, make it deep
And let me die without a peep.

He closed the shower door and turned on a full blast of hot water, something to help numb his senses. He kept his eyes closed for he didn't want to see it coming. He tried to hum the tune he had heard at a funeral some time back, partially to make a noise so he wouldn't hear the shower door open. This gave him some comfort in the last moments of his impending death and he tried to remember the words that went like--

When life has passed this worldly state,
When time has come to cross that river,
When life has passed into the clouds
MMMM mmm mm cut my liver.

Of course, he tried to think otherwise, but he could feel the knife enter his back and cut deeply into the vital parts.

When he ran out of hot water and was still living, he had to think again about where Al and Jeannie were. Perhaps they would have a car wreck and both be killed. Terrible thought, but a new way to look into the future. Maybe, Diane had not heard and there was some hope for me after all. With this new thought, he dried himself and hit the bed at top speed and again thought, Carpe Diem, seize the moment. Ted had been without sleep for many hours and when Diane had taken the jitters out of him, he fell into a deep sleep that was almost like death. Morning found Ted rested in body but not quite rested in spirit. He had all of this Sunday to worry about Al and Jeannie. Will they make it home or will we hear of their terrible accident? Ted felt miserable to think that he wished them harm, all to allow him to live. Their death would be the perfect answer, but, certainly, he never gave a thought to anything except an automobile death for them. Hoping his friend would have some form of cure, Diane watched him suffer with something that he could not or would not name, so she tried sending him out for a golf game with Doc.

Before they got to the sixth hole, Doc stopped for another beer and asked Ted to set in the shade for a conference. He had noticed the worry on Ted's face the first few minutes and had been trying to discern the meaning of downcast eyes. Thinking, as doctors and friends do, he ruled out a medical problem and felt it necessary to pry a little. "Is it a woman, Ted? Have you jumped the fence and now find yourself too remorseful to face another day on earth?" He took Ted by total surprise and before Ted could reason this question out, he blurted the name, Marla. Catching himself, he quickly stated, "I'm not guilty." That was all Doc needed to wade into the private life of Ted which was not private any more. Doc got only the basic facts but enough to feel sorry for Ted and to offer some advice; "Never admit to anything, Never."

Al and Jeannie were due back in about a week, and, the closer to that return time, the more worried Ted became. Nothing Diane could do would help and she began to wonder what kind of trouble he was facing. Was he losing his job or had he been gambling and lost everything they had? The truth was that he had gambled and lost. Not only did he have to face the return of Al and Jeannie, he had to face Marla on his next call to Mega Manufacturing. He figured the only way to face that was to be the cool salesman he should be and allow her anger to slide off his back. The most he had to lose was a good customer and the ire of Bud Billings.

As for Marla at Mega, he did as he had planned and gave her the cold shoulder.

To her credit, she understood at once and went along with a ploy that they had never met. This worked to her advantage in that she could arrange for a quick meeting with the proper buyer or confuse the issue till Ted never got to see the right person. Sales quickly went to zero and Ted Billings went ballistic. He told Ted he needed to go up there and see them about the loss of business, and this gave Ted another bout of abject terror. There went his job if Marla talked and even held the possibility that old

Billings would give Diane a call. First, the job, then his home, then his life, for by then he would have shot himself. Terror will do that to some----

Friday night, Al and Jeannie returned from their vacation, tired and ready for bed. Diane had a very brief conversation with Jeannie, only long enough to set a time in the morning when she should "Come over" to see what Jeannie had purchased on their trip.

Ted had tried to listen without allowing Diane to know how curious he really was. All he got for his trouble was that they would talk Saturday morning over late coffee. This gave Ted about fourteen hours to suffer and to wonder if the two of them would plot his death and the time of it. Meantime, he would be treated as if Diane really loved him enough to put on the front of a devoted wife.

All of Friday night was taken by wide-eyed staring at the ceiling and contemplating a method of denial and possibly escape. Morning rolled around and Diane brought coffee to his bedside, which scared him even more. Was he being given a sedative so he would put up little resistance to having his heart cut out? Might as well accept it and drink the coffee which he did with some distaste. He was certain it had a bitter taste and he was trying to remember what he had heard about sleeping pills or liquid sedatives. In either case, he finally went down to the kitchen for bacon and eggs, just as he liked them, and hot oven-baked biscuits. Everything he tasted had a foul taste or odor, and he forced it down as if he had no choice. It was inevitable that he should die. So be it.

Just before noon, Diane returned from the visit with Jeannie. She seemed to be happy and Ted could only assume the die was cast. Plans were solidified for his death and body disposal. Until now, he had not heard from Al, so he supposed Al was in on the master plan. Perhaps, if Ted went out to the back lawn, Al would join him and leak some of the plan to give his friend a chance to run.

Ted was pretending to dig around the base of some flowers when Al came up behind him and spoke, "Good morning, Mr. Teddley". Ted did not look up from the base of the flower he was digging around for fear he would do or say something he would regret. As it was, he did the right thing for Al said he understood, and he said he was willing to bet that Ted had had a bad night in the bridal suite. Ted just grunted which Al took as admission of guilt or forced innocence. Either way, he was guilty of something which Al and Jeannie were willing to overlook providing-- providing what? Al said they were willing to keep it quiet if Ted made the promise never, never to attempt to jump the fence again. This did not mean that he got off Scott free. There was yet a price to pay. Ted learned the price at the Saturday night card game when Al made the comment several times that it was good to have the Teddley's for neighbors. Jeannie said she loved to visit old hotels. Do you like them, Diane?

Poor Ted had to sweat through many Saturday night card games and, from then on, he was a constant loser. Now we know the terror of Teddy.

Almost the end!

Sequel.

Some of my readers and my editor have asked what happened to Teddy in the end?

Well, in the end---

Just as Teddy opened the front door after five long days on the road, he heard the last dish in the kitchen hit the floor in a pile of already smashed Dinnerware. Diane was doing the dance of the betrayed, angry, and murderous wife. She had just received a phone call from Marla, asking if Teddy was going to meet her again this weekend at their favorite old hotel. Teddy was quick to pick up on the source of her anger and his next thought was,

Where did I last see that S&W .38 I gave her three months ago?

Of course! In her apron pocket.

How the he** can I get outa here-----?

BANG ! Right in the end----------------------THE END, END.

The Beans

As can happen in late November in the mountains, storms can catch the hunter far from either a road or a camp. About 1970 I was given a taste of what could have been tragic for me and certainly was for two other hunters. They were lost in the storm and when located a week later, both were frozen and showed signs of panic which undoubtedly sealed their fate. The search party found both of them huddled as close as possible, just under the edge of a rock over-hang.

It is hard to understand why they had removed their underclothes and tried to start a fire with them. Still, with a foot of new snow covering everything, there would be no branches or dry grass to use for that purpose. They had abandoned their rifles which were never found. It was speculated they had fired all of their ammo in the three shot distress signal and realized the rifles were then useless and extra weight.

Fred and I were long time hunting and fishing buddies and thought we were well in control of our ventures into the wilderness. I was well trained for living off the land by the military but Fred never had that pleasure. As was usual for us this particular season, we were well prepared, we thought.

Just why we felt we had to hike into unknown territory escapes me now, but we could not be satisfied to elk hunt close to camp. It was rare for either of us to bag an elk since we were too smart to kill one five miles from camp and our desire to see the other side of the mountain took care of that.

Most mornings we were up and, on our way, well before daylight. It was not unusual for us to leave camp in the valley as early as 3 AM so we could make it to the mountain top for sunrise. There we could and did hold a short Sunrise Service, being thankful to God for the privilege of seeing the beautiful mountains and the freedom to roam.

As a safety precaution, I had supplied us with small hand held radios that had a range of about one mile through the woods in a reasonably straight line. Over the mountain, the signal tended to fade rapidly. On this particular morning, it looked as if it would be a clear but cold day. We moved out and up the mountain about two hours before daylight, heading for a place the game warden had told us was a beautiful place of cedar and fir trees.

Perhaps the best part of our hunting trips was seeing places where others had not spoiled the scenery with roads, trails and trash. We arrived at our destination about an hour after daylight and after three hours of tough hiking. We ate our lunch early, just because it was such a pleasant place to be and decided to spend the day there. As was usual, we split up staying in touch by radio contact every two hours.

As weather changes in the mountains tend to occur, heavy clouds rapidly turned the day dark, windy and almost at once started a heavy snow fall such that I had never experienced before. The blast of arctic air caused both of us to be ready to get back to camp as soon as possible. It was about eleven AM when we made radio contact, Fred high on the mountain and me at a lower elevation. I was closer to camp and asked Fred to start toward me while maintaining radio contact. Losing contact in this blizzard could be disastrous so while I waited on him, I placed a poncho over my head and spread out the map and compass. It was apparent that downhill and to the west was toward camp.

As we communicated, the signal started to fade which told me something was wrong. I asked Fred to reverse his direction and check again. Even though Fred did not want to walk down the mountain, he continued insisting that we would just have to walk back up again. I got worried about Fred because I knew he had lost his sense of direction and somehow ignored his compass. We did agree that above all else, we must stay together, even if we were going in the wrong direction. When we finally did get together, Fred relied on his sense of direction and almost refused to follow me back to camp. He relented only when I reminded him I had military training and was not likely to go against all that I had learned and successfully used in some very hazardous situations.

By this time the snow was well above shoe tops and blowing sideways with great force. Since it was impossible to see more than a few feet before us, we had to struggle through ever deepening snow and over fallen logs. On entering this area, we had used game trails that made walking much easier. Now that the trails were covered in snow, there was no way we could take advantage of them and this left us to navigate in as much of a straight line as possible. Fallen trees were a very great obstacle as well as hidden crevasses between rocks that could break an ankle or a leg. That would spell disaster for both of us since leaving one with no method of keeping a fire going would mean freezing to death in a few short hours.

After an hour or so, we had to stop and rest. Now we were sorry we ate too soon because it looked like a serious hike through the storm. From here on, it was push for 15 minutes and rest for 10. Snow covered fallen logs and filled ditches in such a way as to keep us in a continual state of trying to stand up again. Hot drink was impossible even though we had military heating tablets for this purpose. Hours later and it was still snowing but the wind had died down a little and we were exhausted.

Darkness was to be soon on us and we had no idea how far we had to travel. By this time snow was up to our knees and we were becoming much concerned that we might be stuck for the night in a blizzard with not much more than a poncho for overnight cover.

We were both worried and although we had not mentioned fear, it was beginning to creep up on us. My thoughts were that I had pulled a major boner by taking it for granted that a nice morning would stay that way, at least until we could make it back to camp.

Usually I did not venture into the back country without a pack, rifle, water, flashlight, extra batteries and extra food. This day, I placed too much trust in the radios and my ability to walk out in about the same time it took to walk in. Never did I consider an injury or a blizzard. Either one could have been the cause of my death.

Even the stupidity of depending on dry matches only for a fire was now causing me to worry. How can I build a fire when the blizzard has dumped nearly two feet of snow and still coming down sideways? It would take all of my training to gather dry material to start with but more than that, it would take some doing to keep a match lit in a wind of this magnitude. It took all of my mental strength to hold fear in check and now that it was almost ten PM, I was on the verge of real fear and Fred was closer to that stage than I was. He still trusted his sense of direction and I refused to listen to him. With vision cut down to less than ten yards, it was impossible to tell if we were headed into a mountain or a valley.

In the beginning that morning, we had followed a forest jeep trail used by the forest ranger and some game trails. It wound around through thickets and heavy forest in such a way that it was impossible to find in snow. We had depended on seeing that faint trail for our return trip. Following the compass was much different and led us up to places we could not possibly climb. When we encountered a place such as that, it was necessary to guess which way was best to skirt the obstacle. I think this alone added miles to our return trip and piled on the worries of a night in a blizzard.

Then, I got a small whiff of cooking beans. There is no other odor on earth like cooking pinto beans to a hungry man. I asked Fred if he smelled them and he said no. Perhaps it was because he was a smoker and I was not. At any rate, we stopped until I got another whiff and the direction of the wind. Forget the compass, walk into the wind which we did. It must have taken us at least an hour to locate the source but when we did, we came to a clearing and what looked like a collapsed tent under the snow.

In front of this heap, there was a large place where there was no snow and from the center, a little steam. Closer inspection revealed a sheet of tin over a large iron pot set down in a hole dug and filled with coals. The pot was covered with a heavy iron lid and the coals were just about finished but still hot enough to put off steam.

That beautiful pot held about three or four gallons of pinto beans. These experienced campers had set that pot of beans so they had cooked all day, what a treat. No tracks around convinced us they were also lost so we dug through their collapsed tent for plates and spoons.

One quart of beans for each of us were life savers and we were two grateful campers. I still relish the memory of that hot pinto bean soup going down into a chilled stomach. We stayed there long enough to add water to the pot and build up the stock of coals before we were ready to move on. Never was I more grateful for pinto beans.

While we were eating those delicious beans it got a little lighter with reduced snow fall and through the tree line I could see we were in what looked to be a logging trail. Hurray, we had a clear place to walk, even if the snow was knee deep. It mattered not where the road or trail led, we followed it for about a mile before we came to a place that we were familiar with. From there it was another mile or so to our camp and just after midnight when we arrived.

I had very bad time with Fred since he never gave up the idea we were in the wrong place. He thought for several minutes when we did get to our tent that it belonged to someone else and was just like ours.

We never knew who the hunters were that had provided the salvation of pinto beans but they may someday read this and I want them to know, a better dinner was never served and will not be in the future until the Lord's supper in the Heaven to come.

The Bird

One bright morning when the sun's rays were filling the trees with glorious light and a gentle breeze lifted and tossed the leaves so the bird could see the newness of its surroundings. The nestling stood on the edge of the nest to better see the strange sights of its world. Let us call the bird Mr. Cheeps for that is the name Dixie gave him or it when she picked it up from where it fell to earth. He, if that was truly what it was, had lifted its new wings for the feel of the breeze and a gust caught it unawares, lifting and dropping it to earth. Stunned to the point of near death, Mr. Cheeps was fair game for the local cat but Dixie had seen its frantic flutter of wings not yet ready for flight just in time to rush to its aid.

Near death, Mr. Cheeps lay in her cupped hands while she gently covered it with her warm breath and I am certain she was praying for one of God's creatures for that was her way. I watched, fascinated at the gentleness of her hands as she coaxed life into that baby bird and I must say that I was thrilled when I saw it open its beak and utter a small squeak. Over the next two or three hours, Dixie sat on the back lawn, wondering what to do since the nest was far too high for me to climb and replace the bird in its nest. Now it was hungry and it was up to Dixie to feed it. I watched the love and care of that bird as she crawled through the flower garden looking for tidbits for Mr. Cheeps. I also watched as she converted its diet from bugs to bread dipped milk, pieces of steak about the size of a bug and other items of food from our table.

Days passed and Mr. Cheeps began to take on the character of a bird, crossed with the human trait of love.

I found it hard to believe that Dixie could train that wild bird to act at her command, but she did. In the beginning, Mr. Cheeps would eat and while perched on her shoulder would relieve himself, leaving an unsightly mess on her. With gentle scolding and taking the bird to a cage, I saw it learn to eat then quickly fly to the cage for relief. All of this time, weeks, Dixie kept the bird with her in the house but eventually, she took it out to the back lawn where others of its kind flitted happily through the trees. Mr. Cheeps did not want to leave her shoulder but to encourage it to fly, she would gently toss it into the air.

Most of that first summer, Mr. Cheeps spent his days on her shoulder and nights in a cage next to her bed.

Dixie tried in vain to introduce it to its family in the trees behind our house. Nothing worked. The love they showed for each other made me just a little jealous. Silly huh? I often watched those two in what seemed to me to be a conversation. Mr. Cheeps perched on her hand and as she spoke to him, he would often answer with a cheep, cheep. I don't think that bird had yet learned to talk bird talk even though he had heard it all summer as he sat happily in Dixie's shoulder in the back lawn.

Fall and then winter came and the birds of Mr. Cheep's kind disappeared. I suppose they went to Florida or perhaps to the gulf coast but Mr. Cheeps was quite happy to remain in the house with Dixie. On occasion during the winter she took him outside and since there was no other birds in the trees and no leaves to block view, Mr. Cheeps delighted flying to the tops and sailing from tree to tree. I have watched in amazement when she decided to go in, she would call and Mr. Cheeps would leave his perch and fly directly to his place on her shoulder. We never heard that bird sing but from what we could determine, he came from the thrush family and should have been more vocal than "cheep-cheep".

Dixie had a deep love for all small animals and birds. She often told me about the pet crow she had as a child. It seems she came by that bird in much the same way. She rescued it from a nest that was felled by the lumber company harvesting trees. She liked to tell me that her mother would not allow it inside but she would raise the window in her upstairs bedroom and commune with "Blackie" until it got dark and then the crow would fly away for the night. She told me the crow was with her for three years and was hit by an automobile when she called to it. The crow was flying to her from across the road and did not see the car speeding toward it. Dixie said she cried for days over seeing her pet hit and killed.

Spring came and Mr. Cheeps was a year old, still dependent on Dixie for food, still not in the mood to sing although I could tell he was very happy. Others of his kind started drifting in for the summer, flitting from bush to bush and again making use of the bird feeders Dixie had placed all over the back lawn and on into the woods behind our home.

Our library on the second floor had a very large picture window such that tree limbs were almost touching. I had to eventually cut back trees because they became too large and was doing damage to the roof. One of the most amazing things about that was the Humming bird nest that was built so close to the window that we could see the eggs not more than two feet from the glass. Directly below was where Dixie kept several humming bird feeders full from early spring until the birds were gone for the winter. We watched the hatching of three little ones and watched the growth of them until they outgrew their space. The most thrilling thing to see was the little birds work their rear ends up over the edge of the nest and fire a shot that kept the nest totally free of any sign of their presence. I think

Dixie must have spent at least two hours each day watching those birds. Love is like that.

Near the end of the second summer, Mr. Cheeps did manage to visit with others of his kind but not for long. It seemed he would mostly stand clear and watch, never trying the sounds they made. He was happy with cheep-cheep, still baby talk we presumed. Dixie would be in a lawn chair and her bird would come set on her shoulder. Some of Mr. Cheeps kind would follow him to the flower garden near Dixie but would not land on her chair arm as Mr. cheeps did. Dixie would talk to the birds and it was something to see how they would stop, look at her and seem to listen.

It was one of those times when her bird started trying to talk to his peers. It was comical for me to be well away from them but close enough to see and hear the conversation. There was no doubt in my mind but that Mr. Cheeps was trying to tell them she was his mother. Dixie never said so much but I understood there was so much love for that bird that she would have fought a wild cat for Mr. Cheeps.

Cool evenings in that second fall caused some change in the relationship with other birds. Sometimes he would fly with them into the woods but in just a minute or so, he would return to Dixie, almost as if to say, "come join with us". Very soon all of his feathered friends were gone for the winter. Dixie became more of a doting mother than before and I had to ask her about it. She said she loved that bird so much it would hurt to see him leave but at the same time, she felt sorry for him being alone from his kind.

Early spring of the third year Mr. Cheeps was more active than ever when he heard the chattering of what was surely his relations. Dixie took him outside and encouraged him to fly by tossing him into the air. It seemed to me that he was reluctant to fly away from her but he did eventually go to where others of his kind were. As the weeks progressed into fall, Mr. Cheeps had gradually spent more time with his kind but still sat perched on Dixie's shoulder whenever she had the time to set on the back lawn. By this time she had reluctantly taken to leaving him outside at night and ignoring him when he sat at the kitchen window at dusk. It was very difficult for her and I have often seen her at that window with tears on her cheeks.

Cool nights arrived and Mr. Cheeps spent more time at the kitchen window and on her shoulder when she was outside. She was heartbroken but did what she believed was for his good. Soon the day came when he did not come to her call. Most of the birds had left and none of his kind was to be seen. Dixie took it hard that winter and talked much about where she thought her baby was and of course, I missed him as well.

Spring came at last and as soon as it was comfortable, Dixie would set outside and look to the trees and to the southern sky. When it happened, it was almost unexpected that Mr. Cheeps did not stop anywhere before he landed on Dixie's shoulder. He hopped from the arms of the lawn chair, to her shoulders and back again with such a happy chatter that it reminded me of a child returning from the first visit to a circus. Mr. Cheeps was filled with chatter and all of this time three other birds like him sat in the flower bush near Dixie's chair. It was as if they were waiting to be introduced. I happened to be doing dishes at the kitchen sink when all of this took place. I watched in fascination at the glad reunion and knowing Dixie and the birds, I took three slices of bread out to her. For an hour, she sat there and hand fed those four birds. I finished the dishes and still I stood at the kitchen window, filling my eyes with the scene of true love. God's creatures surely have a built in penchant for love.

As I now remember that last fall when Dixie and her birds were so close I can't help but shed a tear. Soon after Mr. Cheeps left, Dixie followed in death and there is emptiness in my soul that will remain for all of my life. I spent only four more days in that house before leaving it, forever behind. I often wonder if Mr. Cheeps returned and if so, how did he take the absence of his adopted mother? With thoughts of their relationship, it is not difficult for me to see in my mind's eye, Dixie in Heaven with birds all around and to believe that God has made it possible for them to communicate.

The Cat House

Elmer, one of the newest members to our hunting party, brought an extra-large amount of his private well water to camp this past year. We could not help but notice that Elmer was suffering from fresh sunburn and this was the Thanksgiving hunt in November 1986 with snow and bitter cold here in the mountains of West Virginia. Someone, expecting to receive an explanation and glowing report on the sunny south mentioned it to him. Well, we were disappointed for Elmer said nothing, and, in fact acted as if he failed to hear the question, if that was what it was. Camp was set up on Saturday and Sunday was used to look over the mountain in search of deer runs and feeding grounds. Monday morning, gun season opened and all of us were out well before dawn, returning late in the evening, too tired to talk much. I think one deer was brought in that day, but not mine. For me, I would rather see the country than have to drag a dead animal all the way back to camp so my deer hunting was never much more than to gather an education. Now that may seem like a useless statement since no text books were in camp and few were blessed with more than high school to their credit. Me, I never finished high school. In fact, I never went near the place, so most of what I hear in deer camp is an education.

Most evenings when we had a roaring camp fire and spirits were high, tales were told.

Now when I said spirits, I meant that to cover more than one. Some spirits came from out of the nether land, some from the state controlled store, and some came from the pure and cold mountain water that few places have to rival West Virginia's coal fields and streams.

Now we did know that Elmer had been way down south and we wanted to hear all about it, but we had to wait till the spirits moved him. Saturday night was a good time to set up camp and gather fire wood but not much for talk. Sunday night was better but most of us wanted to bed down early for a fresh start the next morning.

Monday evening when all were safely in camp, sore and tired, the camp fire did what only a good fire can do. Arthritis had hit all of us and needed to be medicated. Prescription meds were brought out and shared with all who suffered from the pain of arthritis. Exactly how this medication works is not clear to me but I do know it loosens the joints, relieves pain, loosens the tongue and causes the eyes to water.

It did not take long to tell of the happenings of that day's hunt and mentally file them to experiences of life. Now this is what I came for, an

education that can only be attained in deer camp and after proper medication. All of us wanted to hear about Elmer's sunburn so when he spoke, all shut up and waited. When he spoke it was as if his mind was elsewhere and he promised us this would be a short story, a warning to widowers, by giving us the benefit of his experience. I quote verbatim ----
--

Now, I have been known to fib a little but never outright lye. (notice the spelling). So when I relate my experience of the past thirty days, you may as well believe it happened just as I am saying it did.

My longtime friend, Bill, lost his third wife about three years ago. He left his first two when he said they would no longer bring him his beer when needed.

In fact though, I believe they left him when they found out what a slob he really is. It has taken me almost twenty five years to really get to know him as they did---the slob part I mean.

Well, I lost my wife of forty years about three years back and I have suffered the life of the damned, learning to get my own beer, food, clothes, etc'. Before she died, I was doing much of the kitchen work and enjoying lots of free time to take her places and living in a clean home. Both of us made an effort to keep the house clean, so when my friend, Bill, decided to spend a month with me after my wife died and after his third left him, I welcomed the company. One thing I noticed while he was in my home was that he was a man of leisure. He really enjoyed good hot meals, three times a day and I did notice that he picked up some extra pounds while here. I also noticed that he loved my recliner and seldom got out of it except when I announced that lunch, breakfast or dinner was ready. I took that to mean he was worn out from all of the activity back home, for how many women can a man of his age satisfy?

Since we talked by phone every two or three days, I was constantly hearing about his many lady friends. He was telling me how great it was to be free of #3 and free to play the field again. I kinda thought it was my good deed for this year to feed and rest him.

Bill had lost #3 almost three years back and he has had the house all to himself since then. Now, I did not mean to say he was all alone for there was a lot happening there. He often referred to Becky, Babe, and Marie and told me about some of the things over long distance phone, and I almost came to believe he was having a good time. ALMOST.... Bill is in the change of life that should come at age eighty and because I have my own experiences to relate to his, I double doubt he is one hundred percent truthful. Of course, I expect all old men to be as truthful as I am, so why should I doubt him?

Well, here it is late October and nights are already getting cold enough for a fire in the grate, so it's time for me to return the thirty day visit since he seems down in the dumps. He lives down in south Florida and I thought it would be a good time to for me to depart for a month of sunshine. He has been alone long enough to really feel the loss, and I can tell by his phone calls that no woman has decided to move in with him on a permanent basis. He has been asking me to visit for at least two years so when I decided to do so, I set it in motion to make it a full thirty days. As I said, Bill has a big house with bed and bath in each end, so I am expected to occupy the spare bedroom which has its own TV. More on the TV later since that's a story in its own right.

I traveled the fifteen hundred miles in two days of driving so I would arrive late Sunday evening. Bill had given me good directions on how to get to his country home from Homestead, Florida, so I had no trouble arriving there just before dark. I arrived very tired and with expectations of a good hot shower and perhaps some form of dinner.

Even a sandwich would have been welcome. Not so. Bill had plans to go to the local McDonald's which we did, even before the shower I needed and before I had time to take my luggage inside. We left at once and when we ordered the usual greasy hamburger and French fries, Bill discovered he had left without his billfold. He said it was still in the pocket of the trousers from when he changed. From the looks of what he was wearing, that must have been about a month ago.

On returning to his place, I discovered that Bill did not live alone. By this time it was dark so I did not notice that I was walking across his porch and through a heavy layer of cat hair. I did notice when I arrived that cats ran everywhere, mostly under the house. Bill spoke to Becky to assure her I was a friend. At this time, I should have returned to my car and skedaddled out of there. But no, I thought it would be good to visit with my longtime friend and perhaps he would clean off the cat hair the next day. Perhaps he did not like working on Sunday and would do it tomorrow. Still, it should have been obvious to me that cats can't shed that much in less than a year.

Bill was suffering from the recent loss of his close companion, Phiado. Also a shedding, long haired mutt which he allowed the run of the house. Unlike the cats, Phiado was allowed to sleep with him, probably since his third wife left him or perhaps before. I had to wonder if Phiado was allowed to sleep between them or did he or she or it have to sleep on the outside next to Bill. Right away I got the feeling that the loss of Phiado weighed heavily on the mind of my friend. His recent death was too traumatic for Bill to tell me about at this time. I never learned if Phiado was male or female but I did learn that Phiado had shed hair all over the bed assigned to me. It took more than a week for me to learn that Phiado did not die. He or she or it left in the middle of the night and I could only suppose that he or she or it had decided enough is enough of the competition with twenty five or thirty cats. Fortunately there was a sweeper in the closet in my bedroom. I found it worked after I cleaned out the filter. I doubt it was used after his third left him but it served to pick up another bagful of hair----and bugs.

Now I have to tell you about the bugs. Never since I was down in the South Pacific in WWII have I seen such monsters. They came out as soon as the lights went out, and the first night, I got my gun out to defend myself. I thought there was a big animal or a man creeping up to do me harm. I was still awake so there was no doubt in my mind that I would have to shoot it, whatever it was. I listened for a minute or so and determined it was safe to turn on the light. When I did, there was a scramble of bugs as long as my finger. It looked like the traffic trying to depart Daytona 500 after the race was over. They headed for the cracks in the floor, under the bed and the Lord only knows where else they were headed. Would you believe I was scared? Well, anyway, I saw they were not climbing bugs and could not carry me away, so I turned out the light and fell into the arms of Morpheus, too tired to care.

Well, now, I have to tell you about the TV's. There is a large TV in every room in the house, all tuned to the same cable input box. When I first arrived, I thought there was something wrong in his house for the walls seemed to vibrate and I could hear a man telling me to buy gold and the world is about to end--- all this from out in his yard. Incidentally, the grass out there was well into becoming a prime source of hay for some farmer to gather for winter cow food. I soon learned that he had the TV control at his recliner with all seven units running from the same control, and since he has lost eighty percent of his hearing, the volume is set on "BLAST".

I found that he does not trust just any channel for the truth. It must come from FOX news. So the channel never gets changed and neither does the volume. Now keep in mind that the TV in my room is also on Fox, full blast. He explained that he could not sleep unless the TV was on. Well, I could not sleep or think with it on. The solution was apparent; I had to unplug the dang thing since I had no way to reduce the volume. This was another time I thought that I might have to use my gun; that is, until I realized I could unplug it from the power source without causing a fire or some other calamity. Before I got there, I assume the bugs relied on the TV Fox channel for their entertainment. I asked Bill if he was aware of the monsters that had invaded his home and he looked blank and asked "What monsters?"

I told Bill that I had used the bathroom that first morning and when I went to brush my teeth, I couldn't find my tooth brush. I looked all over the place and failed to see it until I looked in the corner behind the commode. There, I found one of his bugs using my toothbrush to scratch its back. Bill just had a blank look on his face as if I had lied to him. Of course, I told you in the beginning that I don't "lye."

Come daylight Monday morning, I needed to go to my car for another cardboard box containing my stuff. Then was when I got a good look at the porch floor. In the distant past, he had covered it with indoor/outdoor carpet. At the same time, Bill was in the process of feeding his cats and this made it easy for me to determine what caused the carpet to appear lumpy and smelly. His cat food was made up of milk over some form of biscuit, quickly sloshed out on the carpet from cat greed and promptly smeared all over the layer of cat hair. As I say again, I won't mess with the truth but it made me sick to walk across his front porch. When you have to dodge 25 or 30 cats in order to get through a feeding frenzy, you will understand.

While I am on the feeding part of this narrative, I need to explain why Bill is a walking stick of skin over bones. When I first arrived, I was thinking, poor Bill, he must have some form of disease that is sucking the life out of him. Now five days later I know the truth. His malady is all in the mind and is sometimes known as "lazy". When I attach that diagnosis to Bill, I must explain his eating habits and this will take some time.

I might add that I stayed two weeks of my planned 30 days, so I had ample time to confirm my diagnosis. The truth is that Bill fed his cats much better than he did himself.

They required five gallons of milk each week, plus the best brand of cat biscuit. I must also tell you that local milk would not do because it contained both BGH and HGC (whatever the heck that is).His cats had to have whole milk without that dangerous additive (if it was added or the cow was infected with it) and for this, he had to drive thirty five miles each way, every week to a farm where the dairy would sell him stuff, fresh from the cow.

On his return from the milk run, Barbara, Alice, Joan, Kittie, Valerie, and twenty five more cats that I can't remember, all were waiting for him on his return with fresh milk. I wondered how he got more kittens since he had none named Tom or Henry. I have heard somewhere in my past, perhaps in grade school, that certain things have the ability to reproduce themselves. In my latter years, my memory is not what it used to be so it could well have been cats.

Back to my story about how Bill eats.

Chapter 4 of Matthew in my Bible, Verse 4 states ----

IT IS WRITTEN, MAN SHALL NOT LIVE BY BREAD ALONE, BUT BY EVERY WORD THAT PROCEEDETH OUT OF THE MOUTH OF GOD.

Bill has his version which is-------- man shall not live by bread alone. He must have peanut butter. He must truly believe this since that constitutes about 85 % of his diet.

Since I am used to cooking and since Bill told me to make myself at home, I did.

There was nothing in the fridge except milk and bread so I went to the grocery store and bought a good stock of meat and potatoes, among other things. Now, figuring Bill must be hungry, I set about cooking a good country meal even though he said he was not.

All of this time he was sitting before the blasting Fox news with peanut butter in one hand, spoon in the other. I watched him "lick and dig, lick and dig" until I almost lost my appetite. Well, to shorten the story, I placed a very large plate of country cookin' where I figured he would sit. With my plate generously heaped--"it has been a long time since the greasy hamburger." I sat down and started to eat. Of course, Bill was no slouch when it came to food someone else prepared. Wow! Could he ever put it away?

Over the next several days, I continued to cook when I got so hungry that I had to.

Several times I asked Bill if he would like to go downtown with me for a restaurant meal. He always said he was not hungry but would go with me. Being the gentleman that I am, I would offer to buy, in which case he would say, "I'm not hungry but I will order something with you." That something always turned out to be enough food to last him until I cooked again, perhaps two or three days. He was still wearing the same trousers so I had to assume his wallet was still on the floor by his bed, still in the same pocket. Now I must admit that I cheated a few times. Under the pretext of going to the post office, I sneaked another greasy hamburger and allowed him to return to the peanut butter. At one restaurant, I discovered he loves baked potatoes with lots of bacon, cheese and sour cream so I bought big potatoes, shredded cheese and sour cream, but no bacon.

I figured if he wanted bacon, let him buy it. Well, he did not because his third wife left him with a pantry full of canned goods and there should be something there to put on a baked potato. "Fine" I said. "We'll see what you have".

Now again, I must tell you there has been no sign of a cleaning party there since Hector was a pup or since wife #2 left him years ago. When he showed me the pantry door, I expected to find a dozen or so cans, but there were at least fifty or more. I picked up the first can in front which happened to be green beans. It was so light that I shook it and heard a dry rattle. Looking at the bottom, I saw rust had eaten through and liquid had run across the shelf, causing every can on that shelf to be spoiled, either rusted through the bottom or bulged top. No way am I going to eat out of that pantry. I did notice in another area that there were several cans of chili w/beans. I asked about them and Bill said "every now and then I get hungry for good country cookin'." That evening, we had a split baked potato with chili/beans in the crack, concluded with desert of an extra glass of water.

After a week there, I was beginning to get homesick. I was getting tired of cleaning hair off everything I had to use. The second Monday after being out all day in the heat of a late October, I walked into my room which I had managed to get kinda clean by now.

Since the door is usually closed to keep out more hair, I opened it to a horrible stench.

Something died in there. At first I thought it might be a colony of big bugs hit by the heavy spraying I had given them about a week ago. Since it was really bad, I opened a window in the bathroom and another on the far side of the bedroom. Last week I had seen a window fan in the pantry room, so I got it and placed it in my window and turned the speed up to cyclone. In about two hours it was getting dark and turning cool outside. The stench was mostly gone so I turned the fan on lower and went to work on my computer. By 11PM it got cold in the room and still I had the odor to contend with, so I turned on the electric heater. Now I must explain that the air conditioner and the central heat for this house had failed years ago. Bill had done nothing about it, but just bought electric space heaters, notorious for their high consumption of electricity and low efficiency. Bill came to my room about the time I had both window fan and space heater going. He did a double take and promptly climbed my frame for the stupidity of heating night air for the entire county. When I gave him the reason, he said, "Don't let it bother you. The stink will go away in a day or two." By the end of the following day, I was certain the odor was coming up through the bathroom floor since air was coming through the bedroom and out the bathroom window. When I went into the bathroom and closed the door, it was quickly over powering. With this certainty, I told Bill and was stunned by his answer. It seems that he was missing "Blinky," the little sick cat, and it was his conclusion that "Blinky" went to the usual place to die, under my bathroom. Now I had to wonder why he did nothing about burial services. With his devotion to his charges, I would have thought he would make arrangements with the Methodist minister where he attended church once each month or so.

The next day I used a long handle shovel to remove "Blinky's" remains and did the burial services alone. No tears. While removing that member of the family, I saw bones of others there, indicating the possibility that cats are much like elephants are thought to be. They all try to go to the family plot to die, and I suppose Bill did not want to disturb the tradition of his family.

Today was beach day and time to enjoy the surf. I had looked forward to this since leaving the cold of West Virginia, and I had brought a pair of cutoff jeans for this purpose. I learned long ago to stay out of water deeper than my knees. It just ain't safe to be where things can crawl up your exposure. I learned this in the South Pacific in WWII, and I classify all water over ankle deep as dangerous. The beach did have great attraction though, not the sand and water but the people who used it. For several hours, I splayed myself out on a big blanket and watched the scenery stroll past. This was also a part of my southern vacation that I had looked forward to and didn't get enough of. Exception to this was that I got too much sun; so much, in fact, that I could not go back for a few days.

Now I was in the middle of the second week and I truly believe my welcome was wearing thin. I know my desire to stay was even thinner but I determined to stay until the next weekend. Actually, I failed to make it to Saturday as planned. Bill got angry with me again Wednesday evening and I excused that episode due to the fact that I had not fed

us for two days. Peanut butter, as his usual diet, was not as satisfying as before I arrived.

He had become used to solid food from my cooking or from my taking him to the local diner. He seemed to have a hard time remembering where he left his wallet. I was also growing short tempered from the constant blasting of TV, Fox news. Even after I pulled the plug on the TV in my room, I could still hear it loud and clear from the living room. I wished several times I had brought my ear protectors from the shooting range.

It might have been uncomfortable wearing them while trying to sleep, but better it would have been than going unconscious from the noise level.

As I started to say, Bill got angry with me Wednesday evening since I had removed "Blinky" and still insisted on running the window fan and the space heater all night. The cost of heating the entire county was touching his "money nerve." I listened with my mouth closed but my mind was working overtime. Bill went back to the living room and placed himself in a sprawled position before Fox news.

I went into high gear packing my suitcase which incidentally was two cardboard boxes. I placed all of my clothing possible into garbage bags so as to trap the colony of bugs desiring to go home with me. It must have been about two hours for me to shower and pack before I took the first box to my car. Bill was sound asleep with Fox filling his head with news of the night. I almost forgot to tell you that Bill claims to know everything about everything. He is well informed from the FOX point of view but if I asked him a question about something else, his standard answer was..."I know everything but I don't know that, yet." Well I got the last box and garbage bag loaded shortly after midnight and Bill was still zonked out in his chair. He was absorbing FOX and learning everything about everything by that process of sleeping while the textbook is being read to you from the pillow speaker. I suppose that's the way it works. He found the next morning that his cook was gone.

Fifteen hundred miles later, I arrived at my home and proceeded to fumigate and disinfect. Before I entered my house, I unpacked outside and shook out my followers, as many as possible. Then, I carefully carried clothes in small loads, straight to the washer. Since I live in the country, it was no problem to strip to the bare skin while still in the backyard, shake myself like a wet dog then run into a hot shower. November is a cold time to be nude in your back yard but a good time to shed bugs since they probably will freeze to death.

Now I have told you of this experience for the sole purpose of warning widowers to stay away from peanut butter and cats. If you want a cat house, choose the two-leg variety since they don't usually shed all over the house. If they do, most of them will be able to run the sweeper, and, at least, if you are lucky, they can cook.

It might also be worth a word to the wise, do not throw away the TV control after you set it on FOX NEWS.

Elmer concluded his tale by taking a very long slug of Mason jar water and with a swipe of the back of his hand across his beard, headed for the sleeping tent. There was nothing more to say since none of us had a better tale to tell.

Good night.

The Dodge

No doubt some of you will doubt this story and I can't blame you. It is rather out of the way, as stories go, but I did the only thing a thinking person could. I must admit, though, very few men would have acted so quickly to cover the evidence as I did. Now, fifty years later, I wish I had done it another way as you will see.

The story

1956. My job was such that I had a lot of free time. I worked as emergency x-ray repair and that meant I worked lots of nights and weekends but had many free days.

About this time, Dad bought a small valley piece of land at the edge of town where he proposed to build a home as well as sell off house seats. To develop the valley into reasonable places for houses, he bought a bulldozer for me to use in my free time. I spent many days cutting a clear road into the back side of the property, and, in the process, cut out and leveled places where about 12 houses could be placed.

At this same time, my younger brother, who was eighteen, worked in Detroit at the Chrysler auto factory. He shared an apartment and also worked with a young man his age who lived somewhere in eastern Kentucky. That man had recently purchased a new Dodge, 4-door Sedan and offered to drop my brother off at his home before continuing on to Kentucky. They arrived Saturday afternoon, and, later that evening, a local friend of my brother picked both of them up for a night on the town. Sunday morning found my brother at home in bed with no sign of his Detroit friend. The following Monday, he had not returned and my brother decided not to return to Detroit. Instead he took a job with the railroad which took him in the opposite direction. Now the valley my dad had purchased was narrow at the point of leaving the highway but widened as it continued deeper into the valley. Dad had built his temporary home near the main road and used the road up into the valley as his driveway. It was rather restricted in width and could not be widened very much without destroying his home.

The new Dodge was parked in that narrow driveway up into the valley. It left little room for entry by large trucks that now had to use the driveway. It sat there for several weeks, and my brother never got an answer from the address where they had shared an apartment in Detroit.

He tried to contact his buddy by writing to friends in Detroit but never got an answer. That beautiful four-door Dodge sat there gathering dust and with the windows up and locked. We could do nothing to protect it from the sun and weather. After about two or three years had passed, it became necessary for me to open up the road to several new house seats I had cut out in the valley. That automobile was still sitting there and Dad would not allow any of us to touch it. He was fearful of being responsible if the boy came for his car and it was not there. It was on private property and had not been too much in the way so dad was trying to be a reasonable man with other people's property. All of this was good until I needed it moved before I could complete the road and cut the last two new house seats just a short way up the valley.

Just a mile or so from the property, the West Virginia State Police had their headquarters. This was a small community and they were well familiar with dad's property, so I needed to ask them what to do with the Dodge. The answer I got was not what I expected, "You can't do anything with it." They said it would be theft if we tried to sell it or any part of it, so I said I would just push it down to the main road and let the state remove it. "You can't do that since we would have to arrest you for an abandoned vehicle on state property." They suggested I give them the tag number for ID and write to the owner for permission.

A week later I wrote to the address they gave me. Another two weeks passed before I got a return from his mother stating he was in the Kentucky Federal prison. She gave me the address and I followed with a letter and an offer to buy. Another month passed before I got a letter from the warden.

Dear Sir,
This is to inform you that "Blank Blank # 359867" is in our care and is not permitted to buy, sell or trade any article, either inside or outside the confines of this prison. Furthermore, his sentence is life without parole.
Sincerely,
**** ****
Warden, Kentucky Federal Prison System.

Now I am in a no-win position of "Can't sell, can't junk, can't give it away."

Back to the west Virginia State Police and another wall of, "can't help you.."

By this time I was afraid of the State Police. What if that car was reported stolen or the finance company did come looking for it. There were several "What ifs" on my mind and I wanted no part of trouble over it. I wanted to be able to say the last time I saw it, it still had the doors locked and the windows closed and say no more. What a shame that a new 1954 Dodge Sedan is such a burden, but I had the answer in a bull dozer and the ability to dig a deep hole where there is to be a house seat. Not even dad would know where it disappeared to.

As it happened, this was already a very low place that needed to be filled in, so I needed to dig deep enough that if there were to be a basement there in the future, the new owners would not find a new Dodge grave site.

I did not open the automobile to check the contents so I had no idea what might be in the trunk. Since the owner was in prison for life, I have often speculated that he might have been a mass murderer and there could have been a body in that trunk. I suppose I should have told the people that lived in the house over the grave that the sounds they heard on some dark nights might be ghosts. Or maybe I should keep my mouth shut?

You be the judge!

The Helmet

Chapter 1

As previously stated, I give George Washington a run for the money. He never told a lie and I never tell a lye. (NOTICE THE SPELLING) In fact, I try not to hear a lie.

Just in case, I carry a little salt in my pocket since I have been told that you are supposed to take some things with a grain of salt. Also, I have been told from my youth, that if one's lost in the woods it is possible to survive on rabbits. All I have to do is sneak up on one and place salt on its tail which makes it easy to catch. But the main reason is that salt helps me get through the news from Washington every evening. The pile behind my recliner is growing quite large as I have a habit of throwing the salt over my shoulder even before the newscaster announces that the president will speak.

All of this is just to let you know that I am not well educated in science, except in the course of my life, I have never missed a chance to attend hunting and fishing camps. Around the campfire at evening time, the true facts of life come to surface and, from the time I was twelve, I had a burning desire to learn from these older men. Just what made them open up and talk about their secret desires and hidden thoughts, I am not sure. I have pondered this phenomenon for years and have concluded that it must be brought on by medication for arthritis or rheumatism and always by the doctor's orders.

Now as you must know, the average hunter does little exercise and when he get out in the woods, he overworks muscles that have had little or no use for the past year.

Tramping through the woods, up and down the mountain, and carrying a heavy rifle will take its toll so everyone needs to be doctored as soon as the camp fire is hot enough. Arthritis will do this to the strongest of men. As I said, prescription medication comes in many forms, most of it from a licensed source, but not always. I remember the old man that brought the water from his well back home. He brought it in Mason fruit jars, carefully packed so as not to run out of his own well water. To hear him tell the story about how his well water has been tested pure time after time, a gift from

God, it brings tears to his eyes. His story is so sweet that I almost shed a tear with him.

Since I have grown older, I have been able to buy an old farm that has a well similar to the one owned by that old man. As I think about the purity of my well water, I get thirsty and need

to take a few minutes from writing to go draw another Mason jar of that cold, clear water. Now some of you may not know that creek water found up high in the mountains in a secret place, secret from the federal revenuers that is, becomes Mason jar well water when mixed with corn. It takes a lot of work to get it right and when well done, is prized and protected. As for mine, I keep it in a jug with a small rope through the handle and stored deep in my well. That way it is always cold and not likely to be found by them, the revenuers that is. The nature of the water wells here and in the neighboring state of Kentucky surely must have something to do with coal in these mountains. Here in West Virginia, this water seems to be plentiful in the areas where coal is mined. This makes me thankful to be a Western Virginian, if nothing else.

Well, I had to tell you about the hunting and fishing camps in order to get to the point of my story, the Helmet. I think I was thirteen when I was in a deer hunting camp near Richwood, West Virginia. It was Thanksgiving evening and everyone was filled with venison stew and had taken an overdose of their arthritis medication early. All had gone to the big tent to rest their arthritic bones except the old man Cartwright that had so much to say. As I said, I was eager to learn and he had much to teach me. I believe this was about 1913 and he seemed to be in his late eighties which made him born around 1828. He told me he was about my age when he found the Helmet. As best as my limited education can place this, it must have been around 1840 or so. Anyway he was a mountain boy with little education at that time. He told me he was from a mountain-top farm out back of Ranger, a place he called Leet, West Virginia, where people were as scarce as teeth in a chicken. Having traveled that area later in my life, both hunting for deer and searching for the helmet, I can understand the relationship to chicken teeth.

The old man told of reading about Indians placing their dead, along with prized possessions in earthen mounds. he had heard of the mounds being opened for treasures, so he was curious to see what was in the mound on their land. He said the mound was not large but it was unusual in shape and was placed on top of the highest point, aligned with the North Star. Curiosity got the best of him, and, even though he shunned work, he took shovel in hand and started digging. From the first, it got scary and troublesome. He would dig all day and return the next morning to find most of the dirt replaced. Since the dirt was already loose, he was determined to keep digging and soon found bones and arrow- heads, indicating he was digging in the right place. Days later, he had found all of the skeleton except the skull, and determined it was moving away from where he was digging. The skull seemed to be going deeper, so he dug faster and soon caught up with it.

When he found the skull, he was surprised to see that it was wearing a Helmet of something that looked like the shell of a very large turtle, with exceptions. The interior was similar to that of a sea shell, all iridescent colors of green, blue, pink and white. Amazing enough, it seemed to shine on the inside. On the outside, it was dark and rough in color, much like a turtle shell that he first thought it was and it had two places on the sides where a chin strap had once been. From all appearances, it had been worn in battle. There seemed to be cut scars on the upper left side where a sharp flint had grazed off without doing damage to the wearer.

Now that he had it, he was fearful that some older boy would take it from him or that the circuit preacher might do so, calling it a sin to desecrate a grave. Knowing preachers, he could just see the preacher trading it for more of that cold, clear well water he so desired. He said he could sympathize with the preacher since it helped him tame the rattlers and copperhead snakes he had to deal with, but not with his helmet. No sir. Let him draw his own well water.

The old man's story was so vivid in the telling that I could feel the excitement of having such a wonderful treasure. It took another long draught from the Mason jar before he could continue and as he did so, I scooted my section of firewood seat closer so I could catch every mumbled and slurred word he spoke. He had begun to slur his words as if he needed more time to think of the past and to get it right. Of course, I was anxiously holding on to every pause and wanted the story to go faster.

Now that I look back on that night, I am glad he took so much time to think for it gave me time to record on my memory, every nuance of truth he uttered.

Nothing would do for him except he had to try the helmet on his smaller head than it seemed to be made. Being a very loose fit, he held it by both sides to keep it on straight and from the moment he placed the helmet on his head, his whole world changed. His body became lighter than air and would not stick firmly to the ground. He found he could lift his arms and float gently upward, just a little or enough to skim the earth as if he were walking but not moving his feet. By just the act of serious thought, he could go higher and move faster, or stop in midair and look down on where he had been digging. At first it terrified him that he could go higher than the tree tops because he knew if he fell, it would do serious harm to his body. He was holding tightly to the helmet in fear of it falling off and allowing him to fall to earth. It was certainly sticking to his head in such a way that he did not need to hold on and hold up his weight but he was also afraid if he turned it loose, it would climb alone and leave him stranded. When he determined by an act of thought, he found he could think himself to earth.

When his feet were firmly planted back on solid ground, he removed the Helmet and cleaned the grave dirt off it and gave it a minute examination. As he tilted it to light and looked inside it, there seemed to be imbedded in the iridescent shell surface

some form of writing or squiggling marks like none he had ever seen. Then he remembered hearing from some old folks in his church that robbing a grave was bound to send the robber to Hell.

As he sat on the ground and pondered the outcome, he decided to return the Helmet to the skeleton and cover it as well as he could. But then he thought, why not keep it for a few days and enjoy seeing his daddy's land from above? Even seeing what this old mountain looked like, possibly going high enough to see the big Guyan River. Temptation was too great and Hell was too distant. Later in life, he would come to realize that this is the attitude of almost every living person. As he sat and contemplated the wonders in store for the holder of this marvelous Helmet, dusk reminded him of chores he should be doing. So, it was time to head for the barn, but what should he do with the treasured Helmet?

Taking it to the barn was too risky and taking it to house was out of the question. Momma had found the quart of wine he had set in the barn well before he had a chance to taste it. In fact, it had not fermented yet, but Momma had a way of looking into his mind for sins thought of but never carried out. He was only following the directions of an old man who had been making wine and other stuff for many years. This was his first try and it was a total failure, thanks to Momma.

Well, it was an absolute truth that the Helmet had to stay in the woods and he had the perfect place to hide it. Not far away there was a small rock outcrop where he had once watched a skunk bring out her brood of young ones from the hole underneath. The hole was a perfect size for the Helmet and it smelled bad enough so that no one would venture to stick a hand inside.

After milking old Bossie and feeding the pigs, he was free to carry firewood in for Momma's cook stove and wash up for bed. He could not afford to let Momma see his excitement and worm out of him the reason for it. He had to fake being tired and going to bed early so he could ponder and cogitate without interruption. During sound sleep that night, he dreamed of the entire world being under his command. He could wave his magic wand and make things appear and disappear. He dreamed of wearing a robe of purple silk and having the finest horse to ride, of servants and a house made of brick he had read about. As dreams go, there was no end to the magic under his hand. He even dreamed of hot biscuits, frying bacon, and the sound of a skillet on a cast iron stove when he realized it was no dream. Momma was making breakfast.

Keep in mind that this story took place about 1820 or 1825 and he had little knowledge of the world outside his daddy's land and the church which also served as the schoolhouse. " Nearby" in those days meant a mile or three.

So he had little schooling--- not much in picture drawings of what the world looked like. Pencil drawings of other places only served to whet his appetite for seeing with his own eyes. Someday, Poppa promised, he would get to see the big city of Barboursville or Logan and the tall buildings made of brick and stone.

Chapter 2

Barboursville was not formed until 1813 when James Barber, Governor of Virginia set the name. It was previously known as Merritt's Mill due to his grist mill being located at the mouth of Mud river. Near the head of the mighty Guyan River was the settlement known as Aracoma, Which was accessible only by canoe and river boat and then mostly in high water days. In 1907 when coal mining boomed and a railroad was opened, the name was changed to Logan after the old Indian chief Logan who was said to have lived on the island mid-stream in the Guyan. It is also of note that the tribe Chief Logan ruled was named Guyan. Towns like these were not at all like the log house they lived in, but until he found the Helmet, he never dreamed he would be able to perhaps see things that Poppa had not seen. Poppa had also promised to take him on the all-day ride to Hamlin in their wagon pulled by their team of matched bay horses. Poppa had to make the arduous trip about four times each year for things that the farm could not supply. It was a two day trip and required sleeping under the stars which was much to his liking. There was very little open land so not much grass feed for the horses on the way. They had to carry hay to feed and sleeping in the wagon on a load of hay was great excitement. Poppa would soon have to go for supplies but for now, he had to stay with Momma and take care of the chores.

Today was to be the most exciting day of his life. He vowed to try out the Helmet with a piece of raw hide harness string under his chin to keep it firmly on his head. During his night dreams, he gathered courage as well as a desire to see just what the Helmet would do for him. He rushed through the morning chores, taking great care that Momma did not see his excitement and question him. It was a bright summer day and, without a doubt, the best possible time to go aloft and see the world from where the birds were flitting happily across the sky.

Withdrawing the Helmet from its hiding place gave him the shivers and caused him to wonder again about Hell and if that's where the Helmet would cause him to go. Never mind, today was worth it. Placing the string through the holes on each side and firmly securing it under his chin, he felt the lifting effect with a degree of fear. What if---if he sailed off into the sky and lost control, where would he go? Certainly not to Hell for it was in the other direction. Just a little bit at a time---just float over the tree tops as he did yesterday and perhaps float down over his house and see it as the birds did.

With the thought of floating upward, his feet left the ground, and, since he was so fearful of going too high, he thought SLOW. And so it was.

Here we sat across the campfire from each other and the old man was finding it necessary to wet his whistle more often with his Mason jar of well water. This was taking time from the story telling and I was becoming impatient to hear more of the story. He used this excuse to prompt me to add more wood to our fire and I suppose, time for him to recall the details of that first flight.

Being young, I was prepared to stay by the fire all night if it took that to hear his story. When the flames of renewed fire gave good light, I could see tears in his eyes and I was thinking that something tragic had happened and this was the reason for the pause and the fruit jar. Not so. They must have been tears of joy for he resumed by telling me how he ventured all of the way down and off the mountain to the river and beyond.

After he floated up to clear the tree line and mountain tops, he found he could move his arms and guide his direction, as well as height. It was so easy to float over his house and see Momma down in the yard where she was bent over a #2 tub doing a washing. He was tempted to call out to her, but, on second

thought, he was afraid she would either faint or make him come down where he would lose the Helmet. No, better he keep quiet and use it for an education. No sense in tempting Momma and possibly be the cause of her going to Hell with him.

Flying was so easy that he decided to go on down the mountain toward the river where he had been only once in all his twelve years. He had been with Poppa that time when Poppa wanted to see the timber rafts on the Guyan River. Loggers were cutting timber and building giant rafts anchored to the river bank. These rafts were being built all along the river for miles, waiting on the winter rains to flood so the logs could be floated down to the town of Guyandotte and several sawmills. There the lumber was to be shipped on by river boat and rafts to Cincinnati and beyond. He wanted to see this from above, and, when he did get there, he was so shocked by the size and activity that he continued on up river for several miles. As he followed the river, he could see places where some horses and wagons were traveling along dirt roads near the river. It did not seem to be a continuous road but it wss curved away from the river to cross a mountain where the river valley was too narrow. After flying up river for many miles and seeing all of the activity from timber cutting and road building, it was amazing to him to see the devastation of woodland and how the creeks were changing to muddy streams.

Now that he had seen all of this from down low and had gained control of flight, he lost some of his fear and decided to climb higher so he could see over the mountain. When he had gained height enough to see over the tops, he was surprised to see it was just more mountains and less people when away from the river.

He also found it to be too cold up there for his overalls and thin shirt. Even his bare feet were feeling the cold. The higher he went, the colder it became and he was forced to return to his original flight path. It also occurred to him that he could get lost and perhaps never find his way back home. How could he land and ask someone the way back when he didn't know how to tell a stranger where he lived? The thought occurred to him that he could build a large, smoky fire up on the hill above the house and barn, and, from the smoke, find his way home.

On second thought, he remembered seeing a lot of fires from where people were clearing land. That idea was out but he still needed some assurance that he would not be lost here on earth as well as lost to Hell for desecrating the gravesite.

Returning in good time to do his evening chores, he was so filled with the desire to tell Momma and Poppa about what he had seen that he was near to bursting. Surely God would not send him to hell for seeing the wonders of nature and the way man was destroying this beautiful land. He still held some fear that the warning about robbing a grave had some merit and there was the possibility it was true. Don't take a chance of sending Momma and Poppa to Hell by telling them about his find. He would use the Helmet and take his chances, for the rewards were too great to part with and Hell was too far in the future.

As he lay in bed that night, he considered that if he got too cold at the limited height he reached, he must find a way to dress warmer before going higher. He had found height so exciting. He must find a way to go very high and this would take heavy clothing that he could not buy, even if he had money.

As we sat by the fire that night, I lost all track of time and would have followed the old man to dawn and all the next day and the next night, if necessary. Old man Cartwright took such a long pause that I thought he was finished with the story, but, no, he was remembering his school days, all forty of them. After several hours thinking about the problem, old man Cartwright came to the conclusion that only a bear would be able to stand the cold up there. He told me about the teacher's story concerning the Englishman, Sir B.H Hodson who was the first to record the sighting of YETI. This was the name for that creature which looked like a large man/ape. He walked like a man and was covered with hair much like an ape. Days later I did some research and learned that he was right about YETI. We later came to know it as the Abominable Snowman since other sightings have been in the Himalaya Mountains where snow covered almost everything, and in Nepal, India, and Tibet, it was considered fact that the creature existed.

Leaving the helmet in his hiding place for the next few days was necessary because he needed to quell his excitement so Momma would not pester him for information. Also, it would give him time to hunt and to kill a bear or two. Up to now, Poppa would not hear of him going bear hunting alone, and, if he even thought it might happen, he would have removed the rifle from its usual pegs on the wall.

It took great courage for the boy to face his first bear all alone, except for Old Ring, his constant companion. The woods were full of bears, all sizes, and he did need a big one and a small one. His first bear was a big black with full fur and would make the coat he needed. Being trained with the rifle ever since he could hold it up for the shot, that first bear didn't have a chance.

Carefully skinning and processing the hide, almost intact, he came up with a suit that was a little too loose but with buttons all the way down the front where he had opened the bear. The suit fit as well as a Sears & Roebuck coveralls could do, or so he thought. While this suit was in the curing stage, he caught a smaller bear to make into a hood which would leave space for the helmet and leave only his eyes showing. Three weeks later, he was on the mountain with his new suit and had located a suitable hiding place for it. He was careful to keep it where he could use it and never be seen by another human as it was possible he could be shot for a bear.

Finally, the day came when he was to use the new suit. He chose another beautiful day and donned the helmet and the suit. With this on, he could float at ground level, and, by moving his feet, it almost looked as if he was walking with very long steps. He practiced this floating walk to make certain he would have control when he went up into higher altitude.

The flight that first time in high altitude was perfect. He soared to an altitude that allowed him to see all the way to Aracoma and a hundred miles in all directions. It also allowed him to get a mental map of his place on earth so he could not get lost. He had left early in the morning, and, by late afternoon, he had seen both Aracoma and Barboursville which was the extent of the Guyan valley. Till now, he was afraid to lose sight of the river and, possibly, lose sight of home. He saw an even larger town in the distance, west of Barboursville, but was afraid to venture there on this first high altitude flight.

On the way home, he became so hot and thirsty in that heavy bear suit that he had to go down for water and to relieve himself. He chose a dense patch of woods where he saw a small stream and no sign of people. He landed in a small clearing where he had to walk about fifty yards to water. In his walking gait, where his feet moved but his steps were yards long, he proceeded to water.

After drinking his fill and relieving himself, he started back to the open area where he could go up without passing through tree limbs. It was then that he saw a man, rigid with fear watching him. He did the best he could by running to another open spot and zooming up to head for home. After all, he did not want to contribute to that poor soul's astonishment by leaving the earth in plain sight. But his greatest fear was the possibility the man was a hunter and would mistake him for an ape or a walking bear, in which case he might take a shot at him. His most disturbing thought was that this abominable suit of bear hide could be the cause of his death, and yet he had to look like YETI in order to fly high.

For months after that close encounter, he remained earthbound. Fear that he could have been shot and sent to Hell caused him to suffer great trauma and ultimately put him to bed. His Momma worried over him all of those months but never got out of him the cause of his illness. Perhaps, this worry could have been the cause of his untimely death had it not been for the preacher, when on many of his visits, brought his pet snakes and held short services.

Then it was customary for a preacher to use a lot of well water which he brought with him in Mason jars. Now as you must know, preachers seldom have to do manual labor and the creation of first class "well water," also known as White Lightning did require much labor. However, the preacher was well liked by his congregation, meaning he was well supplied with no labor involved. So, after a year in bed, his Momma approved of the preacher starting treatment of a generous dose well water every day, and that did the trick. Not only did it cure him, it caused him to lose a part of his memory, the part where he had hidden the helmet.

Some of you better educated may know of the so called, first sighting of a creature tagged with the name of Abominable Snowman seen in Himalayan mountains of Nepal, India, and known as YETI. Well, I want it to go on record that the first sighting happened in West Virginia. All of those educated nincompoops in India failed to understand the contribution of West Virginians to history, science and whatever else is needed to explain where we stand in importance of this wide, wide world.

Chapter 3

I relive that exciting evening almost every night when I pull the covers up under my chin in preparation of restful sleep.

Old man Cartwright has gone on to his reward and my prayer is that he went up, not down. I doubt there is anything to the story of Hell being the final resting place for those who rob a gravesite. It just does not make sense to me that something so important as that Helmet should remain in the grave for all eternity. So, now you also understand why I have spent the past fifty years searching that part of West Virginia known as BIG UGLY PUBLIC HUNTING GROUND -------for that special Helmet.

The first thing I have to tell you in this second part of my story is——-I lied to you. I hate to admit to such a dastardly deed as telling a blatant lie, but I did and with much shame, then and now. With this admission out of the way, I will try to set things right with the truth, unadulterated and straight from the heart. Now that I am approaching ninety years of age, I recognize the fear of Hell that the old man felt when he first donned the Helmet. I certainly don't want to go there and I have done enough to warrant that judgment without telling you another lie.

I was forty years of age when I found the Helmet in its almost perfect hiding place. It was carefully wrapped in an almost totally decayed bear skin. Under the rock ledge was the old man's choice and a good one, for I had been poking into holes and under rocks for over twenty five years before I finally poked under the right rock. This bears consideration. The bear skin had provided the right amount of cover to protect it from easy access.

Now that I had it, shivers ran up and down my spine like a squirrel harvesting nuts in a tall tree. I was just as fearful as the old man was when he first tried it as a boy. The difference was that he had told me how to use it.

He also told me he was fearful of Hell since he had robbed a grave for it, and, I must admit, I had a smattering of the same fear. Now that flying saucers were in vogue, I had the additional fear of being seen for an outer space visitor. Knowing all about high-powdered rifles and the desire of people to become famous for shooting down the first visitor from Mars, I had to be extra careful.

Not exactly expecting to find the Helmet after all the years spent looking, I was not really prepared. I had no chin strap and no sea grass string on hand to secure the Helmet to my head. Now I recognize the vast forest surrounding the place where I found it, but I also recognize that most locals carry a rifle with them at all times. Even though the chance of being seen floating above the tree tops is almost nil, I had to try just a little bit. Carefully holding on to the sides and resolving to end the first trial at just above the tree tops, I placed the Helmet on my head. With just a thought of lifting off, I arose to the astonishing height of tree top level.

Again my spine did a shiver that almost unseated the Helmet. Then the awful thought occurred to me as it did to the old man so many years ago. What if the Helmet got away from me and I fell seventy feet to earth? No doubt I would die there in the "Big Ugly Public Hunting Area" where men don't usually go until hunting season. By then, if I was found, it would be only bones picked over by the vultures. Not a happy thought.

My home is in Barboursville, West Virginia, where I live alone so there's no one to grieve for me, no one to care so I can take the Helmet home with me. In fact, I have a gun safe where I can store it in safety. I will decide later when and where to use it. I also want to photograph the strange squiggles and writing inside so I can have some learned archeologist tell me what it means. I just hope it doesn't say "The user of this head gear is on his way to hell".

About two thirty Sunday morning when the entire town was sleeping, I was wide awake in anticipation of my first major flight. The place I wanted to go was back where the old man told me was his first flight. There, I had no fear of light aircraft that I might have to dodge, not at this time in the morning anyway. One thing I found out on this first flight was that speed was regulated only by my mind. I could out-run any aircraft, other than military that broke the sound barrier. I found this out the hard way by thinking fast without thinking how fast. I found there were no limits, and, before I was able to change my mind, the wind had stripped me naked. Talk about cold, a thousand feet up, naked in zero weather in a three hundred mile wind. Did I ever learn fast? I should have remembered the bear skin suit and, at least, put on some heavy clothes. Good thing it was night. A naked man streaking across the sky would have caused the National Guard to be called out or perhaps the ladies home auxiliary.

My friend David wears a suit on his motorcycle that keeps him warm and doesn't come off in the wind, for which we are both thankful, especially David. I'm gonna get me one of those suits Monday or, at least, before I venture into the wild blue again. I think his is heated by motorcycle's battery, but mine will just have to go it alone.

At the motorcycle shop, I had some trouble with the clerk. He wanted to fit me with what he considered a proper suit, but I wanted it extra-large since I wanted to carry things with me, inside the suit. I finally convinced him that my brother would also wear the suit and he weighs a hundred pounds more than I do. I promised not to lie but sometimes it can't be helped.

He told me at least ten times that I needed a helmet to be safe and inside the law. I assured him I had the finest Helmet in the world and that set off another series of questions. Why can't I keep my trap shut? I also bought a hand held GPS so I wouldn't get lost, and, again, I had trouble with the clerk. He insisted that I needed to secure it to the handle-bar and I hated to tell him I didn't have handle-bars. Of course, he had to ask what kind of motorcycle I rode, and I told the truth when I said I didn't have one. Was that ever a mistake? I have to tell him another lie, my brother has one but I don't know what kind it is except it has two wheels. Now he wants to know if they are in the front or the back. Some people just force you to lie.

Well, I finally got out of there about 800 bucks lighter but with the secure knowledge that I can fly high without frost bite and I probably won't get lost on my night flights. For a time, until I gain some experience, night flights will have to suffice, and

since I will be flying without light markers, I will have to stay well below radar--500 feet. When you can't see the ground on a dark night, there is some risk. For now I plan to follow the rivers so I can see the moonlight glow on the water. Perhaps, I need to buy an altimeter but not yet.

The next Sunday morning, I was dressed in my new suit and with the GPS strapped to my arm. I even placed a fruit bar in my pocket since I had a pocket and might get hungry before dawn. I planned to be in well before daylight but one never knows with a new travel vehicle. With a near nervous fit, I went out in my back yard and thought, "Up slow and easy." It worked and, before I was at the right flight level, I changed my thought to head for the Ohio River where I was familiar with the territory. I thought it would be dark there, but did I ever get a surprise. That river was lit like a carnival for miles and miles.

I cruised along at about a hundred or so miles per hour and saw no end to lights. I passed several small towns and some really big ones that I never thought were there. Good thing I had the GPS since I failed to recognize any of them from the air. I was truly lost and had no idea where home was, so I turned back with hopes I would find the place where I entered the river flight. I suppose I passed it without realizing and by the time I could see the GPS,

I had failed to bring a flashlight, I was well down-stream. Now I was fearful of being seen and, at this low elevation, where I should create a lot of excitement. I thought it was best that I climb higher where I wouldn't be so noticeable. Now I am at about a thousand feet and, before I know it, I am being chased by a small plane.

Sunday morning is the day all students and plane lovers go for a dawn flight and I am caught. No problem for me, though, I just think faster and made a rapid turn. I left him so fast he never had a chance to figure it out.

Now that I can read the GPS, I head across country for home. Day flying is for me. The beautiful things I can see from up there make me want to go slow and take it all in. I hated to end it, but the sight of my house down there was a relief. Strange how I thought I could not miss it, and, even there, it was hard to tell if I was in the right place until I was almost on the ground.

There is a saying that you can take a boy out of the mountains but you can't take the mountains out of the boy. That must be true with me for I want to make future flights to see the rugged mountains of West Virginia. There are so many places I have camped and hunted in the most remote places I could find, and now I have the means to see those places from the air. Not much chance I will be discovered or have a conflict with an airplane if I am touring the areas I love. The next warm weekend will be the one for me. I can leave home at that magical hour of two a.m. and be there at dawn. GPS coordinates are available on the internet close enough for me to find Middle Mountain just out of Elkins, West Virginia. I well know the highways leading there from Elkins, and once there, I can record the location for rapid return at later dates. The second Sunday in May is perfect since there is no hunting season at that time and it should be a deserted mountain road. No spring campers yet and the trees will be leafing out well. I will have food with me and the place to enjoy all to myself for the day.

Dawn brought a shocking sight of mountain tops removed and massive scars everywhere. Funny why I never noticed this destruction from the ground and not even from commercial flights of which I have made many in my business life.

I understand the government forces the mine operators to reclaim the land but no one has been there to tell the mine owners. I found the sight so sickening that I spent much more time looking at the destruction than I did at the beauty of what's left untouched. Never the less, I spent a wonderful day in the wilderness. Sometimes I would bare-foot wade a mountain stream or walk a game trail. Taking my lunch by a waterfall that ran full with spring rains was the highlight of my peaceful day. Dusk brought the end of my time to be at peace with nature and the necessity to return to the grind of living among people and all of the noise that goes with this. Gathering my gear for the return to my home, I was ready to make the flight by leaving just late enough that people on the ground were not likely to see me even if they were looking up. It would also let me arrive home in about an hour since the direct line is only about one hundred, twenty-five miles. Now that I carry a GPS and a flashlight, I will not be passing over many populated areas. I feel safe in flying above the highest mountains in the area and even if radar from Charleston picks me up, they won't be able to identify me or do anything about me. I will be at home before anything can cause me trouble. After all, I am a licensed pilot and understand the rules of the sky. I recognize the dangers of being in restricted areas and can avoid them with no trouble. I hold a VFR ticket and this means I am not supposed to fly on instruments but so what? I am not a registered aircraft and can fly so close to the ground, I can avoid even the sophisticated radar located at the Charleston and other city airports.

Several weeks and many short flights later, I was getting confidence in my ability to see the eastern half of the USA without being discovered. I was also well aware of the restricted zones where non military aircraft were in danger, both of being challenged and of being hit by fast moving aircraft. These were places I steered well free of since I could travel at very high speed and skirt those zones with no trouble. I particularly wanted to see the Gulf coast of Florida and Mississippi, but both places were dangerous to me as there were too many military bases along that part of the USA. This was the cause of my decision to make an over water trip to the South Atlantic for a look at the islands.

Summer is past and cold weather is here, making flying a little more uncomfortable. I have learned to protect myself from cold and heat and realize that some conditions will result in the icing of my head gear and he loss of vision due to ice on my face mask. This is the perfect time for the planned trip to warmer weather. My decision was to fly to Charleston, SC, for a look at the place where I used to live on Sullivan's Island and from there set off on a course of '160' degrees for Adelaide, Nassau. From there I will set a SSE course of '125' degrees for the island of Grand Turk, United Kingdom.

I believe this to be the final destination and a place where I can truly see a southern island where tourists are scarce. I had no trouble in finding my destination but I was sorely disappointed in finding it over-run with tourists. It seems there is no place left on earth that man has not defiled with trash. Even so, I found several places where I could find a room for the night, and since I could carry my flying suit as if it were my duffle bag, I was taken for a sailor or a fisherman. I did enjoy taking in the local scenery by walking most of the day. Bicycles and scooters were in plentiful supply but I need nothing except feet. I did keep my Helmet handy though as it was possible for me to make a quick exit, if needed. Even though the English language was common, it was not the language I heard most of the time. It would be better for me to move on now that I had satisfied my curiosity.

Chapter 4

Early morning with the sun barely lighting the eastern sky, I was down on the beach where I could dress and take off without being seen. I still had the desire to see more of the South Atlantic islands and had hopes of finding that perfect, uncluttered place. During my work years, I had seen all of the places I had just visited and hoped they were still as I remembered them. Not so. Trash and multiplied humanity had changed for the worse. Now I decided was time to head deeper into the southeast islands. I set a course of '120' degrees for the French holding of Guadeloupe. I never expected to find rugged country there, but the western half of that island was just that. It made a good place to stop for an hour to study the world map I carried and to set a new destination course. From there I planned to follow the string of islands down to Kingstown and to turn due east to Bridgetown. My reasoning was that since that, island was off to its lonely self, it would be deserted, or nearly so.

Unlike so many of the places I had seen from a few thousand feet, I was not disappointed in Bridgetown, Barbados. In fact, it turned out to be such a beautiful place that I considered making it my permanent home. Barbados has beautiful cities, well- manicured fields of cane, and all kinds of vegetables. I was even surprised to find that my credit cards were all I needed to enjoy

the best of the island. My major problem was that I could not and

would not turn loose of my Helmet. Although I enjoyed the beaches, I dared not go near the water. Just the thought of losing my Helmet made me stay away from any place where I might fall or drop it.

After a wonderful week there, I decided it was time to move on. I wanted to see more of the south Atlantic, and since I could travel at any reasonable speed, I decided to take a course of '350', almost due north, which would take me to Nova Scotia where I had friends to visit.

It would be cool there but not unpleasantly so. I calculated the distance at close to 2,700 miles, and since I could comfortably travel at 300 or perhaps to 500, I would have no trouble making it in eight or nine hours. I know the sound barrier is off limits for me, but 700 MPH is fast enough to rip my suit apart. Even so, 300 might be all it can stand. I had previously traveled at well over 250 so I did not doubt the ability of the suit to hold together.

Again, I chose to leave just before dawn, in part not to be seen but also to arrive in Nova Scotia in time to land before dark. I had been there many times and had decided to land south-west of Springfield where I would spend the night in the back country. The next morning just before dawn, I would move down S.E to Cherry Hill where my friends lived. How to explain dropping in on them with no visible form of transportation was a problem I placed behind me. I would deal with that as I traveled north and had a lot of thinking time.

About four hours into my travel north I became very uncomfortable and realized I might have made a mistake in so much over water travel. It became so much of a problem that I started looking for a ship where I might set down for a rest stop. How to explain my presence was the least of my worry as time brought more discomfort. It was during this time of acute stress when I began thinking of the Bermuda Triangle stories, ships and airplanes going into the Bermuda Triangle and never being heard of again. Not too many years ago, I did a study on the Sargassum weed which was proposed as a product that could be turned into bio-fuel. Although I did not remember much about that article, I did remember the details of the Sargasso Sea where so many ships had entered and never were heard of again.

I had read many stories of this place where it was said to be a grave-yard of lost ships, lost in a parallel dimension and time orbit. I also read that Christoforo Colombo in October of 1492 spotted this mass of weed and steered clear of it. This is the first recorded sighting of what was later named the Bermuda Triangle. History has changed his name to Christopher Columbus but the Sargasso remains the same.

As discomfort increased, my speed increased to the point that I thought my heavy leather suit would be torn off. Keeping my head into the wind to keep the Helmet from being torn off was of prime concern. Even so, it began to press against the top of my head until I had to slow down. It was about this time that I saw the first edge of the matted Sargasso weed that comprised that place referred to as the Sargasso Sea.

From my altitude, I could see no end to the mass of sea weed, and, for the first time, I could understand how a ship could be trapped in that weed jungle and remain there forever. I did read that the sea weed was forever on the move with the ocean currents but always in a circle and miles across.

As I moved across that matted surface, I could see that it formed something like an island with small hills probably piled up by winds from a recent storm. In with this massive gathering of seaweed, where thousands of glass and plastic bottles rejected by passing ships and washed down a hundred rivers by people who cared little for the environment. By this time, I felt real pain in my stomach and my back and was becoming desperate for a place to stop for a few minutes. Since the Sargasso weed was so piled up, I reasoned it would hold my weight for an hour or so until I could take an Aleve tablet for my pain. Being just a few short weeks short of my ninetieth birthday, I am used to pain and always carry a good supply of pain medication. Now, I am glad I have it with me.

Carefully, I let myself down until my weight was firmly planted on a high hump of Sargasso weed. There seemed to be solid footing and I took a few tentative jumps to assure myself of the

safety of lying down there for a few minutes, until the Aleve did its work. I must have dosed off in spite of the danger and of how much I had reminded myself to stay awake for when I opened my eyes, it was dark.

I had placed the Helmet on my chest before I closed my eyes but it was not there now. I felt all around in the dark but there was nothing except more sea weed. Panic, the unremitting, primeval fear that makes the bladder relax and the mind go numb, like nothing else on earth. In fact, I felt that I was no longer on earth except for the mass of sea weed I was tangled in. I would have tried to run, run away from that assiduous fear that gripped my heart.

I tried to relax enough to think, but all I could do was realize that the wind was picking up and a storm was bearing down on my island of fear. Lightning zinged across the sky and headed in my direction, each bolt becoming more hazardous to my position atop the mound of sea weed. I fell to my face on that pile of sea weed and called out to the God I hoped was in charge of the lightning and begged that he would have mercy on me. Every bolt of lightning lit the island of Sargasso weed like the morning sun and gave me the hope of locating my Helmet.

I looked in every direction with each new bolt, but there   was nothing except the rolling weed like the waves underneath. There was no sign of anything except obscure shadows all around me.

About an hour of this stormy condition and I had become used to seeing those shadowy figures all around me, growing more distinct with each bolt of lightning. As the wind began to die down, I realized there were sounds from those shadowy figures, like whispers in a large auditorium where there were many but none defined. By this time I had given in to my imminent death either by starvation or the lack of water.

Fear had receded to numbness of my heart and I could no longer feel my heart beating. Minutes ago, it was pounding and racing as if it would burst the walls of my chest, but now it was so peaceful that I could no longer detect motion and certainly the heavy feeling of fear was gone. My heart was at peace.

Then I heard a whisper near my ear which I could make out to be a welcome. "Welcome to our place," it said. I turned to look at the whisperer and found myself looking into the vacant eyes of what appeared to be a very old sailor. Unbelievingly, I turned to look in the other direction and their forms began to take shape in the murky twilight. What I saw were people of all sizes and shapes and even the outline of a sailing ship in the ghostly distance. I turned back to the whisperer and asked, "Where am I ?" "Welcome to the ethereal holding place of the ghosts of the Bermuda Triangle," it said???????

The Hog

Once again I need to assure that I don't lye about important matters and certainly about my wonderful state of West Virginia. There is the matter of pride to be considered and I am proud to be back home in the mountains after being away for over fifty years. I have worked all over the world, lived in several states and hunted deer in West Virginia for at least thirty of the fifty. I have traveled thousands of miles over those years, just so I could be in West Virginia over the Thanksgiving week of deer season. My non-resident license fees for hunting and fishing trips alone would be enough to make a lot of people happy. Even so, I consider this money well spent for where else could I have obtained so much for so little?

My hog story starts when my great granddaddy held me on his knee and told me about the hog he had a run in with as a young man. He said "Best I can remember it was 1857 before the timber was cut away round here". Grand Pappy was born in 1839 so I suppose he was about 93 when he told me this hair raising story. I remember how scary it was because Momma had to change my diaper. Now you might not believe that part of my story but his encounter with a wild boar made him need and believe in Depends.

Granddad lived somewhere on a mountain near the present Marlington, West Virginia so he told me. It was not uncommon then to run into a bear or a mountain lion every time he ventured into the woods. As it was then, trees were so thick and so big it was hard for the sun to ever touch the floor of the woods. In fact, he said it was almost dark all day and the nights were so black that seeing a star or the moon only happened when he was in the clearing around their cabin. He was a true Virginian that had traveled across the mountains looking for a place he could call his own and get away from the tax man. He and Grandma had a horse, blankets, an axe, cooking pots and little else. His rifle was his prized possession and the only thing that kept them in food and also the only thing that kept them from being food.

The first people over the mountains brought hogs and some never made much of a home before falling prey to cat, bears, Indians or just plain, thieving robbers. Some men would kill you for a good cooking pot. Anyway, hogs went wild and had the best food in the world. The woods were filled with chestnut trees and butternut trees. There is little that a hog won't eat if he can catch it and snakes were prime food for hogs to fatten up on.

Before I continue with Grandpa's story, let me tell you that there is no meaner animal in the wild than a hog. Hog hunters today go well armed and stay close to a good tree to climb if all else fails. A mean old hog has teeth that extend out four or five inches with which it can rip a leg off of a man in seconds. Now I am not talking about the cute little pot-bellied pigs some people lead around on a string. I refer to the big ones such as. a record kill registering a whopping 1,051 pounds, about the same as a big cow. How would you like to meet one like that some dark night when it was hungry? That's what happened to Grandpa.

Well, it wasn't dark but grandpa was picking up chestnuts in a very dense forest of very large trees, he failed to see the wild hog approaching him. It was a female hog that probably had pigs to protect. Grandpa said it stood waist high on him when he stood up. First, it probably appeared to that big momma hog that Grandpa was an intruder on her private realm. To the hog with poor eyesight and with Grandpa on his knees, I can see why he might have been mistaken for another hog. When that big hog was probably let out a squeal and charged, Grandpa stood up and looked for a place to run or a tree to climb. Running was the only option since every tree within sight was much too big to reach around and the first limb was three times over his head. Now, I don't know the speed of a hog but I do know I would not like to be faced with that problem. Grandpa did the only thing he could and that was to play "Ring around the rosey" with that hog. He was much more agile so he could make sharper turns around the trees and not being fat as the hog was, he was able to keep it up longer.

Uncle Henry being fourteen and still not cautious about anything was close enough to hear the pig squeal and Grandpa doing likewise. He ran toward the confrontation and before he had time to take in the total scene, the hog changed direction and now Henry was doing the tree dance. While Grandpa caught his breath, Henry was losing his. Salvation came with the same thing that would happen to most any overweight human or animal. That hog literally ran itself into a heart attack. Just like little David, the giant killer, who used the giants sword to cut off the giants head, Grandpa cut that hogs head off. Unlike David though, he had to furnish his own knife. Meat for the winter fattened on chestnuts.

Closer to home, my experience with a very large and a very mean hog came about when I was about forty and full of confidence. My neighbor on the adjoining farm had a very large boar hog he had kept for breeding purposes for several years. This hog ran loose in about a half acre pen and was so dangerous to people, no one dared to get in the enclosure with him. This neighbor wanted to take all of his hogs to market and get away from raising them. Now it is a fact that old boar hogs have such strong meat they are not fit to eat and the market will not buy them. The neighbor had called a veterinarian to have the hog castrated. After about three months, the hog would gentle down and could be sold at the market. The vet refused to go near that hog so the alternative was to shoot him and bury. I happened to stop by his place just before this was to take place and I offered to do the castration, no charge. My neighbor thought I was crazy to attempt what the vet was afraid to do but he gave me the go.

Now I am a wood worker and always carry an extra sharp knife. That day was no different and I had almost all the tools I needed. I asked him for an ice pick, a near empty feed bag, a can of tractor starting fluid and a can of salve he used on his injured cattle. In wonder, he brought all of the items and watched as I performed surgery.

First, I cut a slit near the bottom of the feed bag then I opened just enough of the fence to allow the bag to be pushed through the hole. By pushing the open end of the feed bag

through the fence, that hog bullied his way to the front and promptly stuck his head in for the feed. Next, I punctured the starting fluid can with the ice pick and dropped it through the slit.

All mechanics know that engine starting fluid is ether and the stuff doctors previously used to put patients to sleep. It also works on hogs. This hog tried to get away by running with that feed bag over his head. That only served to make him breathe deeper and quickly go into a sound sleep. He made it for about fifty or sixty feet before legs failed to carry him.

By the time his owner and I got to him, he was totally under so neighbor held one leg up while I did the surgery. When we got to him, we had immediately removed the bag and fanned him some fresh air. Even so, he slept for about twenty minutes and when he did recover, poor thing just sat on his injured rear end and looked around for well over two hours.

A week later, I was at my dentist office and told him the story. I heard him in the next room, on the phone telling someone that was the first time he had ever heard of starting fluid being used as stopping fluid. When he did get to me, he was still laughing and told me he had to call his brother to relate the story to him.

I need only add that my neighbor kept the hog for another four months then took him to the sale barn. He was a very gentle hog and sold for a very good price.

The Key

Believe me, this is no "lye". Truth in all things is what I, Jess Stover strives for, and, if you should find error in this story, don't believe it. Please read it to the end to find the moral of this narrative, and believe me, there is one. Riches come in many forms, and money is the least of all for the Bible tells us that "The love of money is the root of all evil."

Richwood, West Virginia, Ramp capitol of the world, in the head waters of Cherry River, and, used to be the state's largest producer of clothes pins and cherry lumber. In 1950 when I was at the bright age of sixteen, my troubles started when I dropped out of school, and I did this because I thought I knew it all. My friend George, also well educated, he thought, was helping me at the only job we were qualified for, grave digging. People die and need to be placed under ground, and where we came into the picture was that flat land was in short supply. Burial plots were easy to come by but, only on the side of the mountain where it was too steep for machinery to dig.

My real love was for the forest. The mountains around Richwood were filled with the remains of destruction from timbering. It was sad for me to think that I would never be able to see what these mountains looked like before sawmills chopped it into lumber and dust. The Richwood mills screamed night and day in an effort to destroy the last vestige of beauty, the last majestic tree. I spent every day of my free time, searching deeper into the mountains for some semblance of the glory of yesteryear. Gone were the days when giant cherry and chestnut trees covered the slopes of our beautiful mountains, gone forever.

George and I were in no great hurry to complete this lowly job since it was a bright and hot day. We were two white boys looking to get the first rays of summer since a good suntan would set well with the girls down at the swimming hole. We were on the sunny side of the mountain and from where we were digging, the slope of the land rose sharply upward. It was difficult to keep the removed dirt from rolling down, and away, and it would certainly be needed tomorrow to cover the casket. We had dug down to about where we could call it finished when the bottom caved in and I fell through. I landed on my feet with the empty hole above me just out of reach. Just enough light came in over my head for me to see that I was in a manmade tunnel, running in the direction of deeper into the mountain. Of course I was terrified and George was not much better off, but I did get him to understand that I needed a ladder, rope and flashlight.

Thirty minutes later, George returned with these items, and with an additional flashlight. He had heard, and seen enough to want to explore as I did. He lowered the ladder and for purely safety reasons, he tied the top of it to a large tree nearby. When he came down with the lights, we saw an amazing sight, totally beyond our limited education to comprehend. The walls, including the floor and ceiling of this tunnel were done in fitted stone, so carefully done as to cause us to run hands over the wall trying to feel where joints were.

It was almost as poured concrete would have been, but we understood from the first moments that we were the first people down here in hundreds, if not thousands of years. Just the odor of antiquity alone would convince anyone of how long this tunnel had been sealed.

To our right which was down the mountain slope toward town, the tunnel became so small it was almost as if the builders had become smaller, and smaller as they worked their way out. By the flashlight beam, it was easy to see that the tunnel ended well short of reaching the surface of the mountain. To our left and into the depths of the mountain, the tunnel became much larger, and certainly more complex in structure. It also sloped downward to the point that it almost needed steps. At this point, George lost the desire to explore. Really it was nothing more than plain fear and I was about to lose it also.

George decided one of us had to remain on the surface for safety reasons and he, being slightly older decided it should be him. I had no objections to this since I had spent so much time exploring the mountains alone, I could not resist going to the end, regardless of what the end may entail. I was so excited that nothing short of death would have stopped me. As I continued another few hundred feet, the tunnel increased in size and eventually ended at a blank wall. The disappointment of a dead end almost made me cry.

Why would any being, be they people, angels or demons, choose to form such a perfect tunnel and ending in a blank wall? There had to be a reason and I decided to search a little more carefully. Then I saw it!

One stone of a different color and not cemented in place as were all the others. With shaking hands, I pried and pulled at that stone until I worked it loose. I expected it to yield a great treasure but I was sadly disappointed when it turned out to hold only something similar to a large key made of stone. I sat down on the stone I had just removed from the wall and I must admit I shed a tear of disappointment. But then something spoke to me, from that key it seemed. A voice that was not a voice but a deep rumbling that made itself understood by me, one that I would only have understood with that key in my hand. What it said to me was not too difficult to understand, it was offering me one wish and one only. It informed me that

I could have anything I wanted, so long as it did not contain a wish for riches or gain of any sort.

I sat on that stone for a very long time trying to think of what to wish for. Every thought seemed to end in a desire for riches, now or in the future. All were rejected as not acceptable to the key.

At last I had the answer to my past day dreams, I could see the mountains as they were before man destroyed timber and rivers. My wish was to return in time to when men had the freedom to roam the woods without government interference, taxes and general need for education. I could see the world as a white trapper and explorer found it back before destruction. When I declared my wish to be a young man, one hundred year ago, it was accepted.

Back on the surface, George became mighty fearful when darkness fell and he had heard nothing from Jess Stover. He called for some time and heard nothing. In desperation, he left for down in town where he raised the alarm. Very soon, half the town was trying to peer down the hole but the mayor took charge and formed a party of three coal miners who were used to underground labor.

With their miner's lamps and lots of rope, they descended into the tunnel. None knew the need for rope but caution caused them to also carry oxygen and first aid equipment. Radio communications were arranged for in order for the mayor to keep the people informed and since Jess had no immediate family, it was the mayor who spoke for Jess.

As the three miners approached the tunnel end, their bright lights allowed them to see there was no Jess and no way out. It became a profound mystery though, why was the rope, flashlight and clothing of Jess Stover placed as it was? Rope and flashlight on the floor of the tunnel and clothing draped over the stone as if in a setting position. Shoes neatly placed side by side at the end of the ragged jeans Jess had been wearing.

On returning to the surface, the three miners were suitably shaken and declared a reluctance to return to the tunnel. The mayor could find no one who would again inspect that fearful place. In order to quell panic, he made the public statement that Jess had played a trick on the town and left naked while George was in town raising a search party. He gave the police department, both of them, orders to arrest Jess on sight for public nudity. A series of man hunt, x that out, boy hunt orders were posted and the town searched for the next three days. An all points bulletin went out all over the state for a naked young man on the loose. Every widow in three counties around joined the hunt on a twenty four hour basis, but no sign of him was discovered. Most people around town soon decided it was no great loss since Jess was just another school dropout but most of the widows continued to hope and look.

Several weeks went by with no sign of Jess and the mayor tried once more to get men down into the tunnel for a closer look. He had hopes he would show himself as a strong and compassionate man by renewing the search party for Jess, but no volunteers were available. His efforts only induced greater fear that whatever happened in the tunnel to Jess might exit the tunnel and prey on the town's people. Fear began to grasp the hearts of mothers with small children. If the thing in the tunnel could eat a big boy like Jess, what could it do to my little Suzie? The mayor was in a dilemma, action of some kind was needed to save his position and his reputation, what there was of it in the first place.

Of course, put the city workers to doing something except leaning on shovel handles he thought. Organize a work party of city workers and call for volunteers to fill that much feared hole on the mountain. Make it so news worthy that the county seat in Webster Springs would give him a write up in their paper and perhaps send some money to help with the disaster. No use letting the disappearance of a school dropout go to waste for he needed all he could get for the next election.

Now it was too difficult for trucks to get up to the tunnel site so it was perfect to arrange dozens, if not hundreds of people to carry baskets of Cherry river rocks up there. Besides, there was a serious need to clean out the river bed and where else could he get an extra vote or two. This was well known as the way to kill three birds with one or a dozen river stones. Richwood had a great following of cooks that specialized in preparing massive amounts food for the Ramp festival so why not utilize them to set up a survival kitchen.

Volunteers would be fed at city expense and an appeal to Webster Springs for money and help could be extended to Charleston. Who knows, this could get him re-elected, maybe even known over in Charleston.

Several weeks later, the tunnel existed no more and the scare was over. Whatever ate that poor young man down there is forever covered in river stone. Cherry River now flows clean and the mayor can tell, for many years to come, the story of how he handled the crisis.

Backward to the year of our Lord, eighteen hundred and fifty six, just six years since his transformation, a naked young man now known as Jase was in dark Africa with his brothers of about twenty other blacks, at least he thought of them as brothers since they called him and each other bro. They were running and hiding from men, both black and white who caught his brothers and secured them in chains. Jase had no idea if any of these people were really his relatives because he had somehow lost his memory. He just knew he did not want to be caught, for any reason.

Eventually, they were surrounded, caught and placed in chains. He soon learned it was to be his fate to take a long voyage in the belly of a sailing ship. Next stop was a great relief for him since he was able to stand outside and breath fresh air in a place he heard called Baltimore. He did not know it yet but he was in the hands of slave traders and was to become the property of a land owner and put to doing work. That was the one thing he had always desired to stay clear of and would fight to keep from soiling hands with it.

The following day he found himself being prodded and poked by men who gathered around him and his brothers. They were placed on an elevated platform so they could see over the heads of several people who all looked at the man on a higher platform. Much talk and much prodding him and he was soon released from his brothers and taken away by another much larger black man. He was placed in a wagon along with three other people in chains and the big black man who watched them at all times. The driver was a fat white man who seemed to be the boss. Late that night they arrived at a place where there were many buildings, one of which they were locked into for the night.

The next day he was taken to a field where tobacco was growing in long rows, as far as the eye could see. The big black man showed him what he was to do by gestures and prodding, repeating the action by a slap on the head when he thought Jase was not paying attention. Jase was paying attention but determined not to do what he saw as work and no amount of head slapping would change his mind. After a time he got the point across that he was not going to work, now or ever. Then came the time for his first hard lesson from the big man he soon learned to call "Yassa BossMan". He was taken back to the clearing where he was bound to an upright post and where Boss Man taught him his second lesson. The whip changed minds with twenty lashes and another ten for firmly seating the memory. The very next day, Jase was taken to the field and he needed no instruction as to how to sucker the tobacco plants. He was very glad to join his brothers in serving Boss Man and the planter.

Jase worked and schemed for the next several years on how to become a Boss Man himself. He saw this as the only way to escape the torture of work. He learned the language and the most important words in it were the ones he learned his first day there which was "Yassa Boss Man". Eventually he gained the trusted position he sought and found what he had been working toward for years, a chance to escape.

As all slaves had heard rumors of the Underground Railway, so it was that Jase determined to find freedom by this route. Not that Sunday was a day of rest but it was a day when the plantation owner fed them a little better. It seemed he went to church and was likely to have other church goers visit on Sunday afternoon and he wanted to make a good impression. Show his magnanimous nature by having slaves well fed and resting in the shade when there was work needed to be done. Never mind, they would have to catch up tomorrow or feel the whip. It was just such an afternoon when Jase slipped down to the river and started his trip to freedom. The mighty Delaware River was almost too much for Jase but he made it to the other side where there were not so many people and from there he cautiously moved north. Moving at night and with extreme caution, he gathered and ate from the fields where farmers had gardens and grain crops. Jase had no real idea of his destination, only the desire to move as far north as he could and to get away from the hated Boss Man.

As he stayed east and away from the river, he met few people and had the advantage of more farm land where he could find food. He had heard there was an Underground Railroad working out of Philadelphia and that city was to the north and freedom. Sleeping deep in the woods by day and traveling by night allowed him to reach the edge of what appeared to be a large city, but now there, what to do next?

Seeing a group of black people working a field without a Boss Man in charge gave him the idea he might get some food and help from them. He waited until near dark and seeing them split up and leave in different directions gave him the courage to approach an older black man. As it turned out, this was his salvation for the old man was a free black and anxious to help a brother. After feeding and hiding Jase for another day, he had the time to give exacting directions to a place where the station master, William Still lived. Not too far away there was another free black brother that had a team and wagon he hired out for freight. It was such that Jase was placed with this free black for the slow and dangerous trip toward the railhead. After all day and part of the night, Jase rode the wagon under a load of corn headed for the grist mill in Philadelphia. Sore and almost suffocated, he made it to the place known as the Railhead where Mr. William Still took him in for several days.

From there, many sympathetic white people took in runaway slaves and passed them on to another safe house. Keep in mind that there were rewards offered in thousands of dollars for the return of runaways. Persons helping them could and did have to pay fines of large amounts and even serve jail time so it was very risky to take in Jase. Eventually, he was passed to a Mrs. Harriet Tubman, a free and much sought after black woman. There was a reward of forty thousand dollars on her head, posted by the planters who were losing slaves to her and her Underground railway to Canada. Mrs. Tubman lived most of her time in St. Catherine, Ontario Canada with frequent and very brave trips to Pennsylvania. No wonder the planters were willing to pay for her capture. Jase traveled under her guidance and in her care for the next three weeks and then was given his freedom in Canada.

In the year of our Lord, eighteen hundred and sixty one, Abraham Lincoln took the reins of president of the United States of America. On April 12th that same year, the war started when the Confederate army fired on Fort Sumter, South Carolina. President Lincoln immediately called for a volunteer army and the call reached Jase and many other black men now living in Canada. Jase was not so much ready to fight for freedom since he was already free, but he had a grudge against plantation owners who had mistreated him and his kind. His thought was to get a gun and go kill, even the so called brother who had whipped him. The following years were made up of marching and more marching. Hundreds of miles on foot and never a shot fired by him, that is until eighteen sixty three in a place called Gettysburg. Jase was lucky enough to survive that bloody conflict and with a much reduced army was marched for another hundreds of miles. First east then north, then south by west. It seemed their officers had no idea where to go next.

Finally he found himself with the army of General Grant at Appomattox Court House on April 12th, 1865 when General Lee surrendered and ended the war. Jase had the option of leaving the army where the last battle was fought. With no money and little food, he and others decided to go west where it looked to be a safer place to live and also where he could find land to call his own.

Since he was in the ragged uniform of the defeating army, he was allowed to take some liberties in gathering food while in Virginia. Their course west included passing through Lynchburg and Lexington, Virginia where the food supply was very short but as they continued west, they found Clifton Forge to be a little better supplied. Not much was known about the trails ahead of them but as they continued, it was possible to learn from residents that there was a pass though the mountains and into the western part of Virginia.

To this time, Jase had not found any of the plantation owners that he desired to punish. It seemed he was out of the country where plantations were scarce. Crossing the mountain pass and finding themselves in land that was becoming rolling hills and very pleasant land at that, it seemed all was taken. It was necessary to keep moving west. They soon arrived at the very attractive town of Lewisburg and learned they were now in a place that had removed its self from the confederate states and wanted it known that they were now, West Virginia. They were proud that the town was the location of fort Savannah in 1770 and that Colonel Andrew Lewis was the founder. Actually, the town was officially founded twelve years later in 1782. Land here was far too valuable for the displaced soldiers to even think of remaining so they moved northeast for a few days. Soon it looked as if they were heading into territory that was too populated for their limited ability to buy land. Then they discovered a break in the mountains that looked promising and so they turned north. As they traveled on this northward course, people became friendlier and there was far more open land they might be able to settle on.

Jase and his companions were all from the wild African territory and had long ago learned how to live off the land. This seemed perfect to them, woods and streams as far as they could see. Not used to the mountains but they held no danger to the group. Each had the rifle they were allowed to keep when they left the union army. Now they were in no great hurry to move on for it was a dream fulfilled for Jase. Somehow in the back of his distant memory, he had wanted to see the grandeur before and all around him.

He had time when lying by the camp fire at night to study his mind, searching for the elusive thought that he had been seeking this very time and place for years. During the day time when the men were resting or bathing in a mountain stream, Jase asked each of them if they had the feeling of being home, if the mountains reminded them of their home across the seas. None had the feeling Jase was trying to describe and none truly felt at home here in the wilderness.

Slowly they moved their camp sites north as the game became scarce where they had hunted and disturbed the tranquility of the deep woodlands. As they moved further north, Jase became more and more filled with the feeling of being home. He tried to explain the feeling to his companions but they had no way of understanding the turmoil in the heart of Jase.

Many days later they struck the upper reaches of a fast-flowing stream and decided to follow it down to deeper pools where they might be able to catch trout for a change in their diet. It took them several weeks to work their way down and by this time, winter was about to show its bared teeth. Camping at night with the increasing cold was not to the liking of men that had been raised in Africa so they decided to search out a wide place in the river bottom and build a winter cabin. Now they picked up their gear at first light and proceeded downstream, searching for that ideal place. When they found it, there was a minor problem, others were there before them. Even so, they were welcome and in short order, built their winter residence.

Now Jase was in deep trouble in his mind. Loss of sleep had him on the verge of insanity.

Why did he have the feeling of being here before? Why did he feel he was an outcast as a black man? Why did he seem to feel the pull of returning to the same spot every day he was out of the cabin? Several times he tried to discuss the feeling with his companions but there was no answer. Now Jase was no infidel and he had learned the catholic faith while in Canada and now he turned to asking God for answers. He also attended the only church in the settlement of this town which he had learned was called Richwood. He was told it got its name from the richness of the smell of burning fire wood of the cherry trees.

The mountains were covered with the glory of millions of giant cherry trees and game was plentiful for the taking. In fact, Richwood was paradise on earth. The river was filled with trout and nothing was troubling to the residents of Richwood. He was asking himself again and again, why trouble yourself with unanswered questions?

Then one night in a dream of terrifying reality, he found himself deep underground in a long tunnel. He was a white boy in misery because he could not see this valley as it was before man cut all of the cherry trees. Now he understood. He got his wish of seeing back in time and the cost of that was that he had suffered time as a slave and was now a black man.

The moral of this story is that you should be intoxicated with happiness for what you have, thanking God every day for who you are and where you are.

The Missionary, Jacob Hatfield

The Reverend Doctor Jacob Hatfield was secure in the native hut that had been constructed for him when he first arrived at the mission designated clearing in Avakubi, Congo, Belgium territory of Africa. It was now November, 1909 and he was weary of travel having left New York last May, 8th, 1909. His mission was to establish the Baptist church teachings to natives that had very little contact with the white race and were, in fact, hostile. He had joined the expedition of Lang and Chapin who had been commissioned to study the flora and fauna of the rain forest along the upper reaches of the Congo River. His church had taken advantage of this expedition to insert a missionary, and Jacob was their choice. He was newly graduated from medical school and was ordained as a Baptist minister. He was also single, with no immediate family to hinder a long period on the mission field.

Jacob was twenty three his last birthday, just a month ago. His friends at the church had placed a great deal of responsibility on him but that was because he had been very active in church work since his early teens. Jake had little time for girls and there was no shortage of them after him. He was too busy with his medical studies at the college and working as an apprentice with Doctor Abrams who was also a leader in their church.

Jacob had a good life except for the loss of both parents in an accident just two years back. His father had large holdings in the local bank and a lot of land which left Jake a wealthy young man. No wonder the girls used every excuse to get near him and his money. When Doctor Abrams heard about the need for a doctor to accompany the Lang/Chapin expedition to Africa, he immediately thought of Jacob, the perfect fit. When he brought it before the church elders, there was total approval for the church body to finance his extended stay as a missionary. Although the expedition would cover costs as long as he stayed with them, when he left for other than church duties he would be on his own. Jacob did not need funds for this but he did need the church to support him with supplies such as medical equipment and a hundred other items that he did not yet realize he needed.

Depending on his supporters to help, Jacob amassed the mountain of supplies he would need for perhaps years in the jungle. It was shocking to him to see what they had gathered at the port of New York for his trip. Not the least of which was at least twenty cakes baked by the local belles of his church. He took all as if it would accompany him all the way to Africa, but he knew a major part of everything would have to be left behind.

Leaving New York aboard the SS Zeland, complements of King Leopold, and headed for the port of Antwerp, Belgium, Jacob was filled with misgivings. What if he was to fail his church and all of the people who pledged to support him with money and prayers? What if he got sick while deep in the jungle and had to depend on a witch doctor? All of these questions made him wonder if he was really qualified until he changed ships in Antwerp and again set sail on the ship SS Leopoldville. From then on to his destination of Boma, which was a hundred miles up from the mouth of the Congo River, he had to change his thoughts to, "There is no turning back now."

The Lang/Chapin expedition had been the project of the American Museum of Natural History and was financed, in part by King Leopold 11, William Rockefeller, and J.P. Morgan. Doctor Jacob Hatfield was a welcome member to the expedition and his church family was happy to finance that part relating to his extended stay. James P. Chapin was newly graduated from Columbia University and was the same age as Jacob. This resulted in a firm and friendly relationship. The bond between James and Jacob made the trip into the unknown parts of Africa more pleasant and allowed them to study things of mutual interest together. Language seemed to be the greatest problem Jacob faced when he was finally left behind by the expedition, but there was no way to know what dialect would be used. He was told that English was common and there would be no trouble until he left the river for the interior.

Two weeks of sailing down from the North Atlantic to the South Atlantic gave Jacob ample time to prepare for the isolation he would face in the upper reaches of the Congo River. Jacob spent much of that two weeks hanging over the rail, too sick to care if he made it or not. Being a doctor gave him no license to ward off motion sickness, so he lost weight from not eating much and losing most of what he did. After they left the open Atlantic and started up the Congo River, motion sickness left him and he began to enjoy the trip.

Their destination at Boma would require another two weeks to organize the trip upriver. Although the Belgium Government had supplied transportation in the form of a 56-foot sternwheeler, it was not ready when they arrived. Minor repairs, so the captain said, but it looked to them that he just wanted time ashore. They all faced more than a hundred miles of river travel to Stanleyville, but he had the return trip which made him reluctant to start. Loaded as the boat would be, he could not hope to make the trip in less than two weeks, and this did not include time he would be tied up for unloading freight and loading fuel.

While they were stranded at Boma, James and Jacob spent much time asking questions about the interior and the people. They were told many times about how the natives would not work and how lazy they were. Of course, this kind of information came from the white population, mostly French and Belgium people. None volunteered that the Belgium Colonial whites had enslaved the natives for the past fifty years in order to harvest sap of the rubber trees. None mentioned the fact that thousands of natives had died due to forced labor, slavery and sickness introduced by the infusion of the white race.

At last, they were all aboard and ready to head up stream. Jacob, with the help of Herbert Lang had sorted through the mountain of gear and reduced it to a more manageable amount. Many items were either sold or abandoned at the dock in Boma. They depended on Belgium authorities there to help them adjust their needs for interior travel. The items Jacob could not allow anyone to sort or exclude were his medical supplies. He believed he could do much good for the natives, and, at the same time, teach them about God. There they learned they would need native bearers to carry everything around the rapids at Stanleyville. One hundred fifty miles over the mountains would require at least two hundred men, and the cost would be up to their bargaining power.

Travel on the stern-wheeler steam boat was slow and hot on the wide Congo River. Being near the equator meant every day, nights included, would be hot. It would take some getting used to and Jacob was constantly thinking of the more pleasant spring weather back home. He had to shake off the feeling that he was making a great mistake and make himself look forward to helping the native people to a better life. Food was now more appealing to him since he was past motion sickness but there was not much to look forward to on the old riverboat that slowly paddled its way up stream. A break came when they reached Matadi where the captain had made previous arrangements for fuel. Although they would be docked for only an hour or so, James and Jacob made a quick trip into the settlement for no other reason except to look. There was little to see except unsanitary conditions in every direction. They decided living in a jungle camp, away from the natives, would not be so bad after all.

As they approached Stanleyville, excitement started to build for it was here they needed to locate native porters and start the overland portion of their expedition. It took a week to hire and organize the 200 natives required to carry all of their gear. During this time, much was lost and some things were discarded, but Jacob's medical supplies were intact. The long march over the mountains and around the rapids took another twenty days which served to acquaint Jacob with the kind of camping he was to experience for the next several years.

Above the rapids, the Congo River became wide and placid again.

There, Herbert Lang set about buying all of the boats available and building more until they had enough to continue for another several hundred miles. About half of the natives stayed with them to man the boats, and to help with camp chores at night. Places along the river that were wide enough and clear enough were scarce, so these men were a great help in clearing places for night stops and tents.

Several days later, they reached the broad expanse of the Congo where the combined rivers of Lomalar and Liuiaka flowed quietly into the main stream. At this point, Jacob was to leave the expedition and go deep into the rain forest for his work as a missionary. Five of the native bearers decided to accompany Jacob and this was mostly because Jacob had made firm friends with them. His love for the people was evident from the start, and when they were injured along the way, Jacob's skill and love won them as lifelong friends. He did not miss a chance to tell them about his God and he proved his faith by courage when times were extremely hard on all of them

Breaking off with one canoe which was sufficient to carry the six men and his supplies was a sad and somewhat lonely parting. Jacob would miss his friend, James, but the natives with him made travel upriver interesting. From them, he learned much about their language and customs. One of them had been this far up river before, and, being an older man, he assumed the position of leader and boss. All of them spoke very little English and could understand Jacob well enough to need very little bossing. They were eager to please which made Jacob believe God had arranged their decision to follow him. One day up river, they came to the village of Kinshasa, the last place where Jacob met a white man who knew the country. His advice was to go no further up river as the natives were not friendly to black or white. Just as Jacob had hoped, there was promise of a fertile field for introducing God and medicine.

Early the following morning, Jacob's loaded canoe headed up river. His destination was the interior of the rain forest and the place where he hoped to build a following and perhaps a hospital. Two days before they found the junction of the two rivers and decided to go up the Lomalar. There was no particular reason, but it was just that Jacob had prayed about it and felt God had directed his path. One more day upstream and the valley opened up to some cleared land and three small grass huts along the water's edge. As they beached the canoe, small children came out to see them but no others. Jacob's men were cautious, as if expecting an attack, but only women followed the children, only after it was apparent to them that the canoe men meant no harm.

Unloading bare essentials while the old man boss talked with the women, it was learned that the village men were on a hunt and would not be back till night. This was a real break for it gave Jacob time to make friends with them and shower them with gifts brought for this purpose. Well before darkness fell, his men had pitched his tent and set up a hut for themselves. It looked as if he had found a home base, and, with the help of his men, had a cooking fire going. With canned items brought from Boma, the last place where these items could be purchased, a large dinner was prepared for him and his men. Even so, it was not large enough for the children had to be fed and this made Jacob happy. It meant that he was making friends, instead of enemies of a people he had been told to fear.

When the men of the village returned that night, it appeared they were more than ready to dispatch the intruders. Of course, the children were running happily among the newcomers and it took only minutes for them all to be friends. Jacob thought again how amazing it was that God was here before him and had laid out the red carpet of friendliness.

Over the next few weeks, Jacob was busy treating minor cuts and abrasions on the children and winning the trust of their elders. He was also busy with the local men hunting in the jungle for herbs they used and to watch them hunt with their poison dart blow guns. During these excursions into the jungle, he was taken across the mountain toward the Liuiaka River which was about two days travel. There he was introduced as a friend and treated to much welcome. He also had a chance to treat some of the children's cuts and sores. He immediately recognized a chance to set up another camp where he could treat sickness and preach about his living God. On the return trip, Jacob made many notes of the trails used for he intended to return on a regular basis, with or without a guide.

Over the next few months, the local tribal doctor made his rounds complete with ointments, feathers, rattles and much dancing. Jacob stayed well clear of him for fear of exciting rivalry. He did not need an emy in the medical profession. But the day came when one of the village men was carried in with a massive wound from the horn of an angry water buffalo. With the puncture wound as well as broken bones, this man had little chance of survival. Apparently, jungle drums had summoned the witch doctor for he arrived at the same time as the injured man was carried into the village. He set about treating the patient with first a prolonged dance and fanning campfire smoke over the patient. Jacob had no choice but to stand by and watch helplessly as nothing done would have helped the man live. He deduced the witch doctor was giving him the last rites since he made no effort to set the bones of broken arms. An hour or so later, the witch doctor left without medically treating any part of the open wounds. It was the children that took him by the arm and led him to the injured man. They knew he could do miracles with open wounds, and now, he was called on to do his medicine.

First, he had to determine if the puncture wound had damaged internal organs that he had little hope of doing anything about, or if it was only a matter of infection from a dirty horn. Yes, the man was badly mangled but there was not much internal damage. Jacob treated him with the insertion of antiseptics and laudanum for his pain. He then set the broken arms with splints of reeds quickly cut to order. Next he treated the superficial wounds with bandages and tape which went a long way toward giving the patient confidence and helping him to recover quickly. Now he had an enemy of the witch doctor.

Two years passed quickly and Jacob had made friends with most of the local tribes. He had established what he called his hospital at the clearing on the Lomalar River and an outpost treatment center on the Liulaka River. He made the trek across the mountain once each month by spending one night on the trail each way. He traveled alone for the most part since he had become used to living in the jungle. In all of this time, Jacob had never had to use the rifle he carried for protection from animals. There was no need to protect himself from the natives, or so he thought. At the midway camp site, he would build up a large fire to keep away large cats and other animals that could do him harm, then he would lie beside the fire and sleep through the night.

Jacob did know he had one enemy in the witch doctor but he did not fear him for he had too many other friends. Like people all over the world, there will always be those that will do anything for money, even murder. Jacob was not secure from people like that and the witch

doctor made use of two of those who were willing to dispatch Jacob for money. It was planned for one of the monthly trips over the mountain to his treatment center. Jacob was followed by these two men.

Jacob did not expect the native carrier from down river to arrive with a package and instructions for him to return to the USA. His church had made arrangements for his return by placing travel money in the package for him and a larger amount in the Belgium bank at Boma. His instructions were to return for a period of ninety days furlough while he gave the church a report. He was also expected to select a companion for his return to the Congo River, either a doctor or another minister. With these instructions, Jacob wasted no time in preparations for the return trip. Actually, there was not much to do except load a canoe with a few articles he wanted to show his church and many notebooks and pictures. With three of his friends, he left with promises of returning.

Weeks later Jacob stood before the congregation of his church with stories of his life in the jungle. He told how it was difficult to win the natives over to God for that first year because he did not understand their belief in magic. When he later understood the language, that belief in magic became clear and he was able to prove how God had sent and protected him.

He told of the last week he was there and on his way to the outpost over the mountain. He told of how he made camp that night as usual and how he felt it necessary to be on his knees and openly pray for protection that night.

On his return to base camp three days later, one of the natives came to him privately with the following story. "My brother and I were paid by the witch doctor to kill you while you were sleeping on your first night on the trail. We followed you all day, and when you had a great fire going, we saw you kneel and call out to your God to protect you through the night. We thought nothing could protect you from our knives when you were sound asleep. We retreated into the jungle to give you time to fall completely asleep, and, when we returned well before dawn, your fire was bright and there were twenty warriors standing guard around you and the camp fire. We now know your God is greater than ours and we want you to help us to know him."

After the service was over that evening, some of the church elders came to Jacob to ask about that incident. They wanted to know exactly what morning that took place. When they had the date pinned down, Jacob had become very curious about their questions. When he asked for an explanation, the minister told him that one of the elder gentlemen of the congregation had interrupted the service that evening with a request that all men form a circle and pray for Jacob. He said it was a feeling that Jacob was in danger and he understood that prayer was all that could save him.

Ending the story with the line "Prayer was all that could save him" was foremost in my thought as I wrote the story of Jacob Hatfield. I believe I have been in Jacob's shoes as I have faced the open end of the gun that intended to kill me. Now, it is difficult for some to believe in the power of prayer. Some will believe an incident such as Jacob's to be pure fiction. Not so!

I write this story just as my wife Dixie and I heard it from one of the very old deacons that stood in that circle. We were staying in a small town in the mountains of the northwest for a summer month of what we liked to call vacation time. While there, we attended the First Baptist church services in the town where we were staying. We met several wonderful people and this deacon was one of them.

I did have to take some liberty in the construction of the time and location of this story for the deacon did not give us all of the particulars. Doctor Jacob Hatfield was a real person and our visit to that church did take place around 1972. I took the liberty of placing Jacob in the Herbert Lang and James Chapin expedition for this is also fact. The facts are also that Jacob did have a base and an outlying treatment center over the mountain trail. He did have the experience just as I have written it. He did win those people to Christ and that is all that really matters.

Author Note

This book has done much for me in allowing me to hold on to sanity.

My sweet Dixie passed into eternity on the twentieth day of December, just six days before our fifty-ninth anniversary. I have spent a thousand hours in regret that I failed to tell her everyday how much she meant to me.

I do believe I will see her again in the Heaven God has prepared for all that love him, and I can hardly wait.

This story is almost all true. The exception is her disappearance and return, plus, the location of a twin sister. The peculiar part is that I saw the part of a twin sister story and her disappearance in a dream. This dream was more peculiar in that it occurred two nights in succession, as if to pound it into my troubled brain. In either case, I do not understand the power of love. I just know God has placed it in our hearts to love, and, when we fail to keep this commandment to the limit, we will have to suffer.

May you who read this, have, and give love to the fullest measure allowed.
Bernie

The Mystery of Love

This is a mystery of love, never ending
February 19, 2013

How can I possibly have all of the emotions at the same time? Love, despair, anger, fear and unspeakable joy. Enough to make my knees fail and leave me helpless. It started with beautiful girls with superb costumes which was due in part to the wealth of Barksdale. Friday night football at our high school was a time of great merriment, even if we lost the game. We were a small village in western Virginia known as Milltown and were located just eleven miles from another small village high school known as Barksdale. You can imagine the intense rivalry between these schools and it centered on both the bands and the football teams. Our band, the Milltown band was usually considered the best since we had more members and made the most noise, but Barksdale had the blue ribbon in cheerleaders. Wow! Did they ever have it in that category. Their football team was also blessed with the latest and best red and white uniforms. They made our blue and whites look dingy on the playing field so we had to make them look bad in the scoring department. After the game ended, all was well except for one or two hot-heads that just loved a fight, even without a reason. The rest of us mingled and bragged about winning, if we won, and made excuses if we were the unlucky losers.

This was the beginning of my senior year and, as a band member, I was usually in with the band crowd from both high schools. We did not have the same feelings about a lost game as did the football team, and we did not have to meet in the locker room for congratulations or a chewing out from the coach, depending on a win or loss. The band members could meet at the local hotdog drive-in, and, by the time the football team arrived, there were virtually no parking places left.

The year was 1942 and not many boys had transportation and even if they did, gasoline was strictly rationed so every car was filled to capacity. This particular game was last in the season and our last game with Barksdale. Milltown had only one traffic light and one city cop, so his job was mostly "to stay out of the way" and watch the traffic light. By the time we were gathered at the hotdog stand, those that liked to slug it out were long gone and there was just good fun and lots of courting. We boys were just like boys have always been, on the lookout for the most attractive girl in the group and I was right in there with the crowd. Back at the game at half time, I saw the most beautiful creature God had ever placed on earth. She was one of eight cheerleaders on the Barksdale team, and I wondered why she had to be from Barksdale where I had limited chance of ever getting to know her. At the stand, I was looking for her with high hopes of just learning her name.

My luck did not hold and I just got a glimpse of her in the back seat of a Barksdale car as it pulled out into the direction of home. Little did I know about how the future would tear into my life with a combined state of anger, unspeakable joy, and heart break, all at the same time and all because of her. And this, my friend, is one of the mysteries of love.

After graduation from Milltown, I decided to go to work for the summer and perhaps go on to college if it was possible to save enough for my needs. I became very good at my summer job and loved the work to the extent that I was undecided about college. I had turned eighteen the last December and had to register for the draft. The war was in full blast and troops were needed so it was almost a certainty that I would be called into service with little choice as to what branch of service I would be sent. After talking to a sergeant at the recruiting station, I found I could enlist and choose my branch of service and even select the type of service I liked. At the recruiting station, the sergeant told me it was possible for me to study college courses even while on active duty and this really appealed to me.

My work the past summer had been in the electrical communications field and it was a first choice for me. It also turned out that there was a need for soldiers with my qualifications so my enlistment was complete. I began active service after notifying my summer job boss that I would be leaving in a week. My choice of communications left me with much free time in which I could do little except wait for the next breakdown in communications and study for the monthly exams. Many times, I was at a loss for something to do except dream of the time the war would be over and I could go home. In the meantime, I studied for the federal communications radio license examination which would allow me to communicate with other radio operators around the world. The armed forces had an educational program that was called USAFE and would allow any member of the armed forces to study for any degree of education he desired. It was free and conducted in such a way as to allow students to escape many duties such as KP or guard duty. I took advantage of everything this program had to offer and the end result was a chance to take the final months of my army duty in the university located just four miles from the base. Obviously, I was left with not much to dream about except the job I would return to and the girl I had fleetingly seen.

My short time in the tropics gave me more time to think since sleep would not come because of the and the loneliness. My state of mind caused me to dream of a time when I could have a family, and the image of her was always in my mind. We would have a small country home with plenty of room for the children to play outdoors and with horses to ride. I would teach my son to hunt and fish by the river that would be near but not so close that I would have to worry about floods. I did love to do these things and there was no doubt that my son would also be a lover of the outdoors. I would also teach him to love God and to do his best to live a clean life just as my mother had instilled in me by setting the example. I always did my best to fulfill my duties of service to my country which usually got me the best jobs and accounted for the company commander's choice of me for his jeep driver.

Several times I wrote to my friends back home to enquire about *that girl* but the answer was always the same. Perhaps I was dreaming too much since by this time I had placed her on a pedestal of angelic proportion. I realized this was happening, but I determined to hold on to the hopes that one day I would find her and she would truly be the girl I held in my mind. As I dreamed of her appearance, the thought would come to mind that she would be about sixteen and would come from a secure family background. I also guessed she would be in her last year of high school and might be going off to some distant college where I would never see her again. This troubled me more than I liked to admit to myself. Why should I allow a vision to ruin my life? Why should I become upset over something that could possibly never be within my grasp? Even if I fell deeply in love with her, how could I expect her to fall for me? After all, I am only a country boy who has little hope of anything more than to return to my old job and barely make enough to live on. I know the GI bill will allow me to attend college where I could have a graduation as students usually have but it made no difference to me. I had the university certificate of completion that was issued to military personnel. Besides, all I had missed was sports, some courses in public speaking, and such things that I did not need. I also know the GI bill will pay for my extended education as I work on my old job. There are still some things I would like that was not available in service so I did take advantage of correspondence courses in photography. The best part of this is that I will advance in the position where I work at the same time I am paid to work.

In July 1946, the army decided they did not need Tech Sergeant Bernie any more since all he ever did was eat, study and dodge extra duty. I was discharged with six hundred dollars in my pocket. By this time, I had decided that the army was a good place to be for twenty years and then retirement. I could leave for a six-month period and then return for a four year enlistment with full rank. Now that I had credit for three plus years, that meant that I could retire in seventeen years. Retired at age thirty-eight certainly was a happy thought. I would take the six months and look for *That girl as I* worked the job I had left behind and gather some savings before returning to the US Army.

All went well on my return to the old job. Wages were good and I fell into the bracket where I would have been had I not left. My army experience and education fit well into the job. Perhaps it did not please some of the men I had left behind because they did not like my being placed in a slot above them. Their thought was, "Why?"

I have stayed here and worked up to this position and now he returns and takes my place.

As it was then, the law said that I had to be returned to the position I was when I left. Now it was up to me to prove that I was capable of holding up my work load. This made it difficult for me since I was not liked by most of the other employees and my boss wanted to find reason to fire me. He did in fact have me sent to an examination board in an effort to have me disqualified. At this hearing, he was to ask the questions and I was to answer since this was an oral exam. To his great disappointment and embarrassment, I passed with flying colors and a 100 percent grade.

Charles, another of the returning veterans worked near me and we became close friends. Working with him set us aside from most of the other men because of our experience in the military. We had much to talk about that left the others out, even though we did not want it that way. Unlike me, Charles had waited to be drafted and had no choice where he was to serve. His time was spent in the Navy, mostly traveling on board ships from one island to another. Another of my very close friends had also waited to be drafted and lost his life in the last few weeks of the war The military left him in France at the close of "The Battle Of The Bulge." I have no other way of looking at my service other than that God was with me. For what reason he spared me, I will not know in this life for it is a certainty that I did not lead an exemplary life. What I do know is that my mother stayed on her knees in prayer for me and I am truly grateful, for it has been an exciting and rewarding life, except for some major, unexplainable occurrences. These will soon be evident and will explain how one can be angry, overwhelmed with joy, sick at heart, and confused all at the same time.

I had been back on the job for only ninety days and all of my spare time had been spent in looking for *that girl* of my dreams. Nothing had been working out for me in that field even though I had visited the high school in Barksdale. With no name, either my description was faulty or I had not found the right person to ask. Charles and I had talked about our desire for a wife and his lady friend seemed to be the one for him. Back in high school, he had told me he wanted to find a wife that was beautiful, rich and would let him be the boss. Now he tells me he has found the right one but she is poor and rather bossy, but that's OK because he has fallen in love. Another mystery-----

He does have a problem, though; her mother won't allow her to date unless there is another couple along on the same date. That was not unusual in those days. Mothers thought it was dangerous for their daughters to date army men before they were twenty one as if that would make a difference. I suppose the thought was that army men had been around" and might take advantage of their daughters. I doubt this was the case in city people but remember this is country, before television and before most people had traveled more than fifty miles from their home. Indeed, I had my first glimpse of a major city only after the US Army took me there. Well, Charles had the problem of taking his intended out of the house and away from mother unless he could arrange for another couple to go along. Charles and his lady, Fay,had the answer in that she had a first cousin the next farmhouse down the road. As it happened, Monday of this week was some sort of holiday and Fay was able to arrange a proper date. Charles put the pressure on me to accompany him as the blind date for this occasion. He had the automobile washed and polished as well as a nine year old car could be polished. His car was not in perfect condition but at least it was clean and would take us there and back, It was about twenty miles from where we worked and over some twisty country roads.

Darkness set in well before we arrived where Fay lived. Charles brought her to the car and made the introduction in almost total darkness since there were no interior lights and certainly no street lights. From there, we drove another mile to the house down the road. Fay went into this house and brought out a rather petite girl whom I could only make out in the parking lights of the car. I got out of the car and stood by the back car door for the introduction and Fay introduced us as if it made no difference what we were called. No last names were mentioned. Again, introductions were made in almost total darkness and from there we decided to drive to the Milltown hotdog stand that we all knew as the meeting place for all couples. There was no other place to go in a town this size.

So, Charles was driving slowly so as to extend the time we would be able to spend with the girls, and I spent the time by asking questions.

Now I had dated several girls before, I dated one while the army had me stationed at a semi-permanent location, one that I met in a local church. Maxine was a senior in high school and the daughter of one of the deacons. This was while I was attending the university and had plenty of free time. With my week ends totally free, I chose to attend church in town rather than the "All Faith" services the military held. Dating Maxine was almost serious but we just never quite fell completely in love. Perhaps she did but I was still looking for that dream girl that I remembered in Milltown. Maxine's mother and father took me in their home almost as one of the family and I suppose all that saved me was a transfer to places beyond reach.

Being on a blind date was almost more than I cared for since there was a surplus of young ladies at that time. So many boys failed to return from military service that there was a shortage and I had a wide field to choose from. I had even dated several times since I returned but all of those dates turned out to be short lived. Never more than two or three times. My standards were very high and I would settle for nothing less than someone very close to the girl of my dream or finding her.

As we drove away from her home, her name came first- Dixie Cummings. Then I learned that she had just finished high school from Barksdale and had plans for college but needed to work a year for funds. During this time, I learned she was a Sunday school teacher for children in the six-year-old bracket. Her father worked for the same company that employed me but in a different location and with a different type of work. Her mother was the pianist for her church and her father was a deacon, bothwere active in church work. Both her mother and her father were slender and tall people. Her father loved to hunt and fish and he also had a large wood working shop I had used my spare time in service by studying every subject the army made available to us and there were many books about wood working. I had found these books to be pleasant reading and they had given me a desire to have a small shop of my own some day. All of this was much to my liking and I pressed her for more details while telling very little about myself. Of course, she had learned a great deal about me from her cousin, Fay, who had heard much about me from Charles.

Dixie must have thought I was nuts to ask so much about her family and hardly give her time to answer the last question before another. I learned much about her family but little about what she looked like. Again, there were no street lights and no passing cars. After all, this was country roads on a dark night. At last we arrived at the hotdog stand and I turned to look directly at her under the drive-in lights and promptly lost my capacity to breathe. After three years of having her in my dreams, here she was beside me, the girl I was hopelessly in love with. I must admit that I remember very little of what was said during the next two hours. I was having trouble thinking as well as breathing. This lovely creature beside me was responsible for my blacked out memory so I really can't tell you how that two hours went. What I can tell you is about the last ten minutes

I spent with her on the concrete walkway leading to her front door.

I do remember the clouds had rolled back to reveal a sky full of very bright stars at the time I took her by the hand and stopped her from going on into her house. I remember the night breeze being so gentle that her long hair was blowing across her cheek and that she had pushed it back from her face in a slow movement that seemed to be calculated to hold up her hand for a time. It was almost an unconscious movement to prevent me from touching her cheek and Heaven knows I wanted to. I had no idea whether her mother was looking out at us or not. At this time I had done nothing more than hold her hand and then only from leaving the hotdog stand all of the way home. I had lost control of my thinking process or I would never have been so bold as to say what I did next.

Dixie, please don't let this shock you to the point of sending me off forever. I have fallen totally in love with you and plan to marry you. Don't say NO; just wait until next Saturday evening when I return and then I expect you to say YES."

Without a word or a gesture, except to remove her hand from mine, she walked two steps up to the porch level and without a backward look, entered and closed the front door.

I believe my heart fell the equivalent of a mile. I was stunned at what I had said and her reaction. Charles was sitting in the car with the motor still running and the lights still on. The first thing he said was, "I didn't see you kiss her good night." I had no answer since God only knew how much I had wanted to and why I failed to take her in my arms as I had so desired for all of the past three years.

The following day, I did my work without thinking, and it is a wonder the boss did not fire me as he surely would have liked to do. My mind was elsewhere and my hands refused to cooperate, causing a few mistakes. Charles asked if I was feeling well and I could only say that I was not and did not give an explanation. Somehow, I got through that day and, as soon as possible, I, wrote Dixie a letter, trying to apologize and at the same time trying to express the sincerity of my statement. Dixie's home had no telephone and, I now believe, that was to my advantage. Her mother might have answered it and told me where to go, a place not to my liking. To end the letter, I continued to act the fool by not asking but by telling her what I wanted. I ended the letter by writing that I would be at her home at 7pm next Saturday, that I wanted to meet her parents, and that if she would not marry me, please say nothing at this time. I was willing to wait all of the years necessary in order to win her hand and her heart.

Charles asked if I would join him on his next date and told him I had other plans. I did not tell him the true reason for my reluctance. It would not have been understandable to him that I wanted to meet Dixie's parents. I worried all of that week that Dixie would not see me at all, that she would not be at home, or that she would find some other reason for rejecting me. After three years, I don't think I was man enough to live through a rejection from her, and, yet, after the way I proposed, should I expect less than total rejection?

My work week was a disaster in every way. Thanks to Charles, he did a masterful job of doing my work as well as his own and covering for me. Then I didn't know how a man was supposed to act when he was hit with a love as strong as this, but I do know now, these fifty-nine years later.

At last, Saturday evening came and I was dressed as well as my shaking hands would allow. I was in no condition to eat the dinner my mother prepared and even she thought I was sick. I suppose she had an idea since I dressed in a way that I had been reluctant to do since I returned from service. After all, I had taken a sworn oath never to wear another necktie, not after the army made me wear one in tropical heat. Now here I was, dressed in a silk necktie and looking as if the world was about to end. She never told me what she thought, but it must have been very confusing since she knew I was not on my way to a church service.

I drove to Dixie's home very carefully so as to be there exactly when my letter had said I would be. As I approached her home, I did so with my heart in my throat or perhaps a better way to say it was with a pounding heart. What would I say if she was not there and I had to explain to her mother why she was avoiding me. Or what would I say if her dad came out with a club to greet me? I still wonder to this day why he did not greet me with that ball bat. As I came in sight of her home, I saw someone in the front porch swing and that lifted my spirits, even more when I saw the bright colors a lady would wear and not the dark clothing her dad would be wearing. I cannot explain the feeling I had when I realized it was Dixie, dressed in a flowered skirt and pink blouse. Her hair was neatly done as if someone helped her do it right. Her cheeks were a rosy pink and I wondered at that time if it was added coloring or if it was natural to a beautiful young woman. With a wave of her hand, she indicated that I was to sit beside her on the swing, and, as soon as I could get my breath again, I did so. Although I had dated several other ladies, never before had I experienced the feeling that I should not touch. It was almost as if I might break the spell and I would be in a dream. Such a lovely lady to invite me to sit beside her. No wonder I was slow to speak or to move as I was almost paralyzed with the thrill of being invited to sit next to her. I was even afraid of taking her hand because this might cause her to stand up and head for the front door.

We sat in the swing for well over an hour with no meaningful conversation, just trivial stuff about school functions and when she was a cheer leader. She asked about my military service and I gave her the short version, mostly focused on the time I had spent in the classroom. I learned that she was part of a school dance team called the "Dixie Debs" and being the leader, she was known as Dixie. Her real name did not seem to matter and I think I did not know it for several weeks. Conversation was running slow and I was thinking only of how I could get another direct look into her eyes. She seemed to be staring off into space and that gave me some degree of fear that she was trying to gather courage to tell me to "Go Home" Not knowing what to expect next, I would have appeared to some as a complete idiot, not gifted with the power of speech It was at this moment when she turned to face me and said one single word-----"YES." To this day I still find it hard to believe that over sixty years ago, I heard it right. I believe there can be no greater joy for me on earth and the only time in the future will be when God will say, "Welcome Home."

I had known Dixie for over three years and, to think, she had known me for less than one week. Surely God must have had us in mind when he created the human race.

Later that same evening, Dixie's mother came out and when I stood up to greet her. Dixie made the proper introduction with one minor fault. She said, "Mother, I would like you to meet Bennie," and of course my name is Bernie. I did not correct her and I was called Bennie for the rest of the evening. For years to come, Dixie liked to tell the story of how she got engaged to marry Bennie and in the confusion, married Bernie.

I won't spend much time talking about our whirlwind courtship, but, needless to say, it was not to the liking of her father. She had just turned seventeen and he still considered her a child. I will tell you that our courtship was difficult since we always had to take her little brother, who was about eight, with us and he was a very difficult pain in you know where. On leaving the driveway, his first words were, "I want a hotdog and a milk shake."The second statement was the same with the added words, "I will tell mother what you did to Dixie if you don't get me a hotdog". Now I do not believe for a minute that he knew what he was going to tell his mother, but I do believe he was coached. Eight-year-olds did not know what sex was before Television and Momma had to tell him what watch out for. I suppose she did not want her daughter to follow in her footsteps, so I hold no grudge. At any rate, little brother made certain to use the threat to get well fed and then stuffed with more. All of this started in the first ten minutes. It got so bad that we could not talk because of his demanding "payoff" gifts for not telling mother lies. Of course, both Dixie and I wanted a Christian marriage in her church, but this became unbearable after a few months.

To the credit of her mother, I was invited to Sunday dinner with them many times over the next few months. Sunday dinner with Dixie and her parents was truly hard for me because I had learned so much about them that I had become a little afraid of her mother. I was afraid of saying something that would cause both parents to turn against me so I said very little. I did know that her dad loved to hunt and fish so most of my conversation was with him. He made it easy for me by letting me know he was a devout man and his only hobbies fell in line with mine. I always attended church services with Dixie and her parents, and, in fact, I became a member of their church. Already it was understood that some day in the distant future, Dixie and I would marry. I do wish to this day that we had made it clear to her parents that her little brother was driving us toward a secret marriage. Perhaps Dixie would have had the church wedding that she missed so much in later years.

I always intended to give her a wedding on our fiftieth anniversary but that year was one of the busiest I ever had. Somehow it slipped up too soon and then it was too late, so I set the sixtieth as a renewal of our marriage vows in a formal church wedding. Alas, too late for the Angels took her six days short of our fifty-ninth. Now I live with my memories and the wonderment of those years and how fast they passed. It makes no difference, though, I will love her till God allows us to start over in eternity. Ah ! The mystery of love eternal.

The new year started with no improvement in the escort service from the back seat. After six months of this, we decided to forgo her church wedding and get married at another church, very quietly. I have no words to express my joy when I heard her tell the minister, "I do," but I feared the wrath of her father and mother, Ken and Virginia Cummings, for I had stolen their daughter. I firmly believe her mother was upset mostly because she was losing her housemaid and servant but her father was of another mind. He truly loved his daughter and I did him wrong. I broke his trust in me and it was several years before he became my father as well. I truly loved him, even more than my own flesh and blood. I know he forgave me even though I never forgave myself. We learned to work side by side in his workshop, and he taught me to become a master craftsman in wood. I have no doubt he felt toward me as his son and gave me far more time than he did his own flesh and blood. Many times I have taken him to work with me when it meant I could make the trip in less than twenty-four hours and it was his day off. We shared many good times while on the road, and I got many laughs from his wisdom.

He was a frugal man and hated to pay the price for hotel dinners which were usually priced too high and had too little in good country cooking. Although I never allowed him to spend the first dollar, he would reluctantly accept the dinner with these words,

"I suppose I shouldn't care about cost as long as I'm not out nuthin.'" His English was better than that but he used slang to get me to laugh after a hard day on the road.

I will never forget the time I took him on a fishing trip to Canada. Up to this time, he had never fished for anything other than bass, a three-or-four-pound fighting fish. His fishing gear was all light weight for this kind of fish so I encouraged him to leave it behind. There was plenty of gear available for the larger game fish in Canada, usually northern pike which usually runs in several pounds and could be as long as four feet in length.

We rented gear and bought lures for what I thought would be the most exciting fishing trip my father-in-law would ever experience. That trip lasted almost two hours in the canoe, just until he hooked a monster fish far too large for our net. He became disgusted that the bass would not strike his lures and the pike bothered his efforts. He quit then and there.

Many good times were spent with him, fishing the rivers as we floated a canoe down stream and casting a lure to either bank. Bass was the game fish we wanted and we always caught all we wanted. Most of our memorable trips would start at dawn and we would float and fish until late afternoon. Sometimes we would stop on a sand bar in late morning, build a small drift wood fire and grill fish for our lunch. Nothing was needed except perhaps one of us would have thought to bring along some salt in a small medicine bottle. I well remember the time Dixie went with us which made the canoe a little unstable but we did not worry about being spilled in the river. It would only serve to give us something to laugh about. On this trip, we did have the driftwood fire and we did have salt. We also had several ears of fresh yellow sweet corn. When thrown into the red ashes for about eight or ten minutes, it would cook to perfection. Then peeling off the shuck and eating it with roasted bass, there could be no better food on earth. Dixie loved camping out in the mountains and down by the lake shore. Any place where we could be alone was perfect for her.

As for Dixie and me, I could spend hours at the keyboard telling of our trials and tribulations and our many wonderful days and years together. As so often happens, I had not saved enough money to start a marriage off with sufficient money to take care of our wants, just our needs, and that was a struggle. My job paid well enough but the strain of being relocated many times caused our budget to fall by the wayside about every three months. That continued until I changed my profession to engineering design and sales in the electrical industry. Only a shortened version will do by saying that I changed employment to Westinghouse Electric Corporation, and, from there, to forming my own business in another city.

In winter months, we became tired of cold weather and of the way

Westinghouse was using me. It was then, and because of this, that we decided to start a new life in Huntsville, Alabama. We had no friends or acquaintances there and no job to go to. While working for Westinghouse Electric in Pittsburg, PA, I was being sent all over the country to complete jobs others had failed to do on time or doing x-ray repairs too difficult for the local man. This was causing me to leave Dixie alone for as much as two weeks at a time and was not sitting well with either of us. The alternative was to change jobs, and, at the same time move to a better climate. We chose Huntsville, Alabama because it was the center of the space industry at that time. There were over fifty companies located there, all of them engaged in some form of manufacturing and mostly electronics connected to NASA. . We sold our home in Ohio and, with a bank account of over sixty thousand, we had little cause for worry. I had been driving a company car, so the first thing was to buy a new Buick. There was no reason why I would not be able to obtain work there, so we moved without having made much of a plan for work or living space. The major trouble was the lack of available housing in Huntsville. Building contractors were doing a rush job, so all we could do was get on the list for a new house. In the meantime, we were able to find a small apartment well outside of town. Within a few days there, I saw the need for an engineer to make available information on the latest electronic components to all of these companies. This was the start of my business as a manufacturer's representative.

By hard work, I became the representative for several companies in the USA as well as in many other countries. My job required me to do factory visits which took me to places such as Frankfort and Munich, Germany, where we had the pleasure of touring the Rhine River and touring several castles along the Rhine.

I had the pleasure of representing General Electric International from my location in Huntsville, Alabama. The area I was assigned was the eight southeastern states and for component items only. Almost any electrical item that would be used to manufacture a finished product came under my contract and this made me a very busy man. Dixie was my constant companion and, on many sales calls,, she would accompany me to the engineer's office and sometimes carry the conversation which always helped me make the necessary sale.

We loved it and as business grew, we hired another lady to do Dixie's job and she began to travel with me all over the world. By this time, it was not unusual for me to be "on the road" for two weeks at a time, and Dixie made the travels something of a joy instead of work. We found our travels almost to be at the expense of IRS since she was considered an employee and we wrote off all of our combined expenses. We made it a point to visit the companies I had under contract on a Wednesday. After that, we would be able to do as we pleased for the remainder of the week, and still calling it part of the business trip. We were, in fact, guests of the IRS.

We visited many other companies and places and we always managed to find a few days to enjoy the world where we were at the time. Dixie managed to continue her education in college, both in Ohio and in Alabama. She became well respected in interior design as well as a top notch accountant. Her total time working as an accountant, though, was less than two years and it ended because we loved to travel. The place where she was employed as accountant was about thirty people in a woodworking shop where they made speaker cabinets. What the owner did not know at the beginning was that Dixie had a lot of experience in both her father's wood shop and in mine. Her office was in a room at the top of a stairway containing only two offices. Hers was a glass-walled office looking down on the work area where she could see every person at any time. It soon became apparent to Dixie that wood products were being wasted because of mistakes in cutting. Pieces like this were being sent to the furnace instead of being used in a place where smaller parts could be cut from the waste. When she told the boss about this waste, he corrected it but the word got out that "ole eagle eye" upstairs was watching you. It first made some of the employees resent her, but, in time, all was well and she was much loved and respected. Her boss became so dependent on her ability that he started staying out for days, leaving the business to her to run. He paid her a little more but nothing like he should have.

After about a year of this, the company was not making enough profit and was near bankruptcy. Her boss told her not to pay the federal payroll taxes, that he would take care of them later. She insisted and so he wrote her a note of instruction, do not pay the taxes as I will take care of them later. Dixie became much concerned and wrote him a memo about it and copied the bank that carried their accounts. Dixie was on the books to sign all checks except payroll and taxes. Even so she was worried. The day came when an IRS agent came in without notice and without knocking. Showing a badge, the agent said she was there to examine the books and asked if Dixie would mind. Her answer was short and to the point. The boss is not here but I am glad you are. Here is my note from him to withhold payment for taxes, and the office is yours. I am going out for lunch. You may guess the end result. Bankruptcy and the taxes were paid the same week.

Dixie loved her work and was sorry to lose her job.

Through the fifty-nine years we were married, we lived in several different communities and several states. We never failed to attend the local church and Dixie was almost always in the children's classroom before we were members for the first month.

Her personality was such that she was forever calling me to "come meet my new friend. " She was definitely an asset to me when I visited my principals, those companies I represented. It seemed someone was sure to invite us to tour the plant, and dinner invitations were a certainty. Many of the companies I represented would place calls to my home for me but would talk for long minutes to her before finally asking some mundane question of me. I was aware of the ploy but I was delighted in having her as my wife. Needless to say, I was proud of her.

Dixie did have her strong feelings about several subjects but was very quiet about politics. No one ever heard her make a choice of either party for any given office.

The strongest words I ever heard from her were that all politicians had a streak of greed or they would not be in the running. It leaves us with the choice of voting for the lesser of two or more evils. I suppose I have always agreed with her so we never had cross words on this subject. She also had strong feelings of competitiveness but did not like ball games. In this, we shared the same opinion. Ball games were a total waste of time to her. For me, the thought of ball games made me recall the time in grade school when our ball field was a cow pasture and I was tackled at lunch time and hit my head on a rock. I was knocked silly and totally blind. It was two days before I could see light enough to make out my hand before my face. This was about 1938 and the last time I ever watched a ball game or had anything to do with either throwing or catching a ball. Golf was OK since it was a form of exercise. She was very good on the course and I more or less acted as caddy since I could drive a ball a mile but always in the wrong direction.

Dixie was fascinated with toy trains, perhaps because her father was a railroad telegrapher. He always worked alone in a station by the tracks and directed movement of trains in his area. He chose to work the evening shift, from four to midnight which allowed him to take Dixie to work with him when she was a young girl. We had toy trains at our home and she was the one that bought them and I set them up. Many years back, we found the place in north Florida on interstate 75, just south of Lake City I believe. It was something like Christmas in July with all displays and products forsale pertaining to Christmas. In the upstairs level, there was a very large toy train display which Dixie would watch for hours, or until I insisted, we move on. I would shop a while and wait in the car for a time until I could stand no more. In my opinion, this has some bearing on the future of Dixie and, of course, my future included.

So many thoughts come to mind that I have trouble sorting them out and placing them in the right order. The truth is that Dixie took many secrets to her grave, and, although I have searched to the limit of my ability, there may never be answers. So many times in my long life, I have heard people say, I would die for her or him, as the case may be. If they really meant it, that would be a case of Agape love as the Greek language put it that explains the love of Christ for everyone. I truly would have died for Dixie. Even as she lay on the hospital bed and struggled for her last breath, I would have gladly given my life to allow her a few more days. My love for her was such that I gave her credit where credit was not due and I excused any and all her actions that did not please me. Love will cause forgiveness when perhaps it should not and that is the mystery of love.

Dixie was a lover of animals, particularly horses. For her and against my better judgment, we purchased a farm of two hundred acres in Tennessee walking horse country and built a small cottage suitable for our weekend visits. The place already had a nice barn which I converted to a stable for several horses. We then undertook to buy the perfect horse for her and it seemed none would please her. She was looking for the perfect quarter horse and we tried many places with no luck. After buying several horses with none being perfect, we continued to search until one day we found the place where several were brought out by a little black boy. All got the thumbs down by Dixie and the stable manager said he had no more to show. The little black boy said, "What about Danny Boy?" I think by this time the manager was tired of us and, as a joke, told the boy to go get him. Moments later, the boy was leading a decrepit old horse out that seemed ready to fall at any step. Dixie walked over to that gelding and when she did, the horse laid its head on her shoulder. That did it. The manager changed in a flash and started telling about how many blue ribbons this horse had won and how valuable he was. Dixie heard none of this, but I heard only the price going up as Dixie patted that horse and spoke to it as if it were her sick offspring. The end result was a super high price for what I thought was a dead horse because the manager admitted they had forgotten Danny Boy and left him to winter on a bare pasture.

Danny was in the last throes of starvation, much too far gone to move to our place.

Never mind, Dixie took up residence in their barn for the next several days. First the vet was called for shots, pills and a tube feeding. From there, Dixie pulled choice grass to feed Danny for several days. I had to care for her by insisting she leave him for a shower and food. Several times I took lunch to her and we would sit together and admire the lines of that horse. Now me, all the lines I could see was where the bones were protruding and about to break out of the skin. I have no idea what Dixie saw in that horse but neither do I understand why that horse came to love her as it did. I watched a miracle occur when only a week later we were able to move Danny to our barn and the tie that bound Dixie and Danny was an even more profound happening.

I will close this part of my story by telling you that they were so close that Danny would allow no one to ride him except Dixie and he did perform to her highest expectation. They were close like this for another several years until Danny died of old age.

Again, I had a front row seat to the mystery of Philos love, that which the Greek language used for the love of friends and animals. I have no doubt that Dixie held some sort of attraction to all people that I will never understand. Babies who would normally cling to their mothers breast and resist even a smile from a stranger would, without fail, reach out chubby little arms to Dixie. I have pictures of her feeding wild birds from her open hand-something I have never seen in another human being. Only God knows the answer to that. At one time she took on a pair of miniature pigs, so small she would hold them to her breast and talk to them as if they understood English, in a baby form of speaking. Soon they became adults and soon there was a litter of six more, followed by more litters, Since we lived on a farm and the woods came almost to our back door, Dixie turned them loose to roam the woods. Again I have pictures to show how a call from her and fifty little pigs less than the size of a football and almost as round, would come rolling out of the woods to be at her feet.

I tell you all of this just in order to let you know how attached I was to her. I got extreme pleasure from being with her in church services, both as she taught the children's class and in the main service afterwards. Her classroom was directly across the hall from the kitchen and I was one of the church cooks so I had access to it. On Sunday mornings, we were there very early so she could set up her classroom and I would prepare a small breakfast for children that would arrive on the church bus. Many of them were from families that could not or would not feed their children before sending them off to school during the week or to Sunday school. Dixie and I got much pleasure from feeding them first from the kitchen and then from the Bible. Later in the main service, Dixie's place in the choir was front row where she could look down on me, usually about the third seat from the front. It was not unusual for her to wink at me and give that smile that everyone in the congregation would know it was for me. As the choir left their places and joined the congregation, I would stand and hold out my hand for her. She would take her seat beside me and everyone there knew I was truly in love with this woman.

One day at the mall, Dixie ran into a lady that had been coming to our church for the past several weeks. She and her husband usually sat in the same place which was about five or six rows behind us. This lady was laughing when she told Dixie what her husband had said last Sunday in the parking lot after services. He had watched me hold the car door open while Dixie was being seated and had said to his wife, "I sure hope Bernie wins her hand in marriage because he is trying hard enough," She said he was speechless when she told him we had been married for several years and still acted like we were courting. That really sums up how I adored her and treated her as I did. It also lets you know that although I had every reason to be jealous of the attention other men paid to her, I was secure in my belief that I was the only one, now and forever.

Early in our marriage, we lived in Columbus, Ohio, for about five years. We never came to like that area but my job with Westinghouse Electric demanded it. While there, we did not have a lot of money since we had bought a large home that needed much in the way of repairs. By the time the repair bills were paid and the mortgage was secure, we had little to spend for clothing and other goodies. The results was a lot of shopping and little buying. One Friday evening, we were doing the usual at a department store which I recall as "Larsons," in the ladies department. Dixie did need clothes but was a very careful shopper. She had tried on a pink suit that looked grand on her but was too far out of her price range, so she rejected it for another which I thought looked the price-- cheap. While she was busy looking, I motioned the clerk out of Dixie's hearing and bought that suit and had it wrapped so as to be underneath the suit she chose. When Dixie got home late that evening, she prepared a late dinner for us before opening the package. I could tell that she was not too excited about the purchase she had made so I could hardly wait for the surprise she would have on opening that box. I was not disappointed. I think it was one of the best gifts I ever gave her.

Another gift did not turn out so well,-- the wedding band I ordered from Kaes Jewelers. When we were married, I bought a very small, yellow gold band called "Orange Blossom". Not only was it small, it was thin. So thin that it was wearing out fast. One day I went to Kaes and, with the description of the ring, ordered another of the same design but very heavy and certainly more costly. I paid twenty percent holding with instructions that on delivery I would pay cash. At this time, I was working for Westinghouse and they had been sending me off to distant places which might require I stay out for two weeks. On Tuesday of this particular week, an invoice arrived from a finance company with payments set up for a year of payments for the Kaes purchase, not mentioning that it was for a ring. Dixie opened this and first thought it might be for a gift for her. When I phoned her that night, as I did every night I was away, she hinted she knew she had a gift coming soon and, of course, I denied having anything for her. After all, it was to be a surprised for our next wedding anniversary. She said no more but I noticed a coolness when I called the evenings after that. Trouble started the moment I arrived home on Friday evening. She handed me the invoice with a demand that I confess to a woman friend and who and where she was. I had to confess to the ring and I still have my doubts that she totally believed me. Of course, I raised the roof with Kaes and got the return of my deposit as well as a letter of apology. Even that never really convinced Dixie of the truth and I had to wonder if this episode had any bearing on what happened years later that made me so angry and broke my heart.

One of my major accounts was located in Waukegan, IL, where the latest and best switches came off the assembly line by the millions. They were one of the first to take me on with a contract to sell for them in all eight southeastern states. A very large part of my income came from commissions here which required me to visit their plant at least every ninety days. I always took Dixie there with me because most of the office people knew her from business conversations and from past visits. It was a short vacation for both of us as we were so well received. It always meant a good evening with the sales manager and his wife and always a joy to be with them. Jack liked to tease Dixie, so he chose the Playboy club for dinner this particular evening. As we pulled into the parking lot, he told Dixie he chose this place because Bernie always asked for it when he visited alone. He got a great laugh from this joke but he did not know the incident of the ring from Kaes still smarted with Dixie.

I waited until his next week to travel with me for their customer visitations. He usually rode with me over at least two states in order to call on their customers, just to say hello and thank you for your business. I had just recently purchased a new Buick, and with the switch samples they regularly sent me, I chose two that fit my plan. I had mounted one just under the floor mat under my left foot and the other in the door arm rest. With one touch of either switch, I could cause the wiper blades to activate for one or more passes a cross the windshield. I never told him about the switches but sure enough, one of the days we were in Georgia, a very light rain started with just random drops. Perfect for my joke. As these random drops hit the windshield, I would step on the floor switch for just one wipe. I did this several time before Jack asked about it. I told him it was a new Buick option, a water sensor for automatic wipe. Of course he did not believe me and told me to stop. I pulled off the road and he got out and spit on the windshield. When it wiped for one time only, Jack told me to "Get out of the car" I stood at the side with my hand still on the arm rest and when jack spit, it worked again. Now he was convinced. On returning to the plant, Jack told his boss about the new Buick option and, of course, his boss called Buick and got the truth. This made Jack the laughing stock for a day or so.

Our visit to this plant went very well and we did a very large amount of business.

We could laugh at our practical jokes and look forward to the next trip in three or four months.   In a few days from our return to Huntsville, we had a trip planned to Nova Scotia where we were to be the guests of a family that Dixie had first come into contact with. On one of the so-called business trips we were on, we had to take the ship across from Portland, Maine to Yarmouth, Nova Scotia. As much as I hate ocean-going boats, I was well aware that I would be sick. Accordingly, I booked a cabin for the trip, even though it would not be an overnight run. Dixie had the stamina of an old sailor so she liked nothing more than to visit the dining room for the cuisine available on this Canadian ship. As usual for her, she left me to sleep the several hours of the crossing while she toured the ship and made friends. Among them was the French speaking couple, Marie and Claude Bouche, who were returning home after a vacation in the lower USA. They had been in Huntsville to visit the space museum of NASA, and this gave Dixie and them a lot to talk about. When we neared the port, Dixie and Marie came to the berth to arouse me for the docking. I was very groggy and hardly understood what they were talking about but since they were in a state of laughter, I soon came to realize we had new friends. In Yarmouth, we heard Claude tell Marie he had to see about the bus schedule to Spry Harbor and home. Dixie was quick to stop him by asking them if we could share our automobile and, of course, we had passengers for the next two hundred miles.

It was late in the evening when we docked at Yarmouth, so we decided to spend the night there for an early start up the east coast. This would be a very long day since Marie wanted Dixie to see so many things and to make so many stops. We had no time schedule so this trip was one of our best ever. Our hotel room was very nice but on the expensive side and Dixie would have preferred a motel. Otherwise it was enjoyable to visit with the Bouche couple and learn more about their home country. At the time this happened, there was quite an uprising between the French of eastern Canada, including New Brunswick and Quebec. It seemed that these people wanted to secede from Canada and form their own country. Claude gave me an education concerning our proposed continuing trip to Montreal. When traveling through that area now, it was going to be difficult if we did not speak French, which we did not. We later found out it was very difficult because even though most of them spoke some English, they refused to serve us. Buying food was almost impossible until we showed American dollars. Strangely enough, most of them became fluent in English at the sight of green bills.

Dixie and I have laughed many times over the McDonalds incident. At noon time in Quebec, we pulled into this place and went inside since we expected a language problem.

To make it simple, we both wanted a Big Mac and a coke. Ordering it just as we do here, I got a blank stare. I repeated BIG MAC and still got a blank stare. Of course, everyone in that place was speaking French, and by raising my voice I got the attention of many people and several grinning faces. It seemed we would leave hungry, but when I dropped a twenty in US currency on the counter, the girl looked at it and said, "OH! You want a Big Mac, do you want fries with them?" I suppose the French speaking people were trying to drive the English westward by starving them out. USA money and people were welcome.

Back to the friendship with Claude and Marie and the trip north. It did take all of the day and well into the night to go the two hundred miles. We made several stops to see places they thought we would be interested in seeing. They made it a very enjoyable trip and took us to some of the best sea food restaurants we have ever been in. We were also introduced to some seafood dishes that we had no idea what kind of swimming or crawling things were cooked, but, I must admit we totally enjoyed.

We arrived at their home about ten pm and expected to find the place dark. Dixie and I had reluctantly agreed to spend the night with them and were totally surprised to find the house lit up like Christmas and several cars parked in front. Their home was just a short way inland from the docks at Spry Harbor and behind them was just open country. Since there was no other house close to theirs, we knew the automobiles were family or friends. As it turned out, their late teens daughter was still living at their home and was expecting us from a phone call Marie had made last night. The family had gathered in for a late dinner and was prepared for us to stay the night. They had wine on the table and the main course was some of the largest Bay Scallops I had ever seen. This family made their living on the ocean so we had a memorable experience with them. We were enthralled with their stories and experiences, and enjoyed listening until the wee hours of the morning . Late the next morning we were treated to very rare seafood for breakfast, available only to those that regularly took their food from the sea. Braised Abalone did not sound much like the breakfast we were used to, but, I assure you, it was a very real treat and one that we will remember as an unusual and wonderful meal with new friends.

From there we drove north to cross the land bridge from Truro, NS, to Moncton, New Brunswick. This trip was made memorable by the size of the speeding ticket I got just as I entered new Brunswick. I was in a line of cars almost bumper to bumper and was driving a new Buick. I was easily spotted as a car from the USA, so the end result was that I got picked out of that line for a trip to the magistrates' court for a very hefty fine. Needless to say, I don't like New Brunswick but it was necessary for us to continue on to Bangor, Maine where I had a principal to call on. I failed to mention that I represented a small company in Truro that made line cords for appliances. There were only twelve people working there, all of them part owners. I was able to sell their product in Mississippi to a place that made electric blankets. Their quality was very good and prices were low because all were owners and, I supposed, worked for very little pay. Output was also limited, so I never had the pleasure of finding another customer for them.

Being now well set in Huntsville, Alabama and traveling as we did, we had a small company in Columbus, Ohio, under contract and a need to visit them about an order.

Accordingly, we made the visit on Wednesday and used Thursday and Friday to visit with old friends. On Friday evening, we had dinner at a place on Olentangy Road which I believe was called Amiel's. We planned to leave the next morning for the drive home which would take about twelve hours. Saturday night we would stop at any place along the way and finish the return on Sunday. It had been a good week and we were anxious to be at home for a few days before our next planned trip to Minneapolis where I represented a plastics manufacturering company. Friday evening after an early dinner, Dixie mentioned she would like to visit the downtown location of Larson's again since it held some good memories for her.

We had an hour to let dinner settle before going to the hotel, and I thought Larson's would be a good place to spend that hour. Perhaps I would be able to buy Dixie something that would make her memory of this trip really special. As I look back at the sequence of things that evening, I am amazed that things took such a path as to be almost identical as before.

While Dixie was busy trying on clothes, I managed to pay the clerk for something we agreed she had liked. It was wrapped and we waited for such a long time that the clerk went to the changing room to see about her. When the clerk returned, she had a very troubled look, and I immediately thought Dixie might be sick in that small room. There was only one entrance and it was so near to where we had been, I knew she was in there and needed me. Without asking, I broke past the clerk and went directly into the changing room.

There on the bench lay her purse but no other evidence that she had been in that little room. I ran out of the room and into the main store, yelling her name as if I was mad.

Which I almost was. Closing time was still two hours away and several shoppers were all over the store. I had a good photo of Dixie in my billfold and I was showing it to everyone, asking if they had seen her. No one had. I ran through that store from end to end and had the manager with me asking everyone to look for her. One clerk took the photo to the office and had copies made to pass out.

The manager placed a message over the intercom that all employees were to meet him at the store front before leaving. He then asked all of them to look at the picture and let us know if any one of them had seen Dixie, at any time. Some did remember her from the time we first entered the store but none saw her afterwards.

It was with a sick heart that I reluctantly allowed him to close the store.

This was late summer and the weather was quite warm so I thought she might have gone outside for a breath of night air. The store was overheated and it made sense for Dixie to want to cool off outside. Of course, I was searching for the proverbial needle in the haystack. She had to be close, she just had to------

Nothing worked and after the store closed, I figured she might have gone to the car. She did have an extra set of keys and did know where we parked so I wondered why I had been in such a panic as to forget the car until now. I ran as fast as my legs would allow, praying that she would be there and knowing the chance was very slim. I had carried her purse with me since I picked it up in the changing booth, and more than one person thought I might be a purse snatcher, but no one bothered me. Then at the car, I remembered that her keys would be in the purse I was carrying and it was then I fell to my knees in a fervent prayer, one like I had never prayed before. Why me, God? Why Dixie, God? Have we not been good to honor you with our tithes and our efforts to teach little children about you? I sat there on the concrete and cried until a city patrol car stopped for the drunk I seemed to be. They did not believe me until I showed them the picture which was now wet with tears. They told me that a missing persons report was too soon but they would take me to the station where I could make out a report and at least all city police would be on the lookout.

On leaving the police station, they took me back to my car and from there, I started walking the area, calling her name, The initial panic had now changed to shock, disbelief, and a form of anger yet to be understood. I loved her too much to be angry at her but I was angry that she had disappeared from me. I was angry at the store for reasons that I could not understand. Surely they had nothing to do with her disappearance but the fact that she was not there anymore made me all the more angry at the store manager and the employees. I just had to feel angry at the unknown and my anger was natural to run parallel with fear and the awful loneliness that had set in.

I walked the streets all that night, calling her name and, in between sobs of grief, I would be on my knees on the sidewalk in pleading prayer. What few people that were out that night must have considered me a drunk and left me strictly alone. By this time I had cried until my face was swollen and ugly, almost as if I had been in a bar room fight. No wonder people left me completely alone. Very early Saturday morning, I began calling all of our friends, asking if they had heard from Dixie. My phone credit card took a large hit that Saturday morning, but no one had a clue and, of course, all wanted to know what happened. I made the explanation as short as possible and moved on. By mid day, I was so tired it was necessary for me to rest. I did not want to waste time by going to a bed, so I

spent an hour in my car as I hoped Dixie would awaken me by knocking on the car window. It was a wild thought but it was necessary for me to once again go and look in that changing booth. There had to be a way out of there that was not evident, one that had

been cleverly arranged just so a criminal could snatch a woman from there without anyone knowing or hearing any strange sound. I went to the manager with this accusation and he was good enough to bear with me for my inspection of that changing booth. I thought he might also have a suspicion of something like that for he examined the booth as well as I did. We did all but tear out the walls, until we were both satisfied it was just like all the others.

By now the local TV station had word of the strange disappearance and a reporter chased me down. I was very glad to give him a copy of the picture and tell him exactly how it happened. Perhaps someone would recognize Dixie on the nightly news.

Hopes were high with me that evening and I went to the hotel room we had not used because I could lie down for a short nap after the news cast and wait for the phone call someone would make to tell me they had Dixie. I fell into an exhausted sleep after the news cast and knew nothing until Sunday morning.

My first call that morning was to our minister in Huntsville, asking him to place Dixie and me on the prayer list that morning. There was no question but that I expected God to answer our prayers. He had to because he had said in his Isaiah 41:10 for me to *Fear not for I am with thee; Be not dismayed; for I am thy God.*

The thought came to me that he may be God but He doesn't know fear as I do. Gut wrenching fear, the kind that makes you think you can't control your bowels, the kind that makes your heart pound till you think you can stand no more, but where else can I turn?

All day Sunday, I roamed the streets looking for any sign of Dixie, still thinking she might be walking from nowhere to nowhere having lost her mind. But how did she get out of the changing booth? I stopped by the police station several times to inquire and finally wore out the patience of the front desk lady. Still no word and no hope of much

help from them, I was told there must be a body or some sign of foul play before they could do much. I suppose this was normal but my Dixie did not fall into the normal category, and I had no intention of allowing them to forget it.

By the end of the day, I had run out of people to call and places to look. I had even returned to the house where we used to live and worried the occupants into allowing me to look through their home. Sunday evening I attended the church services where we used to be members and where we had spent many happy hours. Of all the places in Ohio, I thought Dixie would most likely show up there. I made a plea there for them to be on the lookout for Dixie and to pray for both of us. Only two members there remembered us and the lady was good enough to speak to the congregation about Dixie and the need to pray for her return. At the close of the service, I was invited to the home of the minister, both for prayer and for what he considered advice. Neither seemed to be what I needed, so I determined to go home that very night.

The next two or three days are a blur in my memory. I would drive a few miles and stop where I could get on the phone again. I called so many people and awakened so many, there must have been some that wished I might also disappear. I would show her picture and ask total strangers if they had seen her. Mostly people were kind but some told me to "Hit the gutter, old man." There was no doubt that I looked the part of a bum and I did not blame them for their mistake. I called my office almost every hour, as long as my secretary was there to answer the phone. After that, I called my telephone answering service all through the night. Being tired was an understatement if ever there was one. My mind worked even when I was in a coma of sleep and true rest never came. Going back over the past days before she disappeared, I was looking for some hint of trouble or for a reason why she would do such a thing to me. Not only was there no reason, it was evident that her disappearance could not have been planned. We had not been apart for more than a few minutes for several days, neither at work or as we traveled. Some mysterious force was at work and I doubted I would ever find the answer but never would I give up.

On returning to my office, I had much sympathy and many calls from customers that had already heard. I have no idea how news traveled among my customers so fast but I was grateful. Perhaps one of them would hear from Dixie, and, in some form of miracle I would find her again. From that day on, I never did another hour of business with or for my customers. I had a thriving business and there was no shortage of potential buyers for it so it took me all of three days to reach an agreement and move out of my office. My home was another matter for I could not stand the thought of living in that house again. We had built the house out in the suburbs, based on the sketch Dixie had put together. She had been in the contractors hair the entire construction time and every detail spelled Dixie. I did not need to sell it but I did need a place to call home so I moved into an apartment down town. Closing the house and leaving it just as Dixie had just before we left on the trip to Ohio meant that I did not have to face the disposing of her things.

It also gave me the hope that some day she would return and until then, I had no need to ever enter that house again.

Although I had heard Dixie say many times that she was through with her siblings, I thought it would be well to at least call them in hopes she did return to Barksdale.

She had classified her brother as lazy, whiney and lower than dog doodoo. Her sister fared not much better , being classified as nosey, gossipy and a trouble maker. Knowing what Dixie thought of them, I figured there was no point of returning to Barksdale to look for her since her parents had passed away some time back. All of her school friends had long since married and moved away. She had not remained in touch with them so there were no leads from that source. Leaving no reason for a visit to Barksdale, I did call both of her siblings and, as I expected, there was no news and neither of them gave any sign of sympathy. Since I expected nothing, that is what I got and it freed my mind of another place I need not check again.

Now that I was free of a business and no house to care for, I determined to retrace our trips from the past year. I wanted to see the same places and the same people if possible. Perhaps, somewhere, there would be a clue and I might have a road to follow to locate her. I would not believe there was another man involved unless he took her by force. If there was a man in the past capable of such an act and if he had designs on Dixie, I vowed to find him. Now the worse of my anger surfaced and all I could think of was finding him and killing him slowly. It became an obsession with me to remember any man that had ever shown undue interest in her. Try as I might, none came to mind but that did not keep me from searching our past for that elusive contact , perhaps the start of it all. I discovered that anger can develop into a sickness, so I saw a doctor for nerve settling medication. Anything that would allow me to stay on the road as I retraced our past year.

One of the companies I had under contract was located near Boston, and we had such good luck selling their product that we had visited their plant at least every ninety days for the past five years. From there, we sometimes continued on up to Portland, Maine, where we would take the ferry across the Bay of Fundy to Yarmouth, Nova Scotia, where we had several friends. One family we were close to had a lot of acreage that was in low country and was perfect for growing Christmas trees. Ken and Elsa had one small son that was too young to help much, so both of them worked the year around, planting and harvesting Christmas trees for shipment to the lower forty-eight. I found it very interesting that Ken had made two trailers from two truck axles with the differential somehow connected . The tractor could pull and the power takeoff from the tractor connected to the trailers would cause all wheels to pull together. With this rig, he could go into the swampy area, load, and literally crawl out of the mud to higher ground. Tree cutting began the first of November and trailer loads of trees were shipped to central points in Chicago and Atlanta. They were a very industrious couple and very good friends, but I had no time to spend with them on this trip. An overnight visit with them would be enough to clear my mind that Dixie had not been there without me. It would be another dead end to a long journey if I were to cover the many places and friends we had made over the years. When Dixie and I made this trip, it meant we spent a lot of time driving but we would manage to continue north until we crossed the bridge at Quebec. There we would spend some time sightseeing and visiting friends that would enjoy being with us for the evening. So far this trip, I had the chance to visit two families that Dixie and I liked very much. I found no clue to her having been in touch with either for the past year. Before leaving Maine, I had spent a full day in Bar Harbor where Dixie and I had spent several weeks in the cabins run by the Thompson's. We had loved the place for its location on the water and because we could have lobster every day, fresh off the boat. I thought she might visit there but again, no luck.

The next day, still feeling much too sick to be a safe driver, I headed out for Buffalo, NY, where Dixie and I had spent some wonderful times. We never tired of this place and I had high hopes of finding her at the motel where we always stayed when we were in that area.   On arrival, I checked in and went directly to my room. There I broke down in prayer and tears. I cried until I must have passed out on the floor. Sometime in the early morning, I was still on the floor and was awakened by a car door slamming. People were beginning to check out and I was still too sick to be hungry. I had run out of tears and my face was too puffy for me to be seen in public, so I took a hot shower and fell across the bed.

Late that same afternoon, I felt a little better and realized that real sickness would take me out if I did not eat something. My stomach was calling for food but my mind was screaming for Dixie to show up in the crowd of tourists all about the place. I went outside with them and my eyes were on every woman that was the size of Dixie. Several times I would see the back of a woman that would look similar enough that I had to run to her for a closer look. In my state of mind and the way I looked so desperate, more than one man took the position of protecting his wife from the mad man I must have looked like.

For three days, I looked among the tourists and in the local restaurants. I must have asked a thousand times, "Have you seen this beautiful lady?" I had more copies made of the only picture I had with me and passed one out to every hand that opened in front of me. By this time, the police had heard of me from many sources and had checked me out, had checked my story, and then agreed to place her picture on their "LOST' board. Each night when the tourists went to their hotel rooms and the locals went home, I would fall on my knees in that lonesome motel room and cry and pray myself to sleep, usually on the floor.

Having exhausted all hope of finding a clue in that area, I continued on to Cleveland where Dixie had a first cousin that had been keeping in touch at Christmas time. Although she had lost her husband the year before, I found little sympathy there since she made the remark that perhaps Dixie had reason to want to get away from me. I had no idea what she was referring to but I did know that she and her husband had lived a stormy marriage. Perhaps she was thinking that she might have been better off had she left her husband long ago. At any rate, I could not stay and listen to her endless complaints when, in just another few miles, I might find someone who could help.

I still called my telephone service three or four times each day and the answer was always the same. They had received many calls from my recent customers and from companies I used to represent. None had anything except sympathy and a promise to pray for me and for Dixie. I became so sick of mind that I started thinking that ending my life would be easy. I considered the many ways to do it and all except putting a gun to my head seemed too slow, and, besides I did not like the idea of leaving my brains scattered around for someone else to clean up. Why I should worry about that eludes me. I suppose it was just a way for my inner self to avoid doing the job.

With all of my travels and searching taking me everywhere but back home, I determined to visit a church every Sunday. It was truly amazing to find the difference between the several churches I visited. Even in the Baptist churches that I was so familiar with, there seemed to be endless differences. Some were just friendly Christians meeting to share the Agape love of Christ with all who would listen, and others didn't care if a newcomer was greeted or not. I do remember two churches that people didn't greet me or express any desire for new members or visitors. These were the cold churches that I was happy to leave behind without asking for any news of Dixie or anything else. I also attended services at Methodist and Presbyterian churches and always asked for a few minutes in the pulpit. I remember one Baptist church I visited in rural Canada which left me wondering where the so called Christians of this community were.

I arrived late and since it was likely the only church I would find this morning, I entered thinking the service had started and the quietness indicated a prayer was in progress. To my surprise, the congregation consisted of two older women and none other. I did join them in a short service and left without telling them the reason why I stopped at their church. At the many churches I visited, my story brought many tears, and several times, I was asked to look for a lost daughter or wife from another grieved soul. Before long I was carrying pictures to stick up wherever I could, and it was shocking to me to learn that so many had been lost. This information was distressing and made my search seem more difficult than ever. I did visit Catholic churches two times and was well received except I detected a hint of reserve since I did not know proper protocol.

Weeks had passed and it was by the generous help of a close friend in my church back home that all of my bills had been paid and mail was taken care of. He had caused my home to be winterized and my utilities to be cut off. We were in touch by phone every few days, both to keep in touch with my affairs and to hear of any news he might have heard. I had no idea when, or if, it would end, so I am truly thankful for his help and the support of his caring wife. Without them, I have no idea how I would have survived this terrible ordeal. Several times when I was in the depths of despair and very close to ending it all, his wife and he would join me in a telephone prayer. I am certain their prayers helped me face many dark days and gave me the strength to continue on down that dark and lonely road I was on.

On leaving Cleveland, I started driving south with no idea of the road I was taking. I was like the explorer that just had to know what was over the next hill. Around noon that day I remembered that five or six years back, Dixie and I had a summer home for three years in a small town called Mexico Beach, about thirty miles southeast of Panama City, Florida. We had spent many happy months there, fishing along the gulf and loafing in the sun. It was not much of a tourist town but there was a seafood restaurant not far from there that we visited almost every day. I loved to read and write and she loved to read so we were very busy and had little need to go into town. We did make the twenty mile trip to Panama City every few days, mostly for groceries and when we did, it was always a movie at the theatre. Normally, we never thought of seeing a movie but being isolated as we were, it was fun. Now as I drove south, I thought this might be the place where she would remember as her home. If she was wandering around with faulty memory, she just might remember this place as home.

Our little cottage stood well back from the gulf and had some rising ground behind us. The town was only about four blocks deep from the water's edge and we were in the last row on the back side of town. There was a small motel down on the main road that was the only place for tourists to stop for many miles and fishing from the beach was not so good. Really, there was not much reason for anyone to stop here and that was the reason we liked the place. It was close to some shoals and quiet water where mullet could be caught with a throw net and that was about the extent of my fishing. I hated offshore fishing because just the thought of a lifting wave and I had to lean over the side and empty all of that day's and last week's food. There is really no word for the deathly sickness that came when I got into an offshore boat. When I went netting for mullet, Dixie stayed on the sun porch and read. Her love of books never ceased to amaze me for it included every form of writing. If she rejected anything, it was modern poetry. It had to have rhythm before she would even classify it as being a poem.

By noon I realized I was half way toward Cincinnati on I71 so it was just as well that I continue to pick up I75 toward Atlanta. We had lived in Norcross for several months while I was doing a special job. While there, Dixie had worked at the Gwinnett County mall in the Hallmark card shop. She had loved the job there and was well thought of since she never met anyone that could resist her sales personality. The shop owner hated to lose her but the time came when I had to spend some heavy time in the office in Huntsville.

Surely Dixie would still have good memories of that experience, so it would be good for me to check it out. Two days later I was back where we had rented an apartment. Of course no one remembered us there so I went to the mall card shop. Naturally, it had changed hands and no one remembered Dixie there. I spent a few days in the greater Atlanta area, passing out her picture and looking at every lady that passed me, searching, searching and still full of hope that one of them might be Dixie.

Please, God, give me the strength to continue looking and help me to find her before I lose my mind. It was certainly close, that moment when my mind would take no more abuse. I even thought it would be a blessing if I did lose my memory. At least there would be an end to the agony of lost sleep, the anger when I thought I was incompetent and my losing weight from improper eating. I was well on the way to the end of my life and seemed to be rushing toward the end.

Two weeks in this area produced nothing except more despair so it was time for me to continue on to the other side of the fence. I had heard the grass was always greener on the other side so I needed to go see. As I drove on southwest, I had nothing but that numb feeling of failure. By now it was common for me to stop at truck stops, road side restaurants and any place a group of people gathered. I would hand out her picture to any and all, begging information and offering a large reward. By this time, I had my name and how I could be contacted along with a reward notice of one hundred thousand dollars, all printed on the back. I had passed out hundreds of these photos and not one believable phone call had been received. I had arranged to pay the six ladies hat worked three shifts around the clock, a little extra for handling my phones, . The switchboard where two ladies were always on duty was a private telephone answering service. All of the ladies that worked there knew my circumstances and were trying to do their best for me. I did make a habit of calling them for a report at all times of the day or night so they all knew my voice. I had also promised to pay a bonus to the one that took a call leading to Dixie's location.

Almost six months had passed and not a single clue to Dixie's whereabouts. Mexico Beach produced nothing in the week I spent there. One good thing did happen though.

I made it a habit to visit the seafood restaurant where Dixie and I had enjoyed so many good meals. At first, it was in hopes of finding some trace of her there, but I found myself enjoying the wonderful food they served. I had also handed out pictures to any and all which gained me a good customer status with the waitresses and assured me a full plate of the best they had. In that week I gained pounds but, more than that, I regained my determination to press on. I was at a loss as to which way to look now that I was between places in Florida that I wanted to look and places in Texas I must go.

With a flip of a coin, I headed deeper into Florida to visit with neighbors that we had become close to in Huntsville. Fred and Ethel Turner had lived next door to us for about two years. Fred was an army major, retired and, later, a buyer for General Electric. Because he was both a neighbor and a buyer of my company wares, we had become fast friends. On retiring from GE, Fred and Ethel moved to Daytona. While in Huntsville, Fred and I had both taken the examination for a ham radio license with the intention of using that to stay in touch. Fred soon dropped out since he loved to fish and had no time to radio surf. Even so, Dixie and I spent long weekends as their guest and our friendship continued. Although I had called them when Dixie disappeared, I wanted to be there just in case some small happening might have slipped by them. To spend a few days with them would help me settle my nerves and might also lead to finding a tourist along the beach that might have seen Dixie back in Timbuktu or wherever they were from.

Ethel was a good cook and Fred was a good fishing buddy so my visit was the first pleasant time in all of the past lonely months. Even though Dixie and I had friends in Fort Lauderdale, I chose not to go there at this time. I had represented a company there called UID Switch Manufacturing Company and they were the cause of our spending some time there. We did become friends with some of the employees there but nothing lasting. I even doubted I would be able to locate them now. Most of the time when I had to do a plant visit there, Dixie would stay with Ethel for the two or three days I had to be in Fort Lauderdale. Not having her with me at the plant meant I did not make many friends of the kind she would have made.

Now that I had exhausted every potential lead in Florida, I decided to head for Texas where we had some very close friends, so close that we had stayed in each others home's many times over the past several years. The Britt family was down to just the two of them now as all three children were married and long gone. I had spoken to them two or three times during the past six months and knew they would have called me if anything had come up. I just had the desire to be among friends who would help me forget if only for a few days. Chuck Britt had been a close friend and had shared many hunting camps with me in years past. We would still do the hunting camps if not for age and a little arthritis but we had enough good memories that we could relive them for hours, or even days. I looked forward to spending time in their home and discussing Dixie's disappearance with them. Perhaps they might cause a new thought that would lead to my locating the love of my life. A week with Chuck and Reba Britt renewed my faith in God and his wonderful power. I left there confident that God would soon answer the prayers of my many friends and that he would dry the tears that coursed down my cheeks every night at bed time.

I left Texas for another town where Dixie and I had visited and loved so many times.

My old college town of Joplin, Missouri, still held a close attraction for me, and I had taken Dixie there many times to visit old school friends. We had loved dining at a restaurant in Neosho and several times we continued on to Branson for overnight and a show of one kind or another. We both loved music, so it made little difference where we went; music was everywhere. Again, I stayed in Branson but did not take in a show. My heart was not in it and my time was spent handing out her picture. I determined to leave the next day for Huntsville, Alabama, since I thought it was time to see the friends that had been so faithful to care for my home.

Before leaving the motel, I called my answering service once again as I would be on the road for hours and would not find it easy to call from just anywhere. Wanda answered the phone and, immediately I knew she had heard something. She was so excited I thought I would never get the story. But of course, I was too excited to shut up and give her the time to tell me what she had learned. At last I got the word that a lady in Seattle, Washington had called to tell us that she knew where Dixie was. It seems she was a checkout clerk in a major grocery store, Safeway, on Othella street, and that Dixie had been coming in every Friday evening for the past few weeks. There are words to describe almost all feelings but none to tell you how I was feeling as I hung up the phone. Joy unspeakable, elation, bliss, euphoria, ecstasy, rapture and intoxicated exhilaration all swirled through my brain and, all of these combined, failed to convey my feelings. I was almost unable to move but move I did. I managed to book a flight out of Joplin that afternoon for Los Angles . No direct flights were available but, by this route, I could be in Seattle the next day around noon. I left my car at the airport, so excited that my memory is not very clear. I just know I made it to Seattle by the following evening before five when Dixie usually came in. At the store, I found Marie, the checkout clerk, waiting for me in the office as we had agreed to do. She said Dixie was due to come in between five and six, always alone, and she usually bought very few items and those the lowest priced the store had. This would fit Dixie since I had found her check book and credit cards back in Columbus so many months ago. Of course, I wondered how she had made out with no money and no identification. How did she get so far away and what did she do for food? I refused to believe she would sell her body for support. I knew she would willingly starve to death before this would happen. Someone had to help her and while we waited, I wondered who and how this could be..

Until this time, I had no real promise of ever seeing her again, but I had received a phone call some weeks before from a crank that told us they had a message from Dixie and would sell it to me for a price. Not willing to let any possible clue get past me, I did meet with that woman with the intention of paying for information. I met with her in Cincinnati, Ohio, at a place she called her space laboratory. It was a small room, complete with shaking table and the usual glass ball in back of her house, and set up for palm readings. She gave me a ridiculous price before she was willing to tell me anything so I asked one question before leaving. Did you get your information from the glass ball or the cards? The world is full of people who will take advantage of any person that is hurting. I do know my God will deal with these people in time, so I just walked away and left it to Him.

Five o'clock passed and no sign of Dixie and I was beginning to wonder if this was just another attempt to scam me for dollars. I thought about it for a few minutes and then realized that Mariehad not asked me for anything. Surely she was being truthful and was trying to be helpful, so it was wait another hour if necessary. From many pictures I had made of Dixie while times were good, I now carried a small picture album which I had shown to Marie. Her statement was an absolute positive identification. I was as convinced as she was that Dixie was here. When I saw her come in through the front door, I thought my heart would burst with joy. Never had she looked so lovely, even dressed in cheap street clothes. I did not know whether to rush to her or approach quietly because she did leave me and perhaps she would run on seeing me. Marie saw the adoration on my face and asked why I did not run out and grab her with a big hug. My God knew I wanted to but there was that fear she would run, and, perhaps, I would never have this chance again.

I waited until she was in the back side of the store where I believed I would be able to catch her if she did run. I walked slowly up behind her and touched her on the shoulder so she would turn without fear. At the same time and in a soft voice, I spoke her name as I

had so many times in the past, "Dixie, my love". My heart was about to jump out of my chest and tears were streaming down my face. People were looking at me as if I were out of my mind, which I almost was. I expected her to turn to me and open her arms in the same kind of love I had for her but this was not to be.

I had called some of my friends this same afternoon and had given them the good news. It looks positive that I have located Dixie. By this time, dozens of my friends had passed the word and I know there was much joy that Dixie would be coming home. We would have a celebration like no other had ever been and our church walls would be bursting outward from the joyous occasion. Never again would I allow Dixie out of my sight, never again would I allow a day to pass without telling her how much I appreciated her. What wonderful plans rushed through my head as I waited for her to turn to me with open arms.

She turned with these words, "My name is not Dixie". Right then I realized that was so. She spoke in a deep voice that had obviously been damaged by the use of cigarettes.

As I looked closely at her face, I saw the mole on her right cheek was missing. Otherwise, she was a double, both in size and in the way she held her posture.

I was out of tears by now and apologized and tried to explain. I must say she was a lady and listened without interruption. As we talked, I noticed her teeth were not as perfect as Dixie's. This lady had not been so careful or she had not had the money for good dental care. We could not stand in the aisle and talk for long, so Marie asked us

to use the store employee break room. Both this lady and I wanted to know more about each other but, first, I wanted to know her name. She told me it was Virginia and that struck me as peculiar since Dixie's mothers name was Virginia. Dixie's mother had died four years back and had never given me or Dixie much of her early history even though Dixie had tried to get as much information as her mother would allow.

Virginia, Marie, and I sat in the store break room for an hour, exchanging information

and it occurred to me that I was hungry. I asked both of them if they would take me to a place where we could eat and talk. Marie declined as she had children at home that needed to be fed but Virginia accepted the invitation. It was apparent that she was also hungry and in no hurry to go anywhere. We sat in a booth in a small restaurant a block down the street, ordered, and ate a very good dinner. It appeared to me that Virginiahad not fared so well and I was careful not to ask embarrassing questions. I understood that kindness on my part would get all the information I so desired. But first, I had to tell her why I was looking for Dixie and why I was so determined to locate her. She did not seem to understand a love that would last until death for it soon became clear that she had never had such love. Virginia had known only the love that the Greek language called Eros and we know as erotic. That fades fast as Virginia was well aware.

As we sat there talking, my mind was racing back to the early years with Dixie. I believed her mother was beautiful and also much too young to be the mother of Dixie. Her father was obviously senior to her mother by about fifteen or twenty years and it was obvious he adored Dixie's mother, even though that adoration was not returned in kind.

The longer Dixie and I were together, the more I learned about their relationship. Dixie had questioned it in her high school years but never got much satisfaction from her questions. All I gathered was that Dixie was not the apple of her mother's eye. In fact, she seemed to be a slave to her mother, and Dixie was missed most because she was no longer the one to do the house work, laundry, and all of the chores her mother should have been doing. Some time in the first few years of our marriage, I came to the conclusion why Dixie said "Yes" to me so quickly was that she wanted away from her mother. As time passed, it also changed our relationship to a point where I was positive that Dixie loved me as deeply as I loved her.

Dixie had also wondered about her parents' age difference and had, by searching, found the correct age of her mother. From there, she found her birth certificate and her mother's age listed as fourteen. She also found the record of their marriage, Ken Cummings and Virginia Akers, but the dates did not match. Dixie was a bastard for three months before the marriage took place. This explained to her why her father cared so deeply for her, far more than her siblings. Even though the mystery of her birth was solved, it did little to cure her desire to know more. We both decided this was the reason her father said nothing when we slipped away for a secret marriage.

Virginia and I talked far into the evening and I asked if it would be O.K. if I walked her home. At first she was reluctant but finally decided it would be safer to have a man with her than to face the dark streets alone. We walked about four blocks into a dark and dingy neighborhood to where she said she lived alone in a second floor apartment. I gathered that she was running away from a bad relationship in a city not far away. Her job here was clerking in a second hand clothing store and it was evident she had very little income.

I know it will seem that I was courting Virginia, and, perhaps, I was without realizing it.

After all I could barely control the urge to take her in my arms and speak those words I was so used to: "Dixie my love." All the next day I spent on the phone trying to tell my friends I had found a double for Dixie but the search was still well under way. I did not know the location of the store where Virginia worked; otherwise, I might have walked in just to take another look at that face so like the one I would die for. I could hardly wait for Virginia to show up at the restaurant where we met the night before. It was to be a good dinner for her and a good learning time for me. It would have been so easy to take Virginia as a replacement for Dixie and my search would be over. I would quickly get over the slight differences in them but, then, there was the inner beauty of Dixie that I knew Virginia did not have. My search was to continue until death if it took that long.

At dinner that evening, Virginia told me the truth about her life and I had much pity for her. She was the adopted daughter of Ben and Helen Kelso, a career navy man and a mother who followed the navy men from port to port. Her mother never seemed to miss her father when he was at sea because she was always in the company of a sailor, sometimes for only one night. When her father did come ashore for a few days, it was stormy and Virginia was mostly ignored. Her schooling was fragmented-- schools from Seattle to Baltimore, coast to coast. She never stayed in one place long enough to make the usual school buddies. On retiring from the navy, her parents made Seattle their permanent home because it was a shipping port and her father could ship out as a deckhand any time he chose. This meant he was still gone most of the time but, at least, Virginia did have a steady school long enough to graduate from high school. She also found a steady boyfriend that meant some relief from a missing father and a mother who seemed never to care.

On leaving high school, Virginia felt lost and relied on her boyfriend to relieve the tedium of her mother's drunkenness. Before mid-summer, they decided to slip over into another state and get married, very much as Dixie and I had done. Unfortunately for Virginia, Jimmy Hobbs was a totally different person once he had control over her. He was jealous and a bully which led to his beating Virginia whenever he felt she had done him wrong or when things did not go well at work. A few years of this caused Virginia to leave with nothing except the clothes she was wearing. Virginia had to escape the brutality of a man who got his kicks out of striking a woman. Jimmy had never allowed Virginia to have money of her own and had always made certain the money he gave her was returned along with a sales slip, proof of where she spent it. His temper came to a head one evening when she lost a grocery sales receipt and could not account for about one dollar. Since he would not allow Virginia to work, she was a prisoner in every respect. So, with no money and poor prospects, she left him one night and continued walking all night. By morning, she was cold and tired which caused her to stop at the used clothing store for perhaps a coat. The owner felt pity for Virginia and gave her the coat and a job to keep her alive.

Soon I had to be on my way in the search for Dixie but I could not think of leaving Virginia in such deplorable conditions. I asked her if she would like to move to Huntsville, Alabama, and although she had never heard of the place, she quickly agreed. I understood it would be dangerous for me to be caught with her by her violent husband but I wanted to do everything I could to rescue her from such a deplorable relationship.

I called my attorney in Huntsville for advice and decided immediately that he was right. I must take Virginia through Nevada for a quick divorce before continuing on to Huntsville.

As we drove south, I was in a continuous silent prayer asking God what this meant. Was Virginia meant to replace Dixie? Then, why, God, did you lead me to her in such a way as to have me on a mountain top one minute and in the depths of despair the next? Of course, God does not answer the prayer at once. I suppose he gets his fun out of leaving someone like me to guess. In a rented Ford, we left Seattle as soon as I could arrange for the car. We did not even stop by her apartment for fear Jimmy might have traced her this far. We drove down the coast, about four hundred miles on our way to Reno, Nevada. I figured this would be far enough to lose Jimmy if he had somehow figured out where Virginia was, and, besides, we were exhausted. After a good dinner, we went to our rooms and I fell into what I called a death sleep. By five in the morning, I was up and knocking on her door. It was necessary that we complete the trip today and be prepared to seek out the divorce court tomorrow morning. All went as planned and by noon the following day, Virginia was single again. By way of celebration, we stopped at a shopping mall for some new clothing for her and clean underwear for me. Our next move was to turn in the Ford, to catch a flight for Joplin where I could pick up my own car, and to continue our trip to Huntsville and a new life for Virginia.

We arrived at Huntsville International airport very late Friday and took rooms at the airport motel since my apartment would be dark and would have no food , not even coffee. Saturday morning I introduced her to as many of my friends as I could get to in one day. Late that evening, I took her to the home of my friend, Steve Henderson, giving him her maiden name of Virginia Kelso. Steve owned and operated NAVCO, Inc. in Huntsville and employed about thirty people in the business of manufacturing navigation electronics. He had been a good customer of my company as well as a good friend. He had lost his wife in a car accident some time back and then devoted his time to the business, making it very successful. Dixie and I had found him to be entertaining company and had him visit us many times for horseback riding and dinner. Steve was looking for acreage near ours but, in the mean time, he made good use of ours. We welcomed him there, even when we were not able to be there with him. Steve knew Dixie very well since our time together stretched out over several past months.

When he saw Virginia, he was more than astonished. He was speechless.

I told him the story in short form and that I expected to help her with an apartment and in locating a job. Steve quickly stated that she already had a job and he would help with the apartment.

That same day we located and contracted for a furnished apartment In the Hay Stack complex, just a few blocks from Steve's place of business. From there we headed directly to the mall on the west side of town where we delighted in buying clothes for Virginia. I was amazed at the way she selected things that I know my Dixie would have chosen, and I was fascinated at how Steve doted on her. It was evident to me that Steve had fallen in love just as quickly as I had when I met Dixie in the back seat of my friend's car. My own emotions began to surface, that I was a mite jealous of Steve. Just to think, I could have had her to replace Dixie and I could now see that it was too late. The more time I spent with Virginia, the more she began to act like Dixie, and it was noticeable that she had stopped smoking and was beginning to use much better manners.

Later that night when I was in my own apartment, I really had time to think. Dixie was still foremost in my mind and not even Virginia could replace her. For this, I was truly glad that Steve would have her and our relationship would continue. No one would ever replace Dixie, not in this world. Other thoughts came to mind that night and I got very little sleep. I was still lonesome, even more so now that I had been with Virginia for the past few days. I must start looking again, but where?

As my thoughts drifted around the world that Dixie and I had known, places where we had found the most pleasure, none came to mind as the perfect place to look. So near morning, I decided to ignore known places and start at the beginning. Richmond, where Dixie was born, the hospital, the courthouse and any place that might have a record of something new to me.

During the following week, I had a wonderful time with Virginia and Steve. It was a whirlwind of sightseeing and meeting people. Steve had to spend a lot of time at his business and I had Virginia all to myself. I must have been mad to have spent so much money on clothes for her. We soon ran out of closet room in her apartment. I took her to all the local spots of interest, such as the space museum, and, of course, to the best restaurants Huntsville had. I did all the things for Virginia that I could not afford for my true love Dixie when we were courting. I wanted to feel like I was courting Dixie all over again, but now I had cash and could treat her to the very best. I think, by this time, both Steve and I were experiencing more than a little jealously. The difference was that Dixie never left my mind, and I was determined to follow every lead on earth for the rest of my life. Taking Virginia to the homes of several of my fellow church members caused quite a stir. Now that she was well dressed and groomed, not one person would believe she was not Dixie until I called attention to the mole on her right cheek. Nothing would do except I bring her to church the next Sunday, which I agreed to do. Neither Steve nor Virginia had ever attended church and neither knew of the saving grace of Jesus Christ. Because I asked, both were enthusiastic about attending their first church service since it would please me very much . Word got out fast that we would be in church, and the following Sunday was a record breaker. I had asked our minister to give a sermon on the saving grace of Jesus and to place emphasis on Heaven and Agape love, the unrelenting love of Christ for all of us. At the close of his sermon, he gave the invitation for anyone to approach the altar for a prayer of thankfulness. To my surprise, both Virginia and Steve followed me to kneel at the altar. It was evident that their hearts were filled with love for everything around them.

That is part of the mystery of love.

The following Tuesday I left Huntsville with some reluctance. I had become a follower of both Steve and Virginia. What a wonder it was to see a love bloom that was surely as rich as mine was for Dixie. I did not leave until I had assurance that they would wait for me to return before any lasting bond was sealed.

On arrival in Richmond, I made my way to the courthouse to look for birth records.

Dixie had given me her birth certificate that was made in Richmond showing she was born there, but she knew nothing more to tell me. She had no living relatives that could or would tell me, even if they knew. It was a simple matter to locate her birth record by using one of the courthouse employee's help. Though I had found county employees not usually too helpful, this was a new experience. I had all of the help I needed. I found she had been born to Virginia Akers with no father listed. The delivering doctors name was there, Dr. Jacob Weinberg. The second hospital I visited turned out to have the records of her birth and from there I found the name of the attending nurse. I also found that lady was still living nearby.

I found Miss Anna Keeler to be very sharp of mind even though she was in her late eighties. After talking to her for a short time and sharing one of her special cookies and a cup of tea, she did remember well the little fourteen-year-old girl who had had such a very hard time. She had much pity for her since she was totally alone and obviously the victim of some older man. Doctor Jacob, as she called him, seemed to be distracted that day and did very little to help the girl she remembered as Virginia, no last name. The delivery of a four-pound six-ounce girl was very difficult, and Doctor Jacob told her to clean up and then he left for the day. As Anna was cleaning the girl and the baby had been taken to the nursery, Anna saw the beginning of a second birth. And with no one to help her, she did all the right things and delivered another girl of nearly the same weight. Doctor Jacob had already filled out the birth certificate and left with it to be filed on his way out. Anna had little choice but to place baby number two in a nursery crib with no identification, except the tag she had marked with the mother's name "Virginia" attached. She had to return to the task of cleaning the mother and it was very late in the evening when she finished. She then did what she could for Virginia no-name and took her to the ward for recovery from the sedative Doctor Jacob had administered.

The next day, Anna was due to go back on duty at four p.m. and the first thing she did was to look in the nursery for the no-name baby so she could tell what happened. To her shock, there was no baby number two. A wave of fear swept over Anna for it was likely she would be charged with something and at least lose her job. She knew any word of dereliction of duty aimed at Doctor Jacob would result in her having to prove it, and she realized it would be her word against his. It could even get her some jail time so what choice did she have but to remain silent? She also learned that an older man by the name of Ken Cummings had come in for the Akers girl and her baby. He had paid the hospital bill and left no forwarding address.

For the next several days, she watched and listened for some indication of another person would know what had happened. Three days later she had the answer but was still bound to silence for it would be evident that she was party to the theft of a baby. Her answer came when she learned that the night nurse, Helen Hutchinson, was assigned to the nursery that night and had resigned without notice. Although it had been many years ago, she still had the name of that nurse written in her Bible and she had kept track of her and knew she had been married two times, the last to a sailor by the name of Ben Kelso.

Next, I had to start searching the records in Seattle for any information available on the man named Ben Kelso. It was easy to find because he had a police record of several minor skirmishes with the law, bar room fights resulting in arrest for disturbing the peace and resisting arrest. Traffic citations and DWI seemed to be his worst offense and resulted in ninety days to cool his heels and sober up. After this, he managed to get into the International Longshoreman's Association (ILA) which was the Sailors Union of the Pacific, International. Going to sea was a way for him to dodge the responsibility of caring for a wife and daughter. Helen and Virginia had it rough for the next few years with very little coming from Ben and the jobs Helen could hold were of the lowest pay scale. Primarily she did poor work and spent much of her free time at the local bars on the lookout for a few dollars and a load of headache material. Many times Virginia was left alone for long evenings, from the time of her first memory until she was old enough to go out on her own.

Now AnnaKneeler knew it was a case of lost records and there would be no investigation, nothing she could do without the possibility of finding herself involved in a kidnapping charge. As time passed for Anna, she finally stopped worrying and soon forgot except when she saw the name in her Bible. As for me, I was somewhat free to continue my search for Dixie but not free of aching loneliness and debilitating heart ache. Being in Richmond was sort of a central point along the east coast, leaving me with a difficult decision as to where I might have the best chance of finding Dixie. We had so many places along the coast that we had spent time and loved the place, it was almost a flip of a coin. As I thought about it, I realized it might not have been the place but that Dixie and I were so much in love, any place was near heaven on earth. I did remember that we always found more secluded places back in the mountains where we could have a picnic and enjoy a fast running stream. Places where most people would pass by with the comment that it "Sure was wild" and would keep hiking along to the next stream. We loved the wilderness and took pride in our ability to name the trees and wild flowers. We were able to camp out under the stars in places where others would classify as "spooky" and where we could be totally alone with God as our keeper. I remembered such a place where we spent two nights in a tent along the fast flowing stream called Kent's run in western Virginia. Spending another day or so at the same location would help me relieve my mind as well as possibly give me a lead to where I should look next. Driving all day found me in Elkins and with enough time to purchase some food at the Kroger store and a sleeping bag at Sears. I set off into the mountains. Just before dark, I found the place where Dixie and I had camped beside a timbering road that was more trail than road. No improvements had been made since I was last here and I knew that rain during the night might keep me stuck here until it had a chance to dry out again. I did not have a tent in case of rain but I could move into the back of my van. There would be just enough room to get some sleep but not enough to stretch out in comfort.

When Dixie and I were camping here, we had such things as a cooler and a camp stove. We had plenty of hot food and drink as well as the comfort of a good tent. I now had cans of beans, cheese, cold cuts of ham and other such processed meat. Not really appetizing but enough to get by on with a small camp fire for hot instant coffee. All went well until I was fed and in my sleeping bag, then I was hit with a wave of loneliness and grief, such that I could not stop the tears. I cried myself to some form of sleep where I did not rest. Even my dreams that first night were such that I would awaken and cry again. I called out to God all night long that he remove the suffering and allow me to either forget or find Dixie. Even death would be welcome, and I asked Him to please take my life this very night. I now believe that I was so close to taking my own life that God did interfere and held my hand in check. He would know the future and he was not finished with me.

Two nights in the mountains and I was now ready to look where my dreams had seemed to point. Normally, I do not put much stock in dreams but there are times when the dream is so overpowering that I can't get it off my mind for days. I do know that in the millions of miles I used an automobile in my business, on two occasions a dream probably saved my life. One outstanding occurrence took place on a rural road in Georgia, near the town of Rome. I had a dream the night before in which I saw myself being removed from a pileup of several cars and trucks. It was so vivid that I was uncomfortable the next day and somewhere along the way, I had the feeling that I was riding in a vehicle that could take my life. Nothing would do except to pull off the road and try to shake the fear of the unknown. Twenty minutes later, I felt somewhat better and decided to proceed with caution, not my usual way of driving because I always had many miles to go. Just as I turned the last curve to go onto a main road, the sight of many cars and trucks piled all over the intersection told me it had happened less than a minute before I got there. How could I not believe in dreams?

I was over an hour at that location, doing all I could to help and watching the last victim leaving as the road was being cleared by wreckers. In this case, I had to trust in a dream and leave these West Virginia mountains for the mountains of Montana.

Not too many years back, Dixie and I had spent a few weeks in the foothills of western Montana. We were in a cabin that belonged to a close friend and allowed for travel each day into a new area. Each morning we would drive out with a different destination in mind and return to the cabin well into the evening. We toured many abandoned mine sites and towns that had been long ago filled with life and activity. Our exploration of these sites gave us much to talk about for many months afterward. I have been an avid photographer for many years, and, of course, I had taken loads of pictures which we could sort and label later. We had visited a mining operation where the tourist could dig for gems and where we were very lucky in finding several of value. These I had made into jewelry for my love, Dixie, as a reminder of the wonderful time we spent together.

One thing of interest that consumed two days took us to the university of mining in Butte, Montana. The story starts when my father worked for the railroad company several years back. He was always looking for a way to turn their junk into money since they sold off un-needed equipment to employees on a closed bid basis. Dad had bought many items such as air compressors and even trucks that he sold at a profit after cleaning and repairs, if necessary. The time came when the railroad placed a gigantic crane up for bid. This was a crane capable of lifting a derailed locomotive back on to the tracks. I have no idea what it weighed but it far surpassed that which was allowed on US highways. Part of the bid rules was that the successful buyer had to remove it from company property in less that sixty days. This crane was located in one of their salvage yards, still on the tracks and capable of being moved by a standard railway engine. My father had bid one cent per pound, thinking he could have it cut up and sold for scrap metal at five cents and make lots of profit. Mother almost had a heart attack when he told her of his latest toy but he had a plan. While trying to line up a crew to salvage the metal, he also tried calling heavy construction companies all over the nation in an effort to sell it, as is. One call led to another lead and another call. Eventually, he was put in contact with Anaconda Mining Company in Butte, Montana. Their copper mine in Butte was one of the largest in the world, with a pit in the earth almost a mile wide and several hundred feet deep.

Anaconda needed just such a crane and bought it at a very good profit to my father.

Within a week, the Anaconda crew arrived to secure the crane and prepare it for a rail trip to Butte.

When Dixie and I made the trip to Butte, we were surprised to find that Anaconda had recently closed that mine and moved on, to where was a good question. No one seemed to know and what happened to all of the heavy equipment was a mystery. With nothing left to do in Butte, we decided to visit the museum of mining. We found ourselves the lone visitors and much welcomed by an apparent dedicated curator. The displays were fascinating since Montana is rich in precious stones as well as copper, silver and gold.

We had the pleasure of seeing the second largest gold nugget ever found, one which was 27.41 ounces and measured over eleven centimeters in length. I do not remember the name of the person that did this for me but, after making a few phone calls, he told me the crane had been shipped to their operation in South America.

Another very interesting mining story came from our visit to Mule Retirement Ranch.

There we saw several mules in the best of pasture lands and with very nice shelters. Our questions revealed these mules had served their time in underground mines which was most of their life, without ever seeing the light of day. They had been taken down the deep shaft while still young, with their legs bound to their body so they would fit inside a man-sized shaft. In my opinion, they deserved the comfort of retirement such as we saw at the ranch. Our stay at the friend's cabin was such that we never stopped talking about that wonderful trip and how we would never be able to repay our friend for the loan of his place. My dream was that perhaps Dixie loved the place so much that she might have gone there in a state of mental confusion. But still I had to wonder how she got out of the dressing booth at the Larson's store, and what did she do for travel money? Needless to say, I would go anywhere in this world if it seemed to have a small chance of holding a clue to Dixie's whereabouts.

Today my call to my friend who was collecting my mail and paying the normal bills told me of a ransom note. Apparently someone or ones had sent the note demanding ten thousand dollars for the release of Dixie. Of course, he wanted to turn it over to the FBI but was reluctant to do so without my approval. When he told me the note said "Send us" and that the note was words cut from a newspaper, I did not hesitate to tell him to call the FBI. It became immediately noticeable that the writer had little education and had to be an amateur. The note asked that the money be in fifty dollar bills, left in a black trash bag and dropped beside the road just east of the intersection of Tennessee highway sixty four and the interstate. The first thought to come to mind was that the reward totaled more than ten times that which was asked. Obviously an amateur that would not last long under the scrutiny of the FBI lab . It gave no other instructions, so I left it up to the FBI and thought little more of it. I did learn a few weeks later that two juvenile boys were taken into custody. I never learned or cared what the courts did with them.

More weeks of travels across the United States, stopping at every truck stop and every homeless shelter gave no clue. Not even a clue as to where to look next. I took a break from travels and visited Virginia and Steve in Huntsville, mostly because I wanted to spend a few hours in the company of Virginia while Steve had to be at work. Somehow I took comfort in the belief I would once again have the same quiet time with my Dixie.

Virginia renewed my desire to find her because now Virginia was almost as anxious as I was to see her sister for the first time. Steve, Virginia and I spent a few evenings together discussing my next move, where and how I was to search. From these discussions, it was decided that I should start all over again, going back to Larson's in Columbus and back to the same ladies' department. I could see no other possibility and after a year of searching, I felt it necessary to renew my resolve to find her.

I arrived in Columbus on a Thursday evening in early October and found a room at the local Marriott. Because I was retracing our steps of a year ago, I had dinner at the same restaurant on Olentangy road where Dixie and I had our last dinner together. I believe this was the worst dinner I ever tried to eat. It was not the restaurants fault but mine for I could hardly swallow the food for being almost ready to break out into free-flowing tears.

I determined to sit there until I regained my composure and not embarrass myself or the waiter, and, against my better judgment, I consumed several ups of coffee. Knowing that one year ago tomorrow would be the anniversary of our last meal together, here and perhaps at the same table, I managed to finish a small part of the dinner, not knowing what it was and not caring. Leaving for the hotel and in hopes of sleeping off the tiredness I felt and dreading the next day at the store made me feel even worse. I could think of nothing to be gained by putting myself through the same misery as I had felt a year ago but true to my promise to Virginia and Steve, I had to do it.

Sleep never came. Perhaps the coffee and the dread of putting myself in the same place today that I was a year ago was at fault. In either case, I dressed and went down for the coffee and to be among happy people. No doubt they were all happy by my standards for I could set the standard for unhappiness this morning. More than once I thought that to give up would be a little easier because I would still be able to visit Dixie's sister. She might be married to Steve but I could still dream of times past and get by for another day.

As I sat there among other humans that had no obvious worries or concerns except the coffee before them, I had to ask God again, Why ME Lord? I know some people near me saw the tears falling to the table and must have wondered, but none cared enough to ask if I was O.K: This seems to be the way the world is going this day and time, all for me and you take care of yourself.

Because of the dread of seeing Larson's store interior again, I did everything I could think of to put it off. I drove past the place where I used to have an office and past the place where Dixie and I had lived. All this did for me was to make me sadder and lonely and drove me closer to taking my life in my own hands. I had stopped keeping a gun in the car as it was too tempting for me to use it on me. The thought came many times that the bridge abutment ahead of me is solid concrete. At seventy miles speed, nothing would hurt. It would end in a second, end forever. Usually, this thought brought me back to a prayer to God for help. One more mile and I think I can handle it for another day.

As time never stops, surely it did not today and I had to face it. Larson's, an hour before closing time found me wandering toward the ladies' department, barely able to drag my feet to that awful place. Since it was near closing time, there was only one clerk and two customers. I went to the clerk and asked her if it would be OK for me to look in the second changing booth on the right side. Of course, she wanted to know why and I had to come up with something about my wife lost a small object in that booth earlier. She told me the customers would be leaving very soon and that I should wait for a few minutes.

While waiting, I decided to tell her who I was and the reason I wanted to look. She knew the story and expressed her sympathy and, of course, cleared the booth area at once.

When she came out of the area, she was followed by a woman who caused me to fall to the floor on my knees. I was speechless, numb and unable to move. All I could do was stare at Dixie and at the same time I heard the clerk tell me I could go in now. She was not aware of the person following her out of the booth area.

Dixie spoke in a rather harsh voice, "Bernie, what are you doing on your knees? Are you sick?"

As she walked up to me, I grabbed her around the legs and pulled her close to me with a sob that could be heard all over the department. I was crying so hard I could not speak and I certainly could not tell her how happy I was. The clerk was as astonished as I was and she could not speak either. It was some time before I regained my voice and could ask, "Dixie , where were you?" She looked as astonished as the clerk and I when she said she must have fallen asleep and asked why we did not awaken her.

I tried to stop crying long enough to thank God for the miracle of Dixie's return. People from all over the store had gathered to find out what the excitement was all about. They all heard me thank God for returning her to me after a year of extensive searching and some of them remembered the original disappearance. Dixie was the most confused person there for she thought she had been asleep for just a few minutes, and she could not grasp the joy I felt and the desire I had to hold on to her. I would not let go, now or forever more.

The store manager and several customers had gathered and there was no way the store could close on time. Some brave person had called the newspaper, and, very soon a photographer and reporter arrived. Never had I seen such a confused person as Dixie was and it seemed that I would not be able to get her out of there until the reporter got the story he wanted. By this time, Dixie realized that she had been gone for a year and this left her more confused than I was. It was necessary for me to take her by the arm and force our way out of there. We made it to the car and from there, I was afraid to go to the Marriott for fear the crowd would follow and I would not get to talk to her for hours. Both of us wanted to be alone so we drove off out route forty and down forty- two toward Cincinnati, Ohio without checking out or picking up my baggage. That could be done by phone at a later date. There would be no hurry to get anywhere so I drove rather slowly so we could talk. She said she just fell into a deep sleep and could not understand why we did not awaken her. I told her she had been gone for one year today and she could not believe me until I reminded her that I had lost thirty pounds and now had some gray hair. Not only that, I had a different car from the one we drove to Columbus in. Once she was convinced that a year had passed, she wanted to know what had happened to me, what did I do. She had a thousand questions but I had many more that that. If she was just sleeping, she had to have had some brain movement in the form of a dream. What did she dream about? Did she remember the time she fell asleep, and, if so, how did that happen?

Dixie gave that some deep thought and took several minutes before speaking. She said she had put her clothes back on and was sitting down and leaning over to put on her shoes. Then the weird thought hit her that one half of her body was approaching death and that Bernie could find the cause. She thought she must send Bernie out for the cure and then she fell into a deep slumber. She remembers nothing more until she heard me talking to the clerk outside. I had hopes she would remember more after hearing my side of the story and that would take many hours. But first, I just wanted to pull into the next safe place to stop and give her the greatest hug ever. I wanted to tell her what a princess she was to me and how I wanted death when I thought I had lost her forever.

We stopped at a convenience store that had a phone outside and I made a call to Virginia and to Steve, then to my pastor in Huntsville. I knew he would be up for hours in order to call every one on the list. The good news is that Bernie has found Dixie, safe and sound. They are on their way home. I made two more calls. Texas and Florida friends had to hear the good news from me. We continued on to Cincinnati before we became too tired and hungry to stay on the road. A Waffle House took care of the hunger and we stopped at a motel that for the life of me, I can't remember a name for it.

I hate to admit it but I did not want Dixie to go to the ladies' room unless I stood at the door. Even then, I had uneasy feelings about her being out of my sight. I had to hold onto her every step we took outside the car and even in the car, I would keep a hand on her arm. My love for her knew no bounds.

The first thing Saturday morning was a call to Steve to let him know where we were and to give him some estimate of our arrival in Huntsville which would be around five. I do believe Steve was almost as excited as I was. He had trouble with words but was trying to tell me about the big party tonight. Many of our friends would be at the Shogun on University Drive where we have a table for forty reserved for seven p.m. This would be a night to remember for everyone wanted to see Dixie and Virginia meet for the first time since birth. Until now, I had not told Dixie about finding Virginia, and I wanted it to be a surprise, the greatest of her lifetime. Obviously, I wanted to drive fast and get there in a hurry but I also understood the need to be safe. A long day in the car with Dixie was like old times for we had done this for many years. Never with the excitement of this trip though, holding hands as we did when we used to sit on her mothers porch swing. There is a certainty of love between two people but no one could explain the exuberating love I had for Dixie on that long ride home. Every mile I drove gave me a tingling feeling in my fingertips and the urge to shout out the window that Dixie is back. More than a thousand times that day, I gave thanks to God for the return of my life and my sanity.

This drive was about nine hours and allowing for ten, we had plenty of time to stop by my apartment in town for a change for me but there was nothing for Dixie. As I thought about that, I had to call Steve and have him buy some things for Dixie since she was the same size as Virginia. He assured me he would fill the closets for her with the help of Virginia and if we happened to be a little late, never fear. The party might go on till midnight.

Dixie was confused when we went to the apartment instead of our home and I had to explain that I had not returned to that house since she disappeared. She was worried about all of her things, but I assured her everything was just as she left it but for a time, we would stay in the apartment. I told her about Steve setting up the welcome home party and right away, she worried about having nothing to wear and no time to shop. Did we ever have a wonderful surprise for her, new clothes and a new sister.

At the apartment, I led her in with the thought I should have carried her over the doorstep for she surely was my bride. She took it all in quickly making the comment that I did not seem to need much in the way of furniture. The room was almost bare for I spent so little time here that I needed nothing except a bed and a TV for the news. Even the kitchen was almost bare. Again, all I needed was coffee, toast, and once in a while, an egg. Now that she mentioned it, I had lived a very skimpy life this past year. One thing was certain, though, the refrigerator was full to the top, things Steve and Virginia had brought in so we would be able to enjoy a honeymoon for a week if we so desired. Dixie asked me about the female touch Steve must have had in order to gather all the right stuff. I had a hard time dodging that question. She would know in a very short time.

Dixie was fascinated with the changes in the Huntsville streets in only a year. I believe it took the sight of the many changes before she could really believe she had been away for a full year. Construction was everywhere and many streets were changed and /or closed.

Buildings had been removed and new ones built. Where our old office used to be located, there was now a new office complex. She asked me if we were still on Memorial Parkway and when I assured her we were, she asked about our office. Until now, she had not asked me about the business and was surprised to hear that I had sold everything. She was having a hard time facing a year of absenteeism which had not become so apparent to her until we were back where she was familiar with everything. Her next question was about the farm in Tennessee and about Danny Boy. Again I could assure her old Danny was well taken care of and the farm was secure. She could hardly wait until tomorrow to drive up there and once again hug her old horse. I hoped he would enjoy it as much as I enjoyed a hug from Dixie. I was reasonably certain she would forget all about old Danny tomorrow. Virginia would take the next few days of her time. They both had a lot to talk about and more to come.

As we entered the Shogun at seven thirty that Saturday night, we were met at the door by at least a dozen people who all tried to hug Dixie at the same time. Of all of them, I think Steve got the most sincere hug. Perhaps it was the love in his eyes that he felt for Virginia that showed and Dixie felt it as Virginia would. In either case, I was glad Steve had Virginia for I could see some competition for the love of a woman. I was just glad for both Steve and Virginia. We were led back to the large dining room where everyone was milling around as if covering up a secret., which they were. When Dixie was cheered and greeted, the crowd opened up and there stood Virginia. I don't know if Dixie momentarily fainted or if she was in shock, but in either case, there was not a sound from anyone in that room for what seemed to be minutes When Virginia spoke, "Hello, my sister" Dixie slumped in my arms for a few seconds and then the crowd went wild. Both girls lost their composure and rushed to each other to embrace as only seeing a lost loved one could cause. Tears flowed all over the room, and I must admit I cried more than most. I shouted in a very loud voice, "Thanks be to our God of mercy and love for Dixie is home".

The party lasted until midnight and it would have continued except the manager asked us to please close it down. Dixie and I were glad it ended for we were so tired and wanted some rest before church tomorrow, or perhaps it was already tomorrow We wanted to be in Sunday school at ten a.m. and church services at eleven. Dixie wanted to visit her class of little ones even though she doubted many would remember her. Oh, how wrong she turned out to be. She was mobbed by all of them, even though some of them had never seen her before. Church services at eleven found standing room only, something that had never happened before. Many of our customer friends were there and some of them had never been in a service before. Steve and Virginia had become very active and took their places in the choir loft and my heart was about to burst. There stood, side by side the two most lovely women I had ever had the pleasure of knowing---and one of them was mine.

At the distance from the choir to where I was sitting, I could not make out the mole on her cheek but I had no trouble caching the wink Dixie gave me. Never have I heard such heavenly singing as the choir did that morning. That was one time I could not sing because I had a lump in my throat that would not allow anything but a sob.

After church services, nothing would do except we were taken to the church dining room where a banquet had been catered. No doubt the largest one our church would ever have again. As much as Dixie wanted to be alone, there was no free time that wonderful Sunday. After the banquet, it was necessary for us to go to Steve and Virginia's home for a question and answer session. They were filled with questions and Dixie had no answers but she did have a multitude of them for Virginia. It was during this evening that I became so tired I fell asleep and into a deep dream, at least I think it was a dream. Perhaps this is the way God talks to us. The three of them continued talking and allowed me to dream on for over an hour. I shared the dream with them later and all agree that it was God giving me the reason for my misery this past year.

In the dream, I remembered that while Dixie was in the Larson's booth, she had felt that half of her body was dying It came to me in the dream that it really was. The half she had never known except in the womb was close to death from the anger Jimmy had and the beating Virginia was about to receive just a short time after I took her off toward Cincinnati.

Therein lies another mystery of love. Dixie's love for a sister she never knew and, across space and time, the need to save her came to the surface. Only God had the power to create this kind of love. This is both Agape and Philos love, not fully understood by man.

Nothing would suit Dixie the following day except she had to go to the farm for the reunion with Danny Boy. Both Steve and Virginia wanted to be there to see what that horse would do, so we set off soon after dawn for a Waffle House breakfast and the farm.

For the past year, the horses had been cared for by my neighbor's teen-aged boy and the automatic feeder I had made for them. Steve's horse had been with them from the beginning and Steve had been at the farm almost every week since Dixie had disappeared.

This morning the horses were still loitering around the barn when we arrived. Calling for Danny, Dixie jumped out of the car almost before it stopped and ran toward the barn..

The results were amazing. Those two met at the gate and again I saw Danny Boy lay his head over Dixie's shoulder. The difference was this time we all saw tears fall from Danny's eyes as well as Dixie's. Another example of the mystery of love.

Dixie did not want to see the cottage. She cared nothing for it at this time. All she wanted to do was saddle Danny Boy and to ride him out to the far pasture. Of course all of us had the same desire including Virginia. She had never been close to a horse and was afraid of them before Steve had taken her by the hand and led her to his horse which was a very gentle horse. He nuzzled Virginia's hand, looking for that sweet that some people sometimes offered him. Steve had been prepared with a box of raisins and gave Virginia a handful. That made Steve's horse a follower of Virginia, but he had another smaller mare which he had bought for Virginia. By now, she had become a lover of horses and did her own saddle work. My horse was the odd one in that I had not groomed him for the past year. He did not like the saddle so I had a little trouble being ready when the others were ready to head out. For the next two hours we rode the full farm, two hundred acres of mine and three hundred of Steve's.

Steve had been a good customer of mine from the beginning of my business and we had become fast friends. In those early days, Dixie and I had invited him to the farm for weekends and most of them had been to ride the hills adjoining our property. We had two hundred acres and had built a small cottage for our comfort and with a small guest room. Steve was alone now that his wife had been killed in a car accident. After her death, Steve had devoted all of his time to building his business and it was a very great success. Having him with us on the farm allowed him to relax but in some ways it made me cautious. It was evident that he thought the world of Dixie but it was also evident that he would never allow it to show, if he could help it.

While Dixie was away, to where we could only guess, another three hundred acres came up for sale. This was property next to mine and Steve bought it without delay. Behind both of our places there were at least a thousand acres of woodland and a small river. We could not have chosen a better place to have our weekend hideout. We never bothered to find the owners of that wooded acreage since it was open for us to ride and to picnic down on the river. It was just a beautiful place to be.

After a ride that lasted much longer than we had planned, we were hungry and decided to have a cookout at the cottage. Dixie and I had left little in the cottage, but Steve had been using it for the past year so it was well stocked on all the essential items. There was gas for the grill and sauces in the refrigerator. Salad makings were there but no steaks. Steve and Virginia volunteered to run into town for those while Dixie and I built an outside fire. We used to build a fire outside in the summer months and keep it flaming up to ward off bugs. We also liked to sit on stools made for this purpose and tell tall tales or just reminisce about the good old days. Of course, we were in the very best of good old days that started the day I found Dixie again.

By the time Steve and Virginia returned, we had the grill hot, salads made, and a roaring fire just a short piece from the grill. Steve did the honors of grilling since I was out of practice for a long year. We ate the best steaks ever grilled in the state of Tennessee and in the best company in the USA. After they were finished and the plates were washed, in the fire, but not the silverware, we sat back to talk and enjoy the night that was filled with stars and a gentle breeze. I doubt there ever was a happier group of people anywhere this side of Heaven. The subject came up about dreams and I suppose I started that because I am a firm believer that God still communicates with us through that media. As so often happens, each of us had a favorite dream, remembered from years or just days ago. My dreams were many and profound, all about Dixie and her disappearance. This was obvious for me but others had more pleasant dreams. It was time for Dixie to tell us about one she remembered.

There was a very long pause before she spoke. When she did, it was in very low voice, almost a whisper. She said, "I have had recurring dreams about being surrounded by ghostly figures." She could not elaborate on this statement even though we waited in total silence for minutes. I was thinking she was in pain or something because she was leaning back on my shoulder and I could feel the shudders of her body, as if she was very cold.

I became afraid for her so I changed the subject to church functions. I had a funny story to tell that Dixie was familiar with and would get another laugh out of it. A few years back, Dixie and I had invited four young couples from the youth group to come to our farm for a Saturday night wiener roast. I had arranged a large fire to be built between two logs about a quarter mile from the cottage and near the woods. Placing bales of hay around the fire location gave everyone a place to sit in comfort one of the young men, Andy was in on the joke I planned and he brought his pick-up truck to a place near the fire. I also placed mine close to his. With the tail gate open on both trucks, we had the necessary tables for food and drinks. This fire was just on top of a small hill and next to the trail down to the cottage. My truck had a topper over the bed and his did not. To set it up, I had previously made what the old timers called a bull horn. It was just a small nail keg with a heavy string attached to the outside bottom. The string was soaked in heated pine tree resin, and when stretched tight it acted like the string on a bass fiddle. By anchoring the keg to a tree and pulling the string tight, it was possible to make a very loud roaring sound. The pitch was controlled by pulling the string tighter for a higher pitch. When they came, I was wearing a pistol with blanks, and I gave Jimmy a shot gun, also with blanks.

I told them it was precautionary since we had been seeing a very large animal around the farm.

After we had eaten our fill and was sitting around the fire, Andy started the story- telling session by telling of his last hunting trip in the mountains of the Great Smokies. The story goes that they lost one of their dogs to an animal too large to be stopped by the little guns they carried and that they had to run. I told them I had to go down to the cottage for something and left the fire. As soon as I was well out of their sight, I made a detour to where the keg was ready. Andy knew what was about to happen so he placed himself between the fire and the woods. When I pulled the string and gave it a screaming roar, I fired my blanks and Andy fired his. We never expected the following. All four of the girls left the hay seats at the same moment and all four dived over the tail gate and into a pile in my truck. To this day I am amazed there were no broken bones and no bruises to speak of. It did take about two weeks for them to forgive Andy and me.

The next Monday, Steve had to go back to his business, leaving Dixie, Virginia and me to our desires. Virginia wanted to take Dixie to her apartment in the Hay Stack complex and it was evident that I was not wanted. I was not hurt as I might have been but I was scared stiff at the thought of Dixie being out of my sight. I dared not intrude on their time together but nothing could keep me from hanging around the front door. I suppose I had a form of love sickness because I wanted nothing more than to hold on to her hand.

For the rest of our lives together, I drove the car with one hand on her left knee or holding her hand. I could not bear the thought of another separation like before. I never allowed her to grocery shop alone again and never in the shopping mall. I must have appeared jealous but this was not the case at all. I trusted Dixie with my life and I was absolutely certain that she loved me as much as I loved her. It was not jealousy, but it was abject fear. Many of our church friends made jokes about what the kids in Dixie's class called me. I was widely known as Mr. Dixie and I loved it.

As soon as we settled down to near normal living, we decided to build our permanent home on the farm and sell out in Huntsville. Dixie drew the rough plan of the house she wanted and I reluctantly agreed to it. The only thing I did not like was the three floors I would have to navigate Bedrooms all top floor, living rooms and kitchen first floor and my study and living rooms on the lower floor. I wanted it spread all over an acre or more, but, alas, I lost that round. Virginia was in on the decision because Steve decided to build his new home at the same time. Virginia wanted what Dixie had drawn so Steve and I both lost. I already had a good guest cottage and a very nice stable for six horses. Steve had to build all but he had plenty of money to do anything Virginia desired.

First came their cottage which was to be their home when the wedding took place two weeks away. That was a very short time to build a dwelling, but they did not want much of a cottage and they did not want to go elsewhere for a honeymoon. They had everything the heart could desire as it was.

The wedding invitations were sent out at once, setting the date for the first Saturday in June. It was to take place at our church and the reception would follow in the family building on the church grounds. There was room for at least three hundred and Steve planned to have the caterers provide a sit-down dinner for that many, with a 20 percent over run just in case. The caterers were experienced in this business so Steve gave them the go on a complete set up, including flowers for the church and the reception.

Dixie, as the maid of honor, and Virginia had a ball choosing dresses for themselves and the six bridesmaids. There was no mother to worry about so it was fairly simple to arrange, and they got to it with great anticipation and sisterly fun. Steve worked very hard at the office in order to be free for a week or two after the wedding. I had my hands full in caring for the horses and supervising the building of their cottage. The cottage just had to be completed on time and nothing would be allowed to go slack. Because it was to be their permanent guest house, it had to be right even though it would only have a master bedroom and one small room that could serve as a child's room for a few days.

The great room would contain a kitchen and dining area in one end and the other open end would serve as the living and TV room. The bath would be modest but would have a tub as well as a shower. All of this was left up to me to see that it was done right and on time. It had to be finished, in time for me to have the plumbers finish and the appliances installed.

It would, in fact, be a complete home except on the frugal side.

The builders did a wonderful job, in part, because there were to be two new homes built following this. They expected to get the job of doing those, so it made good sense to do an impressive job. Dixie and Virginia made the choice of the refrigerator and washer/dryer. They also bought all of the furniture and set the delivery for the Friday before the wedding. Linens were bought and taken to our house because Virginia would be giving up her apartment as soon as possible. She had very little in the way of personal articles in the apartment except mounds of clothes. The place had been rented, fully furnished so there was not much to move. Until their house was built on the farm, Virginia would be moving to Steve's apartment. It might be crowded but neither of them planned to be at home that much so it made little difference.

The Saturday morning of the wedding came all too soon. Even though all seemed to be going well, we were all nervous wrecks. The wedding was set for four p.m. and dinner at five. Dixie and I were almost too busy and Virginia was no help at all. The caterers did give us a lot of help and suggestions so all went well in spite of our nervousness.

Our minister stayed out of the way until thirty minutes before the ceremony because there was nothing he could add. Friday afternoon the minister had all of us in for a rehearsal and it seemed to go very smooth so he was confident of a near perfect wedding. And so it was!

The number of attendees was amazing. Some of my customers and Steve's showed up from distant places. It was a good thing Steve ordered a twenty percent over run because there were over three hundred there.

Our church grounds did not have the parking space for that many cars but we did have permission to use the hay field adjoining our parking lot. Fortunately, there was no rain so we had no mud to contend with. Dinner was more than we expected and it was served to the table hot. Our family center had a wonderful kitchen, complete with warming ovens and everything commercial grade for a large restaurant. Before I lost Dixie, I served as one of the cooks, and it was a pleasure to prepare meals for our congregation. We did not have a walk-in freezer but we had every- thing else, including a commercial grill and double ovens large enough to bake bread for two hundred at a time.

Earlier Friday morning, Dixie and I had used one of the young men from the church to move the last of the things Virginia wanted from her apartment to the cottage. We also stocked the refrigerator, and, as many as we could remember, we put spices in the cabinets. Coffee, sugar and salt as well as a dozen other items and still I knew we would have missed something important. Silverware, china and cooking utensils had been purchased by Virginia and Dixie the past week. It was a matter of placing them where we thought Virginia would like them. What a pleasure it was to have the money to buy everything needed, nothing like when we started our marriage. The young man with us helped me set up the bed and helped Dixie place the linens on it while I set up the TV and music system. We had to start early and work right up to the time of the church rehearsal.

During the ceremony, I did something so strange that people asked me about it later.

I cried! Big tears rolled down my face and I could not help it . The memory of my meager wedding for Dixie and the remembrance of the many times she had said she wished we had waited for her church wedding, was all too much for me. My love for her was such that I could not help but look at her during the wedding and think that it was for us the minister was speaking. I had lost her for a year and this served to make me even more regretful and yes, love her even more.

The gowns of the ladies were in a very light blue and Virginia carried a bouquet of light red roses. The blue of the tuxedos worn by the groomsmen were of the same shade, and, in the lapel, there was the same pale red rose. I don't think I have ever seen such a wonderful combination of colors and happier people than I saw that Saturday afternoon.

Virginia and Steve were a loving couple and for them, my heart was filled with joy. Both of them had been served a short stick in their first marriage-- Steve by her early death and Virginia by having chosen a brute, a dangerous bully. No two people I ever knew deserved a new chance as much as these two did. In a way, I have a second chance, that is to show my Dixie even more love if that's possible.

Following the wonderful dinner, Steve and Virginia spent very little time mingling with the guests. Before we were aware of it, they were gone. Because I was responsible for the church building, I had to be the last to leave. Dixie and I were almost too tired to do our job well but we did.

It was just before midnight when I locked the door, and, even though the parking lot was well lighted, I had a creepy feeling. I might add that for several years, I had carried a hand gun concealed on my person or in my car. This seemed to be necessary when I first started my business for I had to carry large sums of money and be on the road for a week with it. I had the states of Alabama, Mississippi, and Georgia to travel in and some parts of those states were less than law abiding. I had stopped keeping it with me when I was searching for Dixie for fear that I would use it on myself. This creepy feeling made me realize that I did not have it with me and that I should not be without it from now on. My fear was in part due to many drug users and the other was that so many nights I had been on the road late at night in places where it was definitely not safe. Now I had a new fear to contend with.

Since the decision had been made to build our new home on the Tennessee farm, I decided that we, Steve and I, would need a wood shop and a place to loaf. His hobby like mine, was in radio communications and a small room in the building would serve as the electronics lab. My desire went far beyond this for since Dixie's dad had taught me to love working in wood, I had a desire for the best shop money could buy. I also understood that the wood shop would be very helpful when we started on the two new homes we wanted to start right away. As soon as the wedding was over, I contacted a supplier of metal buildings and purchased a steel building, fifty by thirty feet in size. The concrete slab for this building was to be poured this next Monday. In addition to the slab for the building, I was having an additional slab poured for outside work. It was a continuation of the main building slab and was to extend another twenty feet. I had in mind to do spray painting of my finished furniture outside on nice, clear days and to store some rough lumber under a shed roof over this slab. It was a very busy time for me, and Dixie stayed at the cottage where she liked to read. She was also running back and forth to check progress and to bring me another coffee in the mornings and cold drinks in the afternoon. I might also add that while Steve and Virginia were having a quiet honeymoon at their cottage, we were not wasting the time in ours.

Thursday evening was to be a dinner for the four of us. Dixie had not asked them to come yet but she planned to do so in the late afternoon. It was to be the first contact with them since the wedding and Dixie decided they must be hungry by now. She was doing well with that plan until she found she was out of a necessary article for dinner and had to make a run to the store in town, about ten miles away. She asked if I would mind her picking up Virginia and going to town without me along. I was so very busy and also beginning to feel secure in being out in the country where we saw only the people working for us, so I gave my OK.

Dixie drove to the cottage for Virginia and found them to be gone, probably for a walk in the woods behind our properties. Thinking there was no reason to drop the trip to the store and having nothing to fear, she decided to continue alone. At the super market, she parked near the front door since it was not too busy today. She took only about ten minutes to make her purchase and returned to the car. Seeing no one close to her Buick, she clicked the electronic entry button and all doors unlatched . On entering the car, she was in the process of fastening the seat belt when the passenger door opened and a strange man jumped in with a gun in his hand. He had been hiding on the off side of the car where Dixie and no one else saw him until it was too late.

Well, bitch, thought you could get away from Jimmy Hobbs didya?"

Dixie knew at once that Jimmy had mistaken her for Virginia and probably did not know there were twins. She quickly came to the decision to bluff it out with the lie she was glad to see him. She followed with the statement that she had been kidnapped and only this morning had been able to get free of that man. Keeping her wits about her was one of the most difficult things she ever had to do, but she managed. Jimmy ordered her to drive toward Nashville, which was over an hour away, leaving Dixie time to think of a plan to defeat Jimmy and get away.

Virginia and Steve had walked to the woods and continued until they were back of the construction site. They were walking toward me when I realized Dixie should have been back and that Virginia was not with her. I think I might have passed out for a few seconds for I fell to the ground on my knees and remained there until Steve picked me up. I could not talk and tears were already streaming down my face. I could not talk to Steve and Virginia but they heard me in a prayer to God, "Please don't put me through this terrible burden again. Please let Dixie come home now." Then they knew Dixie was gone again.

Dixie did not know all of the particulars of Virginia's escape from Jimmy but she did know most of the details. Virginia had not talked much about it but she had most of the story from me and my first-hand experience. Because she was so familiar with the escape, she had to fabricate a reason for working at the clothing store where I found Virginia. They were now on I65 heading north and approaching Franklin, TN, exit and something had to happen in Nashville or the chance to get away from him may not come for a very long time. Dixie had convinced him she was anxious to return to Seattle and had enough money to pay for gasoline but not enough for food and motel bills. Jimmy wanted to know how she had managed to get such fine clothes and have a nearly new Buick. She told him she had been a prisoner of a wealthy member of the crime family in Huntsville and they were so loose with money it was easy for her to steal. She explained the car as being one given to her by her captor but never allowed to use it without one of the women loyal to her captor being with her. Today she had been able to slip away but had no idea where she could go. She told him that the man's name was Steve and he was near the top in the crime family. She said it would be difficult to get lost from him and that Jimmy's life would be in danger from this day forward as was hers. Jimmy started bragging about his ability to kill anyone that came after him, so Dixie played it up as to how smart Jimmy was. She told him that if he applied himself to the kind of crimes she had learned about while with Steve, they could be rich. Jimmy relaxed some while thinking over this new proposal.

This gave Dixie the chance to unlatch her safety belt without Jimmy knowing it was loose. He did not know the city and that there was a bypass around town and by now Jimmy had almost become convinced that she really did want to return to Seattle. Dixie did not take the bypass exit but continued through the middle of town She hoped to get in a lane of slower traffic for just a short time and,. if not, make a mistake and be on an exit ramp. They were now beginning to see evening traffic pick up and some slower lanes. Also Dixie knew where there were exit lanes that were "must exit" and she was trying to maneuver into one of these without Jimmy being aware. When she did manage to get on one right in the heart of Nashville, she took the exit at too high a rate of speed. Just as she was clear of the main road, she made one fluid motion of releasing the seat belt, opening the door and threw herself out. She hit the pavement at over thirty miles per hour and rolled off into the grassy area at the side of the road. The Buick continued and caught Jimmy by surprise so that he never got his belt loose til just before the crash.

The end result was a crash into the concrete curb at the end of that exit and Jimmy did not have a seat belt to save him. He was unconscious when the police arrived, and Dixie was also unconscious but reasonably unhurt. She had lots of bruises and minor cuts but was too groggy to tell the police anything other than that she jumped to get away from him. Both of them were taken to the hospital but, for some reason, the ambulances were of different companies, so they ended up in different hospitals.

Five hours had passed before Dixie would be able to phone us to let us know what happened. Neither of us was near the phone so we did not get the message. My heart was acting funny and I was too dizzy to stand alone. Steve and Virginia had taken me to the local hospital where I was given a sedative and they had notified the state police with a description of the Buick and Dixie.

It took only a short time after Dixie was able to talk intelligently before the state police in Nashville notified the police where we were. Needless to say, I needed no further hospital treatment. I needed to be on the way to Nashville with Steve driving as fast as he could without being arrested for undue speed and possibly endangering our lives. Meantime, Jimmy was not detained since Dixie had not been able to give them the full story. By the time the police did get to it, Jimmy had managed to get up and away. Now I understood the uneasy feeling I had in the church lot a few days back. Jimmy had been there and had no doubt traced Virginia to me since my description and my name would have been on the hotel register in Settle. He would believe me to be the man Dixie referred to as Steve as he now knew she was telling one monster lie. Not only did he feel foolish for falling for it, he now felt murderous toward me and Virginia. We would have to be exceptionally alert until Jimmy was caught and we hoped that would be soon. There was an all points bulletin out for his arrest on the charge of kidnapping and attempted murder. He was assumed to be armed and dangerous so we believed he would be caught before he could leave Nashville.

Several days passed and Jimmy was still on the run. We had been extremely watchful, both Steve and I had made electronic alarm systems that would let us know if anyone approached the cottages during the night hours. The system worked very well and set off the alarm inside the cottage but was silent outside. I believe Steve thought as I did, that we did not wish to catch Jimmy but that we wished to kill him. We had notified the state police of the alarm system and told them it was not necessary to have the sheriff's

department to patrol our road at night. They had thought that thier driving by every hour or so would deter Jimmy but we knew better. The only trouble with the alarm system was deer. They usually roamed the grounds at night and this caused us to be up and watchful many times during the night. Both of us had purchased night vision glasses but, due to the enormous expense, had bought less than was needed. We could usually spot a deer if it was less than thirty yards away and we knew if we saw deer at all, that would mean that no human was close. It was when we did not see anything, that we went on high alert.

We had been on alert for a week before we got a clear view of a man outside at night. It could have been a night hunter but we had to be very certain of the identity of anyone before taking any kind of action. At this time, neither of us had a sure and certain plan. It was to be "action as needed" at the time. Any-thing to protect our wives and our homes and one of the things we feared was that Jimmy would encircle our cottage with gasoline and set it off, burning us to death. We also feared explosives since Jimmy had served in the marines and would be very familiar with ways to obtain the right kind and amount of explosives to destroy us and our cottage . Because of the threat of this kind of violence, we lost much of our sleep at night. We hoped Dixie and Virginia were able to sleep through it all and give us nap time during the day.

While all this stress was bearing down on us, we were talking to the builders and both of us had signed contracts for new homes. I was stuck with Dixie's tri-story house but Steve had managed to have his way for a sprawling one-floor plan. Virginia was not difficult to please since she had never had a home, nothing more than rented flats or apartments. It was a joy to me to see her delight in what was under construction for her.

Of course, Dixie was just as delighted since this was a house of her design and she was rightfully proud of it. I photographed construction of both houses every day, and from time to time, Dixie would get involved with minor changes. One of those was a laundry chute from the third level to the basement that she had overlooked in the original drawings. Of course I had my hand in it also because I wanted a secret room underground for the safe keeping of my gun collection. I had them do all except make the passage way from the basement to that underground room. Much later, I hired two men I could trust to help me open up the connecting passage way. I did not need help in constructing the secret door but needless to say, it had to be secret and yet easy to get open. I solved this problem by using powerful magnetic latches that I could slide a metal shield between the magnets and the latch. It worked as planned and I later made it our safe room for items that needed to be protected from fire.

A month passed and our homes were nearing the finished mark. Steve and I were very busy installing our own security systems in those houses, and we spared no expense to get the best. We understood that Jimmy would always be a severe threat and in case we moved into the new homes and he was still at large, we needed to be certain he could not get to us.

Early one Sunday morning after we had been out to a party that lasted until one a.m; we were tired and not too watchful on arriving home. We were still living in the cottage and it was well locked so we had no fear of returning at this time in the morning. We went in and turned on the lights and the security system. I took one long look at the exterior grounds and saw nothing moving. The electronic alarm was silent, so we prepared for bed . Just as we fell into the bed, the alarm went off and at the same time the front door gave way to a loud crash. Jimmy had been just outside and just around the corner where the alarm did not pick him up until he started for the front door. This gave me just a few seconds to pick up my .45 from the night stand. As he was a silhouette in the open front door, I fired six quick rounds into his chest.

Steve heard the shots and called 911 before he jumped in his car for a quick trip to our cottage. When he arrived, the flood lights had our place lit up like a Friday night ball game. I was still standing in the door with my .45 in my hand and Jimmy was twenty feet out from my front door. Of course, he was dead and would have been dead after the first shot. Five more were totally unnecessary. We could hear the sheriff's patrol car siren coming from a mile away, and, as I stood there, I could feel nothing except satisfaction. I was still standing just outside the front door when the two deputies came up to me and took my .45 from my hand. I told them what had happened but both of them felt too important to listen. They decided right then and there that I had shot Jimmy outside and that he was not armed. Even though there was a small gun on the ground beside the body, one of them picked it up and asked if I had thrown it on the ground. Steve had to admit he had just arrived and that he did not see the shooting. It made no difference to the two deputies when we told them Jimmy was wanted for attempted murder. I believe they were too filled with their importance to see or hear anything. They just loaded me into the back seat and delivered me to the county jail. In spite of all Steve and the two women had to say, I was off to the cell for the rest of the night.

Keep in mind that we were Alabama residents and property owners in Tennessee. To the deputies, we were to be treated as criminals to let the court decide tomorrow. We tried to get the deputies to call their sheriff but they refused to do so since it was about two thirty in the morning. It would have to wait till Monday when he arrived for a new day. Steve could not get an attorney and there was no way for bail to be set, so I had to spend the rest of the night in a holding cell. I was still wearing only my shorts, and I was so very cold. The cell already had a drunk sleeping on the only bench with the only blanket there. I asked for a blanket but was ignored. I fairly screamed at them for something to cover myself with but they gave me no blanket. Instead, they threw me a piece of black plastic and it was colder to touch my body than nothing at all. I sat in the corner the rest of the night with my back to concrete blocks until someone arrived to take me out for a hearing. I was taken into a small room where Steve and two other men sat. Steve handed me a wool army surplus blanket and told me the two men were a bail bondsman and a preliminary hearing judge. I answered his questions and Steve verified everything. The deputies were no where to be found and I now believe the sheriff sent them off to be clear of this hearing.

The hearing judge took very little time to ask questions before he set bail at one hundred thousand. Steve said he would put up the money or property instead of paying a bondsman. This meant I had to wait until the courthouse clerk could verify Steve's property had no lien and the value was such as to cover the bond. As we were leaving, we had to stop at the front desk where we were told I would be notified of the trial date. We went home so I could get clothes, then returned to the sheriffs office for information. He would not see us and we were unable to find the person or persons that investigated the so- called murder. It seemed very odd that one man at seven a.m. could set bail without going over the circumstances of what happened. Of course, this meant I had to obtain the services of a local lawyer. Nothing made sense but the lawyer told us it was all a formality and the charges would be dropped after the investigation. To this day, we never heard anything from an investigator or the sheriffs department. The court notified me of a trial date and time which was almost two months out. My attorney said again, forget it, the charges will be dropped but they were not and I went before a jury of my peers.

The day of the trial, the charge was read as murder in the first degree and the prosecutor made the opening statement that I had shot Jimmy six times and that I had rigged my home in order to catch him before he could get away. As he spelled it out, I did look guilty because he never allowed for the broken door or the pistol on the ground. My attorney then told the jury about Jimmy's stalking us and about his being wanted for kidnapping Dixie just a short time back. All of this seemed funny to the people in the court room since my attorney played it up as a comedy and everything the prosecutor had said was refuted . This trial lasted most of the day, and, to make a long story short, the charges were dismissed. In the early afternoon, the prosecuting attorney announced to the judge that he refused to prosecute me on the charges laid out and then he asked to be dismissed. This was the only way he could get off the hook of losing a trial, so now we know what the sheriff was saying when he said the charges would be dismissed. It appeared to Steve and me that the entire thing was rigged in order to take us for all the money they could shake us down for. Even before the trial started, my attorney, who was local, told me it would be dismissed and he would only charge me the price we had earlier agreed on. As the trial ended, my attorney said, "I am afraid I will have to have an extra thousand since this went on longer than I expected." To us, that was proof of a crooked legal system out to take us for a ride, but there was nothing we could do about it.

As the weeks passed, we found so much pleasure in our new homes and our horses that the memory of Jimmy slowly died. Dixie was having a wonderful time in teaching

Virginia all the things she had never had access to. The girls were having a ball decorating our homes and both chipped in to help each other. Steve and I were left to our wood shop and I had the pleasure of teaching him how to build furniture of the early American variety. Dixie spent many weeks teaching Virginia many things she never had the opportunity to learn. They became twins in more than the usual way and it appeared they became one. Steve and I had developed a friendship such as if we were more than brothers, so, when we decided we needed more tools and shop space, we had the time and the money. We increased our shop and bought the best tools on the market. Steve sold his business and we became well known for our fine cherry furniture We had a dream shop and it was made perfect by two lovely women keeping us supplied with coffee, iced tea and far more food that we needed. They also had a very long list of furniture we were to build for them.

Love continues to increase in intensity even after Dixie, my love, left for her place in Heaven. Even though I have lost Dixie, I still have Steve and Virginia and may God allow me a few more years to enjoy them.

And that, my friend is the mystery of love. It never ends.

Bernie McMellon

The Old Man

Once upon a time, not many years ago, a real tragedy came into my life, that left me totally destitute. It looked as if I might have to find a place under the nearest bridge to lay my head. Having spent my life with everything I needed and wanted up to the age of seventy-nine, life was perfect. And then to be cast aside as a broken old man, I leave it to you to decide the terror, the fear, the hopelessness, and the desire to die. I need not tell you that I had the feeling of JOB, the bible character who lost everything except his life.

He was my brother in the sense that I lost everything except loyal friends that came to support me through eighteen months of court trials.

The start of this was the loss of my wife, in death, and my children's greed, followed quickly by the loss of my home and my life's savings. I did not have enough left to travel several states away to move in with a widowed sister. The support my sisters and the members of my church family gave me was all that held my life together for the following three years. Death was my only desire for most of that time, and only my faith in God and the knowledge that suicide was forbidden held me at bay.

It was at this time that I remembered the many weeks I found an old man sitting in the sun on the courthouse lawn. I used to go there on city and county bid openings in order to see that my bid was entered and to keep the bidding straight.

On these days, I went early and sat with him, just to be certain that I would not be delayed and miss the opening. I must admit that I went as early as possible for I wanted to hear more of his story. I well remember a time when he was telling me about the last few days his wife lived. I could not help but shed a tear with him. Perhaps I did not fully understand the loss of a wife then, but I do now. I stood by the side of a hospital bed and held the hand of my loving wife while she struggled for just one more breath. Perhaps others would have words to describe this kind of grief, but I don't.

THE OLD MAN

I was curious to know why he sat so still,
controlling his sobs with an effort of will.
With age on his shoulders and hands all a tremble,
fingers all knobby and no longer nimble.

I watched until certain he needed a friend.
Perhaps I could help with something to lend.
I spoke with concern to the ancient old man,
offering with love, my outstretched hand.

He looked at me grateful and with some surprise.
He saw my concern through his faded blue eyes.
I listened with love to what he would say
as he spoke of friends, long since passed away.

The story he told has made my heart sad
as neither family or friend the old man had.
He was lonely and tired of living his life
for his days had been filled with worry and strife.

And now, he informed me it was time to die.
No one to grieve him, no one to cry.
His worldly processions he would soon leave behind,
farm lands and buildings of numerous kind.

So now he has moved to that promised land,
after passing some wealth into my hand.
But of gold and silver, I would pay no heed,
if I could no longer help a friend in need.

This old man, Mr. Stearns, as I knew him then, had struggled for well over sixty years in order to secure his future and his last years. I did not realize at that time how closely I would fit the mold of this poem. My work had taken me all over the world and caused me to spend many weeks away from my family. Then, I felt it necessary in order to secure a good living for my wife and children, as well as to provide for our latter years.

I had great pity for this old man and his kind. I still do today and in a way have joined his ranks. He has passed on to eternal rest and the courts have taken control of his wealth. Money did him little good when it came down to those last hours.

Thanks to courts and lawyers, my home and my worldly possessions, down to my clothing and an old farm truck were sold at public auction. After the sale, the money grabbers disposed of everything I had struggled for except about ten percent that I had to fight for. I thank God for my Christian friends and siblings.

Just to obtain the services of an attorney required an upfront payment of five thousand dollars which was so far out of my reach that I had given up. My sisters who were not well off at all, managed to raise the money and wired it to the attorney. From the first day, it seemed like a lost cause for even my attorney could not believe there was so much greed in one small family. He took my case only because he was willing to work for me as long as I kept him paid in advance. This meant five to ten thousand dollars every so often-- money that I had no idea where it would come from.

About 1970, I shared a campsite with four other men. One of them came from the same small town I lived in at that time and where this incident took place. Perhaps four blocks from where we lived, a retired couple had it made to the point that they could close their
home for a summer in Europe. This man had it all, including a wood shop that was the envy of every man in that town. He was well known for his generosity and willingness to build furniture pieces for the needy and he never built pieces for sale.

His shop was a large concrete block building with the back side facing an alleyway. There was only one window in that building and it was small, about six feet above the alley and just large enough for light when entering the building from the front. During their summer in Europe, two boys in their early teens, I believe they were both thirteen, chose to use a ladder and enter that rear window. While in that forbidden shop, one of them lost an arm. On returning from Europe, the couple learned a suit was against them for having "An Attractive Nuisance" in a residential neighborhood. Never mind that it had been there for twenty years. Never mind that it was built there in such a way as to keep noise in and boys out. Lawyers being quick to see the possibility of stripping a friend of his life's savings by ambulance chasing got on this one fast.

Several months and many thousands in attorney fees later, this aged and broken couple left town with their total wealth packed in the back of their car. I was left with my old farm truck containing my clothing piled in back. Since my time in hell on earth, I have had only one thought to hold on to and that is "GOD will getum".   More recently, I have heard of several unlucky people who have faced destruction by the hand of fate and ambulance chasers. It is my opinion that the destruction of this nation will come about through greed, primarily by our elected officials who are almost, if not all---lawyers.

I need not go into details but it is enough to say that my children decided that I had so much money that I should share it while they were young. My son made the statement that if they did not take it from me that I would just get married again and leave them nothing. There had to be about a dozen lawyers in our county who would jump at the chance to get into a pile of money like this. Of course, there was no shortage of outstretched hands. Just as a point of reference, the court closed the transaction by the judge awarding his secretary a sum of thirty- seven thousand five hundred dollars. I never got an accurate accounting of where it all went, but you may guess that the system got the greater percentage by far.

Now, almost six years later, I have been blessed just as the Bible character JOB was. I have the love of my siblings and my church family. I am secure in my little home and have no need for anything material, and, if I did, I could manage. Most importantly, my health has improved dramatically. It is a mystery to me how God has blessed me and replaced my broken heart with peace of mind and the love of people I never really knew. Just as I have forgiven others for their actions against me, God has forgiven me for my many sins and failures. After six years of being five hundred miles from where my home was and my children still are, neither of them have bothered to check on my health or welfare. I have only one prayer which is that they will see the error of their waysbefore their time to face God and eternity.

What more can I say or do except remember those that are aged and hurting.

It is noteworthy that many I have helped in years past did come forward in my time of need. Today, I have friends all over this country, some that I thought had totally forgotten me. Then I underestimated the power of God because I thought he had forgotten me also.

The Old Man I wrote about was Henry Aaron Stearns and as I got to know him over the next few weeks, I learned he had inherited about five hundred acres in Pennsylvania that turned out to have a good oil deposit. As a young man, he had no money to do much with the land but he did have the desire to work and save for the day he would. His first job as a helper in a machine shop that specialized in well drilling equipment was in 1900 when he was fourteen. Oil was discovered in Pennsylvania in 1859 but it took some time for the real value of this discovery to be widely used. The job he was given there was to work in the wood shop to form spokes for massive wheels used in the drill rigs. These wheels were much like wagon wheels, exception being they were sometimes as large as ten feet in diameter.

Henry was assigned to forming the spokes since he was a strong, young man and could handle the large timbers these were cut from. During his time there, he learned all he could from helping wherever it looked as if he might be useful. As a good worker, he became familiar with the entire operation of making drilling rigs. Four years as an apprentice and Henry was ready with savings and knowledge to start a new shop. He chose a town where new oil fields were and drilling was building a need for new rigs.

In 1912, at the age of twenty six, Henry was successful and a much sought after bachelor by several young ladies in his church family. Henry was very faithful in serving God and had little time for courtship, but the day came when he did make a selection of the most desirable lady in his church congregation. Not one to delay progress, he took Lucille Adams in marriage and, at the same time, began the construction of their new home on his five hundred acres. Lucy was the daughter of Joseph Adams of Adams Mercantile and Feed Store. Henry did not consider this at the time of choosing Lucy but it did work out to their advantage.

Not long after Henry had built the fifth drill rig for other men, he started work on his own. It was to be quite different from the normal and would incorporate many advancements that he had learned of but could never sell to an established drilling operator. Their theory was that the old way worked so why tamper with a known design.

His new design worked so much better that Henry decided to use it on his five hundred acres even though to date, no drilling had been done in this area. He was told he needed the opinion of a trained geologist and, that without one, he would never find oil.

Still, Henry had the best geologist the world has ever know or would ever know. He had God and prayer on his side. After he drilled to the usual depth and finding nothing, other drillers were telling him to quit while he was still ahead. They did not know of the improvements Henry had incorporated into his rig, so they did not know he could go down another five hundred feet without strain on rig or budget.

Now that their house was finished and Lucy had made it into a home, Henry delighted in returning to a good evening meal and a cheerful wife at the close of the work day. Many drillers were working by moonlight or fires built some distant from the rig, but Henry had complete trust in God and had no need to work around the clock.. He certainly knew the danger of a fire even though it might be some distance from the rig. He had seen other places go up in flame from the drill bit striking a gas pocket. So much gas in such a short time resulted in an explosion that would kill the operators and burn the rig. He had no desire for that kind of a loss.

Late Monday afternoon, the drill rig was shaken with what seemed to be an earthquake. Henry and his man had no time to run before a stream of sweet oil shot up toward the heavens, far above the height of his rig. Preparations for just such a geyser of oil had been made and Henry quickly took the necessary steps to control the flow. It was now evident that Henry was rich from two directions. He had discovered a way to drill deeper and had found the layer of oil called "Sweet Oil".

Before the day was out, Henry had orders for several drill rigs of his new design and he had to turn most of them away. He now had the need for his shop to become a factory and to produce more rigs than one at the time.

That April evening in 1914 when he arrived home, Lucy greeted him with more good news, at least she thought so. Henry thought otherwise but only because he was too busy to contend with a new baby in a new home and a new factory starting immediately. Henry hardly had time to sleep with all of the design problems of a new factory running through his head. He did not recognize how helpful Lucy was to him, soothing his nerves, feeding him the best and keeping his books and records straight. He just did not know the hours she contributed toward his success. now, Lucy had given him two sons and, also by this time, the stock market had reached an all-time high. Everyone was becoming rich, on paper--buying stocks in everything under the sun, including oil wells and speculated oil fields that had never been drilled. The world was being set up for a mighty crash. It was Lucy who saw the madness and gave Henry a solemn warning to solidify their holdings.

Black Thursday came on October 24, 1929, which started the downhill slide of the market and the economy. More than 8.5 billion dollars was out on loan to investors.

By the following Monday morning, which is remembered as Black Monday, investors in droves were trying to cash out and banks were swamped and some were closing as soon as the crowd arrived. Black Tuesday followed next day with the announcement by President Herbert Hoover that he would veto the Hawley-Smoot tariff bill which might have helped for a time. That same day, 16 million shares were traded with a record loss of 14 billion dollars. That week alone saw a net loss of 30 billion dollars, more than ten times the annual budget of the USA and more than the total cost of World War One.

Through it all, Henry sat back with great concern, but having made Lucy and his business safe, he was free to buy when the bottom was reached. He accumulated far more wealth than he could ever spend so he invested in larger factories and more land. It was about this same time that Henry Ford was in the picture of contributing to the success and fortune of the Sterns' family. Oil was the lubricant of the future of America.

There would never be another product from the earth that rocketed this world into such prosperity.

By the urging of their mother, both boys made great progress in their studies The first born was named after his father, Henry Aaron Sterns II and completed his education at Harvard Law 1n the spring of 1933. From that day forth, he worked with his father in causing their many endeavors to succeed. The second son, Peter Michael followed Hank Stearns in graduating in the spring of 1935. He also joined the Stearns Empire and their fortunes grew along with the recovery from the 1929 crash and into the rush toward World War Two.

Henry Stearns had made his fortune from the land and its resources, so it was a natural for him to invest in more land in Pennsylvania as well as the state of West Virginia.

Oil and gas had been discovered as well as millions of acres of timber and untold numbers of coal seams protruding from the sides of mountains. The Stearns Empire had to place their profits somewhere and this seemed to be the ideal place for their investments.

In 1938, the name of Adolph Hitler made the evening news more and more frequently.

President Herbert Hoover lost the bid for re-election to the president's chair and the new president, Franklin D. Roosevelt very quietly made preparations to face the coming war.

One of his first actions was to create the CCC or Civilian Conservation Corp where all eligible men could join what looked like a workers' army. This served the obvious need for money to starving families and at the same time prepared these men for what many saw coming as a war with Germany. There was a great need for educated men to set up this Corp and to see that it was well trained in work as well as regimented action, when the need did arrive.

Hank Stearns II was sent for by Henry L. Stimson, Secretary of War under President Roosevelt. Of course he went immediately to Washington for the meeting that would change all of their lives. Secretary Stimson came to the point without hesitation, "He said Our country needs you" This left Hank Stearns little choice, so he became a member of the United States Armed Forces and was placed in charge of building the CCC into a regulated body, not yet called an army.

December 7, 1941, was a day our President would regard as a day of infamy. We were at war with Japan, and, before the smoke cleared, Adolph Hitler declared war on the United States. That week was when Hank Stearns realized his duty and devoted himself to the destruction of Japan and Germany. That week was also the same one that his younger brother, Peter Michael, "Pete" enlisted as a major in the US Army. Lucy Stearns was broken hearted at the loss of her two sons from their home. Neither had married, in part because they were, like their father, too busy to seek a bride.

The war years wore hard on both parents as news mostly came to them from radio broadcasts. Neither son could write much about where they were or what they were doing. Both were in very important locations, both near the front. Hank, being the senior officer in that part of France where both were assigned, could and did arrange for a jeep to take him to see his little brother during a time when both could be free of duty for a 24-hour period. Hank had relieved his driver for this trip since he felt it was not the duty of an enlisted man to go with him for his personal reason. That reason was to get Pete away from the battle for a day since he understood the strain his brother was under. Hank had no trouble locating Pete and removing him from duty for the few hours it would take to travel to a stable area of France for a good dinner. He chose Lourdes, a small town the Germans had by-passed, and this left the town almost as it was before the war. This town had a small restaurant that Hank had heard about and considered safe where the two of them could relax, at least for an evening.

Unfortunately, the town did have a deserted German soldier that had come to regret his desertion and wanted to go home, via his regular outfit some miles away. As soon as he saw two high ranking US military officers enter the town, he formed a plan. If he could claim the life of both of them and returning to his commanding officer with evidence, he would not only be welcomed back but would receive the prestigious Iron Cross award.

During his time in the town, he had made friends under the pretext of hate toward the Third Reich and all German army aggression. He had even found enough friends to allow him to gather stolen explosives for the day when he would use them against his own countrymen. Under cover of darkness that evening and while Hank and Pete were enjoying the last of their wine, this soldier used the explosives to mine the jeep so both would be in it at the time of the detonation.

The town's people were so afraid of retaliation by the US troops that they made no report of the visit of the two men. They did very quickly dispatch of the German traitor by hanging him the very same night. Both Americans were buried in a common grave and the wreck of the jeep was towed to town's edge and left. Many days passed before the Army discovered the jeep and traced it to General Stearns. It was now only a matter of asking before the entire story came out. Both bodies were removed and sent home for placement in the Arlington National cemetery where their parents were presented with the Medal of Honor to each of their sons.

Lucy's health began to deteriorate the moment she first received word of their being missing in action. Henry became more attentive to her needs and began to turn his business over to those he trusted. It seemed that he could do nothing to ease Lucy's worry and pain. So far, she had not spoken of her pain and Henry thought it was only the boys she was worried about.

Just two weeks later, official word came that both had been killed in action. No details were given and there was no mention that they were together at the time. This was the point of no return for Lucy. She lost the will to live and nothing Henry could do or say nothing that would alter her diminishing health.

Eighty seven days after her boys were placed in the Arlington National Cemetery, Lucy went to bed for the last time. I don't have to imagine the agony Henry suffered for I know first-hand and I believe it is the very worst time in the life of any human. Lucy did not want to live so it was a very short time before she also was placed in her final resting place. Henry spent very little time in his business from then on. There was no reason so far as he could see, so the board of directors took control and Henry took to the courthouse lawn. He never explained to me why he chose this particular seat and at this location, but for the next two years, when I was back in town, I would stop for an hour with Henry. He was there even when the cold and snow was too much for me. It was most as if he wished the cold would kill him. The last time I saw him, he did have a very bad cough, and even though I urged him to seek medical treatment, he refused.

Even today, many years later, I still drive by there for just one more look and one more regret that I could not do more for the THE OLD MAN.

The Saucer

Because some of you might tend to consider this a lie, it is well to tell you in the very beginning that I do not *lye*. My friends will tell you that lying is not my forte', I don't do it well. My lifelong buddy, Fred Engle, would tell you this except he has gone to heaven and I can no longer depend on him to verify my veracity. I even had a little trouble with him in deer camp because he sometimes forgot my reputation for truthfulness and would clam up when I asked him for verification. Well, you will just have to believe me that strange things do happen and this could be one of them.

My home is in West Virginia at the base of some small mountains, small as related to the Rockies, but still steep enough that we have some switch-back curves that slow us down to a crawl around those KYA curves. For you uninformed,

KYA means kiss yur own a**. When my children were small, I used to take them across the mountain to be with their grandparents for a day and sometimes two. One day we stayed much too long and it was very late before I could get them loaded and on the way home. My wife had made me promise to have them home by ten, but it was already midnight before we were under way. About five miles from the grandparents' home, I came to the first mountain that had two switch-back curves on the way up. I had slowed to perhaps ten miles per around the last of those curves and just as I got the car straightened out for the long and last climb, there before me was the thing.

My son was in the front with me and still wide awake. He was about six and curious about the animals we usually saw along the roadway at night. This particular night he was standing in the floor with his chin on the dash where he could look out better than sitting. We both saw it at the same instant and he let out a loud "whatisit daddy?" I was dumbfounded and all I could think of to do was shut off the engine and turn out the lights. Now on this road, there is practically no daytime traffic, and, for certain, no night time traffic at all. We were in deep woods with a very narrow road through and since it was over a mountain, the county barely kept up the gravel layer that made it passable during wet weather.

I was scared, seriously afraid of what we saw and what it might do to us on this lonely road in the middle of the night. There it was, suspended over the road about twice as high as the tree tops, moving ever so slowly

374

as to first appear to be still. It moved from my right to my left and was in sight for several minutes. Since we were almost on top of the mountain, we could watch it as it moved away for perhaps a half a mile. The most notable thing about the movement was that it moved up and back down as it passed over higher or lower trees. At the time it was directly in front of us, I had the time to study the length and shape, and I do believe I was a good judge of distance and size. Now that I really have had time to think about it, I realize that I was below it by about two hundred feet and another two hundred feet until I would have been directly below it. his means that I had a forty five degree line of sight, and it would have allowed me to see the shape of a disk object as something more like the shape of a football. Even this could not describe the true shape.

As I first saw it, I thought it looked something like a short and fat cigar, perhaps ninety feet in length. I used this guess as to the width of the roadway being about thirty feet wide at this point. I did go back later and measured the road width which also served to make my memory much clearer about the tree line height. It did appear to be three times the width of the road, and from, this assessment, I guessed the height to be about fifteen feet. As for lights, I have trouble trying to describe something that I have no earthly thing to compare it to. The best I can do is to say that it appeared to have a ring around the lower edge that looked much like blue lights covered in a thick layer of fog. This ring seemed to pulse at near the same rate as my heart beat and that was very rapid that night

All the time this was in sight, my son was speechless and that is something very out of character for him. Of course I was totally silent and I believe it was fear of that thing hearing me and perhaps coming back for me and my children. It had been reported in upper West Virginia that people had been abducted by space vehicles and I did not like the idea at all. Others had reported the loss of electrical systems in their cars at the time of sightings and I can't vouch for that since I had turned my engine off out of fear. I believe we sat there for a full half hour after it was out of sight; again it was fear. I have told very few of this sighting because some people ridicule the story regardless of the veracity of the teller.

My father –in-law believed me and this is why we made our own UFO.

For several years after the close of WW11 every town worth the name of town had an army surplus store named Mike's Surplus or perhaps Joe's Military Surplus Goods. In my line of work, I traveled over three states and had little to do in the evenings. If Joe had a surplus store near the motel, I did my shopping there because I was a veteran and knew the quality of stuff being sold. I might not need it now but I bought it while it was cheap.

I lived in the country and there was a never ending need for something being sold at these stores.

One evening at Mikes Store in Columbus, Ohio, on north High Street, if I remember correctly, I bought a weather balloon said to be twenty feet in diameter. I really can't say just what I was thinking but it came to me later that it would be perfect for a practical joke. My father-in-law was a railroad telegrapher and station master where he worked the eleven p.m. to seven a.m. shift. He was located where trains had to slow or stop at the intersection of two lines, and, because of this, the railroad supplied his location with lantern batteries by the case. Trainmen and conductors would frequently stop there for new train orders, and while there, they would renew the batteries in their signal lights. There was always an over run of batteries so he brought a dozen home for the joke he was now with me on and very enthusiastic about. Over the next few weeks, I gathered the proper twelve volt bulbs and put together a circuit that would allow twenty four of them to flash on for a period of two seconds and go dark for about twenty seconds. When laid out in a row, the appearance was flashing at random over a string of about eight feet. We were waiting on a very dark time of the moon when the sky would be nearly cloudless before releasing our UFO. For the batteries, we had taped them together for attachment to the neck of the balloon, and just below them, we had a cane fishing pole eight feet long with the lights strung out in a horizontal line. Just after darkness set completely, we took the balloon to a line where he had free gas from a well on his property. Filling the balloon was no problem and, well before it was filled, it was trying to leave the earth. There was a very gentle wind that night and it was blowing in the direction of a small town about eight miles southeast of us. Perfect.

Very proud of our accomplishment, we released the balloon and sat back in lawn chairs to watch it gently climb into the dark night sky, very proud of our accomplishment. I suppose we were at peace for about fifteen minutes when we heard the first siren over on the highway, about a mile from us.Now, most of you know how sound travels at night. It seems to have no interference from heat waves that go up from the earth while colder air is settling back to earth. Well, that worked for us that night for we were very quiet and listening. Sure enough, we caught the sound of the volunteer fire department siren in this small town going full blast. More sirens on the highway a mile from us. Wow, we had created some action and we hoped it would never be traced back to us. Neither of us considered the possibility of injury or damage from that joke, but as we sat there listening to the commotion in the night, we began to wonder if something had gone wrong. All we could do was think, listen and wonder. If it had caused damage, would we be liable, would they be able to trace it to us?

The next morning we did something unthought-of since it was a

Sunday. We did not go to church but instead went to town for a breakfast at the only diner for many miles around. We would never consider missing church and certainly never, never buy breakfast when we had better at home. What we bought was information and the eggs were thrown in free along with the toast. The information was plentiful and all around us. Every person in that café was talking about the UFO and what it did to the old Mason place over on Two Mile Creek. It seemed some people from the National Guard had taken it on themselves to shoot it down, and, apparently, they were successful. It appears they were using tracer bullets and one of them hit the UFO whereupon it burst into flame and fell on the abandoned Mason house, burning it to the ground. The fire department was too far away and too late to save any part of the UFO or the building. According to the local news, the site had been sealed off until the federal government could do a thorough investigation. It was expected to release the findings in about thirty days.

Knowing the federals, my father-in-law and I ceased worrying since it would be common knowledge that night hunters frequented that old place and lantern batteries would be expected, along with old lantern bulbs. We were very proud of our National Guard troops for their decisive action in protecting the public from any threat of little green people.

Now that I have told you about one UFO that I know was real, even though I can't prove it and one that two of us built and sent aloft, now for one that you must judge.

It must have been 1951 when one of my invited guests failed to show for that November hunt. We were to meet at the service station junction of route 219 and route 33 in Elkins, WV, where he was to leave his car for the next week. From there we planned going east and south to the heart of Laurel Fork wilderness area. We waited for several hours past his due time, and, since cell phones were very scarce then, (Ha, non-existent), we continued the hunt without him. When I returned to my job and called on him about a month later, he made no excuses and acted as if it had never happened. Of course, I did not ask for fear of an embarrassing him.

Several months passed and we were friends and doing business together. I believe it was about the first of October when he brought up the subject of hunting the next Thanksgiving in West Virginia. Again, I did not want to ask about last year but I thought I would enjoy his company, so I asked him if he could join us next month. I was surprised that he accepted without a word of apology or any reference to his failure to show last year. We made all the usual arrangements and arrived at the campsite Friday evening, nearly a week before Thanksgiving. Fred, my long time hunting buddy and one other invited guest, Bill, made up our camp this year.

Around the campfire on the third evening, we were just about ready for the sleeping bags when he said," Fellows, I believe I owe you an apology for my failure to show last season. I also need to tell you how embarrassed I was and why I have said nothing till now.

Hey, Fred!, pass me a whistle wetter from that Mason jar over there, I need it to get through this tale."

Last year one of my buddies and I were out on the lake in western Kentucky doing some night fishing when we saw what I know was a flying saucer. That thing came down from over the trees and skimmed across the water toward our boat. We ducked, expecting it to hit us but it slowed down as if undecided what next, then went straight up about ten feet and resumed its flight across and then back into the sky.I don't mind telling you we were two scared bimbos, and right then, we threw the rest of our Jack Daniels overboard. We wondered if it was just that we were too pickled to know what we saw. Now you guys know a lot of strange things have been showing up in the sky in the last year or so. Some, if not all, have been explained but not this one."

Well, we know we left work Friday evening to go fishing and got to the lake just after dark. By the time we got the boat in the water, loaded our gear, and got to our favorite fishing spot, it was close to midnight, Friday. The curious part of this is that we always catch some very nice fish here but not this trip. Not a single minnow except those we had brought along for bait. Shortly before dawn, we motored to the dock, tied up the boat and walked to the diner about a half mile down the road to grab some breakfast. This diner always opens about 5 a.m. in order to accommodate the workers that go to the early shift so we were there well after opening time. When we got there, it was apparently still closed and we just thought either their clock was wrong or Jim's watch had to be. I didn't have a watch, but I was hungry and willing to wait till it did open.

When we got to the door, the sign said CLOSED SUNDAYS. We looked at each other pure amazement and fright. Here it was Saturday morning we knew because we went out on the lake Friday evening. This can't be right. Did we over-do the Jack Daniels or what? Fred, pass me that Mason jar again, my mouth is kinda dry."

Fred, Bill, and I sat in total silence, fearful of breaking his narrative. We had heard of flying saucers but never had contact with anyone that had seen one that close. It was obvious that Hank was under great stress and some of his agitation was telegraphing itself to us, so better to keep quiet and listen.

Hank continued from when they were in front of the diner, twenty-four hours later than when they thought it was. It truly had to be Saturday morning but the sign on the door told us it was Sunday. "Now we realized we were terribly hungry and had nothing at the boat to eat. Go back to the car, sit down and talk this out. There had to be some explanation if only we talked about it. Hungry we were but more important was the lost time to talk about. Several minutes in the car and Jim asked me if I thought the nurse was pretty. "What nurse?" He turned in the seat and stared directly into my face, and said, "you mean to tell me you don't remember flirting with the nurse that took care of me? "When were you sick or hospitalized?" I asked, "cause I don't remember the nurse or even the hospital." Then BANG, it hit me. He was off his rocker. "Don't you remember when lightning knocked me down last week?"

Now I know he's nuts because we were at work together all last week and lightning came nowhere near the plant. To humor him and perhaps get a little more of what he was thinking, I asked where it hit him and he opened his shirt front to show me the burn scar.

Sure enough, there was a long burn scar from upper center of his chest, down to well below his belly button. I was astonished because I had seen his chest many times at work and he did not have a scar. Since this scar was as straight as an arrow, I failed to see how the zigzag of lightning could have done that.

While asking Jim more questions, it suddenly dawned on me that we were discussing the missing 24 hours before this came up. About then I realized that there was an itch on my chest that I had been scratching without thinking about it. With some fear of what I would find, I slowly opened the buttons of my shirt and lifted my T shirt. Sure enough, I had the same scar. We looked at our scars and became totally quiet for at least an hour. It was impossible to believe, but we had been abducted and opened up for inspection, or insertion, of something, or just to see how we were put together.

Well, of course, we had no desire to fish and really no desire to eat, even though just an hour ago, we were at the point of starvation. All that remained was to hook up the boat trailer and go home. Monday morning, we both arrived at the plant on time but too worried and preoccupied to be of any value to the company. We did compare notes and found neither of us had been able to sleep. We were almost zombies that first day, going through the act of staying busy but not really aware of what we were doing. Monday passed, and Tuesday was no better. On Wednesday the foreman wanted to send Jim home as he was too too sick to work. Jim said he felt fine, just as I did except we were filled with thoughts of if what had happened. Never the less, the foreman sent Jim on his way and told him the doctor wanted to see him right away.

After work, we met for a beer or six, and, as we relaxed it began to clear our minds and we were able to remember some of the strangest things, one of which was the beautiful nurse. I had no memory of her until that Wednesday evening when the sixth beer started to work. Now I have never been able to tolerate alcohol before this but that changed.

"Hey Fred, pass me that Mason jar again; I have developed a need for the hard stuff,especially after Jim left in a flash of light. Now I don't mean to say he disappeared by flying off into the sky or anything like that. It was just the way it happened. That has me all torn up in this nervous state and in need for a dose of FORGET IT water"

The nurse you asked? Well, she was in that bright room with Jim and me while the doctors were patching up Jim. She was the only one that spoke to me and, really, the only one that I could see the face. The doctors were all covered from head to foot, and, in fact, I never saw their eyes. The nurse seemed to be there not to help Jim but to keep me distracted. She didn't have too much trouble with that since I never have seen such beautiful curves, and she all but climbed into my lap while I was seated on the couch against the wall. Jim was under a half sleep and did not talk to me or the doctors, but he did watch me all of the time he was on that table. I do remember her more than anything else, and I now believe that was the reason she was there. It must have worked since I have not been able to remember anything else. As Jim told me later, he saw me on the table and she did him the same way, even to the point of several juicy kisses. Jim thought he was cheating on his wife and didn't tell me about this part for several days.

By the end of the week, Jim was so upset that he decided to go to a friend that worked in the x-ray department at our local hospital and have him do an x-ray not recorded by the hospital. Sunday afternoon when all was quiet there, Jim, the technician, and I met in the hospital and Jim got his x-ray. The technician and Jim were so astonished at what they saw, the technician insisted on Jim's seeing the radiologist after hours next day. By this time, Jim was so near starvation and worry that he could not sleep and definitely could not work, so he agreed to visit the department late the next evening.

Doctor Adams, the radiologist, got a rundown from the technician, and a look at the x-ray that made him so curious that he agreed to keep the visit off the record and not to make charges of any kind. Jim was delighted that there was hope in returning to normal and he was urging me to see Doctor Adams at the same time. Me, I would rather wait until I see what they come up with in Jim's case.

Doctor Adams had studied the computer image and still could make no determination as to the use of that "thing" in Jim's chest. He needed more information, so he persuaded Jim to allow a dye injection that would let him see the blood circulation in and around the box, as we were now calling the "thing".

Next evening, after hours, Doctor Adams had arranged for a cardiology friend to accompany him in case there would be a reaction to the die injection. I was allowed to be there only because Jim wouldn't go through with the examination without my presence. The doctors did not know I shared the experience with Jim, but, by this time, Jim had told them about the saucer episode. Both doctors were excited over the prospect of retrieving an object from outer space, one that would make them famous. They were careful to keep the discovery off the record and secret from their peers so the surprise would be that much more astonishing to the world. Famous they would be.

Doctor Patel, Doctor Adams, the x-ray technician, Jim, and I met in the x-ray department after hours on the following Sunday evening where he was to receive dye in the blood stream. The injection went well, as far as I could tell and Jim seemed to be OK with the procedure. Doctor Adams tuned up the scope and all I heard from the doctors were several sounds, hummmmmm and again hummmmmm.

Now I am not totally ignorant about x-ray images and I did get a glance over their shoulders. What I saw was a tube similar to an oversized cigar container, like five dollar cigars come in. I did see where the dye marked blood vessels entered and left the box and I did see several tiny wires running all up and down Jim's torso. Of course, that scared the s---out of me since I knew I had the same contraption in my belly.

After about three hours of sitting with Jim while we waited to make certain he would not have a delayed reaction, the doctors were in the radiologist's office studying over the computer screen. Finally they came out to speak to Jim and both of us were on edge. Their diagnosis was that it would have to come out and to do so, secrecy was imperative.

I still did not want them to know I shared the experience and Jim still kept my secret.

They had come to the conclusion that the hospital operating suite was out of the question. In part, it was the cost and, in part, they did not want the chance of contamination in case Jim's "BOX" was laden with something from planet ZZopilingareloper. Speculation was that was where it came from since the box kinda had the shape of the star group ZZopilingareloper. I guessed at least one of them was an astronomer and had a powerful telescope that star gazers were known to use.

In either case, they decided it could be done in the doctor's office, an operating area of Doctor Patel. He was known for his compassion and did many operations in his office in order to save the patient the cost of the more expensive hospital O.R. No doubt he did it solely for protection of the patient's purse. I had my own theory about the selection of his office but did not bring it up with Jim. I still believe it was a case of those doctors wanting to write a paper on the first successful recovery of a flying saucer artifact.

Doctors Patel and Adams made arrangements for the necessary supplies and for the coverage of their patients while they would be out of touch for the following Monday and Tuesday. In spite of Jim's insistence, I was not allowed to attend the operation. Doctor Patel said it was because his operating room was too small for another person to be on the premises, so I reluctantly gave in and went on to my job at the plant.

Jim had not told his wife Susan about the encounter for fear the episode with the nurse would slip out. Susan might take it that we had been spending our weekend fishing trips by fishing for something else and that could ruin their marriage. It was good that he had played it this way, for now he could claim a week-long fishing trip with me. All I had to do was stay out of sight until Jim recovered.

Doctor Patel's office was at the outside edge of town and since he had a very lucrative practice, it was situated near the center of his five acre, well-manicured grounds. His office was about ten miles from my home, so I accompanied Jim to Patel's place and left him to his ordeal while I went on to the plant for a very stressful day.

About noon that Monday the local radio announced a mysterious explosion just out of town. I paid no attention to that since my mind was filled with concern for my friend.

I was so concerned for Jim that I did not watch the evening news. I spent the evening in my basement cleaning my hunting and fishing gear until almost midnight. Tired to the point of exhaustion, I fell in bed and did sleep until the clock got me out in time for work that Tuesday morning. As I drove to work, the radio news told about a gas explosion at the office of Doctor Patel and my heart sank. Immediately I turned around and headed to the doctor's office where there were several cars and official vehicles. As I had to park quite a distance from where the office building used to be, I got out with the intention of walking up to one of the policemen and asking what happened. Before I had even closed the car door, I looked down and saw the mangled remains of what I knew to be the tape recorder of my friend, Jim. Knowing Jim was no more and with tears in my eyes, I lovingly picked up the recorder remains and placed them on the floor of my car. At the site of the explosion, I found a friendly fireman who said this was the most unusual gas explosion he had ever heard of since there were no gas lines running to the property.

To make a long story short, I need to tell you that the ATF people worked the site for several days and found not a trace of explosive material. Nothing could account for such a violent explosion. Not only had the building been totally destroyed, even the metal tools the doctors used had been melted into a mass of unusable junk. Two trees that used to be about thirty feet on each side of the office were so badly mangled that even the roots had been lifted out of the ground and destroyed. There were only two holes in the ground where the roots used to be.

The remains of that tape recorder lay on my work bench for several days before I discovered it had been hurled through the sky with very little damage inside. I carefully opened it and found the tape intact. Knowing my friend Jim was a nut about photography and tape recorders which he used to record details of pictures he took, I wondered if he had taken it to the operation in hopes of hearing the doctor's discussion while they peered into his insides.

Yes, he had turned it on and, yes, he had their conversation from the moment they started. I listened with fascination as they described the opening and exposure of the "BOX." I heard Doctor Patel say it was rigged to filter all of Jim's blood and it was a masterpiece of surgical skills, designed to intercept and diagnose Jim's blood. It was apparent that whatever device they used, it was possible to cut a blood vessel and seal it back again in a matter of seconds. Then I heard Doctor Adams say that was nothing compared to the wiring that had been connected to his kidneys, heart, liver and all other vital organs, including those running to his scrotum and attached to each testis. I listened with fascination while they described the layout of that "BOX" and all of the functions it seemed to be able to perform. There was no doubt, so Doctor Patel said, it was capable of transmitting information to outer space. Otherwise, why place it inside Jim? He also said the wiring running from the base of Jim's skull and down to his crotch had the appearance of a short wave antenna. "Yes, doctor, we will be famous."

Well, it was time to remove the "BOX" so it could be studied and so Jim could return to normal life. Doctor Patel said it appeared to be easy to remove the wiring simply by cutting the wires close to the "BOX," but that it would be a little more difficult to take it out of the aorta. Since this was the main blood supply, they would have to be careful and act fast. Better to cut all of the wiring first which would not take much time, then work on the aorta. Doctor Patel said. "Hand me the wire cutters, please----thank you" ---pause ---snip –*BANG !*---silence.

Now I have the facts. I am wired to something from the planet ZZopilingareloper which will explode and blow all of us to kingdom come if just one wire is cut.

"Fred----Please pass me the Mason jar again."

Time Travel

My name is Bill and I am here today because my great, great grandson Matthew, in the year of our Lord two thousand, one hundred seventy-five, made arrangements for me. At the age of sixty, he worked as a scientist in the world renowned laboratory of Space Travel in Huntsville, Alabama. He had been assigned the project some thirty years prior to this date in order to find a way of controlling time for the purpose of space travel.

As Matthew looked back over the years, he could not help but marvel at how time was determined by the movement of the sun and the moon : how the rotation of the earth, the moon, and the sun was held suspended in space. He was well aware that failure on his part was out of the question for to fail meant that he did not exist. To put it in the proper perspective, if he failed, then his great-grandfather Bill, would not have existed; therefore, no grandfather and no father. His entire family would not have had a place in this world.

Several years back, he had read a poem about the way God had suspended the stars and had made the universe to work in an orderly fashion. This he believed and the more he studied the poem, the more convinced he was that time travel was quite possible. From his high school days, he pondered the phenomena of sound travel and had thrown at least a ton of rocks in the lake near his home, just to study the action of waves. He had the word of renowned scientists that sound waves, once started, would never end. If so, then why not be able to reach out from a distant space craft and record the actual speech of George Washington, or even Moses? Why not transmit these voices back to earth for the real character of those men?

Working for the One World Government was very difficult even though there was an unlimited supply of funds, but there was not unlimited forgiveness for failure. Comrade Glozovol was constantly looking over Matt's shoulder and reminding him that he must produce. Failure was not permitted in the glorious communist party.

He was constantly bombarded with speeches about how the communist father of this world held the key to all things, including the right to live. This great communist father, the Supreme Comrade, had his palace in Moscow, but he was seldom there since he did not really care for the winters there. He could be expected to appear at any time and at any place and with him came the power to take life without regret. A hint of failure when the Supreme Comrade appeared could result in immediate death. Because of this fear, my great grandson was under great strain.

Was there truly a God that could place the stars in suspension, or was it pure chance?
Did the poem really have meaning as the writer must have felt?

LAWS OF THE UNIVERSE

There are those who study the location of Mars,
 directing their life by the movement of stars.
And there are others with crystals to see,
 where fate and the gods would have them to be.

Some people will trust in the all mighty dollar,
some only wish to be a great scholar.
Some have a desire to live as great kings,
 others care nothing for earthly things.

Some people live as if today is their last,
with death being final, all things are past.
But others believe in physical reincarnation,
elevating their body to a higher station.
3
Some people meditate and study inner spirits,
expecting a divine message, if only they could hear it.
Let your conscience be your guide is the message they receive,
 which allows them to structure what they believe.

The laws of the universe hold the stars suspended,
just as the creator originally intended.
But the stars are mindless and will surely obey,
not like we humans who seek our own way.

For a time in this life we may choose our own bed,
until the death of our body, when the spirit has fled.
And then we face God and the laws we have broken.
Too late, too late, the Master has spoken.

Matthew came from a long line of men in his past all named after the Bible character and were called Matt for short. Did this mean that his ancestors were true believers in the Bible? Even though that book had been banned and destroyed many years ago, a few people like him had carefully hidden and read copies of it. How could it be that so much of it seemed to be a history book and still written many years, even centuries before it came to pass? By pressure to find the answer to time travel placed on him by Comrade Glozovol and by the wonderment of the words in his forbidden Bible, Matt was a very troubled man. His wife was no help because he was not free to discuss his private thought with her. Mary had been assigned to him by the party and he had not been allowed a choice. Even the privilege of children was denied except by party choice. He and Mary were allowed only two children and those had to be a boy and a girl. All other pregnancies were terminated by the party doctor. Mary's loyalty to the party made life very miserable for him and made it easier for him to stay at the lab very late at night.

Then came the night when he was alone in the lab that something strange happened.

He turned on the dilathermography unit and directed its rays, along with intense light from the sodialblume, toward the chamber holding zerconal gas. The unearthly glow filled him with wonder, not only because of its appearance, but because it was what he had been searching for during the past three years. He understood the use of this mixture could be very deadly, but, at the same time, it could unlock the secret of time travel. It was his theory that time existed in the minds of man, and, if the mind was properly excited, it could transform the body. It was a known fact that the mind could cure an illness and also generate an illness that could end life. Medical science had discovered many years past that if the patient truly wanted to and believed in healing his own body, it could be done in most cases.Age seemed to be the only obstacle to extended life by mind over disease or matter.

As Matt studied the gas before him and pondered the life he had with a wife that he did not love,he considered what it would mean to his children if he should cease to exist. There was no reason to consider them since the state owned them and his disappearance would have no effect on wife or children. Why not keep the secret of the gas to himself, and if it failed, what did he have to lose?

Matt closed down the lab after placing a volume of the gas in a compressed container.

He knew he could produce more of it but, for reasons he could not explain to himself, he wanted a supply of it outside the lab.

That night was one of the longest Matt had ever known. He lay in bed for the entire night with thoughts of how and why and where and when, on and on his mind raced. By morning he had decided to use the gas the next evening when he would again be alone in the lab.

One thing the party did not prohibit was the reading of history, and Matt was a real history buff. His favorite part was the great world war of 1941 through 1945. In the history books distributed by the party, it was well documented how the great Soviet Union had won the war and secured peace for the entire world. Now Matt was more than educated. He had a mind that searched for facts among the lies. How could this be true? Where could he learn the real truth? Perhaps the Time Gas would hold the answer for him. Again, he had nothing to lose so his decision was to try to return to those war years for answers. While there, if possible, perhaps he could find his, Great-grandfather.

Comrade Glozovol left him at the lab at his usual time, around three in the afternoon since he had a party speech to attend. Party speeches were necessary in order to hold the people in their place. Everyone had to be brainwashed every day and only a few, like Matt were excused from attendance due to the nature of his work. At three fifteen, Matt donned the clothing he thought would be more fitting for where he hoped to go. If it worked, as he believed it would, he would take the pressurized gas bottle with him and the several gold coins he had been able to hide. In his mind, he would find

Dr. J. Robert Oppenheimer at his lab in Los Alamos, New Mexico.

Dr Oppenheimer was in charge of the effort to develop the Atomic bomb for the United States and had almost 1,500 people under his direction and on this project. According to the Soviet Party, it would have been a total failure had not the Soviet Union sent their great minds to help work out the final details. Matt doubted this but wanted to find first- hand truth, if possible. Dr. Oppenheimer had been on the atom Bomb project from early 1942 until its use in Japan on August 6th and 9th of 1945, and Matt wanted to join his lab crew.He felt he could just "drop in" since he might not be noticed among 1,500 workers.

Matt chose, in his mind,the date of Saturday, January 6, 1945 at 0900, knowing the holidays were just over and the confusion of a new face in Los Alamos would not be too noticeable. Also this would give him the chance to sell some of his gold coins for money of that time and let him buy clothing that fit the place where he intended to be. Matt sat back in his most comfortable office chair and closed his mind to all else except the date and time he chose to arrive in down town Los Alamos. He was afraid to open the gas bottle for a breath of gas for fear it would work and transport him before he could close the valve. So that he did not lose control, he carefully filled a latex glove and then closed the gas valve. The gas container was small enough for him to place it under his jacket and close the zipper tightly for he wanted it secure for his return trip, if there was to be one. With all in readiness, he placed his nose to the glove and slowly opened the end of it.

Zero nine hundred, January, 6, 1945, found Matt looking for a place called a pawn shop where he had read of as being a place to sell gold for cash. He was just a little early, but when the owner opened the grill work, Matt was at the right place. He did have a little trouble convincing the owner that he did own the coin, even though the owner had never seen one just like the one Matt had. His next move took him to a store called JC Penny where he purchased clothing recommended by the young clerk. Also, from him came information on where the lab buildings were located and where to catch a bus for the compound on Monday morning.

Matt spent the day looking over what he believed to be a typical city of that date but it was far different from his home in Huntsville, Alabama of 2075. Huntsville was about the only place he was familiar with since the Party did not allow travel, and very little information was allowed, not even pictures unless approved by the party. Sunday morning he was awakened in his hotel room by church bells, something he had never heard before. Even so, he had read about them in forbidden literature that was saved by his father along with the poem he had. Matt hurriedly dressed and found his way to the church that was almost filled when he arrived. It was unbelievable that so many people would choose to attend a speech without being forced as the party would have it.

When Matt found a seat, it was near the front for it seemed everyone wanted the back.

This was nothing like a party speech. All party members wanted the front, not because they wanted to hear better but because they wanted to be seen by the party leader. To survive in the communist controlled government, it was necessary to act as if hearing party lies was a great privilege. Accepting the same lies told every day was the only way to advance in the party, even to stay alive.

With computers, there was instant communication and even some mild jokes passed, but it was a death sentence to send or even receive banned material by computer. What Matt saw and heard in this church service over the next hour was baffling to him. These people were truly happy. Their warm smiles and hand shaking was surprising since they were losing the war and were soon to be prisoners of Germany unless the Russian army arrived in time. The Russian history books told how the American people were on the brink of losing the war and were only saved by the arrival of Russian relief. Of course, Matt had already discovered the wealth and strength of America and that the party lies were too outrageous to be believed.

After church services, Matt returned to his room where he found a Gideon bible and began to read where the minister had told the story of

Christ in John 3:5 where he said,

"Except a man be born of water and of the spirit, he cannot enter into the Kingdom of God"—"Marvel not that I said unto thee, Ye must be born again". Hours later, Matt began to understand the poem, "And then we face God and the laws we have broken,

Too late, too late, the Master has spoken".

Monday morning with hundreds of government employees returning from the holidays, Matt was able to ride the bus through to the lab area without being challenged. At the front desk, he made the report that he was arriving from Atomic Energy Commission in Oak Ridge, Tennessee, and needed to see Dr. Robert Oppenheimer at once.

He was so knowledgeable and convincing that they gave him a badge for entry to Dr. Oppenheimer's office. When Matt arrived at the doctor's office, he found the man was to be out for the week which was the break Matt needed.

Since he seemed to have more knowledge than the average scientist there, he was welcomed as one of them. For the next three weeks, Matt supplied so much new information to these men that he was considered tops in his field and given access to the entire facility. There he learned what he desired; that there was not a single Russian scientist there, none even allowed near the place.

Now the next chore he had placed for himself was to find me, his great-grandfather.

Matt had some family history and knew that I was serving in the army of the United States. With the clearance of his Los Alamos badge and identification supplied at that lab, Matt was able to enter army records, and, within hours, had located me at the port of embarkation in San Diego, California. At the time, I was in the final stages of training for the invasion of Japan. It was to be a bloody invasion with every citizen of Japan ready to die for hisemperor. Even little children would be entering the fight by carrying spears made of bamboo or boys of eight and nine carrying rifles. Just the thought of having to shoot a child was almost too much to face.

My company of combat engineers, of which I was designated the Pioneer, was due to ship out on May 7 and the invasion was to be Thursday, June 7 1945. My chance of survival was about one in one hundred and Matt saw this at once. I do not have knowledge of when I met Matt, and if I did, he did not choose to give me his real name.

I just know a high-ranking officer showed up at my compound one morning with orders cut to have me transferred to the University of Missouri for extensive training in radio communications. Exactly how Matt knew I was interested in radio communications is far beyond my knowledge, but he did know, and he set about using that knowledge in order to save me, and therefore himself.

Matt returned to Los Alamos with the desire to expedite the completion of the atomic bomb. He quickly became a close associate of Dr. Oppenheimer, and, with knowledge one hundred and forty years advanced from the scientists in Los Alamos, his input was vital to the rapid finish of the bomb. My great, great-grandson pushed as hard as possible without giving away his secret because it was vital to him to finish the war and get me home safely.

In closing, as the minister would say, Matt returned to the church services every Sunday he was free from work. On his return to Huntsville, Alabama and during the year of our Lord, Two Thousand , one Hundred and Seventy Six, he carried the Gideon bible under his jacket along with the pressurized gas bottle.

Chapter two, Time travel

The year is Two Thousand, One Hundred and Seventy Seven and I have just returned from the year of our Lord, One Thousand, Nineteen Hundred and Forty Five where I was

instrumental in the rapid conclusion of that war of the worlds referred to as WWII.

My great, great-grandfather was in danger of being terminated and, therefore, I would not have existed. It was a rare chance for me to discover the means of saving the lives of my ancestors, as well as myself. The discovery of Zerconal gas in my laboratory has allowed me to alter my mind and, therefore, alter my position in time. This gas was discovered after many years of searching under the control of the ONE WORLD GOVERNMENT and controlled by the glorious Communist party with headquarters in the supreme palace located in Moscow, Russia. The discovery and use of this gas has been kept a closely guarded secret from my supervisor and fellow workers. I have found it too important and too exciting to share with the world as it was my only means of escape from the oppressive Communist party. Being able to keep this secret is due to my lazy and ignorant party supervisor, Comrade Igor Glozovol. Due to my advanced age and my very great knowledge, the state does not consider me much of a risk and, therefore, allows me the run of the military compound in Huntsville, Alabama.

This place was a natural for my research in time and space travel since it has been the original site of the United States National Aeronautic and Space Administration, NASA for short, for the past two hundred twenty-five years.

My immediate supervisor, we lovingly refer to him as "Iggy." has no idea of the work that is done here. He was assigned to see to our party obedience and attendance to party functions. Iggy has been told that I am completely trustworthy and need not attend the party speech as my work is vital, and I am to have complete freedom to roam the base. This is just another reason for keeping the secret that I have uncovered. The gas allows me to be gone for weeks, and Iggy thinks I am at party headquarters.

Since the original discovery, I have been modifying the method of storing and carrying Zerconal . Fear of losing it while in another realm of time has caused my research to come up with another form of storage. Loss of the gas container was my greatest fear, and perhaps the need to leave a place of danger quickly meant a more secure way to carry it.

Through much work, I have been able to compress Zerconal into powder form and therefore into pill shape. The only remaining problem was storage and carrying a goodly supply without having it taken from me by some overzealous police or just in a plain robbery. Believe me, robbery in this so called perfect world has not been eliminated. The death penalty for being caught in robbery has only made the criminal mind much more crafty. The need to protect myself and my invention has been the focus of my work over the past two years.

The capsules I now carry with me at all times consist of powder compressed Zerconal covered with a secure and water tight plastic shell. If need be, I can swallow several of the capsules in complete safety. I can also carry one in my mouth where it is possible to crush it and immediately inhale Zerconal that is released by the moisture in my mouth.

This is definitely a last resort as I would not like for a human in the past or the future to see me disappear.

It is a fact that I do not wish to and will not alter the future again, or so I tell myself. I just want to see with my own eyes the things I have heard about and confirm the stories the supreme communist leader is telling the people. One rumor is that he is wrong about the entire world being under his rule. One whispered rumor is that a little nation calling itself Israel is still free and that no amount of pressure has subdued it. This I wish to see for myself. In fact, I may find it such that I will remain there because I have read in the Gideon Bible that it will remain forever. This Bible is against all communist rules and all Bibles have been destroyed that have been found. It is the death penalty to be caught with one and I would only have this Bible because I brought it back from the year 1945 when I saved my great, great-grandfather from certain death in Japan.

I had such an overpowering desire to discuss this Bible with someone; I cautiously mentioned it to an associate and was shocked to hear of a

Bible society underground here in Huntsville. The state religion is Islam, and compulsory prayer has been a thorn in my side for many years. I detest the sound of million-watt speakers shaking my brain loose from my skull with the call to prayer. From my associate I learned that the holy Koran cover was also used to contain the Bible of the one true God. Being caught with it was certain death by the removal of one's head from the body. I have decided to join this group as soon as I return from my next venture into the unknown.

But first, I wish to look into the future for just a very short time. I will not venture into unknown areas for there is too much danger in finding myself where I may not be able to return. The past has been and it is safe to say that venturing there will allow me to learn about the here and now; perhaps it will help me better the world or even some small part of it.

Just for a starter, I would like to see the city of Moscow and all of the riches there. Almost every party speech I have heard is filled with praises for that great city. I can't help but wonder if this is so, and, if it is, why does our supreme commander spend so much time here and in the south Atlantic. Later I will go there to see for myself. All I need to know is when and where he will be and I can arrange to visit with little or no danger.

It is now a bright and sunny day here in Huntsville as April usually is. Now would be a good time for me to visit Moscow as the weather should be mild enough for the clothing I have on hand. One thing is certain and that is the type of money they use there. The OWP, as the One World Party is referred to, would be using the coins and bills all over the world. With what I am paid, I have nothing in reserve and no cash to take with me, but, there is a way. You may call it dishonest but I call it necessity and can muster up no guilt feeling over what I plan to do.

At compound headquarters where the party bank is located, I have noticed the vault being open and only one trusted party member on duty during all open hours. I have also noticed that there is a rush and a very busy time for the banker on Friday evening from four until five when he closes the vault. At four, the rush is for payment to be made to officials and this is done in cash. Even the small pay I receive is in cash. This is a perfect time for me to use the Zerconal and allow myself to appear inside the vault. I only need a very few seconds to load my pockets and transport myself out to safety. With ample cash on hand, I will be able to stay at the finest place in Moscow and to partake of the wonders the party chairman tells us about.

My plan is to arrive in Moscow at 8:15 a.m. on Friday in order to see the work day take place and in order to do this, I must leave at 1:15 a.m: I have chosen to arrive in the shopping district since I have plenty of cash and may find myself in need. Tthis would be the best place to go unnoticed.

Moscow, 10:00 a.m. and the state-run shopping center is open. I have been walking just to pass the time. This center is just off Red Square and is a continuing center for the past two hundred years. OKHOTNY RYAD has been the shopping center for the masses where they have banking and many other services in three, underground levels. GUM is the other shopping place for the masses and is also over two hundred years in business.

For the elite and upper party members, their store is also located right on Red Square.

TSUM is the central universal store and the place where I intend to buy clothing when it is open. I have plenty of cash and the clerks will fit me with the finest which is necessary to help me penetrate the Kremlin. If I am dressed properly and carry myself with an air of authority, I doubt I will be questioned. It is a fact that the fear of immediate death keeps security at a low level for who would venture into the lions mouth unbidden.

Looking at the city, I see no sign of the opulence we are told about back in Alabama. All I have seen so far is regimented people with a look of fear on their faces. It seems as if none of them will really look at me, and they should for I am underdressed and stand out like a beacon in a storm. Just in case I am found out, I carry a capsule of Zerconal in my mouth ready for my departure in seconds.

At TSUM, the clerk was at first reluctant to serve me. All I had to do was speak in a very threatening and authoritative voice and the place was mine. Cash speaks of high- ranking party members and this solidified my position and I could leave dressed as the best of the best.

On entering the Grand Kremlin Palace, I was suitably impressed with the grandeur of such a building that had stood the test of time. After all, it was designed by a team of architects under Konstantin Thon in 1837 and completed in 1849. It was built on Borovitsky hill, the original residence of the ruling princes. I was truly amazed at the size, 82,000 square feet, about the size of sixteen football fields. It was also apparent the building had been well cared for, and no doubt, with free labor down through the ages.

I wandered through the offices with little interference, noting the difference in worker and party offices. Nothing seemed to be missing for the comfort of the ruling class. It did not take me long to get my fill of such a place, and I wanted only to see the rest of that ancient city. My best chance of taking in the real city was to hire a driver of what I am told is a Gipsy Taxi. These are private auto owners and need to be hired by the hour.

Normally, it would not be safe in certain parts of the city, but since I am dressed as one of the party ruling class, I find it works well for me. I spent the rest of the day touring a city that has been in existence for over eight centuries. It is a mix of all I expected with the ruling class occupying a very distinct area away from the working class. When I arrived in Moscow, no one would look directly at me since I stood out as a poor worker. Now no one would look directly at me because I stand for danger, dressed as a top party official.

I had intended to spend the week-end in Moscow but I found it too depressing and decided to return to Huntsville instead. There is little in Huntsville to attract me but there is a homing instinct on all animals, and I sometimes feel that I am classified as one by my party supervisors. I do need to spend a few days in my lab so my associates will not begin to wonder at my absence. I also need to be very careful of all the cash I have. By now the missing OWP cash at the party bank has been discovered, and even though there is no proof of a robbery, anyone with a lot of cash would be convicted with no proof necessary. Now I wish I had left the Gipsy taxi driver a rich man since I have unlimited cash any time I choose to drop in on the bank.

The HBS group is openly known as the Help a Brother Society but it is secretly known as the Home Bible Study group. I have thought a lot about the study group since I returned from Russia. There, the state religion is compulsory Islam, and it is too depressing to be considered by any thinking person. The woman is nothing, even less considered than here in Alabama. The woman assigned to me is intolerable and I stay away from her as much as possible. By the state religion, I can put her away and take another of the state's choice but there is no promise of anything better. I find the lab a labor of love and a place where I close my mind to the atrocities of the state religion.

My first meeting at HBS is with my associate who introduced me to the group and told them about my secret Gideon Bible. Although I am fearful of having it outside the secure safe at the lab, I promise to show it at some future meeting of HBS. At this first meeting, I heard the story of Jesus, the Christ, and decided he was for real. Why he allowed this world to fall into Islam was too much for me to grasp, but I was assured by those knowledgeable students, this was not forever. They were all convinced Israel was the key to the return of Christ and the end of Islam. All expected this to occur at any moment and urged me to study the book of Revelation for the answers I needed. They pointed out the book of Zechariah, Chapter 14 that states that "all the nations will gather against Jerusalem to battle and the city will be taken, the women ravished and half the city shall go forth into captivity. Then shall the Lord go forth and fight against these nations".

The little nation of Israel, the last place on earth to hold out against Satan and his evil dominion of earth. Secretly in my heart, I knew I had to visit such a brave nation. I had the means, the time and desire to know more about how the true God allowed them to hold fast against the entire world of Communism and Islamic domination. Monday at the lab, all talk was about the great investigation into missing money at the bank. Speculation was that a very high party official had been there when the bank was closed and had found temptation too much. Only two or three had access to the bank other than the lowly teller and he was easy to eliminate. A thorough search of every place he had access to had not revealed a single OWP coin or bill that he could not account for. That left the high ranking official to be investigated and of course he had all kinds of bribe money stashed away as all high party members had. He could not prove himself innocent or give a reasonable account for the large amount of cash he had in his home. Of course, he was replaced, beheaded we surmised.

I much doubted Israel would be using OWP as their monetary exchange, so I had to study carefully what I was to do about money when I did visit that nation. I did know they used their currency which dated back well over one hundred years: The Agorot being the smallest, the Shekel, the largest coin up to 10 Shekels, and, from there, paper up to 200 Shekels. My needs were 50 and 100 Shekel notesor gold coins left over from the free times of Canada. My obvious move was to visit a bank in that nation and plan after seeing the way banks were still run. Of course, I could go to Israel and do the same trick but, somehow, I did not feel right about that. There was a great difference in stealing from a nation of communist and Islamic rich people. First, I needed to see if the bank of Huntsville had gold or silver coins. A quick change would give me this answer, but now I had to concern myself with the possible installation of recording cameras inside the vaults. All that meant to me was that I would have to dress totally in black before entering the vault. Obviously the appearance of a person or thing out of thin air would give the authorities something to discuss and would no doubt result in the complete change of the camera system. It made little difference to me so long as I got the gold or silver I needed.

After successfully visiting the Huntsville vault and seeing no cameras, I found no gold or silver, so I took nothing. Before deciding on a visit to Canada, I reconsidered Israel and the limits of my stay there. Perhaps one day there would satisfy my curiosity and for that I would need no money. Hunger for twenty four hours would do me good, and if it should turn out to be longer, I had a good supply of Zerconol tablets and could go anywhere, even to a restaurant kitchen after hours.

For my visit to Israel, I chose to arrive there at 9:00 a.m. which meant I had to leave Huntsville at 1:00 a.m. I chose May 14 because that is their national holiday of independence and one which I would gladly celebrate with them. My desire for independence is felt by most of the people in this world but especially in the former America. They slept while it quietly slipped away; while their elected leaders in Washington sold their souls for power and then lost it all. I know it will be tempting for me to remain in Israel but my lab means too much for to me to leave it.

The first thing I did when I arrived in Jerusalem was to join the crowd who was in a very festive mood. Friendly was the perfect word and I soon found English speaking people gathered around a free coffee table. Although my English had suffered from Russian dominance, I was able to join the conversation and soon have friends. Of course, I was full of questions and had to answer many from them. They assumed I was from Russia, but when they were assured that I was from the former United States of America, they openly discussed the freedom they shared and the sorrow that America had lost hers. From them I learned they still had a mixture of English law with the Knesset laws set down by the committee of Law and Justice. I also learned that they all belonged to the armed forces and were never without their rifles and side arms, dedicated to the preservation of their freedom, as young as eleven and as old as ones still able to stand.

The sad part about the loss of freedom in the old America was the way people allowed just a very few communists to take the freedom of bearing arms away from the majority.

The loss of freedom under the second amendment of the constitution was sneaky in several ways and not the least of those reasons was by allowing a very few ignorant people to control the Environmental Protection Agency. Due to that group, America became slaves to Islamic nations who sold oil to America when America had more oil than it could use in a hundred years. That oil money sent to the Middle East was converted to arms which were used to subdue America. Other reasons are easy for all to see in looking backward. Because too many demanded free money from those who had to work for it, the system failed. No doubt America would still be free and strong if the real working class had just said no to the greed and communist leanings of their elected leaders in Washington. By the time they were awake to the danger, all honest people had lost their guns and their ability to fight.

How I envied the Israelis and their happiness at being able to choose their mates and travel without restrictions across the country. All of the simple things America used to have. Freedom to choose their religion was also apparent for they totally rejected Islam' and a great number of them had converted to Christ. I had no doubt that conversion to

Christianity accounted for the reason they were still free. America gave up Christ for free will, free speech, free sex, and freedom from seeing the cross of Christ on church buildings and in cemeteries. It makes me sad to read of the millions of Jews slaughtered in that war of 1938/1945. I know this occurred because they had lost the freedom to bear arms, and, without them, they were like cattle led to slaughter. Of course, the millions of children slaughtered by abortion is no less vile in the eyes of the God I now read about. America had to pay the price for the freedom of a few short years of "do as you will" and the price was no freedom at all. It makes me very sad to be an American in the chains of communism.

I spent two happy days in Jerusalem with the kind of friends who could show true love for a fellow human. As much as I hated to leave, my friends had to return to duty after the holiday and I had to return to my lab in Huntsville, Alabama, Republic of Russia.

My associate from the lab who took me to the first meeting of HBS told me he and the home Bible study group had been praying for me and earnestly desired my return to their group. I was touched and came to believe that they were able to direct my thoughts through prayer. I was beginning to wonder how I might be able to help the world with my invention. Before this I thought only of how I could use it for my escape and my gain.

Now I realize there is little I can do about changing the course of history but perhaps I can find another way to help my fellow human race.

Joe, my associate, took me by the arm late Friday afternoon and led me to where he could speak of the HBS meeting. There he told me of their desire to locate copies of old manuscripts that were written by Bible scholars of a century ago. He asked if I would attend the meeting that night, and, without hesitation I agreed. Perhaps this was a prayer answered even before I had really asked God for direction.

At the meeting I was greeted as if I had been a part of that group for all of my life and it almost seemed as if I were back in Jerusalem. I became a true believer that night and had the most wonderful feeling of my life. I now knew I had purpose and direction; that of gathering old manuscripts for this group and, perhaps, for the world that was in bondage.

Before I left the meeting that night, I asked if they had a way of re-printing old documents and distributing them without danger to themselves. Of course, the answer was danger is ever present, but they did have access to the old presses of the now defunct Huntsville times.

My next move was obvious. As a start, I had to return to Jerusalem where there was bound to be freedom of speech and a library full of old documents. Money was the problem now. I refused to think of stealing from the Israeli's, but how I was to obtain funds escaped me. After much thought, I decided to let the HBS group know I had access to documents in Israel but that I would have to pay for them and money was the problem.

I dared not let them know that I would be traveling there, and, so I had to refuse to answer questions about how I could arrange it.

Two weeks later the meeting took place again at a member's home in south Huntsville.

I was there and filled with desire to learn more about God and what the group had in mind. By this time the number had grown to include some of the very old Jewish people who had roots in the former NASA--those whose fathers had worked for the United States government. They turned out to be the answer to prayers of where can funds be found?

One of the old men had saved Israel'money from fifty years back and was glad to put it to good use. There was a wonderful trust placed in me that he was willing to pass money to me without an explanation. I had no idea what I would be able to find and if it could be bought or copied, but I had to trust God that if He wanted us to have them in Huntsville, He would provide. So far it seemed He was making provisions with no help from us.

Back at the lab, I was so happy that it was not possible for me to contain my joy with the new days before me. My associate warned me to be careful of Iggy. He might become suspicious and have me followed. He might even accuse me of subversion or some form of crime against the party since we were not supposed to be happy. I took the warning to heart for it would destroy my new purpose to be thrown out of the lab. Fear of death no longer came to mind since I knew all I had to do was open a Zerconol tablet in my mouth and disappear to another time zone and start a new life under more pleasant living conditions. But now, I have a purpose and I do not want to lose the chance to help my fellow members at HBS and all the others that might need the help. With money and purpose, I made preparations for leaving the lab in my associate's able hands for three days. Of course, I could not tell him of my intended journey to Israel, so I hinted about a secret trip to Nashville where I thought there might still be religious literature available.

Now that I had friends in Israel, I planned the transformation to be such that I would arrive there mid-morning on Saturday. I felt they would be willing and able to help me locate some good literature. So far as they knew, I had plane travel documents and could take only a limited amount back. They were very careful not to question me about my home and why I was in Israel, but I did my best to assure them I was a Christian and on a very peaceful mission. During the afternoon, they took me to a book store that had hundreds of volumes on the things of God. Of course, I could take only items printed in English.With their help, we located four books that I knew would be welcomed in Huntsville.

The Complete Dead Sea Scrolls by Geza Vermes

The Archaeology of Qumran and the Dead Sea Scrolls by Jodi Magness.

The Community of the renewed Covenant, The Notre Dame Symposium of the Dead Sea Scrolls.

Eschatology, Messianism and the Dead Sea Scrolls by Evans and Flint.

With these books properly secured, I had spent very little money and felt this to be enough for this trip. When I told them it was time for me to return, they insisted on accompanying me to the airport. Now what? I couldn't possibly make the transformation in their presence and I had no papers to allow me near a departing plane. Stalling for time to think, I asked them for one last coffee at the beautiful coffee shop in the Dan Panorama Hotel. I would have enjoyed that much more if not for the strain of leaving and not telling my friends of my plan.

When we were ready to leave, I told them that I must stop at the Russian Consulate on the way to the airport. Of course, they were afraid to enter that imposing place which was part of my plan. I knew they would wait for me for a short time and when I did not exit, they would assume I had been detained. When I entered the building, I went to the first door marked as a toilet, entered the first stall and immediately broke the Zerconol tablet.

With this, I transferred myself to the tiny sleeping room provided for me in my lab, the one place where I could be certain of privacy.

The following Wednesday night at the weekly meeting of the HBS group, I presented them with the four books and returned the money I did not have to spend. They were overjoyed at the selection and I could tell they were filled with questions but in the society we were living in, asking nothing is the only safe way. Like Christians down through the years, there was great pleasure in having verification of their present Bible. My pleasure was beyond description-- that I could use the discovery I had made to guarantee me eternal life. I would never have known about Jesus without that and the dedication of people who would gamble their lives to meet and discuss Jesus and what he did for us.

I am nearing the end of my life here in Huntsville and on earth which I do not fear.

In fact, I have thought so much of what the Bible tells me about Heaven, I am anxious to see it. I have led a wonderful life since the discovery of Zerconol, and I believe it has brought many lost souls to Christ. For this, I thank my God and I pray you will also come to know Jesus and eternal life in Heaven. As I prepare to leave you, I have made the necessary arrangements to destroy all records of my lab work. My Soviet earthly masters would not use it for the good of mankind.

Good Bye and God Bless you

Yesterday's Roses

Alex sat in the kitchen chair with the shotgun in his hands. He had removed one shoe and had tied a string to the trigger and to his big toe. His mind was numb with grief and loneliness.

As he looked across the table for the last time, he saw the tall glass container that held two wilted and forlorn roses. Last week they had been red and full of life, still on the rose bush that he had helped Dottie plant several years ago. Now they were gone, just like Dottie. Before he used the shotgun, he had one last chore to do. He had to dig up the rose bush and destroy it. Dottie had cut those two roses for her pleasure and for his and it was the last act she had performed in her kitchen. Surely no one would want to see roses from that bush hurt them as it was doing to him now.

He took the shovel to the flower garden in which Dottie had spent so many happy hours. It was spring time and everything was in full bloom. Every bush and vine meant hours that Dottie had turned the soil, and had watered and trimmed until she was satisfied her plants had the best of care. Alex had sat on the patio and watched her work that flower garden for years, and his love for her was so strong that sometimes he would find himself near tears of joy to think that she belonged to him. Just two weeks ago, he had watched out the kitchen window as she kneeled to work the soil around that rose bush.

It was in his mind now that she looked as if she were in prayer. Perhaps she was. Dottie had never complained of feeling bad. She hated going to see a doctor and even refused aspirin when Alex knew she had a headache. Perhaps she was in pain and in prayer, using that hated rose bush as her altar.

Alex had married her fifty-nine years ago in a whirlwind courtship. It had been love at first sight, and he had shocked her into silence when he proposed the same evening he met her. Needless to say, Dottie did not give him an answer that evening but just one week later, she said yes. Fifty-nine years were unbelievable to most people since the usual was anywhere from three months to three years until the first divorce. Alex thought the moon and the stars were at her command; that no other woman had ever been so desirable to a man. Even Alex could not believe fifty-nine years had slipped by so quickly and that a love so strong could bind two people together so firmly.

As he leaned on the shovel and stared at the rose bush, his mind raced back to their first Child when they were really unable to afford children. Their son was born just one year after they were married, and in many ways, Alex regretted the arrival since it meant he had to share her love with another.

Two wonderful years later, the second child arrived and by the time this child arrived, Alex was used to sharing Dottie and had come to love the sharing of children.

Dottie blossomed to a more beautiful and desirable woman as she left girlhood behind.

Alex prospered and was able to give Dottie a good home and supply their children with more than they needed, perhaps too much more.

Alex closed his eyes and remembered taking Dottie and the children to the beach for the first time. He could almost feel the warm sand on his feet as he and Dottie held hands at the water's edge. A week at the beach with beautiful children and a gorgeous wife was a memory planted in his mind and was filed in the "Extreme Pleasure" folder. Of course, there were many trips to the beach and many trips to the mountains. Dottie and the children loved camping and sleeping in a tent on "blow up" air mattresses since this was part of the fun. The air mattresses were not too dependable and usually would lose air and leave the sleeping one flat on the ground. Many times, when all was quiet in bed and neither Dottie nor Alex was yet asleep, Dottie would make the sound of blowing in an air mattress that had lost air during the night. When she did, Alex would start laughing until both of them were in fits of laughter.

Alex bought a large boat when their children were ten and twelve, just because they wanted time with their children while they were still young enough to be enjoyed. The only lake near enough for them to visit on weekends was just far enough away till they had to use a camping tent and sleep on the ground. Alex had very little experience with boats and this boat was a powerful one with two large outboard motors. It was excellent for water skiing and Dottie and both children learned to do it well. When Alex bought the boat, he got instructions on starting and running it from the dealer but not on the water. He had much to learn. The first weekend they were at the lake, the boat was moored at the edge of the lake, just twenty feet from their tent.

During the night a very heavy rain storm came and by morning it was clear again. The tent had been excellent shelter and all had slept dry and well.

Alex had not expected the rain and was surprised to see the boat was very low in the stern. There must have been well over a hundred gallons of water settled back where the weight of the motors already had the stern low in the water. Rather than bail, Alex decided to do as the boat salesman had told him on how to clear water from the boat. He said to run the boat slowly picking up speed and remove the bilge plug in the bottom center, just forward of the motor mount. This way the water would be sucked out and no bilge pump was needed. As Alex stood looking at a near sinking boat, another camper from nearby came over. He had the same advice on draining the boat.

Well, OK. His twelve-year-old son took the knee deep position by the bilge plug and Alex started one motor and headed out. When he got the boat up to a good speed, his son pulled the bilge plug and at that instant, the motor coughed and died. Alex was screaming to put the plug back in and his son was yelling, I can't find the hole. All of this time the visitor was standing on the bank with a blank look at bumbling idiots. Alex had enough presence of mind to start the second motor and all looked well--- for about fifteen seconds. Water was being sucked out just as the visitor said it would. Then--the second motor coughed and died. Then I heard the visitor still on the bank yelling, "Open the gas valve". Salvation came just in time. With fuel, both motors ran and the boat was saved.

Bless her heart, when Dottie saw Alex do a stupid thing forever after, she would yell--" Open the gas valve".

Alex again started to push the shovel in under the rose bush when he remembered Dottie's horse. How she had loved that horse and placed the output from him in her garden. Danny Boy was special and everyone would admit she made him that way by her special kind of love. It is well to remember that to be loved, we must first love, and never was this more pronounced than the love Dottie gave Danny Boy.

After running that through his memory, Alex was shedding tears that prevented him from seeing more than the outline of the rose bush.

He had to find a seat on the patio for time to clear the tears away. Through the veil of tears, Alex could see the outline of Dottie leaning over that hateful rose bush. He now believed she loved it more than him. Then his mind raced back to the first year of their marriage and how they had to do without so many essential things, like a washing machine and a sewing machine for her. There was no doubt that Dottie loved him because he remembered when she had so lovingly taken care of him when he was sick. Many times during their marriage, she had shown her love by doing unpleasant things for him, so how could he doubt it now? Then he looked around at the other flowers in her garden and realized her love was big enough to cover them all. Surely he could not believe that her love stopped at the rose bush. It was too broad and sincere for that.

It seemed there were at least ten thousand memories of things Dottie had done for him. Things she had done only because she wanted to show her love for him. His mind raced across the years and it seemed to stop at the many times he had failed to tell her how much he appreciated her love and her efforts. It was too late now and Alex heard the line from an old country song which said, "Give me the roses while I live". Oh, how it hurt to remember those times when he could have given Dottie bushels of roses to show his love, but he had failed. If only he could call back just one hour, to hold her again, to place a rose in her hair, to

My Dottie, my love

If God but grant that we could talk
 and through the garden, one more walk,
That I could see your happy face
 and hear your laughter in this place.

The day you left with the Angels in white
has made all my days as dark as night.
Though tears I shed won't bring you home,
I must suffer in silence, all alone.
My bedtime tears have delayed my sleep
while I place my soul for my God to keep.

Alex ran these words through his head until there were no more tears to shed. He was numb with grief and there was no cure for it, no medication that would help.

As he sat looking across the lawn and into the woods in back of their house, he could just see Dottie on the riding mower with her dog, Bo, short for Beauregard. Alex gave her the pup when it was young enough to cry when it was left alone. Dottie had carried it in her lap as she ran the mower and Bo had come to regard that as his personal property. As he gained too much size to ride in her lap, Alex made a platform over one side of the mower where Bo could sit. Love between Dottie and that dog was just one more example of how a bond could be forged to exclude all others.

No matter how hard Alex tried, Bo would not go near the mower when Alex used it. There was a bond between Bo and Danny Boy, too. When Dottie took Danny Boy for a ride, no matter the distance, Bo was right beside her.

As Alex looked across the back lawn, he could see the peach tree in full bloom--another reminder of those endearing memories of Dottie. He had planted peach trees for her almost as a joke because of their early marriage mistakes. Dottie was very much in love with her home and always tried to make it more comfortable for Alex and their children. She was a very good cook and considered it no problem to take up canning.

Alex did not know anything about canning but he did know Dottie was good at everything she did.

Alex helped Dottie with canning a bushel of peaches, and when the job was finished, both of them looked at next winter's supply with some degree of pride. What Dottie did not know was the cooking time of the finished jars, so three weeks later, it was discovered they had peach brandy.

The uncooked peaches and sugar mixture had fermented. Sick at the loss, Dottie and Alex took the peaches to Mr. Barber's hog's at the next place down the country road. The three of them watched those hogs crowd to the feeder where all four got roaring drunk. Alex could see the hurt in Dottie but his love for her was magnified at her determination to can another bushel and do it right.

When he came home with another bushel of peaches, he also had four seedling peach trees meant to show his love for Dottie.

Enough of this. Remembering the love he shared with Dottie was too much to bear. He returned to the kitchen where he had left the shotgun. He sat at the table and shed more tears until he could no longer see. It was such a short time since Dottie had filled this kitchen with her lovely voice and her industrious clattering of pots and pans. How could Alex bear the loss? Why not use the shotgun and join her wherever she was? Still, remembering caused Alex to think of the many years Dottie had been a faithful teacher of little children in their church. How many times she had filled this kitchen with the odor of baking cookies for her class. He thought of the many times she had set a party for her Sunday school class, to meet and enjoy food she had prepared for their pleasure. Yes, Dottie was loved by many children as well as adults she had taught as far back as thirty years ago.

Now, Alex had to wonder if he would be permitted to join Dottie if he used the shotgun. He realized he was not worthy of the love she had given. Perhaps he still had to do something to earn a place beside her.

Alex was so alone, so lost in grief he could not think clearly. He had to wonder why he had children living nearby and yet neither of them seemed to care enough to be with him, to help him overcome his mourning period.

As he sat there in deep thought, he had to face the fact that neither his son nor his daughter ever showed much love for anything except money. Alex had been very successful in the business he started and had run for over twenty years. He had been generous with his children, perhaps too much so.

Now that he had retired, he had taken Dottie over many parts of the world and certainly they had visited every state in the USA. Discussing some of these trips with their children had left them wondering why neither had shown enthusiasm for their parent's travel pleasures. Suddenly it dawned on Alex that his children were greedy and upset that he was spending money that should be left for their inheritance.

With this revelation, Alex again looked at the wilted roses and thought of them as his children. It appeared to him that these represented how his children looked at him--faded and of no further use. Now he made the decision to return the shotgun to the gun case and re-write his will. He had work to do. He must build his bank account to the place where his children would someday regret dropping him in his time of need.

The rose bush took on a new meaning for him, and, the two wilted roses were exchanged for one bright red one in the center of his table. Every time he replaced the rose, he felt that bond of love he held dear to his heart for Dottie. She was still with him in the care he could give that rose bush and, with care, it would be with him until the wonderful time when he would again hold his dear Dottie. He was certain Dottie was in charge of the rose garden in Heaven, and someday, he would be there to help her take two for the table.

THIS IS A VERY TRUE STORY. ONLY THE NAMES HAVE BEEN CHANGED.

Doctor Laurie's Story

As doctor John looked over his shoulder, he could still see the smoke of his beloved city, Atlanta burning. His two daughters were very quiet for they understood the tragedy of leaving home, forever.

All they owned was beside and underneath them in the wagon that was pulled by their horses.

Doctor John Dexter had planned well for this day, in great hopes that it would never come. Dr John had made the necessary arrangements by having a wagon fitted for long travel through what might be enemy territory. A canvas cover to allow dry and warm cover for his daughters, as well as cover for his stock of medicine and medical implements.

The yankee army had swooped down on north Georgia, burning and looting everything. Atlanta had been sacked two days back, and no place was safe, not even if you claimed to sympathize with the northern army. Dr John thought his best chance to escape with his two lovely daughters, intact, was to use his occupation as a cover for moving freely through either army lines. Having the daughters acting as nurses in case of running into a battleground, with wounded to attend to.

Laura was a lovely sixteen, and Candice or candy as she was known, a beautiful eighteen. Both were well educated by Atlanta standards. Laura had just begun training as a nurse while Candy was more interested in fine arts. Dr John had done all he could to keep them at home and educate them In what he knew of medicine. He had been well educated for his time since he had attended the medical college of Edenborough, Scotland. After ten years in the new land of America, he was well established and very happy, then tragedy fell on his happy home. Eveanna, the mother of his children fell into an unknown lethargic condition that rapidly claimed her life. Nothing in his past training had prepared him for such a physical condition. Now it seemed his life was over, and the advancing army of the north gave him reason to move for the safety of his daughters.

This Sunday morning in Atlanta was not the usual happy time of a free city. This family had been faithful in attending services, both on Sunday, and evening services each Wednesday. . Now that the family had been reduced to three, there was little joy in meeting with friends at these services. Candy was the one that mostly missed the Sunday morning service. She had an eye for the young man who was always looking toward her. It appeared the feeling was mutual, and under normal conditions would have developed into a serious courtship. Dr John was much respected in their church for he was a devout Christian. He often lead services from the pulpit for he was a well-read bible student. Candy had a great love for children, and was constantly looking for ways to teach them the love of God, and the saving grace of Jesus Christ. Laura was some-what a tom-boy which made her the center of attention with both the boys and the girls.

Dr John had made certain his daughters were the best dressed in all of Atlanta. Now that he had lost Eveanna, he was much more certain to watch how his lovely daughters acted and dressed. As was usual, men sat on one side of the church, and the ladies sat on the other.

Dr John was aware of the eye courtship of Candy with the young man across the aisle. He was determined to keep it at this level, and no more. Losing Candy to this young man would completely upset his plan to move to the northwest. His fear was that Candy, being a very strong-willed woman, would fall into the trap many young men would set for such a beautiful prize. Never the less, the day came when the young man approached Dr John in the church yard. He came directly to the point, asking for permission to call on Candy at their home. Even though he was expecting it, Dr John was speechless for a moment. To say yes would undoubtedly wreck his plan, and to say no would require some fast thinking, and possibly alienate both Candy and the family of this young man. He gave it much prayer over the next week, but still had no reasonable answer. Sometimes, this is God's way of saying, wait and pray a little longer. The following Sunday, Dr John feigned sickness and asked his daughters to stay at home with him. By Monday, God had given him the only answer he could have used. It was time to tell the girls of his travel plans and the reason he could not possibly let this young man in on the plan. Candy was excited over the plan to move west, even though she did not understand the rigors and danger of this kind of move. She did understand the fear of an approaching army which gave her cause to start the planning stage with her father. While they could still find and buy suitable heavy garments and shoes, the three of them set off for the shopping area of Peachtree street, down-town Atlanta.

Dr John had purchased a very large amount of the best-known medicine of his time, cocaine. and following closely, heroin, with the word, addiction, unknown. Either could and did make pain go away for a time. Dr John was using cocaine for such things as amputation, persistent coughing, and any number of aches and pains. Little else was needed to have a medical practice in late eighteen hundred. Even so, Dr John had learned by doing and by study of the occasional corpse that had no relative to claim it. Laura was the only one of his daughters that had the stomach to learn with him.   Medical books and papers were in short supply, and soon to be nonexistent to them.

In order to avoid as much of the war as he could, Dr John had planned to travel northwest, with the ultimate goal being in Kansas City, far from the war that was tearing America apart. General Sherman took Atlanta in 1864, but Dr John had seen the future of the south long before then. He had made future plans by converting his earnings to gold coins, quietly buying needed supplies, and having a wagon built to his specification. His income was due to the fact that his practice had been in the north end of Atlanta where the wealthy gathered. Part of the wagon construction was a secret panel underneath where he could carry gold and important papers. He had a place for an extra rifle and two pistols, all loaded at all times.

Even though it would be dry under there, he vowed to change powder frequently in order to prevent being caught unarmed. Both of his daughters had rifles and due to his insistence, they had learned to load and shoot. His next great concern was a safe, and comfortable place for his daughters to sleep. For his bed, he chose to sleep under the wagon where he could be more in touch with danger, should it approach during the night. He had no doubt that there would be times when men would see his wagon as a source of wealth worth taking. Of course, he had great love for his daughters, and knew he would have to always be aware that certain men would try to take them by force.

Although it was a very hot August, Dr John decided to move out while the roads were still open in the country north west of Atlanta. Leaving from his home near Sandy Springs had to be done as soon as there was enough light to see. He planned to stay clear of traveled roads as much as possible, even using open fields to travel through when available. Marietta was well populated and he had to pass through there as quietly as possible since there would be yankee soldiers there. He was prepared to stay there until he treated the sick and the wounded. It would be a great help to have this work out in a day or so since it would help to have their travel blessings. The second day he approached the town carefully so as to not be noticed, but even so, he was stopped. He had painted his name and profession on the side of the wagon so it was that he was asked to treat some wounded, southern solders from Atlanta. They were on the run from Sherman's army, traveling to Chattanooga in hopes of joining the remains of their comrades who left Atlanta two days before. It worked out very well as they were in shape to travel and decided to join Dr John. Perhaps this was well, but could be very bad if they were to encounter yankees. That could mean death, and certainly capture of the valuable wagon load of food and supplies. Obviously a traumatic, and serious experience for the two young ladies.

Two more days of travel through hot and dry country side found them at a place called Rockway, and approaching rolling hills that sometimes needed to be traveled around instead of over. Laura had taken it on herself to treat the wounded as well as she could. None seemed to be infected, so Laura could wash the wounds in heated creek water they would camp beside. She had great compassion for those men, and listened to many sad stories of lost family members. Dreams of going home was foremost in their minds, and mother was the name most often mentioned in all of their conversations. Of course, those men also reminded Laura of her lost mother, and of the home they had just left. Dr. John had little notion of where their next home would be, except that it would be in the far west. A new life far from war was his goal. How could he know that war was in the mind of almost all men, and nowhere was really a safe place to be.

A place west of Rome called Coosa, Georgia was to be their last town in Georgia, and it was the beginning of more hills to give trouble to the traveler. Dr John had talked to many men who had made the trip across here into Alabama. He had been told the mountain crossing here was the best for many miles, and from there, they would be traveling due west, and across north Alabama.

Dr John had been following the war as much as he could, from Atlanta printed papers and some local print shops. It seemed that no-one really understood the army's movements, not even the officers that gave marching orders. The hills were rapidly giving way to mountains that divided Georgia and Alabama. Crossing this far south of Chattanooga would be less hazarders from armies and from territory too rugged for the horses. No doubt, north Alabama was not excluded from battlegrounds. The only good thing was that mostly, they would encounter only southern troops. Much more likely to be friendly. Also, the land would be more easily traveled by their horses. Over the next five days, they were not stopped or questioned as to their destination. It seemed that a fourth of the people were on the move to somewhere else, many not certain of the next day. Uprooted farmers and their families that had lost all of their winter supply of food for their family and all of their cattle. Where ever armies had been, there was a shortage of everything. Dr John had little to go on without maps, other than what he could beg or borrow from soldiers. Most information came from friendly soldiers that had lived in this country. He was advised to travel a little more in a southerly direction in order to miss the most difficult mountain's, and possibly find a better crossing for his wagon. The Tennessee river could be difficult, but along the way some men had rigged rope crossings where a wagon could be carried across on a raft. After a long, two-day struggle, they found their way southwest to a small town known as Sutton. There was a raft crossing there which Dr John gladly paid toll for. Now that they were clear of the most rugged mountains, travel was relatively easy. Another two days, and they were in the thriving cotton town of Huntsville, Alabama. By this time of the year, cotton fields had been stripped but there was still enough hanging on dead plants to make the fields look white. For as far as the eye could see, the fields had produced a bumper crop. Cotton bales were stacked near the mills ready for shipment, but no way to ship, and no place to go. Normally, cotton would have been shipped to large factories in places such as Massachusetts. These mills would turn the cotton into garments and return them to the south. Now, much transportation had been cut off, and cotton bales were left to rot, or to be burned by the invading yankee army.

Huntsville was a very rich city with factories producing goods such as shoes, saddles and many other leather articles. The city had been built around a very large spring that made a very attractive water flow out of the city. It was a strange site, just to see a large volume of water coming from what looked like a protruding rock shelf.

Cotton farmers from a wide area had settled here for the trading and banking economy. The government had set up a powder and explosive manufacturing facility just a few miles west of Huntsville. This site was selected due to the Tennessee river and hundreds of acres available along its bank. Powder manufacturing had to be done in widely scattered buildings due to the likelihood of an explosion. Several miles of cotton fields surrounded this area which made it the perfect place to manufacture explosives. Huntsville had not seen a battle within the county it lay in. It was therefore a very peaceful city which made Dr John decide to stay there for a short time. It was a good place to restock both food and medical supplies. He found lodging in a comfortable home known as a "Bed N Breakfast", giving his daughters a way to bathe and dress as ladies for a short time. It was also a wonderful time to visit with another doctor, and allow him to share information on the treatment of battlefield wounds. Of course, Laura was by his side as these things were discussed, adding the nurse's viewpoint when applicable.

Two days later, they all attended Sunday morning services, held under the reverend Jacob Miller. Being a southern Baptist community, what else other than a Baptist church, and having a large lunch prepared for after the service. Weather permitting, this was usually held outside on long tables, and with seats scattered everywhere. The good doctor Carl Elkins had a surprise for them, held back to just before lunch was served. He had given it much thought and set it up with the hopes that Dr John might decide to stay in Huntsville. He needed help in setting up the first hospital in north Alabama. He already had one doctor ready to join his practice, and this was the time to introduce him. He envisioned a team of three doctors and a twenty-bed hospital, the very best for many miles around.

When he called the participants together for the big introduction, nothing he planned happened as he wished. The moment Candy laid eyes on Dr Colin Moquin, she was lost. from then on, she heard little and retained nothing. Dr Moquin was the picture of intelligence, and educated bearing, so it goes without saying that Laura also fell under the spell. I doubt either of them could later tell of the delicious food that was served. Dr John saw his trip west falling apart, seeing both of his daughters forgetting him. Dr Elkins was overjoyed to see the anchor attached to Candy. This meant he would for certain have Dr John join him. Obviously, he would do all in his power to encourage the relationship between Candy and Dr Moquin.

Monday morning, he asked Dr John to accompany him on his rounds through the greater Huntsville area. He had in mind to show him the building he had chosen for his first hospital, and to tell him of his great plan. Dr John was not interested simply because he could not rid his mind from the thought he was losing Candy. He questioned Dr Elkins as much as he dared, concerning Dr Moquin. Looking for some reason to reject him , and to cause Candy to do likewise.

The following week saw the two young people together as much as possible. In practice, Dr Elkins took care of the house calls while Dr Moquin cared for the patients calling at their office. This meant that Dr John and Laura were with Dr Elkins while Candy was doing her best to act as nurse for Dr Moquin. Candy's lack of experience did not show to Dr Moquin since he could find no fault. The fall season "Cotton Ball" was just two weeks away, and Dr Moquin lost no time in asking Candy to the Ball. This was the most important dance of the year in Huntsville, Alabama. It was the usual time for young lovers to announce their engagement, and set the marriage ceremony date for Christmas. His mind was already made up for the beautiful Candy to be his bride. Short the engagement might be, it made little difference to either of them. Time for Dr Moquin to ask Dr John for his daughters hand in marriage. DR John knew it was coming and tried to think of some way to delay or to stop it altogether. Nothing came to mind, so he appealed directly to Candy for the sake of the western dream and for the unity of their family. He had no intention of staying in Huntsville, and made it quite clear he would never change. This placed a great burden on Candy. She did want to continue the dream west and to stay close to her family. Dr Moquin had no family in America so now, it was up to Candy.

Over the next few weeks, Candy agonized over the thought she had to make a decision between her family and Dr Moquin. Nineteen years with her father and ninety days with her chosen partner for the rest of her life.. It was a terrible dilemma, one she thought would drive her to insanity. Her efforts to bring it up with her Colin were almost more than she could face. And yet,, it had to be done, and the sooner the better. Her decision came after much prayer amd meditation. She could never talk to her father about this, and certainly not to Laura. That left only God. The date was firmly fixed in her mind the following Sunday morning when the minister said, "All things are possible when God is the leader". With that thought in mind, she determined to have her husband and to continue the trip west as planned. Now, all she had to do was convince Colin the westward trip would be what he wanted, not hers. Poor guy never knew what hit him. He just knew he was thinking about it when Candy brought up the subject.

December 29, 1867 A sunny but cool Sunday morning. A perfect wedding day.

The first Baptist church of Huntsville, Alabama never hosted a more beautiful wedding to this time. It appeared that half the city turned out for the affair. Everyone knew and loved Dr Moquin, and had quickly learned to love the Dexter family. Now the town knew they were losing both and as a last-ditch effort, were there to try changing their minds. Several ladies of the church had pooled their talents and constructed a bridal gown that had no equal. In addition, they had decorated the church in so much finery, there was no Sunday service. The gown made for Candy was something to behold. Each church lady had contributed cloth and or lace they had been holding back for something special. This was special and all set about with their best efforts to have their contribution incorporated into the gown. The straight across bodice allowed just a hint of cleavage. From the waist line upward, a bold and spacious white on white embroidered needlework embellishment spot-lighted her wispy figure. From the waste to the floor, ruffles and ruffles circled the expansive lower gown. The sleeves were three-quartered long and slightly puffed at the shoulders.

The wedding service was over. Candy and Colin were on their way to the adjoining river town of Decatur, perhaps an hour or possibly two if they stopped for any reason. They had been offered a small cottage belonging to one of the members of their church. They planned to stay there for about a week, as weather permitted for the return trip. Generally, the weather this time of the year was balmy, but there couch be a cold spell of a day or so possibly snow flurries. Colin did not want his bride to return to Huntsville looking ragged from bad weather travel.

Conditions were right for a Sunday return trip, so they left about nine that morning. Of all the people looking for them, Laura was the most excited. She wanted to know everything, and she did mean Everything. Of course, she was terribly disappointed. One thing that Colin wanted to talk about was the river traffic. The few he had a chance to speak with indicated a westward travel, with Memphis being the final destination. Dr John had been busy the past week, questioning all who had traveled westward. He found the most likely way to their final destination was to ride a river boat from Memphis to as far north as possible, Minneapolis as far as he could determine. This would save many weeks, and hundreds of miles of hard travel on his daughters. The possible problem was that travel from then on would take them through eight hundred miles of Indian country. He determined to start this journey trusting in god to protect them, and trusting fellow travelers for information about the future roads. He was certain the river boat captain would be able to advise him on where to end travel by boat.

Colin and Candy had discussed the westward move, but Candy did not know very much. Laura had been the one to discuss it with her father and help with the planning of the next day or weeks travel. Colin was very anxious to know of these plans so he could prepare for travel articles, as well as a separate wagon for his family and doctors supplies. He had much to learn and it must be learned before early spring. Dr John wanted to be well on the way by mid-March, and it would take a full sixty days for a wagon master and blacksmith to build a suitable wagon. They would have the benefit of Dr John's wagon to copy which would be a great help. Of course, Dr John did not want them to know of the gold container, so he had to empty it in secrecy. This led to the possibility of someone finding the secret stash, so he had to let them know only that this compartment held only guns. From then on, he had to carry as much as possible in a money belt, and never let anyone get close enough to him to discover the bulge. Some he entrusted to his daughters to hide among their personal things. It was quite a worry, but better to have it and worry than to have none to worry about.

Early march found the wagon ready and Colin well prepared to load it with all necessary tools and some medical equipment. He did not want to load all medicine for fear there might come a freezing spell and ruin some of his supplies. Colin and his bride had made a last-minute run on clothing and extra shoes. It was possible that they would not have this chance again for another year, or more.

March 15, 1868

Wagons west, so Colin called out in fun. He was very excited to be under way, having no idea that he was starting on a very tiring and sometimes dangerous journey. The morning air was crisp, but with the promise of a beautiful day ahead. When they were well clear of town, Dr John called a halt to their journey. He and Laura walked back to the wagon where sensing trouble, Colin and Candy had started to climb down. Dr John called for them to relax, no trouble. It was just time to halt for prayer. Dr John wanted them to be clear of towns people so they could commune with God without interference.

He wanted to thank God for the means to travel, for the beautiful morning to start, and ask his blessing on the entire trip. Of course, all were in favor of this short prayer service. Laura said she thought this should be a morning ritual, regardless of where they were. Candy and Collin quickly agreed. With only

The Tennessee river to cross and no rough ground to speak of, they made remarkable time. Just three years back, a violent earth quake had hit western Tennessee. Because of the restricted water flow and the time of the year, the river was very low and would present no problem in crossing. They had traveled almost ten hours with only a short stop to rest the horses. There was a surprising amount of fresh grass along the way, and many places where they could rest them for an hour. A light lunch brought from Huntsville was quickly consumed, and only Dr John found it restful to stretch out on his back for a few minutes rest. Two full days were required to cover this part of their journey. They did well to make more than one half of the trip on this first day. They made it to the western border of Alabama for the night , and there found many places to camp along a small stream. Dr John had heard that Mississippi was a desolate place at night. He did not know exactly where the border was, but he did know the area they were in did not look all that prosperous, and neither did he feel safe. Even though he was very tired, he decided to remain awake in his bed beneath the wagon. Normally a light sleeper, he thought it was best to stay awake for the first hour or so. In order to keep their camp as safe as possible, he had all fires extinguished well before dark. Since they were well off the beaten trail, he could not feel enough danger to keep himself awake. An hour before dawn, Colin had built the breakfast fire, so the smell of coffee brought all of them out. Candy was first at the fireside and first to have bacon sizzling in a hot skillet. She also knew how to make wonderful biscuits at any fireside. By full dawn, Dr John had the horses harnessed and hitched to the wagons. Then it was time for the morning travel prayer in which Colin led this beautiful dawn.

Good morning God,

First, we wish to thank you for a safe night in which we all slept well. We thank our wonderful savior for his protection during the darkness of night. We also want to give you our praise for making this trip possible and for the comfort we have along this long and dusty trail. Our travels this far have been possible without incident. Perhaps that is because we know you ride beside us in both rough and smooth trails. We praise your holy name, and ask that you give us guidance should we encounter others that may not have the comfort we have. Thank you, dear father, for your love and mercy. Amen

All were in good spirits when the wagons started to roll toward Memphis. Dr John thought this was the most desolate country he had ever seen. Of course, he had no idea of just far the word" desolate" could go. This would have to wait for some future day of their travels, somewhere in the northwest. As full light came, they had already covered many miles. The trail they were following seemed to be deserted, but as the sun behind them came on strong and their shadows reached out far ahead, they met others on their way to somewhere. Dr John always tried to speak on very friendly terms, asking of the road ahead, and injecting a word or two on the love of god. Always, they found the travelers to be locals on their way to work or trade. Being slower than a two-passenger buggy they were soon caught up with people who were headed to Memphis. From these, he learned the road ahead was usually clear of trouble. He also learned of the best way through the city to the river steamers was not through, but around the south side of town. They continued west until early afternoon before stopping to prepare a meal. Dr John was in hopes of making Memphis well before dark, so he asked them to eat lightly and save room for a grand dinner of jambalaya, a New Orleans dish but also very popular in Memphis. The main ingredient of this dish was crawfish or river shrimp. Also ham, sausage and many vegetables cooked with a generous covering of tomato sauce. His destination was Beale street where he was told good food and lodging was best. This street was the meeting place of many negro musicians who came here to meet others of their liking, but also because it was a way to find work on the river. Many were looking for a way to escape the stench of slavery, perhaps finding a way to travel safely to open northern lands.

First, he had to find lodging for his horses and his family. Both needs were to be found along poplar street, not so far from the river docks. Tomorrow would be soon enough to find river passage and to determine their needs for the long trip up river. As he stabled his horses, the blacksmith who was busy placing new shoes on a horse came over to see Dr John's horses. As they talked horses, the blacksmith had placed a value on the two horses, and offered to buy them. Dr John thanked him and told him he might sell later in the week. It depended on the transportation cost of taking them to Minneapolis.

A boarding house that looked clean and had a reasonable charge was located near the stable, so Colin and Dr John began the task of moving necessary items. For help, there was at least a dozen black men looking for a way to earn pennies. Just before dark, the two men joined the girls on Beale street to listen to some string music and to find the dinner they had promised themselves. In a way, it was sad music since much of it was about picking cotton and the cruelty of a strict master. Most of them knew first hand about both issues since almost every field south of Memphis had been in cotton and worked by slavery. The war had ended in May 1865, but that did not end slavery for many families. Many were too poor to do anything except continue to work for the same master. What did change was the freedom a man had, that could take his family and leave. But, where did he have to go? Gathering in places such as Memphis, looking for work and food for a family. Looking for a way north.

Dinner turned out to be one of the most pleasant times they would have on the entire trip.

They were very hungry from almost nothing to eat since dawn. Jambalaya, Memphis style left nothing to be desired. There was no doubt the cooks were experienced from having served in New Orleans, part of the migration north.

Going to their new quarters on Poplar street turned out to be somewhat of a problem. It had suddenly become dark and they were without lights in a strange city. Both men were carrying pistols so they had little fear of robbery. Even so, their fear was walking in a dark city, and locating their boarding house. Some homes did have lanterns outside their front entrance which made it possible to carefully walk and eventually find the right house. Colin and Candy had the large room and Laura had a very small room to herself. Dr John had decided to return to the stable where he would sleep in their wagon. Protection of their goods was of primary importance, not to mention the stash of gold he still had untouched. At dawn the following morning, he walked the short distance to the boarding house for a wonderful breakfast of ham, eggs and country biscuits, with ham gravy on the side. The best of this was not the food, but the enjoyment of being with the only family he had. Of course, morning prayer was the only way to start the day.

All four of them walked down to the docks where they found a small office and a man who sold tickets on the boats. Dr John had a multitude of questions and it was fortunate that the agent had plenty of time. No boats were entering or leaving today, so Dr John started by telling him of his plan to travel to Minneapolis. Questions came so fast the agent hardly had time to answer one before the next came. Was it possible to buy passage for the four of them, one cabin for Colin and Candy, and one for Laura. He planned to sleep in his wagon but to take meals on the boat with his family. Yes, this was all possible. Now to the time to make Minneapolis and the fare. According to the agent, time was somewhat due to river conditions, and could not be pinned down to the exact number of days. The trip was close to a thousand miles and should take about thirty or forty days, again depending on river flow. Dr John thought the fare was very high and asked if there was any way to reduce it. The agent explained it was because the two wagons took so much deck space. Perhaps he could leave one behind? Giving it no thought, he said no. He would take both wagons and leave the horses behind.

During the following week, the four of them toured the waterfront, the city and much of the outlying farm area. Waiting for a suitable boat to take up river was not wasted time for they learned much. Many people in Memphis had been as far north as Minneapolis, just for the boat ride or some as traders. The trade in furs, mostly in bison hides was brisk. Northern lands were not yet able to produce much in the way of food and or clothing, so the traders were doing a brisk business. Some had left the river towns and ventured inland. These were the ones Dr John was most interested in talking to. From them, he learned to expect almost anything, including Indian trouble. The native people were very disturbed over the slaughter of their natural food supply, the buffalo. It would be wise to travel carefully and to have a good supply of trade items such as knives, cooking pots and beads of many colors and sizes.

At last, the right boat arrived. The MISSY QUEEN was new and much faster than her sister boats. In addition, she was built with a flat bottom so as to navigate more shallow water. This boat also had more deck space at the bow which was perfect for the two wagons to be placed crosswise, just forward of the cabin area. The captain could see across the tops of them for an unobstructed view of the river ahead. The wagons were loaded and secured to the boat deck. The girls were assigned to their cabins, and Dr John set about arranging his bedding for the best

view outside. Colin's wagon had been carefully loaded with most of their trade items as well as food supplies that would keep for the next year. June 14,1868. At last, the steam was brought up to normal for travel and the order was given to, shove off. The passengers, about thirty of them, stood at the railing to watch Memphis slide out of view. Most of them were on this trip for the first time, and were filled with questions for the experienced travelers. Making new friends was foremost in the minds of both Candy and Laura. Laura knew her father would be careful to take care of them, and to choose the right road in whatever lay before them. For her, it was the first time in her life that she did not have a multitude of duties to perform. She felt a freedom like never since childhood. Dr John also felt a measure of freedom, for a short time. Only Colin and Candy saw no reason to look toward tomorrow since they felt they were in capable hands. Dr John had called for all passengers to gather with them at the start of the journey. He wanted to have a community prayer for the safety of all of them, captain and crew included.

JULY 10

By early July, they had traveled over 300 miles. St Louis was a thriving city with a lot of trade taking place. The Missy Queen was tied up at the dock for three days. Unloading freight and taking on more for upstream. It was also a place for refueling that took another half day of loading many cords of wood. The two doctors took the girls off for a night in town where they enjoyed a wonderful dinner of roast beef, with all sorts of trimmings. This was the beginning of cattle country and because beef was very low cost, Dr John decided to purchase several pounds of dried beef. It was something he hoped would save them time when they were finally on the trail again. Moving out on the fourth day was exciting all over again. Their next overnight stop would be in Peoria, Il, about four days in the future. So far, the spring rains had not caused the river to rise above manageable levels. For this they were thankful. High water and floating trees were very scary to Laura, and of course, they were all thankful for the relative calm river.

Taking on fuel and a light exchange of freight at Peoria resulted in only one night at this port. Neither of them found this exciting enough to spend more than a long evening on a wonderful dinner. One thing was certain, this place knew how to prepare many different dishes containing corn. They were all very happy with the food, and the welcome in Peoria. By this time Dr John had been successful in establishing an evening prayer service. It was never a long service. Just long enough to thank god for the safety of the trip so far. To also ask for his protection for the remainder of their journey.

Back on the river for the long, and last leg of the boat ride. Soon to be traveling over land into the unknown.

Dubuque, Iowa was not much more than a stop to unload the Dexter party as they were known. Unloading the wagons and saying their good byes, sad to part with new found friends but exciting to look forward to new ones. The usual August 68 heat was rapidly changing to cool nights, pleasant for now, but a foretaste of winter weather to come. Fourteen hundred miles to go across unknown plains with winter coming on. Not a pleasant thought for any of them, but a real matter of concern to Dr John.

His first concern was the purchase of horses, and that turned out to be a difficult task. He was fortunate to find a friend in the stable business, an aged old man who insisted he had only one name, Roper. Perhaps this came from his cowboy days and he had long forgotten his real beginning. Roper had spent his life on the western plains, and had lots of very good information for Dr John. First of all was, don't plan to travel past Rapid City with winter coming on. Perhaps you should consider wintering at Sioux Falls. In either case, stay off the plains after the first indication of snow. Storms out here with just wagons for shelter will surely result in four dead bodies. If you plan to stop over there, then horses will do fine. Otherwise, look for oxen since they can take the weather much better. Dr John thanked him profusely as he concluded the purchase of two teams of fine horses. He had brought his harness from back in Memphis, and that required little adjustment before they were ready to start the westward journey. Last but not least, buying grain for the animals and extra salt for meat should they be forced to take deer or antelope along the way. He took the advice of Roper and purchased a small heating stove that had a small top surface area where a cooking pot could be used. Roper insisted that he might be forced to stop in a place where there was no shelter. He also cautioned Dr John to stop along the way for firewood. Where ever he could find good hard wood, cut as much as he could reasonably take with them. Near a settlement, most easy to gather firewood had long since been depleted. Dr John made certain he had an extra axe and two good saws of a type that could be used by one person.

August 68

Leaving Dubuque at dawn the following day was exciting for the girls. Colin was not so excited for he knew he was entering a time in his life where there would be no help, even if he really needed it. He had listened to the morning travel prayer from Dr John, and thought he heard some apprehension in the plea for travel guidance and mercy. He thought of the immense responsibility of caring for the girls should something happen to Dr John. This made him shiver with the fearful thought, and send up many extra prayers for their safety. Four hundred miles to Sioux Falls, and seemingly no way between here and there to call for help. At least ten days without meeting a town or settlement. For the first time on this trip, Colin asked himself, what have I gotten myself into? Then, all he had to do was look at the lady beside him and know, whatever it took, he would protect her with his life.

Day two was well underway when they came into a terrible odor of rotting flesh. For several miles, it became more unpleasant. As they passed over a small rise in the land, there before them lay the carcasses of two or three hundred dead buffalo. Now they understood the reason for wagon loads of hides being loaded on the boat in Dubuque for down river shipment. What a waste of animals. How could a man do this? It was no wonder the words of warning were being passed of the possibility of Indian trouble. From this point on, Dr John would not allow a large fire at night. Only a smokeless, small cooking fire was allowed. Nights from then on were cold and lonely. Leaving in the mornings was even before dawn, trusting the horses to see the trail or the dangers ahead. Breakfast was usually cold bread and dry meat with a small amount of coffee done on the smallest of camp fires. Even these were built in lower depressions of earth so as not to be seen for any distance. For the next few days, no sign of man had been seen until they were near Sioux Falls. No Indian trouble had been reported in this settlement. After visiting some of the people there and learning all he could about the land ahead, he bought some additional grain to replenish his supply.

September 1868 found them just outside of Sioux Falls, stopped for the morning travel prayer It was still dark and somewhat chilly in the damp morning air. Both of the girls were wrapped in their sleeping blankets where they had decided to set together in their fathers' wagon. Dr John had decided to travel on toward Rapid City, 425 very long miles ahead. He was thinking if the warning given him by Roper back in mid-summer when cold weather was the last thing to think of. Now it seemed time to think well. Ahead lay a large river to cross and then the beginning of mountainous terrain. Dr John began the morning prayer just a little different than in the past.

Dear God, you have protected us along some treacherous ways. We know there was danger that we never saw, because you were there ahead of us. Now we are undertaking perhaps the most difficult part of our journey, and we hesitate to continue unless there is positive word from you. We believe you answer every prayer for the good of those that love you. Father, we do love you and trust you will guide us through every moment of the remainder of our lives.

Dear God, we thank you for your attention to the troubled four of us. We pray In the lovely name of Jesus.

Amen

With the prayer finished, Dr John climbed up to seat himself beside his daughters As the horses started to move out, Colin was heard to call Wows to his team. As he called out Dr John immediately stopped his team and climbed down to fine Colin, already looking at the lead horses front hoof.

For a reason not immediately evident, the horse was lame. The trip for today was cancelled. Dr John looked to the heavens with these words, thank you God for so prompt an answer, Amen. On returning to Sioux Falls Dr John really looked at the settlement for the first time. There seemed to be no empty buildings, no place to put up for the winter. In desperation, Dr John went to the trading post which was a large log building owned and operated by Dennis Carter. DC as he was known welcomed them to look around while he did some checking outside. When he returned, he had a happy grin. Everything is taken care of, he said. My brother Jimmy has the bar across the road, and we came up with a solution. Jimmy has very little reason to stay open during the winter. He lives in the back store room, and only then so as to keep the fire going through the freezing months. He also has another storage room, quite small, but well heated. We decided that he would move in with me and you can have his place. The married couple can have his office and bed room, Laura can get by with the smaller storage room and you, Dr John can have the entire bar to yourself. Jimmy knows you wont drink up his supply of liquor, and you might even hold a church service there while the weather permits. Jimmy and I will enjoy living together for the winter since it gets so very lonely living alone.

For the few remaining days of September, they were very busy moving things around and taking items that could not be left to freeze, inside for the winter. Moving their stock of horse feed to the stables where the blacksmith had agreed to care for them, and making certain their horses were in a safe place. Parking the wagons as close to the building as possible, they used canvas to seal both ends well enough to keep out most of the snow that was soon to come. Dr John wasted no time in setting aside times for prayer. He also invited the brothers to come over at any time they had to spare, particularly at their prayer times. Neither showed any interest in prayer meetings but they did like the idea of visiting, and of course, returned the invitation.

By mid-October, snow had covered the ground and travel was impossible. Now Dr John could see that making Rapid City would have been impossible. He and his family would have been caught on the trail, and probably have frozen to death. What a wonderful god, to see this in advance and temporarily lame his lead horse. He could not thank God enough for the way he stopped them from such a horrible death. For the rest of his life, he will recall how fast and certain God stopped him after he prayed for guidance. Now that cold, winter air was seeping in through every crack, it was necessary to do all they could to stop the cracks and to keep the fire ahead of the cold. Thank God they did not have to stop on the trail to Rapid City and cut firewood. It would be up to Dr John to replenish the wood they were burning, and he was in hopes he could hire this done. He hoped to be on their way as soon as possible, not held up to cut fire wood.

Time passed so very slowly, and before they were ready, Christmas was on them. They had nothing to give the Carter men since every thing was battened down in the wagons. With so little to give, the girls decided to prepare the best Christmas dinner they possibly could. Even this was almost impossible due to the fact they had nothing to work with. Giving up the thought, it was up to Dr John to make Christmas special by telling the Christ story. The day before Christmas, the carter brothers arrived with their version of a party. The brothers knew of a hunter who could and did bring in a winter elk. For the past two days, the brothers had tended an outside fire pit where the elk was being roasted to perfection. Now they invited the Dexter party to join them out back of the trading post. Dress warmly and be prepared to be outside for some time. When they arrived back there with the Carter brothers, they were surprised to find several people standing close to the fire pit. Anxiously awaiting their arrival. What a wonderful surprise. A table had been set up for a few dishes supplied by the only women in the community. Three kinds of bread, some potatoes fresh from the fire pit and two pies made from berries picked last fall. Dr John could hardly return thanks for the lump in his throat. He had so much to thank God for and he made it known that these new friends were the best.

Now that Christmas was past, time moved ever so slowly, seemingly standing still. January, February and March of 1869 found winter so very cold, it was hard to visit, and rarely did any of them venture outside. The first arrival from the east was hide hunters moving ever westward in search of dwindling buffalo herds. Their travel was very difficult and done in order to be ahead of many more hunters that would soon annihilate the buffalo. All of this was fueling more Indian trouble as it was wiping out the food source they had depended on for centuries. The new arrivals were telling of the coming railroads that would connect the two oceans. They would also open up places like Sioux Falls to thousands of people wanting to leave the war-torn eastern part of the united states. It would be another twelve years before this town would become a city of two thousand inhabitants. Before then, many wagon trains would become targets for inflamed Indians.

April first 1869. Dr John had moved his family out of the bar and on to the wagons. He had made a deal with the blacksmith to see to the replacement of firewood.

He had paid for wintering his animals and restocking his wagons with more grain for the trip westward. Except in higher elevations, snow had disappeared and now it was the rainy season they would have to endure. For about the next month, there would be some creeks to cross and in about two weeks the Missouri river would create a problem. For much of the trail they were following now, it was traveled by many, both wagons and animals. Dr John had heard about this river and was told he might find the ferry raft in operation by the time he arrived. That would be a blessing for he had no experience fording a river, even though his wagons were built like boats. It was still very dangerous, even for an experienced hand.

Moving out to the last edge of the settlement, he called a halt to offer up the morning prayer. His concern was not so much for himself but for his children, of which Colin was now one of them. Through many muddy places, and a few creeks, they made good time. Over the next twelve hours, they traveled almost sixty miles, not stopping for a noon rest. This was not good for the horses and Dr John realized this only when he noticed one of his horses with his head hanging down. Usually when they stopped, the animals were looking all around, but not this time. He felt so bad for this error he vowed to never let this happen again. That night was a long sleep for all of them since Dr John was not going to punish his animals by starting before they were well rested. They lost the time gained by staying on the trail for a full twelve hours.

Day five and they were approaching the Missouri river. They met a wagon of freight coming from the river, heading for Sioux Falls. The men on it told them the good news that the ferry was in operation. It would take two trips and would cost ten dollars each. That sounded like a lot, but Dr John was overjoyed. Even at twenty, he felt it a real bargain. He felt even more so when he saw how it worked and estimated the cost of setting it up. A large pulley had been anchored on each side of the river, well back from waters edge. An endless rope had been placed through the pullies with the connecting knot at a place where the barge was attached at the extreme end. To cross from east to west, the knot was secured to the front of the raft. The river flow from north to south pushed the raft downstream. As the raft angled up stream, water pressure on the side caused it to travel across to the other side. This required no effort on the part of the operator except to secure it to the bank for loading or unloading. Before an hour was lost, both wagons were on the trail west.

May 1st 1869 , Rapid city, South Dakota was in sight. Dr John had no plan to stop there for he needed nothing he could not find on the trail. Grass was high and horse feed was no longer needed, except for the treat that caused the animals to always stay close. Passing Rapid City was a great milestone for now they only had two hundred and fifty miles to Sheridan, Wyoming. By June first, they would have been through most of the plains and soon to be approaching hills and then mountains. None of the mountains would give them any trouble for the most part, the bad ones started after they reached their destination of Butte, Montana.

Rapid City was large enough to have a small hospital with two doctors in attendance. Dr John's services were not needed here, and besides, he had an eye for the mining town of Butte where he was told there was no doctor. His last information was that Butte had amassed well over two hundred citizens. Anaconda had opened a small mine to take copper from deep mines, and it was speculated there would be more. Butte, Montana was a large hill of almost solid copper it looked to have no end to the supply. Copper was the new metal for cooking utensils as well as casings for munitions. America was growing at a very rapid rate, and new things were coming that needed copper. The civil war had almost depleted the copper supply, so anaconda saw the market opening for much more than was readily available.

There was a shorter route to Billings, Montana than the one he chose. Dr John had asked many questions as they passed wagon trains moving east. Most of them recommended the longer route through Sheridan, Wyoming, simply because it was well traveled. More help should it be needed. He also considered his daughters need to see other people, especially women. With only about two hundred and fifty miles to Billings, Montana, he felt there was no need to overwork his horses. Their strength would be sorely needed when they approached Butte, and the hills just east of their destination. With six hundred miles to go, Dr John estimated they would be there no later than August fifteenth, plenty of time to set up for the winter

May 23,1869, Sunday morning, and a beautiful day. One that all had decided to take the entire day off in order to hold a prayer service. God had protected them over some dangerous territory with never a hitch. No sign of trouble and only God could cause this to happen. They had passed through some territory where many Indians lived, and never an incident except where Dr John had stopped the wagons to treat a small boy who had been seriously injured. He had no way of knowing what caused the injury, but he did know how to stop the flow of blood,   and to treat the little boy from the symptoms of shock. He had just finished treating the boy and Laura was cleaning up when several older Indians arrived. At first it looked as if they were very angry and might cause harm. But then the boy spoke in a very rapid tongue which caused everyone to relax. As they were getting on the wagon with intention of leaving, one older man brought Laura a blanket with many beads and stitches. It was beautiful and Laura could not hold back tears of gratitude. For the next several miles, Indians rode ponies beside their wagon. All laughing and calling out to others they were passing. Now that they were clear of the Indian village, Dr John called the halt for their Sunday service. They were singing and praying when several older boys came up to their service. They did not interrupt, just took a seat on the ground out side of the wagons and listened. Dr John made certain they knew he was praying by holding his arms to the sky and looking up. The others stood with heads bowed but Colin was watching from the corner of his vision. After about an hour, Dr John motioned for the young men to join them. They reluctantly moved in closer but would not come within touching distance. While they were there they prepared a lunch. Candy was best at doing this and Laura was best at trying to communicate. Dr John was busy in their wagon, digging for beads and knives. He was determined to leave them as friends of the white race, and to let them know about his god. Lunch was successful as the young men did decide to join them for some of their food. All went so well; they were hesitant to load and move on. As the young men passed out of sight, Cindy, in a loud voice thanked God for the experience, and prayed God's blessing on them and their families.

May 26, 1869

A beautiful day in Billings, Montana. They were so glad to see the settlement since there had been little to see over the past twenty-five days. A very few travelers, and a lesser number of home sites. This was a very direct route across the western plains and Dr John thought there should have been more travelers. What he did not consider was that almost all were moving west, just as he was. The few he did meet heading east had many questions about the trail he had just passed over. At Billings, several stores were open with trade goods, but little to offer in the way of food they needed for the last section of their trip. Their needs were nothing to be concerned about, but Dr John was the cautious type. He did not wish to arrive in Butte without enough to care for his family for several days, or possibly weeks. Spending only the remains of the day they arrived there, and one night was enough. By this time all were anxious to see the place where it looked to be the last place they would ever live. Colin was the first to refer to Butte as "home". Already he was thinking of the place he would have children, and a loving home to come to at the end of a day's work. When he did start to tell Candy of his dream, he was met with silence. The following evening when the two of them were in the quietness of their bed, Candy gave him the news. She did it in a loving way that shocked Colin. Her good night prayer was just a little different.

Dear God, you have been a wonderful God, to care for us so well through many dangers, many that we were not even aware of. We face new dangers every day of our lives, and we do so with the knowledge that you are there to hold our hands through it all. As we approach the end of this journey, we need special care for the addition to our family that is soon to be. Precious Lord, we ask in complete faith, that no danger come the way of this new life you are giving us.

We love and praise you, our heavenly father, in the name of your son and our savior, Jesus Christ.

Amen. Colin was speechless, except to say, Amen

Leaving Billings on the 28th of May saw them very excited. ready to face the difficult part of the westward move. Already the hills were beginning to grow in height, giving the horses just a little more trouble in starting the wagons to roll. Dr John was confident there would be no trouble with mountains, or even high hills. Every traveler he had spoken with assured him all would be well, providing he did not plan to continue on to the west. From Butte to the west, great mountains could be seen from long distance. Some with snow on top in mid-summer. To this point, Dr John had managed to handle the wagons well in crossing small streams. Nothing had been lost and no one had caught so much as a cold or cough. All of them were thankful and gave God credit for their health and good traveling. Now saw the horses having to struggle on some grades a little steeper than they were used to. Travel time was reduced from ten to twenty-five miles each day to some times less than ten per day. Even so, it looked as if they would finish by mid-June. Dr John told them at the evening stop that all seemed very well. He told them he had been in contact with anaconda while they were still living in Atlanta and had made arrangements to be the company doctor. On arrival there, they could expect a home, already furnished with a waiting room, examination and operating rooms ready. This being the first Colin had heard of the Anaconda reception gave him great joy, knowing Candy might be the first to deliver in the new place. He had been in a state of worry over the need for a home for her. He really had no idea of what to do, and was depending on Dr John to guide him. He also knew Anaconda had no way of knowing that he, another doctor was with Dr John. What if there was too few people to support him as a doctor? This was a real worry for him until one day they met another traveler that just came from Butte.

Colin had many questions, first was there housing available, and then what was the population? The housing question brought a definite, none available. Population, several hundreds coming out of the coal fields of Pennsylvania, having been hired by Anaconda there and given travel help to Butte. Now at the near half way point, Dr John saw his estimate of about twenty days extended to perhaps thirty days. Even so, he thought they would be there by July first, plenty of time to get set before winter.

He was right in extending the estimate. The trail was more rugged and very difficult for the horses. Some days he could not see forcing them into more effort unless they were well fed and rested. The delays were costly in time, but very profitable in the long stretch. As they approached the town of Butte, all were completely surprised at the number of well-constructed buildings. They arrived in the late afternoon, Saturday, July 3rd, still enough time for Dr John to ask for and find the only Baptist church in the area. Dr John had directed his team through the middle of town, looking for the offices of Anaconda. When he did find them, he was somewhat surprised at the meager accommodations. On entering the building, he found only two clerks hard at the books. Introducing himself caused one of them to quickly leave his desk with words of welcome.

Anaconda was expecting them, but not so soon. Their home was ready though, and this young man, Charles Childres told them he would lead the way. They were taken to the northeastern edge of town where it looked to be near the mine entrance. Dr John and the others were very surprised at the size and quality of the new office/home. Charles told them there seemed to be no empty homes available for Colin and Candy. But since there were no patients for the doctor's office just yet, he thought it would be fine for them to move in until something was found. For the next two days, the wagons were unloaded of all the items needed to make it permanent. What was left was consolidated into Dr Johns wagon. Colins was to be sold while there was a steaming market for such wagons. Dr Johns bedroom was closest to the examination room while Laura had to take the small storage room. Her bedroom next to Dr Johns was assigned to Colin and Candy for a time. For the next two weeks, all were busy setting up their home as well as the doctors office. The doctors sign had been painted and someone had hung it over the front door.

DOCTOR JOHN DEXTER
HOURS 10 AM TO 5 PM
NO SUNDAY HOURS

Colin had hoped to join Dr John but was not surprised when he heard of the Anaconda plan. His office was to be on the other side of the mines, in order to make it more convenient for an injured miner to get help. It was also decided that Dr Colin was to be more responsible for the families of the miners. He would be expected to make house calls and tend to women and children. In this role, candy would be of enormous help since she loved children, and would soon have one of her own.

Their first Sunday there was July 4th 1869. The entire Dexter family walked into the First Baptist Church of Butte promptly at 10 am. It seemed they were already late as bible class started fifteen minutes ago. It was unusual that no member had stopped by on Saturday with an invitation to attend. It seemed most thought them to be too tired after months on the road from Atlanta. Yes, they had been told about them and expected them Dr John and his daughters, but wonderfully surprised to hear all about Dr Colin.

During the first month in their new offices, it was a wonderful experience to be meeting new friends, and to be setting up procedures. All four of them were having a wonderful time of learning the people and the town. It was also very busy with many people having the need to see a doctor, and some calling just to fulfill curiosity. Dr Colin had mostly the children, and mostly colds or unexplained rash being the cause. Dr John had many men with injuries that needed treatment, some quite serious due to previous lack of sanitary care. Altogether, the past month had been very rewarding, and gave the promise of many more to come.

Before they had time to really think of the passage of time, the year was gone.

1870 went almost as fast with little change except the courtship of Laura. Soon after they had opened the office last year, Jacob Miles started his routine trips to Dr John's. office. He was there to help set up the company books, so he said. Even if he did help, it seemed his eyes never strayed far from Laura. She was aware of the attention, and encouraged it to a point. She soon learned Jacob was an attorney as well as a major stock holder in Anaconda. He was from Pittsburg, PA; and had been educated in Harvard. His job was one of his choice and had been a temporary location, until he saw Laura. Then, he saw to it that the job was as permanent as he would like to stay in Butte. The courtship lasted until Laura had her twenty fifth birthday in 1876. It was then she consented and married Jacob Miles. By this time, the railroad had been completed, coast to coast, passing just to the south of Butte. Jake, as Laura had started to call him, insisted they take their honeymoon on a train trip to meet his family in Pittsburg. Dr John was forced to hire a new nurse, and Jacob retired as Anaconda accountant. As could be expected, they started their new family which turned out to be a girl named Laranne.

We are told that time behind bars passes ever so slowly, that every day seems to the prisoner to have no end. We also know that time seems to fly when we are in a very pleasant place or when we are having a wonderful visit from friends. So it goes that the Dexter party has had years of the most pleasant experiences. But, as time passes, so do the lives of our family members. No amount of love can hold back the clock of time, and no amount of love could hold back Dr John. Jacob and Laura decided to build their home next to Dr Moquin and Candy. Jacob decided to open a new business as attorney for private practice as well as representing Anaconda. Of course, he was growing older and needed to curtail his activity. Now he had grandchildren that needed his attention while Candy did her best to keep up. Their children had been sent back east for the education not available in the plains of Dakota. Some of them had moved back to the Butte area, but like all children, they had to make their own way in life.

It seemed natural that at least one of the girls of each family would follow the footsteps of their mothers. Something in the genes of mothers wanted their children to follow in the desire to care for others. Each of the following generations of both Laura and Candice became doctors or nurses, thus following mom's example of love for fellow man. Though scattered across the expanded United States, they remained in close harmony as their great grandmothers would have had it.

Migrating families had a wide country to choose from when seeking a place to work and to live. Train, plane and automobile made the USA so very small, causing some of the Dexter offspring to wonder about their roots in the southeast. So it goes that Linda, another of the dexter offspring that had turned to nursing, decided to research her family tree in hopes of learning about her past. A good start would be to spend a vacation week in Atlanta. She was doing family tree and found almost a dead end with John Dexter. As she suspected, the burning of Atlanta in 1865 had destroyed records of many people. No way to search back from there, so she decided to use the week to visit the greater area of north Georgia. She liked what she found and decided to stay.

She knew she had an aunt living in St Louis and figured this a good place to start. This aunt was on her sister Cindy's side and well informed about the family, perhaps this would lead her in the right direction. This lady was the grandmother of Cindy and had kept many records of the family. She had records written in a diary by the daughter of Dr John Dexter. This lady was known as Candy and she had written many short passages about the crossings of rivers, and dangerous places. It seemed that she was afraid, but it was impossible to determine if she was afraid for herself or for little sister, Laura. The diary gave great details of the wagon trip across barren lands and only a little of what Linda was looking for. It did tell her that Doctor John came from Scotland, leaving there alone, and with little except an education. He had left his parents only because they were old and not able to stand the trip to America. It also told her that Dr John had been a land holder in the southern part of greater Atlanta, now known as Griffin. Linda decided to check out this city in hopes of finding the land that one of her great grandfathers had owned. Now that she had something concrete to look into, Griffin was her next move. On arrival in Georgia, she went directly to Spalding county for the land records. She was in a gold mine of information.

There she found that Camp Stephens, named after Alexander Stephens, the vice president of the confederacy covered much of the old city. Researching old army records, she found Dr John Dexter was the camp doctor for the entire training camp for southern soldiers. She also found the land her ancestor had purchased was on the same site and was confiscated by the union army at the end of the civil war.

Linda had found so much to satisfy her curiosity that she found her free time was short. Sunday morning found her as a loss for solid plans, so it was time to find a church. It would do her soul good to worship with other people and to trust God to give her direction. She had no trouble finding a good solid Baptist church which made her welcome as another child of god.

Being alone caught the eye of an older man and his wife. After service, Linda was invited to join this couple for lunch. When the couple found how traveled Linda was, they kept her busy until church time that evening. She had little time to ask questions, but she did get in a few. One of which was about hospitals in the area. By the end of that Sunday, Linda had made up her mind to stay in the south. Griffin was to be her home since it was close enough to live there and commute to a hospital in Atlanta.

Finding a job in nursing at Emory University hospital in mid Atlanta was just what she was after. A choice job in a choice city was such that she was well liked. A beautiful young lady could not stay single for long, not when she showered love on all of her patients.

Then Tony Wilson shows up under her care. Nature took over and before she was aware of it, she was in love for the first time. Several wonderful months later, a beautiful daughter arrived which was named Laurie.

True to the genes of her mother and grandmothers, Laurie learned to the care of others. Instilled in her was also the love of God. This was from the beginning, just as her parents had taught her. Laurie, as a child showed enormous talent in the arts. Her teachers encouraged her to become an artist by telling her she could make a good living with a set of pencils. That did not fit into Laurie's love of people and the love of god. It did make her more determined to become a nurse or a doctor. It quickly made her realize she would have to seek the help of God and trust him to make a way for her education. Being very active in her church, she became a very close friend with the minister and his wife. With their help and some other members, Laurie was given a grant to attend college. With top grades, she had no trouble finding help from a north Georgia medical school in obtaining a federal education loan.

Laurie, like many students of higher education had to depend on student loans. She was in constant prayer concerning her grades and her needs. Still, she found time to attend church,

and to continue learning in her love of art. To this time, she had great talent in pencil art, but nothing as she wanted it to be. She could draw animals and many other things, but not faces of people. Her prayers never let up in calling on God to help her with the great load on her shoulders. God answered her prayers in a dream. He told her to write while Satan was telling her it was of no use. The next morning, she went to the typewriter and wrote what she was told in the dream. As she wrote, she was told to obtain the list that she needed for the art work she was started in. After purchasing these articles, Laurie found she could do pencil portrait faces to perfection, to almost fulfil her dream.

Then the day came when Perry Stone held a revival, one that she attended every evening. During this time Perry had the vision of helping others by setting up a conference sale, similar to a flea market. Laurie saw this as a chance to perhaps earn some much-needed cash. She took several of her drawings to the Saturday sale, one of which was the face of a young girl. When she did it, she was so disappointed that she was going to discard it, but her mother was not about to let that happen. At the sale, her drawings were set up for all to see. She watched as people looked them over, wondering if one of them might sell. As she watched, Perry Stone stopped before the drawing of the little girl. He stood quietly for some time, and then tears ran down his cheeks. He bought the picture. A year later. he told on his show that he had recently lost an infant daughter, and god had told him this picture was what his daughter would have looked like had she lived. He told his audience that Laurie Wilson was the best artist he had even known.

Laurie first attended medical school in a less well-known university located in Georgia. Later she attended Tulane university in New Orleans, always in very close touch with God. Again, with top grades, she found a place in Marshall university, Huntington, West Virginia where she did her residency. Today, Doctor Laurie Wilson can be found serving as a loving doctor to the sick and the wounded. Her relationship to God has grown with every passing year, and she is much loved by staff and patients alike.

Cindy's parents gave their children no choice. While Cindy was still in grade school, her father was transferred to Lexington, Ky: Cindy was tops in her classes, all through high school which allowed her to find entrance to the University of Kentucky. Her love of the arts was to control her life in many ways. It won her a scholarship into the arts program, later a doctorate in fine arts. In later years, she found her place in the teaching profession, although not remaining in the classroom. Dr Cindy has been the host on radio shows and has traveled over much of the world, always boldly speaking out on the love of God. At this writing, she can be found as Dr. Cindy Herzog , working in the school system of Louisville Kentucky. God is the caretaker of all that love him.

Pencil drawings by Dr Laurie Wilson

God holds me in his hand